BELOVED SON

THE UNTOLD STORY OF JESUS CHRIST

A Mystical Adventure

SAGE RAINBOW

BELOVED SON

THE UNTOLD STORY OF JESUS CHRIST

© 2015 by Sage Rainbow

Published by:
META INSIGHT PUBLISHING
3101 Peninsula Road
Suite 314
Channel Islands Harbor
Oxnard, CA 93035

belovedson.sagerainbow@gmail.com

www.SageRainbow.com

First Printing, 2015

Printed in the United States of America

ISBN: 978-1511572965

CONTENTS

THE ARRIVAL

JERUSALEM, THE YEAR 30

The black-bearded man's pace through the marketplace was nearly frantic. His eyes darted back and forth scanning the throngs of people. He stopped suddenly when he saw the back of a man wearing a tattered tunic with his head coverings drooped between his shoulders. The long hair didn't look the same, *but could it be him?*

The black-bearded man's heart pounded in his ears. He approached the tunic-clad figure that resembled the vivid image in his soul-stirring dream. He remembered the image of the tunic with a tear on the right sleeve. The tunic-clad man turned.

"No," the black-bearded man blurted to himself. "His nose is too long and hooked. His sleeve is not torn." No one around him paid any attention. Disappointed, but propelled by the powerful impulse of his dream, he continued to search. It was mid-afternoon, and he had already canvassed the other more prosperous parts of the city, making his way toward this poorer crowded marketplace. The heat was oppressive. His legs were weary from the relentlessness of his search and his early morning start. His shoulders slumped as he approached the southern entrance to Jerusalem. *This is the last place. He must be here,* he thought. Beyond the city's south wall was only the vastness of the desert.

At the end of his dream, it had happened: an intense, blinding white light caused a shocking loss of his physical senses. He had opened his eyes, yet he couldn't see the walls, the floor, the ceiling, or the bed. Instead, there was only dazzling white light, more intense than the brightest desert sun. He had bolted up, sitting ramrod straight, acutely disoriented, panic coursing through him. *Have I died? Is this the afterlife?* He extended his arms, flailing about like a blind man who has been spun around repeatedly and then thrust into an unfamiliar room.

For a few moments, he couldn't feel anything, his senses filled only with the all-penetrating brightness of the light. Slowly, sensation returned to his hands. He reached down and could feel his legs and chest. He patted his bedding. *Yes,* he thought, *I'm still in bed.* He opened his eyes, yet the dream images of "white within white" were all that he saw. He stood up, aware that his feet had touched the floor; he reached for the wall and pressed his body against it for reassurance that he really was in his room.

As the soft moonlight faintly illuminated the room, his sight returned. He knew it had been a dream, but like no other he had experienced before. He looked down at his hands. He couldn't stop them from trembling. He remembered that in the seeming nothingness of the white light, there were faint images and outlines of people in patterns of light. The different intensities of light formed the patterns and shapes. A final image of a gaunt, tunic-clad man with a light beard had captivated his soul in a mysterious way that he had never before experienced.

He had seen the light of God. That is what had compelled him to look for the tunic-clad man, that and the all-powerful voice of God that shook his body: FIND HIM TODAY!

The sounds of a commotion from behind grew closer. He turned around. People shouting curses in the marketplace scurried to the sides, creating a path for the bleating goat being chased by a robed man who was caning it.

The black-bearded man quickly stepped aside but checked his impulse to curse the frightened goat, as was the custom of the times. On special occasions, to cleanse the sins of a congregation, their rabbi would ritualistically place his hands on a chosen goat's head and say a prayer that was supposed to transfer the transgressions of the people to the goat. The goat would then be chased and cursed by the people and driven into the desert to die, relieving the sinners of their guilt.

If only a cursed "scapegoat" could purify Jerusalem's sinful ways, but it never has, he thought. His dark eyebrows rose, causing the horizontal furrows of his high forehead to deepen as his eyes followed the frightened goat's path toward the broiling desert.

He continued walking toward the city's outer wall; the heaviness in his tired legs and despairing heart slowed his pace. He thought, *Was it just a fool's dream?* He wiped off a few drops of perspiration that had collected on the pointed tip of his prominent nose.

Near the high stone wall, a gathering of thirty people were listening to a gaunt man with a light beard preaching on a makeshift platform. The black-bearded man stopped and stood attentively. The preacher on the platform was wearing a whitish-tan tunic. The black-bearded man's heart once more beat hard and fast. He walked toward the back of the group, just another of the numerous such groups he had witnessed earlier.

A young woman with scraggly black hair in the middle of the crowd called out to the tunic-clad speaker, "If you are the Messiah, can you heal my leg?"

"Come to me," he beckoned as he stepped off the platform to greet her as she nervously limped toward him.

She was apprehensive. He grasped the woman's shoulders and shook her vigorously. Her startled eyes opened wide. He placed both hands on top of her head and exclaimed, "Sinner, now be healed!"

The woman fainted, falling to the ground. Those nearby helped to revive her. As she came to, the preacher ordered, "Stand up."

She stood before him. He said, "Now walk."

She hesitated and then took a few unsteady steps. Her steps became normal, and she turned to face the preacher. "I can walk! I can walk!"

The preacher pointed to a cup on the platform and addressed the crowd. "Give your coins to me so that I may live to heal others, and my prayers for you will save your souls." No one in the skeptical crowd made an offering. A hunched man with a cane winced with each step as he approached the preacher. "Heal me. I have been in pain for three years." The preacher again shook his subject vigorously by the shoulders, put his hands on the man's head and proclaimed, "Sinner, heal!"

The man staggered a moment and then stood upright with his chest out.

"Cast away your cane and walk," the preacher ordered.

The man let his cane drop to the ground. He took a step forward. Then on the next step, as his other foot touched down and bore the weight of his body, he grabbed his leg and cried out, "Ouch! Ow! Ow!"

He fell to the ground and reached for his cane.

The crowd booed and hissed the preacher.

Infuriated, the preacher retorted, "This man is not a believer in me. His sins are so great that God will not forgive him."

The crowd booed louder; some yelled, "Faker! Fraud!"

The preacher raised his fist in anger. "Believe in me and I will take your sins from you and carry them to my death. Those who do not believe in me and who mock me will burn in eternal damnation. Those who follow me to God's kingdom shall forever live a life of purity. Hear me all, for I am the chosen one! I am Jesus of Jerusalem!"

The black-bearded man frowned in puzzlement. Two of the speakers at similar gatherings had also called themselves Jesus. Unlike the others, this preacher resembled the image of the man in his dream, but still he felt doubtful. He moved closer to the preacher to get a better look.

The preacher had a tear on the sleeve of his tunic. It was on the left arm, though, not the right. A long, red curving scar covered the back of the man's right hand. The preacher glared at the black-bearded man.

"Why do you look at me so?" the preacher shouted and then pointed a finger at him. "You are the greatest sinner of all. Damn you!"

Dejected, the black-bearded man stepped back, turned, and then walked hurriedly away. He ran to the outside of the city wall. He sat on the ground under the shade of a single palm tree. He pressed his index finger and thumb into the deep furrows between his eyebrows and thought, *What does all this mean? What am I supposed to do?* He covered his eyes with his hands and wept.

Exhausted and dejected, he looked beyond the barren desert sands to the horizon. Hazy mirages danced on the hot sand, blurring and distorting the contours of the landscape. A point of intense white light suddenly flashed in the distance, so bright that his head jerked back. He shuttered his eyes and then uncovered them, searching for the light. It was gone, perhaps an illusion of the sand and the broiling sun. But he had never seen anything as dazzlingly bright before.

The intensity of the light made him think of his dream. It was too overwhelming to comprehend what he had experienced. He closed his eyes and remembered more of his dream. The white light was neither hot nor cold. It was silent, yet seemed to contain all the sounds that could be imagined, all vibrating at once at endless frequencies. It was formless, yet all forms seemed to exist simultaneously, each with subtly different intensities that rapidly appeared and disappeared. It was allness and nothingness and terrifying.

He leaned his head back against the wall and looked skyward. "Am I going insane?" he asked himself.

With a forlorn sigh, he looked back toward the source of the light. From the haze and shimmering mirages of the desert's floor, two distant figures emerged. He squinted, trying to discern more. The figures came closer. It looked like a man walking beside a donkey.

After a while, he saw that the approaching man wore a tattered tunic. Instead of heading for the gate of the city, the man and his donkey headed straight toward the black-bearded man, who stood as the man and the donkey stopped within a few feet of him. The donkey carried a simple wooden saddle with a rolled blanket tucked behind it and a water bag slung over the saddle horn. The man was gaunt with a light beard and skullcap; the right arm of the man's tunic was torn. The black-bearded man's pulse quickened. Simultaneously the two men each pointed a finger at the other and said in unison, "You're the one!"

Motionless, they stared at each other for a timeless moment. The black-bearded man was surprised and puzzled. He asked, "Why did you say that I was the one?"

"Because you were the one in *my* dream whom I needed to find today."

The black-bearded man protested, "No, no, no. You were the one in my dream whom I was searching for today."

The stranger laughed. "Then we should be grateful that both of our dreams have been fulfilled."

"But what was the purpose of the dream?"

"To give us the insight and guidance to seek each other."

"Why do we need to meet?"

"So that we can fulfill our missions."

"What missions?"

"You ask many questions. The flame of curiosity burns strong within you and spurs your yearnings to search for answers. I have answers for your questions. I am a Rabbi."

Perplexed by this response, the black-bearded man frowned. He wrinkled his pointed nose and sniffed the air near the Rabbi's shoulder. His face turned to revulsion, and then he asked the traveler, "What happened to you?"

The man smiled graciously. In a soft voice he answered, "I became lost in a sandstorm; then I was found."

"Who found you?"

"My Father," he replied softly.

"Where is he?"

"He is everywhere!"

"You talk in riddles. Where are your sandals?"

The stranger smiled again and replied, "They were lost in the furious sandstorm. I wandered alone for a long time." He turned up the sole of one foot and brushed off the sand. The black-bearded man winced. The foot was covered with bright-red, blistering skin.

"Doesn't that hurt?"

"Not anymore, not after I found my Father," he replied with no trace of discomfort in his voice or face.

"Why are you walking instead of riding your donkey?"

"After I found my Father, this donkey found me. I have the energy and desire to walk. It is a way of attaching me to this body."

"That doesn't make any sense to me."

The black-bearded man sniffed the air again and declared, "You stink! Why is your tunic so large and ill fitting?"

"Before my journey, it was very snug on me because this body was heavy with flesh." He turned and pointed to the east. "As I transcended from there," he turned and pointed to the ground, "to here, I was cleansed and shed the excesses and toxins that this body possessed. What you smell is what my tunic absorbed."

The black-bearded man shook his head skeptically, then looked at the donkey and pressed his hand to the water bag. "You say you came from the east. The only water in that direction is a river, thirty miles away. Why then is your water bag full?"

The stranger replied, "That water is not for drinking. It is healing living water. I was not thirsty on my journey, but this body, now cleansed, can use some water and nourishment."

"You are a strange one. There is a water trough on the other side of this wall. Come, Rabbi; I will take you there. My name is Judas Iscariot. What is your name? Where are you from?"

"I am Jesus of Nazareth."

2

The two men and the donkey walked through the gates and entered Jerusalem. Judas noticed a white tuft of fur in a star shape centered on the donkey's forehead. Pointing to it, he said, "I've never seen markings like that on a donkey's hide."

Jesus replied, "That's why I've called my desert companion "Star," because my Father's gift to me of this donkey was my guiding star, which led me to you." Judas raised his brows in disbelief.

They walked on and passed a new gathering of people who were listening to the preacher with the torn left sleeve. He sternly addressed those gathered: "I promise you that one day, you will bow down before me and pray to me as your savior. I will accept all of your sins as my sins, and you shall be cleansed and purified so that you may enter heaven."

Jesus looked kindly at the speaker. Judas scoffed and said in a low voice, "He is just one of a flock of deluded prophets who clutter the city."

The preacher raised his voice. "The power of my God has planned my destiny. Nothing can stop His will and my rightful place as His chosen one. People from all lands will think of me as their Messiah. I have come to fulfill the prophecy that everyone speaks of."

Many of the listeners booed and hissed.

Judas leaned closer to Jesus and spoke low so as not to be heard by the others. "Do you believe him?"

Jesus replied, "There are many who speak only threads of truth that have yet to be woven into the greater tapestry of God's full glory."

Judas shook his head and said, "Do you think so? You should know that there are many more would-be prophets in this city who are claiming the same thing."

The preacher raised his voice to the gathering: "And I tell you all that when I die for your sins, I will be resurrected from death because God's power can never die: it lives eternally."

Judas looked away from the speaker, studied Jesus's features, and said, "You resemble that preacher, but there are definite differences in your manners. Do you also share similar viewpoints?"

Jesus replied, "I don't believe that anyone should die for another's sins."

The preacher stopped talking. He stared at Judas and again pointed a finger at him. "The day will come when you will kiss my hand with tears in your eyes." He then addressed the crowd, "Those who mock my words, like that man, will burn in eternal damnation. Those who follow me to my Father's Kingdom shall forever live a life of purity."

Judas grabbed Jesus's arm and said, "I've heard enough nonsense. Let's get your donkey some water."

The donkey drank from the lower trough. The two men bent over the higher drinking trough and scooped up the water with cupped hands. Jesus took one sip and spit it out. "It's wet, but it tastes foul."

Judas poured the water over his head. "It's better just to refresh yourself. I have a clean well at my home." He bent over the trough again with cupped hands and dipped them into the water. Behind them, they heard the soft sound of horses' hooves on the packed sand.

CRACK! The sharp sound of a biting whip suddenly cut across Judas's back, ripping open a gash in his flesh and staining his robe with blood.

"AGGH!" Judas cried out in pain and bolted upright. He turned and faced a Roman centurion on horseback who was rolling up his whip. He was accompanied by two helmeted soldiers with shields, spears, and belted swords. They all were laughing. One pointed at Judas and said to the other, "He jumped like he was thrown into a skillet of boiling oil!"

"Out of my way, Jew. My horse is thirsty," the centurion ordered. Judas's face was red with anger, his eyes glazed with pain. He took a menacing step toward the centurion, who unfurled his whip in a challenging pose, ready to strike again. Jesus pulled Judas to the side and said, "For now, be calm."

A soldier said to the centurion, "You like to play with your toys."

The centurion nudged his horse, pushing Judas aside, and made his way to the upper drinking trough. His horse noisily slurped up the water. The sun's rays glinted against the centurion's polished metal helmet. Jesus pulled Judas further away, and the donkey followed. Judas winced in pain. He reached behind his back and felt the ripped cloth. He looked at his hand and saw his blood. "It hurts like a thousand bee stings."

Jesus took his water bag from the saddle and said, "Pull down your robe and let me see."

Delicately, Judas pulled back his robe, wincing again as the cloth brushed against the bloody gash.

Jesus said, "I shall give unto you healing living water." He then poured a small amount of the water over the wound.

Judas grimaced, anticipating a stinging pain. Jesus gently patted the water over the open gash. Judas's face relaxed; surprised, he said, "That soothes the pain."

He turned and faced Jesus, "Whatever you have in that water is magic."

Jesus smiled as he slung the water bag back over the donkey's saddle horn and replied, "It's a gift from my Father."

Judas clenched his fist and angrily eyed the back of the centurion, who ignored them. "If only your father could take away the pain that the Romans inflict on our people, which would be a greater magic. My family is wealthy and has status. They could file a complaint of his violation."

Jesus spoke softly, "Forgive them, for they know not what they do."

"Forgive them? I hate them!" Judas retorted.

Jesus put a hand on Judas's shoulder and said, "Do not hate your enemies, or even be angry at them. Forgive them, lest your hate and anger diminish the gift of love that God freely bestows upon you."

"They have defiled me. How can one forgive their cruelty? Why should I?" Judas replied bitterly.

"Because it is better for you and the better thing to do. For what defiles a person is not what comes from without, but what arises from within."

Judas shook his head. "I don't understand you. He spilled my blood!"

Jesus affirmed, "In time, you may understand that the taste of revenge is bitter to one's soul."

Judas sighed dismissively. He looked down at Jesus's tattered robe and again sniffed its foulness.

Jesus smiled and said, "Yes, I would like to wash the desert dust from this body."

"How did you know that I was about to ask you if you wanted a bath?"

"I can see that you are a man with a hospitable nature. Surely that is what you were thinking."

Judas, perplexed, stroked his beard. "Hmm...I wonder..."

Jesus said, "I also see that you are a kind, loyal, and generous man. You seek the greatest truth, yet you are skeptical, which prevents you from being fooled. You act gruff at times, but your heart is golden."

Judas, surprised, stiffened. "You seem to know me."

Jesus nodded. "I am in you and you are in me."

Once more Judas rolled his eyes, sighed again, and then said, "More riddles." He looked into Jesus's eyes and felt a deep sense of compassion flow through him. "You will be my guest. You can bathe, and then we'll share a meal with my companions."

Judas, Jesus, and Star walked through the marketplace that was teeming with workmen, tradesmen, and pilgrims as well as servants and slaves shopping for their masters. A cacophony of voices haggling back and forth between sellers and buyers, often shouting and teasing each other over prices, blended together, expressing the exuberant activity of an average day in Jerusalem's crowded city center. Copious displays of fruits, vegetables, clothing, souvenir trinkets, and some fine goods and luxury items filled blankets laid on the ground and tables under shade cloths. Beggars and thieves, many without work, and other unemployed poor who had migrated to the great city in hopes of bettering their lives mingled with the population. The smell of domestic animals being sold for food or sacrifice mixed with the odor of hot oil that was cooking meals to be sold, adding an aromatic heaviness to the market air. In the background stood the massive walls of Jerusalem's temple, constructed of impressive stones, some of which weighed 100 tons.

They made their way up and down narrow hilly streets and soon entered a dense middle-class section of the city There they approached Judas's home, a one-story stone house with a flat roof and an eight-foot-high stone wall surrounding its perimeter. The street side stone wall had a high wooden gate large enough for a cart or wagon to pass through. Next to it was a heavy wooden door.

A man who had curly, reddish-brown hair, a long beard, a long nose with wide nostrils, and wore a skullcap was standing by the wooden door. He greeted Judas and, looking disdainfully at Jesus, said, "This can't be the one you went looking for."

"He needs a bath, Peter, and new clothes," Judas replied.

Peter protested, "Not another homeless beggar."

Judas said sternly, "He's a rabbi. Be respectful. His name is Jesus."

Peter smirked, "Just what Jerusalem needs, another Jew named Jesus."

Once inside the perimeter, Peter lifted a heavy wooden bolt and slipped it between two sockets on the inside wall, firmly securing the outside door.

Judas led Jesus and the donkey around to the back of the house past a courtyard to a stall tucked into the rear corner. The walled courtyard was barren except for a well and a parched palm tree with brown, wilted leaves. After they settled the donkey in the stall, Judas latched the stall's gate and they entered Judas's home.

The furnishings were sparse, neat, and humble. A large low dining table with mats on the floor for sitting on took up much of the space in the main room. Adjoining it was the kitchen with a stove, pots, and cooking utensils on shelves; and on work counters were a mixture of pottery and wooden bowls, some filled with nuts, lentils, barley, olives, and figs. Large jugs of water sat on the floor.

Above the jugs on a counter were baskets of many festive foods to be cooked. An open curtain hung from a six-foot-high rod separating the main room from the kitchen area. Windows around the house let some light in, and the flame of an oil lamp on the dining table added additional illumination. Down a narrow hallway were Judas's bedroom, two guest rooms, and a bath area.

A short time later, Peter came into Judas's room and said, "The Rabbi is about to take his bath."

"Good," Judas replied. "Let him have a good soak. I'm exhausted; I need to rest." He bent over to take his sandals off.

Shocked, Peter exclaimed, "Judas! What happened to your back? Your robe is torn and bloody."

Judas reached his hand behind his back to feel the tear. "I almost forgot about it. A centurion flayed my back with his whip."

"I'll get some aloe. Let me see it first," Peter said.

Judas delicately removed his robe and turned his back to Peter. Peter examined him, then rubbed his hand over Judas's back and said, "There is a little bit of blood, but there is no wound. Your skin is not even broken."

"Impossible. I felt the flayed skin," Judas said as he turned to face Peter.

The two men stared incredulously at each other.

3

"Wake up," Peter said as he shook Judas's shoulder. "Your rabbi friend has been in the tub for two hours."

Judas sat up and asked, "Is he all right?"

"I've checked on him five times. He barely has his face above the water. The first time I checked, I thought he was dead. He didn't seem to be breathing, but when I poked his head, he took a breath and whispered, 'Please leave me.' Not too friendly a guest."

Judas got out of bed and said, "I'll check on him."

"Ask him where he found that water. It's still hard for me to believe that your skin had an open cut," Peter said.

Judas knelt before the tub; Peter stood at his side. The submerged man did not move. His nose and mouth were at the still water's surface, his eyes closed beneath. Judas noticed that the water was crystal clear with some sand and sediment on the tub's bottom. A mild fragrance wafted in the air, like a gentle spring rain.

Judas gently nudged Jesus's arm, "Are you all right?" he asked.

At first, Jesus didn't respond. Judas nudged him harder. Jesus shook his head and then sat up and opened his eyes.

"Are you all right?" Judas asked again.

Jesus turned to him and smiled, "Surely. I was in my Father's Kingdom. I now know more about my mission."

"Where did you get the healing water from?" Peter blurted.

Jesus looked at him and then at Judas and asked, "May we speak alone?"

Judas looked up at Peter and nodded. Peter frowned and wrinkled his long nose, flaring his wide nostrils. He turned to exit, annoyed, muttering, "It's your home."

Judas turned to Jesus and asked, "Do tell me about your healing living water. I know it worked on my back. What well or spring did it come from?"

"It came from my Father. As I told you, I became lost in a desert sandstorm without any water. This body was sure to die. Then the donkey appeared with the water bag. I immediately grabbed the bag and was about to drink of it when my Father spoke to me. 'Drink not of the water you hold, for it is the healing living water for your mission. Have faith that I will sustain you.' And as you can see, He has sustained me."

Judas raised his bushy eyebrows skeptically. "It's a very, very long journey from Nazareth to Jerusalem without any water. Why did you leave?"

"I was told to leave. The townspeople thought I was insane."

"What made them think that?" Judas asked.

"Because I was able to silence the demons of those possessed. Then I admonished the people not to turn away from those afflicted or lock them in darkness, but to give the afflicted shelter, love, and kindness. They didn't understand. They became angry at me and accused me of being in an alliance with the demons." Jesus's shoulders slumped. "My family was ostracized because of me. My brother James, whom I love dearly, asked me to leave Nazareth for fear that I would be attacked..." Jesus stared at the empty space before him and then said sadly, "And I'd brought shame to my family. I was an outcast. I felt deeply depressed when my family abandoned me...I didn't want to live in this wretched world any longer."

Jesus sat up straighter; he cupped a handful of water and poured it over his head. He smiled broadly. "But I am no longer the 'I' that I was. I retain all of this body's feelings and memories as if they were of my life, yet it is not my life, for my new life has begun."

"What do you mean?" Judas asked.

"The man Jesus had given up on his life. His will to live was diminished down to his last breath." Then Jesus paused, closed his eyes, and his head and shoulders shuddered as if in response to a sudden loud voice; his face contorted. A few moments passed, and then a peaceful glow filled his face.

"Then what happened?" Judas asked anxiously.

"Then my Father bade me to go forth in this body as His Son, to offer forgiveness for mankind's sins."

Judas shook his head, "This is too much for me to believe. You are a man in a bath, not a god."

Jesus looked into Judas's eyes. "You are half right and half wrong. For now, I am both man and the Son of God in transition."

"In transition? To become what?" Judas demanded.

"To become fully realized, within myself, as God in man and to be realized by man that I am the Son of God."

Judas stood and pointed his finger at Jesus. "No, your living water may have healing powers, but I see you as just a man."

Jesus lifted his leg and turned the bottom of his foot upward. "Look at my foot; feel it."

Judas saw that the grotesque red blisters were gone. Hesitantly, he reached down and felt the soft, smooth skin on the sole of Jesus's foot and said, "That's remarkable. You do seem to have a gift for healing, but a God? No! Almighty God cannot be contained within a human body."

"You are right, Judas. All of God is not in this body. I am of God, the Son of God in transition, within this body so that I may know what it is to be human and so that I may teach man of my Father's Kingdom."

Judas knelt again. "No, I've heard too many others who have claimed to be the Messiah. I admit, there is something very different about you that I have not experienced before, but for you to say that you are the one, that you are the Anointed One who is the Messiah, no."

"Judas, please remember your dream last night. Remember when you first saw me at Jerusalem's wall: you pointed at me and said that I was 'the one.' I am the one."

"I meant that you were the one in my dream. You also pointed at me and said that I was 'the one.' Am I a Messiah too?"

Jesus laughed. "You are playing word games with yourself. You are 'the one' to help me complete my transition and fulfill my mission. Think for a moment; how is it that I know what you dreamed of last night? How is it that I know that your mind is locked in disbelief but that your heart feels the truth? Poor Judas, you suffer from so much conflict. Think about your dream. What did it mean to you?"

Judas's high brow furrowed in confusion. "I don't know how you know such things. Some people are very intuitive; some people can read the thoughts of others, but they are not gods."

"That may be true, Judas, but what meaning did your dream have for you?"

Judas closed his eyes and spoke. "What I remember is the intensity of the whiteness. It contained all forms that could exist simultaneously as subtle but different patterns and outlines of light intensity. The forms spontaneously appeared and disappeared. I've never had a dream like that before. It was as if I had died, but I felt more alive than ever before. I don't know what it meant," Judas shivered, "but I do know that it frightened me."

Jesus smiled, "You experienced the Light of God. What did you see at the end of your dream?"

"For a flash of a moment, I saw you," Judas replied.

"And I saw you also. We were sharing the same dream. Judas, have you ever wondered whether you, in this reality, form your dreams or your dreams form this reality?"

As Judas stroked his beard in thought, a quick knock on the door diverted his attention. A tall, lanky man with straight brown beard and hair carrying a blanket entered. Judas asked, "What is it, Luke? We're busy."

"Judas! The Rabbi's donkey is gone. All that was left was this blanket rolled around a white tunic," Luke replied.

Judas stood. "How is that possible? I know that I latched the stall's gate. Were the stall and front gate left open when you checked?"

"No, the front gate and door were locked as always."

Judas took the blanket in one hand and held the garment in the other. "Where's the saddle and water bag?"

Luke shrugged his shoulders. "I don't know."

Jesus stepped out of the tub and walked to Judas. He took the tunic from Judas's hand, pulled it on, and nodded. "A perfect fit."

Judas asked, "But what about the healing living water? It's gone!"

Jesus picked up a pitcher and filled it with water from the tub. He pointed to the tub and said, "Save this bath water." Jesus put on his skullcap and walked out.

Judas followed. Luke stood bewildered. Judas called back to Luke, "Do as he said. Save the water in the large jugs."

Luke, perturbed, called back, "Save the water? I burned his other stinking tunic. Why save his stinking water?"

Luke walked to the tub and saw that the water was crystal clear. He put a hand into the water, then lifted his hand to his nose and smelled the wetness. It had a refreshing fragrance. He touched his fingertips to his tongue. His eyebrows slanted in puzzlement. The water had a pleasant, sweet taste.

Judas followed Jesus into the courtyard. They stopped under the wilted palm tree. Judas said, "Well, I can see why they kicked you out of Nazareth. You haven't been here a day, and the only two people you've met in my house don't like you."

"Each person will color his experience of me in a unique way based on their individual perceptions. In time, their perceptions will change."

Jesus started to tip the pitcher he had filled from the tub and poured the water onto the base of the wilted palm tree. Judas grasped the pitcher. "Don't waste the water. The tree is dead. The earth beneath does not sustain any plants. We will be drawing lots to see who will cut it down and cart it away."

"Please allow me to pour this," Jesus said.

"Reluctantly Judas replied, "It's your bath water."

"Jesus poured out half of the water in the pitcher, then set the pitcher down at the tree's base. Judas went to the empty stall and examined the latch. "The latch is still closed." He turned, knelt, and studied the earth. "I don't understand it. There are hoof prints leading into the barn but no hoof prints leading out. How is that possible?"

Jesus replied, "My Father giveth and taketh away, and He giveth again in many ways as surely as His divine love giveth us breath and taketh away each breath and giveth another breath again."

"You talk in circles but don't really give me the answers I want."

"Perhaps I give you the answers you need," Jesus replied. "In any event, I am learning to meet the challenge of your resistance and skepticism, which will help me to master the challenge of connecting the thoughts and actions of our people to a higher plane of divine love."

Jesus placed his hands on Judas's shoulders and said, "I stand before you with all my material possessions, only a skull cap and tunic, not even sandals on my feet, and I say to you that I am the richest man in Jerusalem; for I am one with my Father and His glorious kingdom."

Jesus raised his eyes upward toward the late afternoon sky, "I have accepted my Father's mission to impress upon our people that their striving for more power and material things should be directed instead to improving the plight of those less fortunate. That is God's way."

"Rabbi, if you want to impress the people as the Messiah, the King of Jews, then you will have to wear the crown and garments of a king and not those of a common man."

"No, Judas. A true king of man is measured by his deeds, not by the garments and opulent jewels of royalty. A crown of thorns is more befitting false kings than one of gold."

Judas stepped away. "You want to accomplish the impossible."

"If it is my Father's will, then it is the impossible that I will strive to accomplish."

"You would have to perform miracles," Judas challenged.

Jesus replied, "Now you are beginning to understand."

"Now I don't understand at all," Judas retorted. "Only God can perform miracles."

"Exactly. That's the truth, Judas."

A short, chubby man emerged from the back door and walked toward the two men. Addressing Judas, he said, "Please introduce me to the rabbi with the magic water."

"Rabbi, this is Matthew; he lives here with his ten-year-old son, Little Seth, who is short for his age. Matthew is a tax collector for the Romans."

"I hate it!" Matthew declared. "But it's something I had to do to support my family. That was before they died of the fever, except for Little Seth. Most people hate me for being a tax collector. But Judas has given us shelter, and I am grateful for his kindness."

Jesus looked above Matthew's head at his aura, then looked into his eyes and said, "You are also a man searching for great truths."

"All of us in this house are. John is in the kitchen preparing dinner. He's the most righteous one." Matthew turned to Judas. "Everything is clean and ready for tomorrow. All we need is the wine delivery." Matthew smiled at Jesus. "Maybe you can show us some magic at dinner. I've got to help John finish preparing our meal." Matthew walked back into the house.

"This has been such a maddening day for me," Judas exclaimed. "I almost forgot about tomorrow. We're hosting a wedding reception for John's daughter and her husband-to-be."

Jesus looked skyward and said, "Thank you, Father." He then said to Judas, "Wedding parties can be very enjoyable. This one will help me adjust to my transition."

"Adjust to what?" Judas asked.

"To pleasure," Jesus smiled delightedly; then his face turned solemn, his shoulders slumping.

"What's wrong, Rabbi?"

Jesus said sadly, "This body still retains heavy emotional remnants of pain and suffering. It now needs the balance of pleasure."

"Our people have endured pain and suffering for centuries," Judas commiserated.

"In Nazareth, the poor have struggled so hard to survive that they have lost their sense of purpose in life. It is even worse for those here in Jerusalem. They see the riches of others, and their blood boils with envy and jealousy."

"That is true," Judas replied. "I have been helping those I can, but there are so many poor people that my efforts feel futile."

Jesus stood tall and said, "I am here to help you, and you are here to help me. Together our mission will serve a great purpose and renew hope in the souls of the hopeless. It is not enough for me to cleanse myself of this body's toxins of pain and despair. In the next phase of my transition, my Father wants me to experience the pleasures of being human so that I may breathe joy into the lives of the joyless. Our people taste mainly the bitter from the bittersweet cup of life. The bitter is intended to heighten the sweetness of life's wonders but not to be dwelled upon. Pleasure can be derived from seeing the good and doing good."

"Dear Rabbi, you are a puzzle to me. Let's go in and enjoy the pleasure of a good meal. John is an excellent cook."

The large dining room adjoined the kitchen that was in the far corner. A half-closed curtain separated the areas. Candles burned on the dining table. Judas sat at the head of the table next to Jesus. Matthew and Little Seth sat on one side next to Luke and John and Peter on the other. After saying their prayers, they commenced eating.

Jesus finished his last bite, pushed his plate away, and said, "That was delicious. You are an excellent cook indeed, John. It was as if my tongue were tasting food for the first time."

John, who had a small nose and large ears, smiled and nodded his acknowledgment of the compliment.

Peter exclaimed to Jesus, "You ate like a glutton!"

Judas retorted, "He needs to gain weight," and then pointing to Matthew, added, "unlike our portly friend."

John addressed Jesus. "You should thank Judas, not me; he paid for the food and all the trays of food I've prepared for tomorrow's festivities."

"I thank you again, Judas," Jesus said.

"Judas has been our generous savior in many ways," Luke added.

Judas sat up straight. "My family is wealthy, but my only interest in money is as it serves me to help others."

Matthew added, "Judas believes in living a humble life and only gives us enough money so that we also may live humble lives. It would be nice to live more comfortably."

Luke reached out his long arm and pointed at Matthew's belly. "You look comfortable enough to me."

Peter leaned toward Jesus and asked, "Tell us about your healing living water magic."

"What do you want to know?" Jesus replied.

"You said God gave it to you and then took it away – with your donkey. Of course, I know how some magicians work their tricks. But I also know that Judas is very hard to trick. So how did you get him to think there was a whip gash on his back? Did you put the blood on his robe?"

Jesus sat back. "I see what you're thinking. You should know that I did not make Judas think anything. The pain from the whiplash was real, and his anger toward the centurion overwhelmed his thoughts."

Judas clenched his jaw and nodded in agreement.

"But where did you get the blood from? I saw it on his robe," Peter probed.

"The blood was Judas's blood. But it doesn't matter what I say to you, for you will believe what you want. This is only our first supper together. By the time we share our last supper, you will believe."

Seth stared wide-eyed at Jesus and said, "I believe you."

Jesus turned to him and said, "The eyes of a child can see simple truths that the skeptical eyes of an adult refuse to see."

The rising sun cast a golden glow over the city of Jerusalem. Seth woke up before his father and began his chores to help prepare for the wedding reception. He took the empty bucket from the kitchen table to fill from the nearly dry well. When he opened the back door, he saw Jesus sitting on the ground facing the palm tree, his back to Seth.

Seth dropped the bucket in disbelief at what he saw. He ran to Matthew's bedside and shook his father's shoulders. "Wake up, wake up! Come see!"

Groggy with sleep, Matthew mumbled, "What is it, Seth?"

Seth grabbed his father's nightshirt and pulled him up to a sitting position, then struggled to get him to stand. "What are you doing, Seth?"

"Come see," Seth said again. He pulled his father's arm and led him to the back door.

Matthew's sleepy eyes opened wide and his jaw dropped as he approached Jesus.

"How is it possible?" Matthew asked.

The brown, drooping, parched palm leaves were now green and full.

Matthew looked down at his feet and saw small green shoots of new grass sprouting from the ground.

He grabbed Seth's hand and ran back into the house to Judas's bedroom. "Wake up, Judas! Wake up!" he yelled in a panicked voice.

"What? What is it?" a sleepy Judas replied.

"Your Rabbi isn't a magician; he's the Devil!" Matthew exclaimed.

"What do you mean?" Judas asked.

"Come, see for yourself."

The commotion awakened John and Luke.

Soon, the five household members stood by the back door watching Jesus facing the palm tree. The morning sun was higher, and the green leaves appeared even more luxurious than they had a few minutes earlier.

The four men and the child cautiously approached Jesus. They marveled at the green of the palm fronds and the new shoots of grass.

Without turning around, Jesus stated simply, "This is my gift to you, Judas, for your hospitality and to honor John's daughter's wedding day."

Jesus then turned around and looked at everyone's stunned faces. He smiled and said, "I have given the tree and the earth healing living water."

Jesus stood, reached for the pitcher of his bath water, and poured more of its contents onto the palm tree's base. "There. That should do for now." He smiled at everyone and said, "Shouldn't you all be going to the synagogue soon for the wedding ceremony? I'll keep Seth company here as he completes his chores."

Jesus casually walked to the house; everyone else stood bewildered. After a few moments, Judas said to Matthew, "He is not the Devil. This gift of green life is not a curse; it's a blessing. There isn't much time; let's all get ready and let's all be thankful."

At noontime, Seth walked out of the back door toward the palm tree where Jesus sat on the new grass shoots, leaning against the trunk. Everyone else had left for the wedding ceremony at the synagogue.

The boy's adorable face was slightly smudged with dirt, and his shoulders drooped from his non-stop chores. Jesus patted the ground and said, "Sit here. We both deserve a rest."

Seth plopped down next to Jesus and sighed. "Thank you for helping me with my chores, Rabbi. When Judas went looking for you yesterday, his chores were left undone, and I had to do them and the extra work for the reception."

"You are an excellent worker, Seth. I have a treat for you," Jesus said. The boy perked up. "What is it, Rabbi?"

"Yesterday you helped John prepare all that food for today's celebration," Jesus said, patting his stomach, "and I know those dishes are delicious."

Seth licked his lips. "Yes they are, and I'm starving! I can't wait till we eat!"

Jesus smiled. "What is your favorite part of the meal?"

"Dessert!" Seth declared, his delicate eyebrows rising high over large sparkling brown eyes.

"And what dessert that John made do you look forward to having most?" Jesus asked.

Seth's eyes opened wide and he exclaimed with glee, "The honey cake!"

"Hmm," Jesus stroked his beard, "I thought so." Jesus leaned forward, reached behind his back, and brought forth a two-by-two-inch square of honey cake that was four inches high. The crust was brown, and the cake was golden yellow. He offered it to Seth.

The boy's eyes opened wider. He sat up on his knees and eagerly started to reach for the cake, then sat back. "No, I can't. John and my father made me promise that I wouldn't eat any of the food until everyone was here and the blessing for the food had been given."

"You're a faithful and loyal son. That's why you should be rewarded. I am a rabbi, and I have given this cake a special blessing." Jesus again offered the cake to Seth.

Seth licked his lips and swallowed empty air. "Thank you, Rabbi, but I promised. I can't."

"Last night you said that you believed me." Jesus put his hand on Seth's shoulder and said, "Believe me now. This piece of honey cake is a gift from my Father to you. As a rabbi, I promise you that John and your father will say not a word of reproach to you. It is I who give this cake to you and not you who takes the cake from the kitchen. Believe in me." Jesus reached over and held the cake under Seth's nose. "Here, please enjoy it."

Seth breathed in the rich, enticing aroma. He looked at Jesus and grinned ear to ear. He said, "I believe you," and eagerly took the piece of cake. "This is my favorite." He broke off a small piece, put it in his mouth, and let it dissolve. He looked up at Jesus and smiled. "Thank you, thank you. This is the best honey cake I've ever tasted."

"Thank you, Seth, for believing in me."

The hot noonday sun heated the parched ground of the courtyard. The shade of the palm tree helped, but Seth's forehead soon built up beads of perspiration. A drop landed on the top of the cake. Seth wiped his brow with his sleeve and said, "It sure is hot."

"Yes it is," Jesus replied, "but I think I feel a breeze building up from the west." Jesus raised his hand toward the west and made a beckoning gesture.

Seth looked up at the dead-still palm leaves, then toward the west. He felt a gentle, soothing breeze on his face, and the leaves swayed gently above them.

"How did you know a breeze would come? We hardly ever get a noon breeze."

"I just knew," Jesus said.

"Except for Judas, the grown-ups call you a magician, a faker, even the Devil – all because of your tricks."

"My dear Seth, they aren't tricks. They are happenings that my Father helps me with."

Seth put another small piece of cake in his mouth and savored the flavor. Jesus looked at him and said, "There are questions on your mind that you want to ask me. It's okay. Ask what you want; I'll give you the answers."

"It's my chore to sweep this back yard and smooth the earth. I always make patterns with my sweeping as a way to play with my work. Yesterday I was extra careful and neat and made perfect straight lines for the wedding reception today. I know your donkey never left the stall because there weren't any changes in the patterns except for the hoof prints going into the stall. How did you do it? Was that a trick?"

"What do you think?" Jesus asked.

"Judas told us that you said God, your Father, gave you the donkey and took it away. How is that possible?"

"I don't always know how my Father works, but I do know there are divine reasons for all that He does. I have a deep faith and belief in my Father and His deeds. I accept them as blessings, as you joyously accepted the honey cake that is soon to disappear like the donkey."

Seth swallowed the last piece of cake and smiled. "Can I ask you about your healing living water?"

"Of course," Jesus replied, "what do you want to know?"

"Why do you call it living water?"

"Because each drop of water is alive with God-life. God is in all things, even in this empty space between our faces," Jesus said as he touched first the tip of his nose, then Seth's nose.

"Is God in me?" Seth asked.

"Of course God is in you. God is in all people, but very few realize it; many even deny it. My Father in Heaven has given me a special mission to awaken people to realize that He dwells within them. He has also given me the gift and powers to use His 'living water' for healing and in any way that will help me accomplish my mission."

The breeze grew stronger, rustling the green palm leaves. Seth reached down and touched the tips of the grass shoots. He looked at the pitcher of water beside Jesus and said, "Is your bath water in the pitcher also living healing water?"

"You are a smart young man, Seth," Jesus said and poured a small amount of the water on his hand and then wiped the dirt smudge off of Seth's face.

Seth closed his eyes and said, "That feels soothing. Your hand feels tingly."

"I have been in communion with this water. When I was in the bath, I fell into a deep state of prayer and meditation. I became One with my Father in Heaven."

Seth leaned toward Jesus and said, "And because God is in every drop of water, the water and you and God became one. The water is now holy water."

Jesus leaned back and laughed, "You are very wise for one so young. Now you had better change into your clean clothes, for your guests will soon arrive."

"They're here!" Seth yelled out from the back door to Jesus, who was still sitting under the palm tree. "Will you help me open the big gate?"

The two of them removed the long wooden bolt and opened the gate. John walked through first, leading the horse that pulled the bride and groom's cart. Thirty others followed on foot into the courtyard. The entire wedding party was hot and tired from the morning's events and the torrid noonday walk from the synagogue.

Seth took the bridle rein from John and led the horse to the stall. Jesus stood at the gate, nodding and bidding *shalom* to the wedding guests as they passed through. The wedding guests looked at Jesus curiously; some whispered to others, then giggled or smirked. He overheard someone say, "That's the would-be messiah magician."

Judas came to Jesus, grabbed his arm and said, "Come, let's go in, eat and celebrate. Everyone is hungry."

Inside, the men spoke together in groups while the women, under John's direction, took the prepared foods from the kitchen and set them on the large dining room table. "Rabbi," Judas called, "please meet my friends, who share many of my aspirations. This is Phillip, Nathaniel, Andrew, Thomas, and Saul."

Jesus nodded to each. Saul pointed at Jesus and said snidely, "I've heard some interesting things about you."

Andrew chimed in, "I hope you will show us some of your tricks."

Judas held up his hand. "Please respect the Rabbi. He is a sincere man."

Jesus said, "I sincerely hope to enjoy the feast John has prepared."

The men smiled and nodded in agreement. Nathaniel pointed to himself and said, "I sincerely hope to enjoy Judas's fine wine. He always serves the best."

"Yes! Yes!" the others agreed in unison. "My mouth is parched; let's get the festivities going, Judas," Phillip said.

"Simon hasn't arrived yet with the wine. He should be here any moment," Judas replied.

The men's faces turned dour. "He better get here soon," Thomas said. "Everyone can use a good uplift."

Andrew looked Jesus up and down and said, "Rabbi, I hear that you can heal a whip-flayed back and turn brown leaves green. What else can you do?"

Jesus replied, "I do what my Father in Heaven guides me to do."

"A very political answer," Nathaniel said, "but what does your Father guide you to do?"

"To teach brotherly love, forgiveness, and tolerance toward all people," Jesus replied.

Saul laughed, "That won't do much for you when Roman soldiers take what they want from you and beat you." The others also laughed, except Judas.

Jesus replied, "You should know, Paul, that no one can take from you what is most precious."

Saul raised his thin eyebrows and said, "My name is Saul, not Paul."

Jesus replied, "I know your name."

The front door opened, and in walked a short, balding man who appeared distraught. He approached the circle of men. "J-J-J-Judas," he stuttered. "I-I-I…"

Judas put his hands on the man's shoulders and said, "Take a deep breath, Simon. It's okay. Try to speak slower."

Simon took a deep breath, but the worry in his face did not abate. He spoke with his lifelong stutter. "J-J-J-Judas, th-th-th-the wh-wh-wheel of the c-c-c-cart came off at the t-t-t-top of the-the hill. All th-th-th-the j-j-j-jugs of wine fell off and b-b-b-broke."

The men were incredulous and disappointed. Phillip asked, "All the jugs?"

Simon looked down at the floor and responded, "Y-y-y-yes, all th-th-th-the j-j-j-jugs."

Saul looked at Judas. "What kind of celebration will this be without wine?"

Jesus stepped away from the complaining men and walked into the kitchen behind the pulled curtain. A buxom woman whose hair was covered by a headscarf, only her pretty face showing, followed him and picked up a large bowl of cooked chicken quarters. She smiled at Jesus and said cheerily, "Good afternoon, Rabbi, my name is Hannah."

Jesus stared at her a moment, then said, "Good afternoon, Hannah. You have a radiant glow about you."

Hannah blushed and smiled. "Thank you for the compliment. You'd better get your seat at the table; this is the last bowl of food coming out of the kitchen."

"You go ahead. I'll be right there," Jesus replied.

She turned and left him alone in the kitchen area. Jesus knelt down on one knee next to the six jugs of bath water on the floor under the worktable. He uncorked the first one, stuck his index and middle fingers into the top of the jug and immersed them in the water. He closed his eyes for a few seconds, then took his fingers out and re-corked the jug.

He repeated the procedure with the remaining five jugs, then stood up and went into the main room, taking a seat at the dining table with everyone else.

Bowls of hummus, tahini, and olive oil for dipping were spread around the table. A very large loaf of challah bread was in the center. The fragrant smells of cinnamon, thyme, cardamom, and nutmeg permeated the air. Large serving plates with braised lamb, chicken, and beef with garlic were near the center of the table. Mixed vegetables and a beet and pomegranate salad filled other large plates.

The bride and groom sat at the head of the table. John sat near his daughter on the long side of the table, beaming proudly as the father of the bride. The groom's family sat across on the other side. Judas sat next to Jesus at the foot of the table. John looked down at his empty wine glass and looked back up and across the table at Judas. Judas shook his head, shrugged his shoulders, and raised his empty hands palms up. John got up and walked over to Judas, who whispered to John of Simon's mishap. John's face fell in disappointment. He scowled at Judas. "But what about the blessing? This marriage must be blessed, and this celebration must be happy. We need the wine!"

"I'm sorry. And disappointed also. But there is nothing I can do," Judas said.

John stomped back to his seat. Jesus leaned toward Judas and whispered in his ear.

Judas looked at him incredulously and whispered back, "You're insane. There is only your bath water in those jugs."

Jesus stood up and walked over to Hannah, who was seated near the middle of the table, and spoke to her. Hannah spoke to the women seated on both sides of her, and then the women all went into the kitchen. The three women came out, each carrying a pitcher that they had filled. They began pouring their pitchers' contents into everyone's cups.

Judas's frown deepened as his cup was filled. He looked down suspiciously at the red fluid. Perplexed, he looked up at Jesus, who sat next to him.

Jesus smiled and said, "As the host, aren't you going to give the blessing for this celebration?"

Judas gave Jesus a cold stare and said, "I think not. I don't even know what's in my cup. You give the blessing, Rabbi."

Jesus stood and held his cup in front of him. The room became silent. He said, "Judas has asked me to give the blessing over the wine. Please join me."

All of the guests picked up their cups. The men who knew of Simon's mishap were puzzled but dutifully held up their cups to the bride and groom. Simon was quivering; John was still scowling.

Jesus raised his cup higher and solemnly said, "Blessed art though, O Lord our God, King of the Universe, who creates the fruit of the vine." He extended his cup toward the opposite end of the table and said, "Congratulations to the bride and groom. L'chaim." Jesus took a sip of the wine and smiled with delighted satisfaction. Judas hesitantly raised his cup and sniffed the liquid. He jerked his head back and studied the liquid a moment, then sniffed again. He took a small sip, raised his eyebrows, and turned to Jesus in disbelief. Jesus smiled and said, "Drink up, Judas; it is a true blessing."

John had already sipped his wine and called out to Judas, "Because this wine is the most delicious I've ever tasted, I can't be upset about your practical joke. Thank you, dear Judas, for being such a gracious host."

Simon quickly downed his full cup of wine and sighed with relief. He held it out to the woman nearest him with a pitcher, beckoning her to refill his cup. Everyone drank and ate and drank and then drank more of the wonderful wine. The strain of the earlier part of the day's events turned to rejoicing and great merriment although periodic glances of suspicion were cast upon Jesus by some of the men.

As the dinner party progressed, people rose from their chairs to talk with others seated at the other end of the table. John, Saul, Peter, and Matthew leaned down in conversation with Judas, who was still seated next to Jesus. The wine had filled everyone's heads with lightness as all the talk blended into a joyous din. Only Seth was fidgeting in his chair after finishing his dinner.

John beckoned to Seth. When Seth approached him, John said, "It's time for the honey cake. Go into the kitchen and bring the tray here."

Seth said reluctantly, "No, no. Do I have to?"

Judas said sternly, "What's wrong with you? Listen to your elders."

Seth looked at Jesus who said, "It will be all right. Do as you're told." Jesus smiled and winked at Seth.

Knowing he would be reprimanded for the missing piece of cake, reluctantly and with slumped shoulders, Seth went into the kitchen to fetch the large tray of honey cake. He pulled off the protective cloth from the top of the tray and stared down at the cake in amazement. The honey cake was perfectly intact. Not a crumb was missing.

Seth brought the honey cake to John, who took it and placed it on a cleared section of the table. He picked up a knife and began cutting two-inch squares, then announced to everyone, "Dessert is ready." He turned to Seth, saying, "Please bring in the figs and dried fruits."

Seth replied, "Of course." He turned to Jesus and smiled broadly at him. "Thank you, Rabbi. I will always believe in you."

Jesus nodded and winked at Seth again.

Everyone was feeling joyous, and the men felt rambunctious from the copious amounts of wine consumed.

Hannah was pouring wine nearby and had been glancing curiously at Jesus throughout the meal. She came over to Jesus's side and touched his hand to offer him some more wine. He felt the softness of her hand and without looking up, knew that it was Hannah. He looked up and their eyes met. He shifted in his chair uncomfortably. Hannah leaned over to fill his cup. Her plump breasts pressed against his arm and shoulder. He turned his head and stared at the nape of her neck and its smooth white skin. Instantly, the lap of his white tunic stirred as evidence of his arousal.

Peter noticed it and pointed to Jesus's lap. Saul, Matthew, and Judas looked down also. Peter said, "Our Rabbi appears to like Hannah!" The men looked at Jesus with disdain. Hannah looked down, surprised. She blushed a bright red and accidentally spilled some wine on the table.

Hannah quickly straightened and hurried away from the laughing men. Jesus turned to see Judas's flabbergasted face and then looked up at the men staring at him. The men shook their heads at Jesus in disgust. Saul, repulsed at what he saw, turned and walked away, his shoulder dipping to one side due to his persistent limp.

Jesus stood, perplexed, and said, "Excuse me." He walked out the back door to the quiet of the courtyard and leaned against the palm tree. He wondered, *Why did this body react that way?*

9

Jesus paced back and forth in deep thought for fifteen minutes. The sweet sound of a songbird delicately pierced the silence of the courtyard. Jesus stopped in his tracks. He looked up at the palm tree and saw the little bird, then took a deep breath, relaxed his shoulders and sighed. In a moment of realization and gratitude, he knew the reason for his surprising reaction to Hannah. "Thank you, dear Father. Now I understand."

Judas walked out the back door toward Jesus with a serious look on his face. As Jesus turned to face him, Judas demanded, "How did you do it? How did you get the wine in the jugs? Seth said you never left the house. Where did you get the wine from?"

Jesus put his hands on Judas's shoulders and said, "Calm down, take a breath, and listen to the songbird," pointing to the bird in the palm tree.

Judas stepped back. "I don't want to hear a bird sing. I want to hear you tell me how you got so much wine into those jugs."

"Why can't you just accept the wine as a blessing without having to know why or how?"

"Because it bewilders me. Everyone is talking about you. They think I've played a joke, a trick with you. But how could any of us have known Simon's cart would throw a wheel just before dinner was to start? There was no time for you to get wine elsewhere. You must tell me where the wine came from!"

"I will tell you although no one will believe you." Jesus folded his arms across his chest. "But first, you must feel gratitude for the divine gift of wine and the pleasure that you received. You must also allow me to feel gratitude for my realization that my Father is guiding me to fulfill this body's need for pleasure, just as the songbird calls to us to receive the pleasure of its song."

"I am thankful. But I don't understand what you mean about your body," Judas retorted.

Jesus pointed his finger at Judas. "You say you are thankful, but those are only words. You do not *feel* thankful. You diminish your pleasure in the blessings given you when your thoughts do not allow you to bask in the grace of gratitude."

Judas clenched his jaw and pointed a finger back at Jesus. "Who are you to tell me how to feel thankful?"

Suddenly, a dragonfly dropped from the sky and hovered between the two men's pointed fingers. Judas froze, captivated by the blurring motion of the dragonfly's wings, its steady stillness in mid-air.

He heard Jesus's gentle voice. "Take a breath, Judas. Let it go. Be here with me now."

Judas took a deep breath and then retracted his pointed finger. He breathed out, allowed his arms to drop to his sides, and relaxed his shoulders. The dragonfly held its position. Judas took three more breaths. He finally relaxed his facial muscles and grinned. The dragonfly turned in the opposite direction and faced Jesus. It paused a moment, then quickly darted away.

The two men's eyes met where the dragonfly had been. Judas said, "Forgive me for not showing you my gratitude for the wonderful gift of wine."

"I forgive you. But it is God's forgiveness you should ask for because it is your feeling of gratitude for His blessings that you should be grateful for. A true feeling of gratitude will lead you to a state of grace."

Judas bowed his head. "You make me feel ashamed."

"Just feel gratitude, Judas." Jesus reached out his hand to Judas. "Come."

Judas stepped forward and the two hugged. Judas said softly, "Thank you, Rabbi. Now are you going to tell me about the wine?"

"Of course, Judas, of course."

The sun had sunk lower in the sky, and the palm tree's silhouette of shade grew longer on the ground. Jesus and Judas sat together on the new grass. Judas stroked his beard and said, "So you can commune with water because to you, the tiniest drop is alive and aware that it is a part of God. Then in a spirit of love and oneness, you are able to have the water particles agree with your request to change their vibration, their state of being, to appear in different ways, such as wine, to our human perception." Judas rolled his eyes. "No one will believe this."

"Maybe not that part, Judas. It is enough that you will tell them that I turned the water into wine. However, I wanted to satisfy your curiosity so you'll believe in me. Believing in me will inspire you to instill my Father's message into your group of friends."

"Because of what I have seen with my eyes and tasted with my tongue, I am believing more, yet it is all unbelievable – a rabbi who talks to water! What else can you do with that connection to water?"

"With the power of love and my perception of the oneness of all things as a manifestation of God, I am discovering that water can also connect me with people's bodies because their blood and body parts are formed mostly of living waters."

Judas shook his head. "That's more than I need to know about you and water."

"The simple way for you to understand is that first I acknowledge that in love, I am connected to God and God's love connects me to His creations. Love is the bridge that connects all things." Jesus pointed up at the green palm leaves and said, "The water that I gave to this tree was vitalized by me, and now it gives love and vitality to each leaf. The living water has the power to heal and make whole that which is weak or sick."

Jesus pointed to the green grass shoots and said, "You now sit on the ground that has also been vitalized and gives new life. The earth is alive and draws up the water from springs below to nourish and sustain the new plant life just as God's love nourishes and sustains all life."

Judas held up both hands. "Enough. I don't understand it all, but I believe you. I must go back to my guests, but I have to know about your reaction when Hannah leaned on you. The way you eat, drink, and dance, everyone's saying that you're too rambunctious to be a rabbi."

"Let them say what they will for now. As time unfolds, they will learn more, just as I am learning more about myself. And I am allowing myself to enjoy the feelings of celebration and pleasure."

Peter, Andrew, and John, their heads filled with wine, came out the back door and approached Judas and Jesus. "You must come back in," John demanded.

"We want to see what you will do next," Andrew chided.

Peter teetered, almost losing his balance. "The women will want you to 'rise' to the occasion again." Andrew and Peter looked at each other and burst into laughter.

"Go back in. I'll be there shortly," Judas replied. But the three men stayed and leaned against each other.

"Go. Go on. I'll be there," Judas said more adamantly.

Reluctantly, the three left, laughing.

Judas turned to Jesus. "If you are to be the Messiah, how can you then be affected so easily by the flesh of a woman?"

"I have asked myself the same question, and my Father has answered me. To help mankind learn more godly ways, I have to experience the ways of men through this body. To do that, I have opened up my senses to receive all of people's thoughts and feelings without judgment, as I have for you, Judas. That's how I know that your heart is good and generous and that you seek God's truth."

"But what happened with Hannah?" Judas persisted.

Jesus closed his eyes as he spoke. A smile formed on his lips as he recounted his experience. "Hannah's maidenly, maternal instincts were greatly stimulated by the wedding ceremony. Her desire to become a mother was intensely activated. I can see people's emotions; each feeling radiates a distinct color. Hannah's aura was a loving pink with deeply passionate crimson bands emanating toward me, expressing her yearning to procreate, to become a wife and a loving mother."

Jesus opened his eyes, leaned toward Judas, and said, "She sensed the intense love that I have for my Father, and that divine feeling of love attracted her to me. Her body exuded a highly sensual scent that this body received. In its memory, that scent stimulated this body to respond. Her scent stirred my heightened senses and momentarily confused me. The scent was pleasurable. When she touched my hand, her skin felt soft and warm; that further stimulated pleasurable sensations in this body. When she leaned against me, her body against mine, this body reacted even more, in a most pleasant way. When I turned and looked into her eyes," Jesus pointed to his face, "these eyes activated the natural response of men in this body, all initiated by her desires. This body felt a wonderful tingling sensation," Jesus said as he pointed to his lap, "and this body had an uninhibited, healthy reaction that was a surprise to me. These sexual areas, when not inhibited, naturally and innocently produce pleasure impulses."

Judas pursed his lips. "The way you describe it doesn't seem sinful, but people will still judge you as a lecher who is unable to control his desires."

"They judge me from their ignorance. They try and act righteous and pious, but they are hypocrites, condemning others for things that they themselves lust for."

"Dear Rabbi, these are the people that a true Messiah must lead."

"I must be true to my Father's guidance. At first, this body's sexual reaction puzzled me. Then I realized that my Father wants me to feel and know the basic drives and desires of man through this body."

"But where will that lead you?" Judas asked.

"It will lead me to greater truth. Now that I understand what occurred, it is unlikely to be a problem in the future," Jesus affirmed.

"You may walk a slippery slope," Judas replied.

"All of man's societies and cultures walk that path. God has endowed all of His creations with the vital urge of sexual arousal, animals and humankind alike. After food and water, the natural urge to copulate and procreate is a primal force to ensure the survival of future life. The forces of natural attraction are driven by love and a desire for fulfillment."

"That is true, Rabbi, but that urge can also cause anger and bloodshed between neighbors, friends, and families," Judas said.

"That is why I must learn more about man's drives, the pleasures of the flesh as well as the pains. This body has enjoyed the pleasures of good food and delicious wine. My Father wants me to continue to understand more of what the body desires."

Judas stroked his beard. "But what about love that does not include sex? The love of a child, the love of a parent?"

"I see there is great confusion regarding love and the morality of sexual pleasure. Part of my mission is to understand the conflicts between the divine and the flesh that often cause men to live in disharmony."

"There's time enough for that. You've been here barely two days. Come, let's go in now. My guests are waiting for us."

"You go, Judas. With their heads full of wine and their preconceived notions, they will only mock me. Attention should be paid to the bride and groom. I need to be by myself."

Judas stood and stretched. The sun was beginning to set. "It's getting late. I must go to my guests." He nodded to Jesus. "As you wish, I will leave you with your thoughts." Judas turned and walked into the house.

The afterglow of the sunset was fading, and stars began to brighten in the early night sky. Jesus was about to leave the premises and close the front gate behind him when he felt a tug on the other side pull the gate open. Seth, with a worried look, asked, "Where are you going? Please stay."

Jesus smiled and knelt down on one knee, facing Seth. "I need to go for a walk. There are things I must do."

"Will you come back?" Seth asked.

Jesus sighed. "I intend to, but not until the party is over."

Seth was relieved and smiled. He said, "I had two more pieces of honey cake. The piece you gave me tasted better. Where did you get it? How did you know I was thinking about honey cake?"

Jesus pointed to Seth's nose. "The space between our noses told me so. In the space around people, I am able to see images of their thoughts and desires created by the intensity of their emotions. That is where I saw your great desire for a piece of honey cake."

"I remember thinking about the honey cake all day," Seth said. "But where did you get the piece you gave me? The honey cake tray was full; not a piece was missing."

Jesus pointed up at the night sky. "My Father in Heaven showed me a way to give it to you as a reward for your hard work and your courageous heart."

"Did your Father give you the wine to give the wedding guests? I saw you stick your fingers in the water jugs."

Jesus stood and said, "My Father gives us everything." He turned to look down the street, then back at Seth.

Seth pleaded, "Don't go."

"Don't be concerned. Always remember, I am in you and you are in me, as the Father is in us. We are one with God." Jesus leaned down, kissed Seth's forehead, and said, "Someday you will become the 'Great' Seth. Tell your elders you should no longer be called 'Little.'"

The eldest priest of the secret Council of Seers knocked on Caiaphas's door. Caiaphas had been waiting for the council's response to the swarm of recent rumors. He picked up his official rectangular gold purse from the side table. The heavy purse was inlaid with twelve large gemstones. Each jewel, such as the red ruby and the green emerald, were highly polished and as large as a small egg. Aligned three across and four down, the gems shone brightly. Caiaphas hung the purse around his neck and felt its heaviness against his heart. The purse reminded him of his heavy responsibility as the High Priest of the Sanhedrin in the Temple of Jerusalem – the seat of religious and judicial authority for the twelve tribes of Israel that the twelve jewels represented.

When the elder priest knocked again, Caiaphas responded, "Enter."

The elder priest, dressed in his tunic of white linen and white hat, had a silver-gray beard and eyebrows. He stood before Caiaphas, who was seated behind a polished mahogany desk. The two men stared at one another in silence a moment; then the elder priest said, "For the first time in over ten years, all of the council's seers have agreed; the rumors are true. He's here in Jerusalem now - the Messiah has arrived."

Caiaphas looked up at the ceiling, then down at his desk. He sighed and said, "So, now it has begun."

He looked up at the seer, who solemnly replied, "Yes, it has begun."

Caiaphas looked up again, this time beyond the ceiling to the heavens above. "Where will it all end?" he implored the seer.

The seer replied, "No one knows how it will end. We only know that turbulent times will follow."

10

Jesus walked the night streets of Jerusalem. He assessed the interactions and thoughts of the diverse mixture of people and their different cultures and beliefs. Two Roman soldiers on horseback patrol approached, looked at him contemptuously, then continued on. The air cooled more rapidly as the hours passed. Jesus stopped at a stable that sheltered two horses. In one stall stood a sleek black stallion, its saddle, blanket, and bridle hung on a partition next to another stall in which stood a large, white horse. On a bench next to the stall were its saddle, assorted wares, and filled cloth sacks. Jesus heard muted laughter from a dilapidated house adjoining the stable.

He walked up to the front door, which was open six inches. A dim light shone from within. The laughter became more boisterous; Jesus opened the door. When he entered, the laughter quieted. Twenty men and women, most poorly clothed, sat at small tables around the large room. They briefly stared at him, and then returned to their conversations. Eight oil lamps illuminated the dingy room. In the corner were two big spigoted wine casks on wooden stands behind a long wood table. Beneath one cask was a wooden bucket with a dirty bar rag draped over the bucket's side. A barkeep wearing a soiled robe sat on a stool behind the table, eying Jesus.

Jesus looked around the room. Next to the long table was the only large round table, at which a woman leaned against a man who was missing his right arm. They sat with three other better-clothed men. There was one empty chair. Nearby, two women sat at a small square table with two empty chairs. At another small table sat a lone woman with one empty chair. And at another table sat a poorly dressed blind man talking with an older man. The other patrons were an earthy mix of Gentiles and Arabs who sat or stood and leaned near each other in conversation at the remaining tables. Three young men with skullcaps sat in another corner. Jesus looked back at the round table, walked directly to it, and stood behind the empty chair.

"May I join you?" he politely asked the five seated patrons.

An olive-skinned man with dark, piercing eyes set below black gull-wing eyebrows stared at Jesus, then mockingly retorted, "May you join us?"

The man's expression turned serious. He looked around at his companions and leaned toward them. His face became strikingly intense, and then his eyebrows rose. His mouth widened into an uncontrollable smile. He and his companions slowly leaned back and then burst into spontaneous laughter.

The laughter was so infectious that Jesus began to laugh also. The short, stout man with the round face seated next to the woman caught his breath and looked around at his companions. He asked Jesus, "Why do you want to sit with us?" Then he broke out in laughter again along with the others. Jesus laughed along also.

The laughter died down. The man with narrow, darting eyes stared at Jesus and said, "Why would a Jew with clean clothes and no money want to be with us?"

The woman asked Darting-Eyes, "How do you know he has no money?"

The stout man answered, "Although he is barefoot, he does possess a clean and finely woven tunic. And as our esteemed, highly professional pickpocket and thief has determined," he pointed to Darting-Eyes and then at Jesus, "he carries no jewelry or coin purse beneath his tunic."

Darting-Eyes nodded his head in acknowledgement of the stout man's words. "First time you agreed with me all night, Merchant."

The one-armed man said, "He certainly carries no weapon."

The woman squeezed the one-armed man's remaining arm and said, "Spoken just like a Roman soldier."

"An ex-Roman soldier," he responded. All were speaking as if Jesus weren't there.

Darting-Eyes looked at Gull-Wing and said, "Maybe he's here to offer you a job."

Gull-Wing's smiling face became deadly serious; his posture stiffened. He looked suspiciously at Jesus. "Are you here to take special care of someone?"

"No, nothing of that sort," Jesus replied.

"So you know about me?" The assassin's demeanor intensified again. Jesus replied, "I know that I would like to join all of you."

"Why us?" the woman asked. "Why don't you sit with that single lady over there? She can show you a good time."

The merchant leaned toward the woman. "Remember, Honey, he has no money."

Jesus said, "I want to sit with all of you because I like your glow."

"You like our glow?" The merchant snorted. He looked at his friends, and they all burst into laughter again.

"What are you up to?" the thief asked Jesus.

"I need to laugh. It makes this body feel good," Jesus replied.

The woman grabbed Jesus's arm and said, "Come on then, sit here." She pointed to the empty seat.

Jesus replied, "Thank you," and sat down.

The assassin said, "Since you have no money, I will get you something to drink." He turned to the barkeep, "Give this man some of the 'good stuff' we keep for new guests."

The barkeep looked at the assassin and said, "You mean the 'good stuff'?"

"That's right, nothing but the best for this fine man who wants to laugh."

The barkeep picked up the wooden bucket from the floor and put it on his long table. He dipped a cup into it and filled the cup to the top. Walking around the long table, he placed the cup in front of Jesus.

Jesus nodded to the barkeep, then turned to the assassin. "Thank you for your generosity."

The assassin smiled, trying not to laugh. He looked at the others, who were also trying to contain their laughter; all eyes were fixed on Jesus.

Jesus picked up the cup and brought it to his nose to sniff. He quickly jerked his head back in revulsion.

"What's the matter?" asked the thief.

"This smells unusual," Jesus replied. They all laughed, and Jesus laughed with them and said, "It feels good to laugh."

"If you want to join us, you must drink up," said the merchant.

"Go on, drink up or we'll be insulted," the soldier prodded.

Jesus looked at everyone, smiled, and then looked into his cup. He put two fingers in as if to pick something out of it.

The assassin asked, "Did a fly get in there?"

The merchant said, "I don't think flies care for that special brew." They all laughed. Jesus laughed too.

He lifted his cup toward the others and said, "Here's to an enlightening evening." He put the cup to his lips. The others leaned toward him in anticipation as Jesus took his first sip.

He held the sip in his mouth a moment, then swallowed and exhaled with a satisfying, "Ahhh, you really don't know how much I am enjoying this."

The others looked at one another, puzzled. The assassin reached up, grabbed the barkeep by his throat, pulled his head down to table level, and said, "I told you to give him the 'good stuff.'"

The barkeep's forehead beaded with sweat. "I did as you said."

Jesus spoke calmly. "Please let this man be. He did the right thing." Jesus took another sip, then looked at everyone and downed the full cup of wine. He placed it on the table and let out a long, loud "Ahhhh."

The assassin released the barkeep and then went to the bucket. He leaned over and smelled it. He quickly reared away from the bucket with a nauseated look on his face.

The others laughed. The assassin took Jesus's cup and filled it himself, then placed it in front of Jesus and said, "Have another one on us."

Jesus smiled. "You are very gracious. I thank you once more." He started to put his two fingers into the cup again when in a flash, the assassin grabbed Jesus's wrist with an iron grip.

The assassin turned Jesus's hand palm up and examined each finger and fingernail carefully. The hand was clearly empty; the others watched intently. The assassin let go.

The thief raised his eyebrows. "We are familiar with those who are 'sleight-of-hand.'"

Jesus rolled up the sleeves of his tunic, spread his fingers wide apart, turned his bare palms back to front twice, and said, "It is important to me to give this very fine wine a special blessing."

Jesus placed his two fingers in the cup again, closed his eyes for a moment, and then put the cup to his lips and took a generous mouthful. The assassin's face, only inches away, followed every movement. Jesus put down the half-empty cup, turned to face the assassin, and let out a long satisfying "Ahhh," smiling broadly.

The assassin incredulously picked up the cup, cautiously sniffing its contents. He looked suspiciously at Jesus for a moment and then sniffed again. He smiled and then shook his head and said, "No, that's impossible."

The others looked on in puzzlement once more. The assassin put a finger into the cup and then brought it cautiously to his lips. "No! How?" Then he took a sip, held it in his mouth a moment, then swallowed and emitted an "Ahhh" and said, "That is really very good wine."

The others looked on incredulously.

Jesus replied matter-of-factly, "Of course. Isn't that the 'good stuff' that you ordered for me?"

The assassin narrowed his eyes at Jesus, grinned, and then laughed. "I don't know how you did it, but it works for me."

The thief reached out for the cup. "Give it to me."

Jesus handed him the cup. The thief smelled its contents, then took a cautious sip, smiled, and then he too emitted a satisfying "Aaahhh."

How did you do it? I watched your hands. I have trained pickpockets. You are a master trickster."

The fat merchant grabbed the cup and took a sip. He rolled it in his mouth, then quickly finished the rest. He also let out a satisfied "Aaahh." "It's better wine than I have had in the emperor's courtyard!" he exclaimed. "But … that's impossible. How can the table spillage squeezed from a bar rag be turned into delicious wine?"

The soldier leaned toward Jesus. "Now it's your turn to buy a drink for my lady and me. And it better be as good for us as it was for them."

"I have no money," Jesus replied. He turned to the nervous barkeep and asked, "But if you don't mind, kind sir, may I have the balance of the bucket's contents to share with these gracious hosts?"

The barkeep backed away in disbelief. "Whatever you want. Have your fill."

The fat merchant, half jokingly, half in awe, said, "Please, please, bless the bucket first." They all laughed nervously. Jesus laughed the loudest.

The other bar patrons had periodically glanced up, curious about the laughing group seated at the round table with a Jewish stranger. The last of the bucket's contents was being consumed as the conversation progressively became more serious. The assassin replied to Jesus's assertions, "Plants fight other plants and rob them of sun, water and earth for their own benefit. Are plants thieves? Animals and fish kill and eat other animals and fish. Are they murderers also? Does your Moses's commandment of 'Thou shalt not murder or steal' make animals and plants sinners?"

Jesus affirmed, "Animals fight in defense of mates or when attacked and kill for food to survive. Men can choose other ways to survive, but they rarely need to kill their own kind. Life is precious. It is a gift of the Creator and should be cherished."

The assassin sat back. "Life is but a short shadow cast on the sand, a brief silhouette in this world, and one way or another is soon gone. I merely shorten the time of men's shadows."

Jesus replied, "Life is an opportunity to create rather than destroy. 'Thou shalt not murder' is God's commandment. Moses was the deliverer of God's message for the misguided Jews of the time who worshipped false idols."

The assassin narrowed his eyes. "So why do the different sects of Jews, the Zealots, the Pharisees, the Sadducees, and the Essenes, pay me to kill for them just like the Romans pay me to kill for them?" The assassin leaned toward Jesus, "Gentiles also pay me to kill for them. I have no desire to kill for the sake of killing. I kill for the sake of making a livelihood for myself."

Jesus replied, "To willingly take a life is a sin."

The assassin cocked his head defiantly and demanded, "Are you judging me?"

Jesus stared at the space above the assassin's head, reflected a moment, and said, "No. I don't judge people. God judges them."

"That's your God, not mine. I am a Bedouin. But if you say you are the Son of God and you forgive sinners for their misdeeds, then you will forgive me, even though I don't seek forgiveness. Besides, you said life goes on after death in your Heaven. So my work only hastens a life from this wretched world to a better world." The assassin grinned. "I should charge an extra fee to those whose transport I have expedited."

They all laughed, and the merchant added, "At least they won't come back and complain that they're unhappy with your services." They laughed louder.

Jesus shook his head. "No. The values of this world have become distorted. I see that you have yet to realize that you are a part of those you kill, and in doing so, you kill a part of yourself. Jesus rocked back in his chair and sighed. "Here I have come to replenish this body with feelings of pleasure, and we are talking about death."

The assassin stared coldly at Jesus. "I will tell you about the feeling of great pleasure. It was when I was fourteen and made my first kill. He was a vile pig, a big, ugly, muscular man. He brutally raped my eleven-year-old sister. She hemorrhaged for four agonizing days, writhing in torturous pain. I stayed by her bedside holding her hand, and each day her grip grew weaker, then limp and colder, then …gone forever."

The assassin lowered his voice almost to a whisper, but his intensity increased acutely. "I knew that pig was camping by an outer oasis. I went there and begged for money to buy food for my sick parents and my brothers and sisters. He spat on me and told me to leave. I begged to stay the night because it was too far to walk in the dark, and I told him I would draw water from the well for his camel."

He stared at me as if I were an inconsequential camel fly. In a silent threat, he pulled open his robe, resting his hand on his hips to display his large dagger. In a most admiring way, I instantly complimented him on how awesome the handle of the dagger looked. It was black with carved, blood-red zigzag stripes running up and down the length. I told him, 'That dagger's blade must be magnificent.' I begged him to let me see it."

"He stepped toward me, towering over me. He stuck out his chest and said, 'When I draw my dagger, blood flows.'"

"The way he said it sent a cold shiver down my spine. He saw my reaction and then laughed at me and said, 'Fetch the water, little flea; then maybe I'll give you a little peek you won't forget.'"

The assassin sat back and grinned. "I cowered, pretending fear to gain his confidence; and as one who is obedient, I watered his camel. Afterward I begged him to see what must be the finest dagger in the land. He said, 'Go home, little flea. Leave me.' But I kept puffing him up until I got the best of his pride. Finally he drew near and stood over me menacingly. He leaned down close to my face, and in a deep, threatening voice, he spoke. 'Do you really want me to draw this dagger? I told you that when I do, blood flows.'"

"My breath became very rapid." The assassin raised his bold eyebrows and said, "He thought I was afraid of him. I answered in a voice tense from the tightness in my throat. 'Please, I really want to see it.'"

"With a sinister hiss, he said, 'Then you shall.'"

"Still bent over me, he looked down at his side at his dagger, and then he started to draw it from its sheath. As he turned to face me, he pulled his dagger up toward my throat and said, 'What do you think of...'"

The assassin paused and looked around the table at his intent listeners and then continued, "Those were his last words. I slashed his throat in one fast swipe with the razor-sharp knife that was strapped to my leg."

The assassin grimaced. "My sister's death was the saddest of all pains I've ever felt." Then he smiled with deep satisfaction. "Killing her murderer was the greatest pleasure I've ever had. To see that bleeding pig's shocked eyes bulge and his massive body writhe on the ground in pain like my sister writhed gave me even more pleasure. Hearing the beast's gasping breath in his open throat as he tried to yell out in pain, but with no air to make a voice, gave me supreme pleasure!"

The assassin turned to Jesus, who was visibly distraught. "My magical friend, you seem shaken."

Jesus breathed in deeply and then exhaled with a sigh. "Your intensity conveyed the feelings and images of your experience in a manner more vivid than you can imagine. I truly understand how you feel."

The assassin sneered, "How can a man like you know of such things?"

Jesus gazed above the assassin's head a moment and said, "I know that after you killed him, you castrated him."

Stunned, the assassin sat back in his chair. He studied Jesus's face and said, "So, you have the gift of 'the sight'?" The assassin sat proudly upright and said, "For what he did to my sister, my only regret is that I had to kill him first and couldn't hear the fat pig's squeals. That would have been the sweetest sound my ears would ever hear."

Jesus placed his hands over the assassin's hand. "Some would say it's revenge; some would say it's justice – an eye for an eye. I don't judge you. I forgive you."

The assassin jerked his hand away. "Forgive me? For what? I brought honor to my family." From under the table, in one swift movement, he drew up a long-bladed dagger with red zigzag stripes carved into the handle and plunged the point deep into the tabletop. He defiantly declared, "And I have brought honor to myself."

The room fell silent; all heads turned toward their table. The assassin looked around the room at those looking at him as he wiggled the blade free, then held the point toward the onlookers. They immediately looked away and resumed their conversations.

Jesus spoke softly. "I understand why you did what you did to honor your sister. It is what you do now for money, not in defense of your family, that I forgive you for."

Indignantly, the assassin replied, "What I do now is my business."

The soldier added defensively, "I've had to kill also. If I didn't follow orders, I'd be tortured and killed as an example." He pointed to his shoulder with the missing arm. "Because I fell asleep one night on guard duty, they cut off my right arm, saying I was unworthy to defend the Empire. Then they sent me away to live as a beggar." He picked up his drink, downed the contents, and laughed to himself, "They didn't know that I was left-handed."

The woman kissed the soldier's cheek and looked admiringly at him. "You are far more 'handy' than anyone I've met with two hands." She patted his lap mischievously.

Jesus focused on a space a foot in front of the soldier's face and said, "I see the reason for your pain and dismay."

The soldier cast a curious look at Jesus. "How can you possibly know how I feel?"

"I can see that you fought bravely in sixteen battles and that you suffered many wounds. You were prepared to die with honor in battle."

Jesus focused more intently on the empty space, then reached over and placed his hand on the soldier's right shoulder stump, saying, "Before that fateful night, you had been up for three straight days. Your commander still assigned you to guard duty because of the shortage of men. You strained to keep your head up. You closed your eyes for what you thought were only a few moments, then fell into a deep sleep."

The soldier pulled back in disbelief. "How could you know that? You do have 'the sight.' What else do you see?"

Jesus replied, "You have unquestionable courage and high ideals. You feel discarded and disgraced, but be not dismayed," Jesus turned to the woman, "for you have a mate who admires the good in you and loves you truly for who you are. She fondly calls you 'one-arm.'"

"Rachel is my true love," said the soldier.

Rachel kissed the soldier's cheek. "That's for sure."

Jesus addressed Rachel. "And you like to speak forthrightly. Sometimes people are insulted when they don't like what you say, but still, they admire your honesty. Many others regard your opinions highly because they are well thought out, yet your heart guides you best. When you were younger …"

Rachel interrupted, "I don't want to hear what happened to me in the past. I am who I am now, and I am content with myself."

"Yes you are," Jesus replied. "However there is one important thing that I must communicate to you."

Jesus beckoned her closer. Rachel leaned close to him. Jesus suddenly poked her side with his two fingers. She instantly pulled back, clutching her side, and burst into hysterical laughter.

Her soldier companion said, "You got her right in her tickle spot."

Rachel caught her breath as her uncontrolled laughter started to subside. Jesus raised his two fingers once more and only pointed them at her tickle spot. In anticipation, Rachel burst out laughing again. So infectious was her laughter that soon all at the table were laughing in a most good-hearted way.

As the laughter subsided, the thief tapped the table with his knuckles. "If you have 'the sight,' what do you see of me?"

Jesus turned toward the thief, whose eyes quickly darted away and then back to Jesus, who said, "I see the time when you were a small boy who never knew his father, abandoned by his mother to survive on his own. You begged for food, and when none was given, you would steal what you could in the marketplace and run. You were caught many times, and many times you were severely beaten."

The thief's darting eyes stilled and became damp.

Jesus continued, "You are quick of wit and plotted your thefts of food more carefully so as not to be caught. Still, your face and reputation became known in the market and you were shunned."

The thief shifted his weight in the chair; his eyes darted around the room, then back toward Jesus.

"You decided to steal money and jewelry, which would sustain you longer when you traded it for food. That would reduce your need to steal daily, thus reducing your chances of being caught. As you grew older, your daring became bolder, and your thefts became more lucrative. In Rome, you stole a jade box containing gold necklaces, bracelets, coins, and other jewels from a senator. You were thrilled that you would be comfortable for the first time in your life, but when you tried to sell a gold bracelet, the buyer, a friend of the senator, recognized it. He alerted the Roman guard, and you were arrested and tortured."

The thief clenched his jaw and stared at Jesus.

"You were to be executed but were able to escape at the last minute. You ran away like you ran away as a child. You've run here to Jerusalem. You constantly look about in fear, like a hunted animal being stalked."

The thief burst out, "Stop! No more! I believe you have 'the sight.'"

"I will say only this: you are smart enough to figure out a way to make an honest living and start a new life without stealing and without fear in this land far from Rome."

The merchant studied Jesus's face, scratched the top of his head, and said, "Remarkable. I've never come across someone like you. I'm fascinated. Can you tell anything about me?"

Jesus studied the merchant a moment, smiled, and said, "You are a rambunctious one. I see you take delight in the finer qualities of life. You have developed a sophisticated tongue for subtle tastes and a gifted tongue for speaking and bargaining. You have an astute eye for knowing whether buyers can afford to pay more and how eager they are to obtain your wares despite their efforts to conceal their desires."

Jesus held up his cup toward the merchant and took the remaining sip of his wine. He let out a satisfying "Aaahh" and then said, "I see that you like wine, and you like women, many women. You also are intrigued by the philosophies and religions of the different cultures that you encounter in your travels. I also see that your appetites are relentless and you often overindulge to satisfy an inner hunger that the material world cannot provide."

The merchant squirmed and rubbed his ear nervously.

Jesus continued, "Your father was always harsh and critical of you. When you were a little boy, he would admonish you for the slightest misstep and pull and twist your ear painfully. He would always assault your left ear, and you would retreat and hide, rubbing and soothing your ear as you do now."

The merchant quickly pulled his hand away from his ear and said, "My father is dead. He can't hurt me anymore. Tell me how you can know these things."

Jesus replied, "I can see your glows; the colors express how you feel. You are surrounded by patterns of light and thought-forms of people, places and events that have been significant in your life. I can experience the feelings and physical sensations associated with your past, the smells, touches, sounds, pleasures, and pains. I can feel your pain at your father's rejection and his disapproval of your young, innocent behavior." The merchant rubbed his ear again. Jesus smiled compassionately at him and said, "I pray that you will believe in my Father in Heaven, who is the Father of all sons and all daughters. He accepts and fervently loves all His children. Accept yourself lovingly, for you are a part of Him."

Jesus put his palms on the table and leaned toward the merchant. "I prefer not to look at people's backgrounds. However, you asked me to do so." Jesus looked at the others around the table. "Other times, I see things because it is important to connect myself to a person's essence so that I may heal or help enlighten."

He turned back to the merchant. "Your father's denying you love in your childhood has played a prominent part in your overindulgences."

The merchant nodded in acknowledgement, then pulled his hand away from rubbing his ear and sharply clapped his hands together. He picked up his empty cup and said, "Enough of my miserable childhood. My adult palette clamors for another taste of your delicious alchemy. We are all wine lovers and appreciate your magic liquid pleasures."

One-Arm and Rachel lifted their cups also. "Yes, yes," Rachel said.

One-Arm added, "Come on, do your God-thing."

Darting-Eyes looked over at the barkeep, who stared mesmerized at the group. "Fill a large pitcher of real wine for us," said the thief. He turned to Jesus. "Do your trick."

Jesus replied, "It's not a trick; it's a blessing."

The barkeep placed a full pitcher of wine in the middle of the table. The assassin moved it in front of Jesus and said, "Now bless us with something very special." Then he laughed.

Jesus replied, "You shall have something very special." And addressing the others, "You shall all have something very special."

Jesus closed his eyes and dipped two fingers into the pitcher. He concentrated for a few seconds and then removed his fingers. He smiled and then filled everyone's cups. He held up his cup and said, "Dear Father in Heaven, King of all gods in all universes, we thank you for creating this fruit of the vine. Let us all say 'Amen.'"

They all tapped their cups together, and all said "Amen."

The other patrons looked on in disbelief. One of the three young Jewish men said to his friend, "Can you believe it? He has them saying prayers."

The merchant brought his cup to his nose, inhaled, and raised his eyebrows. "What an elegant bouquet!" He took a small sip. "Very dry, but extremely smooth. It even has a hint of licorice. Remarkable blend. The very best I've ever tasted."

Rachel said, "No, it's not dry, but it has a sweet taste like wild berries and apricots, yet very delicate." She took another sip, rolled her eyes upward, and said, "Mmmm, delicious. I can even taste a touch of cocoa."

One-Arm said, "No, it's not sweet; it has an earthy, robust taste. That's exactly the way I like it."

The assassin said, "You're all wrong; it has a wonderful bitter taste like the wine my grandfather kept in his favorite jug for special occasions."

The thief finished his sip, took another, and said, "It warms my throat in a most pleasant way. This is a blessing indeed."

The merchant held his cup up to the others, laughed, and said, "This is more than a blessing; it's a miracle."

Darting-Eyes tapped his cup against the merchant's cup and said, "Let's all say 'Amen.'"

The merchant replied, "I'll not only say 'Amen,' I'll kiss the Rabbi's two fingers."

Rachel tapped her cup against Jesus's cup. "God bless you."

Jesus winked. "He certainly has."

———

Darting-Eyes picked up the large pitcher, which was now three-quarters consumed, poured another round, and said to Jesus, "I'm not complaining, but I'm very curious. How is it possible that we all find this wine the most delicious that we can remember, yet we all experience different tastes?"

"Your perceptions color what you see. Your lives are all unique, and you each experience this world from your own point of view. You anticipated something very special in this pitcher of wine, and you received it," Jesus replied. "When I blessed the wine, I prayed that you would all taste it as special and delicious. It was up to God and each of your individual expectations to blend the tastes to suit your expectations."

"You are a puzzling and mysterious man," the assassin said. "Those traits would normally make me suspicious, yet your manner makes me feel that I can trust you."

"Thank you. From you, I know that's a true compliment. Except for this brave soldier who sometimes trusts too readily, and Rachel, who trusts wisely, the rest of you usually trust no one," Jesus replied. "However, I do see that you all deeply trust each other, a rare occurrence in this land. That trust is a result of true friendship."

The merchant lifted his cup, "I trust you enough to have you as my partner. I'll supply the water, you turn it into fine magic wine, and we'll make a fortune."

Loud yelling suddenly erupted at a small table. A man stood and raised his fist to the man sitting across from him. He furiously yelled, "You...you...you cheated me!" His face turned red; the veins in his neck bulged. "I'm going to ..." Suddenly his eyes rolled back. He fell to the floor and curled on his side, elbows to his stomach, and began to convulse. Foamy saliva poured from his mouth.

Except for Jesus's table, all those at the other tables stood up and scrambled to the far corner. One of the prostitutes pointed at the shaking man and shouted, "He's possessed with demons! Stay away! The Devil has him!"

Everyone backed further away, pressing against the walls.

Jesus stood, calmly walked over to the convulsing man, and knelt beside him. He placed one hand on the man's shaking head and held his other hand over the man's chest. Jesus took a deep breath, then simultaneously exhaled forcibly and pulled both of his hands away in a drawing-out motion. Jesus placed his hands a foot over the man's head and abdomen and made fast repetitive sweeping motions as if he were brushing off invisible dust. Then with both hands, Jesus made slower, soft, caressing motions over the convulsing man's body. The convulsions began to subside. Jesus placed one hand on the man's forehead and his other hand on the man's chest and said, "All will be well now."

The man's eyes opened. Beads of sweat dotted his face. He saw everyone looking at him and asked, "What happened?"

Jesus stood up and said, "You are a peaceful man, but your surge of violent anger created a severe inner conflict. It has now been resolved. You will be fine." Jesus walked back to his table.

The man on the ground wiped the foam from his mouth and looked disoriented. His companions helped him up. Slowly the others returned to their tables, casting looks at the disheveled man, then at Jesus, then back at the man.

The assassin asked Jesus, "How did you do that?'

"I'll tell you, although you may not understand. That man's intense anger created patterns of black lightning bolts in his aura. His energy field surrounded him in vapors of dark, ugly, red-brown colors. Those vapors were in stark contrast to his benevolent belief in peace and non-violence. They caused immense turmoil and conflict between his heart and his mind. His anger grew to an unbelievable level; he was about to strike his longtime friend, who had just admitted that he had cheated him. However, his love for his friend prevented him from doing so and 'seized' his body. But his surging anger persisted, and his rapid shifts between love and anger caused him to collapse, taking no action, yet his body could not let go of his conflicting emotions, which were exhibited in his back-and-forth shaking movements."

The assassin persisted, "But how did you help him?"

"With God's power in my hands, I was able to pull away and cast off the dark vapors and bolts of anger that had encapsulated the man."

Rachel asked, "Is that what you did when you made that 'whisk-away' motion with your hands?"

"Yes," Jesus replied.

One-Arm asked, "What were you doing with your other hand over his head?"

"I was directing God's light of comfort and love to shine brighter and replace the cast-off darkness."

"But what were you doing above his body with that wavy soothing motion of your hands? It made me feel almost jealous. I wanted you to do it to me," Rachel added.

"As God's light enters a person's aura, it separates into beautiful colors, like a rainbow, each color vibrating like strings on a harp. I was tuning and harmonizing the color vibrations of his light with the flow of my hands," Jesus replied.

Darting-Eyes pointed toward the recovering man on the other side of the room. "To my eyes, he looked like he was possessed by a demon. That's what everyone thinks."

Jesus said, "A person's own distorted thinking creates his personal dilemmas, which can seemingly become personal demons of sorts. When a person becomes fixated on his distorted, demon-like thoughts and constantly focuses his anger or dissatisfaction or fears on those so-called 'demons,' those images become more intense and embedded in his mind. Those self-created thought-forms are a type of bondage that affects people's personalities. For each person affected, the causes will vary, but inner conflicts will always be present."

"So what can one do if you are not around to help them?" Darting-Eyes asked.

Jesus looked intently at Darting-Eyes and said, "You yourself have the power to un-create those demons that you have created, and in their stead, you can create angels to guide you. You are not the child you were. You are in a different place in a different time, and you can live differently. When you turn away from these demons and you focus on the good in life and devote yourself to acting in ways that will yield mutual benefit to all, then those inner demons will evaporate like a small puddle of water in the hot desert sun."

Darting-Eyes quickly looked around the room, then back at Jesus and said, "Most of these people blame the Devil for their diseases and hardships. Are you saying there is no Devil?"

Jesus replied, "The Devil is a creation of man and has no power over God. Man has used the Devil like a scapegoat to blame it for his problems and absolve himself of wrongdoing." He turned to the assassin and said, "I must apologize to you for having said that your killing was a sin. I am still learning. When I am one with God's light as I was when helping that shaking man, I become more enlightened."

The assassin challenged Jesus. "You say that there is no Devil and there is no sin. But your God says, 'Thou shalt not murder,' for that is a sin."

Jesus affirmed, "You should not murder. Murder that is not for defense of home, family, or life should not be done. There are man-made laws to punish murder. However, killing is still a horrible mistake. But in God's eyes, there is no evil."

The assassin said, "Then are you saying that when I take a life for money, I am not sinning – I am only making a mistake?" He turned to his friends and said, "It's fortunate that I can make a good living from making mistakes."

Jesus's voice became firm. "Do not take this lightly. For in time, in this life or the afterlife, you will become more enlightened to the spiritual laws that supersede man-made laws. Because you are a portion of God, you will have to judge your own actions from God's point of view."

"Does your God expect me to punish myself?" the assassin asked.

Jesus replied, "When you finally open your heart to God's eternal love and feel the oneness and interconnectedness of all life, you will realize the error of your ways. Then you will want to redeem yourself."

Jesus put his hand over the assassin's hand and continued, "My Father is all forgiving, and my Father allows you to forgive yourself. My Father has given you life to create and to interact beneficially with all life. You have free will to create in this world like no other plant or animal. Killing wantonly is a waste of my Father's creative potential, and it's a mistake. You can correct your ways and do more with your life and fulfill the opportunity my Father has given you to be a co-creator."

The assassin stared at his hands in deep thought, then, staring at Jesus, questioned, "You say that I am a co-creator?"

"Yes," Jesus replied.

Rachel tapped Jesus's shoulder. "You speak of your 'Father in Heaven' – what does 'He' look like?"

Jesus's face relaxed. He closed his eyes and passionately said, "My Father is infinite love. He is unlimited creativity. He is here now, and He is in the past and in the future. And He is beyond the beyond. Yet He is much more than that. He is more than can be imagined."

"But what does 'He' look like? Is He very old, tall, or is He good-looking…" she smiled at Jesus and teased, "like you?"

One-Arm grabbed her shoulder, pulled her closer to him, and goodheartedly said, "Hey, you're with me."

"Of course," she replied jabbing One-Arm playfully with her elbow. "I want to know what his Father in Heaven looks like."

Jesus addressed her, "There are no words that can describe Him, for He is not a man, nor is He a woman. He is a Force, not a person. He is an ineffable and eternal power that energizes and connects all life. He is unlimited love. Those are only words that hint at my Father. He is beyond description. Mere words would only diminish Him. He is God. That is why our scriptures had no word for God. He was so sacredly revered and ineffable that no one was permitted to call Him by a name. 'He' could only be referred to by the sound, *YAHWEH.*"

Rachel put her hand to the side of her face, paused a moment in thought, and said, "So you can't describe your God with words, but you do describe the feeling of how His Force moves you. Too bad. I think He would be more appealing if He were a man who was strong, wise, and kind." She leaned against One-Arm. "A man like my hero here and not some invisible force."

Jesus nodded. "I agree that most people think of God as a 'Him' having a physical human form, and that is why I say 'He.' But you asked me to tell you what He looked like, and I answered you. Because God is everywhere in all things, one's eyes can never see more than a fragment of God's expression and then not realize that they are seeing only a part of Him. But your heart has a sense that can feel God." Jesus spoke solemnly, his voice penetrating. "And when you do feel at one with God, as I do, then you will have no doubt."

Rachel's shoulders trembled. "The way you say things makes me want to believe you. You speak openly about deep things in a way that I trust. Can you connect me to your God?"

Jesus replied, "God already dwells within you. It is my mission to teach people that truth. My teachings, healings and deeds are intended to awaken mankind from their ignorance."

Jesus looked at the thief and then the assassin and said, "What I have told you are now seeds of truth within you. As time passes and you give thought and deliberation to what I have said as a possibility, those seeds of truth will blossom in your hearts, enlighten your minds, and guide your actions."

The merchant said to Jesus, "You are a strange one indeed. You are a master psychic and a healer, and you could use your powers to become a rich man, yet all the material possessions that you have in this world are your tunic and skullcap, not even a pair of sandals."

Jesus replied, "I possess the greatest riches that a man can acquire, the bounty of comfort and peace that comes with the knowledge and feeling that I am one with my Father in Heaven." Jesus cast his eyes around the room and then back to the merchant. "I look upon all those here as brothers and sisters – the Gentiles, the Jews, the Arabs, all people from all lands – we are all God's children and of one family – His family."

Darting-Eyes said, "If we are all one family, then we aren't a very happy family."

"At least let us be happy at this table," said the merchant. "Our conversation is getting too serious."

"You are right," Jesus responded. He turned toward Rachel and poked her side just below her ribs.

Rachel instantly broke out in a contagious laugh.

One-Arm drew Rachel's face to his and kissed her passionately. She closed her eyes and melted into him, then slowly pulled away, her face glowing. She turned to Jesus and said, "That makes me feel heavenly, so that must be your God's love flowing through me."

Darting-Eyes said mockingly, "That's lust, my dear."

"God bless lust," said the merchant. "It keeps the body moving in delightful ways."

The assassin asked Jesus, "Do you have a woman?"

Jesus shifted uncomfortably and said, "No, that's why I've come here tonight: to experience the pleasure of a woman's company and to understand why this body continues to have its fleshly urges when my mind sees no reason for it."

The merchant laughed. "There doesn't have to be a reason. Pleasure is the best measure." He called out to the lone woman at the table near them. "Ruth, come over here and meet our friend in need."

Rachel whispered to Jesus, "She's having a slow night, and she's been looking at you."

The assassin said, "Remember, our friend has no money."

Darting-Eyes said with a laugh, "We could take up a collection."

Ruth, a slender, attractive Samaritan, walked over to the group and stood next to Jesus. She put a hand on his shoulder. Jesus sat spine-straight against his chair and looked up at her.

She patted his back. "Relax. We all want a good time."

One-Arm laughed, "He's stiff in the wrong place."

Jesus said, "This doesn't feel right."

Two men came into the room and walked to the table where the two unattended women sat. The women invited the men to join them, and all leaned close together and spoke in low voices.

Ruth's delicate fingers stroked Jesus's hair. His posture stiffened even more.

She said, "You are a handsome and healthy man." Ruth tilted up his chin. "And you have incredible eyes. But you are too tense; I know just what you need."

Jesus pulled his head away from her caressing hand. He turned and looked behind him and saw that the two men with the two women were Andrew and Saul from the wedding party. They looked up and saw Jesus. In a loud voice they simultaneously blurted, "RABBI?"

11

The sun had risen an hour earlier. Beneath the palm tree, which had grown fuller and greener, Jesus sat in deep thought. The new grass was higher, and songbirds perched in the tree, singing crisp, melodic choruses.

Judas opened the door to the courtyard. He saw Jesus and exclaimed, "There you are!"

He walked to Jesus's side. "Where have you been? Andrew came back here after they saw you drinking in that tavern. He left quickly and said it was too late to stay and talk. He seemed very disturbed. I went there to get you, but you had left."

Jesus looked at Judas and said, "Have you ever thought about the 'fullness of time'?"

"The 'fullness of time'? What are you talking about?" Judas asked.

"I needed to step away from man's mind and think in God's terms so that I can bring His thinking to the minds of men. The 'fullness of time' is what God sees as all of history. He chooses a time when His age-old plan for mankind to evolve must move forward. That is why he has sent me as His Son at this time, to deliver His message and plant the seeds of truth to bloom in the future."

Judas looked down at Jesus, puzzled, and said, "Rabbi, the 'fullness of time' may be one thing, but how can you call yourself the Son of God, be a rabbi, and consort with murderers, thieves, and prostitutes? A rabbi is supposed to be a teacher of the Law. Such a teacher must be an example of righteous living and not someone who associates with people so foul."

"You judge me too harshly, Judas. Be forewarned: he who judges harshly shall be harshly judged. You think consorting with those who may appear downtrodden to you is sinful. But then, to whom shall I devote my God-gifted talents? To the rich and pious who perceive themselves to be holy and above the masses or to those downtrodden who live misguided lives and suffer hardships of body and soul?"

"But you don't understand, Rabbi. At the wedding party, everyone saw your arousal with Hannah. Then at the tavern, Andrew and Saul saw a prostitute stroking your hair while you sat and drank wine with a murderer and a thief. Your reputation is badly soiled."

"I care not what they think, for they project their own images of lust and sin upon me. Sin is in the eye of the beholder and is for God to judge."

"But Rabbi, I know that you do have true gifts; why are you squandering them?"

Jesus's voice became firm. "You have not been listening to what I have said. Your mind is fixed on what others are thinking."

Jesus stood up, placed his hands on Judas's shoulders, and said, "Look at this tree above us. Hear the birdsong. Feel the new grass beneath your feet where two days ago there was only dust. Have these gifts to your home been a squandering of my talents?"

Judas looked up at the tree, then down at the grass, and said sheepishly, "No, these are very good things. They are blessings, and I am grateful to you. That is why I don't want your reputation to be tarnished."

"Then don't let the opinions of others sway the feelings of your heart and soul. And don't judge me for what may appear to be a misuse of my gifts. When you receive the benefits of my gifts, you judge my deeds as good; but when others whom you do not approve of may benefit, you judge me as committing wrongful acts."

"I am sorry if I misspoke. I was upset that others are painting you with a dark brush. Your presence is new to me, and I need more time to understand and accept all that you say, for the magnitude of what you say your purpose is…it's often beyond belief."

"You must have faith, Judas. This tree and new grass, the wine for the wedding party that all of your guests enjoyed, were born of my faith and trust in my Father. I ask that you keep your faith and trust in me, for I need your help to fulfill my mission."

"I will try, Rabbi. Please be patient with me. I do become confused by the things you do. After your incident with Hannah, then you were seen with a prostitute stroking your hair. What was I to think?"

"Judas, you should think that in all my actions, however they may appear on the surface, at deeper levels are for the highest good; for it is God's work that is my mission and His divine guidance that leads me to opportunities to fulfill that mission."

"I will try not to doubt you, Rabbi. Can you tell me what you have learned about mankind's sexual compulsions?"

"To begin with, the premise that religious teachings have led men to believe that the flesh is in opposition to the spirit is certainly a false belief, for the spirit and the flesh are one."

"But sexual drives have caused so many hardships."

"That can happen; however, those same drives are necessary to create new life and are as natural as the melodies that emanate from the songbirds' hearts. Man must realize that God has breathed the spirit of life into earth's elements and has created the flesh, which is the physical embodiment of the spirit. The flesh is the spirit manifested and is God's gift to man. The flesh is created from the dust of the earth, and when man stops breathing, the spirit leaves the body and the body decomposes back to dust."

"What has that got to do with sex?"

"It is not animal instinct alone that drives the sexual needs of the flesh; one's spirit also propels and directs that force. The sexual-spiritual compulsion that drives people to join is a way of seeking love and fulfillment, a union of two that can become one in spirit, if only for a brief time."

"But we have been led to believe that the Devil uses sexual urges to manipulate man."

Jesus replied simply, "There is no 'real' Devil."

Exasperated, Judas threw his hands up in the air. "How can you say that?"

Jesus patted the grass next to him. "Sit down, Judas, and hear me as a friend."

When Judas sat, Jesus said, "I will speak to you as the man Jesus. Although I am one with that man, I am not that man. Yet I speak as one with him. When I was stranded in the desert, exhausted and dying of thirst, I felt death was close. I had lived my life trying to teach God's laws, but only a few would listen; all others mocked me. I could not gather enough offerings for the poor whom I served to sustain them or myself. I had to earn money from carpentry work for food. I had always felt a deep inner compulsion to serve God, and at that time in the desert, when I felt life ebbing away from me, I felt that God had abandoned me. I thought that if God could not or would not help me, then I would seek help from the Devil."

Judas looked askance at Jesus, "How could you, a rabbi, turn to the Devil?"

"I was at the lowest point in my life. Desperation and weakness were fueled by exhaustion and rejection from my family, friends, some of those I had helped, and the whole of my town. I felt I had lost everything. In those moments I thought that there was no God, only evil created by the Devil in this life. I called out to the Devil to help me. I pleaded with him to offer me a bargain for a better life."

Judas asked, "What happened?"

Jesus smiled and lifted his palms. "Nothing happened, absolutely nothing. There was nothing left for me to do but resign myself to my last miserable breaths of life and die. That is when I entered into the majesty of my Father's light and he spoke to me." Jesus's expression became serene.

"What did He say?" Judas asked impatiently.

"More important than what He said is what I felt. His white light enfolded and permeated me, not unlike the light that you and I shared in our dream. I felt a calmness within myself that I had never experienced - a depth of peace and serenity, yet at the same time I also felt a magnificent power and timeless wisdom that caused me to tremble, as it does even now."

"What did He say?" Judas prodded again.

"He said that I had lost faith in Him and turned to the Devil but that there was no true Devil to be found. There was only Him, my heavenly Father."

"Then why did He abandon you?" Judas asked.

"I needed to feel what it was like for people to lose all hope and faith, to feel agonizing pain and desperation so severe that even a righteous man would turn to a Devil for help. This was a necessary component of my understanding so that I could help lift mankind from its delusion that all evil is caused by a Devil. God never abandoned me; it was I who had abandoned Him when I lost my faith."

"Dear Rabbi, the Bible speaks of the Devil and his influences and the consequences to people's lives. Are you contradicting what is written? Isn't it your oath as a rabbi to teach the Holy Scriptures?"

"I am becoming a teacher of higher truths, of which my Father has spoken to me. I am not to be a repeater of past interpretations of scriptures that - thousands of years later - have not improved the brotherhood of man with the foundation of love, compassion, and forgiveness that is necessary for mankind to grow beyond embracing hatred, wars, and avarice. Those wretched traits were created by man, not a fictitious Devil."

Puzzled, Judas said, "Through all the ages, the Devil has played a recognized role in man's religious history. Satan tempts man with riches and the power to control others. If one bargains with the Devil, then eternal hell and damnation shall be their reward. This is what we have been taught."

"That's what I also thought, Judas. I questioned God about that, and He laughed and said that a Satan cannot promise man the power to control the world, for the world is His creation and He dwells in every part. God gives man divine freedom to control his lot in life, but no person or Devil can control the world, for the world is God."

"If there is no Devil, then are you also saying that there is no Hell?"

"Oh, there is the Hell of man's creation of a Hell, and as long as man believes in his own creation of a Hell, then it has a reality, but only for those who believe in it. In God's kingdom, there is no real Devil, and there is no real Hell. All That Is is God's Kingdom. Hell is a fabrication of the human mind, and man must contend with his own creations."

Judas pondered Jesus's words and then asked, "So then, the Devil can't take a person's soul?"

"No imaginary Devil can take one's soul because all souls are of God and a portion of God. No entity of any kind can trick away, bargain away, or steal away anyone or anything from God, for all entities and all things are partakers of God. God is in everything, and everything is in God, who offers eternal love and salvation to all."

"Are you saying that the Holy Scriptures are false when they speak of the Devil?"

"It is the interpretations that have not been appropriately explained. All things that man conceives of become reality within his mind to a greater or lesser extent. As a lonely child may create imaginary friends to play with, men may create a Devil thought-form to take the blame for man's misdeeds. The more evil characteristics and powers that man bestows on an imaginary Devil, the more that Devil becomes a greater reality to those who believe it to be so. When large groups believe in their own mass creation of a Devil as being real, then that thought-form becomes a greater collective reality to them, as a child's imaginary friend becomes a reality to the child."

"In time, a child outgrows his imaginary friends, but the Devil still plays an active role in men's lives and has power over men's lives," Judas said.

"Yes," Jesus replied, "because those men have given that power to their Devil and have relinquished their own power and have turned away from God's true power as I did. I must try to help mankind evolve, become enlightened and outgrow its belief in its imaginary Devil as children grow and shed their belief in imaginary friends."

Judas shook his head. "Religion teaches that man will go to Hell as punishment for his sins. If there is no real Hell or punishment in the afterlife for sinful acts, then what will prevent man from sinning?"

"Judas, you have lived long enough to see mankind sin in most ways possible. The threat of damnation and Hell has not ended sin. It is the ignorance of spiritual laws that creates sin, as you understand sin, and it will be enlightenment and the practice of spiritual laws that will prevent man from sinning."

"Then what can make the Devil disappear from the minds of men?"

"Man may always think of the Devil in certain terms as children may remember their imaginary friends when they grow up, but in time, people recognize that their childhood friends were imaginary, and adults do not give those childhood friends any power in their adult minds. For mankind to grow to a higher level of consciousness, man must abandon the unenlightened beliefs that weigh down his growth, and in so doing, man will ascend to a higher level in harmony with my heavenly Father."

"What you say, Rabbi, is hard to believe," Judas said.

"At first it was also hard for me to believe," Jesus replied. "Yet my Father's voice resonated in every fiber of my being in such a way that I could not doubt the veracity of His words. I closed my eyes and prayed for His forgiveness for forsaking Him. I asked if He would help guide me and give me sustenance to spread His Word."

"What happened then?" Judas asked.

Jesus bowed his head in reverence and closed his eyes in silence. Judas looked at him and felt the ecstatic peace of Jesus's demeanor and was imbued with it. A beautiful multicolored butterfly landed on Jesus's shoulder, its large wings gracefully sweeping up and down.

When Jesus looked up and saw the butterfly, he smiled and said, "In answer to my request for His guidance and sustenance, He said, 'A loving father would not give his lost son who has come home a brick when he is in need of food. I will always bestow upon you my forgiveness. You are my Son, and you have asked me for help, and you shall receive what you need.'" Jesus breathed in the sweet fragrance of the new grass and then sighed.

Jesus held out the palm of his hand. The butterfly gently flew from his shoulder, floated down, and alighted on his palm, whereupon Jesus said, "It was then that I opened my eyes and saw the donkey with the wooden saddle, the water bag, and the blanket roll that contained this tunic I now wear. After my Father breathed a new life into me, I was so refreshed and sustained that although I had been but a breath away from the death of this body, I was able to walk barefoot without needing water in the desert for days. I now have undying faith and trust in my heavenly Father."

Peter opened the back door of the house. He saw Jesus and Judas, turned, and called to those inside, "He's back." The butterfly flew off Jesus's palm into the sky.

Peter, smirking, walked toward the two men sitting under the palm tree. Matthew, John, Luke, and Seth soon followed, and all stood around Jesus and Judas. Peter put his hand on his hip and said snidely, "Well, how is our happy Rabbi doing this morning?"

The others were also smirking, except Seth, who said, "It's so good to see you. I was worried that you weren't coming back."

Jesus smiled at Seth and replied, "I said I would. It's good to see you again as well." He turned to Peter and said, "This happy Rabbi is doing just fine. How are you doing after your dreams of Hannah last night?"

Peter's smirk disappeared into a look of vexation. He blushed red, took a step back, and blurted, "How do you know about my dream? Why do you ask?"

"I only ask because what you accuse me of is that which you desire," Jesus replied.

Everyone looked at Peter, who took another step back and said, "You can't know about my dreams."

Judas said, "Oh, yes, he can, Peter. He knew about my dream, as I've told you."

Jesus addressed Peter, "At the wedding party, I also saw projections emanating from your aura groping toward Hannah's breasts. You know that is what you were lusting for."

Peter was aghast. Matthew grabbed Seth's shoulder and said, "Go back into the house."

Seth pleaded, "Do I have to?"

"Go," Matthew ordered firmly.

Jesus said, "Listen to your father, although you are man enough to stay. I'll see you in a little while."

"Okay," Seth reluctantly replied and walked back into the house.

Jesus addressed Peter, "It's natural for man to feel a sexual desire for an attractive woman. Andrew and John shared the same desires and also reached out with their thoughts of fondling Hannah's breasts."

John took a step back and bowed his head. Jesus looked at him and said, "You live a righteous life, and you need feel no shame for the playful thoughts of your imagination, for such thoughts can be a healthy stimulant for your body. You remain honorable despite your thoughts and sexual desires because you harbored no intentions of acting on them."

John sighed with a touch of relief.

Jesus turned to Peter and said, "The same would be true for you, except for your condemnation and mocking of me for displaying a physical reaction to Hannah's feminine attributes. My body's human reaction surprised me as much as it amused you, and I feel no shame for that. I have now learned to control that aspect of my physical body, for I harbor no desire of the heart nor thought in my mind for that kind of engagement."

Peter replied, "I am sorry that I condemned you, but now I have been told that you are consorting with murderers, thieves, and prostitutes."

Jesus responded, "Appearances are not always what they seem to be on the surface. Just as your actions toward Hannah appeared appropriate on the surface, your lust boiled beneath the surface, and you further explored those yearnings in your dreams last night."

"But how do you know such things?" Peter demanded.

"My heavenly Father has given me the sight to see the things that I need to see," Jesus replied.

Matthew took a step back.

Jesus looked at him and said, "Do not be afraid to bare your thoughts to me, for I do not wish to pry into people's minds. Everyone has had so-called 'impure' thoughts of lust fueled by the innocence of basic human nature and often entertained by the mind and explored in the dream state. It's all really more than I care to know about. In this instance, those things that I have knowledge of are intended to help others to dispel their guilt and offer enlightenment – as I hope my words have now done for you."

Peter said, "You do have gifts, and I thank you for your words, but my actions were not sinful." Peter pointed his finger at Jesus and said, "But as a rabbi, your actions and associations at that tavern with people of ill repute are unworthy."

Jesus replied, "Peter, it would be wise for you to consider that when you point your one finger at others in judgment, three of your fingers are pointing back at yourself."

Peter stared at Jesus and then at his hand and his three fingers pointing at himself. He quickly opened his hand and sheepishly put it behind his back.

Jesus said, "There is no need for shame or remorse when you acknowledge basic human nature. Do not judge men or women for their thoughts; instead, place value on their deeds."

Luke said, "He's right. Who among us has never lusted in our thoughts?"

The others reluctantly nodded their acknowledgment.

Jesus nodded back and said, "Now please leave Judas and me to finish our conversation."

Luke said, "Thank you for your words, and thank you for the delicious wine that you blessed us with yesterday."

"You're most welcome," replied Jesus.

The men retreated back into the house.

"I see there are other questions on your mind, Judas. Ask me so that I may satisfy your quest for truth."

Judas stroked his beard in thought and said, "If there are no actual demons and there is no actual Devil but they are just creations of man's imagination as you say, then does that imply that angels do not exist?"

Jesus laughed, "Angels are everywhere, for they are the guiding lights of God's good will toward mankind. At certain times, in moments of dire circumstances, meditation, or prayer, one can sense their presence. In men's minds, it's difficult to translate those unseen forces of God's will that help mankind do what is good into a physical form. So men must give those unseen forces that they sense some human characteristics so that men can identify them in an understandable way. Angels are basically 'patterns of light.' However, men, with their blessed imaginations, endow these forces with an ethereal human form that has wings for flight. Angels symbolize those 'patterns of light' that are lighter than air and transcend time, space, and matter."

Judas surmised, "Then we can feel the presence of those forces but cannot see those patterns of light, so we create an image that we can imagine and identify."

"Yes, Judas. The purpose is served when you accept those guiding forces of good no matter how your mind conceives them. Those forces transcend this material world. My heavenly Father has blessed me with angel-like gifts, but for now, people can only relate to me as a man as I struggle to relate to myself as His Son."

"Why is it a struggle for you?" Judas asked.

"Because I am in human form and I retain the memories of this body and the urges of this flesh, yet I am also intertwined with God's essence and His desired destiny for me, not unlike the Star of David."

"The Star of David?" Judas sat up straighter and looked puzzled.

"My struggle and mankind's struggle are symbolized by the two triangles of the star. One triangle points downward from Heaven to represent the Holy Spirit reaching down to earth. The other triangle points upward to represent the physical elements of the earth. The Star of David is formed when the two triangles are intertwined and interlocked, which represents mankind in its position between Heaven and earth. I am at a similar point, that is, being a man and being His Son."

Judas gazed at Jesus. Judas thought that he had briefly seen a golden glow surrounding Jesus but dismissed the notion. Judas said, "Your conviction that you are the Anointed One, the Messiah who was prophesied to save our people, is a conviction that must be monumentally difficult to accept. It would be impossible for me to accept such an exalted position."

"It is a struggle and a dilemma for me also, Judas. There are times when I have my doubts; then I feel the compelling desire of my Father urging me to accept His mission with grace, and I am humbled. My faith in God has become unquestionable. It is my faith in myself that I struggle to fully accept.

"How can I help you?" Judas asked.

Jesus put a hand on Judas's shoulder and said, "Be my trusted confidant. Let me share my thoughts with you and do not judge me."

"You have already taught me not to judge you or others. What is it that you need to confide?"

Jesus clenched his jaw, looked up at the sky, and said, "It is the powerful sexual urge of this body's loins and the temptations that accompany that urge that may lead me to be in conflict with my destiny. I know that it's a natural yearning to physically join this flesh with another, to feel the warmth, the passion, and the melting together as one in bliss. I am not sure if this compelling temptation is meant to be fulfilled or if it is something that I have to feel so that I can understand temptations in man and then be able to guide others in how to handle their temptations. This pull in the gut, the yearning of my heart, and the ache of my soul to be joined with my physical counterpart cause an inner turmoil that distracts me. I do not like it, but I have not yet been able to fully reconcile it."

"It is something that most people experience. As you have said, 'it is only human' to have such feelings," Judas replied.

Jesus's brow furrowed, "I have come to realize that each one must express and fulfill sexuality in his or her own way and allow others to do the same and to be practical about the circumstances. My personal dilemma is that I am His Son, of pure spiritual essence and yet also of flesh. Each part and organ of mine is richly vitalized with abundant health and vigor, which nurtures that natural, powerfully compelling urge to fulfill the sexual aspect to feel complete."

Judas laughed, "You talk like a teenager. A handsome man, lean and muscular such as you, can surely find a woman to satisfy your needs."

"When we walked through the marketplace the other day and when I walked around Jerusalem last night, I did see many women that this body was readily attracted to. But I also saw many impurities from their minds," Jesus replied.

Judas asked, "Do you mean their past sins?"

"No, it's not a person's past mistakes that disturb me; it's how their harmful beliefs about themselves and how their petty, judgmental views of others stick out like thorns to me so that I cannot think in terms of intimacy with them. Yet my spontaneous arousal with Hannah yesterday demonstrated an outburst of this body's pent-up desires. All of my senses are in a heightened state of awareness, as are my sexual drives. I have now learned to control that part of my flesh to a degree, but that sacred desire to love completely cannot and should not be extinguished, for it is intended to be a rejuvenating force for this body. I must learn to contend with this empty, unfulfilled feeling to join intimately with another."

"Rabbi, don't look so glum. Celibacy never killed anyone. Still, you should allow yourself some indulgence. You don't have to love someone or be attracted on all levels to enjoy the pleasures of sex," Judas counseled.

"That may be true for most men, but I also see the vulnerabilities in women, and I know that if I were to be intimate with them, their unavoidable emotional attachment to me would become heartbreaking, for I would not stay with them. I cannot intentionally harm another."

"Meanwhile, it seems you are feeling heartache. Maybe you are being too sensitive. You deserve some measure of pleasure," Judas said.

Jesus took in a deep breath and said resolutely, "Meanwhile, for pleasure, I will seek to give more love to others, for the giving of love is pleasurable and satisfying to me. I will be open to receiving love from those who give it. I pray that I will be an example to teach others what is of the greatest value. For gold and jewels have no worth in my Father's Kingdom. After having lived this life, the greatest treasure that people can take with them to the afterlife is the love that they have given and the love that they have received."

Seth came out and said to Judas and Jesus, "John has fixed a wonderful breakfast and wants everyone to come and eat."

Judas stood and reached for Jesus's hand to help him rise, but Jesus said, "I'm not hungry now. I need a moment to align my mind with my Father and receive replenishment in His grace and understanding. Please go and leave me."

"Will you disappear again like last night?" Judas asked.

"No," Jesus replied

"I feel it's important for the men to talk with you so they may know you better."

"If asked, I will teach your inner circle spiritual truths so that they may teach others," Jesus said.

"I'll tell them," Judas replied.

As Judas and Seth entered the house, two beautiful butterflies circled over Jesus's head, and the songbird's soulful melodies resonated sweetly in the warm morning light.

12

Jesus sat against the palm tree for another twenty minutes. His eyes were closed, his expression one of reverence. A ring of yellow flower buds had sprouted from the ground and encircled him.

Seth came out of the house to fetch Jesus. "Please, Rabbi, come in now. We can't wait any longer to eat. I'm very hungry."

Jesus opened his eyes and said, "I need to be with John."

"Well then, come in; he's inside," Seth replied.

Jesus smiled and said, "Not that John." He stood up and took Seth's hand. As they headed toward the house, Jesus said, "Our garden needs a bench. I want to make a bench with you like my earth-father did with me."

"I'd like that," Seth replied. "There's a saw and hatchet in the stall."

Jesus said, "We'll also need an adz, a file, a plane, a chisel to shape the wood, a bow drill and bits, and a stone-headed hammer for driving in nails. Can you remember that?"

"Sure. I remember everything – an adz, file, plane, chisel, bow drill, bits, stone hammer, and nails. I'll take the wheelbarrow to bring it all back from the market.

Jesus patted Seth's head and said, "You're a smart young man and your memory's excellent. Matthew is fortunate to have a son such as you. I'll ask Judas to give you money for the tools and plank wood. You'll need to go with Simon and his cart."

Seth's chest lifted proudly as they walked into the house.

Jesus sniffed the air and smiled. "Ahh. The smell of fresh baked bread makes my mouth water."

Pointing to the head of the table, Judas said to Jesus, "Please sit here." John, Luke, Peter, and Matthew sat along the table's sides, their arms folded guardedly across their chests. Seth sat next to his father.

"Will you please bless the bread for us, Rabbi?" Judas asked.

"Of course," Jesus replied as he sat down. "Before I do, I would like all of you to feel more relaxed and not fear that I will read your thoughts and expose what you try to hide. I accept you and judge no one for perceived sins or faults. What I said in the garden concerning Hannah and your dreams was only in response to your false judgment of me and to make the point that judging others is folly, for man's most valuable asset is his imagination and the freedom to think whatever thoughts he desires."

Peter said, "We must control thoughts of sin lest the Devil take control of our minds."

Jesus replied, "It is far better to think thoughts others may judge sinful than to try and stifle your imagination. That only suppresses the thought, which then ferments and intensifies and keeps reappearing until it's resolved. That causes stress and anxiety. Allow your imagination its freedom to entertain all thoughts. Explore their ramifications, their rewards or consequences. Once you do, you'll be more informed and better able to decide what the appropriate action is to take or not to take. That's the best way to avoid mistakes or perceived sins. There need be no shame or guilt in any thought. When inappropriate action that might be taken is contemplated, its consequences can then best be avoided. There is no sin in thought. Thoughts allow you to make better decisions for yourself and all concerned."

The men looked at each other. They shifted their weight and unfolded their arms, relaxing and acknowledging that they did not feel as threatened.

Jesus placed his hand on the bread, bowed his head, and said, "Blessed art thou, our Lord, our God, King of the Universe, Heavenly Father of All That Is. We thank You for the earth that is the womb for the seed that grows the wheat, for the farmers who harvest the grain and cart it to the market, for John who prepared this bread, and for all who have worked in unseen ways to bring this blessing of sustenance to the table before us. Let us all say 'Amen.'"

Everyone responded with an "Amen."

Jesus tore off a piece of the warm bread, held it before his nose, savored the smell, and declared, "This is good." He passed the loaf to the others.

<hr />

Near the end of the meal, most of the fruit and salted fish had been consumed, and not a crumb was left of the bread. Jesus pulled a dried fig from the string that was threaded through a stacked necklace of twelve other figs. The men now felt much more comfortable in Jesus's presence after their mealtime discussion of a wide range of topics.

Matthew sat back, patted his round belly, and with a satisfied expression on his face said, "Thank you, John and Judas, for providing us with a tasty breakfast, and thank you, Rabbi, for your insights."

Peter leaned toward Jesus and asked, "I've been thinking about what you said during our breakfast, that there will come an end of time, an Armageddon – 'the unveiling,' when those who believe that all the ills of their lives and the world were controlled by a Devil will realize that it is they themselves who created those evils. That time will be marked by chaos and suffering because their delusions will be shattered. Can that be avoided?"

Jesus replied, "I am here to help mankind avoid that; however, despite my teachings, many will still cling to the concept of a Devil, for believing in the Devil will temporarily provide a respite from placing blame and responsibility on one's self or others. So the Devil concept will serve a purpose for religions to posit God as good and the Devil as evil, and those religious leaders will seek to control their followers with promises of Heaven if they follow their leaders' dictates and other more sinister promises of damnation and eternal hell if their followers do not give their leaders unquestioning allegiance. To avoid that end of time and its turmoil and strife, I pray that my teachings will enlighten enough people to start a new age of understanding. Those who learn and become enlightened will avoid the pitfalls of an Armageddon."

Jesus looked around the table at each one and then said, "That is why I need your help."

Luke asked, "Help to do what?"

"To learn and embrace God's spiritual laws and to spread The Word," Jesus replied.

Luke stated, "But we already have God's words in the Torah."

"The Torah does contain truth and wisdom and laws to live by. It teaches that to be a Jew is to do God's work and good deeds. But there is still confusion and angry arguing among scholars as to the precise meaning and implications of the Torah. That is why so many different sects of Judaism have sprouted, each seeking to fulfill its own interpretation to convince others that their way is the right way and that other ways are wrong. Each one's perception of the truth is but one spoke of the wheel, and all spokes lead to the hub of my Father's core axis of truth for all. It is my mission to simplify and teach God's 'Golden Law of Life,'" Jesus turned toward Seth, "in such a way that even a child can understand it."

Seth sat up tall in his chair and said, "I'm ready to learn."

"More laws to learn?" Peter protested. "All of us believe in God Almighty. Why doesn't God just wave his hand and erase all the sins and evils and create a Heaven on earth?"

Jesus replied, "My heavenly Father has given man 'The Gift of Choice.' It is up to man to create a Heaven on earth from the opportunities that God provides. Think of all the food that was on our breakfast table or the wedding feast yesterday. Those delicious experiences were tastes of heaven, all produced by people making choices that mutually benefited themselves and others. That is one part of the 'Golden Law of Life.'"

Peter leaned back, confused. "I don't understand."

Jesus replied, "The farmers plant more seeds for wheat than their families can consume so that they can sell the rest to buy clothes woven by weavers who get the wool from sheepherders, and the farmers also buy tools to farm from toolmakers. Carpenters build carts to transport the goods from place to place pulled by oxen raised by other herders. All fulfill their lot in life in an unrealized divine spirit of cooperation, and all earn benefits to sustain and enhance their own lives and in so doing, sustain and enhance the lives of others. When all is done honestly and fairly, all benefit mutually. That is the way Judas has lived his life: to mutually benefit his family's farms and their farm workers and the people in the community. That is God's plan in action."

Judas nodded humbly.

Luke asked, "But most people work for themselves, not to benefit another. Isn't that selfish?"

"It is not selfish for one's labors to benefit himself if one acts fairly and doesn't take advantage of those less fortunate. When one has enough for his true needs and helps those less fortunate, that's of great mutual benefit, for one's spirit becomes more prosperous, as does mankind."

John placed the pit from the date he had eaten in a bowl with other pits and said, "I can see that all things in nature benefit other parts of nature. Even the cow's manure is used to fertilize the crops. Is that part of God's 'Golden Law of Life'?"

The others laughed.

Jesus smiled. "Yes, in God's plan, the animals act naturally, and in doing so, all of nature benefits. Unlike the animals, man has the 'Gift of Choice' that guides his decisions and actions. Man has dominion over the animals, and with that dominion comes the responsibility to be the caretaker for nature's creatures."

Luke said, "An animal is to be used as a beast of burden or to be sacrificed or to be eaten."

Seth spoke up, "All animals are living creatures. They should be treated with kindness."

Jesus laughed and said, "Pearls of wisdom spoken from the mouth of a young and innocent child. All life in all forms, whether used for food, work, or clothing or just enjoyed for itself such as a songbird's song should be revered and loved, for it is a part of my Father's creation and therefore has divine purpose. This is especially true for man's need to appreciate and treat his fellow man with kindness."

Peter scoffed, "I'm not about to revere and love the Romans who have crucified hundreds of thousands of Jews. I don't understand you, Rabbi."

Jesus nodded. "Many things that I say may not be understood or may even be rejected at first; however, as social events and personal experiences occur in your life, the truth of God's 'Golden Law of Life' will eventually have more meaning. When one's intent is to cheat or treat another unfairly, ill will is created and consequences follow."

Jesus looked at Matthew and said, "That means not taking bribes."

Matthew shifted uncomfortably and said, "But bribes to reduce taxes mean less money for the Romans and more money left for the poor Jewish worker to live on … and a little more money for me."

Jesus spoke sternly, "And what will you do when complaints are lodged against you and you are arrested, taken to court, judged guilty, severely punished, and jailed in a Roman prison? Your 'little money' is not worth your peace of mind or Seth becoming a fatherless boy. Be honest and fair, Matthew. Seth needs you."

John asked, "How do you expect people to act the way you suggest? Most people tend to think only of themselves."

"That's true, John," Jesus replied. "That is why my Father sent me here to teach love and kindness, understanding and patience, tolerance and forgiveness in a spirit of true brotherhood."

"That's a huge load to haul, Rabbi. How are you going to accomplish that?" Matthew asked skeptically.

"With your help, Matthew," Jesus replied. He turned to the others. "And with John's, Luke's and Peter's."

"Us?" they all replied.

"What about me? I want to help too," Seth said.

"Yes, all of you, and others who will join us."

A loud knocking was heard at the front door; everyone turned and looked. Judas got up and opened the door. Andrew stood there and saw Jesus at the table.

Andrew whispered to Judas, "Can you and the others, except for the Rabbi and the boy, step outside a moment?"

Judas asked, "Why?"

"Please, just do as I ask, and I will explain."

"I respect you, Andrew, but it is not polite to abandon my guest like that."

"Please, Judas. You'll know why. It's very important."

Reluctantly, Judas went back to the table and summoned the men to come with him and asked Jesus to please excuse the interruption.

Jesus replied, "Seth and I will enjoy each other's company in your absence."

When the men gathered outside the closed front door, John asked Andrew, "Where is Saul?"

"He was disgusted with the Rabbi's despicable behavior and is on his way back home to Tarsus."

"What did the Rabbi do to make Saul leave without coming to say good-bye to us?" Luke asked.

"We all know that the Rabbi is easily aroused sexually, but there is much more," replied Andrew. On our walk last night, we came upon a tavern and went in to get out of the cold. There we saw a prostitute stroking your Rabbi's hair. We later learned that he was consorting with a thief, a Roman soldier and a..." Andrew shook his head and then said disdainfully, "...and an assassin for hire!"

Except for Judas, the men leaned away from Andrew's words as if cold water had been thrown in their faces.

"That's not all," Andrew said. "We learned that before Saul and I arrived at the tavern, your Rabbi had released demons from a possessed man. Your Rabbi is in an alliance with the Devil! Saul and I feel that you should disavow this Rabbi. He has been with you only two days, and we don't know anything about him. Saul said he saw enough to know that he didn't even want to cast his eyes upon him again. Saul adamantly told me that he has turned a blind eye to your Rabbi and will erase him from his mind as if he never existed."

"You are making serious accusations," Judas said. "You should know me well enough to trust that I know who is worthy to invite into my home." He pointed at John, Luke, and Matthew and then at Andrew and said, "I now invite you, Andrew, into my home. The Rabbi has enlightened us about the Hannah incident to our satisfaction."

Judas opened the door and walked back in and waved to the others to follow. John turned to Andrew and said, "We felt as you do, but we're learning that there's more to the Rabbi than what the eyes can see. Don't leave. Come in with us, Andrew." John turned, walked in with the others, and left the door open.

Andrew stood there a few moments, then reluctantly followed.

⊂⊃

Against his protestations, Seth had been sent outside to do chores. Andrew had finished recounting his and Saul's experience at the tavern to Jesus as the other men listened. They all curiously awaited Jesus's response to Andrew's insinuations.

"I see," Jesus replied to Andrew. "But before I speak about my intents and actions at the tavern, it is only fitting that I also speak about your and Paul's intents and actions as well."

"You mean Saul, not Paul," Andrew interrupted.

"I know his name. What is important is what both of your intents and actions were. When you both left this house last night, you told everyone that the two of you wanted to take a walk and get fresh air, but you went directly to the tavern. Two full jugs of wine still remain under the kitchen counter, so you didn't go to the tavern for more wine."

Andrew sat back uncomfortably.

Jesus continued, "The two of you have been to that tavern before and have had liaisons with prostitutes that you met there on numerous occasions, and your intent last night was to do so again."

Andrew's face became flushed.

Jesus said, "When you saw me last night, you judged me with the intents and desires for sexual play that you were experiencing. In passing false judgment upon me, you judged yourselves.

Andrew was taken aback at Jesus's revelations. He defensively retorted, "But what about the prostitute who was stroking your hair?"

"One of the people I was sitting with had called her over, not I. When she started to stroke my hair – not invited by me – I felt very uncomfortable and was about to pull her hand away. That's when you looked at me and I turned and saw you and your shocked faces. Then I got up and left. I never had any sexual contact. The two of you stayed and acted on your intent to satisfy yourselves sexually. You have wrongly judged me."

Andrew became embarrassed and very upset. He protested, "But what about the company you kept? That thief and the Roman soldier? The assassin? That's consorting with those who disgrace your calling as a rabbi!"

Jesus sat back and swept his eyes over the group. "I see," he said. "Whom then shall I seek to help and to teach my heavenly Father's Truth? The rich? Or the pious and righteous who believe that they know all the answers? It is the poor and downtrodden and the misguided souls who need a better path to follow. That and to understand the needs of people are what my time in the tavern concerned."

Again Andrew didn't acknowledge Jesus's words, but accused him, "We were told that you had exorcised demons from a man earlier in the evening. Are you not in alliance with the Devil?"

Jesus replied, "To help a convulsing man feel at peace or to help any disturbed soul to feel better is not a sin; it's a duty. Everyone should feel a desire to help others."

Jesus stood and declared, "I'm going for a walk with the true intention of getting some fresh air," and leaning toward Andrew, "unlike your intention last night. I don't judge you, Andrew, but invite you and the others to join me on my walk so that we can establish a better footing with each other. I think your companions here can tell you what I've told them about the Hannah incident and their own sexual intents so that you'll become more enlightened."

Jesus walked to the front door and opened it. Seth was raking the front courtyard after the previous day's activities. Jesus asked him, "Do you want to walk with me?"

Seth dropped the rake and said, "Sure."

The two of them walked out the front gate. The men looked at each other for a few moments, and then they too followed after Jesus. Andrew walked slowly behind everyone in a semi-stunned state, reeling from what Jesus had told him about his own intentions and actions.

After a while, Andrew fell into step with the others and walked beside Jesus. He said, "Please forgive me if I judged you wrongly."

"You have my forgiveness if you will forgive yourself."

Although Andrew still had misgivings, he said, "Thank you, Rabbi. If there is anything you need, please ask me."

"I need to be with John, the one who wears a camel-hair coat and does the baptizing."

Aghast, Andrew stepped back and exclaimed, "John the Baptist! He's a maniac who lives in the wilderness and eats locusts and honey. Because he's gained so many followers, the Romans feel threatened by him, and all who are in his company are in danger. He also claims to be preparing the way for the Messiah."

"That is why I need be with John," Jesus replied. Andrew frowned.

They all looked at one another, and Judas said, "We should all go with the Rabbi to the River Jordan to see the Baptist."

13

King Herod Antipas sat behind a twenty-foot-long, ornate, marble worktable in the large reception hall of his luxurious palace in Galilee. Royal signing quills, tablets, small sculptures, and beautifully colored glass vessels containing succulent fruit, shelled nuts, and flowers were all precisely aligned along the front edge of the table. Attendants and servants stood ten feet behind him awaiting any requests for food or drink or to fulfill his orders for any whim.

Scribes sat at a row of eight desks on one side of the marble table. Delicately woven baskets atop each desk were filled with blank, rolled up parchments made of sheepskin ready to record Herod's dictates. Rows of quills made from slit reeds were lined up on the desks next to small vessels filled with ink made from a mixture of lampblack and gum. Fragrant lemon grass incense permeated the air.

Herod put his metal quill down on the marble table with a sharp *clack!* that resonated in the silence of the hall. "That's it! No more proclamation signings for a week."

His head secretary quickly picked up the scroll that Herod had just signed and expeditiously rolled it up, tied it with a blue ribbon, and handed it to another secretary who appeared at his side. Herod sat back in his regal cushioned chair and stroked his finely trimmed, gray-speckled beard. His long, hooked nose bent to the left near the tip, giving his late forty-year-old face a gnarly look. He rested his head against the chair's high back and gazed out at his colonnaded courtyard and the spectacular reflecting pools and gardens that showcased imported plants and brilliantly colored flowers from the many lands of the Roman Empire. The polished marble floor in his large reception room mirrored the images of his Royal Guards standing at attention by the entrance. His trusted chief adviser, Octavius, stood next to the king, and the head secretary stood at his side. Herod looked at Octavius, nodded, and said, "I'm ready."

Octavius unrolled a scroll, set it before Herod, and said, "These are the final tallies for next month's military budget." The head secretary handed Octavius another scroll that Octavius opened and placed beside the first scroll and said, "You will see that these earmarked tax collections have exceeded the general's request for next period's military budget. The balance will be transferred to your reserve account."

Herod quickly studied the figures and without looking up, said, "Bring me the accountant's Jerusalem records that I asked for."

Octavius beckoned to the nervous chief accountant, who had been anxiously waiting in a far corner with other administrative staff of the court. As the accountant came forward, two of his aides carried large baskets of scrolls and followed in step as they all walked quickly to Herod's table.

Octavius eyed the accountant and pointed to an empty section of the table. The aides and accountant quickly unfurled eight scrolls and began layering them on the table along side the unfurled budget scroll.

As the scrolls were being prepared for him, Herod gazed out at his view once more. He seemed to absentmindedly put his little finger between his throat and a broad gold necklace that was inlaid with precious stones. He took his finger out and looked at its tip. With a fingernail from his other hand, he bisected the width of his fingertip. He reached behind his neck, unclasped the necklace, handed it to his secretary, and said, "Tell the jeweler to shorten this three-eights of one inch, no more, no less."

Herod stood and leaned over the opened scrolls. The accountant and aides immediately stepped back three paces.

Silence fell over the reception hall as Herod leaned closer and intently studied the scrolls. Standing, he turned to the accountant and said, "Leave us."

The nervous accountant and his aides quickly retreated to the far corner.

"Look at this, Octavius," Herod said as he pointed to one scroll.

Octavius studied the scroll for a few moments and then said, "I see that Jerusalem's tax collections were only five percent higher than last year."

Herod pushed the scroll away and said, "Jerusalem's population has increased over ten percent in the same time period. And I know from the census taken at the gates during the annual Passover pilgrimage that over three hundred thousand visiting Jews were there, the largest turnout we've ever had. All the goods sold and trading done during the Passover celebration should have increased that month's tax collections by at least twenty percent over the year before and not a mere five percent."

Octavius said, "The collections will immediately be audited and investigated." Octavius's tone became encouraging. "Even with that discrepancy, this year's tax revenue projections should exceed last year's gross of two hundred talents - over nine tons of gold from your subjects."

Herod frowned and said sternly, "That doesn't make the Jerusalem shortfall acceptable."

"We have tolerated the tax collectors' lining their own pockets with the people's money as long as they meet their quotas," Octavius offered.

"The pigs have gotten too fat this time. Make examples of those found guilty with harsher penalties and public torture. That should dampen their greed a bit."

"It shall be done," Octavius agreed. He then grimaced and said reluctantly, "The matter of John the Baptist needs to be addressed."

The corners of Herod's mouth turned down. He made a dismissive motion with his hand toward the scrolls on the table. The head secretary and his assistants quickly cleared the work surface as Herod stomped toward the empty center of the grand reception hall. Octavius followed closely by his side. Herod said in a whisper, "This John the Baptist continually becomes a sharper thorn in my side. Tell me what you know, Octavius."

"The Baptist's following continues to grow larger each month. More threatening are the Jewish rumors from the far north of Galilee stretching to southern Judea and beyond to Idumea. They say John the Baptist is the Messiah that the Scriptures have prophesied who would free them."

"I've heard that," Herod acknowledged. "There have been reports of dozens of would-be messiahs. Why is this one becoming so popular?"

"He is rumored to have been born of an elderly woman decades beyond her fertile years, which gives his birth a special godly meaning as predicted in Jewish prophecies. He reaches out to all people and exhorts them to repent and be baptized. Unlike spokesmen of other sects, he doesn't demand any obligation or vows of exclusivity. That gives him a universal appeal to Gentile and Jew alike."

Herod pursed his lips then asked, "Has he made any threats against Rome that we can try him on?"

Octavius replied, "Our informers and spies tell us that the Baptist says that tax collectors may keep their jobs provided they do not cheat the public and that soldiers may soldier if they do not rob or falsely accuse the people. He doesn't even claim to be the Messiah, but he does proclaim that the one who comes after him is at hand and that all Israel shall prepare."

Herod's brow furrowed again. "That makes it difficult to prosecute him. Maybe that's a ploy he's using for now, and when his followers continue to grow at their accelerating rate, he will disavow those sentiments and tell his people to give their monies to him as some other sects have. He could even foment a rebellion. Double the spies and follow up more closely on all the rumors."

Herod stared at the floor a moment, then turned to Octavius and said with resolve, "My instincts tell me that this Baptist bodes trouble for us. We have to handle this very delicately to avoid a rebellion. We cannot permit the different sects to unify around a central figure. Their divisions must be maintained. My power will not be usurped."

Octavius nodded in agreement and said, "So far we have managed to maintain divisions between the Sadducees, the Pharisees, the Essenes, and the Zealots. At present, there are other, smaller sects that have different beliefs and want to maintain their separate organizations of influence."

"So far that is true, Octavius. Their division of beliefs keeps them polarized and creates a weakness that prevents their cohesion and possible rebellion against my rule. But they all share a common resentment of the monies that are due to Rome and to me. This Baptist will have to be dealt with in a delicate way, for if he is killed and becomes a martyr, it may be much harder to destroy his following than if he remains alive."

"I agree," Octavius said. "Divisions of the sects must be maintained, and no central unifying messianic figure can be allowed. It will be done."

"Good," said Herod and looked out at his gardens once more. "Tell the master architect that I want to redesign the north garden. Have him bring me the original plans. And have the palace torturer interrogate our squirmy accountant. He's hiding something more that he's afraid I'll discover. Who's next in the anteroom?"

"Pontius Pilate," answered Octavius.

"You can summon him now," Herod said as he gazed out at his luxurious gardens and the vast green grasses that extended around the borders of his palace.

14

Jesus and Seth walked together leading the group of men who followed a few paces behind. Judas was explaining to Andrew more of what had transpired that morning and Jesus's perspective of the Devil and the Hannah and tavern incidents as well as his revelations regarding the other men's sexual inclinations.

"The Rabbi doesn't judge you; don't judge him," Judas told Andrew.

"He seems like he could be a master trickster," Andrew replied.

"There is something about him that is more than magical," Judas said. "He has an undeniable mystical quality, something very different that I have never encountered or imagined that a possible Messiah would have."

Andrew had difficulty accepting what Judas told him of Jesus's explanations. Peter and John also whispered their doubts to each other. Matthew and Luke were undecided. Seth was convinced.

The group had walked from Judas's middle class section of Jerusalem to the fringe of a wealthier neighborhood with its large mansions and taller walls. Jesus changed direction and after a while approached the section in which the poor and middle-class areas bordered each other.

The streets became more crowded as people walked to and from a busy nearby marketplace. A cart hauling bags of grain approached Jesus's group. "Simon!" John cried as he waved to the cart's driver. Simon pulled up beside the group and followed alongside. He spoke with John as the entourage continued.

Simon said, "I g-g-got a new axel for m-m-my wheel."

As they rounded a corner, Simon's donkey headed for a water trough. Jesus was finishing explaining to Seth how they would build the garden bench, "Also, find some long, curved hardwood branches for the back of the bench."

Just then a blind beggar who had been sitting against a wall suddenly stood up and exclaimed, "It's you! I recognize your voice! You're the one in the tavern who exorcised the demons from the possessed man and turned swill into wine last night." He reached out his hands and walked toward Jesus. The group stopped in their tracks.

Judas approached the blind man, took a silver coin from his purse, and placed it in the blind man's hand. "Here, take this, Ezra, and let us be. We have important things to do."

"Yes, we do," Jesus said, "and what is most important is what this man wants. What is it that you want, Ezra?"

"I want you to heal me, to give me sight again."

The group gathered around Jesus and Ezra and drew curious passers-by who stopped to see what was happening. Peter pointed to the blind man and whispered to Andrew, "Everyone knows that he's been blind for over ten years. His is a sad story. Judas always gives him money."

Jesus put his hand on Ezra's shoulder and asked, "Why can you not see?"

"I don't know," Ezra answered in anguish. "Why is God punishing me? I have lived a righteous life and always helped others before I lost my sight."

Jesus spoke softly and compassionately. "Perhaps you chose to see no more. What is it that you want to see again?"

Ezra's yearning voice burst forth. "I want to see the light. I want to see the sun rise and set. I want to see people's faces, their expressions. I don't want to suffer God's punishment anymore."

"God desires enlightenment rather than punishment," Jesus responded and then asked, "Why do you believe that I can help you?"

"Anyone who has the power to exorcise demons and can turn bar spillage into delicious wine should surely be able to make me see again."

Jesus stepped back and studied the man's aura and then said, "I see. But how much faith do you have that I am able to help you?"

Ezra got down on his knees before Jesus and fervently pleaded, "I believe that you can do it. Please, have mercy on me. Make me whole."

"If your heart is true in your belief, then you shall receive what you ask for.

Ezra's body trembled. He plaintively cried out, "Please help me!"

The growing crowd surrounding Jesus and Ezra suddenly fell silent. All eyes watched as Jesus scooped up a handful of clay mud from the spillage under the water trough. He spit on the mud and molded it into a shape. He walked back to Ezra, who had remained kneeling.

Jesus raised the mud high over Ezra's head and said, "You have asked for your sight and you shall receive it." He swiftly brought his hand down, hitting Ezra squarely between the eyes with the mud, eliciting a loud "*Thwack!*"

Shocked, Ezra tumbled backward from the force of the blow and held his hand to his forehead.

The crowd moaned. A woman yelled out at Jesus, "How could you strike a kneeling blind man? Shame on you! You are the Devil!"

Jesus turned to the woman and said, "All is not as it appears."

Ezra staggered up and rubbed the mud off. He looked at Jesus and exclaimed, "I see! I can see you!" He turned around and faced the crowd. "I can see all of you!" Tears streamed down his cheeks. Ezra took Jesus's hand and kissed it. "I can see! I can see! Thank you, thank you."

Jesus smiled at Ezra and said, "Your faith has made you well."

Ezra pulled a leather cord from around his neck that was attached to his money purse underneath his robe and held it out to Jesus. "Take it all. Please – you are my savior."

Jesus shook his head. "No, I cannot take your money. Your new sight is a gift of your faith to yourself. Use your money to start a new life, and be the best of who you are."

The large crowd looked on curiously. One woman pointed to Jesus and excitedly whispered to another woman next to her. "I can't believe it! He's the one I saw in my dream last night."

Two Roman soldiers on horseback approached the crowd and ordered, "Move along. No blockages allowed near the market. Keep it moving."

Two older men tried to move away from the soldier's horse, but the density of the crowd did not permit it. The soldier kept advancing, disregarding the two men, both of whom were pushed to the ground as the horse brushed against them. One of the three young Jewish men from the tavern who had just witnessed the healing of the blind man hurried away. The other two stayed and mingled with a group of onlookers who followed Jesus as he walked back toward Judas's home.

15

Judas, Peter, John, Luke, Matthew, Andrew, and Simon sat at the large table in Judas's house and talked heatedly for over an hour. Seth sat silently to the side, listening intently to every word.

Finally, Judas pushed his chair away from the table, lifted his palms, and said, "Enough. Maybe he is the Messiah and maybe he isn't. You all know how skeptical I am, so believe me when I say to you that I know that he possesses genuine abilities. Like you, I thought at first that his insights and ways appeared strange and unacceptable and at times, even outrageous. That has proven to be a misjudgment on my part. He has asked me not to judge him, and I am trying not to. I ask you to do the same."

"Why don't you get him?" Peter asked. "Let him answer our questions directly."

Judas stood up and said, "I will."

Judas approached Jesus, who sat against the luxurious palm tree with the birds, butterflies and little yellow flowers surrounding him. Jesus's head was bowed; a hand covered his eyes.

"Rabbi," Judas said, "please join us inside. We want to speak to you."

Jesus put his hand down and looked up with tear-filled eyes.

"What's wrong?" Judas asked. "Why are you crying?"

"Because it's so sad and painful," Jesus replied.

"What's so sad and painful?

"Pain and suffering are a part of life, as are joy and pleasure. I accept that," Jesus said and sniffed at the moisture from his nose as he wiped away a tear. "But I cannot accept the *needless* pain and suffering that man intentionally causes his brothers and sisters. Mankind creates its own torments as Ezra did unto himself. It's ironic that he did so in order to avoid further pain and suffering."

"I don't understand," Judas said. "Ezra had led a pious life. He had a good business and a wonderful family. He was wealthy but lived frugally and always helped anyone who was in true need. He told those to whom he was generous not to tell anyone about his helping them, for he did it out of love and compassion and didn't want any notoriety. He was a very humble and grateful man. It was a shame that those heartless Roman soldiers did such a tragic thing to him."

Jesus sniffed in again and sat up straighter. He motioned to Judas to sit beside him and said, "I cry because it is ignorance of spiritual laws that, once acknowledged and practiced, could prevent unnecessary blindness, pain, and suffering. If not for that ignorance, I would not need to involve myself in healing the Ezras of the world or the whip gash on your back. Mankind could enjoy the pleasures of life instead."

"I say 'Amen' to that," Judas replied. "Is it possible for you to explain something to me? I am so curious as to how you healed Ezra. I want to learn so that I can understand."

"Yes, Judas," Jesus grinned, "you are the curious one who seeks the deeper truths and wants to know how God's forces work."

"Please tell me how your healing works."

"It's different each time and for each person I've helped. So that you may understand what happened with Ezra, I must revisit his circumstances with you."

Jesus closed his eyes and said, "I saw within Ezra's aura the time of his becoming blind when he had been falsely accused of a crime. The Roman soldiers burst into his peaceful home." Jesus winced. "They raped his wife in front of him to mock and humiliate him. When he protested and cursed them, they ran swords through his seven deeply loved children." Jesus's jaw quivered. "Each screaming child's death was unbearably painful for Ezra to behold. Ezra held the love of his adored children as the most precious of all things in his life. It was too much for his nonviolent nature to tolerate. After the last breath left his last bleeding child, Ezra kicked one of the soldiers holding him. The lieutenant was indignant that a Jew should strike a Roman. He drew his sword and approached Ezra. He raised his sword to strike and said, 'Now I'm going to cut off your head.'

"Understandably, Ezra was severely traumatized and heartbroken. He expected death and closed his eyes. With great force, the lieutenant's sword struck Ezra across his forehead, not with the blade's edge, but with the flat side of the sword. With the physical blow of the sword and the emotional trauma of the devastating slaughter he had witnessed and believing that he was about to die, Ezra collapsed, unconscious. One of the soldiers holding him drew his dagger and was about to slit Ezra's throat. The lieutenant ordered, 'Stop. Let him live so that he may suffer and be an example to other Jews so that they do not even dare to think about striking a Roman.' When Ezra regained consciousness, he could no longer see." Jesus opened his eyes, inhaled deeply, and then breathed out.

Judas was moved by Ezra's plight and amazed at Jesus's perception. He asked in a whisper, "But how could you know all of that so quickly?"

Jesus replied, "To you, events take time to experience, but I can now focus my concentration so that I can experience time occurrences simultaneously. I am able to see and feel significant events pertaining to those who seek my help."

"I'm not sure I understand," Judas said.

"All I can say is that time to me is different from your concept of time. All events in time exist at once in my Father's infinite and eternal domain, and I am learning how to connect to events within time."

Puzzled, Judas shook his head. "I'll have to think about that. But with all of Ezra's past trauma, why did you strike him in the head so hard? And why did you spit on the clay?"

"The clay represented the elements of the earth, the source of his physical body, and the physical substance of the sword. The energy in my hands charged those earth elements. My spit was of healing living water. Adding my desire and intent to help Ezra, I impressed that energy and molded the clay into the shape of the sword that I struck him with. With my thoughts, I then suggested that regardless of the torturous horror that he had witnessed, he need not be blinded to all of the good that remains in life. For his emotional defense, to avoid the pain of seeing any more horrors in his life, Ezra had chosen blindness over sight."

"Why did you strike him so hard in the head?" Judas asked.

"So that it would connect him in a similar way to the time just before he was struck with the Roman's sword when his sight was healthy. He pleaded to be healed; he yearned to see again, and he was open to receiving help. I struck his forehead forcefully in the same place as the Roman soldier's sword had struck. The sudden unexpected shock combined with my suggestion and intent to help him and his fervent desire to see again removed the obstacle of his self-imposed blindness. I did not heal him; I enlightened and helped him. What healed him was his faith in me that I could heal him and his desire and choice to see again."

Judas raised his eyebrows and said, "I think I understand, but others would find it hard to believe."

Jesus put his hand on Judas's shoulder and said, "You have asked me to tell you how Ezra's sight was restored, and I did. I am sharing with you the secrets of how my Father's powers work for your enlightenment. It is up to you to choose what to share what I've told you with others."

"I thank you for your insight, Rabbi. I need time to digest all you've said." Judas studied Jesus's face and remarked, "I feel bad for you that you feel so much sadness."

"My sadness is because I see that mankind has created a dark web of thoughts and feelings that covers the land. It's an onerous web of man's own making that shuts out God's Light, the Light that shines within each person but is being suffocated by man's hatred, his fears and his envy. That hatred, fear, and envy are blinding mankind from seeing the good in all things as they blinded Ezra, and this blindness need not be. I need your help, Judas, to fulfill the mission my Father has for me, to open mankind's eyes and hearts, to allow His Light and Love to shine brightly within men's hearts and save mankind from destroying itself."

"I'm ready to help you in any way you ask," Judas humbly replied. "Your Father has given you an immense task."

Jesus sighed and then smiled. "It is a holy and blessed mission. He has told me that He is pleased with me, and He has given me another gift. I no longer need to use living water to help heal. I can now use His greater powers directly through my hands. Now my Father intends for me to heal in more significant ways so that the healing will be more meaningful to those who witness what His blessed Light can do and so that they will believe that I am His Son." Jesus smiled with satisfaction and said, "He has also deepened my connection to all waters everywhere as my connection to all life."

A cold wind rustled the palm leaves. Judas pulled his robe up to his neck and tied it to cover himself. He stood and reached out to Jesus, saying, "Colder winds are coming tonight. You've only a tunic. Come in from the cold. The men are expecting you."

Zadak, the Head Priest, sat alone in his elaborate private chamber in the Great Synagogue - the seat of the Pharisees - located not far from the magnificent Temple of Jerusalem. His priestly robe was embroidered with fine threads woven in mystical symbols. An elegant vestment decorated with gold filaments covered his chest. Tired from his day's long schedule, he leaned back against his regal chair. He rubbed at the dark circles under his eyes, then at his unruly eyebrows. The deep furrows in his forehead relaxed as his eyes slowly closed. He began to drift into slumber when a knock on his door caused him to sit upright. "Enter," he called out.

One of the young Jewish men from the tavern entered. Zadak smiled and said, "Benjamin, my son, what news do you bring?"

Benjamin walked to Zadak's side, bent down, and kissed his father. He was short of breath from his run. "Joseph said that his second dream confirmed that it was him."

"Have you found out his name?"

"We asked his companions, and they said he calls himself Jesus from Nazareth. Father, I saw him perform a miracle!"

Zadak's forehead furrowed deeply with concern. "What did you see?" he asked.

"He healed a blind man's sight. It was Ezra," Benjamin blurted.

Zadak looked at his son incredulously, "Ezra? I've known him for over a decade. You say he is healed?"

"Yes, father, Ezra can now see."

Zadak scratched the side of his head and whispered, "Remarkable, a genuine healing."

"That's not all. After his sight was restored, Ezra offered him all of his money, but Jesus refused to accept it."

Zadak stood up, pacing in thought, then asked, "Did this Jesus make any claim to be the Messiah?"

"No Father. He only bade Ezra use the money to start a new life. Then the Roman guards dispersed the crowd that had gathered and witnessed the healing."

"Where are Joseph and Lev now?"

"They followed Jesus and his companions to Judas Iscariot's house. I came here right away to tell you."

"Him! This Jesus is staying with Iscariot?" Zadak clenched his teeth. "We never know where he stands."

"He's donated money to our synagogue," Benjamin remembered.

"He's given more to the Sadducees," Zadak grumbled.

"Iscariot gives to many groups. Everybody knows that he is dedicated to helping the disadvantaged," Benjamin replied.

"I don't trust him." Worried, Zadak said, "Joseph's dreams have always been accurate. The night before last, he foresaw the exorcism and the turning of waste into wine at the tavern by a man whom the masses would claim as their Messiah and savior. Joseph's second dream foretold that this man would bring light to the darkness in the streets of Jerusalem, and he has in healing Ezra's blindness."

The dark circles under Zadak's eyes heightened his anxious expression. "This healer who rejects money for his services is one who does not respect the wealthy. He could prove dangerous to our political connections with Pilate and our sharing of tax revenues."

"Joseph said that he is convinced that Jesus is a man of truth," Benjamin replied.

"All the more reason to watch this healer more closely," Zadak replied. "Go back to Iscariot's house. Speak not to Joseph and Lev of my misgivings. If Jesus leaves, follow him and report his movements back to me."

"Yes, Father."

⸺

Samuel and Nicodemus huddled together in the courtyard of the Great Synagogue. "It is still hard for me to believe he's really here," Nicodemus said.

Samuel agreed, "Yes, it's difficult for me also. After all this time, we can no longer doubt it. I have also learned that the Secret Council of Seers confirmed that it is true."

"At last," Nicodemus sighed, "the Anointed One is in Jerusalem. Our people's hope for freedom will be restored."

Samuel tugged at Nicodemus's robe and said, "Don't be so jubilant. The council also warned that it's a double-edged sword. Although his presence will bring great glory to our one God, he will also pose a danger to the reputation of all Pharisees."

"We must find him, Samuel! We must!"

The men sat with Jesus at Judas's large dining table. Seth obediently sat to the side. "If you have the power to heal the blind, why don't you just walk the streets of Jerusalem and heal everyone's infirmities?" Peter challenged Jesus.

"People cannot be healed against their will. That would go against the will of my Father. When people sincerely ask for help, then they are best able to receive it," Jesus replied.

"W-w-w-what do you mean b-b-by that?" Simon asked. "Doesn't G-G-God want us t-t-to be whole?"

"Of course He does," Jesus replied. "But people must have the desire and the will to heal and to work and live by His laws and to have true faith that healing is possible."

"So then you aren't the true Messiah," Andrew stated.

Jesus slowly looked at each man around the table. The room fell silent. "I see," Jesus said. "You all have your doubts about my destiny. You have witnessed my deeds. You lean one way wanting to believe, yet you see a man before you who says that he cannot heal anyone against his will. So you ask yourselves, 'How can this man be a true Messiah?'"

The men's expressions hardened.

Once more Jesus looked at each man and then said, "I see that my words alone will not convince you. Perhaps it is because I am still in a state of transition. However, I have already begun to fulfill the prophecies of my coming, and my powers continue to grow. I need your help, your faith, and your love and acceptance to fulfill my Father's mission. You cannot imagine it now, but there are important roles for you to fill. I invite you to join me to learn and to teach others and for you also to become healers of others."

The men stared at Jesus a moment and then gauged one another's reactions. John finally asked, "What did you mean when you said that you want us to become teachers and healers? We aren't priests or messiahs. How can we heal?"

Before I arrived, you came together because you share a like mind, and you are all here now because you share a common purpose," Jesus replied. "I know that each of you possesses gifts that you have yet to realize. Those gifts have been bestowed upon you so that you can fulfill your mission to help enlighten mankind to create new and better ways of living. With your will and desire to learn, I will teach you how to use my Father's spiritual laws so that you will have the opportunity to master His Ways of Life."

Andrew protested, "We already have the Torah with God's words and laws. What do you offer that is better?"

"There is exalted truth in the Torah, if only man could understand it in a more enlightened way," Jesus sighed. "We have had the Torah for scores of centuries, yet with all of its laws and wisdom, the masses have not sincerely embraced it, and our Jewish brothers and sisters have been persecuted for their practice and belief in it. There are many conflicts of interpretation and meaning of the Torah, which has divided the people of Israel rather than unifying us. I have accepted the divine task of simplifying my Father's spiritual laws so that the masses may better understand and one day embrace His intended 'Way' for mankind's glory."

"Are you implying that you are to be the next Moses with new Commandments?" Luke asked indignantly.

"I do not intend to contradict or replace the Torah. However our present times need a new direction, and I must follow the path that my Father unfolds before me. Please join me and call those who are true of heart and have the desire to seek the wisdom of spiritual laws to also join us to meet with John the Baptist."

"What makes you think we want to go with you?" Andrew asked.

"It's my invitation to you. It's your choice to choose to come or not. I cannot make anyone act against his or her will. That is my Father's first spiritual law of The Way."

A commotion of loud voices was heard from the front gate outside, and then it became quiet again. Judas turned to Seth and said, "Go and see what is happening outside our wall."

Seth quickly rose and went outside.

Except for Jesus and Judas, the men got up from the table and spoke quietly among themselves.

Ten minutes passed. Judas stood up and said, "I am going with the Rabbi when he leaves to see John the Baptist. I will provide provisions for those of you who choose to join us. I urge you all to come."

Peter said, "It can get very cold and damp at night by the River Jordan."

The back door swung open. Seth briskly walked in carrying a neatly folded earthy-red robe and said, "I used the stepladder to look over the walls. I counted eighty-seven people including the small groups at the back. They must think that we're going to leave over a back wall. Everyone is clamoring for the Rabbi healer."

Seth placed the robe on the table between Jesus and Judas and said, "I found this on the floor of the stall." Judas began unfolding the robe and lifted it up when a pair of sandals dropped onto the table from within the robe. The binding straps of each sandal were neatly stitched from what appeared to have been previous tears.

Jesus picked up the sandals, smiled, bowed his head, and solemnly said, "I thank you, Father, for your blessings." He turned to Judas and said, "These are the sandals that I had lost in the desert. They're like new." He then picked up the robe, held it to his chest and said, "This is my robe. It is fresh and clean and will give me warmth."

Jesus looked at the men staring at him. He smiled wider and said, "My Father is very pleased with me."

16

The next morning, Judas, John, Matthew, Luke, Andrew, and Peter were finishing the last of their breakfast. Jesus and Seth were talking in Judas's bedroom. A frantic knock was heard at the front door. When Judas opened it, he saw Phillip, Nathaniel and Thomas with anxious expressions on their faces. Without being asked to come in, they quickly entered. Thomas firmly shut the door behind them.

Nathaniel said, "We heard about the Rabbi's healing of Ezra and wanted to confirm what had really happened. We also shared similar dreams last night that have left us unnerved."

Phillip pointed at the closed front door and said, "There's a huge crowd outside your wall. They are saying that the Rabbi is the Messiah."

"We'll tell you everything the Rabbi has revealed to us. How many people are outside?" Judas asked.

Thomas replied, "Go see for yourself."

Jesus came in and said, "Tell the people I will come out to them later."

Judas climbed up the stepladder to look over the wall. To his amazement, there were now over two hundred and fifty people lined up on both sides of the street. A narrow path allowing space for passage was left open in the middle. At one end of the street stood a rotund merchant beside a large white horse. Women gathered around him looking at his wares that were laid upon a blanket on the ground. Four horse-mounted Roman soldiers observed the group from the far end of the street. Away from the crowd, a Bedouin sat proudly upon his sleek black stallion.

A woman outside saw Judas looking over his wall at the crowd below. She called out to him, "When is the Messiah coming out?"

Those nearby started shouting. One said, "We want to see him!" A woman asked, "Is he really the Messiah?" A man declared, "Of course he is! I saw him cure Ezra of his blindness. The Messiah was also in my dreams."

The people who lined the opposite side of the street quickly crossed over and massed below where Judas had appeared. They all began pleading and yelling for the Rabbi to come out. Judas held up his hands and said, "Please be patient. He will come out a little later." Judas hurried down the stepladder and scurried back into the house.

An hour passed as Judas's group spoke about all that had happened. Seth had gone to Jesus in his room earlier and said that Jesus did not want to be disturbed until it was time to leave. Now, Judas excused himself and, knocking on his own bedroom door, went in. Jesus was lying on Judas's bed staring blankly at the ceiling. Jesus turned to Judas and said, "I know, it's time to go."

Judas sat on the side of the bed and said, "The large crowd outside is demanding that you come out soon."

"I know," Jesus acknowledged.

Judas continued, "I need to tell you about some problems. The men have been talking about a dream they all shared last night. You kept appearing to them and offering salvation to them if they asked for it. They are disturbed by the common dream and don't know what to make of it. I told them about the dream I had before I met you. They became more disturbed thinking that you might have been sent by the Devil."

Jesus laughed. "I have told you that there is no real Devil, only God. Dreams till the soil of the mind so that my Father can plant seeds of truth and wisdom. I am here to nurture and encourage those seeds to take root and grow. There is no need for fear or apprehension, for it is up to each one to let the seeds grow or not."

"So you know about the dreams. Andrew also spoke to some of the people outside the wall early this morning. Many of them said that they saw a likeness of you in their dreams healing a blind man and then refusing money, unlike other healers."

Jesus sat up next to Judas and said, "Those dreams prepare people for what they will see."

Judas asked, "What will they see?"

"I'm not certain," Jesus said, laughing, "but we shall see."

⬭

At the dining room table, Peter said to Matthew and Andrew, "We all acknowledge that the Rabbi has genuine powers, but because he has entered our dreams, we must be guarded, lest he try to possess us."

Andrew adamantly added, "Anyone who thinks that he can replace the Ten Commandments and the Torah is not to be trusted."

Matthew shook his head and said, "Don't judge him so quickly. All that I have seen him do has resulted in good. No one has been harmed or threatened. But I also agree with you that he is unconventional, and that makes most people uncomfortable. Still, let us be open."

In a corner of the dining room, Simon, John, and Luke stood and continued to speak with Thomas, Nathaniel, and Phillip. They related what Jesus had said about his mission. They also told of Jesus wanting them to become his followers. Luke said, "It's shocking to me that so many of the people outside claim that he's the Messiah."

John nodded, "Our people hunger for a Messiah to lead them to freedom. They want to believe that the prophecies will be fulfilled and that the time of his coming is now."

John said, "It's too hard for me to believe that he is the one and that we are in his company. He looks and acts ordinary, like a man, not a messiah."

Simon said, "W-w-w-what is a M-M-Messiah s-s-supposed to l-l-l-look like?"

Judas and Jesus came into the room. Judas said, "We're ready." He nodded to Andrew. "Go out and tell them."

The newcomers, Thomas, Nathaniel, and Phillip, looked bewildered. Judas began to explain to them what they were going to do.

Andrew reluctantly opened the front door and then quickly closed it behind him. Within moments, the crowd had surged around him. The Roman soldiers moved closer. Andrew stepped back, his body pressed against the gate. He held up his hands and said loudly, "Please allow us space when the Rabbi comes out, or he will go back in."

The crowd unwillingly backed away a few feet. Andrew said, "Please, leave more room. Stay on the other side of the street. We don't want to block the passage, or the soldiers will disperse us. Thank you." Andrew went back through the gate.

A few minutes later Andrew came through the door again and quickly closed it behind him once more. People began to mass toward him again. "Please, stay back," he said firmly, making pushing motions with his raised hands, and repeated, "If you crowd the Rabbi when he comes out, he will go back in." The people backed away once more.

Andrew opened the door. Judas, Luke, Simon, and Peter came out and nervously looked around. A moment later, Matthew, Phillip, Nathaniel, Thomas, and John came out, and all stood in a semi-circle around the door. Then Jesus came out holding Seth's hand. A woman in the crowd yelled, "It's him!" A man exclaimed, "He's the Messiah! Please fill my empty coin purse!" Another pleaded, "Please put food on my table for my children."

The crowd began to converge on the group of men. The Bedouin nudged his stallion, and in a flash he was at the edge of the crowd. He arced his horse to and fro, creating a large space between the encroaching people and Jesus's inner circle. He turned, nodding to Jesus, and gestured toward the empty path that he had created on the street. Jesus nodded back and walked ahead with a casual grace, unaffected, Seth following alongside. Judas and his companions walked anxiously behind them. The Bedouin followed, the crowd followed behind him, and the soldiers followed them all. The crowd passed the merchant, who was quickly loading his wares into sacks and strapping them onto the sides of his horse's saddle.

After twenty minutes, they came upon a large open square where two large streets intersected. More people had joined the crowd, some out of curiosity, some compelled by their dreams. Six more soldiers of the Roman cavalry had joined the other four. A limping man approached Jesus's group from the opposite direction. The hood of his shabby robe covered his head, revealing only a small part of his face. His raggedy long sleeves covered his hands. He walked directly toward Jesus as both neared the center of the square.

"You are the Messiah," the cloaked man stated in a weak, raspy voice.

Jesus nodded and then smiled. The crowd edged forward and surrounded them except for a buffer zone maintained by Jesus's inner circle. The Bedouin stayed alongside the group and put his hand on his sword, ready to draw it if necessary.

Jesus raised his hands in a gesture requesting quiet. He held his hands up until the tense and excited crowd stood silently. In a soft voice, Jesus asked the man with the limp, "What is it that you want?"

The cloaked man lifted up his arms and pulled the hood back from his head. The crowd loudly gasped, "LEPER!" In horror, they quickly moved back ten paces and turned their heads away although most soon peeked out to see what was happening. Jesus again held up his hands, and the crowd became still.

The leper answered Jesus, "I want you to make me clean again. You are the Messiah and you can heal me."

The leper's disfigured face was covered with raised rashes and grotesque lumps. Half of his nose was gone. One eye was clouded over with a milky white tinge. His clawed necrotic hands were also covered with ugly lumps. Two fingers were missing on one hand and three fingers on the other. Their stumps were red-raw and irregular. The leper took a small knife from his inside belt. The crowd nervously edged back further. He opened his palm and ran his blade across it, cutting a small bloodless slash in the cheesy flesh. He said, "I feel no pain. I feel no pleasure. Please, make me clean and whole. I want to live a life where people no longer shun me, which is worse than the rotting of my flesh."

The crowd now stared wide-eyed at what was happening. Jesus extended his arms to the leper and said, "Come to me." Many people gasped again.

The man limped slowly toward Jesus as Jesus stepped toward him. Jesus's arms were still extended, inviting an embrace. The leper hesitated, as no stranger would ever consider embracing a leper. Jesus beckoned him, "Come. It will be all right."

The leper's tense shoulders relaxed. He stepped closer, and Jesus compassionately and lovingly embraced him. The crowd cringed; tears flowed from the leper's eyes. Still in their embrace, Jesus placed one hand behind the leper's head and the other between his shoulder blades. The leper rested his head on Jesus's shoulder as the two stood motionless together for a minute. Jesus then said, "I welcome you into my Father's Kingdom. You are worthy."

The crowd looked on with disgust. Then their eyes opened wide and their jaws dropped open in amazement. Slowly the grotesque lumps flattened on the leper's face and hands. Jesus stepped back and held hands with the leper as they looked into each other's eyes. The milky white of the leper's eye faded; the eroded half of his nose smoothed, leaving only a slight distortion.

Jesus said to the man, "Look at your hands."

The leper held up his hands and looked at his palms. The remaining red, rough and cheesy fingers had healed. His finger stumps and the skin on his palms were smooth and clean, free of the knife's gash. He touched his face. He wept and said, "My skin feels … it feels clean. I feel clean." He breathed in deeply and stood tall. He smiled, and then tears streamed from his eyes. He fell to his knees, kissed Jesus's feet and exclaimed, "You are the true Messiah. You are my Savior! Bless you! Bless you!"

The stunned crowd cautiously moved closer for a better look. Their disbelief evaporated when the leper stood tall on his toes in glee and all could see that he was clean. The Roman soldiers looked at each other, amazed and disbelieving. People from the crowd called out to Jesus, frantically pleading for healings and gifts of prosperity. As the crowd began to close in on him, Judas's group protectively tightened their circle around Jesus and Seth. The Bedouin assassin drew his sword, extending it outward from his side. With a look in his dark eyes as sharp as his sword, he circled around Jesus and his companions, warding off the encroaching crowd. The Roman horsemen merged into the large crowd that blocked the square. They ordered, "Disperse! Disperse!" as they pushed people to the sides, knocking many to the ground. The outer fringes of the crowd still moved toward Jesus. The soldiers lowered their spears, threatening those who dared disobey.

Slowly the crowd backed off. Judas grabbed Jesus's arm and quickly pulled him back toward his home. Matthew held Seth's hand and hurried along with his fellows, who had encircled Jesus. The Bedouin cleared a path, leading the way to Judas's house.

As they were quickly passing the outer fringe of the crowd, an aristocratically dressed woman broke through the back of the protective circle surrounding Jesus and reached out toward him. Luke's long arm partially blocked her, and as she fell to the ground, she grasped the bottom of Jesus's robe and plaintively said, "I have been severely ill for over two years. Please! Help me!"

Jesus stopped and turned his head, saw her distraught face, and reached down to touch her hand. John pushed Jesus forward to keep him moving away from the encroaching crowd, preventing Jesus's hand from touching hers. The woman quickly pulled herself up to avoid being trampled by the advancing crowd.

Jesus briefly made eye contact with her and said, "Take heart, Woman; your faith has made you well."

Pushed by his men, Jesus hurried along. The woman placed her hand over her heart. Tears of gratitude welled in her eyes from the miracle that she felt she had received. She stood tall and serene as the surging crowd streamed around her.

17

A half hour later, Judas came back into the house and joined the men seated around the dining table. He plopped down in his chair next to Peter and with a sigh, said, "I gave gold coins to four more soldiers." Judas chuckled, "Today I can appreciate Rome's soldiers. The finest money can buy. They will keep the street cleared and people away from the back walls." The men continued their excited conversation.

A little later, Jesus walked into the room and sat on the empty mat at the head of the table. The men's unsettled and frustrated expressions caught Judas's eye. He turned and stared at Jesus, who shrugged his shoulders and said, "Say what you need to say, Judas."

"The men are awed at what you did today. They marvel at your healing powers. They want to trust you, but they feel even more guarded that you can follow their thoughts as if they were naked, and again, they also feel threatened that you can invade their dreams."

Jesus addressed the men in a soft, compassionate voice. "If one's thoughts are for good and brotherhood, then why should one feel shame that others may know them? Think in terms of God's will, and there is nothing to fear. I make no judgment of anyone's thoughts; I only offer absolution to those who ask for forgiveness. You are meant to think of all things that your gift of imagination offers you. The merit of your character is determined less by your thoughts and far more by your actions when you do good by helping others, as Judas has done. It is folly to try and hide one's thoughts, for on a spiritual level, all thoughts are known, and I know not to pass judgment."

The men were silent as they pondered his words. Some relaxed their shoulders. Peter remained tense, saying, "It is no coincidence that most of us shared the same dream last night of you performing a miracle and then all of us being chased by a mob. None of us could remember what the miracle was, but the dreams have come to fruition, reflected in what you did today. That you are especially gifted has moved us. But you have no right to enter our dreams when our will to resist is dampened by sleep."

Jesus replied, "I understand how you would feel if I entered your dreams uninvited. That would be an intrusion. That is not my usual way. My dreams are shared with God, and God offers His dreams to all who seek answers and help. Dreams belong to everyone, but no one can know everyone's dreams. I have told you that I cannot control another's will, be they awake or asleep."

Luke leaned toward Jesus. "But our shared dream came true! That's unnerving!"

His voice still soft, Jesus replied, "Dreams, whether they appear good or bad to the dreamer, need not become a reality. Dreams are meant to be informative; some are curiously remembered, and most are not. Dreams can serve as a guide to life, or they can be ignored. Some dreams can serve as a warning to avoid dangerous circumstances that may cross your path; other dreams can inform you to be alert to an opportunity that may enhance your life because you might ignore that opportunity otherwise."

Andrew asked, "Are you saying that you don't enter dreams and influence people in their sleep?"

"If I see someone on the street who is in need of help, I reach out to offer my help in whatever way I can – especially if asked, as I have responded to the requests of Ezra and the man with leprosy today. I do the same in dreams. I reach out and offer help to those in need who desire my help, although they may not even know of me."

Thomas said suspiciously, "I don't recall asking you to help me."

Jesus sat back, surveying each man's face, and said, "Who among you does not pray and yearn for freedom from the injustices and intolerable hardships that the Romans have pressed upon us? Who among you does not seek to know the deeper meaning of God's ways? Who among you does not want a better life and to end the needless suffering that you see daily?"

The men looked at each other and nodded in acknowledgement that they all shared the same desires.

Jesus continued, "Your wants and desires express certain lacks in your life that yearn for fulfillment and are calls for help. Asleep or awake, I have become aware of your yearnings, and I reach out to offer my help, as I do now. I don't intrude; I am there for you when your yearnings call out, and you can accept the help and guidance I offer or not."

John said, "Experiencing you in my dream bothered me. I saw your image, your face, the way you walk; I heard your voice. I felt the power of your presence. It made me feel good and yet apprehensive."

"Dreams can serve many purposes. They can be unsettling; they can be used to play with possibilities or to create and to experience and even to experiment in so that you can learn and be guided in life to make better choices. Dreams can also rejuvenate and heal. My help is offered to all who ask. But also be open to your own inner voice and listen to its wisdom. It is not complicated; true wisdom is simple and practical."

Simon said, "I l-l-like my dreams. I g-g-g-get to d-d-d-do things th-th-that are fun."

Seth, sitting to the side, said to Jesus, "You can visit me anytime in my dreams."

Jesus smiled, "Thank you, Seth. I accept your invitation." Jesus turned to the others. "Great challenges lie ahead if you choose to accept the invitation that I have extended to you to join me on my mission. I need your help."

"Help to do what?" Peter asked.

Jesus replied, "I need all of you to be my disciples. I will teach you so that you can teach others when I am gone."

Joseph, Lev, and Benjamin sat in Zadak's chamber, continuing their reporting to him of Jesus's doings.

"Why would a Bedouin help this Jesus healer?" Zadak asked.

"He was the one Jesus was talking to and drinking wine with at the tavern. I think Jesus befriended him," Lev said.

"Highly unusual," Zadak mused. "A Bedouin? Are you absolutely sure of the healing?"

Joseph replied, "There is no doubt. The leper's disfigured face and skin healed right before our eyes. No one has ever seen anything like that before. No other healer has performed such a miracle. My dream of Jesus was true. I told you that the Messiah would bring light to the darkness and ugliness of Jerusalem. It was definitely a miracle."

"The healed leper called Jesus the true Messiah and his Savior," Benjamin added. "Everyone in the crowd tried to touch the Rabbi. They were all captivated by what he had done."

"Go back and watch this Jesus and Iscariot closely. Report back to me," Zadak said firmly.

"The Roman soldiers won't let anyone go down Iscariot's street anymore," Benjamin replied.

"Then split up and wait at the ends of the street. I want to know who comes and goes. If Jesus leaves, follow him closely. Now go," Zadak ordered.

Lydia's handmaiden, Nandia, took the long gold necklace from the lavish jewelry box and clasped it around her mistress's neck. Lydia looked into her polished metal mirror and adjusted the necklace over her finely woven purple tunic. "Do you think he will remember?" she asked her handmaiden.

"I am certain," Nandia replied. "You look radiant."

Lydia smiled, and left her dressing room, then entered her husband's study, where he was examining a small gold sculpture of a Roman centurion on a horse. He turned to greet her, his eyes opening wide in surprise. "My dear Lydia, your skin shines as it hasn't in years. What has happened?"

"I've been healed. I feel as I did in my youth," she replied.

"I can't believe my eyes. How is it possible?"

She related how Jesus had healed the leper and how certain she felt that the Rabbi could perform a miraculous transformation in her health as well and how her expectation was fulfilled in an instant when she touched Jesus's robe.

"It's unbelievable, my love. But I can't deny how you look." He stood and placed his hands on her shoulders, examining her face closely. "Your lines of worry and misery have vanished. You are not stooping over anymore." He passed his hands admiringly down her neck, tracing them over the gold necklace. He smiled lovingly and then said tenderly, "This is the necklace that I gave you just before we were married."

"I wear it now because I feel as I did then," Lydia replied.

Her husband hugged her close and said, "It's a miracle. Thank the gods."

"I thank the man who healed me," Lydia replied.

"I would thank him also, but I am a Roman official, and he is a Jew. You mustn't tell anyone about this."

"I already have told Zena, who visited with me when I first came back."

"Zena!" He pulled away, distraught. "You told her? Where is your sister now?"

"She left an hour ago to go back home."

"This isn't good, Lydia. Surely she will tell her husband. You know we can't be seen to have any religious associations with rabbis."

"Zena would never let Pontius Pilate do anything that would harm us. Take heart, my husband, I am well again."

He stared at the floor, clenched his teeth, shook his head, and said, "This cannot be good."

⟨⟩

Samuel was walking fast, pulling his sister, Lois, by her hand. She could barely keep up with him. In the rear garden of the Great Synagogue, they came upon Nicodemus. "At last I found you," Samuel said, catching his breath.

"I was about to look for you," Nicodemus replied. "I've been hearing rumors about miraculous healings."

"And when you hear what my sister witnessed today, you will know that the Messiah is already performing miracles in Jerusalem as prophesied." Samuel looked at his sister. "Tell him, Lois. Tell him about your dream and the leper that you saw the Messiah heal."

18

Later that day, Jesus looked up at the vibrant palm tree that had grown a foot taller. He smiled with great satisfaction. Dragonflies hovered, then darted back and forth as if in a dance with the birds. The grassy area dotted with the small yellow flowers surrounding the palm had grown wider. The air had a sweet fragrance.

Judas sat next to Jesus and stared at him with great awe. Judas had no doubt in his heart that the Messiah sat before him. They had been in private conversation a while, and Jesus continued to speak about charity. "When people are impoverished, sick and in pain and in need of healing, their fears and worries thrust them into a survival mode of thinking, and so they think mainly of their own needs. That is understandable. But when the affluent think only of their own needs and disregard the needs of the needy, that is not in harmony with the laws of my Father and His intent for man to be as one family. It is better to give than to receive, for to give help or money, regardless of one's finances or stature, is an affirmation of one's spiritual wealth that grows larger when what one has is shared with others who have not."

Judas smiled and said, "Perhaps that is why it gives me pleasure to help those in need."

"Yours is a rare soul in Jerusalem, Judas. For you give your money charitably rather than lend your money to make interest to become richer," Jesus said.

Judas grinned and said, "Those who need the most help are the least likely to be able to pay me back, and especially not with added interest. It is better that I tell them that when they are able, they can pay me back. It makes my gift to them feel less like charity and more like a loan. It also helps to preserve their dignity. If I'm ever paid back, it's a surprise to me. I tell them that I'm happy for their success and that with their repayment, I have more to give to others in need and so should they also give to those in need as they are able to do so."

Jesus smiled and said, "To those of true good heart, sharing success and happiness is a true joy. Why don't you use some of your money to buy a mansion in the richer neighborhood?"

"My modest home suits me. This way I don't need servants to take care of rooms I don't need. My friends help me keep up the house, and I help them."

Jesus laughed. "That's why I love you. Your mind thinks in harmony with my Father's intended ways of life. You are a true counterpart to me. You even follow the ancient teachings of the Torah to forgive debts in the seventh sabbatical year."

Judas's forehead furrowed. "I do for those who borrowed for their businesses so that they could become more prosperous and in turn would help others. Since I have taken over running my family's farmlands and manage the money, my loans have become a sore point with them. The Torah says that every seventh year, the land shall go uncultivated, the Hebrew slaves shall be set free, and all debts shall be cancelled. I have no slaves, but every seven years I do cancel debts and leave the fields uncultivated. The crops grow more bountifully the following years and easily make up for the one lost year. But those laws of the Torah are no longer practiced in Jerusalem."

Jesus replied, "In ancient times, to keep money lending from becoming a business, the Jewish community followed the Torah and cancelled debts to maintain giving as an act of aid from one person to another. Now, under Roman laws, the framework has changed."

Judas agreed. "They have a money-based economy, not a spiritually-based one. When the seventh sabbatical year approaches, no one in Judea would lend money if the debts were to be cancelled. Credit would dry up, business and trade would fail, and Rome would lose tax revenues. Now, the law requires that a debtor and creditor make a contract and agree in court before a judge that the debt will not be cancelled in the sabbatical year so that credit and business will keep flowing and so the money lenders and Rome will continue to grow richer. Thank goodness I have no need to follow those ways and I'm financially independent so I can help those I choose to in the way that I want."

Jesus smiled broadly, "You are blessed with your financial wealth because of your natural spiritual wealth and generous nature, which inspire you to give to those who have need."

Judas shrugged his shoulders and said, "I do what feels right. And now I must tell you of the plan that I've made so that we can leave to see John the Baptist. There are too many people waiting for you at both ends of the street. The crowd has doubled in size and is growing larger. I've paid the soldiers not to allow anyone near our house," Judas smiled but then became quite serious. "If you go out and the people see you, they will mob you as before, and the mob grows bigger even as we speak. So this is the plan: Simon will take his cart with Seth to get the supplies to build the bench."

Jesus put his hand on Judas's shoulder, pointed to the barren walls and dark red earth bordering his home, and said, "Have them also get pomegranate and camellia seeds and some fig tree saplings. Your yard needs colorful flowers and fruit trees."

Judas protested, "How can you talk about plantings now? Nothing grows here anyway."

Jesus rolled back his head and laughed. He opened his arms and said, "Judas, look above at this palm and look below at the new grass that you sit upon."

Judas sheepishly looked around and then said with surrender, "I'll tell them to get what you've asked for." His face turned serious again. "We have all discussed the plan and ..."

Jesus cut him off, "I know of the plan. But I do like to hear the devoted way in which you express yourself and see your aura of protection toward me. You are a blessing to me. Your intent to protect me is welcome, but do not fear for me. I do not fear for myself because I have faith that my Father protects me in all ways."

"Then allow us to help God protect you," Judas replied.

John, Nathaniel, Phillip, Thomas, Andrew, Simon, Matthew, Peter, Luke, and Seth came out the back door and stood over Judas and Jesus. Jesus patted the grass and beckoned, "Please join us. We will all talk."

They sat around Jesus in a semi-circle, and then Judas said, "Now we must review what we are going to do one last time.

Pontius Pilate stood on the balcony of his Jerusalem governor's mansion. He surveyed the panoramic view of the vast city below, breathed in deeply, then let out a sigh of satisfaction as he stood proudly over the city of his jurisdiction.

Zena walked onto the balcony and leaned against Pilate. He put his arm around her and said, "Look at them below us. The Jews scurry around like busy ants gathering crumbs of bread. I have the power to crush them as I would an ant at my will."

"There may be one ant that might prove harder to destroy," Zena said.

Pilate stepped back and asked, "Why do you say that?"

"I saw Lydia today. She has made a full recovery."

Pilate scoffed, "Your sister will never be well. She has always been sickly and always will be."

"You are wrong, my husband. She glows with new life. Believe me, I know my sister far better than you do."

"How is that possible? I saw her two days ago, and she was still wan and weak."

Zena smiled. "Now she radiates new life, more vibrant than I can describe. A healer whom the Jews call their Messiah has transformed her."

Pilate scoffed, "In Jerusalem, would-be messiahs come and go. Your sister is always believing in wild cures and trying all kinds of herbs and chants. Sometimes she gets a little lift in her strength, only to fall back into her perpetual sickness."

"This time it's much different. You must see her yourself to believe me, for I wouldn't believe it myself if I hadn't seen her. And all she did to be healed was to touch the Messiah's robe."

"Stop calling him the Messiah!" Pilate ordered, annoyed. "There is no Messiah for the Jews and I will make sure there will be no Messiah for the Jews. No one will try to free the Jews and threaten my domain."

"This one has powers to perform miracles. He cured a leper before a large crowd. The leper's ugly sores and skin healed almost instantaneously. At first I thought it hard to believe, but the way Lydia spoke and how her renewed body and skin radiated vitality convinced me that she speaks the truth."

Pilate laughed. "I heard a report of some soldiers witnessing that. But it was just a hoax that has been laughed at. Your sister has a grand imagination. Instantaneous healing of a leper is nonsense."

"Invite her to dinner tonight, and you will see her 'miraculous' glow for yourself that will convince you of the healer's powers," Zena replied.

"I don't care to see your sister tonight. I have business to take care of," Pilate said and looked away to the city below.

Zena reached up and held the sides of his head. She turned Pilate's face toward her and looked deep into his eyes. In a serious voice she warned, "My husband, this time it's different. You must see Lydia with your own eyes. Then you will believe."

The peaceful ambiance of the palm tree and carpet of green grass that the men sat on as their conversation continued did little to calm their anxieties. Judas said, "We have to act casually, or they will become suspicious."

Luke responded, "We all know what to do." He turned to Jesus. "What I want to know is how you healed that leper so quickly?"

"It was the power of my Father's love within the leper that I was able to amplify combined with the leper's fervent desire to be clean. I connected God's will for mankind to be whole and healthy with the leper's desire to be clean and his belief and sincere faith that I could help him."

"But if it's God's will for man to be healthy, why are so many people sick and in need of healing?" John asked.

"Each person has different circumstances and challenges to overcome. How they go about it and the beliefs that they have about themselves and their interactions with others determine their success or create conflicts that may cause disease," Jesus replied. "In the leper's personal circumstance, it was a matter of self-loathing that had caused his flesh to rot. As a child, his parents were consumed with self-hatred, which caused them to project that hatred to those around them. They never gave him affection or love; instead, he became the main outward focus of their inner self-hatred. As an infant and small boy, he was highly susceptible to his parents' beliefs, especially when they would blame him for their problems and curse him. He grew up feeling that he was of no worth and became guilt ridden as a result of their blame. He became conditioned to expect that everyone would reject him as his parents had. In all situations, he looked for people's reactions of repulsion toward him, and he found those reactions, which confirmed his damaging thoughts about himself."

Jesus looked at everyone individually and saw that they were all following what he said. He continued, "Of course, there were also positive affirmations that people displayed toward him, but because he felt unworthy, he was closed to accepting them due to his parental conditioning. This created great pain and turmoil for the child. As he grew older, as a protective mechanism against further hurt, he became more withdrawn from society. At the same time, he also withdrew the life force from the parts of his body that society could see. As people reacted with greater disgust when his flesh began to rot, it only confirmed his belief that he was loathed and unworthy of love. That accelerated his disease. Society shunned him, and he shunned himself."

Phillip asked, "If that is so, how could you bring about his healing so quickly? It was astonishing."

"My Father has endowed me with His divine compassion. I accepted the man as he was, without judgment. That allowed him to be open. I have learned to combine my will with God's will and connect it to another's will who desires to be well and who has the faith that I can help. As I teach you to be healers, I am also learning to become a better healer. To heal the blind or a leper or anyone's illness, I know that the healing must come from a person's own desires to be well, and then I am able to act as a facilitator of God's will and His majestic power of divine love. The leprous man believed that he was unworthy of love. I was able to transfer the true thought to him that he was indeed worthy of God's love and was welcome in my Father's Kingdom. The man was at a point in his life where he yearned to accept God's love, yet he also felt unworthy of it. In my eyes and in my Father's knowing, the man was indeed worthy. When I said to him that he was 'worthy,' he accepted that truth and opened his closed door to self-love and rapidly reversed his concept of self-loathing.

Phillip asked again, "But how did the healing come about so quickly?"

"His body remembered the natural health that he was born with. I connected that memory to his diseased body and was able to vitalize and accelerate the transformation of the skin and tissues spontaneously."

The men shook their heads, not quite able to grasp the full concept.

Jesus acknowledged their difficulty in understanding his explanation and said, "Surely there were times when you felt weak or sad or sickly or depressed. Whenever you feel that way, you can focus your thoughts on the times in the past when joyous events took place, and then you can feel healthier and happier. That's because your thoughts connect that feeling of your body from the past with your present."

Jesus saw that most of the men were still confused. "I have mentioned these aspects of healing before, although in different ways. Because these concepts are new to you, you will sometimes forget, and when you ask for clarity, I will remind you that the aspects of each person's healing will differ. No two people will have the exact same causes for their problems; however, the essence of healing remains the same. As healers-to-be, you need to know that with your mind, you can learn to connect to another's way of thinking and that will help you to heal that person. But above all else, with love from your own heart, you can always connect with another. Any true connection that you make with the intention to help will always help to some degree, if only to give others the feeling that they are not alone and that you care for their well being. In that act, you become an extension of my Father's love for mankind to the degree of your understanding and desire to help your fellow man. His power will be transferred through you to them."

The men pondered Jesus's words. He said, "For now, I must use words to unlock the doors of your mind that have been closed to greater truths by the words of others before me. Words can be powerful, but without the majestic feeling of love connected to those words, there will be a hollowness to their meaning."

The men tried to grasp Jesus's explanation; some nodded in acknowledgement.

After a while, Andrew asked, "Can you heal any illness?"

"God heals, I help," Jesus replied.

Jesus looked at each one, then closed his eyes and sat in silence for a few moments. He opened his eyes and said solemnly, "Your missions are of greater importance than you can imagine at this time."

Jesus stood and said emphatically, "The way that mankind is acting, they will continue to need healing for the wounds that they will create. That is why it is crucial to illuminate God's love within all people for themselves and their neighbors. I have come not only to heal, but also to teach God's truth and spread God's love so that people can learn how to keep from wounding themselves and instead, prosper and co-create with God's will. I am teaching you so that you may teach others in this new beginning of mankind's next phase of spiritual growth."

Nathaniel said, "I am not sure I can learn to be a healer."

"Many are called, but few are chosen, for they choose not, yet they are able, or they would not be called. I call upon you to learn. You have your free will to choose to accept my call or not. One must choose to be a healer, to help others in whatever way they can, with love, from which compassion flows. Love cannot be forced; it must be given freely from the heart. When you accept your oneness with God, His powers will naturally flow through you to help others. You will be able to perform greater healings than I have."

"I w-w-would l-l-l-like to help p-p-people heal," said Simon. "I know h-h-h-how it f-f-f-feels when you are not w-w-w-wanted."

Jesus smiled warmly. "You are wanted and welcome in my company, and I want you to help others."

Simon sat taller.

Matthew asked, "Do I understand correctly that the way a person thinks about himself affects the way he feels about himself, which in turn, affects his health?"

Jesus replied, "It is more the way people feel about themselves that affects the way they think about themselves; however, the way people think and feel about themselves is the way that they perceive how others feel toward them, for better or worse. That is why love must be foremost in healing mankind's ills, for when love is in our hearts, we are able to perceive love in others and treat them non-judgmentally with kindness and acceptance."

John said, "I feel a calling to help others, but I know I could never heal a Roman. I could never accept or love him."

The others nodded in agreement. Jesus said, "On a spiritual level, all are of one great essence. I know this is difficult to understand; nonetheless, no one person is separate from another. Spiritually, all are connected, and all are one family. God is in each and all - that is what a true healer thinks and feels. That is what empowers a healer."

Peter's eyes narrowed as he asked Jesus, "Would you help a Roman?"

Jesus replied, "Did I ask the leper if he was a Roman?"

In his private chamber, Pontius Pilate spoke with harsh disdain as he addressed Zadak. "You have been appointed High Priest of the Pharisees by a Roman council, and you can easily be replaced." Pilate pointed at Zadak. "You will collect the higher tax rate for the new aqueduct, or your replacement will."

Zadak stiffened. "My people already complain bitterly that their taxes are unbearable."

Disgusted, Pilate said, "They are always complaining." His voice intensified. "Jerusalem needs water to live, to prosper, and to generate more revenue. Rome has deemed the aqueduct a priority. Your people will complain more if their water is rationed or stopped. The new aqueduct will be built."

Zadak protested, "The people will refuse to pay. I will have to deal with their anger."

Pilate poked his finger into Zadak's chest. "I don't care what you have to deal with. I have to deal with Rome. If you don't implement the new tax, then I will take the gold from your temple treasury. One way or another, Jerusalem will have a new aqueduct."

Zadak looked at Pilate with an icy stare,

Pilate stared back. "I have no fear of you. You had better have a fear of me."

Zadak held his stare for a moment longer, then looked away. Pilate smiled with satisfaction.

As Zadak walked toward the door to leave, he turned and said, "Perhaps you do have something to fear. It is being said that the prophecies of a Messiah coming and bringing Rome to its knees are now being fulfilled. He is here in Jerusalem, performing miracles. He stays at the home of Judas Iscariot."

"I know of Iscariot and his wealthy family." Pilate flicked his hands dismissively. "I also know of your Jewish superstitions and the promise of your Messiah coming. Let him come. Rome has no fear of Jewish gods. Rome will always be. Any would-be Messiah who challenges Rome will be a Messiah nailed to a cross."

John walked in through the front door carrying two empty food baskets. He said to the men sitting around the table, "The soldiers said to thank you for the food, Judas. Their shift will rotate at midnight. I told them to tell me when the morning shift takes over so I can bring them breakfast. They said that they'd let us know."

Judas smiled and nodded his approval. He turned to Simon and said, "It's time to go."

Simon and Seth stood up to leave. Jesus asked Seth," Do you remember the list?"

Without hesitation, in one long breath, Seth precisely recited the entire long list of carpentry tools needed to construct the bench. Then with another breath, he added, "We will also get the fig tree saplings, camellia and pomegranate seeds."

The men were impressed with Seth's display of memory. Jesus said, "Excellent, Seth. You grace this house with your presence. Your elders should feel blessed that you are here to help them."

Seth smiled and shyly looked down. He and Simon headed toward the back door to the stall housing his donkey and cart. Jesus said to them, "Also, would you please get four long, old, beat-up wide wood planks."

Peter asked, "Why old and beat-up?"

Jesus said, "I believe we will need them."

In her bedroom, Zena sat at her large dressing table facing a five-foot high, finely polished metal mirror. Two jeweled hand mirrors lay face down on her dressing table; she held another mirror inches from her face and examined the artistically applied patterns of black mascara and eyeliner made from powdered antimony and gum. Zena nodded approvingly at herself. She removed seven precious jeweled gold rings from her fingers and toes, then removed six gold bracelets from one slender arm, leaving the gold serpentine bracelet winding from her wrist to her elbow on the other arm. She turned her head to the side and looked at herself in the wall mirror, scrutinizing the glittering jewels hanging from her ears. She nodded her approval again and said, "I thank you again, my husband. The new earrings are stunning."

"Not as stunning as you," Pilate said as he reclined on their bed. "Come over here so I can see them more closely."

Zena raised her elaborately decorated eyebrows and replied, "I know what you want to see."

"Come here now. You have been in front of those mirrors for a half hour."

"Just a minute more," Zena said coyly. She collected the rings on the table and tossed them onto a pile of other jeweled rings in her large, ornate jewelry box. She then took off her radiant necklace and laid it over two dozen other necklaces.

"Are you going to come here now, or do you want me to come and get you?" Pilate said impatiently.

Zena turned down the oil lamps to illuminate their bedroom with a golden glow. She stood up and faced Pilate. His eyes opened wide with delight as the soft light behind her sensuously defined the silhouette of her naked body beneath the sheer nightgown. The flowing curves of her shapely form were perfectly proportioned, her stance irresistibly alluring.

She suppressed a smile of satisfaction in knowing how to draw a powerful man's attention and fuel his anticipation. Pilate sat up straighter and motioned her to come to him. Casually she walked to their bed as if he weren't there, then settled herself on the bed, reclining two feet from Pilate. He immediately moved to her side. She reached down and brushed her hand over her leg to straighten the nightgown that didn't need straightening.

Pilate nestled his nose in her neck, breathed in deeply through his flared nostrils, then said, "When your perfume mixes with the scent of your body, the fragrance is intoxicating."

Zena leaned down and brushed her leg again without looking at Pilate and then said, "I want to know what you thought of Lydia's recovery and what she told us at dinner about the rabbi healer and her dream."

"Not now," Pilate protested. "It's been a long day. I need to think about it. We'll talk tomorrow."

Zena folded her arms across her chest. Pilate pulled away. She said, "It's my sister." Then she turned to him and gently stroked his arm, "Can't we just talk for a little bit?" She stroked him more sensuously. "Please ..."

"All right," he relented, "but not one of those long talks that go on until you get too tired and then fall asleep or you turn it into an argument."

She softly traced her finger over the side of his face, "Of course not, my husband. Didn't Lydia look vibrant?"

"Yes, yes. She did," Pilate replied. "I must admit I was very surprised. In all the years I've known your sister, she's never looked so radiant or so attractive."

"Attractive?" Zena's shoulders slumped. "Do you find her attractive? I think I shall touch the Rabbi's robe to make me more attractive."

"Don't even joke about being helped by a rabbi," Pilate retorted sharply. "You know your sister does not appeal to me." He edged closer to her and put his arm around her shoulder. "There is no other like you that I have ever seen in all the lands I've traveled to."

Pilate caressed her other shoulder and felt the softness of her smooth, flawless skin. He caressed her slender upper arm, plying its firm and supple flesh. His fingers tenderly moved down her arm to her forearm and touched the long gold serpentine bracelet. "Even the finest beauties in the Emperor's court pale beside you."

Zena placed her hand on Pilate' thigh and gently squeezed it. He edged closer and said, "I see the way other men look at you, even my personal guards. If I turn toward them with you in the room, I see their gaze quickly turn away from you for fear that I will have their eyes plucked out. But it is also a compliment to me that your beauty is so captivating."

Grasping the serpentine bracelet, he lifted up her arm. "Even the Emperor has been taken with you. Why is it that you never take off this bracelet that he gave you?"

Zena kissed Pilate's cheek. "There is nothing to worry about, my husband. It serves as a reminder to me that the Emperor of Rome has empowered you to be governor of all Jerusalem. I wear it in homage to that power."

Pilate asked, "Would you still have reverence for Tiberius if he were just a man and not an Emperor?"

Zena proudly lifted her chin. "I know Rome's emperor is supposed to be thought of as a son of God and not just a man. But that's what he is, just a man. That is why I told you to build the temple in Caesarea in honor of Tiberius. I knew that building the temple in Rome's capital city in Palestine would curry his favor for you, my husband. It was my idea to put both your names on the temple cornerstone, binding you together as one source of power, and he has appointed you Prefect of Jerusalem."

Pilate eyed her suspiciously. "And since Tiberius is just a man, what also might have occurred between you and him in his private quarters to garner his favor toward us?"

Zena pulled away. "I've told you many times, there is nothing to talk about. If you don't believe me, ask Tiberius."

"You know I don't intend ever to question the Emperor. That's why I ask you," Pilate replied.

Zena leaned her shoulder against his and squeezed his thigh again. She caressed his leg and said, "There's no other man like you. All you have accomplished has been brilliant. I know that your deeds and the name of Pontius Pilate will long be remembered in history."

Pilate's chest puffed out, and as he moved closer to her, Zena asked, "What did you think when Lydia told you about the leper and the Rabbi?"

Pilate's chest deflated. "I told you we would talk tomorrow. I would need to see it to believe it. No more talk tonight." He pulled her close and nuzzled the satin flesh of her neck. He moved his mouth up toward her lips and started to pull her head closer. She suddenly reached up to her elaborately styled hair and pulled away as she straightened a small curl that his hand had dislodged. Quite annoyed, she said, "I sat for four hours while three women worked on my hair. Now you've ruined it all. I'm going to need a healer to fix it!"

Frustrated and disgusted, Pilate bounded out of bed and stomped toward the door. Zena called to him, "Where are you going? Come back! I want to talk to you."

In a large hall adjacent to his bedroom, Pilate angrily ordered a sentry, "Get the Commander of the Praetorian Guard. RUN!"

19

As King Herod Antipas stepped out of his morning bath, an attendant quickly held out a fresh robe for him. As he donned the robe, Octavius hurriedly entered his bath chamber. Glancing at Octavius, Herod asked, "What has happened to make you look so worried."

Octavius sounded short of breath. "I had another dream last night that gives me great concern."

"Your dreams have always been prophetic. Tell me what your dream foretold," Herod said.

Octavius swallowed and said, "It was about your beautiful gardens and the green grasses surrounding the palace." Octavius looked down at the floor, his shoulders sagging in resignation.

"What is it, Octavius?" Herod asked impatiently. "Just say it!"

Hesitantly, Octavius spoke, "You always demanded that I tell you of things that are bad as well as the good. The dream portrayed you smiling with pride as you admired your beautiful gardens. It was the end of the day, and you went to bed feeling content. What you didn't see were the thin stems of an all-encompassing vine that had been quietly snaking its way beneath all the grass and plantings. When you awoke the next morning, the vines' leaves had sprouted and appeared everywhere. The garden plantings and grass were withered. The vines had choked off their life force. You couldn't believe how fast your green garden had turned to brown. You were dismayed and angry. You bent down and grasped a vine. You tried to pull it up, but it was too firmly rooted and the damage already done. You became furious. That's when my dream ended."

Herod frowned, paced in thought, and then asked, "Is it a Jewish conspiracy of sedition? Is John the Baptist behind it?"

Octavius shook his head. "I don't know. But of this I am certain – a powerful movement has begun and will spread."

Herod continued pacing. He stopped and pointed at Octavius. "Damn those prophecies and their promise of a Messiah! If there's a movement afoot, then there must be a central figurehead that the people want to call their king." Herod grinned. "If he loses his head, there will be no Messiah to become their king."

"We must be careful," Octavius said. "Remember that your father, the mighty Herod the Great, slaughtered all the male Jewish babies up to two years old in Bethlehem when his psychic advisors declared the Messiah had been born there recently. In trying to ensure that the prophecy would not come true, he almost fomented a rebellion. The people's anger was justified and revenues fell sharply. If a Messiah does become known, we must eliminate him in a way that doesn't incriminate you, lest we incite wrath that might indeed incite a rebellion."

Herod stared at Octavius a moment, then reluctantly said, "You're wise in your thinking." Herod then made a fist and held it high. "If anyone is to be King of the Jews," he placed his palm on his chest and declared, "it shall be me!"

———

Their faces worried, Judas and John entered the house as Seth was cleaning up after breakfast. Jesus sat with Matthew and Peter. Simon was attending to his donkey in the stable. Philip, Nathaniel, and Thomas had left for their homes the night before. John placed a basket full of food on the table and grumbled, "They refused to take 'food prepared by Jews.'"

"This is bad," Judas said. "The Praetorian Guard has replaced the Roman soldiers. I offered them money in gratitude for keeping the streets safe, but they refused it. I don't think we can leave tomorrow. They're patrolling the streets in the front and back of our house. They'll report all our activities directly to Pilate."

"Don't be dismayed," Jesus smiled, "Have faith and be of good cheer. Proceed with your plan." He stood up, turned to Seth, and said, "Come with me. We have a bench to build."

The men looked at each other cheerlessly. Peter said, "The Praetorian Guard surrounds us, and he acts as if everything's just fine."

"Maybe that's because he has the faith that we don't yet have," Judas replied.

———

Jesus and Seth had laid out all the tools and lumber near the palm tree. Jesus adjusted the blade of the plane, gave it to Seth, and said, "Here, shave the rough spots on this plank for the bench seat."

Eagerly, Seth gripped the plane and began to forcibly stroke the wood. The plane made short, jerky motions over the rough spots causing uneven chips to fly about and leaving notches in the wood. Seth stopped and looked discouraged. He asked, "What am I doing wrong? Instead of making it smoother, I'm making it rougher."

Pointing to the grain of the wood, Jesus said, "The grain of the tree has grown set in its way as a man or woman grows set in their ways. To best shape the wood, we have to work with the grain and not against it as you've done. Otherwise, we meet resistance and mar what we're trying to shape."

Jesus took the plane from Seth and with long, smooth, sweeping motions, moving with the grain, produced long, curled shavings. He handed the plane back to Seth and said, "Now try again."

Seth repositioned himself. With a determined expression, he bore down on the plane in the direction of the grain. The plane cut in, yielding a shorter, thicker curl of wood, then stopped, stuck in its path. Seth looked up at Jesus and said, "Why isn't it working like it did for you?"

"Even though you're working with the way the grain has grown, you're bearing down too hard and going too deep to shape the wood. What do you think happens when someone tries to shape a rough person's personality in too harsh a way?"

Seth looked at the plane stuck in the wood and said, "They resist, and progress stops."

Jesus smiled, "Very good! Now work with gentler strokes and see what happens."

Seth did as Jesus instructed, and soon fine, long shavings of wood spun off the top of the plane. Seth smiled delightedly. "This is much easier to do, and the wood's becoming smoother. It looks much nicer."

Jesus said, "And in the same way, it's easier to work with the grain of a man's character than to act against him, for he'll want to fight you. When you work with a person's natural traits, things go more smoothly. You can't change a person's nature, but you can direct it and shape the way that he acts."

They both looked up at the back wall as a Praetorian Guard slowly passed by on his horse. They could see only from the top of his shoulders up. His shiny helmet and the tip of his metal spear glinted in the sun. The guard sternly eyed the boy and man in the courtyard but continued without breaking stride.

"He makes me nervous," Seth said.

"Don't worry about him. He sees us, but he sees nothing to concern him. Just concern yourself with the task at hand," Jesus replied.

Seth shrugged his shoulders and continued to smooth the top of the bench plank. After a while he said, "John wants me to become a rabbi. What did you do before you were a rabbi?"

Jesus laughed and said, "As a rabbi, I earned little money as I tended mainly to the very poor. So before I became a rabbi and even after that, I've worked as a carpenter whenever I could, but more often, I worked as a day laborer because it was the only job available."

Seth stopped in the middle of his stroke and said incredulously, "Just a common laborer?"

Jesus smiled. "There is no shame in working with your hands and back to provide a day's wages, no matter how meager. Keep working, Seth; we have much to do."

Seth continued to plane, then paused and asked, "I'm curious. What did you want those old beat-up planks for? They aren't for the bench."

My Father has placed me in this time and place to fulfill my mission. I must preserve this body that clothes me, and so, with these planks, we'll create a place to help preserve my body."

Seth looked puzzled. "I don't understand."

"You will," Jesus replied. "Keep working."

While Jesus and Seth worked at making the bench, John and Luke left to pick up supplies at the market for the trip to the River Jordan. A little later, Matthew left in the opposite direction. He carried his tax collection pouch hanging by a long leather strap from his shoulder. He purposely spoke to the captain of the Praetorian Guard about tax collection matters to establish his allegiance to the government. Soon after, Peter and Judas left to make the arrangements with friends and family to mind Judas's house in the men's absence. Each time someone departed from the house, the crowds became excited, believing that their Messiah was about to appear, and began to advance on the approaching figures. The Praetorian Guards pushed them back mercilessly with their horses and shields, knocking many men and women to the ground and trampling some.

When one of the household members passed through the crowd after departing through the front gate, people carefully eyed him and shook their heads with disappointment. Someone would say, "No, he's not the one." Others would ask, "Where is he? When will he come out?"

Their answers would only yield shoulder shrugs and replies of "I don't know" from the household members as they squeezed and maneuvered their way through the dense crowd.

As Seth finished the last few strokes with the plane to smooth out the bench seat, Jesus picked up two of the heavy old beat-up planks and effortlessly carried them into the stall. Seth dropped the plane, hurried to Jesus's side, and said, "Those are very heavy; let me help you."

Jesus smiled. "Thank you." He put the two planks down for Seth to lift one end and he the other. Seth grunted with great effort as he struggled to lift his end, then dropped it. "Let's take one plank at a time," Jesus said.

Seth nodded and lifted the end of one plank with Jesus. As they walked to the stall, Seth said, "You're shorter than Peter but so much stronger."

"My strength is growing each day," Jesus replied, then winked. "It must be the company I'm keeping."

Seth smiled proudly. Both he and Jesus turned toward the back wall to see the red plume on top of the Captain of the Guard's polished helmet as he rode by. The captain stopped and carefully eyed the boy and man. Jesus nodded politely to the captain and said to Seth, "Pay the soldiers no heed. Let's continue with our work."

An hour later, Andrew and Simon, carrying filled sacks, entered the stall as Jesus finished his work with the last plank. Andrew said, "It's time for us to go."

Jesus spread out his fingers and then held them against the bottom end of the cart, measuring the distance from the tips of his thumb to his little finger. He nodded his approval. Simon and Andrew placed sacks on the cart and covered them with a large blanket. They climbed onto the cart, and Simon took the reins. He gave the reins a short snap, and his donkey pulled the cart out of the stall. Jesus and Seth remained at Judas's home.

When the cart approached the soldiers, the captain raised his hand and ordered, "Halt!" Simon obediently pulled on the reins, and the cart stopped. The captain slowly circled the cart, then leaned over from his horse and pulled away the blanket that could have been covering a man. He saw the sacks and poked their sides with his spear.

"What's in the sacks?" he demanded.

"J-J-Just some old clothes f-f-f-or the p-p-poor," Simon answered.

The captain pointed his spear at one large sack and ordered his soldier, "See what's in here."

The soldier got off his horse, picked up the sack, and emptied its contents onto the cart's floor. Old clothes spilled out. The soldier spread them around. Satisfied with the contents, the captain ordered, "Check beneath the cart."

The soldiers did as ordered, then replied, "Nothing else here."

The captain eyed the men suspiciously for a moment and then said, "Let them pass."

Very slowly, Simon made his way through the crowd that pressed around the cart fruitlessly searching for their promised Messiah.

⬯

Hours later, Jesus sanded the last of the curved branches on the completed bench's back support. Sitting down on the bench, he leaned back with a satisfied smile. Seth sat next to him and said, "It feels so comfortable."

"It's as it should be," Jesus replied. He then said to Seth, "Bring the seeds and fig saplings; we have more work to do."

A little while later, the captain rode by and looked into the courtyard. He didn't see anyone but heard sounds of digging. He stopped, stood in his stirrups, and looked over the wall. On the other side beneath him, he saw Seth and Jesus planting seeds. He stared at them a few moments. Seth looked up and caught his eye. The captain frowned back sternly. Seth returned to his planting. The captain continued to observe the two for a few moments more, then moved on.

⬯

Jesus and Seth had finished planting the fig saplings near the sides of the stall when Judas and Luke returned. Looking worried. Judas said, "I don't know if we'll be able to make it past the guards. They searched us for weapons on the way back here. They also told me that the captain would be doubling the guards because of the growing crowds. Even if we get by the checkpoints, the people have been scrutinizing us relentlessly. They clamor for you to come out to them. They may arrest you if the people identify you."

Jesus appeared unconcerned. He placed a hand on Judas's shoulder and said, "Have faith that all will be well."

Judas and Luke, knowing the ruthless ways of Pilate's Praetorian Guards, remained very worried.

⬯

The rest of the day, Judas, Luke, Andrew, Matthew, Peter, John, and Seth left the house, either individually or in pairs or threes and at times in fours. Sometimes they would go to the northern part of the closed off street, other times to the south. Simon also made numerous trips back and forth with his cart, bringing goods to the house and taking sacks away, accompanied by different household members each time. Each time the guards searched everyone and recorded their comings and goings. Jesus remained at Judas's house, sitting on the new bench and enjoying the garden. Seth came out and drew ample water from the once nearly dry well that Jesus had blessed. He then watered the new plantings and continued to ignore the probing stares of the Captain of the Praetorian Guard.

THE JOURNEY

20

The next morning Judas left the house, returning in the early afternoon with two of his family members who were husband and wife and who had agreed to care for his home. Judas had to escort them past the Praetorian Guards to allow them entry. Only Judas, Simon, Seth, the couple, and Jesus remained. The others had left earlier.

Judas, Seth, and Simon said goodbye to the couple and went to their backyard oasis where Jesus sat on the comfortable bench under the lush palm tree. The setting was vibrant with songbirds above and the green grass and yellow flowers below.

A short time later, Simon maneuvered his cart out of the stall and through the gate. The cart was loaded to capacity with filled straw baskets and empty goatskin water bags. Filled sacks of supplies were stacked against the cart's high side walls. Seth and Judas sat next to Simon on the driver's seat.

As they approached the captain and four Praetorian Guards, they were ordered to halt and dismount from the cart. The crowds behind the soldiers started to surge toward them, but the guards rebuffed them. The captain ordered the three to the side. He then ordered the guards to empty the cart and search all that it contained. Judas protested but was ignored by the captain. The guards took the baskets and sacks of food, water bags, a few carpentry tools, and clothing, spread them haphazardly on the ground, and searched them. The three looked on helplessly.

One of the guards looked up at the Captain and said, "Just more clothes and food for the poor.

Finding nothing of interest, the captain ordered the three men to be searched, and then he looked under the cart. Everything appeared in order. The captain climbed onto his horse and sternly asked Simon, "Where are you going?"

"W-w-w-we're heading south, t-t-t-toward B-B-B-Bethlehem," Simon replied.

The captain eyed the three suspiciously but said, "You may proceed." He took his small wax tablet from his side pouch and made notations.

The three picked up the strewn goods, refilled the baskets and sacks, and then stacked them back onto the cart. They climbed on, Simon gave the reins a short snap, and the donkey moved slowly into the crowd. A guard sternly ordered, "Let them pass."

The people reluctantly moved to the side to allow them to pass. Some called out, "When will the Messiah come out?" Others yelled,

"Where's the Rabbi?" Their questions were left unanswered as Simon's cart slowly made its way to the end of the street past the crowd toward the southern gate of Jerusalem, no longer hindered by the crowd or the Praetorian Guard.

Joseph and Benjamin had followed behind the cart. Joseph, a handsome twenty-year-old with long, fine hair and intense large eyes, turned to Benjamin and said, "Tell Lev I'm going to follow them to see where they're headed."

Benjamin protested, "My father said we should stay here and wait for the Rabbi."

"I know," Joseph replied as he kept walking. "I'll be back soon. You stay here."

Benjamin grumbled, "You shouldn't leave."

Joseph kept following the cart.

<hr />

Halfway to the southern gate, Simon backed his cart into a stall and got a bucket of grain from the stall's owner to feed the donkey. Joseph had followed them from a distance and now stayed behind a corner of a house, peeking around it to observe the stall. All he could see was the donkey eating with Seth standing next to the donkey looking out at the street.

Simon and Judas took a hammer and pry-bar from the cart. They pried off a short overhang of wood from the back end of the cart, revealing a narrow empty space between the floor of the cart and the old beat-up planks that were added to create a false bottom. There, in a meditative state, Jesus lay on his belly, arms spread out like a cross, head turned to the side, snugly pressed against the top and bottom panels of the false bottom.

They grabbed his arms and gently pulled as his buttocks dragged against the top until he was out. Jesus stood, took a deep breath, and stretched his arms and back. He smiled at Judas and Simon and said, "That's the closest position to hanging on a cross that I would wish to be in."

Simon gave Jesus his robe from the cart. Jesus put it on, covered his head with its hood, and masked his face with the hood's sides. The three men got onto the driver's bench of the cart. Seth took the water bags he had filled and put them in the cart, then climbed onto some of the sacks of clothing in the back. Simon gave a quick snap of the reins, and the donkey proceeded.

Joseph continued to follow behind until the cart approached Jerusalem's southern gate. As the cart left the gate, Joseph ran to catch up with it. When he came alongside the cart, Simon and Judas looked warily at him, and Jesus looked ahead. Joseph, panting, pointed to Jesus and said, "I know who you are."

Simon gave two hard snaps of the reins, and the donkey moved quickly ahead, Joseph running alongside. Jesus held up his hand and said, "Wait."

"Keep going," Judas urged Simon.

"It's all right," Jesus said. "Stop for a moment."

Simon pulled on the reins, and the cart stopped. Jesus pulled down his hood, turned to the young man staring at him, and asked, "What is it that you want, Joseph?"

Surprised at hearing his name, Joseph asked, "How do you know me?"

"You are the dreamer who knows. I am the one you dreamed of last night. This is the cart that you followed in your dream," Jesus replied.

Joseph's eyes grew moist. He swallowed and said, "You are the One."

Jesus turned to Simon and Judas. "He wants to come with us. Let it be so."

"It's too dangerous. We don't know anything about him," Judas protested.

"I do," Jesus replied. He turned to Joseph and said, "If you come with us, you will be leaving much behind."

Joseph replied, "I feel that I will be gaining much more."

Jesus smiled and said, "It is right to trust your feelings when you're certain. That is the foundation of faith."

Jesus smiled at Joseph, pointed to the back of the cart, and said, "Climb on."

Without hesitation, Joseph got on the back of the cart. Seth gave him a welcoming nod and said, "Hi Joseph, I'm Seth."

Judas frowned. Simon snapped the reins, and the cart moved onward.

That evening, the captain stood at rigid attention next to the Commander of the Praetorian Guard in their headquarters. Pontius Pilate's anger could not be contained. Lydia had just left after having been summoned to Pilate's quarters. She had been questioned repeatedly in front of the captain about the Rabbi's description.

Pilate's eyes narrowed at the captain as he asked, "Why did you allow the cart to pass?"

"I checked it myself," the captain answered. "All that was on it was taken off and examined closely. No man with the Rabbi's description had passed earlier, and no one of his description was on the cart; only Judas Iscariot, Simon, a meek man who drove the cart, and a boy. I did see the Rabbi in the courtyard building a bench and planting seeds. He never left the house."

"But how can you be certain?" Pilate asked.

"If the Rabbi left the house, those who had witnessed his healings would surely have identified him. They carefully scrutinized everyone who was allowed to pass our checkpoints. I am absolutely certain he did not pass our surveillance."

The Commander added, "The captain's orders were not to arrest anyone, only to maintain passage of the streets and to note all comings and goings. The men on the cart said they were heading to Bethlehem. When the others who had left did not return, the captain took the initiative and searched the house. All he found were a man and a woman whom Iscariot had asked to care for the house. They said they never saw the Rabbi."

"Impossible!" Pilate exclaimed. "How can a man disappear like that? Where did all the others go?" He faced the Commander and said, "I want you to question the man and woman at Iscariot's home for yourself. There must be an answer."

The Commander replied, "It shall be done."

Pilate clenched his teeth and said, "Now go!"

As the two were leaving, Pilate picked up a beautiful blue glass vase and threw it against the wall, smashing it into small fragments.

21

After heading south for an hour, Simon pulled off the stone-laid main road to Bethlehem and headed east for another two hours on a narrow side road. Seth got off the cart and held the donkey's bridle. He guided the animal off the side road onto a dirt pathway bordered by low scrub and thorn bush-covered hills. They headed northeast toward Jericho, from which it would be a day's travel to the River Jordan.

As night approached, they arrived at a caravansary, an inn used for a caravan's camels and their drivers as a rest spot on their travels. The caravansary was a high-walled square structure, each wall measuring one hundred and fifty feet long. The single gate to the caravansary was only wide enough for a loaded camel to pass through and was shut and locked at night by heavy doors that allowed the drivers to sleep easily, knowing that their wares would be safe from thieves.

Judas went inside and made arrangements for his party to stay the night. The others unloaded the cart's goods and carried them into the caravansary's large courtyard. Simon unharnessed the donkey and led it through the gate to the well, leaving the empty cart outside. He filled a bucket of water and let the donkey drink. The camel drivers staying that night at the inn looked on as they tended to their camels in the stalls. In one stall was a large white horse. A second story above the stalls that lined two sides of the walls was two rows of ten-by-twenty-foot bare-floor sleeping chambers.

The sun had set. Judas, Simon, Jesus, Joseph, and Seth had spread their blankets on the floor of the sleeping chamber and then walked down the stairs to the courtyard below. A pit fire was burning in one corner surrounded by the caravan drivers and a heavyset merchant. The merchant looked up as Jesus and his companions as they approached. The merchant laughed as he pointed to Jesus and exclaimed to the drivers, "This is the one that I've told you about. Come," he beckoned to Jesus, "sit with us."

The Bedouin drivers looked on with intense curiosity as Jesus and his group sat near the warm fire. The merchant pointed to a rugged-looking camel driver with leathery, weathered skin and said, "Jesus, meet Omar; he is the caravan leader and an old friend."

Jesus nodded politely. Omar sat stone-faced. The merchant said to Jesus, "I didn't think you would make it out of Jerusalem. I certainly never imagined that I would see you here, but I am glad that you're here. I've told Omar of your healing talents and your magic with water and wine. Of course he doesn't believe me, even though he trusts me to trade fairly with him."

Omar's stony expression did not change. Jesus said to the merchant, "Only those of true faith become believers." Omar's posture stiffened.

"Don't mind him," the merchant pointed to Omar and said, "He's in a foul mood because Razur, his lead camel, caught his leg in a gully hole a mile from here. The beast was carrying over five hundred pounds, a hundred more than the other camels. Now he is lame and of no use to the caravan. Yet he has been Omar's favorite for over ten years, and Omar is reluctant to turn him into camel meat for his crew and sell his fur for clothing."

Omar shifted uncomfortably and looked into the fire. Jesus said to him, "Bring your camel here so I can help his leg."

Omar ignored him and continued to stare into the fire. The merchant said, "My friend Omar is a good man but very stubborn in his ways. He has no regard for rabbis."

Jesus replied, "All are entitled to their beliefs." Jesus held his palms up toward the warm flames.

The merchant turned to Omar and said, "If the Rabbi offered to help you, you shouldn't refuse. If he fails, I will pay you double for the frankincense."

Omar's eyes opened wide and then narrowed as he said to the merchant, "Do not jest with me; I am in no mood to be played with."

The merchant reached beneath his robe, pulled out a coin purse, and tossed it onto the ground, eliciting a metallic jingling sound. Omar stared at the merchant a moment, then defiantly stood up and walked to a stall. His men looked at each other and shook their heads.

In a short time, Omar returned, leading a limping Razur by a short bridle. He stopped by Jesus's side and tenderly stroked the camel's head below its ear. The camel's right front foreleg was twisted at an angle that didn't permit its hoof to rest flat on the ground.

Simon stood to make room for the camel. Razur snarled at Simon and spat at him. Simon ducked the spit and stepped away from the ornery critter. Omar smiled and proudly patted Razur's strong, muscled neck.

Jesus slowly stood with his open palms at his sides, projecting them toward the beast. The camel took a step back, looked side to side, then stood quite still. Jesus knelt by the camel's lame leg and slowly reached out to it. The camel's large eyes with their very long eyelashes blinked three times, then remained closed. Omar looked on, amazed that Razur allowed a stranger to get so close to his prized possession.

Jesus placed his hands around the twisted leg joint. He held his hands there briefly, then gave a slow, gentle pull to straighten the leg. Jesus stood and stepped away. Razur opened his eyes and placed his lame foot flat on the ground. Omar's jaw dropped. Amazed, his men spoke rapidly among themselves.

Omar led Razur around in a circle testing the camel's stride, which proved to be normal. Omar looked at Jesus and then walked away, leading Razur back to his stall. He soon returned carrying an elaborately embroidered Chinese silk pouch the size of a large coconut. He placed it in Jesus's hands and said, "This frankincense comes from a special grove of Boswellia trees in Africa. It has a magnificent fragrance like no other." Omar grinned. "It was a special order for Herod."

Jesus offered the fine pouch back to Omar and said, "Your camel's health is my gift to you. Healing is a privilege to be given freely. I seek nothing in return."

Omar refused the pouch. He stepped back and frowned. The merchant picked up his coin purse from the ground and then said to Jesus, "You must accept his offering of gratitude, or you and your people will be in trouble."

Jesus graciously bowed his head and said to Omar, "I thank your for you gift." He reached into the pouch and took out a generous handful of the frankincense. He brought it to his nose and smelled its fragrance. "It is delightful! We shall all share in this offering." Jesus carefully sprinkled the frankincense on the glowing embers near the rim of the fire. The fragrance filled the air to everyone's enjoyment. Joseph took a wooden flute from under his robe and filled the night with soft melodies. Omar walked up to Jesus, embraced him like a long-lost friend, and then lifted him up and spun him around in a circle. His men looked on with disbelief as their Bedouin leader was happily hugging a rabbi.

22

The next morning, just before sunrise, the caravan departed. The merchant left with his new wares to sell in Jerusalem, and Jesus and his party headed northwest toward Jericho.

After barely fifteen minutes on the road to Jerusalem, the merchant saw two chariots a hundred yards away accompanied by twelve soldiers on horseback galloping toward him. As they approached, the sound of the racing horses' hooves on the stone road grew thunderous. The lead chariot slowed as it came closer to the merchant. The captain of the Praetorian Guard, who was driving it, held up his hand to halt his platoon and stopped alongside the merchant.

"Have you seen two or three men with a boy on a cart?" The captain demanded an answer.

The merchant scratched his beard in thought, pulled on his ear, and said, "I've seen a herd of sheep, a family of seven with four cows, a goat herder with over thirty goats, but a cart...hmmm...was the cart pulled by a black ox or a white ox?"

"It's pulled by a donkey," the captain responded impatiently. "Did you see it?"

The merchant replied, "I think so. They were headed south toward Bethlehem."

The captain snapped the reins of his chariot sharply and quickly waved his hand forward for his platoon to follow him. The merchant grinned as the sound of the thunderous hooves gradually dissipated as the platoon raced toward Bethlehem.

<hr>

It was Joseph's turn to lead Simon's donkey along the narrow pathway between the hills and the scrub brush. It was a longer and harder path to Jericho than the main road, but it was a way to avoid Roman patrols. Jesus walked alongside Joseph, Simon and Judas sat on the carriage seat, and Seth slept on the soft sacks of clothes and blankets.

"Other people don't understand dreams the way I do," Joseph said as he pulled the donkey's bridle to the left to follow a wider part of the gully so that the cart's wheels would be able to pass through. "My body sleeps, but my mind is awake, and I see many events and symbols that have meaning to me. Some things seem nonsensical and haphazard; others seem as real as this donkey."

"You have been endowed with a gift," Jesus said. "Most people rarely recall their dreams; others recall only fragments. Dreams are as real as the landscape that we are walking on but of a different substance. Men divide the landscape into territories with boundaries that they seek to control as their domain. The dreamscape is without boundaries and can be shared by all. Your inner spirit can soar to all places in the dream state and connect to your earth ego. That's a way that knowledge and information can be communicated."

"That's how I found you," Joseph replied. "But if everyone can get information from dreams, then why has mankind fought to control others for thousands of years when dreams teach that in time, attempting to control others is always doomed to failure?"

"A person can accept or reject information. It's a choice," Jesus replied. "Some people may dream of falling down a mountainside and severely injuring themselves. They may be extra careful on a future mountain hike and avoid such a fall; others may disregard the dream as nonsense and suffer a mishap. Those who try to control others without regard for others' welfare are arrogant or ignorant of my Father's eternal laws, and in time, the arrogant shall fall and the ignorant shall learn. I am here now to teach the ways of my Father."

Joseph said, "Zadak is arrogant and tried to control and use me for his selfish purposes. Now I have run from him to learn from you."

"I hope that you'll learn that your gift is intended to help others in the dream state. You can warn them of mass dangers and guide them to make better decisions. It's good to have a dream walker like you on my journey, Joseph."

"It is my privilege to be with you," Joseph replied. "After I dreamt about you healing a leper, then when I actually saw you do it, there was no doubt in my mind and heart that you are the Messiah."

Jesus stared at the ground as he walked a few paces, and then he said, "You are wise in many ways, Joseph, and you are also impetuous. It's important for you to focus your enthusiasm appropriately, by carefully listening to what people say to you. Then you can respond to them in ways that will help to bring the best possibilities of your visions into their reality."

Jesus sighed and said, "Perhaps it's best for now that you do not refer to me as the Messiah. It obviously offends many people. When a Messiah appears, those people's false doubts reject and curse the one of truth in their midst and vehemently push away that which is good. Others want to grab on to the Messiah as if he were a treasure chest of gold and jewels to be possessed and owned rather than shared for the good of all."

"I will call you whatever you wish," Joseph said, "but the prophecies have told of your coming, and when the people see you heal lepers right before their eyes, they will have seen God's light shine through you, and they will know that you are the Anointed One."

"Perhaps, Joseph, perhaps. But for now, please avoid the term Messiah. Just call me Jesus and treat me normally."

"Yes, Master," Joseph replied.

Jesus rolled his eyes toward the sky.

Zadak sat with his two aides at a dining table enjoying a bountiful late morning breakfast. They all turned their heads at the sound of a rapid knock on the door, which opened before Zadak could answer. Benjamin and Lev rushed into the room.

"What's going on, Benjamin?" Zadak asked.

"They're gone, Father," Benjamin replied.

"Who's gone?"

"The Rabbi Jesus and Iscariot with his household friends and...." Benjamin suddenly became tightlipped.

"And what? Tell me," Zadak demanded.

"Joseph is gone also. He followed Judas and another man on a cart from Iscariot's house yesterday and has not returned," Benjamin replied. "We think Joseph has joined with Iscariot and the Rabbi."

"Why do you think such a thing?" Zadak asked.

"Because Joseph became awed by the Rabbi after the Rabbi healed the leper. He kept saying that the Rabbi was the Messiah and that we should all follow him as our teacher."

Lev spoke up, "I told him we should do nothing but obey your orders to observe and report back to you. Joseph seemed to disregard my words."

"If Joseph has disobeyed me, he is lower than a worm," Zadak said. "Where is the Rabbi?"

"I told you: he's disappeared. The Praetorian Guard searched the house for him but found nothing. Lev and I stayed steadfastly at both ends of Iscariot's street all night and until just a few minutes ago. We saw the guards check everyone who entered or left the house. The crowds of people also scrutinized everyone leaving. The Rabbi never left. He just disappeared."

Zadak grimaced. "This Rabbi Messiah vexes me. If Joseph has betrayed my commands, he shall be severely punished."

The sun had lowered in the sky. It would set in an hour. Jesus and Judas walked together and guided the donkey along the narrow, winding path. Judas said to Jesus, "Don't you want to rest on the cart? You've been walking all day."

"I'm not tired. It's good to work this body. It makes me stronger, not weaker," Jesus replied.

Judas pointed to the others in the cart snacking on bread, cheese, and figs and said, "At least take a break and eat something."

"I'm not hungry now. I'll eat later," Jesus replied.

They rounded a bend and saw a small town ahead. Simon said, "W-w-w-we need t-t-t-to stop soon. M-m-m-my donkey n-n-n-needs to rest."

Jesus stopped walking. He looked at the thick thorn bushes surrounding the town. Most of the homes were darkly shaded from the sun by the high gully walls.

"We need to continue," Jesus said. "This place is not for us."

"Why not?" Judas asked.

"The people here will be hostile to what I say to them," Jesus replied. "Omar said that another town is ahead. That's where we'll stay tonight."

Judas shrugged his shoulders, "If you say so, but I don't know what difference it makes for only one night."

"I do," Jesus replied.

As they passed by the town, two men were leaning against a stone wall and looked suspiciously at their party. Judas waved his hand in greeting to them. One man spat on the ground; the other frowned at Judas.

"These people could learn a thing or two about brotherhood from you," Judas said.

Jesus looked straight ahead and said, "Don't cast your pearls before swine, Judas, lest they trample over that which you treasure."

The sky glowed a beautiful red-orange over the distant mountains as the sun was setting. A golden glow illuminated a bank of wild flowers growing along a nearly dry stream that led to a small village of thirty homes perched on the crest of a hill. Simon walked with Jesus, who led the donkey. The others all slept in the back of the cart.

Simon said, "Th-th-th-there are s-s-s-so m-m-m-many things that I w-w-w-would l-l-l-like to do. M-m-m-my m-m-mind's always th-th-th-thinking."

Jesus nodded in agreement and said, "Your mind's filter is opened wide, and it easily connects to many things simultaneously. When you focus your thoughts in balance with your good heart, you will accomplish much."

"I-I-I-I w-w-w-want to d-d-d-do something important, and I-I-I-I don't want to s-s-s-stutter anymore."

Jesus stopped walking, put his hand on Simon's shoulder, and said, "There will come a day when you will bravely participate in an extraordinary event. Your act of great compassion will overcome your shyness as well as the obstacles that cause your stuttering. You are a good soul, Simon."

"Y-y-y-you say so many b-b-b-beautiful things. It m-m-m-makes m-m-m-me feel good about m-m-m-myself."

Jesus smiled, "To help you feel good about yourself makes me feel good about myself also – for I am one with you."

Simon sighed with inner comfort. He walked a few paces staring at the ground, and then as the path curved around a hill, he looked up at the small village. Olive and almond groves bordered one side of the village; willow trees lined the banks of a small stream on the opposite border. As the sun set further behind a mountain, the sky glowed a soft tangerine that blended into a peach-tinted globe of color that encapsulated the rest of the sky and bathed the landscape with its warm illuminating hue. Simon asked, "C-c-c-can w-w-w-we stop here n-n-n-now?"

"Yes," Jesus replied. "We will be welcomed here."

<hr>

The guards outside one of King Herod's palace's guest rooms made the announcement of Octavius's unexpected visit. Herod pulled down the blanket and sat on the edge of his bed. He said to his bedmate, "Herodias, what could so urgent that Octavius disturbs me as I am about to sleep with the one who brings solace to my heart?"

Herodias was Herod's cousin and his brother Phillip's beautiful wife. She pulled up the blanket to cover her naked bosom, then shrugged her shoulders, expressing both annoyance and embarrassment. Their adulterous affair had become notorious over the last year although they still sought sanctuary for their privacy in one of the palace guest rooms. Herod put on his robe and went out to the hallway to speak with Octavius.

Herod looked sternly at Octavius. Panting from his run to the guest wing, Octavius handed Herod an encased wax tablet and said, "Forgive me for the urgent intrusion. This just arrived by courier from Spartus. The Rabbi is in Jerusalem."

"Spartus? Already? We just assigned him to search for the rumored Messiah," Herod said as he opened the wax tablet and began reading it.

"He's never let us down," Octavius replied.

Herod finished reading the message and then said, "If this weren't from Spartus, I wouldn't believe it. He actually witnessed a rabbi named

Jesus heal a leper right before his eyes. The Rabbi drew huge crowds. Many in the crowd said their dreams foretold the event. Then while being watched by Pilate's Praetorian Guard, the Rabbi disappeared. They think he was headed toward Bethlehem." Herod's brow furrowed. He asked, " How can a rabbi disappear under the noses of Pilate's Praetorian Guard?"

Herod paced back and forth in thought and then said, "Could this Rabbi be the one to fulfill the prophecies? The one who is my nemesis in your dreams?"

"I'm not certain," Octavius replied, "but I do get a strong sense of danger to your throne from this Jesus."

"Send a message to Pilate tonight. Have the courier use the fastest horses. That should take only a day and a half. Tell Pilate to arrest the Rabbi. And have him inform me of all activities concerning this Rabbi who can heal a leper instantaneously. If he's the one in your dreams, then he shall be no more."

Herod removed a ring from his finger and placed it in Octavius's hand, "Seal the letter with my stamp." He briskly turned and closed the door to the guest room behind him. Even Herodias's warm arms did not calm his feelings of dread.

<hr />

Judas hesitated. Jesus urged, "It'll be okay. You can knock on the door."

Judas knocked on the door of the humble wood home with the grass-thatched roof. A moment later, a young woman opened the door and looked at Jesus, Judas, Simon, Joseph, and Seth standing before her.

"May we come in?" Jesus asked.

Standing around a dining table were two families. Lit candles filled the room with a comforting golden glow. A kindly looking older man who was missing a leg leaned on a crutch. He replied to Jesus's request, "My name is Nathan. We have started our Sabbath prayers. If you are of our faith, you are welcome to join us."

Simon pointed to Jesus and said, "He's a r-r-r-rabbi."

"A rabbi!" The old man's face lit up with delight. Nathan pushed on his crutch and took a step toward Jesus to greet him but suddenly stopped and then clenched his teeth painfully. He put his hand to the side of his back and held it there a moment to catch his breath, then walked gingerly, leaning his weight on the crutch. He placed his hand on Jesus's shoulder and said, "Come, come. Be our guests, please."

"Thank you," Jesus said. "Please continue your sundown Sabbath prayers."

Everyone gathered around the table, which was filled with prepared food for the dinner meal. The young women poured a cup of wine for each of the new arrivals, filling Seth's cup only halfway. Seth frowned but nonetheless said, "Thank you."

Nathan held a lit candle near an unlit candle and prayed, "And God blessed the seventh day, and he hallowed it because He rested thereon from all His work which God had created and made."

Nathan lit the other candle, then picked up his cup of wine and said, "Blessed art Thou, O Lord our God, King of the Universe, who created the fruit of the vine. Let us all say 'Amen.'"

Everyone responded with an "Amen." They all sipped their wine and smiled at one another.

Nathan said to Jesus, "Rabbi, please honor us and finish the service."

Jesus held up his cup and said, "Blessed art Thou, O Lord our God, King of the Universe, who hast sanctified us by thy commandments and hast taken pleasure in us, and in love and favor hast given us the Holy Sabbath as an inheritance, a memorial of His creation. Blessed art Thou, O Lord, who hallowed the Sabbath."

Everyone joined in an "Amen" and sipped their wine again. Nathan held out his hand toward the food on the table and said, "Let us all sit for a good dinner and good conversation."

23

Nathan's daughter, Judith, and her sister picked up the last empty platter from the dinner table. Nathan said, "Your company and conversation have been most enjoyable. Thank you for sharing the Sabbath meal with us."

"Your kindness and good food have been most appreciated," Jesus responded.

Judas asked, "May I pay you for your hospitality and your offer to allow us to spend the night?"

Nathan sat back in his chair, held up his palm, and said, "It is my honor to host the Rabbi and all of you. Your company is more valuable than money." Nathan leaned toward Jesus and said, "However, I do have a request. Our small village has no synagogue, and we have not had a rabbi come through here in over two years. As you must know, this small village is difficult to travel to. We don't even have any Roman troops stationed here. But that's a good thing."

Nathan pointed at the two families and said, "We are the only Jewish people here." Nathan's face turned to deep concern. "The Gentiles had accepted us until the wells ran dry and the village's orchards suffered. Now there is competition and strife over what's left of the water from the stream. Our crops are our only source of income." He looked down and shook his head in dismay and sighed. He then looked up and said, "But that's another matter." He pointed to the attractive young woman. "My daughter, Judith," and then he pointed to a handsome young man from the other family and said, "and Samuel are engaged to be married. They were going to go to Jerusalem in two weeks to have their marriage sanctified by a rabbi. Because of my painful back, I am not able to make the journey. It would give me great pleasure if you would perform the wedding ceremony for us."

"Of course I will," Jesus responded without hesitation. "It is obvious that genuine love is equally shared between Judith and Samuel. It will be my pleasure."

Judas shook his head and said to Jesus, "I must remind you that we need to leave early tomorrow and that weddings cannot be performed on the Sabbath, which does not end until sundown tomorrow."

"What's the rush?" Nathan asked and then said, "Your donkey is a beast of burden, and the Sabbath does not permit you to travel or to use your animal during this time."

Jesus agreed, "You're correct, but there are circumstances that sometimes permit travel."

"There are things that you have declined to talk about, and I have extended the courtesy not to press further, but what can be so urgent that you cannot wait another day?" Nathan asked.

"W-w-w-we n-n-n-need to m-m-m-meet our f-f-f-friends in t-t-t-time," Simon replied.

Nathan's face filled with disappointment. Jesus said, "I think it will be fine to leave a day later. There are important things here to be made right."

Judas protested, "What is most important is that the Rabbi's safety is ensured. We must move on."

Nathan looked puzzled. "Safe from what?"

Jesus smiled and replied, "My heavenly Father watches over me. I am safe in His comfort. Let us all rest and take comfort in this Sabbath as our Lord God rested after His work. I can clearly see the depth of your kindness, Nathan; of all people, you deserve to have your desire fulfilled. I will marry your daughter tomorrow."

Nathan lifted up his cup of wine. A tear rolled down his cheek as he said, "Amen."

———

The household awoke early the next morning. Nathan's family had generously surrendered their beds to their guests and had slept on the floor of the main room. At breakfast, Judith said to Jesus, "Last night, Joseph and Seth told me that you have exceptional healing powers. "She put her hand on her father's shoulder and asked, "Is there anything that you can do to help my father's miserable pain? He never complains, but I can see that his constant struggle to move about drains him."

"One's circumstances can always be improved with faith in God's help for those who ask. Speak with all those in your village who are ill, and invite them to come this afternoon for a healing. I will help your father, and all who come will also be helped."

Nathan's face appeared thankful but perplexed. "I welcome your offer to help me, but again, it is against the law to perform healings on the Sabbath."

"Your adherence to the law is righteous and admirable," Jesus replied. "However, do you think that a woman in labor would, in the early hours of the morning, say to her unborn child, 'Not now, you must wait till sundown'? Would a physician of true compassion not help her at her time of need? Or someone bleeding from a wound? To deny help to the ailing and instead yield the blessing of compassion to law is a greater sin. Such a yielding falls short of my heavenly Father's ways of boundless compassion and eternal love. We shall have our morning

Sabbath prayers, and then your family shall go and invite all in this village for a noontime healing service today. The marriage ceremony concerns your daughter, who wishes to respect the Sabbath. The healing service concerns me and those in need."

———

The other Jewish family had come back to Nathan's home for the morning's service. Everyone stood with heads bowed as Jesus recited a Psalm of David for the benediction of their home. "I will extol Thee, O Lord; for Thou hast drawn me up, and hast made my foes to rejoice over me. O Lord, my God, I cried unto Thee, and Thou didst heal me. O Lord, Thou broughtest up my soul from the grave; Thou hast kept me alive, that I should not go down to the pit. Sing praise unto the Lord, O ye His loving ones, and give thanks to His holy name. For His anger is but for a moment, His favor for a lifetime; weeping may tarry for the night, but joy cometh in the morning."

Jesus finished with the morning Sabbath prayers and again bade the two families go forth and gather all in the village who sought healing for a noon service, and so they did.

———

Jesus stood outside of Nathan's home and said to his companions, "Then it is agreed. You can speak of the healings that you have witnessed, but so as not to endanger the people of this village, please do not refer to me as the Messiah."

Judas, Simon, Joseph, and Seth responded simultaneously, "Agreed."

Jesus smiled and said, "Good." He looked up at the sun and said, "It is an hour before noon. Now I need to replenish myself and be one with God."

Jesus walked to a large cypress tree that was nearby and sat beneath its cool shade. A golden butterfly landed on the palm of his hand and slowly moved its broad silken wings up and down. Jesus gazed at its hypnotic, rhythmic movement and admired its beauty. He felt the muscles in his shoulders and back relax. He became one with the marvel of the butterfly's essence and whispered, "Thank you, dear God, for All That Is."

He sighed softly, closed his eyes and felt the peace of the resting butterfly. Jesus's heightened senses felt the butterfly clinging to his flesh as if he were a flower. The butterfly felt Jesus's soothing warmth and his blood vessels' rhythmic pulse and experienced his skin's sweet aroma. Jesus, at one with the butterfly, looked through its eyes and saw himself looking at it. He attuned his senses to the butterfly's mastery of the broad wings that propelled it and the exalted feeling of soaring and gliding to destinations of its choice by using its superb navigational instincts. Jesus's feeling of oneness with the butterfly at once solidified their mutual oneness with God and each other.

He reveled in that ecstatic feeling a few moments, then opened his eyes with the "knowing" of the butterfly's consciousness and focused his love and appreciation on it. He knew the butterfly had received the divine feeling of his wondrous appreciation and love for it.

The playful sound of children laughing caused him to look up. In the glare of the late morning sun, three boys were chasing after three girls, all between five and eight years old. The girls headed toward the tree, glancing back at the boys as they ran. The boys were closing the distance. As the girls ran closer to the tree, they saw Jesus with the butterfly on his hand and slowed to a cautious walk. The boys quickly caught up, and all stared curiously as they approached this stranger. Another golden butterfly landed on the back of Jesus's other hand. The children came closer. Jesus looked up, and then another golden butterfly landed on the top of his head. All three butterflies gently raised and lowered their golden wings, synchronously slow and steady.

The children's eyes widened with wonder. The girls giggled and the boys laughed. One little girl stepped forward from the group. She was clean-faced with a freshly washed tunic that had patches sewn on to cover the worn spots. "I'm Sophie. What's your name?" she asked.

"My name is Jesus. It's a pleasure to meet you."

A little boy a year younger with clean but ragged garments stepped up next to her and said, "I'm Dustine." He pointed to the girl. "She's my sister." His exuberant brown eyes sparkled; his smile revealed a wide space where his baby teeth had fallen out.

"It's a pleasure to meet you also," Jesus responded.

"How did you get the butterflies to land on your hands and head?"

"Oh, you noticed," Jesus said, mocking surprise.

The rest of the children came forward and stood three feet from Jesus. He smiled at them and asked, "Do you all want to see something magical?"

"Yes, yes, yes," they all responded.

"All right then," Jesus said, "but you have to sit down and be very still."

The children quickly sat down in a semi-circle around Jesus. He looked at them and smiled at each one. The butterfly on top kept a perfect wing flutter rhythm with the other two as Jesus rotated his head. "Are you ready for the magic?" he asked.

All the children nodded.

Jesus inhaled deeply, then closed his eyes and held his breath. The golden butterflies on each hand flew up in an arc over his head, crossing over the butterfly on top. Then they alighted on his opposite hands. The children's mouths opened in amazement.

Jesus opened his eyes wide and breathed out loudly. The butterfly on his head flew up a bit, made a halo circle three times above his head, and then landed squarely on his nose, flapping its wings in perfect gentle unison with the other butterflies. Jesus closed his eyes. The butterfly's wings came down and covered his eyes; when the wings closed again, he opened his eyes wide. The butterfly flew a few inches to the right side of his face. Jesus opened his mouth wide and jutted his head forward in an apparent attempt to swallow the butterfly. At the last moment, it darted to his left side as he closed his mouth again. He frowned in mock disappointment, then opened his mouth wide and attempted to swallow the butterfly once more. Again it darted away and landed on top of his head. Jesus frowned again in disappointment at the children. The children stared back in disbelief, then all started laughing.

The butterflies then rose five feet above the group, aligned in a straight row. The children leaned their heads back to look up, their eyes fixed on the synchronized fluttering wings. After a few moments, the butterflies flew down in a straight-line formation to within six inches of the ground and began to make a circle around the group. The children's heads tilted around toward the ground and followed the butterflies' arc. When the circle was complete, the golden butterflies, with their wings still beating in harmony, angled slightly upward, flying in ascending spiraling circles.

The children's heads turned in fascinated unison as their eyes magnetically followed each arc. The golden butterflies soon reached the branches of the cypress tree and flew out of sight into the foliage above.

Jesus said, "Would you all please thank our golden performers?" The children did so, their faces filled with wonder and amazement.

Two village women walked by the group, saw the happy children engrossed with Jesus, and felt the joy the children exuded. They smiled and nodded approvingly.

Sophie said, "That was fun. Can you tell us a story?"

Jesus said to the children, "If you want to hear the story of the rich King and the poor little boy and girl, then come closer. He reached out his arms. Dustine and Sophie quickly sat by his side and leaned against him. Jesus placed his hands on their shoulders as the other children huddled closer to listen.

"A long time ago, in a land not far from here," Jesus began, "there lived a very rich King. He wasn't a bad King, but he was very busy with all the work he had to do to manage his kingdom. And over time, he became very gruff and spoke harshly to those around him. He attended to big problems, like ordering his army to protect a mountain fortress, but the King had a blind eye when it came to noticing the people around him. People began to speak of him as the mean King."

The children stared attentively at Jesus as he continued. "In the King's palace worked a very poor seamstress who was known to sew the most perfect stitches in all the kingdom. She'd been ordered to make the King's new robe for his daughter's wedding.

"The seamstress had a little boy and girl about your ages, and they lived in a poor section of the city away from the palace. That morning the seamstress had finished sewing the King's robe and was about to leave home to deliver it to the palace. She stood at the front door waiting for her neighbor, who was supposed to watch over her children. The neighbor came running to their door and said, 'My husband's mother has just died. I can't watch your children today.' Then she frantically ran back to her home before the children's mother could say a word.

"The little children's mother was dismayed, but more importantly, she had to leave immediately to deliver the King's robe. She turned to her little boy and girl and said, 'There's no time to lose. I can't leave you by yourselves, so you are coming with me to the palace.' The little boy held his sister's hand, the little girl held her mother's hand, her mother held the King's robe and the extra fabric over her other arm, and they all headed to the palace."

The listening children sat wide-eyed and mesmerized.

"When they got there, they entered and passed a palace guard at the servant's entrance. He greeted their mother and said, 'I'm glad to see you. My uniform sleeve tore this morning, and my commander wants it repaired so I can present myself perfectly at today's wedding ceremony. Would you mend it for me?'

"She said, 'I would, but I cannot do it now. The King wants me to deliver this to him personally so he can try on his ceremonial robe when I am there to make any adjustments necessary. I'll do it when I come back.' She hurried along, pulling her daughter by the hand, who pulled her little brother along with her.

"They soon came upon a very long, wide hallway that led to the King's dressing chamber. Palace guards lined the length of the hallway standing at rigid attention. The first guard they started to pass blocked their way and said, 'The children must stay here. They can go no further.' He pointed to a small marble bench against the wall and said, 'They can wait here 'til you return.'

"Their mother told them, 'Stay here until I return. Don't leave and don't talk to anyone. If you misbehave, I will be whipped.' They sat down obediently on the bench, and their mother hurried down the hallway to deliver the King's new robe."

Above where Jesus sat, songbirds gathered in the cypress tree and filled the air with soft melodic tones, and the sun rose higher in the sky, nearing its high noon apex. Jesus continued, "The little boy and girl's mother entered the King's chamber and held out the new robe to him. In a huff, he grabbed it from her and said, 'Well, it's about time.' She bowed her head silently. The King walked over to a full-length polished metal mirror and put on his new robe. A dozen oil lamps on stands illuminated his image. He turned to one side, then the other, looking at his reflection in the mirror. Each time, he nodded his approval. Four manservants stood to one side of the mirror admiring the robe. Then the King took off the robe and carefully examined the stitches. The children's mother stood nervously, even though she knew that each stitch she had sewn was perfect. The King carefully double-checked the stitching, then looked up at the children's mother and said, 'This will do. Go now.' Their mother bowed her head and turned to leave. When the King swung his new robe over his shoulders to try it on again, the corner of his robe caught one of the stands holding an oil lamp. The lamp tilted, and the burning oil spilled onto the robe, setting fire to a corner of it.

"The servants stood frozen, shocked and horrified that the King's new robe had caught fire. The children's mother immediately dropped the extra cloth and hurried to the King. She pulled the robe off of him and threw it to the floor. She then lay on top of it with her worn robe and smothered the fire.

"The King was saddened that his robe was ruined and said, 'Why has God caused me so much trouble?'

"The children's mother picked up the robe and examined it. She said, 'I'm not sure I can mend this, but if Your Majesty will permit me, I will try to repair the damage with the extra fabric.'

"The King frowned at her and said, 'You had better, or else! It must be perfect.' He then stepped out of the room into the hallway. As he stomped down the hall, each guard he passed stiffened in fear and respect. He soon approached the bench on which the little boy and girl were sitting. The King stopped and looked them over, then scowled at them and asked, 'What are you two street urchins doing in this part of my palace?' The children looked up in fear at the angry King but said nothing.

"This made the King madder, and he angrily demanded, 'Are you deaf and dumb? Can you not speak?' The children began to shake with fear and shook their heads in response but remained silent. 'I am the King and I order you to answer.' His voice was so loud and harsh that the nearby palace guards began to tremble. The little boy and girl began to cry but still remained silent. That made the King more furious. He leaned down toward the children and threatened, 'If you have tongues, I will cut them out if you do not answer me.'

"The little boy and girl hugged each other and cried harder." Jesus looked at the children surrounding him; their faces were set in worry. He asked them, "What do you think happened next?"

The children pressed their lips tightly together and shook their heads to indicate they didn't know. Jesus continued, "Well, the King ordered two of his palace guards to take the children to the dungeons. The guards obeyed and picked up the wailing children and began to carry them down the long hallway to the dungeons. The King was so upset that he complained aloud, 'What is my kingdom coming to? My royal ceremonial robe burns, and now maggot children infest my palace halls. How did they even get here?'

"A palace guard nearby who had little children, not unlike Dustine and Sophie in age, was frightened by the King's anger, but his heart made him speak up. 'To answer your question, Your Majesty, your seamstress brought her children and told them that they must not misbehave or speak to anyone or else she would be whipped. If I have misspoken, please forgive me.'

"The King, in his anger, pointed a finger at the guard and was about to reprimand him for speaking without permission. The loud crying of the little children caused him to turn and look at the guards carrying them as they were about to turn the corner of the long hallway to take the wailing little children to the dungeons.

"Their frightened sobbing touched the King's heart. 'What have I done?' he cried. He yelled to the guards and ordered, 'Wait! Bring the children back.' As I told you," Jesus said to the children, "the King wasn't a bad king. He had a good heart but was always so busy that he'd forgotten the duty of a true king, which is to be loving and kind to his subjects. He sat on the bench and said, 'What kind of king am I? How can I, who place the highest value on courage and loyalty, be so mindless as to frighten little children who would not speak under the threat of having their tongues cut out in order to protect their mother from being whipped?'

"The guards brought the crying children back to the King. He said to them, 'I'm sorry that I frightened you.' He patted both sides of the bench and said, 'Here, sit next to me.' The guards placed the trembling children next to the King. He put his arms around them and asked, 'Can you forgive me for being so harsh and rude to you?'

"The little children did not speak, but nodded their heads. The King smiled and said, 'Thank you. I understand why you didn't answer me. You were trying to protect your mother from being whipped. That is a noble act of bravery and loyalty, and you should be rewarded, not punished.' The children stopped crying but remained fearful.

"The King stood up, reached out his hands to them, and said, 'Come with me to see your mother.' The little boy and girl took the King's hands and walked with him to his chamber. When they entered, their mother looked up from her sewing of the King's robe and saw her children holding the King's hands. Their faces were still covered with tears. She immediately rushed over to them and knelt down before the King and bowed her head to the floor, and said, 'Please forgive my children for misbehaving. They are very good children and don't intend any harm.'

"The King said, 'Please rise. Your children have not misbehaved. Rather, they are very brave and most loyal to you. Those are traits that I deeply admire. You and your children are to be rewarded, not punished.' Their mother stood up with tears in her eyes. She opened her arms, and the little boy and girl let go of the King's hands and went to her. She hugged them closely and lovingly. The King's heart was gladdened to see his subjects happy.

"The mother said, 'I am still working on your robe. I need a little more time to make the stitches perfect.'

"The King replied, 'Thank you for doing your best.' He turned to the children and said, 'I'm hungry. I haven't had my breakfast yet. Would you like to join me?' The little boy and girl eagerly nodded their heads but didn't speak. The King said to their mother, 'Please give your children permission to speak to me so that I may enjoy the sound of their sweet voices.'

"Their mother said, 'Of course, Your Majesty.' She then said to them, 'It's all right to speak when the King asks you to. I will not be whipped. Remember, always be respectful to your King.' She hugged and kissed her children. The King held out his hands to the little boy and girl, and they all left for a bountiful breakfast."

Jesus looked at the highly attentive children and asked, "What do you think happened next?" The children didn't know and shrugged their shoulders. Jesus continued, "Well, the little boy and girl were very, very hungry. The neighbor who couldn't watch them was supposed to have given them breakfast, so the little boy and girl ate and ate and ate a great amount of food, even more than the King. He saw that the children were happy, and that made him happy. Remember, I told you that the King was a good man, but he had gotten so busy in his day-to-day affairs that he'd forgotten how to be loving and kind. You see, kings and queens are just people, like your mother and father, who can get so busy taking care of their chores that they too can be harsh at times, but I know they love you, no matter how they may act at times.

"Now, the King was amazed and amused at all the food the little boy ate. When the boy's belly appeared completely filled after he ate the last crumb of bread on his plate and he could eat no more, the King asked, 'What would you like now?'

"The little boy looked up and said 'May I have three more platefuls of food?'

"The King laughed and laughed, then asked, 'How can you possibly eat any more food?'"

Jesus leaned toward the listening children and asked, "What do you think the little boy said?" Again the children had no answer. Jesus continued, "The little boy said, 'I can't eat any more food. But I know my friends are hungry, and I want to bring them some of this wonderful food.' The King sat back and admired the little boy because he was so thoughtful and caring toward his friends, just like all of you should be thoughtful and caring toward each other."

Dustine said, "My mother always tells us to share what we have with our friends." The other children smiled and nodded in agreement.

Jesus said, "Your mother is wise." He continued with the story, "The King ordered his servants to wrap up two baskets full of food fit for a king and had them follow him and the little boy and girl back to his chamber. When they arrived, their mother had finished sewing the royal ceremonial robe and handed it to the King. The King examined the robe carefully and then said, 'You have mended my burnt robe perfectly. I can't see any damage. You're the best seamstress in my kingdom, and you deserve a reward for all your years of good service.' He went to a cabinet, removed a small pouch of gold coins, and placed it in the mother's hand.

"She began weeping with joy and said, 'Thank you, thank you many times over.'

"The King said, 'Don't thank me; thank your brave and loyal children, whom you've taught to be so thoughtful and caring toward their friends.' The King turned to the little boy and girl and said, 'I thank both of you for reminding me that a king also needs to be thoughtful and caring toward all his subjects.'

"With that, the King put on his new, perfectly stitched robe and said to the mother and her children, 'You may be poor with little money and I am rich with a lot of money, yet you are richer in spirit. You have taught me what is of true value. From this day forth, I will be a better king. I thank you.' And the King did become a more thoughtful and caring king for all his people, and his kingdom flourished."

Sophie said, "That was a good story. Can you tell us another?"

Jesus said, "It's getting late, and I'm sure you're hungry and will have to eat lunch soon. But if you would like to know the secret of how I did the magic with the butterflies, I will tell you."

"Tell us! Tell us! Please tell us!" the children begged.

24

"Now I'll tell you the secret of what may have appeared to be magic with the butterflies," Jesus said. The children leaned closer as he said, "The secret to the magic is love."

Dustine scrunched his nose and asked, "But I don't understand. How do we get the butterflies to play with us?"

Jesus's voice became serious, "To get the butterfly to play with you, you must truly love the butterfly; and you must treat it in a very thoughtful and caring manner in the spirit of play so the butterfly will love you and want to play and be with you. Now this so called 'secret' is important to remember in your life: You cannot force a butterfly to love you; instead you must allow the butterfly to choose to love you because it wants to. That also means that if the butterfly wants to be free and fly away, you must let it go, even though you love it and want to clasp its wings together so it can't fly away. If you try to hold on to it when it wants to be free, the butterfly will only try harder to get away from you.

"Now, this is the important part of the magic to remember: If you really love the butterfly with divine love, which is God's love, that means that you want the butterfly to fulfill its desires."

Sophie tugged at Jesus's robe and asked, "But how will we know what the butterfly wants?"

Jesus patted her head and then said to the children, "The 'secret' of what the butterfly wants is to allow it free will to choose what is best for itself. So if a butterfly or someone you truly love wants to leave you, you must open your hand and heart and let go, even if you don't want to. If you don't let go of your grip when they want to be free, they may resent you and surely not want to play with you."

Jesus asked the children, "Do you understand?"

They all nodded their heads and said, "Yes."

Jesus continued, "If the butterfly returns to you, it's because it wants to be with you and has chosen to return. It will always remember your special love that no flower's nectar could give it and will tell other butterflies so that they might choose to come and be with you too."

One of the other boys with a worried expression asked, "What if the butterfly doesn't come back?"

"If the butterfly does not return, then don't be sad, for your hand and heart will be open for another butterfly to come into your life, perhaps one with more spectacular colors that loves you more. And you will love it more than the last one. Be happy for the ones that have left you and wish them well, for if you stay sad or mad, your heart will be closed to another one that will be a better companion to play with than the one that you had wanted to keep in captivity. So you see, the 'secret' of the magic is 'true love,' which means to give and receive love with freedom although 'true love' is not a 'secret'; it's a special feeling that comes from within you."

"Do you think you can do that?" Jesus asked the children. They again nodded yes.

Jesus clapped his hands three times and the children sat up straight. "Let's practice to see how well you can make magic. Everyone, hold out your hand palm up and close your eyes." The children did so. "Pretend that a butterfly has landed on the palm of your hand. No peeking. Keep your eyes closed. Now pretend that you can feel how light and soft its feet are, like the tickle of a breeze. Now remember the secret, and with your heart, speak to your imaginary butterfly and silently tell it how much you appreciate its beauty and wonder. With a feeling of deep gratitude, thank the butterfly for visiting you to play. Tell the butterfly how much you love it and that you want what is best for it and that you wish it no harm, only good."

Jesus observed the children's expressions of concentration. He smiled and looked up at the big cypress tree above, then back to the children and said, "You can open your eyes now, but keep your palms open and be very still." The children froze with their palms extended before them. "Now look up into the tree." All eyes turned upward. "Remember, be very still and continue your thoughts and feelings of love and gratitude for the butterfly that you imagined was just in you hand."

At that moment, six golden butterflies began to glide down from the tree branches. The children's enchanted eyes widened with delight; their open palms remained motionless. The butterflies glided closer to the children. One butterfly for each child flew down and made circles above each child's head, then circled above their palms and gently landed there. The butterflies remained there and slowly opened and closed their golden wings. The children were ecstatic but stayed still as instructed and silently gave their thanks and deep gratitude to their butterfly for visiting them. Seeing that, Jesus said, "The butterfly has accepted your love and wants to play with you. It's all right to stand up if you want to and walk around. Just don't run too fast or jump because that might frighten it."

The children, in a state of trance-like wonder, stood cautiously and slowly moved around the courtyard as the butterflies carefully walked on their palms. A woman carrying a tunic and a robe in need of repair approached them and marveled at the sight. She nodded to Jesus, who nodded back, then called out to her children, "Sophie and Dustine, come;

it's time for lunch." The children walked carefully to their mother as if they were on a tightrope balancing cups of water on their open palms.

"Look, Mother, see my butterfly. It came to visit me because I love it," Dustine said.

She responded, "Yes, I see. It's very golden and beautiful."

Sophie said, "Jesus taught us how to be best friends with the butterflies so that they'll visit us and play." Sophie said to Jesus, "My mother's name is Miriam; she's a seamstress, just like the little boy and girl's mother in the story you told us."

Jesus raised his eyebrows again in mock surprise. "Isn't that amazing?"

Dustine giggled as his butterfly's feet tickled his hand, and he said, "This is amazing!"

Pontius Pilate and the Commander of the Praetorian Guard conversed in the great main courtyard as they walked toward the entrance of the governor's mansion. The hot noon sun caused beads of sweat to form on Pilate's furrowed brow. The Commander was finishing his report to Pilate, "… no sighting in Bethlehem and no valid reports fitting the descriptions of the Rabbi or his group traveling on the road."

Pilate clenched his fists. "He must have gone north, or he's hiding in some small village not far from Jerusalem. Order all available guardsmen to search in all four directions around Jerusalem. Have them fan out into platoons to the smaller villages and question everyone they encounter about anything they know of a healer with great power."

"I'll do as you say, but it's also possible he's camping in the desert or countryside and not in a town, or he may have stopped performing public healings," replied the Commander.

Pilate stopped, turned, and poked a finger into the Commander's armored vest. "If you don't have a better plan to find this miracle-worker-disappearing-trickster-rabbi, then make haste and do as you're ordered."

"It shall be done," replied the Commander, saluting.

The front gate to the courtyard opened, and a centurion on horseback led an elegant purple-and gold-veiled carriage carried by eight heavily muscled pole bearers who'd been rigorously trained to walk in such a fashion that those in the carriage would enjoy smooth, comfortable travel. A horse-drawn cart driven by a sergeant followed, and they in turn were followed by a platoon of soldiers. From within the carriage, Zena parted the curtains slightly and observed Pilate walking toward her. Her friend Cassandra popped a big black grape into her mouth. Zena motioned to her to peek through the curtain, laughed, and said, "Look at him. He's mad and sweaty. Ugh! Men! They are only little boys, just bigger."

Cassandra replied, "For a boy, he wields a lot of control over Jerusalem."

Zena laughed louder, "He even tries to control me, but I know how to control him. I have what he wants – me! I rarely give myself to him so he wants me even more!"

"But he has power over the city, and you want that power," Cassandra said.

"Ah, but I have power over him and his power," Zena replied as she held up a hand mirror and adjusted a side curl. "I want for nothing," she smiled, raising her eyebrows, "except greater power. That's why I help my little boy become more powerful."

The procession stopped, and the pole bearers gently lowered the carriage to the ground without the slightest jarring. The centurion came to the carriage and extended his hand to help the occupants out. Zena turned to Cassandra, winked, and said, "Watch this." She parted the curtain and held out her hand to the centurion, who clasped it, then reached his other hand to her. Pilate arrived and stood next to the centurion as he assisted Zena from the carriage. She was nearly standing, then leaned her body against the centurion in a feigned motion of maintaining her balance. She then stood firmly, placing a hand on the centurion's shoulder, murmuring, "Forgive me. I'm so clumsy." Slowly, caressingly, she slid her long fingernails gently down his arm to his hand and then squeezed it. "Thank you for your guidance today. You made our shopping very special."

Pilate swallowed jealously, red-faced, and the beads of sweat on his brow formed a rivulet. He heard laughter from inside the carriage and demanded, "Who else is in there?"

Zena replied, "It's only my friend Cassandra." She frowned at Pilate, pouting, and said, "You're not being very nice to me."

"Why are you so late?" Pilate asked. "We're hosting the regional luncheon today. Everyone's waiting. I need you by my side with the other wives."

"Well, here I am," Zena replied. She grabbed Pilate's wrist, pulling him toward the cart behind the carriage, saying, "Come see what I bought today."

⸺

Jesus walked from the cypress tree toward Nathan's house. Coming from the house, Judas met him halfway. He said to Jesus, "Everyone's waiting for your healing service. You told me you needed to be alone and at one with God. Why did you spend an hour with those children?"

Jesus replied, "I didn't say I needed to be alone, only that I needed to be one with God, and I was. Children are God's little angels; I was one with their enchanting wonder, and now I'm refreshed."

⊂⎯⎯⎯⎯⎯⎯⊃

Nathan had introduced his twelve neighbors to Jesus as a rabbi who had offered his healing gift to those who now stood by, skeptical but hopeful that their ills could be cured. Judas, Joseph, Simon, and Seth stood behind the neighbors as Jesus was explaining what he was about to do. "...and as an aqueduct brings water to a desert city so that it may flourish, I will act as a vessel connecting my Father's infinite reservoir of love and healing powers to bring health and vitality to those who are open to receiving His blessing. Please know that it is God's love that carries the knowledge for the body to heal."

Jesus bowed his head, raised his hands, and said a prayer: "Heal us. O Lord, and we shall be healed; save us, O Lord, and we shall be saved; for Thou art our praise. Vouchsafe a perfect healing to all our wounds, for Thou, Almighty King, art a faithful and merciful Physician."

Jesus then asked a small boy to come forward. The boy hesitated shyly, but his mother said, "It's okay," and gave him a gentle push. The boy walked with a marked limp, having been born with a short leg.

Jesus bade the boy sit before him. Jesus then knelt down and smiled lovingly. The boy smiled back and relaxed. Jesus grasped the boy's short leg and gently pulled on it. The boy sighed softly. "Now stand up and walk," said Jesus.

The boy started to walk, and then smiled. He walked faster in a circle around the room and explained, "Mother, I'm not limping anymore!" Crying, she went to her son, picked him up, hugged him lovingly, and said, "Yes, yes, I see! You're walking normally." She turned to Jesus and said, "Thank you, thank you, Rabbi. It's a miracle! My son is normal!"

The boy said, "Mother, put me down." She did, and he walked faster around the room and exclaimed, "Now I can run and play with the other boys, and they won't make fun of me anymore!"

The others stood in awe. Jesus nodded to another woman holding a three-month-old infant and said, "Come to me." The woman came forward and fervently explained, "My baby has become so weak with a month-long fever that she no longer eats. Now she's turned cold. Her eyes haven't opened for two days." The mother sniffed, and a tear rolled down her cheek. "My baby is dying."

Jesus took the emaciated infant, whose complexion had a bluish tinge, and held her in his arms. He gently stroked her forehead, and then placed a hand on her tiny tummy. In seconds, the infant's complexion turned pink and her eyes opened. She smiled faintly and cooed sweetly. Jesus handed the infant back to her mother, who hugged her child with great relief. She kissed the child's rosy cheek and said, "She's neither cold nor feverish anymore." Kneeling before Jesus, through tears of gratitude, she exclaimed, "Thank you, Rabbi. Thank you for saving my baby. I don't know what more to say."

Jesus reached down and grasped the mother's shoulders, helping her up, and said, "Thank our heavenly Father, for He has given your child new life."

The woman replied, "You are an angel who has bestowed God's gift of life upon my baby. Thank you. Thank God. Thank you so much."

Jesus graciously nodded his acceptance and then pointed to a teenage girl whose face was almost completely covered with a head veil; only her eyes peeked out from its shadow. "Please come to me," he bade her. The girl turned her head to the side, looked down, and remained in place. Again Jesus bade in a soft voice, "Come. It will be all right." The girl slowly approached him with her head down and stood before Jesus.

He reached up and grasped the sides of her veil to pull it down. The girl immediately clutched his wrists to stop him. Jesus removed his hands and said, "I understand the shame you feel. Everyone feels ashamed at times. Often they can hide their shame, but you feel you cannot. I tell you, the shame that you think shows on your face is not true shame. The thoughts and feelings that you've had as a girl who changes into a young lady are shared by all women, and for that, you have no reason to feel ashamed." In a kind and imploring voice, Jesus said, "It will be all right. Please remove your veil."

The teenager raised her head and from within the shadow of her veil, gazed into Jesus's eyes. He smiled lovingly. The girl slowly pulled her veil back from her face. Many of those present winced at the blistering skin sores, pitted and scarred acne, and red blotches that disfigured her face. Jesus gently placed his hands on both sides of her puffy, discolored cheeks and held them there. Within seconds, her blemishes and scars faded and the swelling receded. The people stared wide-eyed at what they had witnessed.

The girl declared, "Your hands feel so warm and comforting. No one has ever touched my face as you do."

Jesus removed his hands and said, "Now it is time for you to touch your face."

The girl reached up and placed her hands where Jesus's hands had been. "My skin doesn't hurt anymore. It feels smooth and soft!" she exclaimed. Then she felt her forehead, chin, and neck. "My face feels...normal again."

She stood taller and pulled off her veil completely. "Thank you for healing my face! Thank you! God bless you!"

Her mother rushed to her side, examined the girl's face, and declared, "You're beautiful," and they hugged and cried.

Jesus replied, "I thank you for your trust, which enabled me to help."

He then pointed to a ten-year-old boy who stood in front of his mother and father and bade them come forward. They did, and the teenage girl proudly returned to where she had stood before. The boy's right arm hung bone thin and lifeless by his side. The father said, "My son's arm has been paralyzed from birth. Is there anything you can do to help him? He's a good boy."

Jesus knelt on one knee and smiled at the boy, who shyly smiled back. Jesus took the boy's limp right hand in his and placed his other hand on the boy's right shoulder. He looked into the boy's eyes, and the boy looked back. Both began smiling broadly. Jesus said, "Squeeze my hand."

The boy replied, "I can't use my hand."

"Try," Jesus said.

The boy, still smiling, said, "If you say so." He squeezed his hand, and it weakly contracted. "It worked!" he exclaimed.

Jesus said, "Squeeze again, harder."

The boy took in a deep breath, gritted his teeth and squeezed harder. "I did it again! I can do it!"

Jesus patted the boy's shoulder and said, "Yes, you can, and your hand and arm will continue to grow stronger." The boy squeezed Jesus's hand harder. Jesus laughed and said, "Now please don't hurt my hand; I have more work to do." The boy giggled. Amazed, the parents thanked Jesus graciously as he rose from his kneeling position.

Jesus tuned to Nathan, who was leaning against the dining table for support, and said to him, "Nathan, you have graciously hosted us all and have always bestowed kindness and generosity on whoever has crossed your path. Surely you deserve to be relieved of your painful back. Please come here."

Warily, Nathan stared a moment at Jesus, then took his crutch for support and stepped toward him. With each step, he winced with pain and leaned away from the chronically inflamed nerve in his lower spine to shift the pressure of his weight. He forced himself to stand straight before Jesus but cried out, "Ahhh," then leaned his weight against the crutch.

Jesus placed one hand over the small of Nathan's back and his other hand on Nathan's abdomen and said, "Inhale deeply." Nathan did so and then breathed out. Jesus said, "Now take another breath in and breathe in God's light from my hands." Nathan did, and as he exhaled, he stood a little straighter. Jesus said, "Take another breath in through my hands." Nathan complied and was able to stand up straight without supporting himself on his crutch.

"It's gone!" Nathan exclaimed. He leaned to one side, then the other. He held up his crutch to the side and hopped on his one leg six times. "My pain is completely gone! You've performed a miracle, Rabbi! Blessed be God! Thank you!" Nathan smiled with glee.

His daughter Judith rushed to his side and hugged her father. With tears in her eyes, she said to Jesus, "You have given our family a great gift with your healing. We are indebted to you."

Jesus replied, "My friends and I are indebted to your family's kindness, as your community should be, as well as those who stand in your home now." Jesus addressed the neighbors, "Now go back to your homes and live your lives with kindness to others as Nathan has, and you will be blessed in return."

Later on, Judas, Simon, Joseph, Seth, and Jesus all sat around Nathan's dining table. Simon asked Jesus, "Is th-th-th-there any p-p-p-problem that you c-c-c cannot heal?"

Jesus thought a moment and said, "I don't know. I have only accepted the opportunities that my Father has laid before me. I know that my powers are quickening and becoming stronger. Changes within me are occurring as we speak."

Seth asked, "Can I learn to heal like you do?"

The others looked askance at him for asking such a seemingly impertinent question. "You, Seth," Jesus responded, then addressed the others, "and all of you, are healers. You will all learn to heal in your own ways that may differ from mine. It's not so important *how* you help others to regain their health and vitality as long as you are successful in a beneficial way. Because I am in the Light of my Father and you have been in my Light, your abilities to help others will grow in proportion to your desire to do so."

Joseph asked, "But surely you can teach us some of your secrets of healing. Although to do what you've done seems impossible for me to accomplish."

"In all of our talks, I have constantly taught you how to think in ways that will align you with God's powers that in turn will help you to help others. But there is one thing I cannot teach you with words: that is love. I can only be an example of love to help you discover the love that dwells within you that has been there from your birth. Remember what I've said, 'God's love carries the knowledge for the body to heal,' and as you embrace your roles as vessels of love, your healing abilities will flourish."

A soft knocking on the door caused the group to look up. A louder knock followed. Judith entered the dining area and ran to the door as the knocking became louder. She opened the door to reveal a rugged looking man in his forties. "Amal," she declared, surprised. "What are you doing here?"

"I know it's been a long time," he said bashfully. "May I come in?"

"I suppose so," Judith replied and reluctantly showed him in. "I hope your loud knocking didn't wake my father. He's resting from hopping around so much."

Amal glanced at Jesus and then said to Judith, "I heard about your father and the others that the Rabbi helped."

"And your sister, who now has beautiful skin. What do you want?" Judith asked suspiciously.

Jesus got up from the table and walked to the door. "I think Amal wants to ask me something."

"Yes, I do," Amal said. "We are grateful for what you did for my sister. Perhaps you can help my father. He lost an eye in an accident ten years ago. Over the last two years, the sight in his other eye has been going bad, and now he barely sees. He's become very frustrated and mean. It's become impossible living with him. Can you help him to see better?"

"Why didn't he come for the healing service?" Jesus asked.

Amal bowed his head, embarrassed, and said, "He didn't think a rabbi could help him, and ... he refuses to enter Nathan's home."

Nathan came into the room with the crutch walking evenly with a strong stride and said, "Amal! What a surprise. Come in. Come in."

Nathan leaned against the table and waved him in.

Amal, Jesus, and Judith came to the table area. Amal said to Nathan, "You've known me since I was a small boy. You were like a second father to me. I apologize to you that I haven't spoken with you for so long. You know how my father has been. He has forbidden our family to speak with yours and made us promise not to do so. It is not my wish, but I must honor my father."

"Amal," Nathan said, "you were always a good boy. I understand your situation, and I'm not angry at you."

"I apologize anyway. My sister and mother urged me to ask the Rabbi to help. They dared to come here. My sister insisted, saying that she dreamt the night before that she would soon be helped. Then we heard of the healing service, and she said that she was going to attend even if my father disowned her. My mother came also thinking that my sister would be disappointed and sink into despair." Amal looked at Jesus and said, "Of course, that wasn't what happened. You have changed my sister's life." He asked sorrowfully, "Can you help my father to see?"

Jesus replied, "If your father has faith, I will help. But he has to come here to Nathan's home."

Amal shook his head. "You don't know my father. He'll never come."

"It's his choice," Jesus replied. "He must be willing to change his point of view if he wants to see more clearly."

Amal looked dejected and said, "I don't think he will change, but I'll try to convince him. My family will try. We are all grateful for what you've done for my sister."

Amal nodded a goodbye to everyone and left.

Nathan and Jesus sat down at the table with the others. Judith went to the kitchen and brought back a large teapot that had been brewing. She poured the tea for the men, then for herself, and sat with them. She said, "Amal's father, Enid, will not come to this house. Now that his well has gone dry for his olive orchard, he threatens us constantly at the stream's pool, which is also drying up. He prevents us from carting water for our almond trees. He even pushed my father to the ground, causing him to become bedridden with severe back pain for two weeks. A man without a heart who pushes a man with only one leg to the ground doesn't deserve to be healed."

"Judith," Nathan said, "please don't speak unkindly of our neighbors."

Jesus looked above the heads of Nathan and Judith and perceived their mentally projected scenes of the events of which they spoke. "I see," he said and held up his hands. "The choice is Enid's. Give the matter no more thought. Instead, attend to the preparations for your wedding."

⸺⸺⸺

Amal entered Nathan's home first, followed by his mother and sister, who held her father's hand, guiding him to the corner of the main room where Jesus sat in conversation with Nathan, Judith, and Samuel.

"This is the Rabbi who cleansed my face," Enid's daughter said to her father.

Enid squinted in the direction of Jesus but could barely see him and frowned.

"If I help you to see better, will you become a better neighbor to Nathan and his family?" Jesus asked.

Enid became irate and said, "My orchard must have water, or we will have no livelihood. Water is our lifeblood. There's not enough for both our orchards."

Jesus replied, "If I can provide a way, will you vow to be a good neighbor?"

Enid scoffed, "How is that possible?"

"All things are possible with faith in my heavenly Father," Jesus replied.

"You call me a Gentile because I don't believe in your faith." Enid became adamant. "So how can your God help me?"

"It is my faith that matters most," Jesus said. "If a way to provide more water is made possible, then as a man of honor, will you vow to be a good neighbor?"

Enid's daughter tried to encourage her father and said, "Nathan has always been a good neighbor to us. He's always been kind and generous. He's an honest man. Please, Father, say 'Yes' so you can see again."

Enid took a step back and raised his voice. "No! I will not be forced to do anything that I do not want to do. A man of honor cannot be bribed." He turned and started toward the door. His wife and children were dismayed.

Jesus said, "Wait. You truly are a man of honor. You have turned away from an opportunity to have your sight restored because you refuse to be made to do something against your will. To be a truly good neighbor, you must want to be one; no one can be forced or bribed to be a friend. I will help you see better because I want to help you, with no obligations in return."

Enid's daughter pleaded, "Father, please let the Rabbi try to help you. I love you so, and I don't want you to suffer with blindness. Please, let him help."

Enid turned back toward Jesus and adamantly said, "No obligations!"

Jesus agreed, "No obligations. Come here."

Enid reluctantly came to Jesus and stood silently before him. Jesus stepped to Enid's side and placed his hand over Enid's eyes. He placed his other hand behind Enid's head and took a deep breath in, then breathed out and removed his hands. Enid opened his eyes and looked at Jesus. He murmured, "I can see you." He turned to his daughter and stared at her and said, "You look so beautiful." He put his hands over the sides of her face and kissed her forehead. Tears welled in his eyes, and he hugged her tightly. "I can see you. I can see! I can see!"

He turned to Jesus and said, "I can see again! Thank you! I can see!"

"That is good. Now I invite you and your son to come with Nathan and me to his orchard," Jesus said.

"Why?" Enid asked, puzzled.

"Come, and you will see," replied Jesus.

Jesus walked the path that separated Enid's parched olive orchard from Nathan's withering almond orchard. The two men followed him. Behind them trailed both families and Judas, Joseph, Simon, and Seth.

Joseph asked Judas, "Where is he going?"

Judas replied, "I don't know, but I'll follow him wherever he goes."

Jesus stopped and looked toward a hillcrest in the middle of Nathan's almond orchard. A breeze crossed the rows of almond trees atop the hill causing a sprinkling of dried leaves from the wilted trees to fall to the ground. Jesus smiled and walked faster to the hillcrest. Nathan kept up with the faster pace without pain although he still used his cane to support his weak leg muscles. Jesus stopped at the crest, and all gathered around him. He pointed to the earth and said to Enid and Amal, "If you dig here, you will find water for a well that will serve your two orchards abundantly."

Enid protested. "But the well will be on Nathan's property."

Jesus replied, "Nathan has always been honest and generous with all of the people in your village."

He turned to Nathan and asked, "If Enid and Amal dig the well, will you share the water with them?'

Nathan readily responded, "Of course, we all need the water."

Jesus said to Enid and Amal, "Have faith and trust in Nathan that he will do what's right and share the water from this well that you will dig. You are all men of honor, and it's time to honor one another again. Now go and get your picks and shovels and start digging."

Enid asked, "Are you sure there is water on this high part of the land?"

Jesus replied, "Although you can now see clearly with your eyes, you have yet to see clearly with your heart. Do you still lack faith in what I say?"

Enid looked at his son and said, "Let's get the shovels. Our trees are dying of thirst."

The sun had set behind the mountain, ending the Sabbath. The sky was ablaze with waves of golden orange clouds. Nearly all of the ninety people in the village were dressed in their finest clothes and had gathered around the town courtyard for Judith and Samuel's outdoor wedding. Word had spread quickly about the Rabbi's healings and his butterfly magic as well as Nathan's invitation to all to attend his daughter's impromptu wedding. The fragrant aroma of burning frankincense that Jesus had given as a wedding gift filled the air as it burned slowly at the four corners of the village courtyard. Many remarked that its fragrance was the finest they had ever experienced. There hadn't been time for Nathan's family to prepare food for everyone, but the guests brought more than enough. Many of the men carried lit torches. The people were very curious to see the Rabbi, and now he stood under the ceremonial wedding tent with the groom waiting with all those in attendance for the bride to appear.

In Nathan's home, Dustine and Sophie's mother, Miriam, was helping Judith with her final preparations for the ceremony. Almost everything was in order when Judith, in a worried voice said, "Oh my goodness! I just realized I don't have a wedding veil!"

Miriam said, "I have a gift for you." She reached into her garment basket and pulled out a white silk wedding veil. "This is my wedding gift to you. I finished making it just a few hours ago."

Relieved, Judith said, "It's beautiful!" She unfolded it and tried it on. "It feels so elegant. I love it." She hugged Miriam and said, "Thank you so much. You have always been such a close friend to me."

Judith adjusted the veil to hang over her shoulders and asked, "How do I look?"

Miriam stood back and looked at Judith. She said, "You look perfect." Miriam lit a small earthenware oil lamp to carry and said, "Let's go."

The townspeople gazed admiringly at the nervous but beaming bride as she walked down the aisle toward Jesus and the groom. She finally stood by the groom. Samuel looked at her lovingly and then took the veil from her shoulders and pulled it up over her head and covered her face, as was the tradition. Continuing the ritual, he said, "As beautiful as you look today, my love for you is more than skin deep. I choose to marry you not only for the fact that your eyes dazzle me but also because of the values we both share and the warm, loving nature of your character. I can cover your face with this veil and still marry you because your true inner beauty shines through in all ways."

The couple faced Jesus, who then began the ceremony. "We stand under this tent of plain cloth, called a *chupah,* that represents your first home. It is not made of stone or brick but is filled with the radiant glow of your love. For what makes a happy home is not the walls or decoration, but what fills it. It is far better to live in a humble tent full of love than in a large mansion empty of love."

The guests suddenly turned their heads toward loud shouting coming from the hillcrest. They looked at each other questioningly; then they saw Amal running down the hill toward them yelling, "Water! We found water!"

Covered in mud and panting, Amal ran into the courtyard and said, "We dug a hole eight feet down, and then the hole started to fill up with water. We had to scramble out when it came up to our knees. It's now overflowing from the hilltop and down the irrigation rows. Both orchards are being watered as I speak!"

The excited people were delighted with the blessing of newfound water for their village. All shouted hoorays and cheered. Amal said, "I see you've started the wedding. My father begs you please to wait for him. He should be here shortly."

Everyone was excited about the wedding, and the finding of water intensified their joy. Jesus said, "We'll wait for Enid."

The bride and groom held hands. Five minutes later Enid came from his home at a fast pace carrying a small wooden jewelry box. He approached the chupah; his clothes covered in mud, he said to Nathan, "I want you to have this to give your daughter for her wedding."

He handed the small jewelry box to Nathan, who opened it and saw a necklace comprising two entwined gold strands. "Thank you, Enid. This is lovely."

Still panting, Enid said, "The necklace belonged to my mother. She wore it on her wedding day. I've kept it all these years because it reminds me of the precious memories of my mother's love and kindness. Your daughter should have this to remind her always of your kindness."

Nathan thanked Enid and hugged him. He then presented the necklace to Judith. Jesus said, "Under the circumstances, it is permitted to lift your veil to put on the necklace."

Judith held up the necklace for all to see, then said, "Thank you Enid. I shall always wear it in memory of my father's kindness and shall cherish it with great love such as you have for your mother." She put it around her neck, and Samuel covered her face again with the veil.

From horizon to horizon, the sky glowed a spectacular red orange. Jesus said, "We thank you, Enid, for a genuine gift of neighborly love. We know your gift is not to garner favor for the well on Nathan's land, for you are an honorable man who cannot be bribed; it is a gift of true appreciation for Nathan and his family. Let what we have just witnessed demonstrate that a community of true, good neighbors is a mixture of the many Gentiles and Jews who in harmony help each other through the difficult times and celebrate together on joyous occasions as we do on this wedding day. We shall now begin the ceremony."

Jesus began the traditional wedding prayers: "Blessed art Thou, O Lord our God, King of the Universe, who hath created all things in Thy glory.

"O, make these loved companions greatly to rejoice, even as of old Thou didst gladden Thy creatures in Thy Garden of Eden. Blessed art Thou, O Lord, who maketh bridegroom and bride to rejoice.

"Blessed art Thou, O lord our God, King of the Universe, who hath created joy and gladness, bridegroom and bride, mirth and exaltation, pleasure and delight, love, brotherhood, peace and fellowship."

Jesus then said, "The bride will now circle the groom seven times as is our custom." Judith began to walk around Samuel in a circle. Jesus continued, "Just as a circle is eternal, the bride, as she is encircling her groom, is signifying that he will always be the center of her life."

Judith completed the last circle and stood next to Samuel. Jesus said, "It is said that when two people are wed, it is a sacred and divine union, for they become one soul and will share life's experiences as one. And therein lies the true intent of love between two people. For in life, joys shared are doubled, and life's sorrows are halved."

After additional prayers, Jesus addressed the bride and groom: "Judith and Samuel, please face each other. Samuel, with the ring in your hand, repeat after me: Behold, thou art consecrated to me with this ring, according to the Law of Moses and Israel."

The groom repeated the vows. Then Jesus held up the wedding ring and said, "Dear God, King of the Universe, give Your abundant blessings to this vibrant couple whose love radiates for all to behold. And bless this ring that symbolizes eternal circles of love – with no beginning or ending; and bless this couple with health and the energy for all of life's circumstances and sustain their enduring love."

The groom placed the ring on the bride's finger.

Jesus then said, "Please kiss the bride and blissfully begin your marriage."

They kissed, and Jesus then said to everyone, "Let us all together, in grand spirit, now celebrate this wedding night, and let us all say 'Amen!'"

All said a resounding "Amen," and the wedding feast and celebration began; the people danced and rejoiced for the happy bride and groom and also for their village that had been blessed with flowing water once again.

As the celebration continued, the sky darkened, and a new crescent moon arose with the new mood of hope for the village. Joyous music from lyres, cymbals, flutes, drums, and small tambourines filled the night air. Delicious smells of garlic, mint, dill, cumin, coriander seasonings for the the chicken, vegetable and egg dishes lingered as the wedding celebration continued and many consumed generous after dinner portions of cheese, bread and butter, nuts and fruit.

The families of the goat and sheep herders, the olive pressers, the blacksmith, the carpenter, the tanners, the weavers, the grain millers, the farm workers, and others continued to dance and rejoice. Later on, Nathan spoke with Jesus in a quiet place to the side of the gathering. With deep gratitude, Nathan said, "This is the best day of my life. I can move about pain-free, and I have lived to see my daughter married to a good man. Water flows again for my orchard, and an angry neighbor has become a friend again. And you, my dear blessed Rabbi, are the one to be thanked for everything. What more can a soul want?"

"It's important for me to hear you say that," Jesus smiled.

Enid and Amal, who had gone back home to clean up and dress in their finest, came by and joined Nathan and Jesus.

Enid said to Nathan, "Please excuse me for coming to your daughter's wedding all muddy. I was so excited about finding the water and wanting Judith to have the necklace before the ceremony started that I could not delay to wash. I meant no insult."

Nathan patted Enid's shoulder and said, "Your gift to my daughter from your heart outshone any mud on your body. I am gladdened, not insulted."

Judith joined them, adorned with her new gold necklace, took Enid's and Amal's hands, and said, "Come join us in our circle dance."

Enid said, "You and Amal go. I need to speak to Nathan."

Amal and Judith quickly joined the dancing circle of merriment. Enid placed his hand on Nathan's shoulder and said, "Now that I can see clearly, I see my error in going against you for the water. I was losing my sight and my livelihood. My mind was filled with worry and fear. Can you forgive me?"

"Of course, Nathan replied. "We have always been good neighbors, and more importantly, we were good friends."

Enid's eyes became teary as he said, "I rejoice over your gracious heart and our renewed friendship."

Enid hugged Nathan tightly and lifted him off the ground causing him to drop his crutch.

As he put Nathan down, Judith and Amal came up to them. She took Enid's hand and said, "You must join us in a dance. No more waiting."

Enid said, "But I want to thank the Rabbi."

Nathan said to Enid, "Go, it's a celebration. Come back later. I would join you if I could. Go and dance."

Judith held Enid's and his son's hands and led them to join the circle of dancers. Nathan smiled at the sight of his daughter's happiness and her rejoicing with their neighbors. Turning to Jesus, he said, "God has given me so many blessings, and you have delivered them. I don't know how I can thank you enough."

"Your joy is my thanks," Jesus replied. "As was said in this morning's Sabbath prayers, 'Your foes will be made to rejoice over you,' and so it has come to be. Don't thank me; thank my heavenly Father who works through me."

25

The early morning sun's heat quickly dried the night's dew that had collected over the small village. Seth, Joseph, and Simon had finished harnessing the donkey to the cart and loading it with their belongings and baskets of food left over from the wedding. The air was heavy with heat, and small beads of sweat formed on their foreheads. Jesus, Judas, and Nathan came out of the house to join them. A horse-drawn wagon approached them. Samuel was driving it, Judith and Miriam sat next to him on the driver's bench, and Dustine and Sophie sat on the back of the wagon next to baskets of food and sacks of clothes and wedding gifts.

Judith smiled brightly and said, "Good morning. We're going with you."

Judas immediately protested, "That's impossible. We have to travel alone." He turned toward Nathan, who looked down at the ground sheepishly. "Did you know about this?" he asked Nathan.

Nathan nodded and then smiled. He replied, "They had always planned to go to a big city to be married by a rabbi and then start a life there where they would have more opportunity to make a good living and raise a family. Now that they are married, that's what they're doing."

"I'm going also," Miriam said. "There's just not enough work here for me as a seamstress to support my children."

"It's too dangerous for you to be with us," Judas said firmly. "You cannot come."

"I think it will be less dangerous for them to travel with us than you might think," Jesus said to Judas.

"They don't even know where we're going," Judas protested.

"It doesn't matter," Samuel said. "We trust that you'll be traveling near a city soon. That's good enough for us. And we want to be in your company."

Dustine asked Jesus, "Can you tell us another story?"

Jesus replied, "Of course. But later. We must leave now."

Judas shook his head, looking disgruntled. He climbed onto the cart next to Simon. Seth and Joseph sat on the back. Nathan reached out an arm and said to his daughter, "One more hug before you go."

Judith climbed down from the wagon, and Nathan hugged her closely as if for the last time. He said, "I don't know when I'll see you again, but I want you to know that my dearest dreams have been fulfilled now that I have lived to see you married and happy. You've always been a good and loving daughter." He sighed, and his tears flowed as he said,

"Except for the day that you were born, I have never felt such joy as I do now."

He said to Samuel, "Have a safe journey, and take the best of care of my daughter."

"I certainly will," Samuel relied. "I will protect her with my life."

Nathan smiled and affirmed, "As I would as well. Now go safely, and someday soon, return safely to our village."

He turned to Jesus and reached out to hug him. As they hugged, Jesus said, "The light of God shines on you and within you. You have lived your life as His angel. I know that when the time comes, my Father's heavenly Kingdom awaits you."

As they drove off, the water from the new hilltop well ran down the orchard rows, reflecting shimmering ribbons of the golden glow of the low-angled early-morning sun.

———————

Three hours later, as they traveled north, the hardened dirt road leading eastward narrowed as they passed deeper into the desolate, stark, and waterless hills of the barren Wilderness of Judea. Jesus and Judas walked ahead. As the sun rose higher, Judith covered her head with a sun veil, and Miriam did the same for herself and her children. Judas said to Jesus, "In the one week since your arrival in Jerusalem, crowds have clamored to be in your presence, and the Praetorian Guard is now searching for you. In a little more than one day, you converted a parched, depressed village in need of healing into one of hope and harmony. You seem to know when and how to evade the Guard and which village to pass by or stay in. Do you always know what will happen in the future?"

Jesus replied, "Most times, but not always. When in doubt, I trust my feelings. Things may happen in ways that I may not expect, so I am open to all possibilities and have absolute faith and belief that one way or another; all things will work out for the best. I believe that my heavenly Father will always guide me and present before me the tasks I need to perform and the means to accomplish them as long as I have the faith that He will."

"Is the future already destined to be?" Judas asked.

"Creation is being created at each moment, so what we do today creates the next moment and tomorrow's destiny. That's why man has a free will and mankind's future is yet to be created from an endless reservoir of possibilities. I am here to help guide mankind and to make people aware of the possibilities that will create a better future for all."

Samuel called out from his wagon, "The sun is very hot today. Our horse needs water."

Simon said, "S-s-s-so does m-m-m-my d-d-d-donkey."

Sophie said, "I'm hungry."

Jesus glanced over the barren, hilly landscape and pointed to the only two small shade trees within sight. "We'll have lunch over there."

Jesus and Judas led Simon's cart to the trees; Samuel followed. Miriam and Judith laid down blankets on the sun-baked earth under the trees. They took two baskets of food from the cart and set them on the blankets. Joseph wiped the sweat from his brow, then poured water from a goatskin into a bucket that Seth held. Seth then set it before Simon's thirsty donkey, which drank eagerly. Samuel did the same for his horse.

Jesus walked to the top of a small hill and stared pensively at the distant northeastern mountains. Judith approached him and asked, "What do you look at so intently?"

"Those distant mountains and the clouds above them," Jesus replied.

"I wish there were a breeze and that those clouds were over us to block out the hot sun," Judith said.

Jesus smiled, "Yes, that would surely make our travel easier, God willing."

Judith said, "From your mouth to God's ears." Judith stared at Jesus and saw a foreboding look in his eyes as he stared at the mountains. "What's on your mind?" she asked.

Jesus pointed toward the mountains and said, "A destination of great transformation awaits me there."

Puzzled, Judith asked, "I don't understand; what do you mean?"

Jesus said, "Now that you are married, do you feel changed in any way?"

Judith replied, "Yes, I do, but I also feel I'm the same 'me' as before, only different. I can remember when I was a child. That's a part of me, but I am no longer a child. Now I am a married woman, and soon I hope to be a mother."

Jesus smiled, "I'm sure you'll be a good mother indeed. You've gone through many changes of growth, and you have many changes yet before you. So do I. Your marriage was a significant transformation in your life."

"I feel that I am meant to be a mother with all the responsibilities that come with motherhood. And that those changes will serve a blessed purpose," Judith replied.

"I feel they will for you as mine will for me," Jesus said.

Judith laughed, "You won't have the responsibility of motherhood."

Jesus's shoulders slumped, his expression turning solemn. "My Father will offer me a monumental responsibility." He closed his eyes and paused in thought. Opening his eyes, he said cautiously, "However, I feel that I will be able to fulfill that purpose, or He would not offer it."

"Then why do you seem so concerned?" Judith asked.

Jesus replied, "Before you conceive a child, you can only imagine what it would be like to be pregnant with a new life and then give birth. But only when you actually experience it will you really know the burdens and ecstatic pleasures of motherhood. Only when I actually experience that which lies ahead will I truly know the depth of my future responsibilities."

"What do you think the responsibilities are that lie ahead of you?" Judith asked.

Jesus chuckled, "It's not motherhood." He turned serious. "It's the spirit of true brotherhood. It's God's intent and my mission to carry the flame of His love and Light for all people, and I must find ways for that Light to burn brightly in the hearts of mankind so the recurring cycles of hate and war may end."

"That's an awesome task," Judith said.

"It is a task I know I must embrace, no matter the possible consequences to myself."

"What consequences?" Judith asked.

Jesus became solemn again. "I prefer not to speak of that now."

Jesus pointed toward the base of the distant mountains "Soon I will have a transformative union there. That's where my Father will give me the strength to meet my greatest challenges."

Judith looked to where Jesus pointed and asked, "Do you mean the River Jordan?"

Jesus nodded affirmatively.

"Everything changes in life," Judith replied. "I pray your changes will be a blessing for you as mine are for me." She sighed and became concerned. "I do worry about the changes in my father's life. I know he's able to care for himself and that there are many neighbors who will help him, but he will miss me as I miss him. Silly me. I haven't been gone a day, and here I talk about missing my father. I feel sad thinking about him carrying on without me."

"It's not silly, Judith. It's a heartfelt expression of your love for him. When you feel any sadness, think also of his joy in seeing you married, and think of his moment of triumph when Enid, once his foe, rejoiced over him. That was a blessing; your father was doubly blessed because Enid chose to rejoice over him. And so your father was thrice blessed because he also chose to rejoice with Enid. So be joyful for the joyous, and think of your father's blissful moments at your wedding and don't dwell on the fleeting thoughts of sadness that come into your mind."

Judith smiled and said, "Your words help. I feel better about my father. Thank you. And thank you again for all you've done for my village and for me. You are a worker of miracles."

"I pray miracles will suffice to fulfill the prophecies and my purpose for coming at this time," Jesus said wistfully, staring at the mountains.

Judith looked there also and said, "Are we going to the River Jordan from here?"

"No," Jesus replied, "not yet. First we're going to Jericho."

"Jericho!" Judith said excitedly. "My father has taken me there many times. That's where Samuel and I hoped to live someday. I must tell him right away."

Jesus said, "We can both tell him." He patted his belly and said, "This body needs food. Let's eat."

Zadak and Benjamin walked across the Pharisees' Great Synagogue courtyard to a bench and sat down. Zadak said to his son, "Pilate has sent his soldiers to search all of the surrounding towns and villages around Jerusalem. Sooner or later, they will find the Rabbi, and I'm sure Joseph will be with him. Mark my words: Joseph's day of reckoning will come when he is brought back."

"But father, Joseph is my friend. I know he means no harm to you," Benjamin replied.

"He disobeyed me, and for that he will be severely punished."

"Please reconsider, Father."

"He'll be an example to anyone who might think of violating my trust." Standing, Zadak said, "That's final! Speak to me no more of your ex-friend. You are not permitted to speak with him again." Zadak stood and strode briskly away.

The adults were finishing their lunch while Dustine and Sophie wandered around aimlessly, bored and a little grumpy. Jesus caught their eye and beckoned to them. They ran to his side and sat beside him under the small shade tree. The others started to load the lunch baskets and blankets onto the wagon. Jesus asked the children, "Have you been thinking about the butterflies that you played with?"

Their eyes lit up and they nodded.

He said, "I think that's because you truly loved and cared for them, and they so enjoyed playing with you that they surely have told other butterflies how much fun it was."

Sophie said, "But there aren't any butterflies here."

Dustine added, "There's nothing to do."

Jesus said, "There is always something to do when you use your imagination. Close your eyes and open the palms of your hands."

The children immediately did so, and Jesus said, "Now think of how much fun you had when you played with your butterflies. No peeking, Dustine. Keep your eyes closed, and focus your imagination on how much fun you had and how much fun your butterfly had playing with you. Perhaps another butterfly will soon come to play with you."

The children, frozen in their concentration, held their palms open, anticipating and hoping that a butterfly would come to them. Jesus said, "Now open your eyes."

They opened their eyes and looked at their open palms. Nothing was there. They looked all around, but there were no butterflies in sight. They looked at Jesus with disappointed frowns. Sophie said, "I told you that there aren't any butterflies here."

Jesus replied, "There aren't any butterflies here that you can see, but that doesn't mean that they aren't around here."

Dustine looked around again and saw no butterflies and said, "Where are they?"

If I told you that there are butterflies that want to be with you, would you have faith in me that it's true?"

Sophie said, "Yes."

Dustine looked confused.

Jesus asked Sophie, "Do you know what 'faith' means?"

Sophie said, "No."

Jesus smiled and said, "I thought so. 'Faith' means that you believe strongly in something that you cannot see or touch but that you know is there because you can feel that it's there. Do you understand?"

Sophie and Dustine nodded their heads, but their expressions were still unsure.

"All living things have a life-spirit. Your eyes cannot see nor can you touch a life-spirit, but you can feel it. Remember when you pretended that you could feel the golden butterfly's feet tickle your hands. The butterfly did come, and when you played with it, you felt and shared your butterfly's life-spirit. Verily I tell you, if you believe in me and feel my life-spirit and you have 'faith,' then you must not give up the first time you try if the butterfly doesn't come. For if it doesn't come right away, its life-spirit will still feel your life spirit calling out to it, and my life-spirit will always help to connect you to what you seek."

Sophie said, "The butterfly's life-spirit wants us to try again."

Dustine said, "I can feel it tickling my hand."

Jesus saw the children's buoyant auric colors dancing over them. Vortexes of energy radiated from their palms reaching upwards. He looked up into the small tree branches and stared. Dustine and Sophie looked up also. Four red-winged butterflies with bright orange spots descended from the branches. They circled the mesmerized children and then landed on their four open palms. The children were delighted and exuberant. They slowly stood up, carefully balancing their hands in front of them so as not to jar the butterflies. Jesus said to them, "Remember, always keep your faith." He stood up and went to Simon's cart and climbed onto the bench. He looked back at Sophie and Dustine prancing around the small trees with their butterflies, and he smiled with contentment and deep satisfaction.

Miriam called to the children, "Come back to the wagon. It's time to go."

<hr/>

Simon and Judas talked and walked ahead of the cart, Seth sat on the back, and Joseph sat on the driver's bench next to Jesus. Joseph gave the reins a gentle snap and urged the donkey forward. It was early afternoon, and everyone except Jesus was getting road tired. The eastern mountain breeze had become a little stronger yet offered little relief from the relentless baking heat. Hot as it was, Joseph's exuberance would not be contained. He said, "I can't believe I'm sitting next to the Messiah, but I know I am. The healings I've seen you perform only confirm my dreams that you are the one. You are the prophet of prophets - the one who knows. God must speak directly to you. What does His voice sound like?"

Amused, Jesus said, "I thought you weren't supposed to call me 'The Messiah.'" Joseph cringed, and Jesus continued, "When a true prophet says that God has spoken to him, one must not suppose that God has grown a tongue, mouth, voice box and lungs in order to speak in that prophet's particular language. God dwells within you as He does in all people. To hear the Word of God, one does not need ears. God's language is first felt. His message is communicated to you in ways that you'll understand, such as in your dreams or perhaps a passing thought or a sign. Then your mind converts His message into the words of your native tongue."

Joseph was puzzled. "You say that God communicates to me. I'm not a prophet like you are."

Jesus laughed, "Of course you are. Every man is his own prophet to degrees."

Even more puzzled, Joseph asked, "What do you mean by 'degrees'?"

"God's message is universal," Jesus replied. "He continually offers His guidance and constantly gives His love to all who will receive it. But man has free will and a mind of his own to accept or reject my Father's wisdom and benevolence. Have faith and trust, Joseph, that my heavenly Father's thoughts and wisdom are yours to receive. The more open you are to receiving His love and knowledge, the more readily you may become a true prophet."

Joseph stared at Jesus a moment, then asked, "Is that how you acquired your insight, by being so open?"

Jesus replied simply, "I am one with God."

Half an hour later, the cart and wagon slowed as their wheels pushed through a sandy section of trail. Seth jumped off the back of Simon's cart and walked to the back of Sophie and Dustine's wagon. He asked, "May I play with your butterflies?"

Sophie pulled her hands back with the butterflies on them and said, "No! They're mine!" Her two butterflies immediately flew high above their heads. Dustine's two butterflies remained on his palms. Sophie held her palms up toward them and begged, "Come back to me. Please come back." The butterflies remained hovering above.

Dustine said to her, "Remember what Jesus told us. The butterflies don't belong to us. They can choose whom they want to play with." He carefully shifted over and made a space between him and Sophie and then asked Seth, "Would you like to learn how to play with the butterflies?"

"Sure," Seth replied.

"Sit next to me and I'll show you," Dustine said.

Seth quickly hopped onto the wagon and sat between the two. Sophie was still reaching up for the two hovering butterflies. Dustine told Seth, "Hold out your palms and close your eyes. Now pretend that you can feel the butterfly's feet tickling your hands ..."

Jesus turned around and smiled when he saw the two hovering butterflies descending toward Seth's open palms. Joseph said to Jesus, "We're hot and tired, and you look more refreshed than this morning. How do you do it?"

Jesus said, "Turn and see the children."

Joseph did and said, "I see children playing. That's not unusual."

Jesus asked, "What do you feel?"

"I feel hot," Joseph replied.

Jesus said, "I see and feel the joy that the children feel. That feeling refreshes me."

Joseph studied the playful trio a moment, and then he too smiled and said to Jesus, "I remember when I played with my friends as a child. It was a good feeling. Now will you please answer the question that I asked you?"

"Of course," Jesus replied, "The Torah, which is called The Tree of Life, contains truths, as my words contain truths. God's words, in whatever way they may be spoken or written, contain truths. The interpreted meanings of those truths, however, will vary with each person's level of understanding. Different cultures in different lands with different languages interpret the scriptures as differently as do the richer conservative Sadducees and the less wealthy Pharisees. Most people interpret scripture to suit their own needs. However, they often leave out my heavenly Father's supreme message of love. The underlying truth of all truths is that God is love and that all of His creation should express that love with kindness in all deeds."

"That's something that's bothering me and makes me feel guilty," Joseph said. "The Torah says I must honor my father, Zadak, who adopted me as his son. He fed and sheltered me. Benjamin, his son, is like a brother to me. But I have seen a selfish side of Zadak, and he has controlled me in ways that I resent. I don't love or honor Zadak, but I feel guilty because The Torah says I must."

"One's biological or adopted father is not necessarily one's spiritual earth-father. One's true spiritual earth-father will always give love and prudent guidance to his children. He will sacrifice and go without creature comforts to provide for his children and willingly give his life for his child as Nathan said he would do for his daughter. A biological father plays a role in conceiving your physical body so that you may enter this world, but he may not be your spiritual father; and your adopted father may provide basic needs, yet he may not be your spiritual earth-father either. To have a true spiritual earth-father such as Nathan is to his daughter is a blessing, but those who know that my heavenly Father is the supreme spiritual Father of all fathers and mothers and all sons and daughters are blessed. You have no reason, Joseph, to feel guilty about not honoring a man who is not your true father in spirit."

Joseph said, "I feel relieved. I am thankful to Zadak for all that he's done for me, but I also know I have helped him gain power by foretelling events that he took advantage of. I think he has been repaid many times over. It makes me feel better that I am not acting against the laws of the Torah."

"Honor your heavenly Father, and you will be acting in accordance with the higher laws of the Torah," Jesus said.

Joseph smiled, saying, "I will do as you say and as you do." A large storm cloud had pushed its way from the mountains and formed a shade umbrella over them. Joseph pulled off the sun veil that had shielded his head from the hot sun.

Jesus shifted uncomfortably on the bench and said to Joseph, "Stop here. I sense that everyone needs to relieve themselves."

The men walked behind a hill, and the women walked a little to the side of the cart and wagon. The men and Seth lined up facing away from the breeze. Jesus pulled up the hem of his tunic, as did the others. As he began to relieve himself, he closed his eyes, turned his face skyward and emitted out a loud, long *"Whraaahhh!"* Surprised at his outburst, the others looked at him and smiled knowingly as they too relieved themselves. Jesus looked down at his stream as it formed a small puddle in the bone-dry earth. As he finished, he let out a soft-breath "Ahhhh," of satisfying relief. The small puddle was quickly absorbed, and he dropped his tunic. He walked to the side of the hill, and there in the shade was a sprig of broad-petaled yellow flowers. He plucked them and headed back with the others to the cart and wagon.

Jesus pointed toward a deep gorge ahead and said, "We need to go this way."

Immediately, Samuel said, "No, the slopes become steeper, and the passages between them are too narrow for a wagon. That way will take much longer to reach Jericho." He pointed at the trail they were on and said, "This way is shorter and easier. We can be in Jericho tonight."

Jesus said, "That may be true. But," pointing back toward the gorge's entrance, "this way is best."

Judas said to Samuel, "Believe me, when he says which way is the best way, you need to follow him, even if you think he's wrong or that what he says doesn't make sense. After you have followed him as I have, you will learn that when you thought something he said was wrong, it turns out to be best."

Judas climbed onto the cart's driver's bench and sat next to Simon. Judith sat next to Samuel on the wagon, and Joseph, the women, and children climbed into the back. Jesus gave the flowers to Dustine and Sophie to hold. Their butterflies quickly landed and crawled to the center of the flowers to gather nectar.

Jesus and Seth led the way on foot to the gorge. Simon said, "B-b-b-be careful of the s-s-side rocks in the g-g-g-gorge when it n-n-n-narrows so the w-w-w-wheels d-d-d-don't get w-w-w-wedged."

Jesus nodded to Simon in acknowledgment and continued. Seth asked Jesus, "Can you cure Simon of his stuttering?"

Jesus replied, "Simon will learn how to cure his own stuttering, and he will become stronger in himself for doing so."

"I like Simon; he's very nice to everyone," Seth said. A few steps further, Seth started giggling.

"What's so funny?" Jesus asked.

"The sound you made when peeing. It was so loud and long. It makes me laugh to think of it. God is your Father and you are His Son, yet you pee like all men. To me, it's funny."

Jesus chuckled. "It's good to laugh. I often laugh at this body that clothes me. The sounds it makes and the feelings it gives can be surprising and funny. The sound I made when I relieved myself just came out of me spontaneously. My full bladder's pressure followed by exquisite relief and the pleasant tingling feeling of the pee leaving my body resonated in my vocal cords. As I breathed out, a natural sigh of pleasure was released. To stifle it would have diminished the pleasure."

Seth giggled again and said, "Everyone feels that feeling at times, but when we all pee together, usually no one sighs the way you did. We usually pee together quietly."

Jesus said, "It seems a shame to hide one's pleasures, even if they're innocent and natural pleasures. One should bask in moments of pleasure when the opportunity is offered."

He looked down at Seth and said, "I see there are other things on your mind. Do you want to ask me something?"

"I'm thinking about becoming a rabbi like you. My father has been trying to teach me the Torah, but he isn't educated in its meanings like you are. A rabbi in Jericho has been helping me, but I only see him occasionally. I know after we go to Jericho, you will then go to see John the Baptist. Will you still be available to be my teacher?" Seth asked.

Jesus looked ahead pensively, "I would like to do that for you if possible." He paused and stroked his beard. "But if circumstances prevent me from being with you to spend the needed time, I want you to know that my spirit will be with you and will guide you when asked. Becoming a rabbi in our tradition means that you accept the responsibility to be duty bound to follow God's laws. And that you will love the Lord your God with all your heart, mind, soul, and with all of your might."

"Yes, I know that," Seth replied. "I have studied the laws with my father and have been practicing chanting prayers. I also know that to be a good Jew, I must accept my obligation to the poor, the orphaned, and the homeless and see the will of God in all things. Also, I must be a decent human being with high moral values. But..." Seth searched his mind to articulate what was bothering him.

"Just say what you're feeling, Seth," Jesus urged.

"It's just that many of the elders in the synagogue say their prayers and speak of being righteous, but...they don't always act justly. At times, they condemn others for things they themselves do that are wrong. How can they be my true teachers if they don't act in ways that I think God wants us to?" Seth's expression became very concerned. He then asked, "Whom shall I believe regarding right and wrong? Surely not those teachers!"

"It's hard to know what is true based upon what others may say. A known truth is to believe in your inner self, that part of you which captures the whispers of God's true wisdom."

"That's easy for you to say," Seth retorted.

"I faced the same difficulties as you when I studied to become a rabbi. We were encouraged to argue and debate the laws of God's words in the Torah and arrive at reasonable interpretations as to what is right or wrong," Jesus replied.

"What did you learn?" Seth asked.

"That God is 'just' and therefore people should be 'just.'"

"But what is justice?" Seth persisted.

Jesus replied, "It's acting the appropriate way at the appropriate time in the appropriate place. That is justice."

"But was it just or unjust that you did works of healing on the Sabbath even though the Torah says you shouldn't?" Seth said.

"What I did was 'just' in my mind and in my heart. Not to help others in their time of need would be an injustice to the loving will of my Father," Jesus replied. "Each time and each place presents different circumstances. You simply can't have all the answers to each circumstance until it presents itself. You must trust yourself to do what is kind and compassionate in the best way."

"But sometimes it's so hard to know what's best."

"When in doubt, always use the power of love to guide you," replied Jesus. "Becoming a man means you must decide for yourself what is best. The hypocrisies and injustices that you experience will give you natural feelings of right and wrong and what to accept or reject. Listen to those natural inner feelings of your heart to guide you rather than relying on what others may say, be they hypocrites or the pious. When you do, you'll be right more often than wrong."

Samuel stopped his wagon and stood up on the driver's bench to get a better view of the path ahead. He said, "The gorge is becoming too narrow to pass. We should turn back and go the other way."

Jesus walked straight ahead and without tuning around, waved his arm forward and continued. Simon followed in his cart; Samuel frowned in disgust. He sat down next to Joseph and said, "You can go with them if you want to. I'm turning back. It's too hot to be going nowhere. I'll be in Jericho tonight with my bride."

Joseph quickly jumped off Samuel's wagon and walked toward Simon's cart. Judith said from the back of the wagon, "Please don't be hasty, my husband. The Rabbi seems to know what he's doing. I'd rather follow him than be in Jericho one day sooner."

Samuel stared back defiantly. She approached him, and in a soft delicate voice, Judith said, "Please," kissed his cheek, and in a soft, sweet, pleading tone asked, "For me?" Reluctantly, Samuel called to Joseph and said, "Come back. We'll follow the Rabbi."

Joseph hopped back on the wagon. Samuel gave a short snap to the reins and quickly caught up with Simon.

Shortly, the path between the steep walls of the gorge did narrow as they proceeded. The gorge's steep walls allowed only one foot of room on each side for the wagon's wheels to pass. An hour later they came around a bend and then stopped in their tracks. The gorge's path had narrowed sharply and did not permit further passage for the cart and wagon, nor was there any room to turn around.

Exasperated, Samuel said to Joseph, "Your Rabbi is a great healer and he can find water, but his sense of direction stinks. Is my horse supposed to walk backwards for an hour?"

26

Seth looked up at Jesus and asked, "What do we do now?"

Jesus smiled and simply said, "There is always a way." He walked back along the cart holding onto the side of it as he maneuvered his feet between its wheels and the gorge's sidewall. Seth followed. Samuel glared as Jesus passed by his wagon. Joseph hopped off and followed Jesus and Seth back around the bend. One side of the gorge's fifty-foot wall slanted at a thirty- degree angle.

Samuel approached them and said, "You should have listened to me."

Jesus replied, "I listen to a higher source." He added, "Don't be dismayed. We can back up the wagon and cart a little bit and make it up this slope."

"It's too steep and too heavy a load for my horse," Samuel protested.

"If we unload your wagon and all of us push it up with your horse pulling it, we can make it," Jesus said.

Samuel studied the angle a moment and said, "It may be possible, but we'll have to carry everything up that incline in this heat. He looked at the stacks of wedding gifts, all their other belongings, baskets of food, full goatskin water bags and said, "In this heat we'll be exhausted."

Seth said to Samuel, "I'll carry your things if you don't want to."

Samuel narrowed his eyes at Seth as if he were being challenged by the boy to do his work for him. "Okay," Samuel said reluctantly, "we don't seem to have much choice." He wiped the sweat from his brow, turned, and stomped back to his wagon.

Jesus prayed silently, *"Dear Father, help me in this world to have greater patience and tolerance for those who do not see your Light and trust in your ways."* He then looked up at the opposite, steeper eastern edge of the gorge's wall and squinted his eyes against the blazing sun's bright glare. The edge of a large cloud started to cross over it. In a soft whisper he said, "Thank you, my Lord Father, for keeping us in your grace and safety."

Joseph and Seth wondered why he said that since they appeared to be in a precarious situation. They followed Jesus back to the cart. By the time they had backed the wagon and cart to the bend and begun unloading them, the cloud had progressed over the gorge and provided a cooling shade. Samuel looked up at it and said, "I've never seen such a large cloud at this time of the year in these parts."

Jesus said to him, "I pray it will provide you some comfort." He continued to help unload Samuel's wagon.

Samuel gazed at Jesus, looked back up at the darkening cloud, and then looked back at Jesus. He shrugged his shoulders, dismissing the cloud's occurrence and Jesus's words.

Seth pulled the donkey's bridle, and from the back and all sides, all the men and women struggled and pushed the cart up the incline to the crest of the gorge, then did the same for the wagon. Afterward, they labored to carry the cart and wagon's paraphernalia up the grade and reload it all. Dustine and Sophie carried the small things as the butterflies danced over their heads. The breeze had gotten stronger, and the huge cloud had grown larger; both had created a helpful cooling effect that made the exhausting task much easier to bear.

Jesus led the way; everyone else except the drivers rested or napped on the cart and wagon. The air temperature was pleasant. Jesus was alone with his thoughts.

King Herod lay on his stomach as the masseur firmly kneaded the sole of his foot. "Ahhh, that feels superb, Demetrius. You found a good spot," he said.

Octavius entered the chamber and said, "My King, they told me it was urgent. What is it that you need?"

"I'm going to send the whole Third Brigade to Jerusalem. I want that Rabbi in my keeping," Herod replied.

"The latest report is that Pilate has already has sent his soldiers to search the outer perimeters of Jerusalem since there were no sightings in Bethlehem. Pilate will think that you're trying to usurp his power or that you're spying on him," Octavius said.

"Of course he will, and I am. But we'll tell him that we want to reinforce his efforts to find the Rabbi and, in the absence of his soldiers, we need to maintain the security of Jerusalem," Herod replied.

"He will still feel that you're acting to supersede his jurisdiction," Octavius said.

"Pilate can use a reminder that I am still King of Judea. It will also ensure that the Rabbi's fate will also be under my jurisdiction. Have the scribe prepare the orders."

"Are you sure you want to send the whole Third Brigade rather than just a legion or two?"

"I will not have the specter of your dream haunt my thoughts any longer. I have spoken," Herod coldly replied.

Herod pulled his foot away from the masseur's hands and ordered, "That's enough, Demetrius. Now do the other foot." Herod pointed a finger at Octavius and said, "Go and do as I bid."

"Yes, my King," Octavius replied.

—⊂══════⊃—

A half hour later, Jesus was walking at a relaxed pace. He was in a meditative state, his legs moving automatically. The path on the gorge's crest had been windswept, leaving a smooth, hard path wide enough for the travelers.

Jesus had let go of the donkey's lead rein a while ago. The donkey followed his rhythmic pace, and Samuel's horse followed the cart in step. Simon and Samuel barely held onto their reins and periodically closed their eyes from boredom and drowsiness after their tiring work. Judas, Joseph, and Seth napped atop the clothes and blankets in the cart. Miriam and her children slept in the back of the wagon with Judith. A pair of butterflies rested on each of Jesus's shoulders as he led the way.

The huge grey cloud overhead had become much darker. The air became very still. Jesus removed his sandals to feel the living earth beneath his feet and to ground himself from the myriad thoughts and desires expressed by so many people since his arrival. In a few moments, he felt at peace and whispered, "Thank you, dear Lord, for the grace of Your creation that I walk upon."

Jesus heard God reply, *"EACH DAY THE EARTH AWAITS THE LIGHT OF YOUR LOVE AND THANKS YOU."*

In a low whisper that was inaudible to the others, Jesus said, "It's heartening to hear that the earth feels that way. If only man would accept Your Word through me as the ground beneath my feet does, the task before me wouldn't feel so overwhelming. It's only Your love for me and the faith You have inspired in me that keep me on the path of my destiny."

"BE NOT DISCOURAGED, MY SON. KNOW THAT I FOREVER HOLD YOU IN MY LIGHT AND MY PROTECTION."

Suddenly the blackened sky turned bright white as a mile-long flash of lightning reached down and struck a barren hilltop a quarter mile away. The dazzling bright flash of light in the darkened sky caused the sleeping members in the cart and wagon to open their eyes. A split second later a loud, sharp crackling cut through the air, immediately followed by an extremely loud, thunderous *BANG!* and then a rumbling that shook to their core those who had barely awakened.

Samuel's frightened horse reared. Miriam quickly lay over Dustine and Sophie to protect them. Judith climbed up next to Samuel and held on to his waist as he tugged on the reins to restrain the horse. The others trembled even as the thunder slowly ebbed.

Jesus bowed his head and whispered, "I have seen Your Light and hear Your might. Your will be done. I am to be the One."

Under the dark shadow of the huge blackened cloud, Samuel and Judith scrambled to cover their gifts and food on the wagon from the expected downpour of rain. As Simon covered his cart, Miriam put a blanket around the children and hugged them closely. The others pulled up their veils and tightened their garments snugly. A ray of light cut through a small parting of the huge black cloud and shone on everyone. Jesus said, "Why do you bundle yourselves up when the sun shines upon you?"

Samuel pointed to the darkness of the landscape around them, then to the cloud above, and said, "Can't you see? There's a big storm about to pour on us!"

Jesus replied, "It may come or not. But when the light shines on you, savor the feeling! If the dark storm does rain on you, think of the comfort of the light that shines for you now, and you will derive comfort from that feeling during the darkness."

Samuel said, "I can smell the rain!"

Jesus looked up and smiled at the light angling through the small circular opening in the cloud. Beyond the hilltop where the lightning had struck, heavy rain did begin to fall. A glorious rainbow formed from the beam of light, its brilliant colors highlighted against the dark grey clouds as the sun continued shining on the huddled group.

Dustine pointed to the rainbow and said, "It's so beautiful!"

Miriam continued to hold him tightly but then relaxed a little bit and said, "Yes, dear, it's beautiful."

Samuel grumbled to Judith, "Now we'll have to travel through rain and mud. If the Rabbi had listened to me, you and I could enjoy a nice bath in Jericho tonight instead of all this."

"I'd love a bath also, my husband," Judith replied. She kissed Samuel's cheek and said, "Please be patient with the Rabbi's ways. He's done so much for us and our village."

Jesus caught Seth's eye and beckoned to the boy to join him. Seth came, and together they led the party onward.

⬯

Spartus held tighter to the chariot's hand bar as it raced ahead. He ordered Clavis, his centurion, "FASTER!"

Clavis snapped the reins crisply over the two large black stallions, and the chariot surged ahead. He said, "The horses will soon tire if we keep up this pace."

Spartus replied, "Let them drop if need be. The camel driver said the Rabbi was heading in this direction. We have to overtake them."

Clavis turned to look at Spartus as if to question pushing the horses to exhaustion.

Spartus looked ahead and sternly ordered, "FASTER!"

Seth and Jesus walked casually ahead of the cart and wagon. The rain continued to fall in the distance, the sun shone on the dry path ahead, and the rainbow still glowed brightly in the distance.

"What do you want to ask me?" Jesus enquired of Seth.

"When you found the well water for the village orchards, was it because you can see the water beneath the ground?"

Jesus replied, "I feel it. If you pass by a hot pot, you can feel the heat, but you don't see it. I can feel the vitality of living water in all its forms, from vapor to snow."

Seth seemed puzzled and asked, "Why do you call it 'living' water?"

"Because each drop of water is alive. It pulsates with a life-force vibrancy I can sense."

Pointing to the rain in the distance, Seth asked, "Can you talk to the rain?"

Jesus chuckled and said, "I can communicate with the rain and clouds and the water below the ground because all water is alive as is the earth that we walk upon. All my Father's creations are dynamically alive and can be sensed by any who deeply desire to learn."

"Does the water talk to you?" Seth asked

"Everything does," Jesus replied.

Seth's eyes opened wide and he asked, "Can I learn also?"

"Of course," Jesus replied. "Think of the times that you were in a crowded marketplace and everyone was talking at once. You went about your business and didn't pay attention to the constant chatter. But there were times you may have caught a few words that someone spoke. As you concentrated more on what they were saying, the other conversations became distant, and you tuned them out."

"That happens a lot. Most people don't pay attention to a boy. I've heard them talking about cheating a customer on a sale," Seth said. "Their words became clearer as I paid closer attention. I looked away from them so they wouldn't notice me as I listened."

"You have sharp ears, Seth, and you listen and learn with a sharp mind. In time you can learn how to feel living water when you concentrate with the desire to do so." Jesus pointed up toward the far edge of the large cloud and said, "Do you see the border of the cloud against the sky?"

"Sure," Seth replied as they continued to walk.

"Keep looking at the edge and see how it slowly forms a large bubble-puff and how the puffs break off into vapor wisps and then disappear as the sky absorbs them," Jesus instructed.

Seth studied the cloud and sky a few moments, smiled, then said, "Yes, I see it."

"Now look at the edge of that large puff." Jesus pointed a little to the side where the vapors were evaporating. "See how a slight white wisp of vapor forms from the blue sky?"

"Yes," said Seth, "it seems to appear from nothing."

"Keep watching and tell me what happens."

"As the wisp is getting larger, it's forming a little cloud, and the big cloud is pulling it to itself," Seth said. "The cloud's making itself bigger!"

"Very good," Jesus said. Now keep looking and see if you can tell if the edge of the big cloud is going to break away and form a little cloud or pull the vapors to itself."

Seth concentrated his gaze for a few moments and then pointed at a group of vapor wisps and excitedly said, "Those wisps will form a little cloud, and the big cloud will pull it to itself!"

They both watched what Seth had predicted as it came to be. Seth exclaimed, "I was right! It happened!"

Jesus congratulated him, "You are in communication with the cloud. The cloud is living water vapor, and it has spoken its intentions to you in its language."

Seth puffed out his chest and stepped ahead proudly. He asked, "Can I talk to the cloud and ask it to take certain shapes?"

Jesus laughed and said, "Seth, there's a treasure in you, and I'll help you discover it."

Spartus and Clavis's chariot's pace slowed to a walk as it entered the small village that Jesus had left that morning. They approached the village fountain. A nine-year-old boy was filling a large bucket. Now that the Rabbi had discovered the new well that fed the fountain, he didn't have to carry the bucket to and from the nearly dry stream. The extinguished wedding torches were still on their stands from the previous night's celebration. The boy stood and held the bucket with both hands. He saw the chariot slow as it approached the fountain. He saw the big black stallions snorting and sweating. He saw the centurion with his red fringe-topped metal helmet and shiny body armor. When he saw

Spartus's face, the boy dropped the full bucket, wetting his sandals and tunic. He turned away in horror and ran as fast as he could back to his home.

<hr>

"Go ahead and tell him," Judith urged Samuel.

"Not now," Samuel demurred.

Judith took the reins from Samuel and said, "Go now. I'll drive."

Samuel stared stubbornly at Judith. She implored, "Please, my beloved. We are blessed with the sun in front of us. And look," she pointed over her shoulder, "the rainbow is following behind us. It could only be because of the Rabbi's powers. At least thank him for me. Please…"

Samuel's stare faded as he gave in. "All right, I will for you." He stepped off the wagon and walked ahead to Jesus and Seth in the lead.

They had been moving easily along the dry smooth ridge above the gorge for two hours. As the late afternoon sun dipped lower, it shone through a slit in the dark sky with a beam of angled light, causing the rainbow's unbroken arc to grow higher with its ends touching miles apart on the distant landscape. Its radiant colors glowed brightly against the grey shower of the raining backdrop.

Jesus turned and nodded at Samuel as he approached. Samuel sheepishly said, "Judith wanted me to thank you for guiding us on a path that is dry with all of this foul weather around us. She feels it is a blessing and that somehow you are responsible for it."

Jesus replied, "Please tell her she's welcome, but that she should thank my heavenly Father." Seth smirked, and Jesus asked, "How are you feeling Samuel?"

Samuel patted his robe, releasing puffs of road dust, and said, "I feel tired and dirty." He turned and looked at the dazzling rainbow, then sighed and said, "But I must say, I've never seen rain this time of year, nor have I ever seen a rainbow such as the one that's followed us for so long. It must be more than a coincidence that we haven't been rained on and have smooth passage, but to where? Do you know where we're going?"

Jesus pointed ahead as a cloudburst poured down on the path a mile ahead of them. Samuel winced, tightened his robe, and said, "It looks like we are going to get wet after all."

"Perhaps," Jesus replied, "but perhaps not the way you think."

Samuel looked curiously at Jesus and then walked back to tightly cover the goods in his wagon. Twenty minutes later, they arrived at the place where the cloudburst had rained heavily but had dissipated as they neared the spot. The air had cooled comfortably although the path had turned a little soggy. Jesus tapped Seth's shoulder and pointed down into the gorge. Seth looked, and his eyes opened wide with delight.

Jesus winked at Seth and said, "I'll race you down," and then he started to quickly navigate the gorge's steep angled embankment. Seth followed a half step behind. Their momentum built as they neared the bottom. The others all got off the cart and wagon to watch what the two were doing.

Jesus and Seth reached the pool of water that had collected from the rainfall's runoff. It had filled a thirty-foot long bedrock dip in the gorge. They both jumped in at the same time with a big splash. Seth exclaimed, "The water temperature's perfect!"

Joseph, Simon, and Judas happily followed down the steep slope and splashed into the water. Miriam held her children's hands and carefully navigated down the slope, Dustine and Sophie tugging to go faster. Judith hugged Samuel with glee and said, "Even though we're not in Jericho, we get to have our bath!"

Samuel took her hand and said, "I don't know how it's possible, but it's a miracle! Let's do it!"

Everyone was soon playing and luxuriating in the pleasant warm water as the sun shone on them and the brilliant rainbow glowed above in the background. Jesus smiled and felt great joy at the blessings that he beheld.

⬯

Enid's daughter Jessica pounded frantically on Nathan's door, then let herself in before he could respond. He came from his bedroom and stood leaning on his crutch near the dining table. "What is it, dear? What's the matter?"

She ran to him, tears streaming from her terrified eyes, her words tumbling out hysterically. "They killed them! They killed them all!" She sobbed as her body crumpled against Nathan. He put an arm around her, balancing himself on the crutch and asked, "Who was killed? Who did it?"

Through tears and gasping sobs, she said, "Amal, my father, my mother. They killed them. They killed them!"

"Who would do that?" Nathan asked, shocked.

Clavis casually walked through the open door, his hand on his sheathed sword. Nathan's eyes narrowed as he shifted his weight to stand between the centurion and Jessica. Clavis paid them no attention but glanced around the room. Seeing no one else, he stared coldly at Nathan.

"What does a Roman centurion want in this small village?" Nathan asked.

"We will ask the questions, Jew," Clavis replied in a chilling tone.

"Who is 'we'?" Nathan asked.

A penetrating voice coming from the kitchen answered, "That would be Clavis and me."

Nathan quickly turned his head toward the voice and almost lost his balance. He saw the back of a tall figure wearing a black ruggedly woven robe with the hood over his head standing before the bowls of leftover food from the wedding.

"How did you get in here?" asked Nathan.

The hooded man replied icily, "As Clavis said, we will ask the questions." The tall man turned around slowly; he held a chicken leg in his long, thick fingers.

Nathan winced at the man's face as it came into view from the shadow. Half his face, neck, and the top of his forehead were hidden by a large contoured leather mask; the other half revealed hideous layers of white and red scars and a patch of severely blemished skin that hung down from his eyebrow and covered the top half of the one eye that could be seen.

"That's him," Jessica wailed and pointed a finger at the darkly cloaked figure.

The large man took a step toward her and then stopped. In a soft whisper, he uttered the word "Go."

The way he said it sent a chill down Nathan's spine. Jessica, half bent over and holding her stomach, slowly backed toward the door. She bumped against the centurion's armor and quickly spun around in fear and surprise. Then she ran out of the house wailing, "They killed my family! They killed them all!"

Nathan stood transfixed. He stared at the gruesome hooded figure, who took a bite of the chicken leg and slowly chewed it. From behind, without warning, the centurion kicked away Nathan's crutch, causing him to crash to the floor. Spartus grabbed the back of a chair, set it before Nathan, and said, "Sit," and then took another bite of the chicken leg.

Nathan pulled himself up and sat in the chair, perspiration dripping profusely from his forehead.

Clavis took a leather binding from his side pouch and tied Nathan's hands tightly behind the chair's back. Nathan grimaced in pain from the strain of his shoulders' being overstretched backwards. Spartus leaned down and spoke in a low tone in Nathan's ear: "Where is the Rabbi going?"

Nathan turned his head away from Spartus's putrid breath and said, "I don't know."

"I thought that would be your answer," Spartus replied. He went to a side table and picked up a burning oil lamp. He spoke a little louder, but still calmly, "What I like about a small village is that everyone knows what happens, especially when strangers arrive: the newcomers become the highlight of everyone's conversation."

Still holding the chicken leg in one hand, with his other hand, Spartus brought the oil lamp's flame close to Nathan's nose and singed the edge of his beard. The heat of the flame and the smell of burnt hair caused Nathan to jerk his head away. Clavis's powerful hands quickly stabilized Nathan's head in a vice–like grip.

Spartus stated matter-of-factly, "We know that the Rabbi and his friends headed northeast at dawn today. Were they going to Jericho or the River Jordan?"

"I don't know," replied Nathan.

"Of course not," Spartus said as he brought the flame near Nathan's eye, singeing his eyelashes. Nathan futilely tried to pull away from the centurion's grip. Spartus leaned closer, nose-to-nose with Nathan, his foul breath permeating the small pocket of air between them. He said, "If you tell me where the Rabbi and your daughter are going, when I catch up to them, I won't kill your sweet Judith."

"I told you I don't know," Nathan adamantly replied.

Spartus slowly brought the flame against Nathan's cheek under his eye. The smell of burning flesh caused Nathan's nostrils to flare. He gritted his teeth as the pain became unbearable, and he could no longer contain an excruciating scream of agony.

Spartus stood up, looking pleased. He said, "Good. Now we are beginning to make progress." He took another bite of the chicken leg, slowly chewed it, and then swallowed. With the little finger of the hand holding the chicken leg, he pointed to his eye and scarred cheek and said, "I know how exquisite the feeling can be when flame kisses flesh. You will definitely tell me what you know."

Spartus brought the flame against Nathan's other cheek and slowly moved it to his eye. Nathan arched his back in pain but could not pull away. He screamed in pain as his eyelashes and eyebrow were singed, and the tears in his eye audibly sizzled.

Spartus stood and again admired the red seared flesh. Drained of energy, Nathan slumped in the chair. Spartus threw the chicken bone to the floor and leaned down to Nathan, nose to nose once more, and in a cold, expressionless voice, said, "If you tell me where the Rabbi is going,

I will not let Clavis play with your darling newlywed daughter when they are found."

Exhausted, Nathan weakly replied, "Even if I knew where they were going, I would never tell you." Nathan took in a deep breath and then spat in Spartus's eye.

Spartus jerked back in surprise. He didn't wipe away the spittle that hung from the overlapping skin fold, but said to Clavis, "This feisty Jew cripple has told us all he knows." Spartus removed the oil lamp's lid and poured the oil carefully over Nathan's head, covering his hair. The oil dripped down over Nathan's face and saturated his beard. Spartus hummed to himself as he brought the flame under Nathan's long beard and ignited it.

Clavis let go of Nathan's head as the flames grew higher and engulfed the old man's face and head. Clavis could barely hear Spartus above Nathan's tortured screams as he said, "Let's go."

They were about to walk through the door when Spartus stopped and turned to watch Nathan writhing in pain, twisting his bound body against the chair. Nathan continued to scream in excruciating pain. He coughed and choked from the smoke of his burning beard and of his oil-soaked flaming robe. His breathing and screams turned to desperate gasps for air and then stopped. Nathan slumped lifeless against the chair. The air filled with the putrid smell of burnt flesh and hair.

From the hot flames, a red-orange glow illuminated Spartus and Clavis's faces. Spartus smiled with satisfaction and said to Clavis, "We know they headed northeast in a wagon and cart. But they might turn around as they did when they left Jerusalem for Bethlehem to mislead anyone trying to follow. Unlike that main stone road, the unpaved path that they're now taking will be easy to track. Our chariot will quickly overtake their wagon and donkey cart."

The two men walked outside as the sun was almost setting in the west. Clavis looked to the northeast and saw the fading light illuminate the large storm cloud pouring heavy rain below it – the same cloud that had brought water for Jesus's bath. He said to Spartus, "That rain will wash away any hint of a track."

Spartus stared at the distant rain coming toward them and said, "Damn that Rabbi! He's probably going back to Jerusalem. That's the last place he would be expected to go. That's where we'll look for him."

⬯

Jesus lay on his back and looked up at the night sky. The stars flickered, and the moon illuminated the barren hills. He quietly stood up and walked around the encampment. He looked at Miriam, who slept peacefully with Dustine and Sophie huddled by her side in slumber. He passed Judas, Joseph, and Seth, who slept on blankets laid on the ground. Simon was snoring as he lay on his back on his cart. Jesus walked by the wagon and paused to see Judith snuggled against Samuel, her brow furrowed with concern as she slept.

Judith's essence was spiritually intertwined with her deeply beloved father's essence, and she experienced his loss in a dream state. Jesus's strong psychic link with both of them had been established when he had channeled healing energy to Nathan and sanctified Judith's marriage. He sighed mournfully, aware of Nathan's fate, and whispered a prayer: "Our Father who art in heaven, I know You will reward Judith's honored father with enjoyment of his eternal life in Your Kingdom. I thank You for Your blessed grace."

Judith sighed, and her brows relaxed. She snuggled closer to Samuel, who hugged her protectively. As they slept peacefully, Jesus raised his palms over them and whispered, "Bless this loving couple and the child that they have conceived. May the new life that grows within Judith allay that painful loss of her honored father with abundant love and joy. Amen."

Jesus dropped his hands and walked into the night. Troubled thoughts raced through his mind. Nathan's tortured death, balanced against his lifetime of kindness and generosity to all who crossed his path, was absurdly unjust. Jesus walked faster and faster. He ran. Then he stopped and sat on the ground, breathing deeply to still his mind and calm his body. Then he spoke to God his Father: "It makes no sense that this world You have created with Your divine love should contain such willful cruelty. Please help me to understand."

Jesus bowed his head in repose. From within he heard God's words: *"BE NOT DISMAYED, MY SON. REMEMBER THAT MY FAVOR IS FOR A LIFETIME; WEEPING MAY TARRY FOR THE NIGHT, BUT JOY COMETH IN THE MORNING. COME NOW AND STEP INTO MY ETERNAL KINGDOM, YOUR TRUE HOME."*

Jesus exhaled and sensed his spirit leaving his body. In an instant, a feeling of exaltation surged through him. It carried him into a euphoric, infinite vastness of Light. He basked in the bliss of his Father's splendor. Then at once he saw flashes of images that portrayed all possibilities of experience - pain and bliss, laughter and tears, paradise and hell.

The images flashed, then faded, then stillness, then only the soothing, comforting, loving, soft womb of permeating white Light... then His words, *"FRET NOT, FOR YOUR TIME ON EARTH IS BUT A BRIEF MOMENT; MY KINGDOM IS FOREVER. GO ABOUT YOUR*

*WORK AND DO THAT WHICH YOU FEEL THE NEED TO DO.
TRUST THOSE FEELINGS. I AM WITH YOU ALWAYS."*

Judas walked over the hill and saw Jesus sitting on the ground with his head bowed. The sun had risen an hour earlier. Judas yelled out as he ran to Jesus, "There you are. We've all eaten our morning meal and are ready to go." He approached Jesus, who remained motionless. Judas knelt and shook his shoulders. "Wake up! Wake up! Can you hear me?"

Jesus opened his eyes, his face blank. He looked around to orient himself and then at Judas, who said, "We've been searching for you."

Slowly Jesus stood, brushed off the seat of his tunic, and replied, "I have been traveling out of this body going place to place in no time." He grinned at Judas and said, "But I am here now. A moment ago I was in my Father's Heavenly Kingdom. In God's eternal time, it is always 'now.'"

Judas did not understand. Concerned, he asked, "Are you all right? Do you need something to eat?"

"I'm fine, Judas. I have already been nourished in my Father's Paradise. I'm ready to go now."

THE DESTINY

27

Joseph held the reins of the cart's horse as Jesus climbed on and sat next to him. Simon and Judas walked ahead; Seth sat in the wagon with the other children and Miriam. Samuel and Judith sat on the wagon's driver's seat. The men snapped their reins and started toward the day's destination.

Joseph, beaming with excitement, said to Jesus, "Last night I dreamed about a beautiful young maiden in Jericho. Her eyes were beautiful and hypnotic. They captivated me. Her skin looked so soft and golden, I couldn't resist wanting to touch her. I reached for her, but her image faded. I must find her."

Jesus smiled and said, "It's good to hope for love to come your way. But surely you've had dreams about women before."

Joseph grinned and replied, "Of course."

Jesus asked, "What makes you think this young lady is different?"

"I have many dreams," Joseph said as his eyes lit up, "but I have this special feeling." He put his hand over his heart. "I know that this dream was one of my most significant ones, like the one I had about you."

Jesus said, "I see that your dream is of great importance. You're filled with a true, heartfelt, grand hope."

"The rainbow that you made yesterday gave me hope that I will find the love of my life to wed."

"What makes you think I made that rainbow?" Jesus asked.

"You are the Messiah. The sun shone on us while the rain poured everywhere else. The path ahead of us was smooth and firm. The wonderful pool of water at the perfect temperature was a miracle. Surely it was because of you. You are the true Messiah."

"It's better, Joseph, that you think in terms of divine providence that has blessed our path rather than me so that others will not portray me as the Messiah until it is time."

Joseph grinned and said, "That's what makes you the Messiah: wherever you go is divine providence. Nothing bad can happen."

Jesus sighed and said, "Say what you will, Joseph, but choose wisely whom you speak to. Around the time you were born, there was a man from Galilee who claimed to be the Messiah. Roman soldiers crucified him and his followers - one thousand Jews - and left them hanging along the roadway as a warning to anyone else who would claim to be the Messiah."

Jesus turned away and looked behind at the yellow-brown, dry, rounded hills, the last part of the Wilderness of Judea they'd traveled over. He turned back and gazed upon the distant, low-lying city of Jericho and the hills that progressively transformed into high cliffs with ridges and deep gorges that had been cut into the soft clay and limestone by eons of storms.

They continued for two more hours and came to a very high ridge. Seth pointed below and exclaimed, "I see green! It's the Oasis of Jericho!" Just beyond the oasis was the city.

From the River Jordan, Jeremiah climbed the steep path from the base of the mountain. He carried a small basket with a jar of wild honey and a container of dried locusts. He soon came upon the opening of a limestone cave and cautiously peeked in. The cave was barren except for a bed blanket laid upon a platform carved from the limestone wall and a man sitting cross-legged on the floor with his eyes closed in meditative prayer.

"Why do you bother me, Jeremiah?" the man asked, his eyes still closed.

"You've been here five days. I brought you some nourishment. And I must inform you that over a thousand people have collected during your absence and are by the river waiting for you. A delegation of Pharisees have also come and asked to meet with you."

The grisly looking man opened his eyes and said, "Many have come because he is near. The time will be soon." He stood up, his wiry musculature and tall frame impressive. His open camel hair robe revealed a leather girdle that covered his loins. The mangled hair on his head sprang out in all directions, and his unkempt beard bespoke a wild man, except for the intense eyes that pierced beyond the flesh and could look into the deepest recesses of one's being.

Jeremiah pleaded, "Eat something before you see them. You've been fasting and need the energy. There are many to be baptized."

"To deal with hypocrites and the wicked, it's best to have an empty stomach," the man replied as he walked past Jeremiah and out of the cave. Jeremiah followed him, John the Baptist, down to the waiting crowd at the River Jordan.

At the Oasis of Jericho, Seth, Dustine, and Sophie frolicked among the fragrant balsam trees; the adults reclined beneath a cluster of date palms and munched on the sweet fruit as their horse and donkey drank buckets of fresh water from the oasis's well. A sheepherder, his three sons shepherding a flock of over one hundred and fifty sheep, approached the oasis well. The children ran to pet the lambs.

Joseph gazed at Jesus, who lay on his back looking up at the date palm branches above him. Jesus pinched a piece of a succulent date that had fallen from the tree and put it in his mouth. He closed his eyes as the rich buttery sweetness melted onto his taste buds. Joseph smiled as he saw Jesus's expression of delightful satisfaction.

Then Joseph glanced at one of the shepherd's sons who was pouring water into a trough as the dusty sheep huddled close to drink. The lad's father sat under a tree for shade. Joseph puffed out his chest proudly and walked to him, nodding a greeting. The shepherd glanced at Joseph wearily and nodded back.

Joseph said, "This shade feels good."

The shepherd ignored the superfluous statement.

Impetuously Joseph asked, "Do you know that the Messiah has arrived?"

The shepherd gave him a quixotic look, then turned away. Joseph persisted, "The Messiah has come! I've witnessed healings and miracles that he's performed. He healed a leper right before my eyes!"

The shepherd glanced back at Joseph in annoyance, then looked away again. Joseph became incredulous at the shepherd's response and said, "I told you that the Messiah has come! Doesn't that mean anything to you?"

The shepherd turned back to Joseph and said, "My father's father was a sheepherder, as was my father. My sons are sheepherders, as am I." He shook his head in disgust as the wind began to shift and said, "Close your eyes and breathe in deeply through your nose."

Joseph resisted. The shepherd said "Go ahead and do it, and then I will listen to what you have to say."

Joseph closed his eyes and began to take a deep breath through his nose. Halfway through, he scrunched his nose in reaction to an odiferous wave of air. "Finish breathing in, young man," the shepherd urged him.

Joseph finished inhaling and opened his eyes with a nauseated expression. The shepherd asked, "What do you smell?"

"I smell sheep crap and pee. It stinks!" Joseph replied.

The shepherd spoke solemnly, "I can barely smell it. My whole life I've been with sheep as my family has for generation after generation. And for generation after generation, our people have been told that the Messiah is coming; the Messiah is coming to free us Jews and return the land of Israel to us." The shepherd stared coldly at Joseph and said, "When you say that the Messiah is coming, to me your words are like the sheep stench that I barely smell anymore; I barely hear you, much less believe you." Then he stood up.

Joseph protested. "I didn't say he was coming. I said he was here!"

The shepherd mockingly looked around the oasis and said, "Of course he's here." He pointed toward Jesus and said, "That man lying down there must be he. And he's about to enter Jericho, but first he will turn the women and children into mighty military commanders, the men into generals, and my sheep into soldiers. The whole Roman army will fall down at a wave of his hand, and the Romans will pay us sixty percent of all their earnings and will bow to our rule or be jailed and tortured. After all, we are the chosen people." The shepherd turned and began walking away.

"Wait!" Joseph called out. "You said that you would hear what I have to say."

"I did, and from where you now stand, it smells of sheep crap, just like when I hear healers babble and so-called messiahs preach. It all stinks like sheep crap. I've been around a long time, and I've learned to move away from the herd when the wind shifts to avoid the stench of the sheep crap - and the crap of false prophets as well. After your Messiah has created his all-powerful army to defeat Rome, then I will listen to what you have to say." The shepherd walked away faster as the shifting wind was concentrating more of the stench where Joseph stood.

Jesus sat up and saw the shepherd walking away from Joseph. He lay back down and sighed at Joseph's earnest but fruitless attempt, knowing that it would take many miracles for the people to believe in him.

<hr>

Upon entering Jericho, Jesus sat on the back of the wagon with Dustine, Sophie, and Miriam. Samuel and Judith sat on the wagon driver's bench. An observer would assume they were a family and Jesus just another man and not the Messiah that Pontius Pilate's Praetorian Guard was searching for. To avoid being identified as the "wanted group" that had left Jerusalem, Judas, Simon, Joseph, and Seth had entered the city after them and had traveled a different route to their prearranged rendezvous. In the far western part of Jericho was a landmark fountain. At the first synagogue due east of it, they were to meet that day. Judas's group arrived at the middle-class synagogue before Jesus. He knocked on the side door of the rabbinical quarters. A moment later, the door was opened by an elderly, grey-bearded man in prayer shawls. Judas held out his arms to Rabbi Moshe to hug him. The Rabbi abruptly grabbed

Judas's arm and pulled him in. Moshe said. "At last! We've been waiting for you."

Judas embraced him and said, "Moshe, it warms my heart to see you again." Moshe quickly looked out the door and saw the others in his group. He beckoned to them, "Hurry! Come. Come in!"

Judas waved to Simon, Joseph, and Seth to follow him. Once inside, they all took off their sandals and rinsed their feet in the foot fountain by the entrance. Judas had only taken a few steps into the room when Rabbi Moshe excitedly said, "Your other friends arrived a while ago and told me about the Rabbi Jesus. Is it true that he healed a leper? And turned water into fine wine? Can he really be the One?"

Judas nodded and said, "Yes, he is the One. I have much more to tell you and the others about what's happened since we left Jerusalem. But why did you pull me in like that?"

The elder rabbi's excitement faded to concern. He said, "A strange combination of feelings have come over the city. It is joyful for a lot of Jews and eerie for the Gentiles. The Third Battalion has suddenly left Jericho for Jerusalem. Legions of soldiers moving out gets everyone's attention. It's rumored they're joining Pilate's forces to search for your Rabbi. Word has spread quickly among our people that both Herod and Pilate are using all their resources to look for the Messiah; now everyone thinks that your Rabbi must be the Messiah."

Moshe grasped Judas's shoulders and looked deep into his eyes and said, "Judas, I've known you for a long time. You've always been a skeptic, a hard one to fool. You're smart and easily see through things to what is true and untrue." Moshe, needing a final reassurance that his lifelong prayers had been answered, firmly squeezed Judas's shoulders and asked, "Has he really come? Has our age-old prophecy really been fulfilled? Is it really true?"

Judas grasped Moshe's shoulders and squeezed them with each response of, "Yes! Yes! And Yes! "

The elder rabbi beamed, spontaneous tears of joy rolling down his wrinkled cheeks and spilling onto his gray beard.

Peter, Matthew, Luke, Philip, Nathaniel, Andrew, Thomas, and John stood up from the meeting table to greet Simon, Joseph, Judas, and Seth. Judas introduced Joseph to everyone. Moshe poured tea from a large clay kettle, and they all sat and spoke of Jesus's healings and divine powers. After a while, Judas said to John, "I miss Saul. He should be with us. Jesus spoke of him and said that he held Saul in his thoughts. It still sounds strange to me when he speaks of Saul that he calls him Paul, but I know who he means."

Andrew reminded Judas, "Perhaps it's best that Saul isn't here: he said that as far as he was concerned, it would be better to turn a blind eye and speak no more of the Rabbi as if he had never existed."

Rabbi Moshe did a quick count of those present and said, "We have more than ten men, the minimum needed to conduct the evening prayers."

Matthew proudly said, "Soon my son will enter rabbinical school, and we will have one more man." He proudly gave Seth a big hug and kissed his cheek.

Seth smiled as the men held up their cups to acknowledge him. Rabbi Moshe asked Seth, "Have you been practicing the chanting prayers that I taught you on your last visit?"

Seth nodded.

Moshe said, "Good. I want to hear how your chanting sounds."

Judas anxiously looked out the window and said, "Jesus should be here soon."

Moshe leaned next to Judas, peered out, and asked, "Are you sure he knows where to find us?"

"I'm sure. He's been to Jericho many times, as we all have," Judas replied.

"But does he know where the fountain is?" Moshe asked.

"Moshe, please have faith and a little more patience. I'm certain that even if he'd never set foot in Jericho before, he would surely find us."

Judas, Simon, Joseph, and Seth told of Jesus's deeds in the village, the wondrous events during their travels together, and about the rainbow that had followed them that the others had not heard of. They spoke of his ways with people, all people, from caravan drivers to Gentiles and children. All the men were deeply impressed with the seemingly magical quality their Rabbi possessed. They also felt that an exalted time in history was in the making and they were a part of it.

Peter picked up the tea pot and offered, "Another round of tea?" Moshe raised his hand and said, "We can't wait any longer; the sun has set. We must begin the Sabbath evening prayers."

Everyone got up and passed through a hallway to a side door leading into the synagogue. They all paused for a few moments before entering the sanctuary because all worshipers were expected to compose themselves before services. Moshe opened the door and entered. He looked toward the dais and the Ark containing the Torah scrolls and then to the rows of benches on the three sides facing the dais. In the last row sat a man.

The man stood and said, "I've been waiting for nine more men so the evening prayers may begin."

Seth yelled out, "Rabbi!" and ran to him.

Judas said to Moshe, "That's him. He's the One."

Moshe was thrilled. His hands trembled as he greeted Jesus briefly, then unlocked the synagogue's large outer doors to let in the waiting congregation, wondering how Jesus had gotten in. Jesus joined in the evening prayers from his bench but didn't come to the dais to lead any part of the service. In his excited state Moshe could not resist looking up repeatedly from the Torah to glance down at Jesus and almost misspoke during two prayers.

After the service, Jesus and his group went to Moshe's private quarters. Moshe remained in the synagogue and spoke with a few trusted members of the congregation. When they were leaving, Moshe said to them, "Thank you. That information will be very helpful. Praise be the Lord, our God." He quickly joined the others.

Synagogues were more than houses of worship; they served as community centers for all social activities as well as courts for grievances and administering punishments to maintain order and justice. A synagogue was also an educational center, and Moshe's synagogue had an adjacent school. In addition, it served as a place in which one could find work, housing, or receive charity. Moshe had served his community for over forty years and had developed a trusted relationship with almost all the rabbis who led congregations that served the upper and lower classes of Jericho. He was well liked and very often, as a mediator, was able to bridge conflicts between the classes. He also had many valuable connections to the Roman political factions, who relied on him to smooth out problems and work out solutions that most of the Jewish community would accept. Most important at this critical time was the reliable intelligence network that he had established. It constantly funneled inside information from all factions, information such as he had just received from the men who were the last to leave the evening service.

Moshe entered his quarters and immediately told the others, "I have some good news. The remaining soldiers in Jericho have stopped looking for the Rabbi. Herod believes that he's hiding in Jerusalem; that's why the Third Battalion left to find him there. Pilate's soldiers are looking for him in the countryside of Jerusalem." Moshe smiled broadly, looked at Jesus, and said, "But we know that he is right here in our humble synagogue."

Jesus sat at the head of the meeting table and smiled at Moshe. Then everyone raised their cups of tea to Jesus and gave thanks that the Messiah was in their midst.

Jesus thanked his followers for their allegiance to his mission and then said a prayer: "Dear Heavenly Father, Lord of Lords, God of gods, we thank You for entrusting us with the tasks that will be brought before us and for Your guiding Light that will show us the way. We accept Your trust with joy, gratitude, and honor. Your will be done, Your Kingdom come, on earth as in heaven, for You are our Creator and the Creator of All That Is. Amen."

Everyone responded with an "Amen," and then Jesus announced, "Let the word go out that at noon on the day after tomorrow, I will conduct a healing session at the fountain."

Moshe protested, "No! You must stay in hiding or you'll be arrested!"

Judas said, "Perhaps we should wait."

Jesus replied, "God does not wait; God acts. My time among you is short. Tomorrow we will spend our day together so that we may solidify our bonds and so that I can teach you ways that will enable you to teach others; for when I am gone, you can carry the Light and speak the Word for me."

28

After the next morning's Sabbath service, Jesus spoke with his disciples during their midday meal in Moshe's quarters. He emphasized the spiritual principles they needed to master to fulfill their missions. He asked them to go out by themselves and meditate and ponder his healings and teachings and then meet under a large shade tree next to the marketplace.

The day was warm and sunny. The men had dispersed to seek a quiet place, except for Judas and Andrew who walked together as they too sought separate places. At the corner of a street near a small marketplace they saw the back of a tunic clad gaunt man who seemed to be preaching to only three men who appeared bored. They were out of earshot to hear all that the preacher was saying, but when he pointed a finger at one of his listeners and raised his voice they heard the words, "damnation" and "hell". As they passed by, Andrew tugged on Judas's robe and with a startled expression exclaimed as he pointed to the speaker, "It's the Rabbi!"

Judas turned to look and focused carefully then said, "He's looks like the Rabbi, but it's not him. I was almost fooled also when I first saw him. He even calls himself Jesus of Jerusalem."

Andrew squinted his eyes and studied the man's face and posture and said, "I see what you mean. But it was hard to tell the difference at first glance."

Jesus of Jerusalem looked up from the three people who had begun to ignore him and caught Judas's eyes looking back. He pointed a condemning finger at Judas and in a loud seething voice he said, "I know you. The great sinner! There will come a day when you bow before me and kiss my hand with tears in your eyes. But that will not prevent your horrible suffering from your unforgiveable sins."

Andrew was surprised and said to Judas, "He says he knows you. How is that?"

"I saw him as he was preaching in Jerusalem on the morning that I was searching for our Rabbi. He was very unimpressive, but I continued to stare at him because of his resemblance of our Teacher's image that I had in my dream I've told you about. He called me a sinner then and after I found the Rabbi we both passed that preacher again and again he called me a sinner."

Andrew said, "Then he surely doesn't know you."

Judas scoffed, "I'm sure with his manners that he was unable to get a following in Jerusalem. It doesn't look like he will attract a following in Jericho either." The two men walked on.

Everyone had prayed and meditated on Jesus's teachings as instructed and then gathered at the shade tree meeting place and spoke together for an hour. Jesus sat in front; the disciples sat or reclined as he answered questions that they had from the earlier meeting. People passing by paid no attention to them; it was common for men to gather in discussion groups.

Jesus continued his teachings. "You have heard it said that a man who is worth his weight in gold is considered very rich, but gold pales before the brilliance of God's Light that dwells within mankind's being. And from that Divine Light, many characteristics are formed, one of which is the form of the physical body that your physical senses recognize. However, there are many more spectrums of humans' Light that also form ultrafine, colored, mist-like bodies of thoughts and sensations that envelop and complete a person. Those invisible envelope-bodies can not be experienced through the physical senses, but they can be known by your inner senses and intuition."

Jesus cast his inner eye over the auras of his disciples and assessed their level of understanding. He continued, "The psychological envelope-body of Light surrounds a person as patterns of thought that cannot be seen by the eye or touched by the hand, yet I tell you, it exists whether or not you are aware of it, and there are also other bodies of Light that surround you such as the emotional-body that displays intensities of colors that are elicited by your feelings. There is also an intellectual body that calculates in logical ways faster than a lightning bolt. These ultra-fine bodies are never separate from each other and constantly intertwine and permeate one another, including your physical body. And thus, each affects and influences the others, and that's one of the ways the emotional imbalances that are not in harmony with the Light can create physical diseases. Conversely, when your thoughts and feelings are in harmony with the Light, you will enjoy exuberant health. Helping others with kindness and love are actions in harmony with the Light."

Andrew scratched his cheek and pulled on his beard, his face perplexed as he struggled to understand. Jesus looked at him and said, "Ask what is on your mind. Andrew. The answers to your questions will help clarify what others may also be uncertain about."

"How can we identify these different bodies and know their implications so we can do the right thing and be effective healers?"

"First you must have the desire and the intent to help those who seek healing. When you see that the seeker is open to receiving healing and your desire and intent to help are strong and true, to the degree that you are open to receive God's guidance of inner knowledge to help, that knowledge will present itself to you," Jesus replied. "You must allow yourself to act spontaneously and let go of pre-conceived ideas of what a healer should or should not do. Each of you will help to heal in a different way according to your own nature and understanding."

Luke was still puzzled. "I'm not sure what the difference is between the mental body and the emotional body. It seems to me that one's thoughts and feelings go hand in hand."

"They do," Jesus replied. "All aspects of the mind, emotions, body, and spirit are one, and as I've said, each part intertwines with and affects the others. To help one part helps all parts. I've made distinctions between aspects of human nature because each of you may possess strength in one area more than in another. For example, John, Nathaniel, and Simon have a natural compassion for the way someone 'feels,' and they can naturally attune their feelings to the feelings of the person they desire to help."

"I know w-w-w-what you m-m-m-mean," Simon said. "W-w-w-when someone is s-s-s-sad, even if th-th-they try and act happy, I can still f-f-f-feel their s-s-s-sadness."

"And because you can, Simon," replied Jesus, "that becomes your connection to help that person. In God's eyes, all are connected to each other, only to different degrees."

Thomas asked, "What do you mean by degrees?"

"A mother is deeply connected to her child," replied Jesus. "She can look at her child or listen to his voice and know what her child is feeling so much more than a stranger can. In Simon's case, although he would be a stranger to the child, he too would be able to connect to the child's feelings because of his strong, compassionate nature. When Simon concentrates his intention and desire on helping someone in distress, his natural compassion becomes stronger, his connection becomes clearer, and he is better able to help. He identifies with a person's emotional state more than he does with the intellectual aspect."

Philip said, "I must identify more with the intellect because it's easy for me to understand how a person thinks about a bothersome problem, and I'm able to offer advice how to think in ways that will help them."

"You do," Jesus said, "as do Andrew, Thomas, Matthew, and Peter."

Thomas asked, "Does one's mental body include their intelligence?"

Jesus replied, "The intellect concerns the rational thinking process of the mind and the way people understand and use information. Many have acquired distortions of understanding, which have resulted in intellectual confusion. When you can clarify those misunderstandings and shift them so that they are in harmony with the Light, then those distortions and confusions will fade and no longer interfere with a person's natural intellect. People will be able to connect more easily with their inner sight and natural sense of right and wrong."

"Which body does the psychological aspect of people belong to?" asked Peter.

Jesus replied, "The psychological aspect is a result of what a person feels and thinks. This can also be called a person's attitude. The manner in which a person thinks about circumstances determines their feelings, for better or worse. Distorted thinking creates ill feelings, and ill feelings can create distorted thinking. All circumstances, even dire ones, have a purpose and serve to spur action to improve one's circumstances and promote growth. You can help shed light on their distorted thinking to guide them to better understanding. That will improve their feelings, enhance their lives, and improve their health."

Jesus saw the struggles most of the men's intellectual bodies displayed trying to comprehend, but he also saw their emotional bodies intuitively grasping his explanations although the men had yet to integrate them fully. He continued, " The ideal is to create balance and harmony between the emotional and the intellectual bodies so that one's emotions don't over-influence the mind's reasoning and one's reasoning doesn't over-influence one's feelings. When there's balance and harmony, there's health.

"As I said, all the envelope-bodies of Light—the physical, the intellectual, and the emotional—are essentially of the one Light. I've divided them into separate bodies of that one Light so that you can understand the dynamics involved in healing the bodies of mankind. More simply, use your heart, which is the best way to connect with another person. The heart is the way of love."

Joseph blurted, "So love is what's most important?"

"Yes it is, Joseph," replied Jesus. "The love within your heart can connect you to your mate and all of humanity. Your Light connects you to the divine celestial love of your Creator. Many people unknowingly cut themselves off from that divine spiritual connection, which diminishes their health as well as their emotional and spiritual prosperity. You can help others by opening your heart to allow God's divine love to flow through you to them. When you operate on a plane of spiritual love, you will naturally enhance the lives of those who are open to you as well as benefiting yourself from His love that will flow through you."

Peter said, "But just sending out love doesn't always help. Most people need to be told what to do. What is the best way for me to tell them so they won't reject what I say?"

"First, make sure that you're being asked to help; don't intrude. In the future, when people come to hear you speak, they will already be open to receive. Then with love in your heart and your sincere intention to help, speak in simple ways that people can relate to, and always use common sense. You're all beginning to learn some aspects of healing. As you practice the art, your abilities increase. Each of you may work in different ways. Joseph works on a dream level, and his abilities are beginning to mature."

Philip sighed, shook his head in confusion, and said, "The physical body and its needs I can easily understand. I think I know what you mean about a person's feelings and thoughts, but the envelope of Light and dream workings...well, it's more than I can comprehend right now. My head spins."

Jesus gazed at Philip's aura and said, "I see. Don't be dismayed with this new way of understanding, for all of you are in an awakening process. At this time, the doors to your minds have opened, but you have yet to enter the room that contains the greatest treasures of divine wisdom. The seeds of knowledge to guide rightful action are within you. I have been activating those seeds of goodness and enlightenment so that you may awaken the seeds of goodness that reside in others and so that mankind may travel a better path to mutual prosperity, brotherhood, and love rather than a path of mutual destruction. The awakening stages are often confusing, but with time they will become integrated into your thoughts and actions so you may fulfill your greater destiny."

A young woman wearing a robe walked quickly from the public bathhouse and passed behind Jesus. A hood covered her head, and she carried her clothes bunched in her arms. The hem of her robe ended at her tapered ankles. The garment swayed with the movement of her youthful hips. All of the men's eyes turned from Jesus to follow the attractive young woman. A rolled-up shawl dropped from her arms, and she hurriedly bent to pick it up, exposing her shapely calves.

Jesus observed the men's fixed stares at the young woman and shook his head. As she quickly stood, her hood dropped down, as did the top of her robe that covered her left round shoulder and slender upper arm. Her luscious long, dark, silken hair flowed to the middle of her back. She turned her head side to side causing her beautiful, freshly washed hair to sway sensually. She held her clothes tightly against her chest with one hand and with the other, pulled her robe up to cover her shapely shoulder and its golden skin.

Jesus noticed all the men's turned heads as they followed the young woman's every movement.

Joseph stood; mesmerized, his eyes locked upon the young woman. She turned and caught his eye, smiled at him, and quickly walked away. Joseph exclaimed, "That's her! She's the one in my dream!"

Jesus said, "Go to her, Joseph."

Instead, Joseph took two steps back.

Jesus asked, "Why do you retreat from that which you desire?"

"I don't know," Joseph replied. "Maybe she's betrothed to someone."

Jesus said, "Follow your heart, Joseph, and see where it leads you, lest you regret your inaction."

Seth, who sat on the ground next to Joseph, urged, "Go on. She must be the one you've been talking about all morning."

Joseph hesitated a moment, took a few slow steps forward, then quickened his pace, and finally began running toward the young woman as she turned the corner and disappeared from sight.

Jesus began laughing.

"What's so funny?" asked Philip.

"Here I was speaking about the elevated subjects of healing and God's ways," Jesus laughed again, "but no sooner does a man see an attractive woman than his head automatically turns to follow her. The senses and instincts bend the body to follow their whims."

"Is it wrong to look?" Nathaniel asked.

"No," Jesus smiled and replied, "it's a natural, instinctive reflex to look, but what are you thinking and feeling? That's another matter."

John said, "My head does turn when an attractive woman crosses my path, but I dismiss any carnal thoughts that come to mind."

Matthew asked, "Is it wrong to have carnal thoughts?"

Jesus replied, " As I've said, your mind should enjoy the freedom to think any and all thoughts. In the landscape of the mind, you can project any consequences that you may suffer or rewards you may enjoy that will help determine what actions you will take. But when it comes to romantic love between two souls, there is more involved than the mere turning of one's head to follow a pretty woman. Joseph's running after that young woman is a prime example."

Nathaniel asked, "Do you mean his sexual attraction was so strong that he actually chose to follow her rather than just look?"

"For Joseph, it was much more than that," replied Jesus. "As I've said, Joseph's gift is to operate in the dream landscape, and he's learning how to do that. Previously, he'd dreamed of that particular woman and felt a profound love for her. He felt certain that he was destined to wed her. When Joseph actually saw his dream-girl, he also felt a natural physical-sexual attraction as well. All at once, his desires swirled intensely within his emotional body and overwhelmed his thoughts." Jesus chuckled and said, "Of course, as you can plainly see, his emotions affected his intellect and thus his thinking. We've all seen Joseph's usual rambunctious nature, but he reacted differently this time by stepping back instead of darting forward.

"In his heart," Jesus continued, "Joseph knew he truly loved her, but when he saw her unexpectedly," Jesus laughed again, "he became confused about what action to take." Jesus smiled, "Ah, sweet love! You see, Joseph's instincts screamed to him to follow her, but his intellect caused him to hesitate as fears of rejection and disappointment flooded his mind. Yet as we've seen, with a little encouragement, he followed his heart, which in this circumstance was what he had to do, lest he'd regret a possible lost opportunity to connect with his beloved."

Thomas asked, "What about the sexual attraction or lust one may have for another even though no feelings of love are involved?"

"Sexual pleasure without guilt is certainly not a sin and should be enjoyed," replied Jesus.

"What if the moment of sexual pleasure results in a child?" Luke asked.

"A child may be a joyous reward or an unwanted consequence of sexual pleasure," Jesus replied. "A child is certainly a divine gift and a responsibility to be cared for and loved, and that's why one's sexual pleasures should also be responsible."

Peter asked, "What is the responsible thing to do when it comes to possible sexual encounters?"

"If one is tempted to act sexually or socially or in any other way that may result in negative consequences or guilt, then one must pause to reflect and decide whether physical, emotional, social, or mental harm will come to oneself or the other," Jesus replied. "Again I say to you, act with love in all circumstances."

Nathaniel asked, "But isn't it love that drives one to have sex? Why are so many people driven by the need for sex?"

Jesus replied, "Sexual love is the seeking of two people to become one in union with each other on a physical level. People seeking sex seek a way to find love and fulfillment although sex without love rarely brings completeness. Man and woman are parts of God that seem opposite but are intended complements of each other in the One. There is always a basic drive from the two separate complementary male and female divisions of the One to seek union as one. In some people, that yearning is so intensely strong that it distorts their natural sex drives to an extreme.

That can cause serious consequences if their sexual needs become the overriding purpose for finding love and completeness although sexual fulfillment may add immensely to some relationships and may not be necessary in others. God's divine love is non-sexual because as the divine source, it is both male and female."

The men shook their heads trying to fathom the all-encompassing Oneness of God and their individual sexual desires.

"In dealing with sexual matters," Jesus continued, "I tell you that the spirit and flesh are one and that the body is God's gift with which to express that spirit in this world. A person's sexual preferences with their counterpart in life when bound in a union of mutual love is better than a union not bound in love. Judge not another's ways of sex or love, for each is unfathomably unique.

"Feelings of sexual pleasures can enhance the body's vitality; however, where there are inner or cultural conflicts concerning those pleasures, harm may occur."

Phillip said, "You've told us so much that it's hard to comprehend it all."

"I know. As I've said, these new concepts are seeds that will grow within you. But we'll talk more. Have faith that in time you will come to experience more of the divine truth, and after tomorrow's healing session, you'll learn more of what it means to be a healer."

Standing, Judas said, "We're all wary of tomorrow's public session and fear you might be arrested."

Jesus replied, "It's wise to be prudent, but don't fear for my safety, for I'm not concerned."

In the middle of his amphitheater, Herod Antipas stood next to his palace architect. Numerous aides and guards stood far to the side. Herod pointed to the southern top tier of seats and said, "I want twelve more seating sections erected behind that wide arc. That should seat at least a thousand more spectators."

"It will take a lot of stone to build the foundation and supports high enough. That and the labor will cost a lot more than our budgeted building allowance. If we spread the work over three years, our annual expenditures will be less, and we'll still have enough labor for your other projects."

"I want it done in time for next year's Passover Festival," replied Herod.

The architect protested, "That's only ten months away. We would need three shifts working day and night. I haven't even begun to draw up the plans."

Herod narrowed his eyes at the architect and said coldly, "Then you had better get to work immediately."

Octavius, accompanied by two aides, walked rapidly toward the center of the amphitheater. Herod saw him approaching and sternly questioned the architect, "Why are you still here? I said to start immediately."

The architect meekly replied, "Yes, My Lord," and then quickly retreated as Octavius approached. Octavius silently pointed to an area thirty feet away, and his two aides quickly went to that spot and stood waiting.

"What is it, Octavius?" asked Herod.

"An envoy and his procession from the emperor is one hour away," replied Octavius.

Herod looked surprised, then puzzled, and said, "An envoy? No official announcement? That's very unusual. Do you know who the envoy is?"

"No," Octavius replied. "When our soldiers saw them on the road, they asked but were told by Rome's Praetorian Guards that it was a private matter and the emperor's envoy was coming to see you. Couriers raced here to inform you. I've just spoken with them."

"Why the secrecy? What do you suppose Rome wants?"

"I have no idea," replied Octavius.

———

"Your offer of grand hospitality is noted, but a private meeting is necessary at this time," Sejanus said after he was announced to Herod in the palace reception hall. Sejanus was the Envoy whom the Emperor Tiberius of Rome had often praised as the "partner of my labors." Tiberius had given Sejanus supreme command of the Praetorian Guard, which was charged with protecting the ruler of the Roman Empire, and he wielded tremendous authority.

Herod and Sejanus adjourned to Herod's large luxurious private chamber and sat alone. Herod asked, "How is the Emperor doing these days?"

"Tiberius is struggling with the Senate, as usual," replied Sejanus. "He complains that governing Rome is like holding a wolf by the ears. He's already had to deal with two of his armies who mutinied and threatened to march on Rome. That left him unnerved and highly suspicious of everyone. He's immersed himself in astrology and drinks too much wine." Sejanus rolled his eyes. "His mood swings are very difficult to deal with."

Herod raised his eyebrows. "I understand you're the only one he trusts and that you alone are permitted to visit with him regularly."

Sejanus sat up proudly and said, "He does depend on me in every way and thinks of others around him as plotting, toadying courtiers."

"It is said that you are the right hand of Rome," Herod replied.

"It is difficult and tricky work dealing with a resentful Senate, the armies, the picayune citizens of Rome, the scandals, and all the other administrative nonsense in addition to a paranoid Emperor," Sejanus replied.

"Politics can be a tougher foe than your enemy's armies," Herod said.

Sejanus smiled slyly and said, "Especially when it comes to religious beliefs and politics."

Herod shifted uncomfortably and asked, "Why have you come to see me and in such a secretive manner?"

Sejanus noted Herod's uneasiness. Instead of answering, he looked around Herod's ornate private chamber with its perfectly sculpted statues, elaborate furniture, artistic mosaic floor, marble-paneled walls, three-foot-high vases with Grecian figures, and colorfully decorated glass bowls and glasses atop a gold-trimmed marble table. Sejanus toyed with Herod: "For a King of the Jews, you live like a Roman." Sejanus then turned his gaze on Herod and cuttingly added, "All of this and the domain you rule is yours... only by the good graces of the Emperor."

Herod's back stiffened at the remark. He was being put in his place as a subordinate to Sejanus. Even though he was anxious to know the reason for Sejanus's visit and his remark about "religious beliefs," he played the game and changed the subject and asked, "How was your trip? Did you come by ship?"

Sejanus casually sat back, knowing Herod had understood that he was in command, and said, "We made port in Ptolemais in three ships." Sejanus leaned toward Herod, smiled, and said, "I need three ships to transport my personal Praetorian Guard of eighty; and of course, their horses, chariots, weapons, and supplies. Some of my Guard were famous gladiators at the Games. But one who is not in my Guard is a gladiator whom I've personally seen take on ten well-armed men at once. They had ganged up on him to make sure he was eliminated first." Sejanus chuckled, "He killed them all. It was a marvelous show. I sat next to Tiberius and threw a gold wreath at the victor's feet when he approached us and bowed. I was applauded by the crowd."

Sejanus leaned toward Herod and said slyly," Spartus was the name of that heroic gladiator." Sejanus looked to see if Herod's expression changed. It didn't. He continued, "Later that night, at a celebration for him hosted by the emperor, Spartus got very drunk and unknowingly raped Tiberius's favored concubine. He was punished like a slave, severely flogged and tortured with burning oil. When he was to be put to death, he escaped and hasn't been seen since."

Sejanus stared in silence at Herod for a moment, then raised his eyebrows and asked causally, "Would you by chance know his whereabouts?"

Herod shifted uneasily and shook his head. "I do not."

Sejanus smirked, "No matter." He adjusted his elegant robe, adorned with distinguished medals of authority, and continued, "After Spartus's unforgettable victory, what the hungry lions and tigers did to the prisoners was a quick kill. Too predictable and very boring."

Herod, wishing to change the subject, said, "I miss the chariot races at Rome's Hippodrome." Sejanus just grinned but said nothing. Herod could not contain himself any longer and demanded, "Why are you here?"

"Ah yes," Sejanus said, "let's do get to the business at hand. I came for two prime reasons, and now because of new information I have received, there's a third matter that must be discussed. The first matter is to inform you that the present territorial tax rate will be increased by twenty percent."

"Twenty percent!" Herod protested. "We've already levied additional taxes for a new aqueduct to Jerusalem so the city may continue to prosper and produce more revenue for Rome. That alone is causing resentment and talk of rebellion. Additional taxes will certainly create greater unrest."

"Unrest and rebellion are a way of life in the Empire," Sejanus yawned. "That's why we have armies."

Herod shook his head in disagreement and said, "It would be prudent to wait until next year for another increase and let the people get used to our most recent one."

"Rome needs the revenue now, not a year from now," Sejanus replied. "Tiberius insists on a new building spree, Rome's roads need repair, bad crops have raised the price of food to feed our armies, and there's been a shortfall of tax collections in Rome."

"Then raise the taxes for the Romans. Judea can give no more," retorted Herod.

"Raise taxes on Romans?" Sejanus laughed sarcastically and said, "The Roman Senate wouldn't consider such a thing. They want more, not less! The new twenty percent levy will go into effect immediately, and you will maintain order in your jurisdiction and not tolerate uprisings."

Herod gritted his teeth in silence.

"The second reason that I'm here is to order the reassignment of your Second, Third and Fourth Brigades to northern Europe," Sejanus added.

Herod bolted up and stomped back and forth. Sejanus looked at him with amusement. Herod demanded, "How do you expect me to maintain order without my full forces? And why do that many soldiers need to go to northern Europe?"

"My dear King Herod, you are a brilliant, and may I say, a cunning man. Rome is trusting you to use your talents." Then with a hint of mockery, Sejanus said, "We have great confidence in you," but his voice became deadly serious as he said, "but failure on your part will not be tolerated by Rome."

"You must tell me why you need my brigades in northern Europe," Herod demanded.

Sejanus looked away as if to ignore the question; then he sighed and said, "I'll tell you this in confidence. The Germanic tribes are planning a rebellion there as they did before. This time we're sending massive forces. With your brigades and those from other regions, we'll crush them overwhelmingly before it starts. Your troops should return in less than a year."

Herod protested again. "This will cause a great logistical problem in deploying any remaining forces. I've just made a military shift to increase security."

"Yes, I know," replied Sejanus. "That brings us to the third and newest matter. I understand that you ordered the Third Battalion in Jericho to search for a Jewish Messiah in Jerusalem. You must feel that he's a real threat to you, or you wouldn't have deployed so many troops to find one man."

Herod sat down and tried to defray the significance of Sejanus's statement, saying, "Any so-called Jewish Messiah is a local matter and shouldn't concern Rome."

"Rome is very concerned about this matter; and at this time, any interference with the religious beliefs of Judea that may fuel uprisings when we need more revenue must be avoided at all costs, especially when you will have fewer forces to contain any unrest."

Herod sat in silence, digesting what the envoy had said. His shoulders slumped. He said, "You are putting me in an impossible situation."

"You are Herod Antipas, the King of Judea. Rome has given you your kingdom, and Rome can take your kingdom away. You will do Rome's bidding," Sejanus pronounced imperiously.

Herod gritted his teeth, looked away, sighed, and then asked, "How did you come upon the information about a would-be Messiah that you are basing your requests on?" Herod asked.

"I am not making a request. I am giving you an order. As to my sources, never underestimate the powers of Rome. Like you, we have our spies and fast couriers. I always require knowing the current state of affairs of where I'm headed. I don't like surprises. I want to be prepared for any situations or dangers that may be brewing, such as a Messiah who has come to free the Jews from Roman rule."

"He is only a rumor and not a Messiah," Herod retorted.

Sejanus scoffed, "And that's why all of Pontius Pilate's soldiers and your Third Brigade are searching for him, because he's only a rumor? I think not, my dear King. You'll take no action against the Jew's so-called Messiah and do nothing that will invite a rebellion, especially when Rome already has its hands full with rebellions. Instead, you will ensure his safety and make sure that no harm comes to him, at least until our problems in northern Europe are settled and our increased taxes are fully implemented. Then you may rule as you wish."

Sejanus continued, "You are to tell no one of the substance of our meeting concerning the reasons for moving your troops, other than to say that it is for training and maneuver exercises. Mention nothing of the European problem. Surprise is of the essence. You will be notified which ports your brigades will be embarking from and the dates. It will be one brigade a month for three months."

Sejanus grinned in enjoyment at Herod's discomfort and added to it by saying, "Of course, Rome is always grateful for your whole-hearted cooperation."

Herod stared at Sejanus with ice-cold eyes but said nothing.

29

The day before, Moshe had spread the word to his established network that a reputable healer would be holding a session at the fountain in the square the next day. At dawn the following day, people began gathering there and spoke about their dreams and visions as well as the rumors that the Messiah had come. There was still an eerie mood in Jericho that was initiated by the sudden exit of thousands of soldiers who were sent to Jerusalem to find and arrest the Messiah.

By nine o'clock, one hundred and fifty people had gathered. By ten o'clock, there were over five hundred people, and by noon, when Jesus appeared, over twelve hundred people had gathered. Jesus's disciples, with Moshe, Joseph, and Seth, sat on the ground and formed a circular border between Jesus and the crowd. Moshe had also asked his dear friend, the rabbi of Jericho's largest synagogue, to send his temple police to protect the gifted healer from the expected crowd. Those temple police had formed a second ring around Jesus's group. Remarkably, the growing crowd had remained calm and orderly.

On the outer perimeter of the large crowd stood scattered groups of Roman soldiers observing them. Although the unusually large crowd caused concern, the soldiers were not worried; they considered it just another Jewish ceremony that appeared to be causing no problems.

When Jesus was introduced to the crowd, a man called out, as many had in the past, "If you are a true healer, then I beg you, heal my poverty. Fill my empty purse with gold coins so I may feed my children." Others also called out pleading for money and riches.

Jesus addressed the crowd, "I am here today to help those among you who are in poor health and who have faith that our God, My Lord Father, can cure what ails you and make right the wrongs that have befallen you. I am also here to enrich you in spiritual ways that are immeasurably more important than money. I will do so by removing blockages that you have acquired that will then allow the God-given treasure within you to shine outward and brighten and vitalize your health and life. That is a treasure far more valuable than gold or exquisite jewels, for it is your spiritual inheritance. When your inner God-Light is released, your ailments will heal in a miraculous way. Yet I tell you, good health and prosperity are a natural state of being. When you allow God's Light and love to flow through you, His will to see you whole combined with your desire to be healed will make you whole."

Jesus had been healing myriad illnesses for an hour and a half. As in his other healing sessions, the people witnessed astonishing transformations of a person's diseased body to a healthy state, and they were awed.

When a withered fourteen-year-old boy who had been crippled and bed-ridden from birth took Jesus's hand after he had told him to, "Arise." and then cautiously stood up, the large crowd gasped in surprise.

Jesus said, "You can walk now."

Fearing that he would crumble to the ground as always, the teenager dared not move. Jesus's voice was firm but encouraging. "You are standing. Now walk."

The boy took a step, than another. He stopped and smiled in amazement, his face aglow. Jesus said, "Keep going." The boy took a dozen more steps, and then Jesus guided him back to his stretcher. His mother and father were crying tears of joy.

Jesus said to the boy, "You are now whole. Each day walk a little and then rest, then walk again. Your legs have the desire to walk, and they will continually grow stronger."

The temple police had continually admonished the crowd that if there was any unruly behavior, they would be arrested and the healing session would be called off. The temple police enforced the rules of the Jewish communities. Those who broke the laws were tried in Jewish courts and if found guilty, were punished with canings or fines. The Roman authority did not interfere because Roman laws were not being broken; thus, order was maintained.

A short man dressed in an elaborate silk robe and bedecked in gold jewelry with a vestment of sparkling gems stepped out of a finely appointed carriage that was pulled by two groomed horses with braided manes and tails. The carriage had come to a halt because the crowd was blocking the street. He walked to a regally appointed chariot that had protectively followed his carriage and was driven by an aristocratic Roman tribune. A platoon of soldiers and two centurions on foot stood in formation behind the tribune. Two lieutenants on horseback oversaw the rear of the platoon. The short man asked the tribune, "Markus, what do you suppose is going on? Could it be him?"

Standing on his toes on top of the chariot, Markus craned his neck and said, "I'm not sure. Perhaps it is some kind of Jewish ceremony. I'll find out." He motioned to one of the centurions to come forward and then told him to speak with a group of soldiers who had been observing the proceedings.

The short man heard a barrage of "oooohs" and "ahhhhs" from the crowd, but all he could see was the backs of the people who faced the fountain. Not able to contain his curiosity any longer, he climbed a nearby sycamore tree to see what was happening.

From his higher viewpoint, he saw Jesus, who wore a plain white tunic and skullcap. The temple police had just let two people into the inner circle. They wore heavy robes with hoods over their heads and faces. On their knees, they bowed. Jesus began to speak to them, and although the crowd was silent and the short man strained to hear, he was too far away to discern the words.

He saw Jesus motioning to the two figures to stand up, which they did, and then he motioned to them to pull down their hoods. When they did, the crowd and the temple police winced and gasped and retreated a few steps. Many in the crowd yelled out, "LEPERS! LEPERS!" and then turned away in fright and disgust at the grossly disfigured man and woman's faces. Jesus held up his hands to the crowd as they slowly turned back to see what would happen. He then put a finger over his lips to signal silence.

When everyone came to order and there was silence, Jesus approached the two lepers and put a hand on each of their foreheads. The crowd winced again in gut-wrenching disgust at someone actually touching a leper, but they remained silent. Within a few seconds, both of the lepers' grotesque sores began to fade. From atop the sycamore tree, the short man's jaw dropped open in disbelief at what he had witnessed.

A woman in the back of the crowd near the sycamore tree said loudly, "It's him! He's the Messiah! I saw him in Jerusalem. The Messiah is here."

The entire crowd, after having seen one miraculous healing after another and now lepers being healed before their eyes, was soon abuzz, saying, "Yes. Yes. He must be the one! He's the Messiah!" They started to encroach on the inner circle. The temple police lifted their wooden shields to enhance their protective barrier. The disciples stood, encircled Jesus, and moved to escort him toward Moshe's synagogue. The temple police encircled and protected them as the leaders walked briskly ahead.

Markus held out his hand to help the short man as he descended from the sycamore tree to the ground. The tribune asked him, "What did you see?"

"You won't believe it, Markus. I don't know that I believe it myself, even if I just saw it happen before my very eyes. I'll tell you later. Now please take me home. I must check on my sweet little Isabella."

As the short man was being escorted back to his luxurious carriage, Jesus and his inner circle were about to pass them. Luke asked Moshe, who was walking beside him, "Who is that short man with the tribune? He looks Jewish, not Roman."

Moshe replied, "That's Zacchaeus, the Chief Tax Collector of Jericho. He's the most influential Jew here and one of the richest men in the city."

Matthew said, "I know of him. He's a legend among tax collectors. But everyone hates him because he gets a percentage of everything that he collects for the Romans. He often assesses the poor and honest workers unjustified higher taxes so that he can make more money. He deserves to be cursed."

Just then the crowd in front of them that was being pushed to the sides by the temple police to clear a path surged toward Zacchaeus's carriage to get out of the way. The centurion's platoon quickly encircled the carriage and pointed their sharp spears outward toward the crowd. Jesus stopped and looked over at the short man and said to him, "Zacchaeus, you need to invite me as your guest for dinner this day."

Although Zacchaeus wondered why he would be asked to do that and was loath to take strangers into his home, he spontaneously replied, "Come with me now."

Jesus walked unhindered between two spear-bearing Roman soldiers and stood by the carriage door. His disciples were not allowed through, and they vehemently protested. Jesus said to them, "Come by this man's home at sundown. I'm sure that he'll invite you in."

Zacchaeus shook his head *no*. He looked at Markus and then pointed to the carriage door. Markus opened it and held out his hand to help the diminutive Zacchaeus up the first step. Zacchaeus climbed into the carriage and sat down. He motioned to Jesus, "Come, come." After Jesus climbed in, Markus shut the carriage door and then got onto his chariot to lead the way. His troops surrounded the carriage as the driver guided it through the congested street.

The crowd grumbled in displeasure when they heard whose guest their miraculous healer was going to be. A man yelled out, "He's gone to be a guest of a notorious sinner." The disciples stood confused as the carriage pulled away.

Inside the carriage, Jesus and Zacchaeus stared at one another in silence. After a few moments, Zacchaeus asked, "How did you do that trick with the lepers?"

Jesus replied, "You know that it wasn't a trick. You came to see for yourself if my healings were real."

"Maybe I did. Do you know who I am?"

"You are the chief tax collector for Jericho."

"Don't worry, "Zacchaeus said. "I've observed no commerce. You will not have to pay. What else do you know of me?"

"Compared with the meager lives I've administered to, you are wealthy beyond measure; however, compared with their suffering, your pains are also great."

"Why do you say that?" Zacchaeus asked, the pitch of his voice becoming higher.

"You need the protection of a tribune and his troops because you have treated the people unjustly. Rome values you only because you bring them huge revenue. The people despise you and call you a sinner. You're the most hated man in Jericho. To transform that great degree of hatred into love and forgiveness is important for you and the people. That is why I needed to be with you."

Zacchaeus frowned and said, "You will find healing lepers is easier than changing the people's hatred toward me. It's a terrible feeling to be despised for being rich." Proudly caressing the elaborate leather trim that lined the interior of his carriage, he grinned and said, "But it also has its rewards."

Jesus replied, "All of your money cannot buy the things that are most precious."

"And what might those be?"

"Love and forgiveness," Jesus replied, placing his hand on Zacchaeus's shoulder and looking deep into Zacchaeus's eyes, "and the gift of life."

Zacchaeus pushed Jesus's hand away and then put his hands over his face and began to cry. Jesus said, "I know what troubles you. Why don't you tell me about your daughter, Isabella, for she's the reason you came to see me."

Between sobs, Zacchaeus said, "How could you know that?"

"Tell me about her," Jesus repeated.

Zacchaeus hesitated a moment; then the words poured out. "My sweet Isabella, my little sparrow. She was born tiny and frail and has stayed that way. My other eleven children, who are all boys, are big and healthy, but not my dear, sweet Isabella. We just celebrated her second birthday, but she was too sick with the fever to participate. I know what it means to be small. As a child, I was picked on and teased. I couldn't fight back with my fists to any effect, so I used my wits to defeat my hated enemies, who were bigger and more powerful than me."

Jesus nodded that he understood and said, "But now, as a man, your powers and fortune are mightier and far surpass those of the masses. Now others feel 'small' compared to you, and they feel that you are picking on them because of your power to tax them, and you do so unfairly. They despise you in the same manner that you despised your tormentors."

Zacchaeus looked askance at Jesus and said, "Someone who invites himself to be my guest should mind his own business."

Jesus replied, "Your need of healing is my business, but I have no desire for money, only the desire to fulfill my purpose to help, and in that way I am rewarded."

"It is because of my daughter's grave illness that I seek your help. I am used to suffering. It's said that I am being punished for my sins, but then so be it. That is my plight." Zacchaeus's eyes began to tear again. He said, "But why must my innocent little daughter, the love of my life, need to suffer? Why?"

"All things in life have a purpose," Jesus replied.

"To me, sweet Isabella's sufferings are the cruelest punishment. Is that God's way of repaying me? To cause pain to a frail, innocent child?"

"Perhaps I can help," Jesus offered.

"We will see," Zacchaeus replied.

The carriage pulled into a huge courtyard in front of the largest mansion in Jericho. Twenty servants quickly gathered by the carriage as Zacchaeus disembarked with Jesus. Instead of humbly greeting him upon his arrival, as was the required protocol, their somber faces were turned toward the ground. "What is it? What's happened?" Zacchaeus demanded of his head servant.

Hesitantly the servant answered, ""Master, it's Isabella," and then he looked down and shook his head despondently.

Zacchaeus frantically ran into his mansion, followed by Jesus and Markus. Zacchaeus ran up the stairs to his daughter's room. Four servants stood behind a doctor who had his ear pressed against the withered two-year-old girl's chest to listen for her heartbeat. He rose, shook his head despairingly, and then took a polished metal hand mirror and held it against her mouth and nose. There was no breath to fog its surface. The doctor turned to Zacchaeus and shook his head. He said, "I'm sorry. She's gone."

Zacchaeus cried out, "No!" He chided the doctor, "You are worthless. Leave my home at once!" Then he knelt at his daughter's bedside and held her lifeless, pale white frame and wept, "She's gone. My little sparrow. Why? Why? Why?" he wailed. "I'd give anything to have her back."

Zacchaeus laid his head on his little daughter's chest and cried. In a whisper, he said, "I have lost what I loved the most." He continued to cry and then said, "More than all of my possessions, loving her gave me the most pleasure. Caressing her soft, sweet face, seeing her little smile of comfort, and hearing her soft sigh gave me peace and satisfaction."

He sat and looked down at the lifeless body and between sobs said, "Her mother died giving birth to Isabella. Unlike my other three wives, I was the one who cared for her the most and loved her with all my heart. She was my favorite, much more than the older boys. I would have given her all that I owned, but of course, she knew nothing of material things. She only knew the simple joys and delights that any two-year-old would know, be they rich or poor."

Zacchaeus held her tiny hand and raised her arm up, then let it go. Her lifeless arm dropped back onto the bed with the girl's open palm facing up. He stood, backed away from the bed, and said, "Now she has left her frail body and is gone from my life forever. Today I have become the poorest man in Jericho."

Zacchaeus began to cry profusely. He turned away and headed for the door. Jesus put a hand on his shoulder and said, "Wait."

"For what?" Zacchaeus asked.

In a very compassionate tone, Jesus said, "Allow me to help."

Zacchaeus looked incredulously at Jesus and said, "It's too late to help. Your healing powers are useless now."

Jesus sat on the side of Isabella's bed, his palm over Isabella's open palm. With his other hand, he gently caressed her pale, lifeless face. Then he put his hand over Isabella's heart and stared silently at her face. Zacchaeus was about to tell Jesus to let his daughter be, but there was something about the concentration of Jesus's focus and his peaceful and reverent gaze upon his dead daughter that resembled prayer. He restrained himself from disturbing Jesus. Markus looked on.

Jesus leaned down close to Isabella's face as to kiss her lips but stopped an inch away. He gently breathed out between his half-closed mouth into her parted lips. Jesus's eyes became watery, and he trembled. The onlookers thought they saw a faint golden glow surrounding Jesus. He breathed another breath into her mouth that looked like a golden stream of energy. The fine, golden glow surrounded Isabella's body. The servants rubbed their eyes in disbelief, not sure of what they were seeing.

Isabella's body suddenly twitched. Her shoulders shrugged quickly twice. Her head turned to one side, then the other... and then she was still. Jesus took his hand from over her heart and caressed her face again. Isabella opened her eyes and smiled faintly, and then let out a soft sigh.

Zacchaeus's eyes opened wide. He gasped and fell to his knees beside Isabella's bed.

Jesus said, "Your daughter has awakened."

Zacchaeus pulled her to his chest and held her lovingly, tears rolling down his cheeks. He kept repeating, "You're alive! You're alive! Thank God, you live."

The servants and Markus looked on with tears and disbelief.

<hr/>

Jesus had requested that he not be disturbed for one hour and sat alone in meditation. He leaned his back against a palm tree in Zacchaeus's huge, beautifully landscaped courtyard. Zacchaeus quietly approached Jesus, who opened his eyes. Zacchaeus got down on both knees and reverently kissed each of Jesus's hands and then said, "You are more than a healer. You are a miracle worker. You are the Anointed One."

Jesus dismissed the comment and asked, "How is your daughter?"

"Isabella is sleeping now. Her breathing is better than ever. I feel that I have a new life. I don't know what to offer you for returning my daughter to me. Whatever I have, ask, and it is yours."

Jesus replied, "Your daughter is an innocent soul, and she deserves an opportunity to live her life and do good in the world. To know that I have helped is my reward. I ask nothing for myself, but for Isabella's sake, I offer this suggestion to you: Meet with your sons and tell them that you are going to divide their inheritance into equal parts for each of your children. It is important to do so to avoid family conflicts after your death in this world."

"I will do whatever you ask, but how does that concern Isabella?"

Jesus answered, "Children have dreams and premonitions of their possible future. Isabella stayed small and weak because she didn't want to grow up in a family in which her brothers and their mothers were jealous of your devotion to her and intensely resented her for it. Because of her benevolent nature, she would have felt crushed by the weight of their angry feelings toward her and the infighting that was certain to occur by your favoring her in your will. Her fear and anticipation of what was to happen caused Isabella's asthma and breathing problems to grow worse because she no longer wanted to live."

"Hmmm," Zacchaeus murmured as he realized that jealousy did run rampant in his family, often focused on Isabella because he had always favored her over the others. He looked curiously at Jesus and said, "I see what you mean, but how could you know all that?"

"What's important is that you now know it - and that you'll make the changes necessary to avoid the interfamily jealousies caused by your many wives vying for power and money for themselves and for their sons," replied Jesus.

"I do know how jealousy can make enemies and torment one's mind as it did mine."

Jesus said, "And now you have no need to be jealous or have hatred for those who have hurt you in the past, nor toward anyone in your present. You need to rid yourself of jealousy and the hatred of others so that you can truly begin the new life that you feel you now have."

"You're right," Zacchaeus said. "Those harmful traits no longer serve me." Then he frowned, looked down and said, "But it's hard not to hate back when you're hated."

"Change and growth are often difficult, but in time, all things must change and grow," replied Jesus. "With your enlightenment, you now suffer from a troubled conscience and seek forgiveness. You have the power to right past wrongs."

Zacchaeus rose and then paced back and forth nervously. After a while, he stood still and said, "I know I haven't treated the people fairly, and I've made false accusations against them to collect more taxes than they owed. They have every right to hate me and be jealous of my wealth. But what can I do?"

Jesus replied, "As a parent, you know it's disheartening to see your children fighting and cheating one another. On the other hand, it is a wonderful feeling when you see your children respecting and helping each other."

Zacchaeus nodded in agreement, and Jesus continued, "And so it is with my heavenly Father and His children on earth. You, Zacchaeus, need to live an honest life and act fairly and be generous to others, especially to those less fortunate than you. Respect others and be helpful to them, for they are God's creations as you are. Do what is right and what is good with a spirit of brotherly love, for that is divine."

Zacchaeus's emotions were already overwhelmed by the death of his daughter and then the miracle of her resurrection; and now, after hearing Jesus's words, he felt transformed – a forceful feeling that transcended his former manners of thinking and being. He bowed his head, and with tears in his eyes, he reverently declared, "Behold, My Lord, My Savior, I vow to You that I will give one-half of all my possessions and one-half of all my future wealth to the poor. As for those whom I have falsely accused of owing more taxes than were truly due and have charged penalties, I vow to pay them back fourfold."

Jesus smiled, "You have the power to create good with your free will. You now do so not to buy or negotiate for your daughter's life, for she is now healthy; thus, you are freely choosing to act in the spirit of true gratitude with the good intentions that you feel. To feel true gratitude is to be in God's grace. That is the mark of true transformation."

"I can't believe that I said I would give away so much of what I have to the poor, but I truly feel an inner peace knowing that I will indeed do it. My conscience is relieved. I will make restitution to those harmed by my actions. It's the right thing to do."

"Your true repentance has cleansed your soul," Jesus replied.

Zacchaeus smiled with relief. "I feel resurrected without having died. Thanks to you, I feel reborn as a new man. In your honor and for your friends, my cooks are preparing special delights for tonight's celebration. It will be the most glorious feast that Jericho has ever seen.

Jesus, his disciples, Moshe, Seth, Joseph, and his new love, Seffira enjoyed that night's feast immensely, especially the special delicacies. The men were astounded at hearing Zacchaeus's ebullient telling of Jesus's resurrection of his daughter. Joseph was also impressed, but his eyes were even more captivated by Seffira, the young woman whom he had dreamed about and who was now by his side.

He had fervently searched the neighborhood near the baths and nearly knocked her to the ground when they collided as he hurriedly turned a corner of the street. They spoke a while, enchanted with each other. She told him which house she lived in, and he promised to return after the healing ceremony.

She was very taken with Joseph's charm and was highly impressed to be invited to the largest mansion in Jericho, as were her parents, who allowed her to go under such honored circumstances. And now she was being treated to rare delicacies by dozens of servants. The musicians filled the banquet room with joyful music while Isabella happily ate only of the cakes and sweets that were her favorites.

The most highly respected physician of Jericho, who had attended Isabella during her long sickness, had been invited back to attend the celebration. He looked at her in disbelief with her bright eyes beaming as she was happily eating desserts. He had told many people that Zacchaeus's sickly daughter had finally died. The people felt sorry about the little toddler but had no pity for the hated tax collector. The physician's wife, when hearing of the child's expected death said, "At least that dear tiny girl won't have to suffer in that rotten family anymore with that dishonest, greedy little twerp who steals from the poor."

During the meal, Jesus told his followers to enjoy the evening, for tomorrow they would leave for the River Jordan as had been planned before they left Jerusalem.

A crowd had gathered in front of Zacchaeus's mansion. Many people fervently believed that Jesus was the Messiah. Others were doubtful but highly curious to see what other magic the Rabbi might do. Still others were undecided, and many debated the truth of Jesus's being the true Anointed One. Those who had had visions and precognitive dreams of Jesus as the Messiah were convinced of his divinity and adamantly argued with the disbelievers.

Markus had ordered his soldiers to maintain order among the crowd, and a wide perimeter had been formed away from the mansion's front gate and high wall. When Jesus and his group left, Markus and his soldiers, with swords drawn, escorted them safely back to Moshe's synagogue. Moshe soon left to again ask the temple rabbi for additional temple police to guard his synagogue.

Later that night when everyone was about to retire, Jesus asked to be left alone in the synagogue. He walked to the altar and then drew open the curtains of the Ark that contained the Torah. Jesus placed his hands over the covering of the Torah's scrolls. He breathed in deeply and felt the energy and power of all that was recorded in the Hebrew Bible. He stood transfixed in a deep state of meditation. Suddenly, he jerked his hands away as if he had touched a hot skillet. His mind raced as he integrated the Torah's history from the genesis of creation through Abraham, Isaac, Moses, and King David and all of the laws that God had commanded be followed.

Then he thought about Isabella and the image of her sweet, innocent face and her vulnerability. He also thought of Adam and Eve in the Garden of Eden. He pondered their sin of eating the forbidden fruit and suffering death for their transgression against God's dictum – not to eat of the apple tree – The Tree of Knowledge. He questioned the consequences of their "original sin" that would fall on all of mankind.

With deep humility, he spoke in a whisper, "My Father, who art in heaven, I know that Isabella is a blameless soul born of Your creation. In her innocence, she deserved no punishment for the first sin of man that was not part of her doing. Adam and Eve disobeyed You, but surely it cannot be Your manner of justice to condemn the whole human race to damnation for a transgression not of their making. You are my Father and creator of All That Is. I know unquestionably that Your divine love for all of Your creations is infinite and eternal. Certainly You would not condemn all of the innocent babies of the world to die of sickness or war for the sins of their ancestors. Certainly You would welcome all who wish to enter into Your kingdom. I know that You are not vengeful, but rather a loving and forgiving Father, always and forever."

Jesus stood motionless and heard, *"I AM."*

Jesus felt blessed with God's affirmation, but the question was still unsettled in his mind. He asked, "Then why must innocent babies and children suffer death for an original sin not of their own making?"

Jesus closed his eyes and stood motionless in communion with his Father. Answers to his questions were heard within him. When he opened his eyes, he said, "Thank You, my Father, for Your enlightenment." Then he pondered the implications of what had been said to him, and he thought about how difficult it would be to explain the deeper truth of one's soul and its purpose to the masses of people who had already adopted limited spiritual beliefs.

His mind spun furiously and then suddenly quieted as God's words echoed in his mind: *"NO ONE IS CURSED AT BIRTH. ALL ARE BLESSED AND SACRED TO ME. EACH SOUL POSSESSES AN INDIVDUAL PURPOSE FOR CHOOSING THE TIME AND PLACE OF ITS BIRTH. EACH ALSO HAS A PURPOSE AND OPPORTUNITY TO ENHANCE ITSELF AND THE LIVES OF OTHERS. EACH SOUL MAKES ITS OWN CHOICE TO LIVE OR DIE FOR ITS OWN REASONS. WHEN A SOUL FEELS THAT IT HAS FULFILLED ITS PURPOSE OR IF A SOUL FEELS THAT IT HAS DONE ALL THAT IT IS ABLE TO DO AND CAN DO NO MORE TO FULFILL ITS PURPOSE, THE SOUL LEAVES ITS PLACE IN TIME AND CONTINUES ON."*

Jesus thought of Isabella, not as a little child, but as a soul. He thought, *Isabella chose to leave her body because her soul felt that she could do no more in her world to fulfill her purpose, and she thought her future would only result in prolonged suffering and turmoil.* Then he realized that he was able to encourage her soul to return to her body because she anticipated that he would influence her father to create harmony from her family's discord. He also realized that at the time that he had breathed life into Isabella, he had acted spontaneously out of his love and desire to help, not knowing what he now understood.

Again, God's voice resonated within him, *"MY BELOVED SON, YOU HAVE USED YOUR GROWING POWERS AND DIVINE COMPASSSION RIGHTEOUSLY. I AM PLEASED WITH YOU."*

Jesus sat down on the floor and humbly bowed his head. Thoughts flooded his mind of the agony that he had felt from Zacchaeus's torment when his daughter had died and the hardships and agonies of all those he had come in contact with during his healing sessions and their suffering and pain. Then he thought of his daunting challenge—to transform the false beliefs of the masses into an enlightened understanding.

He prayed, "Dear Heavenly Father, everywhere I go there is so much fear and suffering. At times it feels too heavy a cross to bear. Do you still trust me to fulfill the prophecies?"

"DO YOU STILL TRUST YOURSELF? IN TIMES OF GREAT NEED, AN EXTRAORDINARY SOUL IS CALLED UPON TO FULFILL THAT NEED. YOU, MY SON, ARE THAT SOUL. YOU HAVE WILLINGLY ACCEPTED THAT CALLING. YOU DID SO BECAUSE YOU TRUSTED YOURSELF AND TRULY BELIEVED THAT YOU WOULD FIND A WAY TO HELP. YOU MUST ANSWER YOUR OWN QUESTION."

Jesus sighed. He reflected on his time on earth and the conflicting beliefs and feelings of the multitudes based on what they judged to be right or wrong, good or evil, and the needless consequences suffered because of them. He felt severe tension in his shoulders and neck and then realized that his body was reacting to his deep concern. Again he heard his Father's voice, *"COME INTO THE LIGHT OF MY KINGDOM."*

Jesus closed his eyes again and returned to his Father. His body's breath was steady and relaxed as it rejuvenated itself while his soul basked in the grace of God's loving Light.

Twenty minutes later, Judas entered the darkened synagogue. He could not see Jesus. He called out, "Rabbi, are you here?" There was no reply.

Judas looked toward the podium upon which the scrolls of the Torah were placed to be read. From behind the podium, a faint golden glow emanated. Judas walked down the center aisle to the podium and looked behind it. Jesus sat on the floor behind the podium in a trance state, enveloped by an iridescent aura of golden light. Judas gasped at the sight. He knelt and gently placed his hand on Jesus's shoulder. The golden aura faded as Jesus opened his eyes and smiled at Judas.

"You were glowing!" Judas exclaimed. "I saw golden light around you."

"Your sight is evolving, Judas. What you saw were the radiations of my feelings and emotions when I was in communion with my Father. As you look at me now, what do you see?"

Judas studied Jesus's face and said, "I see a man."

"That's what the people also see. I can heal people of ills. I can resurrect a little girl, yet many people only see the man and think he is a trickster. Unlike you, Judas, who have seen me beyond the flesh. You have seen the Light that expresses my soul. Even though others may not yet see my Light, there are those who sense and feel something that they cannot describe because it is indescribable using words. It's my intimate connection to the Ineffable. Those people are the ones who will see me in their dreams and will follow me because of what they feel, as you have, Judas."

"Like my dream about you the night before we first met. My dream instilled in me a powerful feeling that propelled me to search for you. Although I didn't know whom I was searching for, I knew I had to find you. And now I know why: the miracles that I have seen you perform, your magic that entrances children, your ways that mend the wounds of a village, and your reaction to every circumstance that crosses your path make me know without doubt that you are the Messiah who has come to free our people at last. You will make us victorious over our oppressors. That is what the prophecies have foretold, and now you are here." Bowing his head, Judas took Jesus's hand and kissed it reverently. He looked up and was surprised to see tears on Jesus's cheeks.

"Why do you weep? Asked Judas.

"They are tears of bliss, Judas. You give your devotion and unconditional love to me, and I gladly receive it, and it blissfully fulfills my moment. That must be what my Father feels, for it fulfills me in unimaginable ways. It is bliss to give my love and devotion to my heavenly Father and for Him to accept my love and then for Him to return His divine love to me. To give and receive love is the most blissful experience of existence."

Judas smiled and said, "It does my heart good to see you receive pleasure with all that you do to help those who are suffering." Judas's smile grew wider, and he said, "I was also delighted to see that you enjoyed the splendid tastes of Zacchaeus's celebration feast."

"You are a dear and thoughtful soul, Judas. My body's tongue did experience great pleasure, but my heart was troubled as I also thought of the people at the public healing session and their woes and ills and those who did not have enough money to feed their children. That diminished my pleasure. You see, I become one in spirit with all I cross paths with who seek my help. Those who are in distress stir my inner calling to help. My Father has created me with the knowledge that I am of the substance of His Being. It is a divine privilege to be blessed with my gifts, and I am forever thankful for them. It is also a divine responsibility to use those gifts to teach mankind that they too have been created from the substance of my Father's Being and that they also share those gifted-seeds within themselves that are intended to grow and flourish. By my words and deeds, I am to awaken those God-given gifts within all people and infuse those seeds with my Father's spirit of cooperation with all life and His absolute love."

Jesus took Judas's hands in his. He said emphatically, "Man must learn *The Way* so that he will prosper, or those greater gifts of power to create, if misused, will cause man to perish from the earth."

"As our Messiah, will you make the Romans perish from the earth?" Judas asked.

Jesus squeezed Judas's hands and said, "You must understand that in time, all of mankind must change and grow together or perish. If the Romans do not change their ways, they will cause the destruction of their own empire."

Judas involuntarily smiled and then said, "Please God, I should live so long to see the day."

Jesus briskly removed his hands from Judas's. "No, instead you should want to live to see all of mankind live as one in peace, love, and harmony. For you to help me with my mission, you must share my vision."

"I'm trying. Please be patient with me. It will take time."

"I have just visited God's time. Have faith in me, Judas, and believe what I now tell you. I have glimpsed the future and the past and the possibilities of the exquisite joys and horrific tragedies that man can choose to manifest in the future. That is why I urge you to think in terms of oneness with all people, because all of mankind are one and must grow and thrive as one."

Judas asked, "What have you seen of the possibility of your own future success in uniting mankind as one?"

"It will take more time than you can imagine. When I was just in my Father's Kingdom, He told me that I would soon leave this body. After I initiate the changes that are needed, then in the future, I will be given an opportunity to return and finish what I have begun."

"But you are the Messiah. Surely you have the power to make those changes now."

At this time, I can only initiate those changes. Ultimately that power resides in each person to choose to make those changes within their own lives. And when the people as a whole collectively make those changes, the world will change. That's the only way that true beneficial change that endures will occur. You, dear Judas, are the closest person in this world to me; yet when I speak of the downfall of the Roman Empire, your first reaction is your wish to see their deaths and destruction. Your feelings of hate can be understood by common standards, but in time, you must align your standards with God's Divine Way and act not out of hateful feelings, but feelings of love."

Judas thought a moment and then replied, "But so many people are conflicted about what to believe or what the truth really is. Even within our own religion, passions run deep, and viewpoints clash as to which belief is correct or how to interpret it. Far greater differences exist with beliefs outside our religion and in different lands. The pagans believe in false idols, and the Romans have their many gods, all of which create more divisions and conflicts between them and us. Most people are filled with greater hate than I have. It'll take forever to make the changes that you speak of."

"Those changes are possible in a much shorter period than 'forever,'" replied Jesus. "But it will take many generations and many more wars of needless suffering than the Romans have wrought. I must do all that I am able during my time here. Beyond the distorted thoughts of that 'hate,' I see there is still love in men's hearts. I have begun to help that love grow and align man's thinking with the Ways of my Father."

Jesus stood and affirmed, "I shall go forth with faith, love and the power of God's unlimited creativity."

Judas stood and said, "Once more I must ask that you go into hiding. Now that it is known that you have resurrected Zacchaeus's daughter, there will be no hiding the fact that you are the Messiah. If you go to the River Jordan as planned, many people will follow you as the Holy One. There will be no hiding you then. Herod's soldiers will surely arrest you. I fear that you will never be seen again if he is successful."

Jesus smiled and said, "Tomorrow is the day that has been destined for John and I to unite. I intend to meet my destiny."

<hr />

The Roman precinct captain of Moshe's district came into the precinct commander's office without knocking. The commander was asleep on a bunk bed. The captain shook him awake. "What? What is it?" the half-awake commander asked.

"That Rabbi-healer at the fountain square today is the Messiah. He fits the description on the arrest warrant. We verified his curing of the lepers, and he has brought back the life of a dead child," replied the captain.

The groggy commander responded, "Don't you know it's too late in the night to joke with me?"

"It's true. He did bring back the dead. It wasn't just any child; it was Zacchaeus's daughter."

The commander bolted up with eyes wide open. "Zacchaeus's little daughter? Sick Isabella? She died? The Rabbi brought her back to life?"

"It's definitely true," replied the captain. "I just spoke with Markus about the dead child. He witnessed the child's resurrection and told me she's healthier now than ever before. He said it was a miracle."

The commander looked very seriously into the captain's eyes and asked, "Markus? The honest tribune? Really?"

"Yes," replied the captain. "Markus! Really!"

The commander got out of bed. Pacing, he asked, "How can that Rabbi be the Messiah when the Third Battalion went to Jerusalem to arrest him?"

The commander paced faster and said, "But what if he's not the Messiah and I arrest him like those others who were arrested but weren't the Messiah? Will the Jews that this Messiah helped become angrier at me than they already are? But what would happen if he really is the Messiah and I don't have him arrested? Would I get a demotion? On the other hand, if it is him, will I get a promotion?"

The commander pointed a finger at the captain and said, "Don't you think you should order the Sergeant of The Day to take three patrol units and arrest the Rabbi at noon tomorrow?"

"Is that what you want us to do?" the captain asked.

The commander replied, "Why do you question me? Can't you see how certain I am?"

30

Samuel and Miriam stayed in the wagon on the periphery as Judith struggled to weave her way through the denseness of the restless, clamoring crowd. Word had quickly spread throughout all of Jericho of the Rabbi's deeds. She neared the temple police, who were guarding the steps to Moshe's synagogue. Judith pleaded with the police captain to be allowed in to see the Rabbi but was told that no one was allowed to enter the synagogue's premises. She then begged him to ask Judas to come out, explaining that they were friends and that the Rabbi had just performed her marriage to her husband. The captain refused at first but then relented as Judith persisted.

In a little while, Judas came out to speak with her. He told her that Jesus and the others were going to leave in an hour and a half, at twelve noon, to go to the River Jordan. He also told her that the Rabbi had extended an invitation to all those gathered to accompany him to be with John the Baptist.

Judith replied, "The Rabbi told me that it was going to be very meaningful for him to go there. When we heard about the Rabbi's resurrection of the dead girl and that he was here in the synagogue, I had to come. I want to go with you." She pointed toward a wagon near the edge of the crowd. "Samuel and Miriam are over there. I'm sure they want to go also, but her children are with my cousin. That's where the Rabbi asked us to drop him off; we did and then he told us that he was going to meet up with you and the others."

You are welcome to come with us, but we're going to leave promptly at noon. The Rabbi will not wait."

"I'll send Samuel and Miriam to get Sophie and Dustine. Please don't leave without us."

"Hurry and do your best. Jesus said we can't delay. He must see John the Baptist before this day ends."

Judith made her way back to Samuel and Miriam. When she arrived at the wagon, her cousin, Emma, pulled up in her wagon with Dustine and Sophie. Judith saw the dire look on her cousin's face and knew that something was terribly wrong.

"What is it?" she asked. "What's happened?"

Her cousin got off of the wagon with reddened eyes. She hugged Judith fervently. Judith stepped away and demanded, "Tell me! What is it, Emma?"

Tears flowed down Emma's cheeks. She started to cry and then controlled her sobs and said, "Your father has died in a fire."

Judith looked at Emma in disbelief. She shook her head "no" many times. Emma hugged her again. They cried together. Samuel came to them and hugged them both. Sophie and Dustine also began to cry. Miriam held them tightly.

Between sobs, Judith asked, "How did it happen?"

"A neighbor in your village came to tell us that a centurion and another man – a man with the ugliest and meanest face they had ever seen – came to your village to find the Rabbi. They questioned and tortured many of your neighbors. They also murdered Enid, Amal, and his mother."

Judith's face paled, and her shoulders slumped with the crushing weight of shock and grief. In a barely audible voice, she asked, "What else?"

"No one in the village knew where you and the Rabbi were going. Those 'beasts' found out that you were with him and went to your father's home. We think they tortured him also. Then they burned down your home with Uncle Nathan in it."

Judith collapsed to the ground. Samuel knelt to help her; Dustine and Sophie leaned closer to their mother to comfort her as Miriam also sobbed uncontrollably.

<hr />

Because of the large number of devotees who sought redemption from John the Baptist, some of the Jewish sects became suspicious and jealous of him. They were uncertain of his intentions and feared that their own followers would leave them and give their allegiance to John. They periodically sent delegations to determine how best to deal with him and also to curry his favor, hoping that he would not malign them.

The Sadducees' delegation had recently met with John the Baptist and departed. Now three Pharisee priests and their ten aides waited impatiently for him. Earlier, John's disciple, Jeremiah, had told the three priests that his master's first obligation was to those who were sincere in their hearts and sought repentance and renewal; after he baptized the repenters, he would retreat to solitary meditation and then would meet with the priests in the latter part of the day.

When Jeremiah left the Pharisees and was out of earshot, the two priests, dressed in their ankle-length, seamless linen tunics and white linen semi-peaked hats, turned to listen to the head priest, who wore a decorative blue headdress and a blue satin robe over his pure white tunic. He pointed to John at the river administering to those seeking repentance and said, "The Baptist insults us when he says he will see those who are sincere in their hearts first. Does he imply that we are less sincere?"

The short, portly, white-robed priest replied, "The 'immerser' should respect our status."

The head priest nodded in agreement. He shifted his position on the blanket that he sat on to a shadier section under one of the few trees along the green, shrub-lined, muddy banks of the River Jordan. As he moved, the row of small golden bells along the fringe on the bottom of his robe jingled. He adjusted his purple-scarlet, blue-and-gold-embroidered vestment and the attached gold purse that covered his chest.

The other priest, who was tall and thin, said, "The Baptist should know better. His father was Zechariah, one of the longest-serving priests in Jerusalem's temple."

The short priest added, "It's a shame. His father was a good and honorable Jew. And it is said that John was an ardent student of the Scriptures."

"So far our investigation has confirmed that he has not 'technically' violated any Jewish laws," replied the head priest. He motioned to a nearby aide to fan him; the late morning's sun made the layers of vestment, robe and ankle-length white undergarments uncomfortably hot.

The tall priest asked, "Is it true what they say about John's elderly mother? Did she give birth to him decades after her fertile years?"

"That has been verified," replied the head priest. "There is still talk of its being a miraculous and blessed event."

The portly priest pointed to John as he began to baptize a man who knelt before him in the river pool forty feet below and said, "They say he was always strong and very bright."

"Maybe 'headstrong' is a better term," the head priest replied.

The three priests looked down from the only small hill near the baptismal pool as John raised his large hands over his head. He was an impressive figure with his broad shoulders tapering to a narrow waist. His legendary open camel hair coat displayed his chiseled muscular chest. With a clarion voice, he spoke eloquently to the silent multitudes, who had traveled far and wide to receive this ritual cleansing. He spoke passionately: "The day of God's judgment will soon be upon you. Repent, for the kingdom of Heaven is at hand."

John looked toward the sitting priests and said, "The one who comes after me will act as the Hand of God. His tongue shall speak the Lord's words. He will lay the axe to the trees that bear no fruit as those of you will be cast into the fire who do not repent and live a new life that bears the fruits of righteousness!"

John nodded to Jeremiah, who came to him and took John's camel hair coat. John then pointed a finger at the sitting priests and spoke with great vehemence: "All Israel should prepare, for God's intervention is near."

John put his hands on the shoulders of the man who now stood in the water in front of him and looked into his eyes. He then embraced the man and firmly pressed his own chest against the man's chest, heart over heart. In one swift motion, John pulled him down under the water, which quickly sealed above them as if they had never been there. For what seemed a protracted time, the two remained below. Suddenly they burst out of the water. The man gasped for air. John said to him, "Let this moment mark you as one who belongs to the renewed people of God."

Two of John's aides helped the man back to the riverbank. John pointed to a woman on the bank and beckoned her to come to him. The portly priest sighed and said, "There are so many people left for him to baptize. We'll be here all day."

The tall priest added, "I stopped counting after six hundred left to be baptized. He turned to the head priest and asked, "What shall we do?"

The head priest looked disgruntled. He reluctantly replied, "We'll wait."

———

Clavis's whip cracked again. The two black stallions' galloping hoofs raced faster as the chariot surged ahead toward Jericho. The panting horses were covered in a frothy sweat. "Faster! Go faster!" Spartus demanded.

The horses will soon drop," Clavis replied.

"Burn the horses. We know he's now in Jericho. Go faster!"

Clavis clenched his teeth and cracked the whip harder on the lead horse's hindquarters. The chariot lunged ahead at breakneck speed. Spartus gripped the hold bar tightly with both hands. Again he ordered, "Faster!"

———

After it was announced that Jesus was going to leave at noon for the Hajlah Ford on the River Jordan to meet with John the Baptist, Moshe, Matthew, Luke, Andrew, and John went into the crowd to organize those who intended to travel with them. Those who chose to go were the ones who were convinced that the Rabbi was the Messiah. Many others were also convinced, but they were not able to leave on such short notice. Everyone was instructed not to approach the Rabbi and to follow peacefully behind. The disciples also promised that the Rabbi would speak to everyone along the way.

⟨⎯⎯⎯⎯⎯⟩

Five minutes before noon, the procession of over one hundred and eighty followers were aligned and facing the city gate. In the head section were families with children in wagons and carts, followed by those who walked, then those on horse or donkey, then herds of goats, sheep, cattle, and their shepherd families.

A large contingent of Roman troops turned a street corner and marched ominously toward Moshe's synagogue. Everyone's eyes turned toward them. The troops formed a wedge formation with their spear points leveled ahead of them as they proceeded. The crowd around the synagogue quickly opened a path for them. The troops came to a halt at the foot of the synagogue steps. The people who were lined up in the procession and were out of hearing range stared curiously as the Roman sergeant spoke to the head of the temple police who were guarding Moshe's synagogue. They appeared to be disagreeing, then arguing. A man in the crowd yelled out, "They want to arrest the Messiah!" The crowd gasped. Many chanted, "NO! NO! NO!"

The leader of the temple police motioned to his men to double-up behind him and bar entry to the synagogue. They tightened their crossed leather belts across their chests, pulled their red leather skull caps firmly down over their ears, and then protectively held up their wooden shields. The crowd and the people in the procession angrily chanted, "NO! NO! NO!"

The Roman sergeant backed his men up twenty feet and spoke to them. Quickly the troops tightened their wedge formation and then created sharp clacking sounds as they overlapped their long metal shields to form an ominous iron wall of fortified authority. Only the tops of their shiny helmets and their eyes could be seen above the metal wall, a gleaming spear blade protruding from each shield's side.

The crowd around the synagogue steps quickly dispersed and reformed in a semicircle a safer distance away. There was absolute silence as the onlookers held their breath. The sergeant stood at the rear of the wedge formation and drew his sword. He pointed its tip toward the huddled temple police on the steps and was about to give the order to charge.

Just then, the doors to the synagogue opened, and Jesus emerged. All eyes turned to him. The crowd "ooohed" in awe. His disciples followed him and then stood by his side. Jesus lifted his palms toward the police and the troops and motioned to them in a calming gesture. The sergeant held his stance for a few moments as the crowd again held its breath. Then he rested his sword to see what the Rabbi would do next.

Jesus walked down the synagogue's steps. The temple police captain met him, and they spoke. Then Jesus turned to his disciples and spoke to them. They all shook their heads in protest. He held up his palms to them and motioned that they be still. He then resolutely walked past the temple police and around to the side of the armored Roman wedge. The Roman soldiers' shields and spear points pivoted to follow each of Jesus's steps. He stopped at the rear of the wedge in front of the Roman sergeant and then opened his palms at his sides in a sign of surrender. All eyes turned silently awaiting what would happen next.

The sudden sound of a fast-moving chariot drew everyone's eyes. Markus, followed by three of his officers on their horses, was driving. The sight of colorful flags furling from the shafts of four aligned spears attached to the chariot's sides and the unmistakable polished emblem of the Roman Empire gave everyone pause.

When Markus saw the troops in their battle-wedge formation, he slowed his chariot and approached the sergeant and Jesus, who still stood with his hands open at his sides.

"What's going on here, Sergeant?" Markus asked.

The sergeant stood at rigid attention, acknowledging Markus's high official status. He answered, "The precinct commander has ordered this man, the Rabbi healer Jesus, to be arrested."

Markus stepped off of his chariot and stood nose to nose with the sergeant. In a commanding voice but in an undertone, he asked, "Upon what charges are your orders based?"

The sergeant reached into his side pouch, handed a small scroll to Markus, and said, "You can read the arrest warrant for yourself."

Markus took the warrant. He looked at Jesus, who wore only his tunic and sandals and stood with his palms open. He then looked at the throng of spears pointed at Jesus. Markus said to the sergeant, "Unless you feel that this weaponless man poses a credible threat to Rome, then I suggest you order your men to stand at ease."

Again the crowd started its angry chanting, "NO! NO! NO!" The crowd's chanting grew louder; the sergeant stared at Jesus, who stood in a stance of surrender. The sergeant then swallowed and said, "Yes, Sir."

He turned and ordered his troops, "At ease."

Markus unscrolled the warrant and read it. He then said to the sergeant, "This man is charged with two counts. The first is conducting an unruly religious rally; the second charge is suspicion of being the Jewish Messiah based on the standing general arrest warrant of King Herod."

"That is correct, Sir," the sergeant replied.

Markus pointed at the sergeant's chest: "I saw you at the fountain square yesterday when the Rabbi was conducting his service. Did you recognize me?"

"I did, Sir. You are Markus Augustus, the Tribune assigned to Special Revenue Protection from Rome. Everyone in the precinct knows that."

"Everyone on street patrol at the Rabbi's healing service, including yourself, also knows that the service was not an unruly rally. Is that correct, Sergeant?"

"Yes, that is correct."

"Therefore, this warrant is a false charge and invalid. Let this man go free."

"I still cannot allow that, Sir. He also has King Herod's separate warrant against him. Now that I am here, I must follow my orders or be reprimanded, or worse."

"You cannot arrest this man on suspicion of being the Messiah."

"Why is that, Sir?"

"Do you know what a Messiah is, Sergeant?"

"It's someone who heals like this man did. He also performed a resurrection."

"There are many healers throughout the land, but you think that this man is the Messiah. Do you know what else a Messiah is supposed to be?"

"Yes, Sir. He is King of the Jews and is supposed to free them and cause the Roman Empire to crumble."

"Sergeant, take a good look at this man before you."

The sergeant gazed at Jesus a moment, then faced Markus again, who asked him, "Does this man have the trappings of a king?"

"No, Sir."

"Does this man look like he has the power of a mighty army to threaten all of Rome?"

The sergeant looked at the group of unarmed disciples on the synagogue steps. He then looked over at the weaponless common people in the crowd and the harmless families in the waiting procession. He turned and looked again at Jesus. Jesus smiled kindly at him. The sergeant answered Markus, "No, Sir. I don't think Rome need worry about this man or an attack by these people."

"Then you acknowledge that you have no plausible reason to arrest this man," Markus made an arc with his hand toward the angry crowd, "and also that you are aware that your actions may cause a riot and deaths. Do you acknowledge that, Sergeant?"

"Yes, Sir. I am now aware of the full circumstances."

"Then what do you think you should do to avoid making a regrettable mistake?"

The sergeant swallowed again. He raised his sword and pointed it back toward the direction his troops had come from and ordered, "Fall into marching formation." The troops quickly obeyed. The sergeant then ordered, "Follow me. March."

The crowd began cheering for their Messiah as the Roman troops were turned away. Judas quickly walked to Jesus's side, and the disciples followed. They all started walking toward the head of the procession accompanied by Markus, who was followed by his mounted lieutenants. Judas said to Markus, "We are grateful for your help."

Markus replied, "It is I who have come to ask the Messiah for his help. I didn't know that he was to be arrested."

"You came just in time, "Judas said. "What brought you here?"

Markus addressed Jesus, "I came because my loyal servant, Thaddeus, is in the final stages of the fever. Two of our other servants have just died from it. Thaddeus is like a member of our family and deeply beloved by us. I know if you come with me now, you will be able to make him well. Of that, I absolutely have no doubt."

Jesus replied, "I cannot go with you. It is imperative that I leave now to reach the River Jordan before sundown."

Markus's hopeful expression turned to despair. He pleaded, "I can take you to my home very quickly. I know it took only a few moments for you to bring Isabella back to life. I truly believe that you will be able to help Thaddeus. Please come. It will not take that long."

Jesus stopped walking and placed his hand on Markus's shoulder. He stared at the tribune's intense aura and said, "Never have I seen such great faith in all of Israel. Go now, and by the time you get home, your beloved servant will be well."

Markus's dejection turned to relief. He took Jesus's hand, kissed it, and said, "Thank you, My Lord. Thank you."

The crowd looked on in puzzled amazement to see a Roman tribune kiss the hand of their Messiah. Marcus bowed to Jesus, then went to his chariot and made haste with his officers back to his home.

"Rabbi," Judas said, "my heart was quivering with fear for you when the Romans were about to attack."

"Thank the Lord that bloodshed on my account was avoided," replied Jesus. "Markus's faith brought him here. He has helped us, and his need to be helped has been fulfilled."

As they continued walking toward the waiting procession, Judas asked, "How is it possible that you can heal his servant when you haven't even seen him?"

"It was not I who healed his servant; it was Marcus's overwhelming faith in his belief that his servant could be healed that has healed his servant and not I."

"How is that possible?"

"I think by now, Judas, you may understand how it has happened. Marcus has the powerful spirit of a true heart who believes in the forces of healing. Those forces were heightened after he experienced yesterday's events with Isabella. The effect released a wellspring of enormous faith within him, but his faith was based in my power to heal, not his. He did not consider himself capable of being a healer and transferred his faith to me to heal his servant. I was able to see that with the intensity of Marcus's faith and his desire to see his servant well, he possessed the ability to heal his servant. But to do so, the obstacle in Marcus's mind that he believed himself incapable needed to be removed."

Jesus smiled, "When I told Marcus, 'Go now, and by the time you get home, your beloved servant will be well,' those words unlocked the gate to allow his own faith in the power to heal to flow to his servant and for Markus's power to heal him. I never said that I would heal his servant, but that his servant 'would be well.' Marcus then formed a powerful belief and image in his mind that he would indeed see his servant well. That allowed his innate energy that could heal Thaddeus to combine with Thaddeus's desire to be healed. The power to heal resides in all people. That's what I've been teaching. It's only the limitations of doubt within one's mind that dampen one's faith that prevent healing from occurring. Such is the power of faith. So now you know, Judas."

Judas rolled his eyes upward toward the heavens and said, "I only know that I have a lot to learn."

The temple police on the synagogue steps felt both relieved and bewildered at what had just occurred. Their captain said to his men, "We're going to the River Jordan with the Messiah to protect him."

His sergeant objected, "We can't go. The temple priest has not given us permission to leave Jericho."

The captain scowled at him and said, "Can you deny that the Rabbi is the Messiah? He has cured the blind and lepers. He has resurrected Zacchaeus's daughter. He has faced the Roman wedge fearlessly, and we have just witnessed an unbelievable sight: a Roman tribune has kissed the Rabbi's hand and called him 'Messiah.' Our orders were to protect the Rabbi. He is more than a Rabbi; he is our Messiah, and I intend to protect him with my life."

The captain then addressed his men: "If anyone chooses not to follow me, then stay in Jericho." He turned and strode quickly toward Jesus. All of his men followed.

Jesus and Judas walked to the front of the procession, the disciples following closely behind. The temple police walked by their sides. Jesus faced his waiting flock of over one hundred and eighty people and their wagons, carts, and herd of animals. He motioned them closer that he might speak with them. The disciples and police stood protectively between Jesus and the approaching people. Hundreds of others from the remaining crowd came forward from the synagogue area to listen as well.

Jesus stepped in front of his disciples so as not to be separated from the people. He raised his hands above him with his palms toward those gathered and said, "Before we depart, let us bow our heads in prayer."

There was stone silence as Jesus recited the prayer of protection from the Scriptures: "The Lord our God, the Lord is one. Blessed be His name, whose glorious kingdom is forever and ever. We take this moment to give true gratitude for the world that He has created. Love the Lord thy God with all thy heart, and with thy soul, and with all thy might. And let the pleasantness of the Lord our God be upon us, for He is our refuge and our fortress, my God in whom I trust. O Lord, direct us aright and be a shield about us; remove from us every enemy, pestilence, sword, famine, and sorrow; remove also the adversary from before us and from behind us. O, shelter us beneath the shadow of thy wings; for Thou, O God, art our Guardian and our Deliverer. We humbly thank thee, O Lord our God, who art our gracious and merciful true King of Kings. Let us all say, 'Amen.'"

The rapturous crowd responded with a loud, resonating, "AMEN."

Jesus surveyed those gathered and readily saw their hopes and aspirations. He also saw their underlying fears and worries as well as their sorrows and pain. They stood in silence as he spoke. "As we all travel on our path together, I bid you look upon each other as beloved members of the same family, for you all are members of the blessed family of mankind that is God's creation. With that devoted and divine feeling of love, I say to you that you shall love thy neighbor as thyself."

Many of the listeners looked at the strangers among them with some suspicion and wariness. Jesus saw this and said, "I see that it is difficult for many of you to love your neighbors as yourselves. That is because you have not learned the importance of loving yourself. Verily I say to you that each of you is a creation of God's divine love. And because you are of His creation, you are therefore an extension and divine part of Him and not separate from Him. He dwells within you and breathes each breath with you. In your prayers, you give your love and devotion to Him, and so you must realize that to truly honor God, you must also honor and love yourself. Not to love yourself as a portion of God is not to love a part of God, and to not love your neighbor is to not love God. Your neighbor is also a part of God."

Jesus swept his gaze across the crowd and then said, "Look among all who are ready to embark with you and what they bear. Merchants carry goods; herders shepherd goats, cows, and sheep for meat and milk and all that this traveling community of neighbors needs to sustain itself. Verily I say to you that more important than what is needed to sustain the flesh is your spirit of love that will unite this community of neighbors today as one family in God's Light and glory. I bid you all to share what you have in the spirit of God's divine love and grace. Let us all go forth with His spirit as one family in harmony."

Jesus turned and started walking toward the outer gate of Jericho. He bade his disciples and flock to follow him – and they did.

⊂═════⊃

Clavis's lead horse lay lifeless on the ground, covered in a frothy sweat. He and Spartus had left the other horse three miles back after it too had dropped from exhaustion. The walled city of Jericho was now in their sight. Spartus spit on the dead horse and said, "Useless beast." He and Clavis gathered their spears, shield, and other weapons from the chariot and made their way on foot toward the city.

As they approached the top of a small hill, Spartus quickly crouched down, pulling Clavis with him. Spartus whispered, "It's the Rabbi!" Then he pointed to the man surrounded by temple police and leading a large procession of followers and herds of animals. Spartus squinted and said, "He looks the same as when I saw him in Jerusalem."

"You were right, Clavis replied.

Spartus sneered, "I knew he wouldn't be staying around Jerusalem any longer. Not with Pilate's guard and the Third Battalion looking for him there – this one is too crafty. But now he is in sight, and this will be his last day on earth."

Clavis stood up with spear in hand and said, "Let's do our work and be done with him."

Spartus yanked Clavis back down. "Not now. There are too many people protecting him. I'll go alone and join the group. You go into Jericho and get another chariot with fresh horses. It'll be easy for you to follow their tracks. Stay behind them and out of sight."

Spartus patted the dagger on his belt and said, "At night when they sleep, my moment will come, and then the deed will be done. I'll meet up with you afterward."

Clavis grimaced as he looked at the grotesque burn scars on Spartus's face and scalp. The burnt eye socket and hanging flesh still gave Clavis an eerie chill, as it had the first time he saw it many weeks ago. Out of curiosity he asked, "How many people have you killed?"

Coldly, Spartus replied, "In the arena as a gladiator? Or for hire? Or just for the hell of it?"

Clavis stared at Spartus a moment and then turned away in silence. Spartus sneered and then pulled his dark hood over his head, leaving his face in shadow. Standing, he said, "I've blended in with his followers before." Spartus began walking with swift, strong strides toward the procession and melted into the large group of Jesus's followers.

"Why in the world didn't you arrest the Rabbi?" the precinct commander demanded.

"Because the arrest warrant was invalid," the sergeant replied.

"How is that possible? What were you thinking?"

"I was about to arrest him, but Markus the Tribune came by and read the warrant. He said that he and I had both witnessed the Rabbi's service and that we both saw that it was peaceful and not unruly. I had to agree because it was true."

"Are you an idiot? Why didn't you arrest him on King Herod's warrant order?"

"Markus said that Herod's warrant was issued to arrest the Jews' Messiah."

"Why are you telling me that?"

"Because a real Messiah is supposed to be a threat to Rome. The Jews believe that he will have an army that will bring Rome to its knees."

"What has that got to do with it?"

"The Rabbi had no weapons and no army; just common people were there. And they had no weapons. No danger was evident. The Rabbi had already surrendered peaceably. Surely he couldn't be the mighty King of the Jews. Rome has nothing to fear from him."

"Do you want to be demoted to a corporal? Don't you know better than to disobey my orders?"

"There's more. The Rabbi was being guarded by temple police, and the crowd at the synagogue was angry that we were going to arrest him. I was about to attack the temple police to get to the Rabbi when he came out of the synagogue to surrender. That's when Marcus came and read the warrant. My actions avoided bloodshed, which would have caused an official investigation of our precinct and your orders."

The commander raised his voice, "Why do I have idiots for troops? Do you want to become a private?"

"No, Sir."

"Then go back and arrest him or lose your rank."

The precinct captain entered the commander's quarters holding a scroll and said, "This just arrived from the Chief of Jericho's Precincts."

"Can't you see I'm busy? Well, why are you just standing there? What does it say?"

The Captain unrolled the scroll and read, "King Herod has rescinded his arrest warrant for the Rabbi. He has also ordered that the Rabbi is not to be harmed or interfered with by any government agencies."

The commander grabbed the scroll and read it for himself. He scowled at the sergeant. "Why are you still standing here? Go and inform our precinct personnel about King Herod's orders."

The sergeant saluted the commander and said, "Yes, Sir." He then turned and left the commander's quarters.

<hr />

Zena became annoyed. She stood up and said, "What is going on with you, Pontius? I cancelled my massage to fulfill your request that I make myself available for an afternoon 'treat' with you. Now that I'm here, you're perturbed."

Pilate ignored her. His eyes were fixed on the scroll he had just received. Zena bristled at Pilate's disinterest in her. In a huff, she started to leave, but his unusual behavior piqued her curiosity. She quietly walked back to Pilate to look at the scroll. Her eyebrows rose at what she saw.

"It's from Herod. That's his seal, isn't it?" Zena asked in a conciliatory tone.

Pilate rolled up the scroll and laid it in his lap out of Zena's view. She approached the bed and sat next to him. When she put her hand on his knee and seductively squeezed, Pilate acted annoyed.

Zena asked in a low voice with mock hurt feelings, "Is my husband annoyed at me for wanting to be close with him?"

"Don't give me that camel crap, Zena. For the last three weeks, you've had headaches, backaches or stomachaches. You've gone to spend three days with relatives; then you've been too tired or sleepy to spend any time with me in bed." Pilate stalked to his desk and laid the scroll on it.

Miffed, Zena turned and started to leave again. As she neared the door, she looked back and saw Pilate looking out over Jerusalem. Like a compass needle, her eyes fixed on the desk. Zena had to know what the message was that had perturbed Pilate so much.

He glanced back at Zena and saw her staring at the scroll. He said, "Go on. Read it. You are bound to do so sooner or later."

She unrolled the scroll, read it, and then said, "I don't understand this. Herod is ordering the Third Battalion back to Jericho." Zena read out loud, "The Emperor has ordered that the Judean army battalions conduct maneuvers and training exercises to evaluate emergency mobilization protocols."

Zena continued reading and said, "This part is perplexing: Herod is ordering that the Rabbi Jesus should not be arrested and that he be permitted to conduct his religious practices without interference as long as Roman laws are not violated."

Pilate took the scroll from Zena and threw it to the floor. "Damn him!" Pilate scowled. "He thinks like a fox and acts like a worm. Herod is purposely keeping me in the dark to intimidate me. He sends his battalion to Jerusalem to usurp my power; now he calls them back. I order my forces to arrest the Rabbi; he rescinds the order. Herod is doing this to weaken my authority in the eyes of those that I command."

Zena placed her hand on Pilate's chest. Stroking his face with her other hand, she said, "There is no one like you, my husband. Rome has appointed you, and only Rome can replace you. I know that Tiberius would not act against you."

"And how would you know that, Zena?"

She took his hands in hers and brought them to her heart. "I just know. Trust me."

Pilate pulled away and said, "I don't trust anyone." He went back to the window and looked out again. In a subdued voice, he said, "I don't understand. No good can come of this. There must be a plot afoot."

31

Jesus and his flock had traveled for several hours. His disciples rotated visits with him as they walked and talked together. The disciples all asked questions pertaining to their future roles as healers and as teachers of the Gospel – the "good news" of Jesus's message. Jesus instructed each disciple how best to use their personal abilities to fulfill his prophetic roles for them.

After Andrew's session with Jesus, word was passed to the flock that at three o'clock – halfway to the River Jordan – there would be a rest period and that the Rabbi would speak to everyone then.

Seth had waited patiently to speak with Jesus and sat in Samuel and Judith's wagon playing with Dustine and Sophie. Judith leaned her head on Samuel's shoulder as he drove. Her eyes were red from her constant tears over her father's unexpected death. Joseph and Seffira also sat in the wagon with their backs against the driver's bench. Seth kept glancing curiously at them as the new lovers ogled each other and shared clandestine caresses, seemingly existing in a world of their own.

After the last disciples departed, Jesus looked back and caught Seth's eye. He waved to the boy to come to him. Seth jumped off the wagon and eagerly ran to Jesus. Jesus patted Seth's shoulder and said, "Your presence renews me. My head is full of people's troubled thoughts and feelings. It's good to have the Great Seth by my side." Smiling, Jesus said, "I see that you have a lot of things on your mind."

"I do. I..." Seth blushed and then said, "Let me ask you this first. Is it true that you and John the Baptist are cousins?"

"Yes, we are. My earth mother's sister Elizabeth is John's mother. We were born only six months apart. We have lived separately as adults, but we saw each other in our teenage years. It's been a long time since I've seen John."

"Is that why it's important for you two to be together now? For a reunion?"

Jesus patted Seth's shoulder again and said, "Of all the men that I've spoken with this day, you, Seth, have asked the most penetrating question of me."

Seth smiled proudly. Jesus continued, "Our meeting destined for today is more than a reunion; it is intended to be a Holy union. We were both born with special gifts that would awaken within us in time. Those gifts have awakened, and now we are destined to unite."

Seth appeared puzzled. Jesus looked at the boy's aura and said, "Don't be concerned about what that may entail. Speak to me now about your other thoughts."

Blushing again, Seth hesitated and then said, "Joseph has been telling me how wonderful sex is. When I woke up today, I saw..." Seth tightened his lips in silence.

"Don't be embarrassed, Seth. There is nothing to be ashamed of. Please continue."

"I saw that my blanket was wet. I think I spent my seed in my sleep."

"That's something that sometimes occurs in boys usually a little older than your age. It's normal and nothing to be ashamed of. You are growing into manhood."

"But I also have sexual thoughts that are confusing to me. Joseph keeps telling me about things that people do sexually. He also said that I should masturbate when I feel stimulated, but I've heard that it is harmful to do it. I'm not sure what the right thing to do is."

Jesus smiled and said, "It not harmful to masturbate if a person feels the urge to do so. A small child's hands naturally fall to their genitals, and it gives them a pleasurable feeling to touch and play with themselves. They are often told not to act in that way, or as you were told, that it would be harmful. Yet the urge to do so and experience a natural pleasure and fulfill a necessary instinct will still prevail. That can often cause a false sense of guilt and create a conflict between a person's nature and the beliefs of others."

"Then it's all right to masturbate?" Seth asked for affirmation.

"There is no harm in masturbation and giving oneself pleasure unless one feels harmed by it. Masturbation can be healthy for the body, but not everyone needs to experience it to be healthy," Jesus replied.

Seth's confusion turned to relief. He inquired, "Have you had sex with a lot of women?"

Jesus laughed and said, "I can tell you this, that there is a difference between sexual lust and sexual love."

"What is the difference?"

"Sexual lust is the desire to satisfy one's sexual needs. It can give one pleasure, but it does not satisfy the need to love and be loved in return. When one can love and be loved in return, that is blessed unity and wholeness; that is bliss."

Seth thought a moment and then giggled. He asked, "What is the right way or the wrong way to have sex?"

"There is no right way or wrong way, but the best way is with love. Each person must follow his or her own inclinations when expressing sex or love. As long as there is no emotional or physical harm, people should experience sex by following their desires. That's how you'll know what gives you satisfaction and pleasure and what doesn't. Don't be ashamed of your sexual desires and thoughts. Regardless of what others may tell you, give yourself the freedom to discover what you need to fulfill yourself."

From behind them, someone shouted, "Get back here! Get back here!"

"OW!" Seth yelled as a three-month-old goat kid butted his behind.

An elderly goat herder grabbed the young goat's neck. He knelt and held it firmly. Three temple police quickly surrounded them. Humbly, the old goat herder said to Jesus, "Please, Messiah, forgive my errant kid for disturbing you."

Seth, still wincing, rubbed his behind. Jesus said to the goat herder, "You need not apologize. Your kid has brought you to me for a purpose." Jesus knelt and petted the small young goat. Standing, he took the shepherd's hand and said, "Come with me," and led him to the side of the moving procession. The kid playfully followed Jesus, Seth, and the old man.

Jesus held one of the gnarled and swollen arthritic hands of the old goat herder. He slowly and gently ran his index finger and thumb between the man's lumpy finger joints. As Jesus's fingers passed each gnarled joint, the swelling disappeared and the finger straightened. Jesus said, "You have gripped bothersome things too hard and for too long. Because you have held so tightly to your troubles, you have been choking off the life force to your hands."

"What can I do?" the goat herder asked, marveling at the sight of his completely straightened hand.

Jesus picked up the other gnarled hand and proceeded to straighten a finger as he answered, "To prevent your hands from becoming ridged again, I bid you do this: when overly persistent fearful or worrisome thoughts come into your mind, do not waste effort chasing them away. Instead, tell yourself that you will spend a concentrated fifteen minutes each day thinking intensely about your problems and worries; some of them no doubt need attention, although most of your fears will never come to fruition. You harm yourself when worries fill your day. So for the majority of the day, think instead of pleasurable things that make you smile. See more of the humor in life's experiences; you already know of life's torments."

The old man sighed, "But life is so hard."

"If an ill thought crosses your mind, tell yourself that you will give that thought your full attention during your next fifteen-minute worry session," Jesus reminded him.

The goat herder watched in amazement as Jesus straightened out the last and smallest finger, staring at his hands as if they belonged to someone else.

Jesus held the old man's hands up to the goat herder's eyes and said, "Have faith in my words regardless of life's woes, for the truth is that although your hands are now whole, life's problems still abound. Verily I tell you, you are able to find happiness within the world of God that dwells within you. I know that you believe in angels, so if you can't think of anything to smile about, think about this: Angels fly because they take themselves lightly."

The goat herder painlessly wiggled his fingers and thought of them as angels' fluttering wings. He repeated the phrase, "Angels fly because they take themselves lightly," and broke into a broad, toothless smile. He exclaimed, "You are the Messiah! Bless you! Bless you! Please allow me to give you something. Ask me for anything I have, and it is yours."

Jesus grinned. "Do you have two good handfuls of goat cheese?"

The man smiled wider. "That is a request that I surely can fulfill."

"Thank you," Jesus replied. He turned to Seth and said, "Please go with this enlightened shepherd and bring the goat cheese back to me."

Seth and the goat herder headed toward the back of the procession where the livestock were assigned, the baby goat prancing alongside them.

Jesus's disciples had been listening intently to him as he had spoken to the goat herder, and they too were smiling at the vision of angels flying because they take themselves lightly. He said to them, "You are now lighter of heart, and so are your bodies. Run with me as if you were weightless." He then said to the temple police, who were also smiling, "You too." As Jesus began running toward the head of the procession, the men all followed effortlessly. The onlookers wondered why the Messiah and his group were all running and why were they all smiling.

Jesus looked at the sky ahead of him. He saw thousands of Herald Angels streaming down toward the River Jordan where multitudes of Sacred Angels were already there in wait. Jesus sighed, knowing that the Preparation for the Gathering of Angels had begun.

<hr />

The procession continued for two more hours. Jesus led the way, setting a determined pace. Judas said to Jesus, "I'm getting tired, and you seem to be getting stronger. I'm going to rest on Samuel's wagon."

"Go on, Judas; you've earned your rest."

Judas went to the wagon but soon returned to Jesus. "Judith has asked if she may speak with you."

"Of course," Jesus replied.

Judith came to him, and Judas went back to the wagon and lay down. As they walked, Jesus hugged Judith, which gave her comfort. They continued walking hand in hand. Holding back sobs, she said, "I still can't believe that my father is dead. I don't understand...if my father has lived such a righteous life, why was he burned to death?"

"There are many forces opposed to my heavenly Father's intended ways for man to be. But know this truth, Judith: because Nathan led a righteous life, he was rewarded for his goodness each of his days, and the people in your village loved and appreciated him. He lived an honorable life, and for that, God is pleased with him, and he lives again in peace in my Father's Kingdom."

Judith sighed with some relief; Jesus gently squeezed her hand in reassurance. A tear rolled down her cheek as she said, "I believe you." Jesus wiped her tear away. Judith said almost in a whisper, " I am comforted by the thought of my father being at peace, but..." trying not to cry, "...but I miss him terribly."

Jesus put his arm around her shoulder and said, "Your father's love and spirit still embrace you. For a daughter to mourn her father's passing and to feel the pain of grief is a natural emotion that must be expressed. When you grieve, also remember that before he passed, Nathan said that seeing you married was the happiest moment in his life. Know that you gave him the blessings of true joy and that all of his wishes were fulfilled during his time on earth."

Judith sighed again and leaned her head against Jesus's shoulder as they walked. She said, "Your words bring me comfort. But more than your words, being in your presence gives me a feeling - a feeling of conviction that you're right, and that brings me peace, even in my grief. I'll remember what you've said." She hugged Jesus and said, "Thank you, My Lord."

<hr>

The tall Pharisee priest pointed to the multitude of repentants waiting to be baptized by John and said, "Another two hundred people have come. We'll be here for days."

The short, dumpy priest said, "Maybe not. The 'immerser' is baptizing them two at a time, and he's working more quickly."

The head priest scanned the newcomers, then gazed at John, who stood in the river. Two men knelt before him in the water. John placed a hand on each one's shoulder, then pushed then below the water and held them there a moment; then he pulled them up. They gasped for air, then caught their breath and bowed their heads before John. They stood tall as they walked back to the riverbank. John's disciples quickly led a man and woman to John, and he rapidly baptized them simultaneously in the same fashion.

The short, heavy priest said, "I'm hungry."

The head priest replied, "You're always hungry."

———————

Jesus's three o'clock address to his followers was about to begin. The stragglers had caught up, and now all were gathered near him. Most sat or lay on the grassy ground. The wagons and carts were near the periphery, and on the borders were the herds of goats, sheep, oxen, and cows that drank from a stream. A gentle breeze brought relief from the hot sun.

Jesus caught Judith's eye and nodded to her in the large congregation. He then addressed those gathered, and as was the tradition, he asked those to stand whose loved ones had passed on. Judith and the others who had lost loved ones stood, and Jesus began his service with the Mourner's Kaddish Prayer: "Magnified and sanctified be His great Name in the world which He hath created according to His will." Jesus continued the prayer, and when he finished, the mourners and the congregation said in unison, "Let His great Name be blessed for ever and ever."

The mourners remained standing, and they alone gave the responses of the Kaddish Prayer: "Blessed, praised and glorified, exalted, extolled and honored, adorned and lauded, be the Name of the Holy One, blessed be He beyond, yea, beyond all blessings and hymns, praises and songs, which are uttered in this world. May there be abundant peace from Heaven and life for us and for all and say Amen."

The congregation responded with "Amen."

The mourners sat down, and everyone looked attentively at Jesus in silence. He said to them, "There is a needed time to grieve and mourn for the loss of loved ones or for losses of something once highly valued. But after that period, you are not meant to forever dwell in your sorrows and wear your grief on your sleeve as a badge of courage. The world has enough sorrow, so I say to you, strive to not let the world share your sorrow; rather, strive to help others find joy in their lives as you must seek the joy in your own life. Know that when you smile and feel joy, you lessen the burdens of others and yourself as well."

Some in the congregation nodded in agreement; others looked doubtful. Jesus continued, "I know it is hard for many of you to readily accept the challenge to seek the virtues of joy, but I say to you that true joy lies within you because God's Light of love within you shines brightly."

Jesus saw that many were dubious about what he said so he responded to their unspoken thoughts: "It is true that many of your sorrows and grief block His Light from shining through. I ask you all to look up at the sky now." Jesus pointed upward, and everyone looked up and then looked back in puzzlement at Jesus.

He said to them, "When you looked up at the sky, you were not able to see the stars in the daylight, yet the stars are still there shining brightly, and you will see them easily as darkness falls. So I say to you, when you are in the darkness of your sorrow and grief, look within yourself to see and feel God's Light, for it is there and His Light always shines brightly. When you look for God's Light, you allow more light into your world by letting your inner light shine outward as acts of compassion to others."

A man called out, "But what if we have sinned and God is punishing us with sorrows?"

Jesus nodded and replied, "Every adult has sinned at some time in small or large ways. You are not meant to become a slave to your sins; rather, you must acknowledge the wrongs that you have done, then forgive yourself and do what you can to set those wrongs right. You must also forgive and help others to do the same; and most of all, you must turn to God and repent."

Another man called out, "But we know that sinners should never be forgiven for what they have done."

"I say to you, judge no one, not even yourself, for it is only in my heavenly Father's domain that His final judgment may be passed, and not yours. And I know that our Lord is all forgiving." Jesus paused, assessing the assemblage.

"I see that many of you think that you can live your lives falsely and pretend to repent before you die and think that you will surely go to heaven. Know that you shall be judged by all of your days, so start today and strive to act with the intention of love and kindness in all that you do. That is a part of the key to heaven's gate, for it is God's love and kindness that have given birth to you, His creation."

Jesus paused again and studied the collective thoughts of those who remained uncertain about the meaning of repentance. He continued, "And yes, repentance is the other part of the key to heaven's gate. But only true repentance of your heart and soul forms that other part of the key that will fit the lock to heaven's gate. Mere words alone will prove futile."

Jesus looked to where Spartus slouched low and then continued, "Without true repentance your sins shall be your hell." Jesus looked upon the rest of the people and said, "The love and kindness that you give to others shall be your reward in Heaven as on earth."

Jesus continued to answer questions for twenty more minutes, and then he blessed the assemblage. He ended by saying, "The kingdom of God is within you, and so you must have love for yourself; not to do so is to not love God."

Spartus pulled the sides of his dark hood closer around his face and spit on the ground.

Jesus extended his hands toward the crowd and said, "Those who seek healing, come to me now, and I will help you allow God's inner Light to shine out on your world."

Many came forward and were healed. They smiled brightly and walked lightly. The vast majority of onlookers were awed at the healings they witnessed and were convinced more than ever that the true Messiah was in their midst.

Jesus walked quickly. After a while, the procession elongated again. Judith walked beside Jesus in conversation and said, "At first I couldn't help but cry. My father's death was an unexpected shock. I still can't believe he's really gone." A tear fell. "But I believe in what you said. I know that this period of mourning will pass and I will cry less in the future."

Jesus patted her shoulder in reassurance. She said, "We took three more children into our wagon. Their mother was carrying the smallest, and they couldn't keep up with everyone's pace. The little boy, Jason, sat on my lap; her other two children played with Sophie and Dustine. Little Jason hugged me when I cried. Then he kissed me. As sad as I felt, his affection made me feel stronger. If I hadn't reached out to help others, my despair would have continued to grow. Instead, in helping others, I've helped myself."

Jesus nodded and said, "Tell others of your experience so they may understand my words. Many hear what I say; their ears are open, but there are those whose hearts are closed. Your words to them will help open their hearts, and those words will continue to lessen your grief. Your faith will carry you safely through this stormy time."

Matthew, Judas, Luke, John, and Simon walked alongside Jesus. Laughing, Matthew said to Jesus, "For someone who arrived in Jerusalem barely two weeks ago and possesses only a tunic, sandals and a skullcap, you have caused an army to look for you where you are not. Only the Anointed One could do that."

Jesus smiled and replied, "I haven't moved the army; only King Herod and Pilate have done that. I am where the army is not because of divine providence."

Jesus turned to Simon and said, "I see you're still doubting that you'll be able to teach others as I have taught you."

"I am t-t-t-trying, Teacher. B-B-B-But I still have d-d-d-difficulties." Simon bowed his head.

Glancing at the other disciples, Jesus said, "Do not feel dismayed, Simon. Your companions also share those feelings."

Simon looked at the others. They also bowed their heads. Jesus addressed all of them. "Do not expect to heal and teach as I do. I've told you that you are intended to heal and to teach the Word in your own ways. Have faith in the faith that I have in you."

"But, Teacher," John said, "you perform miracles in the way that you heal. It's hard to believe even what I have seen, much less think that I am capable of achieving anything like you have done."

"I say to all of you," Jesus replied, "believe in the Lord and believe in yourselves. Do what you can; do not dwell on what you cannot yet do. If each of you does your share of what you can do, then my Father will be pleased."

Luke offered, "I will try. But, Teacher, I too feel inadequate."

Jesus slowed his pace slightly and looked at each disciple. He then smiled and said, "I have said to you that the seeds and power of the Word have been planted in your souls. Now I see that those seeds are growing in your hearts and minds. Rest assured that night and day, whether you are asleep or awake, like a farmer's seeded soil, those seeds within you have sprouted and continually grow, although you know not how. After today, you will go out on your own, and you will become like farmers who plant the seeds of the Word in others."

Judas's brow furrowed. "What do you mean when you say that after today we will go out on our own?"

"I will tell you more later. Now you must all understand that as farmers, some of the seeds of truth that you sow may sprout but not grow. The worries and fears of this life are many, and they can choke off growth, making your efforts fruitless. Greed, jealousy, and vengeance also suffocate growth."

"What are we to do?" Matthew asked.

"You must keep sowing the seeds of the Word. And take heart and know that the seeds of your teachings, like those sown on fertile soil, will accept the Word and that they in turn will produce a crop many times greater than what you have sown."

Jesus scanned his disciples' thoughts and saw their persistent doubts in their ability to effect changes in others. He said, "Do not underestimate the value of your potential, for you are needed to help me fulfill my Father's mission, which I can not accomplish alone."

Jesus sighed and said almost mournfully, "If I could use my Father's healing powers from sunrise to sunset to the following sunrise, day after day, year after year, I still could not heal all those who seek healing in my remaining time on earth. But as I have said, I can teach you to the degree that you are able to heal; and in your own words and ways, you will heal others. More importantly, you must teach others to live the Word, to think, feel, and act with love and kindness for the good of all. Those who do so will be blessed. That is my heavenly Father's message."

Seth, Joseph, and Seffira came up alongside the disciples and Jesus. The temple police accompanying Jesus's group watched them carefully. Joseph and Seffira walked dreamy-eyed, hand in hand. Seth carried a small pouch on a leather strap that hung from his shoulder. He gave it to Jesus, who thanked him. Jesus took out a handful of goat cheese from the pouch and began eating it. After consuming it, he said, "This is just what I needed, Seth." He smiled and patted the boy's head.

Anxiously, Joseph asked, "Master, may we request something of you that is very important to us?"

Jesus smiled at them and said, "Like two doves in love, your hearts coo with sweet yearning for each other, even when you are together. Seffira, what do you want to ask me?"

Joseph was surprised that Jesus asked Seffira instead of him. It also surprised Seffira, yet she readily replied, "Thank you for hearing our request. I have never met anyone like Joseph. He is everything to me. Judith told us that you recently married her and Samuel. Will you marry us tonight?"

"Will you, Master?" Joseph implored.

Jesus looked at the two lovers and hesitated. Then he said warmly, "Love blooms true in your hearts. If you both want to marry, you should. But I am unable to marry you tonight."

Seffira and Joseph looked dejected.

Jesus continued, "I will soon be gone, but I will return."

The disciples were stunned. Judas asked, "Where are you going? When are you leaving?"

Jesus replied, "There is an important task that I must attend to alone. I will tell you when my time to leave comes." Jesus stared resolutely ahead and quickened his pace.

⊂══════⊃

The sun was lower in the sky, and the air over the River Jordan was cooling in the mountain's shadow. Jeremiah finally led the three Pharisee priests up the mountainside toward John the Baptist's cave. They grumbled as they held up their long robes to avoid becoming entangled in the sharp branches along the narrow, twisting path.

When they entered John's cave, he said nothing but motioned them to sit on the stone floor near him. Reluctantly, they sat with discomfort.

"Shalom," the head priest said to John.

John smiled faintly and returned the one word greeting of hope and peace but said no more.

After a few moments of uncomfortable silence, the head priest stated, "We are here because what you are doing affects the Jewish community."

John stared at the priest but did not speak. The priest shifted his body on the hard limestone floor. He cleared his throat and said, "You could possibly claim to be the Messiah."

John coldly eyed the short, dumpy priest and then stared at the tall, thin priest. John then turned to the head priest and replied, "That would a false claim that the scriptures warn against. I am not the Anointed One."

"What then?" the short priest asked. "Are you Elijah the Prophet?"

John stated simply, "I am not."

The tall priest asked impatiently, "Who are you? Let us have an answer for those who sent us. What do you say about yourself?"

John said firmly, "I am the voice of one crying in the wilderness. I am here to help 'make straight the way of the Lord,' as the prophet Isaiah has said." John then pointed at each priest, and as he spoke sternly, the veins in his muscular neck bulged. "You are supposed to be holy men, yet before me I see a brood of vipers. Neither your birthright as Jews nor your position will serve you unless you open your hearts in true repentance."

The head priest indignantly responded, "Are you offering to baptize us?"

John replied, "I will if you choose, but he who is coming after me is mightier than I. I am not worthy to carry his sandals. If you choose, he will baptize you with the fire of the Holy Spirit."

The priest recoiled and frowned as John continued, "He will choose those of true hearts who follow him because they choose him. False hearts will burn with unquenchable fire."

The priests stared at John, who stared back with disdain. The head priest asked, "Are you implying that we do not live righteous lives?"

"You live lavish lives of plenty." John pointed to the short priest's portly belly, then to the head priest's belly, and said, "Your appearance tells me that you eat more than your body needs. Do you not think it better to share your food with those who have none? How many robes do you have?"

The priests looked at each other and then at their finely woven garments but said nothing.

John scoffed at their silence. The muscles of his bare chest tensed as he said, "If you had only two coats, wouldn't it be best to give one to someone who had none?"

The priests shifted uncomfortably again. The tall and short priests looked guiltily down at the floor. The head priest changed the topic and said to John, "The Romans are suspicious of you and your large following. We want to avoid their wrath toward you and the multitudes you have baptized from affecting the Jewish community."

"Why?" John responded. "For I have said that tax collectors for Rome should be paid if they tax fairly and that Rome's soldiers should do their jobs provided they do not rob the people or falsely accuse them. Why should they fear me?"

The tall priest retorted, "You also maligned King Herod for a fool when you spoke of his carrying on a known affair with his cousin."

John laughed at the priest's accusation and said, "As you say, it is a 'known affair.' I speak of nothing secret, and if I say that such an arrangement appears foolish, that is also known."

"True," the head priest responded, "but to openly speak of that will certainly incur Herod's vengeance."

John laughed again, and his eyes burned into the head priest's eyes as he said, "I don't worry about Herod, for the moment of God's intervention is nearer than you can imagine. The one who comes after me will soon arrive, and all of Israel should prepare, especially you who sit with me now."

Jeremiah entered the cave and in an excited voice said, "Master! I think the ones that you have spoken of have arrived."

John closed his eyes a moment, then opened them wide and exclaimed, "Yes! I feel his presence!" Ignoring the sitting priests, John stood and quickly left the cave. They stood and went to the cave's entrance and watched John hasten down the mountainside toward the River Jordan.

On the opposite riverbank, Jesus stood surrounded by his disciples and the temple police. He said to Judas, "Please get my robe that my heavenly Father has gifted me with, then wait with it for me on the other side of the river."

"You have worn it but once since the day you got it," Judas replied.

"I will be worthy to wear His robe on the outside of this body after He blesses me with the almighty powers of the Holy Spirit."

"I'm not sure what you mean, but I will do what you ask." Judas went to the wagon to get Jesus's robe. He carried the robe to the opposite riverbank and waited.

John the Baptist waded into the river and stood in the middle of it. He bowed his head toward Jesus. Most of the multitude on shore stood up to see, their curiosity heightened by the presence of the temple police and the large number of people and flocks of animals that had accompanied them.

John's disciples had never seen him so humble. John looked up at Jesus as he stepped into the river and walked toward him. Their eyes were fixed on each other. The crowd stood in silence. The Pharisee priests stood above near the cave and looked down on them.

Jesus stood before John and looked up at the huge mass of Angels that had gathered. The Angels extended across the sky as far as Jesus could see. He breathed in deeply and felt their high-pitched frequencies resonating to unsustainable intensity. Jesus then looked into John's eyes and said, "We are as one in brotherly spirit. The time has come for you to baptize me."

"It is I who am in need of baptizing; you should baptize me," John replied.

Jesus put his hands on John's shoulders and softly said, "I need you to baptize me now so that we may fulfill God's purpose and all righteousness."

John stared at Jesus for a moment and then embraced him firmly. In a clarion voice, John declared to everyone, "The one who is with me now is the one whom all should follow."

John then quickly immersed Jesus and himself beneath the murky water, and they disappeared. The wide-eyed onlookers leaned closer, wondering why they were staying under for so long.

The mass of Angels synchronized and powerfully intensified their ultrasonic frequencies, and then, suddenly, a piercing white Light enveloped the river and all those surrounding it. People gasped as all were momentarily blinded by the Light's overwhelming intensity. As their sight returned, John and Jesus were still submerged. The multitude on the riverbank retreated a step in disbelief and fear as the water began to boil, steam rising from the river. At the same time, chunks of ice bobbed to the surface. A man picked up a piece and loudly exclaimed, "It's ice!"

A woman whose feet were in the river quickly stepped onto the shore and yelled, "The water is boiling hot!" Those closest to the river backed away and trembled.

A large vortex of white light formed in the sky above them. Everyone looked up. Some said it was a huge white angel whereas others said it was a massive flock of white doves. But of this, all were certain; everyone experienced a blinding white light. The vortex grew larger, and its white light intensified and began to descend. Many pulled their headscarves over their faces; others turned away and cowered in fear. The twisting tip of the vortex touched the water's surface where Jesus and John were submerged. Another minute went by, and then the vortex of light suddenly vanished.

Jesus and John burst out of the water still embracing each other. A penetrating voice reverberated within their heads: *"YOU ARE MY BELOVED SONS, WITH WHOM I AM PLEASED."*

In a bittersweet tone, John said, "It will soon be my time."

Again they heard the voice of the Lord. *"THE KINGDOM OF HEAVEN IS UPON YOU. THE KINGDOM OF HEAVEN IS WITHIN YOU. REJOICE. REJOICE. I SAY UNTO YOU, REJOICE."*

John and Jesus smiled at each other and both said, "Thank you, dear Father, our Lord, for Your blessings."

Jesus said, "It is done. I must go now."

John bowed his head in acknowledgment and embraced Jesus tightly. He then said, "Go and do our Father's bidding. Remember that you only have forty days. Godspeed is now with you." They embraced again, and Jesus moved toward the opposite bank, where Judas waited.

Judas stared at Jesus with wonder and awe. "Master," he said, barely getting the words out of his mouth, "you are glowing again. This time I see dazzling white light emanating from all around you."

Jesus put on his robe. Judas, still stunned by what he had seen in the river and now witnessing Jesus's brilliant glow, stood nearly paralyzed with weakness.

Jesus said, "Take the disciples and our closest followers to Galilee. Stay with Peter and Andrew's relatives. I will meet you there."

In a barely audible voice, Judas asked, "Where are you going? When will you meet us?"

"I must do my Father's bidding. Just wait for me no matter how long it takes."

Before Judas could ask another question, Jesus started bounding up the mountainside. As he passed near the Pharisee priests, they backed away as if from a flash of fire. Jesus paid them no heed and continued up the steep hillside with ease and speed. From the opposite riverbank, a dark-cloaked man waded into the river and across to the opposite bank. He quickly followed Jesus's path. As he bounded past the priests, his hood fell to his shoulders. The priests gasped at the grotesque features of the man's face.

The short dumpy priest said, "Who's that?"

The head priest replied, "He looked like the Devil."

Spartus ran full speed after Jesus. Even with Spartus's superb natural strength and gladiator training, Jesus was outdistancing him. "He runs like a goat," Spartus grunted as he pushed himself faster. "Like a goat, he will soon be sacrificed."

After twenty minutes, the mountainside terrain grew steeper and rockier. Spartus was becoming short of breath. He could not see Jesus clearly through the brush but was able to catch a glimpse of the back of his robe as Jesus neared the peak of the steep mountain. The path became narrower and then curved around a bend. As Spartus followed the turn of the bend, he looked down at the sheer cliffside drop to the ground over a thousand feet below.

Spartus confidently moved ahead, knowing there was no place else for his prey to go. The path became a narrow ledge of only two feet, then one foot, then only four inches. Spartus leaned against the mountainside for balance, his feet partially hanging over the edge of the path as it continually narrowed around the bend. He smiled when he saw Jesus's sandal prints in the loose debris of the path.

Spartus unsheathed his dagger. He edged around the narrow ribbon of the path more slowly and leaned into the mountainside. He held his dagger in anticipation of a strike. He moved stealthily. With each step, he carefully glanced down at his precarious footing. The path ended; only the sheer rocky cliffside of the mountain remained. On the very small remaining ledge, he saw two sandal prints facing the opposite mountainside. Spartus looked up and froze.

Facing him on a ledge ten feet higher and thirty feet across a steep canyon stood an ibex with sleek fur and striking black and white markings on its legs. At over three hundred pounds, it was the largest ibex Spartus had ever seen. Four-foot-long horns jutted from its head. The horns arced up and curved around with their penetrating points directed at Spartus. The ibex's eyes burned into him. Spartus looked down at the sharp drop below and then back at the ibex, who stared at him with a menacing glare.

Then Spartus saw it. He squinted his one eye in disbelief to make sure. There was no mistake. Next to the ibex's feet on the rocky floor was Jesus's robe. Spartus jerked back, pressing his body against the cliff wall. The ibex continued to stare at him. Spartus eyed the ibex's white throat. He held his dagger by the blade and braced himself against the cliff wall. With a powerful thrust, he threw the razor sharp dagger at the ibex's throat. The blade rotated in its fast trajectory as it neared its target dead on. The ibex stood its ground and kept staring deep into Spartus's eye. As the dagger was about to strike its mark, the ibex casually leaned slightly to the side. The speeding dagger missed the ibex by less than an inch. It struck the rocky mountainside with a loud *twang,* broke apart from handle to blade, and then landed at the hooves of the ibex with a *ting.*

Spartus raised his fist at the ibex and yelled, "Do you mock me?"

He heard a voice in his head say, *"I mock no one."*

In search of who had spoken, Spartus looked to each side, even knowing no one would be there. Then he looked back at the ibex that stared unflinchingly at him. The ibex motioned with a pushing forward of its head and neck for Spartus to go. Spartus stood his ground. Then he heard, *"Go back to John and be baptized. Repent and live a righteous life, or all the horrors and murders you have committed shall be your damnation and fate ten thousand fold in kind."*

"No!" Spartus declared. He raised his fist and yelled, "Damn you!"

Again Spartus heard the voice: *"Now feel your fate but for a moment."*

For the first time, the ibex closed its eyes tightly, then opened them and sharply thrust its horns toward Spartus.

Spartus's head filled with images of the dozens of anguished faces of the people he had tortured and killed. He rubbed his eyes to blot out those burning images, but they remained. Then he simultaneously heard all of their terrified cries for mercy. He put his hands over his ears, but the maddening cries did not stop; they got louder. The pit of his belly felt like a searing hot spear was twisting in his gut. He had to kneel down so as not to lose his balance and fall over the cliff. Spartus let out a wailing cry of horror. He bent forward and put his hands to the sides of his head, shaking it "No, no, no."

Spartus gasped for air. Suddenly, the images and sounds vanished. He was able to stand. Trembling, he held his belly as if in great pain. Again he heard the voice, *"Is that how you truly want to feel for all of eternity?"*

Spartus shook his head "No" again. His tears flowed. The voice said again, *"Repent, Spartus. Repent."* The ibex motioned once more with its head and neck for Spartus to go.

Spartus nodded. Trembling, he slowly backed along the narrow ledge, retracing his steps. His unsteadiness caused him to look down at his footing. When he looked up again, the ibex and robe were gone.

<hr>

The night sky was clear. Moonlight shown on Clavis's chariot as he leaned his back against its wheel. He heard the crunch of a footstep on the ground and reflexively reached for his sword. A dark, hooded figure approached. "You're back. Is he dead?" Clavis asked Spartus, standing and sheathing his sword.

Spartus stood motionless and did not answer. Clavis asked again, "Is he dead? Have you killed him?"

Spartus slowly pulled the hood down from his head and passively looked straight ahead. Clavis stood in front of him, but Spartus seemed to look through him with an unfocused gaze. Clavis asked, "Are you all right? You seem...different."

"I am different," Spartus softly replied. "I am not the man I was."

"What are you talking about? What happened? Is he dead?"

"He, or it? The Messiah lives. What I was before has died. Something within me has been born anew."

"You're not making any sense. Tell me what happened," Clavis demanded.

"I can tell you that I have been baptized. I have been cleansed of my sins. A huge burden has been lifted from my soul."

Clavis laughed halfheartedly, "You're joking with me. Surely you have done away with the Rabbi."

"I joke not. I have come to convince you to be baptized also."

Clavis stared at Spartus in disbelief. He walked around him as Spartus stood passively, his intimidating prowess no longer evident. Clavis remarked, "You have changed. I don't know what's going on, but we must kill the Rabbi."

"Stay the night, Clavis, and be baptized by John tomorrow. Then you will know."

"Are you daft?" Clavis asked. "You can stay here. I must follow my orders. I'll do the deed alone."

Clavis harnessed the two horses to the chariot and climbed on. Spartus remained transfixed, standing in the same place. Spartus looked up at Clavis and said, "You will not find him. You cannot kill a ghost. Repent, Clavis. Repent."

"You are daft!" Clavis declared. He snapped the reins and headed toward the River Jordan. Spartus stood silent and alone in the moonlight. For the first time in his memory, he felt at peace.

32

Jesus immediately left the vicinity of the River Jordan and made haste to the Wilderness of Judea to fulfill his heavenly Father's task. The stark yellow-gray terrain of the stony Wilderness was nearly devoid of green plants. Rugged gorges and endless, desolate rounded hills extended in all directions of the arid landscape. Except for some occasional Bedouin tribes, scorching heat by day and extreme cold at night made the land uninhabitable. A few areas with only sparse water supported life for the hyenas, jackals, wolves, and lions that preyed on wild boars, gazelles, rams, wild goats, and ibexes. Those grazing animals fed on isolated shrubs and scattered tufts of desert grasses.

It was the tenth day in the Wilderness since Jesus's most sacred baptism—the zenith of epiphanies—had occurred in the River Jordan. Since then, his body had not needed water or food or protection from the elements. The supreme omnipotent power of the Holy Spirit's energy more than fueled Jesus's body. So intense was Its energy that Jesus's flesh could not contain that potent might for more than forty days, at which time the body's biological structures would begin to break apart.

That first night after his baptism, Jesus lay on the ground in the comfort of his heavenly Father's robe. With his greater insight, Jesus looked up at the dazzling stars in a way that he hadn't perceived them before. Each star possessed a unique array of pulsing colors that resembled the brilliant auric colors of people. He felt their life force as living entities composed of exploding plasmas of exquisite heat. His miraculous oneness with God connected him in an awesome "knowingness" to whatever he directed his concentration toward. He was one with God and one with his Holy Father's creation of the earth and the heavens and its living stars. His divine senses projected his astral body, and he soared at Godspeed in the spacious sea of the Milky Way. It fascinated him, and he thought of the galaxy as the majestic hand of the Lord that had cast countless billions of seeds of His Light across the night and then given the seeded field of Light a twist in time that in turn had given birth to a multitude of worlds and life.

Jesus intimately experienced how the stars breathed in and out and pulsed in patterns of light, and he delighted as he breathed with them. He smiled and felt an electric thrill ripple through his essence in divine knowing and the ecstatic feeling that all people and all things at their core were individual unique patterns of light.

Back in his body, he picked up a handful of sand and let it cascade through his fingers like water. One grain of sand remained in his palm.

He brought it closer to his eyes and looked deeply into its inner workings. Jesus smiled as he saw vortexes of colored light whirling and twirling and interweaving in a dance that gathered into tiny bits of matter; and that matter did its dance of energy, radiating and gravitating until it grew into a greater mass of matter and formed the appearance of a grain of sand. Everything large and small in the universe exuded life within an infinite ocean of God's Light and Love—the almighty One God within and without all things.

Jesus was enraptured and felt divinely blessed in his humble state of grace. He truly felt like God's Son, chosen by his Holy Father to meet the destined challenges before him. Jesus basked in a supreme state of holy bliss.

In the initial days after his sacred baptism, Jesus began to acclimate to his new powers. At first he felt his body as he had in his lost wanderings in the desert outside Jerusalem before he had first encountered Judas. During those delirious desert wanderings, he had no need of food or water, for his Father's divine Love had been more than ample to sustain him.

In God's grace, he had renewed his faith after he had lost all hope. Then he was given the insight that his life had a greater purpose and a sacred destiny to be fulfilled. Now he was one with the land and the life of the desert wilderness around him. When he moved his arms and legs, he felt as if they were moving with an adroit but slow locomotion through a fluid. Yet when he looked around his surroundings and noted the animals' movements in the wilderness, it was the outside world that moved more slowly. Time and space became relative attributes that he could manipulate, and he was able to transcend the landscape effortlessly with unbelievable speed and agility.

Jesus's consciousness had advanced to an even greater psychic state of awareness than before. His sense of anticipation of each animal's next movement was infallible. He could become one with an animal's consciousness, seeing the world through its eyes. He quickly learned the nature of the animals, just as he had mastered the workings of man's nature.

Jesus knew what it meant to be human, to intimately know the pleasures and pains, the joys and sorrows, the aspirations and agonies, the disappointments and hopes, and all of the bittersweet complexities of life's dramas that made man the human entity he had become. All that Jesus had experienced had blended with his innate spiritual knowledge to guide him to elevate the human spirit so that mankind could fulfill his heavenly Father's intended role for the human species.

Jesus stood and once more looked up at the night sky, gazing in awe at the brilliant colors of the magnificent living stars. His consciousness soared wildly and playfully into dimensions of reality in which physical senses had no meaning. There, only patterns of light and vibrations of sound twirled and whirled, dancing and interweaving, forever creating new combinations of patterns that gave birth to more creations of worlds within worlds and on and on...

Suddenly all faded. He felt a gentle breeze caress his face. He looked down at his foot. A large scorpion began to crawl up onto the top of his sandal. Jesus calmly attuned to the scorpion's consciousness and senses. The scorpion's intention was to continue traveling toward a small stream of water, but it felt unusual warmth from Jesus's foot. The scorpion paused, its curiosity heightened, its stinger tail uncurled with uncertainty.

Jesus projected to the scorpion the feeling that his foot was a cold stone. The scorpion moved in a slow circle on the sandal and rose up a pinching claw. The scorpion paused again, sensing nothing unusual. It then crawled off Jesus's sandal and continued toward the water. Jesus smiled and said, "Thank you, dear Father, for grounding me and for the opportunity to enjoy another gift that you have blessed me with." Jesus felt an exalted gratitude that he was able to faithfully project images to non-human life forms in addition to his ability to project images to men, images such as the ibex that Spartus had perceived to be as real as life.

Jesus looked toward the stream and felt the water's life force. He extended his awareness to follow the living water's path as it dipped underground and circled around a large hill to surface again on the other side, forming a small pool of water near two small trees. The breeze shifted, and Jesus turned his head to sniff the air and identified the scent of a pride of lions a mile away. He was able to discern two males, three females, and five very hungry cubs.

Jesus walked toward the small pool of water. He froze when he saw a young gazelle cautiously approach the pool. He attuned his consciousness to the gazelle's and felt its strong thirst. The gazelle looked toward Jesus but saw no movement and proceeded. After every two or three steps it took toward the water, the gazelle stopped, braced its legs and stood poised to bolt. It instinctively looked behind for any beasts of prey that might be lurking. It saw none and proceeded. When it was five feet from the water, a crouching lioness suddenly sprang from the low shrubs and ran at full speed for the gazelle's flank. The gazelle quickly darted to the side, narrowly missing the attack, then reversed its position and ran full out for its life in the opposite direction. The lioness turned and chased the gazelle for twenty yards and then stopped.

Jesus was fascinated as he became attuned to the lioness's consciousness. She knew she could not outrun or outmaneuver the gazelle once it had gained a certain lead. Jesus felt her disappointment and overwhelming need to find food for her hungry cubs. The lioness turned and saw Jesus. Unlike the gazelle, who looked for movement and searched for scents to detect predators, the lioness's infrared night sight saw what resembled a man; only this man's infrared glow was much different. The lioness slowly approached Jesus and then crouched in her stalking pose. Jesus stood his ground. The lioness edged closer, and when only twelve feet away, felt certain of her kill. The lioness took two quick, powerful strides and sprang with an open jaw and wet fangs toward Jesus's throat. Her sharp claws, fully extended from her large paws, reached out for Jesus's shoulders. The lioness was just inches away from making contact when Jesus disappeared. The lioness clawed at the empty air and then landed and turned around to attack again where she thought the man would be. Jesus had moved at Godspeed and stood between the two trees.

The lioness looked around in bewilderment. She sniffed the air for a scent but found none. She paced back and forth and then pawed at the barren ground. She then walked back to the pool and sniffed the air again. The lioness looked at the bushes and the three small trees nearby. No sight or scent of the man was present. She stared at the trees a moment and then moved toward the hills where her den and hungry cubs waited.

Jesus did not have to change his shape, only the perception of the perceiver as he had done in becoming the third tree to the lioness. He thanked his Father for his humble realization that although he was endowed with superhuman powers and perception, spontaneous circumstances could occur at any time, and he would have to react spontaneously to those circumstances, as he had with the scorpion and the lioness. And in his spontaneous reaction, he had learned more about himself. Jesus knew that he was ready.

Jesus had moved toward Jebel Quruntul, the white-chalk, twelve-hundred-foot mountain in the wilderness, the tallest mountain in Judea. He was soon sitting just below the mountain's peak on a ten-by-twenty-foot rock outcropping. It was an inky black night. Moments passed. Jesus felt a warmth building in his genitals, a pleasant tingle that made him smile. The enticing sexual stimulus was similar to what he had experienced at John's daughter's wedding. Then it had caused an involuntary arousal that his body had reacted to when Hannah's sensual desires mixed with his own newly heightened senses.

He slowly shook his head "no." The tingle and warmth faded, but another, more intense wave of sexual desire started to build. His heart beat faster. The memory of Hannah's voluptuous nature, combined with an image of her softness pressed against him, caused him to shift a little uncomfortably. Again, he smiled and shook his head "no." The sensual feelings ebbed once more.

He pulled the hood of his sacred robe over his head. A ten-foot serpent slithered toward him. Jesus saw a deep crimson aura around it. Jesus nodded at the serpent and said to it, "I've been expecting you. That was a typical way to announce yourself."

The serpent responded, "Stimulating man's primal urges is very effective. It opens the mind's door to more of my thoughts; then the fun begins. But I see that you have acquired an immunity to my lusty projections that stimulate humans to sexual actions that they may otherwise have avoided."

Jesus replied, "On the contrary, I am acutely aware and feel their effects. This earth body still has a basic sexual instinct. I am not immune to those urges, but they are of no benefit and serve no purpose for me, so I have made a choice to dismiss them. My body does not control me. Humans can make that choice also. However, your attempt to manipulate me does demonstrate that, concerning humans' drives, you are very adept at what you do."

The serpent raised its head and upper body three feet above the ground and replied, "Thank you for the compliment: I've been practicing since man walked in the Garden of Eden. Man is simple to tempt," said the serpent, rising another two feet, "and I have made temptation into an art."

Jesus scoffed, "An art of evil intentions, although creative in your realm of activity, is a waste of your resources."

The serpent rose higher, to nine feet tall, then transformed into a red-faced, devious looking angel with broken wings. It said, "My talents are more useful on Earth than in Heaven, where most new souls bow in constant pious prayer to the Lord. It's dull, dull, and dull. Where is man's spark of creativity there? On Earth, I stimulate those abilities that God has endowed man with. That is a great purpose to fulfill!"

Jesus scoffed again, "Using fear, lust, hate, vengeance, jealousy, and greed to motivate actions of revenge, torture, murder, theft, and war is to diminish the use of your potential, for it is far easier to destroy than to create. You are a fallen angel because you fear that you cannot equal my Father's creative powers or His magnificence."

The angel scowled, "I have chosen to challenge the blandness of God's universal love to spur man to accomplish unrivaled feats. You undervalue the fear of the destructive consequences of violence and war. A sword at a man's throat arouses his survival instinct to think and act with all of his mighty resources, much more so than sitting in silent prayer or in humble adulation of God."

Jesus retorted, "It is true that one's survival, when perceived as threatened, is a primal instinct that you use to create the fear that spurs man to act against man. But they are ill-intended actions with consequences that are in opposition to my Father's creation."

The angel barked, "What glory is there in building opulent temples that only certain believers dwell in and deny entry to those whom the temple chiefs deem inferior?"

Jesus answered, "That is not the glory I speak of. When man embraces God's will, he will not deny the sanctity of others, but will act in the spirit of brotherhood and unity to co-create a bountiful life for all. That is the glory I speak of."

The broken-winged angel pointed a finger at Jesus. "You choose to see only the benevolence of God's grace. Do you ignore the passages in your Bible such as that of Nahum, which speaks of the Lord's anger against Nineveh, where it is said, 'The Lord is a jealous and avenging God; the Lord takes vengeance and is filled with wrath!' I am only following in my creator's ways."

Jesus replied, "Then you also know that in that passage, it also says that 'The Lord is good, a refuge in time of trouble.'"

"But of what matter is that?" The angel smiled, revealing fangs. "Man now believes that God is vengeful against his enemies and that He has a jealous nature."

"That is because man has interpreted God's Word from man's viewpoint of the world at that time in history," Jesus replied. "Now man must see the true benevolence of my Lord and act in kind, in God's way, with love and brotherhood as One."

The angel's broken wings opened slightly at distorted angles. "It's too late to change man's belief in what the scriptures have always said, that 'God will put fire to his enemies and all who do not believe in him!' So the pious and righteous who fervently believe and teach and preach those scriptures only reaffirm my 'special' ways to perpetuate those beliefs. They encourage man to act with vengeance against their enemies, as God does."

Jesus shook his head in disagreement. "God has no need for vengeance, for He has no enemies; for no one person nor any army can in any way hurt or wound the Lord Almighty. Man wrote those scriptures and distorted much of my Father's message. Man became the judge of what is right or wrong and what should be rewarded or punished and how. But it is God who has the final rule over all judgments, not man."

Jesus laughed and said, "It is folly to think of God as being jealous. Who would God be jealous of? The richest king with the largest and most powerful army in the world is less than a tiny speck of dust compared to God's heavenly universe. That speck, although less than a drop of water in the vast ocean, is yet a part of God, and so God has no need to be jealous of a part of Himself."

The angel-clad Devil thrust a fist at Jesus and bellowed, "It doesn't matter! Man believes otherwise, and what he believes, he makes his reality!"

Jesus nodded in agreement, "That is true. That's why my Father sent me: to change and enlighten those false beliefs and to teach His true ways. That is why I am here now with you, for you are nothing more than a thought-form created from man's false beliefs."

"So who is right?" replied the Devil. "You see good; I see evil. The scriptures teach both sides of the same coin."

"The scriptures are not complete; more will be inscribed as future generations learn and grow into more highly evolved manners of thinking, feeling and acting with brotherly love. That is my message, yet to be written."

"You, dear Jesus, have your role to play, and I have mine. But I see that you have not eaten in many days, and I know that you enjoy the tastes of delicious food. With your present powers, why not turn those stones before you into warm loaves of fresh bread to nourish your body? Think how delectable that would taste and how it would delight your tongue."

Jesus answered, "It is written that man does not live by bread alone. I have no need of food, for I am sustained by the Love and the Holy Spirit of my Father."

Because the Devil was not able to tempt Jesus with food, he tried to manipulate Jesus in another way. He took him to the holy city of Jerusalem and had him stand on the highest pinnacle of the Temple. He said to Jesus, "You think your Lord protects you. You have such astounding faith that His love for you will prevent any harm from befalling you."

"I do," Jesus replied.

"Then prove it to me and to yourself. If you think you are in the hands of God and that His angels will carry you safely to earth, then jump!"

Jesus smiled and said, "I need not prove it to myself, for I know that my Father loves and protects me always and in all ways. One does not test our Father, our Lord, as you try to test and tempt me, for I am as certain of His love as I am certain that you have no power over me."

The Devil was annoyed. He then led Jesus back to the top of the mountain where they had met. The Devil waved its hand in a full circle around the mountain's base, and all the kingdoms of the world appeared beneath them. Magnificent castles, sheikdoms and harems, treasure chests overflowing with gold coins and rare jewels were lavishly displayed. Millions of people paid homage to their rulers.

The Devil said to Jesus, "What you see is all yours to rule, but for one thing: that is for you to bow down and worship me."

Jesus again burst into laughter, and the Devil growled in frustration. Jesus retorted, "You are a sad Satan indeed. To tempt me to rule the world is total foolishness. Those who take away freedoms and try to rule over others only foment rebellion against themselves. I will not worship you, for I worship and serve only my heavenly Father. Because I am already One with Him and His Kingdom of Heaven, I lack for nothing but to follow the path He has laid before me. It is my honor and pleasure to serve Him."

Jesus chuckled, adding, "To rule the world is a burden you try to place upon my shoulders that I will not bear, for it is intended that all people shall rule themselves and share what is good with each other. You, a would-be Satan nemesis, are just a fleshless thought-form created from man's spiritual ignorance and an unnecessary manifestation of man's imagination."

The Devil smirked, "Yet I do exist, if not in physical substance, then in the reality of men's minds. Furthermore, since you say that God is all things, then I am also a part of God and have my power over mankind."

Jesus shook his head and said, "You only exist because man imparts a power to you. I will bring the Light into that dark part of man's mind, and your dark image will fade in comparison. No temptation that you offer can equal a camel's hair of worth compared with my heavenly Father. You are a foolish fallen angel: be gone with you."

But Satan would not leave. Instead, the white-cloaked angel transformed itself into a twelve-foot tall, red Devil image. Large pointed horns sprouted from its head. Red-orange flames radiated from its body. A long, sharply barbed tail whipped back and forth from the Devil's hindquarters. Angrily, the Devil sneered, "You think that you can banish me with words? Do not forget that all the souls who fear and believe in me have already given me the power to rule over them."

Jesus stood and said, "That is why you fear me. I bring the belief of the power of God's love and forgiveness to those souls. When man no longer believes in your powers, you will fade from men and women's minds and their lives, and then you will be of no more consequence."

The Devil's horns grew longer; its tail whipped violently. Bolts of lightning flashed upwards from its shoulders toward the night sky as it spat, "You cannot destroy me. I will exist forever!"

Jesus spoke calmly, unfazed by the Devil's thunderous display. "It's true that anything once created, even a random thought, will never vanish from the memory of God's universe. But that does not mean that a silly, hopeless, shape-changing Devil such as you will continue to affect man as you do now. When man no longer pays attention to you, for you offer naught of true divine value, your power will shrivel to a faint memory of the past, and those of the enlightened future will discard your legend as a child's myth. The day will come when the masses realize that they control their own fates and have divine power over their present; their lives do not depend on a poor prince of the air such as you."

The Devil's eyes bulged with rage. Its body enlarged twofold, towering over Jesus, and its red flaming arms lit up the night sky as it spoke. "You try to diminish me yet again with mere words. But look below at the magnificent reality of Hell that I have created with the minds of men."

The Devil made a large, sweeping motion with its long clawed fingers and pointed down the sides of the mountain to the view below. It bellowed, "There is my Pit of Souls. They suffer in eternal pain and anguish in my domain, and I am their Lord."

Countless tortured faces stared up at Satan, who stood upon the mountaintop. Their wretched forms cowered in anticipation of great pain. Satan spat a torrent of acid upon them, and the souls uttered screams of burning torment.

Jesus surveyed the multiple levels of the inferno that extended ever downward. Flames from fire and molten lava bubbled up the sides of the pit and flowed down in rivulets, scorching and searing the images of countless souls who were chained to their stations, thrashing and crying in continuous agony. Each soul resided in a shallow or a deep depression in the bedrock of cooled lava that formed their individual "pit" of Hell. The standing souls were all tightly chained by their throats; many others were stretched spread-eagle and chained by all four limbs. The bedrock pits isolated the souls, and each stood in its own urine, feces, and vomit. In many pits, the souls were submerged up to their chins in their accumulated toxins, which would periodically rise up into their mouths and noses with each new emission of their own waste. They would gag, choke, and vomit, and the repugnant cycle of their own making would repeat again and again.

Rivulets of searing lava seeped into the pits and scalded the captive souls. The boiling lava mixed with their pools of nauseating sludge and gave off the epitome of putrid smells that filled the stifling smoky red air.

Grotesque monsters and demons, large and small, poked and prodded the souls ceaselessly with pointed barbs and truncheons, causing the captives to scream in agonizing pain. Their tortured, confused faces were cast in expressions of frenzied bewilderment, lost in an endless maze of horrors and agony.

Jesus looked at the Devil, who stood tall and proud. The Devil smiled with delighted satisfaction. He put his hands on his hips and then swept his arm above the Pit of Souls. "Behold my Kingdom. The harbinger of the future."

Jesus cast his robe to the ground. He raised his hands in the air, and in his white tunic stood in luminous stark contrast to his dark surroundings. Hell's inhabitants became still and wondered who this unusual figure could be. Satan frowned and clenched its fists and then raised them in the air, about to cast out a torrent of ferocious demons intended to divert the pitiful souls' attention away from Jesus and further embalm them in added terror in their tombs of suffering.

Jesus's face became stern. He authoritatively pointed a finger at Satan and commanded, "Be still!"

Satan instantly froze; his raised fists were still, as was his menacing face; he could not even blink an eye. Jesus circled the frozen Satan, then stood before him. All below, the monsters, demons, and souls were stunned by the unbelievable sight of their inanimate overlord. Jesus reached toward Satan's face and playfully tweaked his nose. Satan did not stir an iota. The souls gasped in disbelief, and the demons cringed at the stranger who could mistreat their all-powerful master with impunity.

Jesus smiled kindly at the souls below. He extended his hands toward them and said, "You are asking yourselves, 'Who is this man who can still our mighty Devil like a stone?' I am the messenger of God, and God is your true Lord of lords. The Holy Spirit of God's unlimited forces has been vested in me. As you can see, this Satan who has been frozen by God's command is for now without any power over you so that you may hear your true Lord's message. It is a divine message intended to free you from your bondage of agony."

All below gazed up in awe and listened intently. Jesus spoke with compassion and authority. "When you were embodied in flesh, you were intertwined with the physical substance of the earth. It bound you in limited ways that required food, water, and shelter. You had to think and act in ways that would ensure your body's survival. Now you are free from that blessed and glorious connection to the flesh. Now you have the timeless opportunity to choose a different path leading to a far better destination than you find yourselves in at this moment. Yet you are still bound in an even more limited way to the false beliefs of your mind that you have accepted as truth."

Jesus made a sweeping motion with his hand that arced over those below. At first, the souls winced and leaned away. They trembled, expecting a wave of pain to engulf them as the Devil had done to them countless times. Instead, they felt a gentle breeze of peace embrace them. Jesus spoke, "Verily I say to you that you were more than your earth body when you were intertwined with the flesh, and now, you are more than your minds' false thoughts that have formed dark webs from your beliefs regarding sin and punishment. Those webs of your own creation have ensnarled you in those adhering strands of twisted beliefs."

Jesus paused. Again, he looked compassionately at those below and said, "Be not dismayed, for there is hope. Hear my words. I say to you that any belief that is not in harmony with God's Word and His Way of Love shall have no duration or lasting power, and no soul stays ignorant forever. You must and you will learn that your thoughts and feelings create your future and that you can heal from your past. The Devil in your mind's web of beliefs can only keep you ensnarled in your Hell if you continue to spin those same captive strands of ill beliefs over and over."

"Verily I say to you that in time, one way or another, you will realize this truth. Then you will devote your attention to more worthy tasks and uses of your endowed creativity. Then you will ponder why you didn't shed your erroneous beliefs sooner. Truly I say to you that you can choose to do that now."

The souls in the Pit became confused. Most souls shook their heads "no," refusing to let go of the security of clinging to the self-punishing fate that they had become rooted in, even though it offered pain devoid of any joy or pleasure. However, some souls reflected on Jesus's words and considered the possibility that their fate could be different.

Jesus said with great intensity, "Hear this holy message, for it is from the Almighty power that has created you, and it is this: you can free yourselves. You have forgotten that you have the ability to let go of your prolonged suffering. You have already experienced enough suffering. Through me, or by your own choice, God grants you the option to live in His kingdom. He invites you there to create a magnificent existence for yourself that is in harmony with His Word and to dwell in the blessed aura of His glorious, eternal, and divine love."

The souls stared at Jesus, then looked at the Devil. Even in Satan's frozen state, his image of rage and hatred reminded them of the rage and hatred that they themselves harbored. The red glow of Hell intensified as their collective passions and lust for revenge toward their prior enemies surged.

Jesus responded to their dogmatic reaction, saying, "These feelings of anger and revenge toward your perceived past enemies that you harbor with a vice-like grip now hold you in their grasp. Your old enemies have traveled on, and now you are left to stew in that venom of hatred and revenge that no longer serves you.

"You give victory to your enemies, for although their memory continues to plague your existence, they will suffer naught, and you shall continue to punish yourself in the same torturous ways in which you fervently prayed that they would be punished. Verily I say to you that you can choose to cast off the shackles of the captive emotions that bind you to your needless web of distorted and false beliefs." Pointing to the Devil, Jesus said, "You need not give your power to this frozen image empowered and sustained only by your fear and hatred.

"Your Satan cannot make you do anything that you choose not to do. He will encourage and amplify thoughts that you think are evil. But I tell you that you can dismiss his temptations as mere passing thoughts like the wind that blows around and past you rather than latch on to those evil thoughts and make them steadfast in your minds, like those beliefs that now house your present reality of damnation."

Jesus held his hand up in benediction toward those below and said, "Know that my words are true and that God's love and forgiveness are yours for the choosing. Repent and turn away from all that makes you feel sinful, and you will cleanse yourself of all that makes you feel unclean. Believe in all the goodness and benevolence of God's eternal love for you and His constant offer of forgiveness for all the times that you feel that you have sinned. By embracing His goodness and seeking to emulate His ways, your chains of bondage will fade like snow on hot desert sand. And in time," Jesus pointed to Satan, "this image of a Devil will also fade."

The souls pondered Jesus's powerful words. Many inspired souls understood and took heart from the message, realizing that they were not damned forever. Those souls experienced a blessed transformation. They chose to let go of their past hatreds and transgressions, accept God's forgiveness, and allow God's eternal love to embrace them. The instant they did so, they vanished from Hell. The dense gray-red glow of Satan's domain dimmed.

Jesus said to the remaining majority, "Although you choose to remain in your present state for now, know that my heavenly Father, the almighty Lord of all lords, King of all kings shall keep the gate to His kingdom open for you to enter until the end of days."

The remaining souls then turned away from Jesus and looked at the Devil in his frozen state of rage, his fists held high. His image instantly reminded them of their long-held belief in the need to be punished for their sins. Their fears intensified, and the self-incriminating false beliefs regarding their self-worth reverted to their prior state. Their attentiveness to the Devil's image and all that he symbolized gave a surge of energy to Satan and allowed him to break free from his inanimate state. He was about to bring his fists to rain down on the Pit of Souls as he had been in the midst of doing when Jesus froze him but noticed that the tainted dark-red glow of Hell was dimmer and many souls were no longer there. Dismayed and angry, the Devil turned to Jesus and demanded, "What have you done with my children of captivity?"

Jesus grinned, "They have departed in comfort and peace of mind."

The Devil was furious. The souls below cowered, and searing flames deepened Hell's ominous glow. The Devil raised his fists again to spread his wrath upon those below. Once more, Jesus commanded him, "Peace. Be still." Again the Devil froze. The souls became confused for the second time. They turned their gaze upon Jesus, whose luminous white radiance now commanded their attention.

Jesus smiled and said, "I offer you a pause in your time of chaos and suffering." With both hands, Jesus made large arcs over his head toward Hell's dome. The turbulent red-gray swirls of acrid smoke and jagged, red-orange flames that had filled the dome and the Pit of Souls grew dimmer. In a few moments, the dome faded away, revealing the clear night sky with its wondrous array of countless dazzling stars. The souls gasped in awe. Soon they felt the peace of the calm night's stillness. Hell's blurred red glow dimmed to a faint remnant as the souls' attention was captured by the incongruous view of the Heavens above compared with their hellacious surroundings.

Again Jesus reached down with his palms extended toward the Pit of Souls and said, "What you see above you for these blessed moments is always there. Your beliefs in sin and Hell cloud your ability to see through the dome of smoke and fire created by your self-condemnation. You deny yourselves salvation from this Hell by your continued refusal to let go of your past hatred, jealousies, and need for revenge. Only you can open your hearts to let God's love and light within you shine. I say to all of you that you can repent and forgive and free yourselves."

Many of the souls felt a strong surge within them to heed Jesus's words, and so did the Devil. Jesus's powerful words that people could free themselves allowed the Devil to free himself from Jesus's command to be still. At once, Satan felt many souls' yearning and intention to free themselves from his bondage. The Devil roared voraciously at those about to desert his domain. He spat, "Anyone who even dares to think that they can choose to leave my kingdom will suffer ten thousand fold the pain and suffering that you now endure."

The souls below shuddered from the anticipated horror of Satan's words. The smoke and fire reappeared; Hell's glow increased. Jesus swiftly raised his palm, dispatching a bolt of white light at the Devil. The red Devil's angry image became the frozen image of the angel with broken wings that had previously appeared to Jesus. Jesus walked behind the angel, and with a grin, he gently and lovingly took one broken wing in his hands and straightened it. Then he did the same to the other. He walked around to face the angel and nodded sharply to it. The angel-image awoke; the Devil immediately realized its form had changed. Far more disturbing to the Devil, it realized that its broken wings had been straightened. The Devil pointed at Jesus and yelled, "How dare you!"

The furious angel-image hunched its shoulders, and with one powerful squeeze of its whole body, made a loud cracking sound. The angel-image had re-broken both of its wings. Jesus again thrust his open palm toward the angel, and it froze again. The stunned souls witnessed all that had happened and watched in awe once more.

Jesus knelt down on one knee and leaned over the precipice. He spoke kindly to the souls below. "As you have seen, it is of no use for me to straighten the wings of a fallen angel if he chooses to have broken wings. Likewise, it is of no use for me to make you believe in my message that you have the power to free yourselves if you choose to believe otherwise. And so for now, I leave you with the seeds of truth and enlightenment of which I have spoken. I pray they will sprout in time and that my message will lead you to your 'end of days' in Hell. Verily I say to you, God loves and blesses you."

Jesus stood. His luminous image grew brighter, and his white aura became more intense. Then, with a huge all-illuminating white flash, he vanished.

On the last night of his forty days in the Wilderness, Jesus once again lay on the ground and communed with the stars. His consciousness was simultaneously in waking and dream states. He became aware of a voice calling out, "Master, Master, what shall I do?"

Jesus closed his eyes and was instantly sitting in bright daylight in the shade of a palm tree surrounded by a lush green oasis. Two cups of steaming tea sat on a small low table in front of him. He reached out his hand, and Joseph came to his side. Jesus patted the soft grass beside him and said, "Sit, Joseph. Have some tea."

Joseph took a corner of Jesus's robe and kissed it, then sat. Jesus smiled and said, "What is it that you seek, Joseph?"

"Thank you for sharing my dream, Master. I desperately seek peace of mind. I am both blessed and tormented."

"Tell me what you feel so that you may know your feelings better."

"All my feelings are consumed with Seffira," Joseph excitedly replied. "I touch her soft, satiny skin and my fingertips tingle. I hold her in my arms and I tremble. I don't want to let her go. My head is filled only with her and nothing else of the world. I breathe in her fragrance, and it carries me away. She talks for hours about things grand and mundane, and I am mesmerized by her voice and every word, no matter the topic. I feel the radiance of her soul intertwined with mine. Master, she makes me feel compete. It is as if she is a missing half of me, and when we are together, I feel whole. She is more to me than the family I never had. I... I..." Joseph's face filled with worry.

"Go on, Joseph," Jesus encouraged him. "Let your feelings speak. You can say it."

"I dare not utter my dark thoughts lest they become reality."

Jesus replied, "In your dream state, there are no limitations. You are free to say and do anything."

"Master I... I have had premonitions and dreams that I will tragically lose my beloved Seffira. The dreams are not clear to me, but the feeling of loss is real and tears achingly at my heart. I love her with my life. If I lose her, a vital part of me will die, and my life will surely be over.

"Master, she has only been gone for two days, the longest we've been apart. It's unbearable without her. Her parents are angry with me because we talk all night long and she gets home much later than she promises to. They want her to stay away from me, but we plan to run away and be on our own."

"Are you sure that's what you need to do?" Jesus asked.

"It's impossible not to be together. I've been the happiest with her than I've ever been in my life. She is so perfect for me in every way. But this premonition of dread and danger causes me constant unease. Master, what should I do to still my fears so that I can have comfort in my time with my cherished Seffira?"

Jesus handed him a cup of steaming tea and said, "First, dear Joseph, give thanks to our heavenly Father for each blessed moment that you and Seffira do share together." Joseph took a sip of the tea, and its smooth taste and soothing fragrance calmed him. Jesus continued, "Savor the blessings of your todays, and do not linger over what may or may not happen in your tomorrows. Love is meant to be enjoyed most in the present. You have been blessed to experience a love that is pure and rare, despite the turmoil that it may create in your heart. That is the divine mystery of love, and it has captivated your soul. Cherish each moment with your beloved, for you are creating sacred, treasured memories for your soul that will sustain and nourish you in times beyond the life you now live."

"But I want to marry her and have her carry my child in this lifetime."

Jesus placed his hand on Joseph's shoulder. Jesus sighed and then said, "I can tell you that Seffira will carry your child."

Joseph became excited again and eagerly asked, "Will it be a boy or a girl baby?"

"I will say no more for now, except that it is best that you not fret about the future and instead give your attention to each moment that you have with Seffira; give and receive love in every way possible, for that is your opportunity to experience the bliss of love."

Joseph put his cup back on the table and said, "I will try, Master. Thank you."

Jesus gently squeezed Joseph's shoulder, then said, "Go now in peace."

Joseph kissed Jesus's robe again, then stood and bowed his head. He turned and left. Jesus opened his eyes and looked up again at the stars in the Wilderness of Judea's night sky.

———

Dawn of the fortieth day was nearing, when the endowment of the Holy Spirit would leave Jesus's body lest his flesh disintegrate. However Jesus's greatly advanced psychic abilities and his power to project vivid images that would be perceived as real would remain. Every organ and cell in his body would continue to pulse with perfect precision, spectacularly enhancing all of his physical attributes and agility.

Jesus reflected on the day he first met Judas in Jerusalem and his journeys since then. He thought of the significance of his sacred union with John the Baptist and then the last forty days of the many wondrous experiences infused with the Holy Spirit in the Wilderness of Judea. With his new insight into the possibilities and challenges that lay ahead, he realized that there was one last connection that was needed.

The horizon was turning orange above the coming dawn. When Jesus closed his eyes, an image of Paul's face appeared, and a pathway of communication was opened. Paul looked surprised and confused when he saw Jesus's face. "Why are you in my dream?" Paul asked.

"I need your help, Paul," Jesus earnestly responded.

"You persist in calling me Paul and not Saul. Leave me alone. I want nothing to do with you. You call yourself a rabbi, but you bring shame and disrespect to our Jewish heritage. Your lecherous arousal at John's daughter's wedding reception and then consorting with thieves, assassins, Romans, and prostitutes flout your obligation to live a righteous life."

"Dear Paul, you have judged me falsely. I have come as God's messenger. It is my mission to bring greater honor and respect to our Jewish heritage by teaching that love, forgiveness, tolerance, and brotherhood between all men is God's will. That is the spirit in which mankind must think, feel, and act to avoid creating a fiery Hell on Earth."

"Your actions mock the Torah. Leave me."

"Please, dear Paul, hear me, for I have seen future possibilities that the prophet of the past, Isaiah, has foreseen. As man's powers grow, he will be able to create a heavenly existence. My message will advance the manners in which man may achieve that life. If mankind continues on its present path, the race will destroy itself. I know that I can bring our heavenly Father's message to our people, but my time here will be too short to firmly root His divine Word into the workings of today's societies. Dear Paul, our Lord has given you extraordinary organizational skills to implement His message that I have come to deliver. You are needed to help me complete this mission that God has ordained for us."

Paul reacted with confusion and indignation, "I know not of what you speak. I seek to live a righteous life and want nothing to do with you. Be gone with you!"

As the image of Jesus's face grew larger and brighter, Paul became fearful. Then Jesus's image was blinding, pulsing with countless, intense points of white light. Each brilliant point radiated outward, dazzling patterns of white light appearing and disappearing. Paul closed his eyes to shield himself from the intense brightness. Rather than hearing specific words, Paul indescribably felt the impact of the message within the patterns of white light. The message he discerned was "I am the Christ, the Son of God, our Lord of lords. I am the one who now carries the Essence of the Holy Spirit within my personage. Mankind must open their hearts to share in the joy, intimacy, and glory of God. Above all, the primacy of love must rule, or man will not endure. Paul, you are needed to help."

Paul's fear became anger. "You are not the Christ! You are not the Messiah! You haunt my dreams like the Devil. I wish to erase the memory of you as if you had never existed! Leave me so this nightmare may end!"

Jesus opened his eyes and saw the first ray of sunlight peek over the horizon. The forty-first day had begun.

33

To quell the fires of salacious gossip as well as John the Baptist's continuing condemnation of Herod's adulterous affair with his brother's wife, King Herod Antipas married Herodias. Because Herodias was a princess of a royal bloodline, Antipas also sought to gain favor and greater respect from the people by marrying her. However, the snide remarks and degrading jokes only proliferated, and John the Baptist's vehement condemnation of Antipas's marriage to his cousin to his throngs of followers now served to fan those fires that the king had sought to quell.

Herod entered Herodias's opulent parlor.

Herodias curtly ordered her seven handmaidens to leave immediately. Before Herod could say a word, Herodias blurted, "How can you allow that Baptist John to continue to soil my name? It belittles my marriage to you and my title as Queen." She started sobbing in short, painful breaths. Herod came to her side and put his hand on her shoulder to console her. She pushed it away and said, "Now the Baptist says that your marriage to me is a sin because I divorced your brother, Phillip, to marry you. To permit him to speak of me in that way is to tell all of Judea that anyone may speak of me in the same way."

Herodias's pointed finger was only an inch away from Herod's nose as she demanded, "You must imprison him to silence his tongue." Her sobbing intensified.

Herod stepped back a few feet and said, "It's not that simple. Because of the Baptist's large following, to imprison him would cause disruptions that must now be avoided. Because of the new tax increase, Rome fears that if any of their religious leaders are jailed, a rebellion could arise. That, my dear wife, would jeopardize our kingdom."

"I don't care!" Herodias yelled. "You're so damn smart, figure something out."

Zadak sat in his regal chair and stroked his beard pensively as he listened. The head priest who had witnessed Jesus's baptism by John concluded his summary yet again. "As I've said, the white light not only enveloped everything, it seemed to permeate our bodies and senses. Then when we could see again, the river was boiling with steam and ice."

Zadak sat up straight and asked, "And is that when the vortex of light that looked like an angel or a flock of white doves appeared in a spiral formation?"

"Yes," the head priest, replied, "although no one could be certain of the image because of its brightness, but everyone agreed that it was a powerful and sacred white light that felt like the hand of God."

Zadak stood and paced. "It's been almost two months, and no one has seen the Rabbi or heard of his whereabouts. What do you make of this?"

"After John proclaimed that the Rabbi is the one that he has been preparing the way for, there was no doubt in his followers' minds that Jesus is indeed the Messiah."

The head priest continued, "This can become a problem. As I've told you, it was a revelation to me when I spoke to Jeremiah, who is John's disciple, about how many followers John has baptized. He said that except for the Sabbath, John has baptized fifty to one hundred and fifty people a day for over five years. Some days he has baptized hundreds. That totals many tens of thousands who have sought repentance from the Baptist, perhaps over one hundred thousand. They could all give their allegiance to Jesus."

Zadak frowned and said, "With all that I've heard of this Jesus's healings and miracles, and your experience, perhaps he is the Messiah...but perhaps not. John has called us a 'den of vipers,' so we know he is aligned against us. We must assume Jesus has similar sentiments. I feel that this will cause us many problems if our followers turn away from us and align with the Rabbi."

The head priest replied, "Right after the Rabbi left and ran up the mountain, John beseeched his followers to spread the word that 'the kingdom of Heaven is near.' He clearly implied that Jesus is the Messiah and that he is the one to be followed. Joseph was there, and he had already become a follower."

Zadak clenched his fists and spoke with venom, "That ungrateful betrayer shall suffer greatly for his transgressions against me."

<hr>

Jeremiah sat cross-legged on the floor of John the Baptist's cave. The flame of an oil lamp bathed the cave in a soft glow. John sat above, cross-legged on his limestone slab.

Jeremiah was exuberant. "I can still feel remnants of that surge of energy running up and down my spine from when you baptized Jesus, and then being enveloped by the white light of the Holy Spirit! It was more than amazing!"

John's eyes were glazed with bliss. He nodded in acknowledgement. Jeremiah continued, "Master, the words that you spoke as the Messiah ran up the mountain still echo in my mind: 'Rejoice, the kingdom of Heaven is near.'"

John laughed. Jeremiah asked, "What's so funny, Master?"

"I don't know if anyone truly understood my words." John reflected a moment and then said, "The masses still think mainly of themselves. Their desire to escape their wretched lives and enter Heaven's realm is understandable, even worthy, although self-centered in a way that blinds them from seeing the Christ who was in their midst. He, the almighty force who is our heavenly Father, His pure Essence, was within a man's body, and for that time, His presence of Light permeated everyone and everything with His love. If only others could see and feel what I have! At that moment, dear Jeremiah, the Christ – that sacred and Holy portion of God - was Heaven incarnate in a man's form, and he walked among us. That is why I cried out in ecstasy that Heaven is near!"

⊂———————⊃

"You're my sister, Lydia, and that's why I'm confiding in you," Zena said with a touch of remorse.

"You know you can always trust me, even though you ignore me unless you need something from me," Lydia replied.

"Maybe I haven't been a good sister to you, but I do love you."

Lydia took a sip of tea, then put down her cup and looked around her garden. She said, "My home does not compare to yours, nor does my status in Jerusalem. Because of your beauty, you've always been favored by our father. That made me feel inferior and unworthy of love. I was jealous of you. But since my healing by the blessed Rabbi, I am now comfortable with myself. With all the power and wealth that you have, Zena, why do you seem so unhappy?"

Zena swallowed, then looked down. She adjusted her necklace of cascading strands of pearls and gemstones that were already in perfect order. In a whisper, she said, "It's Pontius. I don't think he loves me anymore."

"Pontius?" Lydia questioned. "He adores you! Anything you ask for, he provides for you." Lydia sat back and smiled "And you do ask for endless gifts and favors."

"I know, I know. But lately, he doesn't give me the attention that he always has. He comes to bed late and says he's tired and doesn't feel like making love. I think I'm losing my hold on him." Zena sniffed back a tear.

Lydia shook her head and said, "Tsk, tsk. My poor sister, the most powerful woman in Jerusalem, can you not see beyond yourself to what is going on around you?"

"What do you mean?" Zena asked.

"Everyone is talking about the Jews' Messiah. He is real. Look at me. I feel wonderful as never before. Herod sent battalions to arrest the Rabbi Jesus and then withdrew them. Everyone in Judea, even my husband, has been pressured to make sure the increased tax levies make it to Rome without the usual skimming. The Jewish sects don't know if they should accept or reject Jesus as the true Messiah. Of course Pontius is upset and distracted. Jerusalem is his command, and his authority is being challenged by Herod and threatened by Rome and the Jews. Where have you been, Zena?"

"I know of those things, Lydia. I fear Pontius's power is threatened and that my power over him is waning. I don't want to lose everything. I don't know what to do."

"Instead of trying to control Pontius like you controlled our father, why don't you just appreciate your husband and support him in the hard work he does and be grateful for all that he provides for you? You have so much to be thankful for, and yet you're always complaining. Pontius loves you, but you don't really love him. You only care about the power he wields and your control over him."

"You wouldn't understand, Lydia. If I love the power that the man has, do I not love the man?"

"Zena, my poor sister, perhaps it is you who does not understand. When you love the man with or without his power or status, then you really love the man. That is true love, my sister."

Zena sat up indignantly and said, "That kind of love is for children, not for important people of the world."

"Maybe you're incapable of feeling love that is treasured on its own without material things that can be bought or garnering power over others." Lydia smiled. "I am now at peace with myself. I have found contentment in my life and feel fortunate to be married to a good man who loves and appreciates me for who I am."

Lydia's husband approached them on the garden path. He nodded at Zena and politely said, "Good afternoon." He quickly turned his gaze to Lydia. Zena saw him smile with delight, beaming with pride. He gently put his hand on his wife's shoulder and then knelt down and tenderly kissed her. Lydia put her hand over his and pressed it against her shoulder. He stood up and looked upon Lydia with sincere caring and love that needed no words, as if he and Lydia were the only two people in the world.

Tears streamed down Zena's cheeks. For the first time in her life, she was jealous of her sister.

⊂══════⊃

"Where can Jesus be?" Seth asked his father. Matthew stood over his son as Seth sat studying his prayer book.

"I don't know where he is, but I'm sure that he'll find us here in Galilee as he said he would."

"But I miss him so much. I don't know if he's all right. I want him to be here."

"Remember what he told you. His spirit will always be with you."

"I know, Father," Seth said reluctantly. "I do feel his presence about me at times," Seth smiled, "and I see him in my dreams. That always gives me a good feeling. But I miss him and wish he were here. He's my best friend."

"We all miss him and wait for his return. Now you must attend to your studies if you want to become a rabbi. That's what he would want you to do if he were here. Let me hear your prayer chants once more."

⊂══════⊃

In the hustle and bustle of Jerusalem's great temple's market place, Nicodemus clandestinely spoke to Samuel between two vendor stalls. "All that I have heard about Jesus of Nazareth confirms what I feel in my heart and soul. That's how I know the time of the Anointed One is here."

Samuel replied, "How can anyone have any doubt after a multitude of people witnessed God's Light and His turning the River Jordan to boiling water and ice. I tremble at the thought. Jesus is indeed the Messiah!"

"I must find a way to protect him. The Sadducees and our Pharisee leaders feel threatened by him. Rome will also want him eliminated when they realize that his powers are real, and as his followers grow in number, they will become a threat to Rome," Nicodemus said.

"It is up to you, Nicodemus. You're a respected member of the Sanhedrin Council that rules over all religious law. The council's police force can arrest, prosecute and punish on their orders. Jesus will be designated a criminal or a heretic by those who feel threatened by him. You must not let that happen."

"I will do what I can. It'll be tricky because if I appear to be aligned with Jesus, I'll lose my sway with the council. We must keep in mind that Rome has appointed all seventy-one council members and thus influences their decisions. I must work delicately between all the opposing factions."

Samuel replied with great urgency, "There are many who sympathize with you and will listen to you. Our people have waited and prayed for this moment when our Messiah will finally come. Now that the prophecies have come true and he is here, you must protect him."

"I'll do my best, Samuel; I'll do my best."

———————

"Are you sure you want to arrest the Baptist John?" Octavius asked Herod. "Sejanus has warned you about stirring up any rebellions."

Herod frowned with worry and replied, "As unbelievable as the reports are of Jesus's baptism by John – that 'white light' and the river boiling with ice – it's just as unbelievable that Spartus sought redemption from the Baptist John. John's huge following combined with the followers of Jesus, the one they call their Messiah, has all become too powerful a force that needs to be decapitated."

Octavius nodded in agreement. "It is indeed inconceivable that Spartus has become a changed man. Clavis had witnessed his torturous ways and his delight when his victims cried out in agony. Clavis couldn't believe that someone as evil as Spartus could change either, but it happened. We must be extremely cautious in dealing with this situation."

Herod surveyed his magnificent gardens and their reflecting pools. He turned his gaze upon his majestic palace, then looked back at the flourishing green plants and flowers. "I cannot forget your dream about the vines that grew beneath my garden and then one day choked the life from the it. I will not let that happen to my kingdom. Despite my marriage, the Baptist persists in insulting my bride - and me. I will not tolerate that any longer. To openly show me disrespect and not suffer any consequences undermines my authority and suggests that others may do the same. I know that I cannot act against Jesus; Sejanus has specified that. But I can and will silence The Baptist in my prison. Octavius, I want you to order the Baptist's arrest immediately.

———————

After Jesus's time in the Wilderness of Judea, he traveled to small towns and villages. There he further developed his abilities and became more skilled at using them. In the first village, he appeared as an elderly, hunched-over man. Only a few kind souls welcomed him and offered him food and shelter. At first, they perceived him as weak and needy. When he offered advice to ease the people's woes, they barely paid him any attention. He could readily discern that they dismissed his words because of his weak and feeble image of an old man. It took persistent effort on his part to open pathways of acceptance in their minds so that they could see the Light. He decided not to hold any healing sessions so that he could measure the power of his words alone. He did not identify himself as Jesus of Nazareth, whose notoriety because of his healings and miracles had already spread among the people. He soon realized that without those deeds, the power of his words too often fell on deaf ears.

Other villages offered more challenges to his spreading The Word, but these challenges only served to sharpen his ability to communicate with disparate individuals. He knew this "testing" would help him to better reach the masses in universal ways that would institute historic changes for mankind's future.

After traveling to many villages, Jesus felt his disciples calling for him to go to Galilee as had been arranged before they had parted. But first, he desired to go back to Nazareth to see his mother, Mary, and his brothers. He also wanted to test his new skills against the forces of rejection that he had incurred when he was forced to leave his hometown in shame. Jesus had also mastered the art of invisibility by projecting his image to others as being a part of the landscape, as he had with the lioness that had perceived him to be a tree.

34

The potter pulled on the reins to bring his cart to a halt. Jesus, now in his normal appearance, got off the cart and said to the driver, "I think that you'll be able to sell all of your wares when you get to Cana."

The potter looked at his cart, filled with vases and jugs. He smiled and said, "Thank you for your encouragement. I want to also thank you for your words about my wife's death. You've brought me great comfort. Bless you on your journey."

"Thank you," Jesus replied, "your kindness in bringing me here is appreciated."

The potter nodded and snapped the reins once. The donkey proceeded on the trail to Cana. Jesus looked up toward the quiet village of Nazareth set on a limestone ridge thirteen hundred feet high. He easily walked the trail to the top, from where he could see Mount Carmel and the Mediterranean coast thirty miles to the west. He looked north to distant snow-covered Mount Hermon.

Jesus turned to the village of four hundred people. He sighed as he thought about his childhood and growing up here in Nazareth.

It was midday and hot, but a mild breeze caressed his face. Jesus walked the familiar narrow streets. The houses in town were small and close together. He avoided the marketplace and chose to walk down the "street of shops" where craftsmen sold their wares. He passed by the mat makers, basket weavers, and potters. When he neared the tanners and leather workers, he closed his eyes and breathed in. The smell of new leather being worked stirred his memories. He knew that his father's old shop was nearby.

Jesus stopped to gaze into a shop at the carpenter who was finishing his work on a wooden plow; the shop had been his earth-father's workplace. Lined up against the wall were finished wooden cart wheels ready to be sold. Wooden sickle handles were in a basket to be carried to the shop next door where the smith was hammering sickle blades to the handles. An iron-tipped plow blade leaned against the wall waiting for the wooden plow to be finished. Jesus thought of his earth-father, Joseph and the carpentry skills that he had taught him with his nurturing ways.

The countryside surrounding Nazareth was lush with greenery and very beautiful. The rich soil and pasturage made Nazareth a highly productive agricultural village, surrounded by fields and vineyards and scattered homes that housed the families that worked the farms. The many varieties of flourishing trees expressed the vitality of the verdant landscape.

Jesus walked to a lone modest house on the town's outskirts. There he sat on the barren ground against the inside corner of a stone wall that enclosed the small backyard of his mother, Mary's, home. The delicious fragrance of fresh baked bread evoked memories of his childhood and his mother's loving care and kindness.

Then he frowned as he remembered the day that his brother James had told him that he must leave Nazareth because of the wrath that had built up against Jesus and his family. The townspeople were aligned against Jesus because of his extraordinary ability to cast out demons from the afflicted. Instead of recognizing him as a gifted healer, they perceived him as an agent of the Devil who could talk to demons.

In the small, poor town of Nazareth where families lived together and all aspects of people's lives were intertwined, there were few secrets. Everyone knew that Jesus was born the illegitimate son of Joseph, and as a child growing up, he was believed to have a tainted bloodline and was treated accordingly.

Jesus shook his head in dismay at the ignorance of the people and the guilt he had felt at the time for bringing disgrace upon his family - and for his own sadness and the deep and painful rejection that he had felt when he had to leave his home town and family.

Jesus came back to the present as Mary hobbled out the back door. With each step, she winced at the pain of her arthritic hips. Mary carried a basket full of raw wool to a small table under an awning that provided shade from the blaring sun. Jesus projected himself to her as part of the stone wall. She laid the basket down and sat in an old wooden chair. From the top of the basket, Mary took out a small hooked rod, a spinner, and a spindle. She held the spinner in one hand, with that arm encircled in raw wool. She began to turn the wool fibers into thread by drawing them out with the hooked rod, the distaff, from the spinner in a continuous twist onto the spindle that stood on the ground by her side. A perforated clay disc whorl weighed down the spindle to help maintain rotation as the wool thread wrapped around it.

Mary fell into an automatic trance-like mode of feeding the wool into the spinner and rhythmically pulling and twisting it into thread as she had done for decades. Her mind pondered the recent rumors that the Messiah, Jesus, had come to fulfill the prophecies. A faint smile softened her face as she thought of the birth of her first-born in Bethlehem.

Jesus sat and viewed her thought-form images as she focused on highlights of those times. It had been a cool, clear night in Bethlehem. The city was overcrowded with people. Rooms were overbooked. Her husband-to-be, Joseph, could only procure a caretaker's workroom adjacent to a stable. Mary, who was then in her late teens, had started with labor contractions. The joy and pain and the sweat and strain of that moment caused her heart to beat faster now as she twirled the wool.

She remembered cleaning the afterbirth off of her newborn son, then rubbing salt over his body to prevent infection. Finally she swaddled him and wrapped him in a soft blanket that she had woven for just that moment. As Mary twirled the thread, her face glowed remembering those tender memories. Her auric colors turned golden with flowing waves of soft pink as she relived that magical flood of maternal love. Jesus smiled at her divine state of love and grace.

Then Jesus saw Mary's thoughts of when Joseph had come to her side and held the swaddled baby in his arms and said to her, "Last night I thought about a dream I had when you were pregnant. I know I am not the baby's father. You have refused to speak of who it may be. In my dream, there were many angels hovering about you in your pregnant state. One angel that the others called Gabriel spoke to me. He said that your pregnancy was by a 'Holy Spirit' and that I should marry you because I love you and because I would make a good father for this holy child."

Mary felt Joseph's love and good intentions for her baby, intentions that he held in his heart and in his spirit. In her thought-form image of the past, she smiled broadly and also smiled now as she sat on her worn wooden chair automatically spinning thread from the raw wool. Jesus smiled as well.

Jesus saw the images of the past when Joseph put an arm around Mary and drew her close as he held the newborn baby and said, "I know by marrying you and naming this baby, I will be adopting him as my legal son. Gabriel said to call our son Jesus. I am honored to do so, and I am honored to be your husband."

Mary beamed with joy. She knew Joseph was a sincere and observant Jew, as she was, and that he would honor their tradition and do all he could to support her and her baby. She felt secure and blessed and serene. She believed Joseph's dream about her baby's inheriting the "Holy Spirit."

Later that evening, suddenly, the door to their small room had been flung open. Startled, Joseph and Mary had sat up in their small bed. Baby Jesus was sleeping in a cleaned trough by their bedside. A large dark-faced man wearing a heavy robe with military ornaments held a large sword in the open doorway. He quickly studied the startled couple, the baby, and the four walls. He grunted, nodded his head, and then backed away from the door. A smaller but more regal man with a kind face appeared at the door.

"Please don't be frightened," he said. "My guard was only checking to see if it was safe for me to come in. May I?"

Mary reached over and pulled her newborn protectively to her bosom. The stranger walked in and closed the door. He said, "Please forgive me, but I had to see what was in here." He glanced around and saw nothing unusual, a couple with an infant and a few meager possessions. The stranger's eyes settled upon Jesus, and he smiled at the comfort and peace that the baby exuded.

Joseph demanded, "What is it that you want?"

"I'm not sure," replied the stately man. "I'm an astrologer, and I have recently been counseling your king. As I've been traveling this night to Bethlehem, I have been transfixed by the bright light of a star that shines above this dwelling. I have studied the stars and their meanings for over forty years, and never have I seen a display of a star's light as I have on this night.

"From the star, a beam of light has pointed down to this area, and I have followed it to this humble room. It is as if a finger of light from night's Heaven has directed me to this destination although I know not why, except that for me, it portends an occurrence of great significance."

Mary said, "Perhaps it is for you to pay homage to this holy child who, as you can see, is surely a gift from Heaven."

The stranger chuckled. "I am from the east, and when a child is born, it is the custom to give gifts to the children, who, I agree with you, are indeed gifts from Heaven."

The stranger clapped his hands twice. The large guard appeared at the doorway. The stranger said something in Aramaic to him. The guard left and quickly reappeared with a small jeweled box. The stranger placed the box at the foot of the small bed and said, "I see by your garments that you are Jews and very poor. Herod the Great harbors enormous fears of ancient prophecies: according to the stars, a Jewish Messiah will soon be born. If this occurs, the child would someday replace him as King of the Jews and sit on the throne of David. Already death squads are being assembled. They will be dispatched to kill all male Jewish children from newborn infants up to two years old."

Mary held the baby Jesus tighter to her bosom upon hearing the astrologer's words.

The stranger cast his kind and intelligent eyes upon baby Jesus. "There is something that I feel is very special about this child and this night and the brilliance of the star. One cannot explain such feelings of wonder and my compulsion to help you. Please accept this box and the gifts within it. You may find the box's contents financially useful as you seek proper protection for your 'holy child' as you travel to safer areas. Please accept my gift and forgive me for disturbing your evening." The kindly astrologer smiled with satisfaction and said, "All things have a purpose, and I feel that the star's light has led me here to fulfill a significant purpose, and now I have. I shall be on my way." He nodded once and closed the door behind him.

Mary's fingers became aware of the last of the raw wool that unwound from the crook of her elbow. She bent over and pulled another bundle of wool from the basket and wrapped it around her arm as before, then reset her spindle and began the twisting-threading sequences again. The air was hot and still. Mary frowned as she thought of the days following Jesus's birth and his secret circumcision ceremony.

Reports of Herod the Great's death squads and his searching legions were sweeping though all of Judea with the soldiers' horrific orders to kill all male children under two years of age. Herod's heinous act was called the "Massacre of the Innocents," and it had terrified Mary to know that soldiers were coming to kill her holy infant.

Mary's thoughts turned to when the cantor had finished the circumcision ritual by holding up the baby and saying, "Yeshua bar Yosef" (Jesus, son of Joseph), sanctifying the legality of Jesus's name and his lawfully designated father, Joseph. Mary had planned to flee the region after Jesus's circumcision, and they left that night.

Mary remembered her relief at their escape. Now, despite the awning, small beads of perspiration formed on her forehead under the high midday sun. They had escaped the sure death of their newborn then, but now she recalled the most recent threat to her son, Jesus. Images formed in her aura of her recent visit to Nazareth's chief rabbi upon his return from a trip to Jerusalem. "Is it true that Herod wants to kill my son?" she had asked the rabbi.

"Yes, it is. Herod Antipas has sent his armies to arrest your son. I am afraid the situation for him is hopeless."

Angst and depression filled Mary's aging, weary face. The chief rabbi's words echoed through her, and then fearful feelings of hopelessness filled her heart. She thought of the overwhelming power of Herod the Great and his relentless murdering of thousands of innocents to protect his throne from her son, and now, Herod's son, Herod Antipas, once again was sending armies to arrest her Jesus. This time she was not able to protect him as she had been before.

Mary clenched her teeth as other old fears surfaced. Images appeared in her aura of Herod the Great's wrath and vengeance against an uprising of protesting Jews. They had looted his palace of weapons from the town of Sepphoris, just a short four-mile walk from Nazareth. The newly armed protesters had created pockets of revolt and opposition to Rome. Mary was only fourteen years old at that time.

Mary stiffened. She pressed her spine against the back of the wooden chair and grimaced as she visualized the overwhelmingly brutal reaction of Rome and Herod as they mercilessly crushed the opposition. Three legions from Syria and auxiliary troops that totaled over twenty thousand burned Sepphoris to the ground. Afterward, all the inhabitants were sent into slavery as punishment. Over two thousand of the men who had revolted were crucified. All of Galilee was in a state of dread from the daily trauma of seeing those dying men nailed to crosses lining all the main roads or set on hillsides to serve as an indelible reminder to anyone who would even think of challenging Rome's authority and power.

Mary visualized herself walking to the market and seeing her neighbor's son nailed to a cross. He was limp with death. She looked down at the ground as she walked on, too sick in her gut to look at the others hanging from the crosses above. As she proceeded, Mary heard a moan and looked up. Her eyes widened in fright as she dropped her market basket. It was her fifteen-year-old cousin, Asa. He had nothing to do with the revolt! Mary cried out, "Asa!"

Asa barely opened one eye. He seemed to recognize her, but she couldn't be sure. She reached out a hand toward him. Asa's face became blurry in her memory's vision, recalling the recent words of the chief rabbi's response to her asking if it was true that Herod had sent his armies to arrest her son: "Yes it is... I am afraid the situation for him is hopeless."

Mary dropped her spindle and in concert with her thoughts, reached out her raw-wool-clad arm as she had then reached out to Asa on the cross. The blurry image of Asa in her mind's vision became the image of her adult son – it was Jesus who was nailed to the cross. Mary gasped.

"NO! Don't think that!" Jesus exclaimed as he stood and approached his mother.

The sudden voice from "nowhere" startled Mary. She turned to see her son coming toward her. She gasped again and said in a whisper, "My sweet Jesus. You're alive." Mary fainted as the last word left her lips. Jesus caught her in his arms before she could fall to the ground.

Jesus carried his mother into her humble home. He passed her loom with its hanging lengths of yarn. He passed her small kitchen area and saw a bowl of olives, a cloth half covering a piece of cheese, and a salted fish on a plate next to the fresh baked bread. Jesus carried her into the sparse bedroom and gently laid her on the bed. He sat on the bed next to her and tenderly caressed her face, recalling the images of Mary's traumatic life that he had just witnessed.

In a few moments, Mary opened her eyes and smiled weakly at her son. She squeezed his arm and said, "It is you! You're alive! Thank God."

"Yes, I am alive and well. You needn't worry or harbor fear for me. I am protected by my heavenly Father." He took her hand and kissed it and then gently stroked the side of her face. He said, "I know of your torment and the sacrifices that you've made for me. The love and protection that you've offered me have served God's will. You've been a guardian angel to me."

Mary sat up and hugged her son. Jesus embraced her and felt her frail body tremble. She pulled him closer and anxiously said, "We must hide you! Herod's soldiers will come and take you; then you will be gone forever."

Jesus held her shoulders and looked into her eyes. He spoke with great conviction, "Most assuredly, I say to you, Blessed Mother, my fate will be divinely guided by the will of God and not by the will of men or kings or Romans."

Mary was chagrined although her voice remained adamant. "You don't understand!"

Jesus saw her mind's thought-forms of the dying, anguished, crucified men lining endless roads and hillsides interspersed with flashes of infants and toddlers being slaughtered. He felt her surge of urgency and panic. He understood how firmly her mind had bonded with her emotions so that now those times were as real as they had been in her past. Jesus spoke softly and compassionately. "I do understand. Truly, I do."

"No one but a mother can know," Mary argued. "You say you understand, but when you were an infant, things happened that I've never told you of. You must now hear me.

"Your father, Joseph had dreams of angels who spoke to him. After your birth, they told us to flee Bethlehem and take you to Egypt to hide you from Herod the Great, who sought to destroy you. He massacred so many innocent babies because one of them might have been you. You were spared. We stayed in Egypt until Herod died. But without a doubt, his sons will use their soldiers to kill you as their father would have if ever they had discovered your identity."

Jesus nodded that he understood her reasons for thinking and feeling as she did. He said, "Herod Antipas and Pontius Pilate have already used all their resources to find and arrest me, but now they no longer do so and I am here with you. I have told you, you need not fear for my safety. I am in the hands of my heavenly Father, your Lord of lords."

Mary sighed, "It's true that you're alive and I thank God, our King in Heaven." She squeezed Jesus's hands and bowed her head in a silent moment of gratitude. Mary looked up into Jesus's compassionate eyes;

she smiled proudly and said, "I knew you were always highly perceptive and gifted in many ways. Now that you are grown, you've become stronger in spirit and filled with greater wisdom. The grace of God has always been upon you – and I have always cherished and protected you with the knowledge that you were the one to become the Anointed One, our people's Messiah." Mary's body shuddered as she spoke the last words.

Jesus felt the awesome burden of responsibility for his safety that she had carried from when she was only a teenager to this day. He leaned over, kissed her cheek, and said lovingly, "I thank you and bless you for all you have done. No one could have done more. I am here now with you as proof that you have succeeded in fulfilling God's will."

Mary relaxed. She smiled and said, "You live. For that, my heart and soul are pleased." Then she stiffened. "But now that other people know of you, I know it's only a matter of time before Herod will take you from me and kill you." She turned away and looked down.

Jesus gently turned her toward him, "Again I say, you need not fear that Herod could ever harm me. All of his soldiers and all of Rome's armies together are less than a single hair on a flea compared to the unlimited power of The Force that has created the heavens and earth and that now protects me."

Mary nodded skeptically. "A part of me felt that way also when I was a young mother to you. I would tell some people who I thought might understand that I had seen angels and spoken with them. Later on, I realized that those people thought me mad. When your father, my dearly beloved Joseph, died, I spoke no more about your birth. I blended in with the people here in Nazareth. I have always lived as quiet and inconspicuous a life as possible. As good Jews, we always followed the customs, even going to Jerusalem every year for the Feast of Passover."

Mary's voice became assertive, "But always, every day and night, I was in fear that people would recognize you as the Messiah and that you would be taken away. That's why every time you showed signs of your gifts, I dismissed them and discouraged you from displaying such 'nonsense.'" Mary kissed Jesus's hand, looked at him shyly and asked, "Remember?"

Jesus nodded in acknowledgement.

Mary continued, "I called it 'make believe' when you said that you heard God talking to you. And I told you that all children say the same things and that it doesn't really mean anything."

Jesus nodded again and said, "Yes, I remember. I believed you, and those beliefs protected me then. Now it doesn't matter what anyone says, for I know that the Word, God's sacred communication to me, is the truest and purest of all things on earth." Jesus kissed her other cheek and said, "Someday people will realize that children do hear God speaking to them and guiding them. Most adults become deaf to His communications because they no longer listen with their hearts."

Mary smiled and said, "Spoken with the wisdom of a child."

Jesus took Mary's hand and kissed it and then said, "I am no longer that child. You must look at me with different eyes."

Mary replied, "You will always be my child." She brought up Jesus's hand to kiss it but stopped and held it before her. Her eyes gazed at the sleeve of his robe. With her other hand, she felt the fine fabric between her fingers and marveled at it. Mary asked, "Where did you get this robe? I've never seen thread spun so perfectly." She bent closer and intently examined the soft cloth. "I've never seen a large piece of fabric woven without the tiniest flaw. Please stand up and let me see all of it."

Jesus complied. Mary got up and limping, walked around Jesus, surveying the entire robe. She faced Jesus and looked curiously at him for a moment, and then she bent over and picked up the hem and studied it. "It can't be!" she exclaimed. Mary lifted Jesus's arm over his head and carefully ran her finger from the robe's elbow past his armpit to his waist. She repeated her inspection on the other side, then put her hand over her mouth in amazement. Mary shook her head in disbelief. She said, "I don't know how it's possible. Your robe has no seams, not even the hem...and it fits your body perfectly in every way."

Mary implored, "Where was this made?"

Jesus smiled and said, "In Heaven."

Mary poked him with her finger and said, "Don't toy with your mother. You must tell me who made this for you."

"My Father," Jesus replied.

"Your father, my dear beloved Joseph, is long gone," Mary said. "Please don't jest with me. Tell me who made this."

Jesus answered, "I did tell you. It was not my earth-father, who adopted me; my robe was created by my heavenly Father and given to me as a gift."

"No!" Mary exclaimed, "you mustn't say such things." She began to weep. Jesus put his arm around her shoulder to console her. She pulled away from him and pointed to her loom with its myriad of dangling threads. Her tears flowed. She said, "The day I heard that Herod had sent his soldiers to arrest you – that was the day I started to make the cloth for a robe for you."

Mary sniffed in her tears. She whispered, "That robe was not to be for you to wear...but to be put on your grave. My final gift to you."

Jesus felt the deep pangs of Mary's years of suffering from the terror of her premonitions that he would be crucified as countless others had been before him. He held her hands tightly and again looked into her eyes. "Please, think no more of any harm coming to me. Would a loving mother or father not do all in their power to protect their child? Do you think that my loving heavenly Father with all of His mighty powers would do less to protect me, His Son? Although your ears refuse to listen, your soul shall know this, and some degree of comfort will be yours."

Mary's disquiet stilled and she relaxed a little bit. The sincerity in Jesus's eyes brought her a moment of peace. He relaxed his grip on her hands. Mary smiled and said softly, "You've always been a God-child to me."

The moment quickly passed, and Mary reverted to her fortress of denial. She held Jesus's hands in hers over their heads and said, "Look at you, a grown man – and too thin. What kind of a mother will others think I am? Come, eat. You must eat." Mary stood and pulled Jesus toward the small kitchen area.

"Have one more slice of bread," Mary said as she picked up the knife and began to slice another piece. She crookedly extended her painful arthritic finger because it wouldn't bend with the other fingers that had grasped the knife.

Jesus reached over and gently held her wrist. He said, "Enough. I can eat no more. But I can help the finger that you cannot bend."

Mary pulled her hand away and said, "Oh, don't bother about me. I'll be all right."

"Please," Jesus implored and reached for her hand. He placed it on the table and then gently stroked the red, swollen knuckle of her index finger.

Mary sighed, "Your touch is warm and soothing."

Jesus continued to stroke her finger, but it remained crooked, red and swollen. He thought of the goat herder and his ten arthritic fingers that were far worse than Mary's. How easy it was for him to straighten out all of the goat herder's fingers, but now he was unable to fix a single finger for his mother.

Mary pulled her hand away. She stood up with a wince of pain from her hip and then took the bowl of olives from the table and placed it on the kitchen counter. Jesus studied her aura as she turned her back to him. He realized that the rigidity of her crooked finger and his inability to help reflected the rigidity of her automatic resolve to protect him from being known as a true healer. He also realized that he would not be able to ease the pain in her hips. Jesus knew that those who needed healing must have the desire to be healed and the faith necessary to receive his healing energy. He could not heal another against their will. Mary's overly strong protective motherly instincts denied Jesus's ability to heal her. Again, he felt her intense worry for his safety harden like a rock.

Mary returned to the table and sat. Jesus took both of her hands in his and said, "I know your love for me is strong and sacred. As my earth-mother, your desire to protect me has been relentless, but I say to you that you may now let go of that need to protect me, for my heavenly Father's love and protection are all I need to carry me safely on my mission."

Jesus gently kissed Mary's hands again and said, "Fear not for me, for I know that His love is true and He will not forsake me regardless of how threatening outward circumstances may appear."

Mary ignored his words and spoke for hours about Jesus's brothers and sisters and some of the neighbors and their trials and troubles. To avoid arousing her inherent fears for his safety, Jesus did not speak of his healings or of John the Baptist.

After a while, they shared tea together, and as the afternoon grew later, Mary said, "I need to get some things for the Sabbath. We should go to the market now before it closes."

At the small marketplace, familiar vendors and townspeople greeted Mary. They also greeted Jesus in a courteous but restrained manner. While Mary was purchasing lentils, Jesus's keen sense of hearing allowed him to hear two women speaking nearby. One said, "Isn't that Mary's boy? The one who speaks with demons?"

The other said, "Yes, it is. Why did he come back?"

Mary put the lentils in her carry basket, and she and Jesus walked on. Two men who had been eyeing Jesus walked behind them. One said to the other, "Herod didn't want him after all. He's only a carpenter, the son of a carpenter."

The other man said, "It was a rumor that he was the Messiah, but look at him: he's only a poor man. Herod arrested John the Baptist. He's the one who must be the suspected Messiah."

Jesus took hold of Mary's arm and escorted her away from the men. He had surveyed the people of the town and was amazed at their lack of faith. He said to her, "Time is fleeting. I must leave for the Sea of Galilee."

"You just got here!" Mary exclaimed. "Why must you go? Your brothers will soon return from the fields, and we can all eat together."

"The work of my Father is a priority that I must attend to. I can do no good here. I must go now."

Mary put down her basket and squeezed both of Jesus's hands tightly. She pleaded, "Please, stay a little longer, at least for the Sabbath. I've been with you so short a time! Please, I beg you."

Jesus sighed and relented, "Just for the Sabbath."

⸺⊂⊃⸺

At the synagogue, it was Jesus's turn to stand and read from the scriptures. An attendant handed him the scroll of the prophet Isaiah, which had been arbitrarily chosen earlier that morning. Jesus unrolled it and read, "The Spirit of the Lord is upon me; He has anointed me to preach Good News to the poor; He has sent me to heal the brokenhearted and to announce that captives shall be set free and that the blind shall see, the oppressed shall be released, and that God is ready to give blessings to all who come to him."

Jesus rolled up the scroll and stood next to his brother James. He said, "Today this scripture is fulfilled in your hearing it from me."

Many were amazed at what they had witnessed. They had heard but had not believed the rumors of Jesus's miraculous healings, and now he read the scroll that was handed to him by their synagogue attendant without knowing its content. One man asked another, "Isn't this Joseph's poor son? Who is he trying to fool?"

Jesus stood and addressed the congregation. "Surely you will quote to me the proverb, 'Physician, heal thyself' – meaning 'Why don't you do miracles here in your hometown as you have done elsewhere?' But I solemnly declare to you that no prophet is accepted in his hometown."

The synagogue's members looked scornfully at Jesus. Jesus continued, "Remember how Elijah the prophet used a miracle to help the widow of Zarephath, who was a foreigner from the land of Sidon? There were many Jewish widows also needing help in those many years of famine because of the absence of rain, yet Elijah was not sent to them."

The members looked at each other with raised eyebrows and scornfully shook their heads. Jesus continued nonetheless, "And you should also remember the time that many in Israel suffered from leprosy in the time of Elisha the prophet, yet not one of them was cleansed – only Naaman the Syrian."

The men became angry at Jesus for implying that foreigners and strangers were more worthy of a prophet's healings and miracles than they – good Jews at a Sabbath service.

Jesus continued, "Because you say the words of a prayer or read Scriptures out loud, you think of yourselves as righteous, but I will tell you a story and let you judge what makes a person righteous and who shall inherit eternal life."

The congregation looked suspiciously at Jesus as he spoke. Some clenched their fists in anger. Jesus said, "It is written in the law that 'Thou shall love the Lord thy God with all thy heart and with all thy soul and with all thy strength and with all thy mind, and thy neighbor as thyself."

Upon hearing the words of the scripture, the men nodded in agreement. Those with clenched fists relaxed them. One man, wanting to justify himself because he felt that he was a good neighbor to those in Nazareth, asked, "And who is my neighbor?"

In reply, Jesus said, "A man was traveling from Jerusalem to Jericho when he fell into the hands of robbers. They beat him severely and then stripped him of his clothes and left him lying half dead beside the road. A Jewish priest happened to be going down the same road, and when he saw the man, he passed by on the other side. Soon a Levite temple assistant came by and saw the man, but he too passed by on the other side of the road. But a Samaritan, as he traveled, came to where the man was, and when he saw the man in dire need, he felt deep compassion for him."

The congregation stirred uneasily. Samaritans were despised. Judeans would have no dealings with them because the Samaritans had rejected the Temple of Jerusalem because in the Samaritans' interpretation of the scriptures, Mount Gerizim was God's chosen place instead.

Jesus spoke loudly and clearly. "The Samaritan soothed the man's wounds with oil and bandaged them. Then he put the man on his donkey and brought him to an inn and tended to him that night. The next day, the Samaritan took out two silver coins and gave them to the innkeeper and told him, 'Look after this man. When I return, I will reimburse you for any extra expense you may have incurred.'"

The congregation stared coldly at Jesus. Jesus looked back and said, "Now I ask you, which of these three men who passed by on the road was a true neighbor to the bandit's victim?"

The congregation of men became riled. They felt that Jesus was proclaiming that they, as Judean men, were not true good neighbors and did not follow the law that prescribed that they should love their neighbors as they loved themselves. Rather, a hated Samaritan heeded the law instead.

Jesus said, "I say to you to do the same as the Good Samaritan."

Upon hearing this, stung by wrath, the men mobbed Jesus. They surrounded him and herded him out the synagogue's door. Jesus did not resist. They cursed him. They pushed and shoved him to the crest of the hill upon which Nazareth was built. There, in the mob's growing anger, they made ready to cast him headlong down the cliff. The crowd surged forcibly behind Jesus as they herded him toward the edge.

At that moment, Jesus seemed to disappear. Everyone looked about in confusion. They only saw each other. Some peered down the cliff and saw no one. Some thought they saw twin images of their neighbors. When they turned to look at the other twin image to confirm what they had seen and then turned back again, the first twin image was no longer there. They searched frantically, looking among themselves. But Jesus passed through the midst of them and went on his way to Galilee.

35

The Sea of Galilee is a huge pear-shaped lake thirteen miles in length by seven miles across at its widest extremity. It is surrounded by mountains and subject to sudden storms and treacherous squalls caused by frequent shifts in atmospheric pressure. The water is sweet and spawns numerous varieties of fish that usually kept the seaside towns such as Tiberius, Bethsaida, and Capernaum prosperous because of Judea's continuous demand for salted fish.

A man rowed in a small boat twenty feet from the shore, a long fishnet tied to his boat. Another man walked along the shore pulling the other end of the net to capture fish that were feeding among the bottom plants. The man on shore tugged hard on the half-filled net, and the other man strained as he rowed parallel to the shore.

The man rowing looked up and saw "him." He trembled and stood up in the boat and pointed to "him." The man on shore called out to the man in the boat. "Why do you point at me?"

"N-n-n-not you, Andrew. It's h-h-h-him!"

Andrew turned around and saw Jesus smiling back at him. Simon sat back down and started rowing to shore. He shouted out to Andrew as he rowed, "It's the M-M-M-Messiah! I t-t-told you h-h-h-he w-w-w-would b-b-b-be here soon."

Andrew dropped the slackening net, letting his captured fish escape. He stood in awe. Simon came ashore and bowed before Jesus. He kissed Jesus's robe and said, "W-w-w-what will you h-h-h-have us d-d-d-do for you?"

"Come, follow me," Jesus replied, "and I will make you fishers of men."

Jesus started walking along the shoreline. Simon and Andrew left their fishnet in the water and followed him. As they walked, Jesus felt the sincere depths of the men's powerful faith and belief in him, unlike his experience with the men of Nazareth. Jesus quivered in humbled exaltation at their affirmation of him as their Messiah, knowing that his mission was proceeding.

In the Wilderness of Judea, when Jesus was fully one with the divine Light of the Holy Spirit, he had realized that to fulfill his mission, he needed to build a critical mass of people who would passionately embrace The Word. In turn, they would be able to initiate forces that would change the course of mankind's misdirected path. Mankind's continued use of violence and might to determine right would eventually lead to the end of man's days on earth. Jesus knew he had to confirm, reaffirm, and solidify the faith of his inner circle and do whatever was necessary to empower his disciples to go forth against all challenges, no matter the dangers. They needed to acquire the power of absolute faith to propel mankind toward greater balance and harmony rather than the doom and destruction at the end of their present path.

As Jesus walked briskly ahead of Simon and Andrew, he felt the power of their belief in him, and he in turn became more empowered, unlike what had happened with the doubters of Nazareth. Jesus, Simon, and Andrew soon came upon a large fishing boat anchored in a deep cut along the shoreline. There, many workmen labored on repairs to the ship. Two men, James and John, were mending the ship's large fishing net and appeared disinterested in their task.

James looked up and saw Simon and Andrew following Jesus. He tapped his brother's shoulder and pointed to the three men. "Look," he said, "it's him! He's the one I dreamed about last night. It's the Messiah!" Jesus approached the stern of the fishing vessel where the large net they were working on was stored. Without hesitation, he called to the two brothers, "Come, follow me."

They immediately dropped the net and their mending tools and climbed down off the boat. Their father, Zebedee, the boat's owner, called out to them from the bow, "Where are you going? There's work to be done!"

Jesus had started to walk on, Simon and Andrew following. James and John ran to catch up. James called back to his father, "We have to leave now. This is the man we need to follow."

Jesus's aura and body had become a vessel of divine Truth – a pure and universal Truth that resonated with an all-penetrating "vibration" that awakened and stirred the "Seeds of Truth" that all people are endowed with as an integral component of their gift of life. That extrasensory and compelling "vibration" was the charismatic attraction that people who were open of heart felt and were attracted to in Jesus's presence.

Within a few hours, the four future disciples following Jesus became eight as the group collected the other members who were scattered in the seaside town. Philip, Nathaniel, Bartholomew, and Mark soon joined them. Luke was the last to be gathered to make it nine. Luke, upon first seeing Jesus, said, "Thank God! You're alive!"

Jesus laughed, "Of course I am – as you can see."

Luke embraced Jesus excitedly and said, "I've hungered for your presence."

"And this body hungers for a good meal," replied Jesus.

Luke said, "I was just about to go back to our house. John and Peter should have dinner prepared by now. Matthew, Seth, and Joseph are there also." Luke looked at the other men and said, "They usually make extra food for the next day. Come, I'll show you where we've been staying."

As Jesus and his disciples approached the small house, a boy was fetching well water in a bucket. The boy looked up and shouted with glee, "You're here!" He ran up to Jesus and said, "I knew you'd come today! You told me so in my dream."

Jesus knelt, embraced Seth, and said, "A part of me will always be with you." He smiled approvingly at Seth and said, "And now you have become a young man who will make an excellent rabbi."

Seth stood proudly and said, "I can say all my prayers and sing my chants without a single mistake to the satisfaction of the chief rabbi. That's because when I was tested, I felt your presence next to me. Thank you for being there spiritually for me."

The men marveled at Seth's faith and gratitude toward Jesus.

That night after dinner, Jesus stood and spoke from the corner of the dining room. All eight chairs in the household were filled, and the rest of the men sat cramped together on the floor. Each one in the room had had recurring shared dreams of Jesus. They all stared with rapt attention as he continued to speak. "...so when you see me in a vision or in your dreams or hear me in your thoughts, know that I am communicating with you in God's way and that I lovingly offer you guidance when asked."

Joseph enthusiastically acknowledged Jesus's words and said, "I know that you have shown me blessed ways to think and feel so that I do not fear for my beloved Seffira. As you've suggested in my dreams, when worry comes to my mind, I think of the cherished moments that I have shared with her, and that brings me peace and comfort. I thank you for your guidance."

Peter asked, half sarcastically, "Have you also been in Pontius Pilate's or Herod's dreams?"

Jesus laughed and replied, "They haven't asked me for help. However, those who know me or will know of me may ask for my help, and in one form or another, they will receive it."

Andrew asked, "But, Master, as others learn about you, how will it be possible for you, as Messiah for all of Israel, to communicate with the multitudes of people who will surely ask you to help them with their individual problems?"

Jesus replied, "The guidance that I give is guidance from my Father. In every instant of the universe, God's words of guidance are available to those who seek it. My Father has embodied The Word in me, and all who desire The Word through me may receive it in prayer, thought, or dreams."

Jesus continued, "The guidance that I give is not to attain power over others nor to attain hoards of gold. My work is intended for people to gain spiritual treasures that will enrich their lives. Again, I say to you that divine wisdom is simple. The message of The Word is universal – and that message is love, forgiveness, tolerance, and brotherhood. To act with love is divine; God is love. So I say to you, act godly by acting with love."

Jesus raised up his palms to everyone and said, "Those are all the questions I will answer for tonight. Tomorrow I will be leaving for Capernaum."

"Why go there, Master?" asked James.

"Because that's where my beloved Judas is," Jesus responded.

Some of the men, especially Peter, felt a tinge of jealousy that their Messiah appeared to favor Judas. Luke spoke up, "Judas has gone to Capernaum to find larger quarters. He told us that you had instructed him to do so in his dream."

After the morning prayers and breakfast, Jesus and eight of his followers, including James and his brother John, got into a large skiff with a small sail and prepared to cross the five miles over the Sea of Galilee to Capernaum. Simon and John loaded Simon's cart with provisions from the house. They, with Matthew, Seth, and Luke, were to travel by land to Capernaum. Joseph went to get Seffira; they would leave together a little later. The others also planned to make arrangements to meet in Capernaum.

The morning sea was calm, and the pristine blue water reflected the clear blue sky. When the provisions were secured in the boat, four of the men took their places on the rowing seats and slid their oars into the oarlocks. As they pulled on their oars, Jesus and his party pulled away from the shoreline. James and his brother John sat in the bow; Jesus sat on the rear seat in the stern. Two hours later, Jesus fell into a peaceful slumber. After a while, a wind began to build, pushing a bank of dark clouds from the mountains over the sea. The men set the small sail and the skiff picked up speed. The rowers were glad to rest their oars.

John pointed to Jesus and whispered to his brother James, "He seems to look like an ordinary man. He sure sleeps like one. Can he really be the Messiah?"

"You've heard the people speak of his miracles as I have," James replied. "And the dream I had was so real; he must be the one."

"But how do you really know?" John asked.

"I just believe in him. Can you not feel his authority when he speaks and how he explains things in a way that gives greater meaning to our lives and destiny?"

John replied, "He does enlighten me, but so have other teachers. Maybe we acted too hastily leaving our father the way we did. He will not understand."

James replied, "If you had had the same dream I had, you'd feel differently."

John shook his head in doubt. "I'm just not sure."

Ten minutes later, the winds became gusty, the full sail strained, and the bow of the skiff undulated in the rolling waves that had formed. After another ten minutes, the winds had become so strong that the sail was taken down for fear the mast would break. The four men rowing pulled with all their strength to keep the boat headed into the waves lest they capsize. Jesus continued to sleep peacefully.

Another ten minutes passed, the sky blackened, and larger waves began to crash over the bow. John and James moved from the bow to the center of the boat for safety and to stay out of the cold spray. They and the others who weren't rowing began to bail out the water that was starting to swamp the boat. Great fear filled them all. Jesus slept on.

In a few more minutes, the winds became furious. Violent whitecaps pushed by the winds covered the sea, and high frothy waves broke over the bow. The men bailed frantically in a losing battle to keep the water from swamping the boat. As their fears grew, faith in their safety evaporated. The rowers strained harder, but they could barely keep the boat headed into the waves. Everyone trembled in fear of their lives, but Jesus slept on.

Peter reached over to Jesus and shook him. "Wake up!" he shouted.

Jesus opened his eyes. Peter implored, "Teacher, don't you care if we drown?"

Jesus looked at Peter and shook his head in disapproval. "You must believe that when you are in my presence, no harm will come to you." Jesus stood; his balance in the roiling boat was steady. His hands rose up to the sky, rebuking the wind and the waves: "Quiet. Be still." In less than a minute the wind died down, and the water became still as glass. The black clouds faded to a light gray.

The men in the boat were awed by what he had just done but were still trembling and terrified. Jesus said to them, "Why are you so afraid? Do you still lack faith?"

The men looked at each other in disbelief. John said to his brother James, "Who is this man who speaks to the wind and the sea, which obey him?"

James replied, "He is truly the Messiah."

<hr />

The men continued to take turns rowing in the calm water. The sail sagged from lack of wind. They were nearing Capernaum, and all but Jesus were exhausted. When the men changed rowers again, Jesus moved to the bow of the boat and sat facing the sea with his back to the others. James said to Peter, "You've seen the Messiah perform many miracles. Don't you feel privileged to have had that experience?"

"Yes, I do feel chosen and special. The scriptures say that our people are the 'chosen' people by God Almighty. And all of us in the boat, including the Master, are Galilean Jews. That makes us more special."

Jesus turned around and asked the group, "And do you know what purpose God has 'chosen' us for to fulfill?"

John eagerly answered, "We have been chosen to destroy the Romans, and you will bring fire and brimstone to burn and putrefy their dwellings and bodies. We will be victorious and rule the land."

The others in the boat nodded in agreement.

Jesus said sternly, "Do not romanticize your calling, for it's a treacherous and difficult path you must walk. Do not feel so special and above others, for all people have their own godly gifts. Your mission is to guide all people to use their gifts in the best way possible, and that way is with acceptance and love."

James said, "But we can't possibly love Romans and Gentiles. Those nonbelievers can't be included."

"I said, 'all people'! That means all people of all nations," Jesus retorted. "Doesn't anyone listen with their hearts to the words they hear with their ears?" He turned his back on them and stared at the approaching Capernaum shoreline.

James and John bowed their heads. All were silent as the tired rowers dipped their oars into the sea and pulled. Soon they were fifty yards from the shore. A lone man was walking toward the sea. Peter squinted to focus on the man and said, "It's Judas!" Peter grinned at the man next to him and said, "He's the only one of our group who is not a

Galilean." Peter sat up proudly and boasted, "All of us in this boat are Galileans, even the Messiah."

Jesus turned, his face scornful. He sternly ordered, "Stop rowing."

They stopped. Jesus stood and said, "I can stay in this boat no longer." He pointed to Judas on the shore and said, "That man listens to me with his heart, and so he understands far better than those of you who think you're superior. When you're ready to listen to me with your hearts, then come ashore."

Jesus sat up on the side of the boat. He turned and swung his legs over the water. His feet touched the top of the glass-still water. Then Jesus stood on the sea's surface, but he did not sink. The men in the boat gasped and watched in stunned awe as Jesus walked upon the water toward Judas.

Judas rubbed his eyes to make sure his sight was unclouded. He stared in amazement as Jesus casually walked on the water toward him. Jesus stepped upon the shore and approached Judas, who stood frozen in wonder and reverence at the unbelievable sight he had just witnessed. When Jesus came within two feet of Judas, Judas dropped to his knees and kissed both of Jesus's feet and then looked up at Jesus and said, "My sweet loving Lord. My life is yours."

Jesus grasped Judas's shoulders, pulled him up to eye level, and replied, "No, dear Judas, your life is yours. It's God's gift to you. I can't take it, for its wrong to take a life in servitude."

"You are the Anointed One," Judas said. "Thy will is my will. To walk on water is a miracle."

"To walk on water is a matter of one's faith. People do not see beneath the surface of all things wherein their Source eternally dwells. They see but a moment of the surface and believe that is all there is to be perceived. What they see is less real than the greater unseen reality. That glorious all-sustaining reality must be felt with the eyes of faith. The depth of my faith allows me to see the Source of all things – and that Source is what I walked upon – which is far more solid than rock or the mere liquid surface that others see."

Capernaum – a town of over five thousand, mainly Jewish inhabitants – was located between Herod Antipas's territories and his brother Herod Philip's lands. The seaside town sat between the cities of Alexandria and Damascus on a major trade route. Commercial fishing fleets made bountiful catches that brought prosperity to the people. Unlike rural Nazareth, the more populous Capernaum was cosmopolitan, and the riches of abundant trade caused many Roman tax offices to be established there. Roman centurions and their hundreds of troops were ever-present. Public buildings were interspersed with private homes in an orderly fashion.

Judas walked with Jesus to the large house that he had rented for their base. The other men followed sheepishly a few paces behind. The stone house was plastered with lime and clay; its roof of reeds and sticks needed constant repair, but overall, the home offered adequate shelter against Capernaum's cold winter rains and the summer's torrid heat. The house's rooms surrounded a large inner courtyard. Green trees lined the town's streets, and lush agricultural fields were nearby.

Jesus surveyed the home with Judas and gave his approval. The two women who had prepared the dinner meal were dismissed, and all ate heartily. The men marveled that Judas knew from his dream that they would be arriving this late afternoon and had planned a meal for them in advance. Jesus instructed his followers to tell no one of his presence until after the others arrived. He said to them, "So that you can teach what my heavenly Father's message is to the masses, I need to unite you all as one with The Word so that you can teach others as I will teach you. There is much for you to learn, and so you shall."

Everyone drank a lot of wine, and their mood lightened after the intense events of their perilous trek across the Sea of Galilee. After dinner, Jesus went alone with Judas to the courtyard. The stars sparkled brightly in the cool, clear night.

Judas had not engaged in the dinner conversation, but had kept his eyes on Jesus throughout the meal. He had retained his reverent state of heightened awe since he had seen Jesus walking on the water toward him. Jesus smiled at Judas and said, "You need not look at me the way you do."

Judas, his eyes wide with wonder replied, "You are unlike any man."

Jesus looked over both of his shoulders and laughed. "I haven't grown angel's wings."

"Master, I cannot look upon you as a man. Before I saw you for the first time in Jerusalem, I had dreamed of you manifesting from the brightest, most intense Light imaginable, and so you appeared to me from the desert as a blinding point of Light. After John baptized you, again the Light appeared, the river boiled with steam and churned with ice, and then you ran into the wilderness and were gone. The next time I see you in the flesh, you appear walking on water toward me. With the countless miracles I've seen you perform, how can I look upon you with anything but hallowed sight?"

"You see me as few do or can. You see beyond the flesh, Judas, because of your sincere love for me. I've told you before that my heavenly Father has given me the gift of Divine Union with His living waters. My walking on water should be no surprise to you. I became one with the water and the body of the sea. That body supported me as it does the countless drops of water that form the surface of the sea. I am of far less weight to the body of the water than one hair on the top of your head is to your own body."

"Master, you say what you have done so matter-of-factly, yet it is still beyond my understanding."

"I know," said Jesus. "Be not dismayed. There are other things you must know that are of greater importance. I want to share with you what my sight with the gift of the Holy Spirit has shown me of God's Light and the greater powers that men will have in the future."

Judas shook his head in doubt, "What could man ever do that would be greater than your deeds?"

Jesus's eyes widened. "Can you imagine a time when man will take a large ship full of people and fly in the sky from Jerusalem to Rome in less than an hour?"

Judas laughed. "Master, I think you've had a lot of wine."

Jesus replied, "Then you would not be able to imagine that in the future, man will be able to speak into a small tile and communicate with another person, or many people using their tiles thousand miles apart from each other?"

Judas stared at Jesus a moment, then laughed harder. "Now you are jesting with me."

Jesus's tone became very serious, "Believe in me when I tell you this, for those days will come, and the world will be in great danger if my mission is not fulfilled."

"What danger is that?" Judas asked.

When in the future, men build flying ships and tiles for distant talking, they will also build weapons with the power of exploding suns that can destroy cities in an instant. In the future, men will be able to bring great plagues against each other. My mission must serve its purpose for the present time, but it also needs to transcend today's times. Love and brotherhood must prevail, or mankind will create an end of days unto itself."

"What can I do, Master, to help you?" Judas asked.

"Continue to be my friend, believe in me, and always give me your loyalty," Jesus replied.

"You need never ask. It is yours 'til my death," Judas vowed solemnly.

Jesus looked at Judas and his aura, then hugged him lovingly and said, "I know what you say is true in your heart."

36

She seethed with anger and vengeance and then burst into a torrent of tears. She stared into the highly polished metal mirror. Gone were the handmaidens and servants who had carefully braided her long, silken hair into one hundred very small braids and threaded each end with a tiny gold sphere. The small braids were gathered and braided into larger clusters that were pinned between fanciful curls. Gone also were the royal cosmeticians who had exquisitely plied their craft on her dazzling young face. All the careful attention focused on her hair and face for the last six hours had been a welcome distraction. Now alone, she stared, transfixed, at her image. Her tears stopped momentarily. She smiled as she recalled the beginning of the session when the master cosmetologist had said, "You are one who has skin so perfect and natural beauty so radiant that it is almost a shame to put any covering over it."

Her smile widened as she turned to look at herself from a different angle. Her jewel-studded headband radiated light from the luminous glow of the flames of a dozen oil lamps. She thought of the last thing that the master cosmetologist had said when she was finished: "When we started, you were a seventeen-year-old natural rare beauty. Now, you are much more. You are more attractive than an exotic queen – the most alluring beauty in all the land."

She now turned to face her full reflection. In the silence of her room, her thoughts focused on the cause of the burning, nauseating feeling in the pit of her belly. Once more, her eyes sparked with anger as she stared at her reflection. Her lips curled in vengeance. Furiously, she pulled the gold-threaded net shawl off of her bare shoulders and threw it at the mirror. She put her hands to her face and again sobbed uncontrollably.

She cried until she could cry no more. She looked up into the mirror at the dark smudges and multicolored smears of make-up that had been exquisitely painted onto her face just an hour before. She clenched her teeth and shook her head violently at the now grotesque reflection facing her. With disgust at her image, she clawed at her upper arm. Her long, manicured fingernails left four bloody tracks on her silken skin.

She picked up the shears and grasped a handful of her decorated braids in her other hand. She raised the shears to cut off her hair.

"SALOME!" her mother yelled. Herodias quickly closed the door behind her and ran to her daughter. "Stop! Don't you dare cut your hair!" She wrenched the shears away. Salome stared at her mother a moment, then fell into her arms crying like a small child.

Herodias hugged her. She felt slipperiness on her daughter's arm and then looked at her own hand. "Blood?" she whispered. Herodias saw the fingernail tracks. "What has gotten into you? Are you crazy?"

"It's that Baptizer, John." Salome said between sobs. "My maidens were talking to each other as they were doing my hair. They spoke of John's disciples who visit him in the dungeon and how they have spread the word that John has condemned your marriage to Antipas. He says what you have done is against the Law of the Holy Scriptures. He has publicly shamed our royal bloodline. People talk and snicker. They make jokes about us." Salome pointed to the many types of finery in her elaborately appointed dressing room and said, "All of this is like make-up. It's a pretty painted cover-up, but if the people think us a mockery, what is the meaning of any of it?"

Herodias felt the sting of her daughter's words, for she, the intended target, felt even more pain and greater outrage than her daughter because of the Baptist's condemnations. She said, "I swear to you, that Baptizer's tongue will finally be stilled." She hugged her daughter again. Then her mind flew in all directions searching for a way to hasten the day when she could fulfill her oath.

Herodias's hand absentmindedly brushed against her daughter's scratched arm. Salome yelped with pain. "I'm sorry," Herodias said. "I'll clean up your arm and put some soothing oil on it." She went across the room and opened a cabinet filled with colorful glass vessels.

"There," Herodias said as she looked at Salome's bandaged arm, "that's better." Herodias took off a jewel-encrusted gold cylindrical amulet from her own forearm and slipped it over Salome's clawed slender upper arm. "Tell no one what you have done. Keep those scratches covered until they heal. Now let's get your face cleaned up. No one must ever see you as you look now."

As Herodias tended to her daughter, a plan took shape in her mind. When Salome was finally clean and refreshed, Herodias admired her daughter's flawless beauty and the radiant sparkle of the girl's youth. Herodias held a cluster of Salome's gold-tipped braids and shook her head. "To cut your hair as you were about to do would detract from your beauty. Losing your beauty is to lose your power."

"What do you mean, Mother?"

"You are the shapeliest and most attractive jewel in the king's court. Herod's eyes always go to you, as do everyone else's." Herodias snickered, "If I'm nearby, he tries to only glance at you, but I catch his lingering looks and…well, I know him only too well. Powerful men have powerful attractions. Antipas has a powerful attraction to you – and that, my dear Salome, betrays his weakness."

"I don't understand," Salome said.

"The weakness I speak of is a weakness of men. That weakness resides between their legs. A beautiful woman's power over that weakness is nestled between her legs." Herodias squeezed her daughter's hand. "You could become a queen."

"What are you getting at, Mother?"

Salome was reluctant at first, for Herod Antipas seemed an unattractive older man to her. But as Herodias reiterated John's tarnishing effect on their privileged royal world, Salome's lust for vengeance against John turned her reluctance into a resolve to follow her mother's plan to silence the Baptist forever.

Herodias sighed, relieved that her daughter understood all she had said. Proud of Salome's willingness, Herodias reassured her, "To be favored by a king for your first experience as a woman signifies your ability to capture his power. To have a king wield his sword as you bid is the greatest power that a woman can possess."

―――――

For two weeks after the balance of Jesus's growing inner circle had arrived in the Galilean city of Capernaum, Jesus continued to teach The Word to them. He would not allow them to venture out of the house that Judas had secured until he felt that they were ready to go forth with the true knowledge of God's intentions and able to teach the Gospel of His good news to the masses.

They had listened, captivated by their miracle worker Messiah and had learned much, but still, the deeper meanings needed to become more firmly rooted in their psyches. The midday air was mild and filled with the sweet scent of the sea that blended with the fragrances of the surrounding trees and growing crops. Jesus sat on a small bench in the courtyard; his followers sat on the ground and listened intently as he spoke. "And so it is imperative to teach the wisdom of our scriptures, our Jewish values and traditions, to the pagans and the Gentiles in a new way – a way that will uplift and enlighten them so that they will know our God and His Word. We will begin here in Galilee and then go forth to all of Judea and to all nations."

Nathaniel asked, "But Galilee is the land of the Gentiles, the non-believers. Why not go to Jerusalem, where our people are in dire need of your teachings and leadership? They have long awaited you, our Messiah, to fulfill the prophecies and bring in a New Age."

Jesus replied, "Because it is the non-believers upon whom you must fine-tune your teaching abilities, and they are the ones who need to be converted to believe in our God, the one God of All That Is."

Luke said, "But, Master, the Gentiles scorn our scriptures and make jest of our traditions."

Jesus replied, "That's because much of the essence of our scriptures' truth has been misunderstood, not only by Gentiles but by our people as well. Our laws have been practiced with too much wrath and malice toward many and not enough love for all. My new teachings separate out the chaff of distorted misunderstandings and emphasize the nourishing kernels of eternal truth."

Bartholomew responded bitterly, "The Gentiles are not worthy of our God."

Jesus stood and spoke adamantly. "It is my mission to convert not only the Gentiles but all of humanity to the 'good news' and The Word of our Lord." Jesus looked at each of his listeners and saw that many were still reluctant to embrace the Gentiles, who had chastised them for their sacred beliefs.

As the men sat in silence, Jesus said to them, "As you have heard from James and his brother John and the others in the boat, I have walked away from them – even on water – when they resisted the concept of inclusiveness for all people. So I say again, you must open your hearts and minds and know God's truth in my words: Gentiles, pagans, all of humanity are sons and daughters of the one Creator, our God. If you believe that I am the Christ, then believe that the Christ is in each of you as it is in all of God's children."

Some of the men shifted uncomfortably at the difficulty of accepting that those not of their faith could be included as God's children. Jesus saw that and reaffirmed the idea. "In time, you will learn and you will know and you will teach those who will listen as you spread this message of inclusiveness that I am destined to bring to mankind. You have been called and have chosen to receive The Word. Now, as my disciples, you must accept God's Word in your hearts, your minds, and your souls and know that God dwells within you and in all of humanity. Although some of you may doubt it now, you will soon go forth to teach and open the eyes of not only our Jewish nation but all the oppressed whom you can reach; and you will empower them with the truth: that God dwells within them and that that divine 'knowing' shall set them free."

Later that night Jesus lay on the ground in the courtyard in solitude, looking up at the twinkling stars of the Milky Way - that huge powdery white blanket of sparkling jewels of light over the Earth. Judas came out of the house, bringing Jesus a blanket, and said, "Master, I know you asked not to be disturbed, but it has gotten very cold, so I brought this for you."

Jesus smiled at Judas and pulled his heavenly Father's robe closer around his tunic and said, "I am warm enough, but thank you for your kind thoughtfulness." Jesus sat up, and Judas sat next to him and wrapped the blanket around his own shoulders. Jesus pointed up at the stars and said, "People don't see beneath the surface to where the source of all things eternally dwells. They see only a moment of the surface and believe that's all there is to be perceived."

"I see the stars," Judas replied. "What is it that you see differently?"

"I see the unseen reality underlying all things. It is greater and grander than the surface of physical substance that merely reflects a speck of the glorious inner wonder of God's life force."

"Do you see into the stars?" Judas asked.

"I feel the inside of the stars as you could see a man's beating heart as he walked and talked if that were possible for you. The oneness and union of my soul with 'All That Is' gives me that ability. It also connects me with a divine sense of time that is simultaneous."

Judas said, "That's like the 'God-time' that you've told me about. It's fascinating. Please tell me more."

"I've always appreciated your curiosity, Judas. You see deeper meanings that most people don't even think about."

"Please, Master, help me to understand how time can possibly be simultaneous."

"As I've said before," Jesus replied, "'God-time' possesses all past, present and future possibilities. Man chooses which piece of time they will embrace and forms their personal and collective reality in a string of flowing moments from those pieces. Each person views and uses their piece of time in their own creative way."

Judas stroked his beard in thought and said, "Except for sinners. They are not creative like those who follow the laws of the Torah."

"Creativity is a divine gift from the one Creator to all life forms. Sometimes sinners can be more creative than righteous men who follow prescribed laws. Waging great wars requires great creativity even if the consequences are destructive. Man makes judgments regarding sin and good and evil. God is All That Is, and all parts of All That Is are a part of God. God cannot sin against Himself, and so in divine terms – not man's definitions—no act is sinful."

"It's too hard for me to think that the atrocities that the Romans have plagued our people with are not sins," Judas said. "The universal love, forgiveness, tolerance, and brotherhood that you teach are very difficult to practice. I've been trying, but I can't emulate your ability to do so. If I'm having so much trouble doing so, then it would take a thousand years or more for mankind to do so."

"Dear Judas, it may take more than two thousand years, but we must begin now to set those changes in motion, and we must do so quickly, for my time in this body is short and I will soon have to leave this body."

Judas frowned in sadness and said, "It grieves me, Master, each time you speak of leaving."

Jesus smiled compassionately. "Do not fret for me, my beloved Judas; for who I am now, I was before my consciousness was called forth to become incarnate in this flesh. My Essence has existed when the earth was first born, I am here now with you; but my presence and message will remain after this flesh of my Essence fades from the sight of human eyes. After I am gone from physical existence, people will speak of an 'end of days' when they believe that I will return and save those who harbor belief in the end of times."

"But you are the Messiah, our savior, who has come to save us now. Why speak of the distant future?"

"The Messiah, the Anointed One, the God-Son, the Savior," Jesus scoffed, "they are only symbolic names given to me by the people of a certain time, place, and language. If in the future I reappear in the flesh again, it will be for the same reasons that I am here now – to serve the needs of that time and place. That is one possible future reality. However, the greater reality beyond this moment in time is that my Essence will never leave; for I am now, I am before and after, I am the Alpha and the Omega, I am for always."

"But, My Lord, to see you in the flesh, to be able to touch you, to embrace you, to hear you speak reassures me that what I feel in my heart is true."

"You must learn to know me not as the flesh that can be seen, heard, or touched, but as my Essence. Know me by your feelings and the voice that speaks to you without a tongue."

Judas sighed, "I will try, Master, but since you've entered my life, I can't imagine this physical existence without you."

Jesus pointed up at the bright stars and said, "I will be up there with those stars and at the same time here on earth, and some day, dear Judas, you will join me."

Judas whispered, "For now I am graced to be with you whatever the future may bring."

Jesus leaned over and kissed Judas's cheek and said, "My Essence will be with you always. Now please leave me in solitude so that I may commune with my heavenly Father. Tell the others that tomorrow morning we will all go forth and spread the 'good news' of the Gospel, and in doing so, they shall become healers."

"As you wish, My Lord," Judas replied.

The next day Jesus led his disciples on a walk. A crowd had gathered around a young man who was violently clawing at his chest and screaming in horror. The man fell to the ground writhing in torment, his head twisting from side to side. The crowd spread out further around the afflicted man. Many yelled out, "He's possessed by demons! Stay away!"

Jesus walked up to the man and raised a hand over him. The crowd gasped. Jesus said, "Demons, be gone." Instantly the young man stopped writhing and stilled. His face became calm. Jesus knelt beside him and said, "From now on, you will be bothered no more by forces that are not truly your own." The crowd and the disciples looked on in amazement.

As Jesus and his disciples continued their walk, many of the people followed. A woman who had witnessed Jesus's baptism by John recognized Jesus and pointed to him. She announced loudly, "He's the Messiah! I saw him at the Jordan River." The people following him had heard of Jesus's healings and the resurrection that he had performed in Jericho, and they knew that Herod's battalions had searched for him. They were awestruck.

As word quickly spread that the Messiah was here in Capernaum, more people joined Jesus's walk. He led the swelling crowd to a field and asked that they sit on the grass. Jesus spoke of the "good news" of The Word as they listened intently. After twenty minutes, ten robed men with their hoods covering their heads and the sides of their faces walked through the seated crowd and stood in front of Jesus. They dropped their hoods and exposed the morbid sores that were the badge of lepers. The crowd gasped. Those seated near the lepers sprang up and ran to the rear of the crowd.

One leper said, "We have heard that you have come. Please heal us."

Jesus smiled warmly at the ten men and then raised both palms toward them. Because Jesus was imbued with the unfathomable power of the Holy Spirit, within minutes, all the lepers' sores were healed. The people gasped again and marveled as others before at the miracle they had witnessed. More people came forth with afflictions of all kinds, and they were also healed. All were certain that Jesus was the true Messiah.

Later, back at the house, Jesus and his disciples ate their afternoon meal and spoke of the morning's events. Their respect for him had soared, and they looked with humble and adoring eyes at his divinity as a god. Jesus again affirmed that they too would become healers to many who would seek healing from them.

Philip meekly asked, "How could we ever do what you have done for those possessed by demons?" The others nodded, acknowledging similar feelings.

Jesus replied, "Is it not true that our Lord, our God, created all things in the universe?"

The disciples nodded in agreement.

Jesus continued, "I also say to you that our almighty Creator has created all thoughts that can be imagined and all emotions that can be felt. How people use their thoughts and emotions is a choice, but few realize this."

The disciples muttered among themselves. Thomas said, "Master, we don't understand. What has that got to do with a person being possessed by demons?"

Jesus replied, "When one is possessed by one's beliefs, whether it's a belief in an angel or a demon, that belief becomes part of that person's reality. Each person's beliefs affect his or her body in ways that engender greater health or more sickliness. Those destructive beliefs can be changed to better ways of thinking, feeling, and acting. Those who were healed desired to be healed and believed that I could heal them. Those seeking healing who will believe in you will also be healed. You now need to believe in yourselves."

Bartholomew said, "But, Master, you touch people, and they are healed immediately – the blind see, the crippled are straightened, and lepers are cleansed. How could we ever do that? You are the Messiah; we are not."

Jesus raised his palms toward his disciples and solemnly said, "Then as your Messiah, I bless all of you with the power to teach those seeking healing and the authority to grant salvation to those who truly seek redemption and healing. They will be the ones who will have faith in you, and with that true faith and their desire to be free of ills and demons, they shall be free."

The men felt a stirring within them. They sat still for a few moments then began to shift about. Luke spoke, "You are our Savior. People see you as their Savior, not us. How can we do what you do if they only think of you as their Savior?"

Jesus replied, "In those circumstances you can inform those seeking healing that I have endowed you with the power to connect them to me, the Christ, to facilitate their healing. You must act with love and forgive their transgressions and sins. That, and your deep compassion and true intent to help will open up channels of God's healing to those who ask you for forgiveness and healing. But heed my words, you must also teach that God dwells within each person and that all healing comes from His power that created the body. They can receive salvation directly from God without the need for an intermediary, for you will not always be there in their time of need."

Jesus surveyed his disciples' thoughts and saw their doubts. He said, "Why is it so hard to understand and feel what I have repeatedly said, that 'God dwells within'? Why must you look outside of yourselves for the truth when that which you seek is within you?"

Judas spoke, "We are learning. You, My Lord, are a complete physician and treat the heart, the mind, the body and the soul. You are the Master; we are your students, and we will strive to learn."

Jesus smiled and said, "And so you shall. Have the confidence that you will do what is best. Believe in yourselves as I believe in you, and my Father will help to guide you. Above all, always keep your faith supreme."

37

Word spread quickly throughout Judea that the Messiah was in Capernaum. Over several months, Jesus had held open healing services for the ever-growing crowds. His miracles were passionately touted by the many who witnessed his feats. Many others who had not been witnesses believed in what they heard, and there were those who remained doubters. But by and large, everyone wanted to know more about the "one" who had been sought by Herod's battalion because his soldiers had questioned everyone in the land and searched their homes looking for Jesus. There were also those who had been at the River Jordan on that epic day of the incredible white light and those who had witnessed Jesus's miracles in Jerusalem and Jericho – they were all adamantly convinced that Jesus was the "Anointed One" – their true Messiah. They, in turn, inspired others to believe that the time had come and that the age-old prophecies would finally be fulfilled. Additionally, throngs of impassioned seekers who had had visions or dreams heralding his "coming" and those with sicknesses who sought healing all flocked to Capernaum to be with the Messiah.

Most people were baffled as to why Jesus could preach and heal in the open without Herod or Rome's interference. Additionally, the people's resentment and unrest concerning the Baptist John's arrest served to heighten the already highly charged atmosphere. The people's daily conversations percolated with speculation and anticipation of what would happen next concerning the Messiah.

Zena opened the door to the tower chamber and stared at Pontius Pilate's back. He didn't hear her enter as he looked out the window from his favored viewing point and surveyed Jerusalem below. Zena walked up behind him and asked, "Why haven't you come to lunch with me?"

Pilate turned around quickly with a huge smile on his face. Holding up a messenger's scroll, he said jubilantly, "Because of all the good news I've received." He grinned. "I had to come here and enjoy my good fortune without being nagged by you."

Zena felt miffed. "You have been so happy and buoyant lately that I thought you were enjoying some new courtesans that I didn't know about. Instead, you're just gloating."

"Why shouldn't I?" Pilate laughed. "Now it's Herod's turn to squirm as I am sure he is."

"Don't underestimate Antipas. He is a clever fox and always plotting. There may be more going on than you're aware of."

"Don't try and take away my pleasure, Zena. I do know that the Jews are even more displeased with Herod since he has arrested the Baptist John. And now their would-be Messiah is in Judea, Herod's domain, and this Jesus travels openly, attracting huge crowds daily. Jerusalem is free from a growing debacle that now festers in Herod's backyard," Pilate exulted.

"But my husband, you don't know why Herod has not arrested their Messiah. He's refused to talk about the withdrawal of his battalion from Jerusalem despite the prodding of his inner court."

"That doesn't matter to me now." Pilate laughed again and said, "But nonetheless, he must feel threatened that the Jews feel this Jesus is their king and not him. Sooner or later, Herod will move against Jesus, and that sly fox will be in a worse predicament. If he were to arrest the Rabbi now, as he did the Baptist, the people would surely rebel." Pilate smiled with great satisfaction and said, "As long as the Jews' would-be Messiah is in Herod's domain, Jerusalem is mine to rule freely without unrest." Pilate turned and looked down at his city.

"Don't underestimate Herod," Zena warned again.

"You cannot take away my exuberance, Zena. I feel too good to allow your nagging doubts to spoil my joy in Herod roasting on the spit."

<hr>

Herodias slid the jewel-studded golden amulet from her daughter's arm. She gently stroked Salome's satiny skin. Herodias nodded her approval, smiled, and said, "Time has healed your scratch marks flawlessly." Herodias stepped back and gazed at her daughter's nude body. Large nipples that jutted out with erect tips capped the young girl's shapely breasts. Her chest narrowed to a delicate waist. Her hips were rounded and in perfect proportion to her torso. Salome's slender and athletically toned legs tapered down to narrow ankles and small feet.

Herodias looked up at Salome's hair, its braids laced with golden threads. She grasped a group of twenty-inch long braids and let them cascade from her hand and said, "Your hair reflects the flames of the lamps like a waterfall of golden light." The queen carefully examined Salome's spectacular make-up, then turned to the attendants and cosmetologists and said, "You have made my daughter more exquisite and captivating than ever before."

The once chatty attendants said nothing but only bowed their heads in acceptance of Herodias's praise and let out a silent sigh of relief; for Herodias had warned them that if they spoke a word of gossip about John the Baptist's remarks or other gossip in the kingdom to her daughter, she would cut out their tongues. She turned back to Salome, who was beaming at her mother's approval. Herodias proudly grasped her daughter's shoulders, looked in her eyes and said, "You're ready. Put the passion of your hate and revenge into your dancing."

Herodias ordered the attendants, "Now dress her."

―――――――

Octavius came into Herod's parlor and said, "Everyone is ready and waiting. I think you will like some of your birthday gifts."

"What could someone give a king that he doesn't already have or that he can't easily get?" Herod replied.

"It's their acknowledgement of you that counts, my Lord."

"Humph." Herod took another large gulp of wine from his goblet, "It's the worried thoughts of my mind that count. They trouble me endlessly."

"It's your forty-eighth birthday, and great banquet festivities honor you today. Now is the time to think thoughts of celebration."

"How is that possible with that foul-speaking Baptist in my dungeon and that Jesus roaming around drawing thousands of people to see him and hear him speak as if he were their king and not I?"

"My Lord, those followers are desperate people searching for a Messiah that does not exist. They even believe that he can resurrect the dead."

Herod's face flamed with anger. He furiously threw his goblet to the floor, wine and glass fragments splattering in all directions. "Never again speak to me of his rumored resurrections. It's ridiculous to think he can raise the dead. He's only a man, not a god for people to worship!"

Octavius stood silently as Herod glared into the empty space before him. Then he quietly suggested, "My Lord, an accident could be arranged so that there would be no connection between his disappearance and you."

Herod got up from his regal chair and poured himself a fresh goblet of wine. "I've already thought of that, but the people would still suspect me. Then I'd also have to kill the Jews who would rebel, which would lead to more rebellion and many more Jews killed. Both Rome and I would lose taxes and a large portion of our free slave labor market – but we know all that crap. And so, Octavius, it perplexes me."

"I know it does. But just for tonight my Lord, try and put that aside. Everyone is looking forward to your birthday celebration. I am told that even Salome has been preparing a special dance – just for you."

"Salome?" Herod perked up. "A special dance, you say?" Herod took another long drink of wine. His furrowed brow smoothed, and the corners of his mouth widened into a relaxed smile. An intense gleam formed in his eyes as he whispered, *"Salome."*

⸺⸺⸺

The royal ballroom was filled with the leading citizens of Galilee – chiefs of estates, top captains, high officials and their entourages; everyone was adorned in their finest garments. All had come to honor King Herod on his birthday. Herodias sat on her regal chair next to Herod, who sat on his high throne. He was immaculately dressed in a purple silk robe trimmed with gold thread and covered by a jeweled vestment. The points of his gold crown were tipped with red rubies that complemented a fist-sized ruby pendant that hung from his elaborate gold necklace.

After having enjoyed a sumptuous banquet of exquisite cuisine and abundant superb wine, everyone was in fine spirits. Conversations blended with the pleasant sounds of the musicians playing from behind a side curtain. The scent of fragrant incense wafted throughout the royal ballroom.

Herodias looked at Herod, who was nervously tapping his wine goblet with his index finger in anticipation. Her lips formed a sly smile. Without any announcement, the music stopped. A loud, slow drumbeat suddenly penetrated the room. The torches that illuminated the royal ballroom were extinguished. Only bewildered whispers of conversation could be heard. Beams of light from the full moon slanted down from the high window openings onto the polished marble floor. The pounding drumbeat grew louder and faster; then it suddenly stopped. The ballroom was silent.

In the dim light, four sensuously costumed maidens holding tall poles that supported black curtains appeared at the rear of the ballroom. The black curtains formed an enclosed eight-foot-square tent. The slow drumbeat began again, and the four maidens walked toward Herod in step with each pounding beat. Herodias faced the approaching curtained square, but her eyes were angled toward Herod. He sat up straight and anxiously leaned forward. Herodias's smile widened.

The maidens stopped ten feet from Herod. The drumbeat stopped. The ballroom torches were relit. The maidens dropped to their knees and laid their poles down, causing the black curtains to fall and revealing a lone figure covered from head and face to toes in an iridescent violet silk veil. From beneath the veil, finger cymbals chimed rhythmically. The maidens gracefully retreated with their poles and curtains. All eyes were on the veiled violet figure. Each chime resonated in the silence of the ballroom. The veiled figure slowly walked around the ballroom floor. The tempo of the finger cymbals became faster, and the mysterious fully-covered figure moved in concert with the cymbals. As the figure approached Herod's throne, the tempo grew even faster. The figure spun around and around, then stopped and stood still in silence. Through a long slit in the side of the veil, a shapely leg darted out, her foot adorned in a golden slipper. Herod's head reflexively jerked back a few inches.

For a few moments, there was no movement; then the figure spun around once, and the violet veil dropped to the floor. There stood the alluring Salome. Her body was covered from her neck down to her ankles with a deep-blue indigo veil; her glorious gold-threaded hair and exquisitely decorated face were dazzling. All the guests gasped at her compelling beauty and divine figure.

Salome bowed deeply before Herod. His eyes stared wide with burning desire into hers. He involuntarily licked his lips. Salome stood up, raised her hands over her head and chimed her finger cymbals three times. A drum responded with three beats. She repeated the chiming, and the drumbeats followed. In unison, the chimes and drumbeats continued as flutes joined in and played a soft melody. Salome gracefully pranced around the borders of the marble floor, captivating her audience. Once again she stopped before Herod. Through the side slits in her long veil, she exposed both of her perfectly shaped legs for a moment, then bowed down again. The room fell silent once more. Herod fidgeted on his throne.

Salome stayed transfixed a few more moments, then rose and chimed her cymbals three times again. A maiden came to her side and grasped a corner of the indigo veil. Salome twirled away from the maiden, unraveling the indigo veil to expose a tightly wrapped sky-blue veil that adorned her body but left her bare shoulders exposed. She chimed her cymbals three times again at a faster tempo than before. The drumbeat followed the cymbals' tempo, and Salome danced seductively around the ballroom floor. She returned once more to Herod and bowed before him.

Herodias saw her husband's legs twitching. She sighed with sly satisfaction.

Salome chimed her cymbals at a faster tempo; the drums and flutes followed. Her erotic dance became more intense, and then she bowed once more before Herod. She arose and danced at an even faster tempo and more seductively than before as the blue veil gave way to a green veil that covered her only from her hips up, revealing her voluptuous, youthful bare legs. In a series of twirls, she shed the green veil, revealing a canary-yellow veil that covered her front only but exposed her bare back. The packed ballroom breathed heavily with delight and admiration.

When she bowed again before Herod, she took off her golden slippers and tossed them at his feet. Herod started to bend down to pick them up but glanced at Herodias and quickly sat back, leaving the slippers at his feet.

Salome stood and stretched her bare arms over her head. A handmaiden came and held an edge of the yellow veil as Salome twirled again, unraveling the veil that revealed her sixth and transparent orange veil. Her lovely breasts were clearly defined as were her rounded buttocks. Her pointed nipples pressed against the light fabric. Gasps were heard from many. Herod breathed in deeply and sat up ramrod straight.

Salome chimed her cymbals at the fastest tempo yet. The drums pounded harder and faster. The flutes shrilled. Salome danced and twirled around the room. Her athletic body moved gracefully and effortlessly. She did cartwheels, then spun on her toes in front of Herod. She threw herself onto the floor, twisting her body in a gyrating frenzy. Her thighs wide apart, she lay on her back before Herod, then arched her belly in the air with her feet and hands pushing her upward from the floor. With each throbbing drumbeat, she pulsed her pelvis before the King. Beads of sweat formed on his brow. He drained the last of the wine from his goblet. His audience clapped their hands in unison with each staccato drumbeat.

Salome turned over and lay on her belly and slithered toward Herod's feet. With each fast-pulsing drumbeat, she jutted her rounded young buttocks up and down. Herod grasped his ruby pendent and squeezed it tightly, his breath almost a pant, his desires on fire.

Then Salome stood. Tilting her head, she smiled at Herod. He smiled back. "You are magnificent," Herod said. "I have never seen such beauty." Salome pulled a small string from the top of the orange veil, and it unraveled from her body. She threw it at Herod's face. He eagerly caught it and grasped it tightly. A skimpy seventh scarlet veil barely covered her pubic area. She arched her back, thrusting her curvaceous bare breasts toward Herod. The drumbeats stopped, and she dropped face down on the floor, exposing only her bare young back and buttocks. There was a deathly silence.

Salome looked up at Herod and in an alluring tone said, "If you want me to continue, you must grant me one wish; then I will grant any wish you ask of me." Immediately the four maidens came to her side and covered her with the black pole veils.

Herod looked down at the black veils covering the object of his flaming desires. He turned to Herodias in puzzlement. Herodias said, "Grant Salome her wish, and she is yours tonight. Completely."

Herod stared at Herodias as her words sank in. The room had become stone silent. All in attendance awaited Herod's decision, and all also anxiously wanted Salome to finish her dance.

In his drunken daze, Herod spontaneously blurted to Salome, "I swear an oath to give you whatever you ask of me – even half my kingdom." Everyone gasped that their king had uttered such an oath.

Salome stood and held the black veils around her body so that only her head and face were visible. She spoke clearly and loudly so that all could hear: "Give me here on a platter the head of John the Baptist."

Herod paled. He sat upright and glared at Herodias, who met his eyes boldly. She nodded to him and then gestured in an encompassing arch toward all the prominent guests who were intently waiting for him to acknowledge his oath, which he drunkenly did, saying, "So be it!"

⊂══════⊃

Jesus had been staring in silence at the glowing fire pit in Judas's courtyard. He put a hand to his throat and closed his eyes. Judas watched him intently. He knew not to interrupt when his Master was deep in thought. The full moon illuminated Jesus's face. Judas saw him wince, and then Jesus removed his hand from his throat and rested it in his lap. He sighed and whispered, "It is done. My beloved John, our Father awaits you in His kingdom and is pleased with you."

38

"The temple police are coming!" Seth exclaimed from his lookout post on the roof. "They're making their way through the crowd."

Judas and Matthew hurriedly climbed up to the flat roof of their house and assessed the approaching platoons. "I knew I could count on Moshe for help," Judas said. He had sent word to Moshe requesting that he send as many temple police as possible from Jericho to Capernaum to help protect the Messiah.

The crowds of people who had made pilgrimages to Capernaum to see Jesus had grown so large that the disciples again feared for Jesus's safety. To date, the people had been orderly enough, but each day hundreds more seeking the Messiah arrived; and at Jesus's healing and speaking sessions, they pressed ever closer to be near him. Roman soldiers were posted everywhere around Jesus's compound, their presence helping to maintain order. As the crowds grew larger, many more soldiers were sent, and a Roman military base camp was set up in a nearby field to house and feed the troops.

The disciples also feared Jesus's arrest. Since John the Baptist's beheading, they felt Herod was unpredictable and could act against their Messiah at any time. Great unrest among the multitudes, those whom John had baptized over the years, had also built up against Herod throughout Judea. In addition, the Sadducees' and Pharisees' leaders were concerned that if the unrest grew too great, Herod or Rome would move against them if their followers supported the Messiah, so they distanced themselves from any direct contact with Jesus, although they had their informers closely monitoring evolving events. So many people had come to Capernaum, where Jesus was, that all the lodging was filled to capacity. People slept in the streets and nearby fields. Merchants in the marketplace were sold out of all of their food supplies. More disturbing, the hauls of fish had dried up. Food prices spiked, and some of Herod's soldiers sold their food rations to pilgrims; those who were caught doing so were severely punished.

Through all the ferment, Jesus continued his healing and teaching sessions and tutored his disciples in how to do the same. Under Jesus's guidance, the disciples were learning daily, yet they remained worried about their Master's fate. After early morning prayers, Jesus reviewed the plans that had been made for the week's highlight session. Word had been spread that that afternoon, the Messiah would be giving special blessings to all who attended.

The men finished their sparse breakfast quickly because there was so little to eat. Luke patted his flat stomach and said, "I don't know how much thinner I can get."

John, who had prepared the morning meal, said, "I wonder where I'll find enough food to feed us all for the rest of the day."

Jesus had sat quietly listening to his disciples' conversation regarding their fears and worries; then he spoke. "I tell you, do not worry about what you will eat or what wrongs may come about. Look at the birds of the air; they do not sow or reap or store away grain in barns, and yet your heavenly Father feeds them. Are you not much more valuable than they? Who of you by worrying can add a single hour to your life? O ye of little faith? So do not worry, saying 'What shall we eat?' For your heavenly Father knows that you need food. First seek His kingdom and His righteousness, and all will be given to you. Therefore, do not worry about today or tomorrow, for each day shall take care of itself and your worry will help no one, least of all - yourselves."

The Sea of Galilee was calm, and the air was still. The sun shone brightly on the water, and the sky was pure blue. Roman cavalry were posted on the top of the high hills that surrounded the small grassland valley. The U-shaped valley, which abutted the sea, was now filled with thousands of people anticipating the arrival of their Messiah. Roman ground troops formed a tight perimeter around the waiting crowd. At the shoreline, the temple police, with their wooden shields, formed a protective barrier between the sea and the people in the valley. Most of Jesus's disciples were dispersed among the crowd fanning out from the shoreline like the fingers of a hand, each one stationed at a knuckle. Empty nets hung from a small fleet of fishing boats on the shore near the base of one hill. A meager group of livestock and their herders and families were the farthest from the shore behind the massive crowd. After a while, people started grumbling about the prolonged waiting and the gnawing of their empty stomachs. Much of the food that was available was forbidden because it was not kosher, and many adhered to religious dictates, refusing to eat it. They began cursing the Roman soldiers to vent their frustrations. The soldiers tightened their grips on their spears and swords.

Then a sleek boat with four fast rowers, a boy sitting in the stern, and Jesus sitting in the bow came along the shoreline. It stopped thirty yards off shore at the crux of the fan of people. Jesus stood up in the bow and raised his arms high with his palms out toward the thousands of people. Word spread quickly that the man in the bow was the Messiah.

Within a few moments, the masses of people quieted, and the small valley was as silent as if no one were there.

Jesus then spoke strongly and compassionately. "I feel your hunger and discontent." Then in a relay-like cadence of his words, the disciples at the first knuckle from the shore repeated Jesus's exact words loudly and clearly. Then the second knuckle of disciples did the same and so on until the multitude in the valley had heard Jesus's exact words.

"I know many of you have shunned food that was unclean and not kosher although you hunger greatly," he said, and his words were again repeated throughout the valley. Many who had eaten non-kosher food looked shamefully down at the ground.

"Please listen," Jesus continued, "and try to understand. Truly I say to you, your souls are not harmed by what you eat, but by what you think and say."

People looked puzzled but listened intently. Jesus continued, "What you eat does not go into your heart. It enters your stomach and then leaves your body. What comes out of a man's mouth is what makes him unclean and defiles him. Evil thoughts from your heart toward others that cause you to curse and slander taint your world in kind and blemish the light and love of your heavenly Father that glow within you."

Again, the disciples repeated each phase of Jesus's message so that all could hear his words. There were many in attendance who heard their stomachs growling instead.

Jesus knew this and said, "I am here to feed your souls, but I know your bodies need nourishment as well, and so by the grace of our Lord, our God, you shall be fed body and soul."

A man yelled out, "We need food, not words!"

Jesus replied, "I beseech you all, if just for today, expect either something good or something better. Learn to give yourself that choice rather than expecting something good or something bad. Have absolute faith that your Lord, our God, will provide for you as I have faith in Him, and so your true needs will be provided for as He giveth to you now."

Jesus then knelt over the boat's bow and reached his hands into the water. He closed his eyes and felt a pleasant tingling sensation emanating from the hundreds of thousands of dendrite nerve endings in his fingertips. The sensation intensified, and Jesus smiled with great satisfaction as the sympathetic vibration of his connection to the water rippled outward. He stayed in that position for three minutes. All watched him, puzzled and perplexed. Then he stood and raised his palms to the mass of people and said, "Fishermen, go to your boats and ready your nets."

The fishermen stood by their boats but didn't climb into them because they didn't understand. There was much grumbling throughout the crowd. A baby's cry was heard, and a woman shouted, "My children's stomachs are empty! We need food!"

Jesus maintained his stance with his palms extended toward the masses. Then the water around his boat began to churn with small baitfish. A minute later, attracted by the baitfish, larger fish jumped out of the water and splashed back into the sea. The fishermen stood momentarily frozen in disbelief. Then much larger fish began to churn the water. The fishermen dashed into their boats to harvest the bountiful catch. The churning and splashing of the waters began to extend farther out, covering a three-hundred-yard radius and then extending even farther. The churning approached the shoreline, and many fish jumped out of the water onto land. People near the edges of the protective semicircle of temple police started loading the fish into baskets. The crowd began to surge toward the shore.

Jesus said loudly, "Be calm and all will be fed. Pass the baskets along to others. There will be more than enough to eat for everyone. Give thanks to our Lord, our God, for the blessings He giveth to you this day."

In little time, the fishermen had filled their nets so fully that they could not haul the heavy catches into their boats, and such heavy loads made it difficult to row back to shore. When they made it to shore, the fish were quickly unloaded into empty baskets that had been passed down from the crowd and then once again filled and passed back up. When the boats were emptied of their bounty, the fishermen rowed out a short distance, refilled their nets, and returned to unload them.

Jesus instructed his astounded rowers to move his boat farther out. He walked back to the stern and sat down next to Seth. The boy's eyes were wide with glee. He said to Jesus, "You have created another miracle. How is it possible?"

Jesus smiled and said, "It appears to be a miracle to those who do not know the workings of God's gifts of life and the elements."

Seth anxiously asked, "Please, tell me how you enticed the fish to come to you when there were no fish to be found by the fishermen."

Jesus replied, "It's good that you want to learn, and I'll tell you because you'll understand what others may not."

James and his brother John, the two fastest rowers, sat nearest the stern and listened intently as Jesus spoke. "I've told you before of my divine connection with my heavenly Father's living waters. When I put my hands into the sea, I was able to create vibrations that mimicked the sound of a school of small baitfish that had become scarce. That attracted a small school of the fish that first churned the water. The larger fish's hunger for the baitfish was so powerful that it didn't matter if only a sound vibration of the baitfish's essence was there and not that many actual fish. It was enough to attract a few of the nearby larger fish that in turn sent out excited vibrations that food was at hand. Those vibrations travel quickly and far in water. More fish were attracted and became excited by the excitement of the other fish, and in turn, they sent out more vibrations of excitement that food was here."

A fish jumped out of the water and landed in the boat at Jesus's feet. He picked up the wiggling fish, smiled, and said, "This is the result." Jesus tossed the fish back into the water and then pointed to the people on land who were frantically filling their baskets with fish from the fishing boats. "I pray that those people truly appreciate my heavenly Father's blessing and gain the faith that he will provide for them when they believe in Him as I do."

"I know how hungry they all must have been. I have eaten very little these last few days," Seth said, patting his stomach, "but many of those people, especially children, haven't eaten at all." Seth's large eyes lit up. "I have an idea. Remember when you first came to our house in Jerusalem and you and I had been working all morning to build the wooden bench? I was so hungry then. Somehow, out of nowhere, you were able to produce the most delicious piece of honey cake that I had ever tasted."

Jesus chuckled, "Yes, Seth, I remember. It was a spontaneous act of my budding ability to project the image to your senses as the reality of what you most desired."

Seth said, "But it was more than an image to me." He closed his eyes and smiled with delight. "It not only tasted so wonderfully delicious, it filled the emptiness in my stomach."

Jesus nodded, "It gave me great pleasure to see your delight."

Seth said, "When you told everyone to have faith and to expect something good or something better…"

Jesus interrupted him, "Yes, I see what you have in mind for the people. It is divine that you were the first one on whom I used my ability when I projected the honey cake to you, and now you have inspired me to give more of my gifted ability to the people. I have told you, Seth, that you were more than a boy, that you will become the Great Seth, and so you are becoming just that."

Jesus instructed the rowers to go ashore near the temple police. At the same time, from the periphery of the crowd, Matthew carried a covered basket and walked through the middle of the massed people toward the shore to meet Jesus's boat. The air was still, and the delicious aroma of freshly baked bread in the basket that Matthew carried wafted through the air and was noticed by the people gathered for Jesus's special blessing. Uncontrollably, the famished people salivated at the new-baked bread's fragrance.

As Jesus's boat touched the shore, Matthew approached carrying the basket, and the temple police cleared a path for him. Jesus stepped out of the boat, and Matthew, with a big smile on his face, held out the basket to him. Jesus and Seth pulled off the cloth covering the basket and looked into it. They saw five loaves of freshly baked bread. Seth breathed in the wonderful aroma and smiled, wide-eyed. "Where did you get them, Father?" he asked Matthew.

"This is a gift of appreciation from an elderly woman whom the Master healed two days ago. Her fingers had been so bad that she couldn't bring them together to hold anything. After her healing, she went to many of her neighbors and gathered sufficient barley flour to bake and was able to work the dough for the first time since her injury – and here are the five loaves of bread that she has made for you, Master."

Jesus took the basket and instructed his disciples to gather many empty baskets. Within the protected area at the shoreline a makeshift four-sided curtain was erected surrounding Seth, Judas, and Jesus. Empty baskets were handed through the curtains on one side. Inside the tented curtain, Seth broke off a few small crumbs of the warm loaves of bread into each basket as Jesus had instructed. Jesus then held his hands over the baskets and said to Seth and Judas, "First, I will say a prayer of gratitude for what we expect to receive." Seth and Judas looked on as Jesus whispered inaudibly, and then they heard a few words clearly: "And give us this day, our daily bread..." The last words of Jesus's prayer were spoken too softly to hear.

Jesus turned to Seth and Judas, who had been staring intently at him. He grinned and told them, "Now we have glorious work before us." Jesus pointed into a basket. The "essence" of breadcrumbs had been multiplied into a vivid thought-form projection of a basket full of fresh, warm, fragrant loaves of bread. Seth and Judas were stunned at what they saw.

Jesus then instructed them to put more breadcrumbs into the remaining baskets. He then repeated his prayer over the other baskets, and in less than a minute, all the baskets were filled to the brim with warm, fresh, fragrant bread. The baskets were then quickly handed out the other side of the tent and passed along to the feasting crowd, who gobbled up the most delicious bread they had ever tasted. More empty baskets were passed into the tent and refilled until each and every person had savored every last crumb of the bread made from the healed hands of the poor woman whose heavenly heart had offered true gratitude to her Savior.

After all the bread had been handed out, Jesus, Judas, and Seth returned to the boat, and the rowers rowed out and stopped thirty yards from shore. The disciples once more fanned out among the masses. The delicious smell of warm bread and seasoned fish cooking on fires permeated the green valley. There was an exuberant atmosphere of jubilation and then relaxation and contentment as the people ate until they could eat no more. The aroma and taste of warm bread was experienced by the multitude, as were the cold stone to the scorpion and the ibex to Spartus perceived as their reality. So satisfying was the "essence" of the bread that the "essence" of the people's hunger was assuaged.

Jesus stood in the bow again and raised his hands. The disciples urged the crowd to quiet down because the Messiah needed to speak to them. The crowd soon quieted; their hunger satisfied, they were much more open to hearing what Jesus was about to say.

Jesus spoke loudly and clearly. "You were told today that you would receive special blessings from our Lord, our God; and now that you have received those blessings, you need to give our Lord a moment of silent gratitude for His gifts. Please do so now."

Except for the sounds of birds and the occasional cry of a baby, the valley was silent. Even the astonished Roman troops paused in silence. Jesus saw his people's thought-forms of blessed thankfulness and true gratitude, and he was pleased. He then said, "You feel satisfied now that your flesh has been fed. However, I say to you that you could eat fish and bread all day and all night but you will still have a hunger if your soul remains unnourished. With the food you have taken into your body, I bid you also believe in the faith that has produced that food intended to nourish your spirit, for it is your spirit that will ultimately sustain you throughout your lives."

Again, each phrase was repeated by the disciples to the now very attentive and appreciative crowd. Jesus continued, "I ask you all to imagine that you are able to reach out and take a handful of God's eternal Light and almighty power – and that that handful could nourish you for the rest of your life. Then do so as you did with the bread as if it were a handful of God's substance, because it is so. Maintain the faith and true gratitude that you feel this very moment for all of your life, and your soul will never be hungry for nourishment."

The amazed Roman soldiers had witnessed everything. Jesus sat down. He felt more empowered than ever before with the faith bestowed upon him by the masses of people who now sincerely embraced him as their Messiah. He told the rowers to row quickly along the shoreline. As they did so, people got into the fishing boats and followed Jesus in their desire to touch the Messiah. Some ran into the water and swam toward him. Many clamored, "Our Savior! Our Savior! Don't go!" The heavier fishing boats could not keep up with Jesus's sleek boat and its fast rowers. Judas said to Jesus, "Matthew counted over five thousand people in the valley." Jesus nodded in acknowledgement.

After a while, the trailing fishing boats were outdistanced as Jesus's boat rounded a bend in the shoreline and was out of sight of the other boats. Jesus told the rowers to bring his boat ashore near a small forested area. There, Jesus stepped onto the shore and instructed Judas and the others, "Now go, and we will meet as planned."

"But I'm sure after your miracle today of feeding over five thousand people, we will be followed," Judas replied.

Jesus replied, "You will all be followed. Tell the others to teach their followers as I have taught them."

"But, Master, there will be spies among them," protested Judas.

"Teach whoever will learn, even spies. The Word belongs to all of mankind."

Jesus hugged Judas and kissed his cheek. He nodded to the others in the boat and then winked at Seth. Jesus turned away and then disappeared into the forest. The rowers sped away, further distancing themselves from the pursuing fishing boats.

<hr>

"I thought you would never get here. I missed you so," Seffira said as she moved quickly to embrace Joseph as he emerged from the darkness. She had been waiting for hours under the lone cypress tree where he had told her that he would meet her tonight. Joseph hugged her tightly and spun joyfully around with Seffira clinging to him, her legs swinging off the ground.

"My sweet Seffira, I missed you so much it hurt." He held her cheeks and drew her lips to his. They kissed passionately. Their young, innocent bodies pressed against each other; their eager hands caressed each other's heads and backs. Joseph's hand slid down to her hip and squeezed her flesh as his lips burned into hers. Their breathing became heavier, then breathless.

Seffira pulled away. In the light of the half-moon, she saw the disappointment and longing on his face. She took his hand and led him to where a blanket lay spread out under the cypress tree. "It's been four days since I've held you; it feels like four years," Joseph said.

Seffira sat down on the blanket and patted a spot next to her, "Come, sit next to me."

Joseph sat and embraced her again. She caressed his muscular back, and again their passion built quickly; his hands started to roam over her body. She pulled away once more and said, "We promised each other that we would wait until we were married. I can't disappoint my mother and father."

Joseph's disappointment deepened. He said, "I know. I respect your promise to them...but I've never had such feelings before! I want you, Seffira! I need you! I love you!"

"And I love you. I need you also. I missed you so much," Seffira said as she tenderly caressed Joseph's cheek, "And I want you too. More than you can imagine."

Joseph smiled, "My dreams about you go beyond imagination." He pulled her on top of him and kissed her. She melted into his arms. Their breathing grew heavier, but once more she pulled away. Joseph lay on his back, dejected; he stared up at the moon.

"Don't feel bad," she said and gently stroked his long hair.

"I feel so many things, Seffira, so many things that my heart and mind constantly swirl in bliss and confusion. You and the Messiah fill my thoughts."

Seffira kissed Joseph's cheek. She said, "He and you fill my thoughts also. When I sat near you in the valley as you repeated his words to the crowd and everyone listened so intently to you, it made me shiver. I wanted to go to you then and there." She kissed his cheek again.

"I saw you and wanted to go to you also," Joseph replied.

"But you had to fulfill your responsibility to the Messiah," she said. "I know the strength of your loyalty to him."

Joseph hugged her tightly. "Then you should know of the strength of my loyalty to you as well."

"I do," she replied and hugged him tighter, "and you should know of mine to you." She kissed him passionately for a moment and then sat up to temper the heat of the moment.

"Don't stop," Joseph pleaded. "It's been four days!"

"It took longer than you said it would. I waited and waited here, all alone. That was hard for me. I'm by myself in a land that I don't know."

"I'm sorry, Seffira. I couldn't help it. The Messiah was teaching us very important lessons, and then he had to tell us of the plans for the special Blessing Session." His eyes widened with wonder and awe. "And it was special – all those fish and that bread – it was a miracle!"

"Did he tell you about the fish and bread beforehand?"

"No, he only said that we should have faith as he had, that the people would be provided for, even if he knew not how." Joseph held Seffira's shoulders and said, "And Jesus's faith created a miracle!"

"Yes," she nodded, "it was a miracle! He is the Messiah!" She grasped his shoulders. "I'm so proud of you that he's taken you into his inner circle of trust." She kissed him and then said, "You stayed away so long."

"I was so torn," Joseph replied. "I had to stay with Jesus, yet I still yearned for you."

Seffira teasingly asked, "Is the Messiah more important to you than I am?"

With deep conviction, Joseph said, "Seffira, my love, you are more important to me than my own life."

Seffira stared at Joseph's handsome face in the moonlight. Her heart pounded madly. She pushed his shoulders to the blanket and leaned over him. She pressed her lips tightly against his. Her body pressed over his. She placed her hand on his thigh and moved it toward his pubic area. He trembled. She pulled up the sides of the blanket to hide them from the night. They rolled back and forth in their sanctuary of love and bliss. Soon, their powerful passions led to complete abandon...

Twenty yards away, like a snake in the tall grass, the dark hooded man, Herod's spy, slithered closer to the young blanketed couple under the cypress tree to hear any information that might lead him to Jesus.

In the privacy of the palace garden, Herod angrily declared to Octavius," I don't care what Rome thinks. He must die!"

Octavius bowed his head and said, "First we must find him, My Lord. The ones he calls his disciples are being followed. They have been seen heading toward the west shore of the Sea of Galilee. It's been over two weeks since he fled – it's still hard to believe that he fed all his people who had come to hear him speak."

Herod's face flushed red. He shouted, "HIS PEOPLE?" and then made a tight fist and held it up to Octavius's nose. "They aren't 'his' people. This is 'my' kingdom and 'my' people. Find him! Jesus must die!"

39

After heading west, Jesus's disciples decided to split up and then traveled in opposite directions around the perimeter of the Sea of Galilee. As instructed by Jesus, they went from town to town seeking those who welcomed them and avoiding those who were inhospitable. To those who welcomed them, the disciples taught The Word and applied their healing abilities to the best of their evolving abilities. From each town, small groups of followers joined them, and then they moved on to the next town. Those not successfully healed were invited to come with the disciples to meet Jesus and have their infirmities healed by the Master, and most followed. Some of the disciples ventured to the bordering country towns to scattered houses to gather followers and then made their way back to travel on around the sea.

Rumors that the Messiah had arrived and of his many miracles preceded the traveling disciples. The disciples told the people that they would lead those who followed them to "him." Many joined in the fervent hope that finally, the prophecies had come true, that a new age of liberation from their oppressors was at hand, and that the Messiah would lead them to the Kingdom of God.

After two and a half months of travel, the disciples and their large collections of followers arrived in Magdala, a fishing town on the western shore of the Sea of Galilee near Tiberius. There, they all gathered at noon at the town square's landmark tower to await the arrival of the Messiah. Luke asked Judas and Joseph, who stood together looking anxiously about for Jesus, "Are you sure this is the right place and time?"

Judas replied, "Joseph and I had the same dream that he would be here today. Keep the faith that he will come."

Luke looked nervously at the more than eight hundred followers who were anxiously awaiting that moment. He said, "I hope you're right, or we'll have to deal with a lot of angry people."

Joseph spoke up, "I know when my dreams are true. He told me that he would be here, and he will."

"Keep the faith, Luke," Judas said. "Keep the faith."

After Jesus's feeding of the masses and then his disappearance, the temple police had been told to camp out in the countryside near Magdala until the disciples called for them. They had been called two days ago and now kept order among the assembled people. Provisions had been gathered from each town that the disciples had taught and healed in, and now those provisions were being distributed among the waiting people as their noon meal. The sky was gray and overcast. It was a cool day, and the smell of the sea permeated the air. Some people put blankets over their shoulders, and many covered their heads with hooded garments.

Joseph tapped Judas's shoulder and pointed to a lone figure in a reddish-brown robe with its hood covering his head and the sides of his face. "It's him! Our Master is here!"

Judas quickly notified the temple police, who ran to Jesus and gathered around him in a circle of protection. The crowd started yelling, "He's here! He's here!" Soon everyone hurriedly massed around the protective circle, many still holding food in their hands from their unfinished meals. The other disciples made their way to Jesus and greeted him warmly. Many in the crowd had been among those who partook of the fish and bread that Jesus had provided for them months earlier and eagerly awaited Jesus – now he was among them. They clamored about him and yelled out praise.

Jesus turned down his hood and raised his hands to the crowd. They cheered him as a true hero. Jesus put his hands down, and the disciples called for quiet. They and the police knelt as Jesus began to speak to the silenced crowd. "I look upon you and see many things. I see in many of your hearts the hope that I will change your life for the better. I also see doubters who are secretly hopeful that their doubts are wrong."

Jesus turned his head to the right as he scanned the last of the crowd and said, "There are others who are here for different reasons. To those who have true hope, I will do all that I can to fulfill that hope."

"Heal me! I bleed from my sores," an old man yelled.

A woman cried out, "Heal me! My head pains me so horribly that I can't see clearly!"

A chorus of varied pleas echoed from the crowd for healing, wealth, and status.

Jesus raised his hands, again requesting quiet. The disciples helped to hush the crowd. Jesus spoke again. "Tomorrow a healing service will be conducted. The time and place will be announced later. Now I will walk among you and give my blessings to anyone who wishes to receive them."

Judas abruptly stood and said, "Master, it's too dangerous for you to walk among the people. They'll maul you."

Jesus smiled and said," Have faith, Judas."

"I do, My Lord. But I am still concerned. Please let me create a path for you."

Jesus replied, "If it gives you comfort."

Judas told the police and disciples to align the crowd on both sides of the street so that Jesus could walk down the middle to bless everyone in an orderly fashion.

The path was cleared, and Jesus began his walk. Judas led the way, peering closely at those kneeling on the ground awaiting Jesus's blessing. Two of the policemen followed directly behind Jesus. Jesus directed his "healing palms" toward each person he passed. As if a torch were being passed along two parallel rows of candles, lighting them, each person glowed brightly as Jesus passed and blessed them. Some of the people gasped, others declared their infirmities healed, and some fainted with overwhelming emotion. Others touched his open flowing robe as he walked by, desperately wanting to be connected to him.

Suddenly Jesus stopped. He pointed to a kneeling man in a dark robe with the hood covering his head, which was turned to the side. The man looked at Jesus with his one exposed eye. Jesus said to the man, "Arise. You need not spend time kneeling in false pretense. Go now to Herod and tell him that I am here."

The man sat up so fast that his hood fell back over his shoulders, revealing his startled face. His stunned eyes wide with disbelief, he stared motionlessly at Jesus for five seconds. The police stood by, looking puzzled. Suddenly, the man bolted to his feet, turned, and ran away as fast as he could. A policeman started to chase him, but Jesus called to him, "Come back. He is doing my bidding." The policeman returned, and Jesus continued his walk, delivering his blessings. The people waited anxiously for their turn. Judas looked curiously at Jesus and then continued to lead the way.

A very pale pregnant woman cast herself in front of Jesus and lay on the ground. She laid both hands on her belly and frantically pleaded, "Please save my baby. It hasn't moved for days, and I'm bleeding from the womb." Jesus knelt beside her and placed one hand on the woman's forehead and the other over her swollen belly. In a few moments, the woman's wan complexion turned rosy pink. She sighed and breathed more easily. She put her hand to her belly, then smiled broadly and cried out, "My baby kicked!" She kissed Jesus's sandaled foot.

Jesus smiled at her and said, "Your baby boy will be born healthy." She crawled back to the sideline sobbing tears of joy.

Jesus continued. A kneeling man held a frail four-year-old girl in his arms. Her legs were twisted in, causing her feet to align toe to toe instead of pointing forward. "She's unable to walk properly," the man said. "My little girl was born this way." Jesus reached down, took the girl's feet in his hands, and gently turned them to align her toes forward.

When he let go of her feet, her toes remained pointing forward. The man gasped.

Jesus said, "Have her stand upright."

The man placed his daughter on her feet. She walked a few steps, then turned and quickly returned to her father's arms. "It's a miracle! It's a miracle!" the man exclaimed.

"It is God's gift and a blessing. Live your life and..." Jesus paused in mid-sentence. His face went blank for a moment; then his eyebrows rose in a concentrated expression. He turned his head and looked behind and beyond the police and the crowd. "My dear Father, is it possible?" he whispered. He closed his eyes for two seconds, then exclaimed loudly, "It's her!"

Jesus quickly stepped through the people on the sideline and ran in the direction he had been looking. Judas and the police ran after him. The disciples quickly followed, and the crowd hurriedly followed them. Jesus dashed through the streets at a blurring speed. His robe flowed behind him like a cape in the wind exposing his white tunic. He sprinted toward the edge of town. A woman's voice wailed in pain, followed by a loud plea, "No! Please, no more. Please."

Jesus ran faster. He turned the corner of the street and saw a woman lying in the center of the town's stoning pit. Her fractured left arm dangled limply by her side. She writhed in excruciating pain. The side of her forehead bled profusely, and blood dripped from her ear. She feebly held up her other hand in front of her face to ward off another stoning attack.

Thirty men encircled her with large stones in their hands. One man cocked his heavy stone back over his shoulder. He grimaced in hate and disgust, and then he prepared to throw it with full force at the prostrate woman. In a thunderous voice that echoed loudly in the pit, Jesus ordered, "STOP! Do not throw that stone!"

The man, taken by surprise, held his stone to his side and turned toward the source of the voice as Jesus ran up to him. The indignant man adamantly declared, "That Jewish prostitute fornicated with a Roman soldier on the Sabbath. She was judged guilty and sentenced to be stoned to death. Who are you to tell us to stop?"

Jesus stood between the man and the bleeding woman and said to the man, "I am the one who knows about you."

The man looked contemptuously at Jesus and said, "Go away, Stranger."

Then he stepped to Jesus's side. He grasped his stone tightly and again arched his hand back, again ready to throw. In an instant, Jesus gripped the man's wrist in a vice-like hold and said, "This man next to you is your best friend."

The best friend nodded in acknowledgement. Jesus continued to speak to the man about to throw the stone. "Your friend has a very pretty wife whom he loves deeply." The friend nodded again but looked oddly at Jesus, who continued, "You like his pretty wife also." The man with the stone brought his hand to his side once more. Jesus relaxed his grip slightly but still held the man's wrist. He said to him, "Last week you met your friend's wife in your stable and enjoyed yourself with her."

The stunned man dropped his stone and looked at Jesus incredulously. He turned toward his friend, who glared menacingly back at him. His friend clenched the stone that he held and brought it toward the man's face. The man turned and ran. His friend ran after him. He threw his rock at him on the run and narrowly missed his head. The other man ran faster.

Judas, the police, and the disciples arrived and saw Jesus addressing the men around the stoning pit. They approached Jesus, who put up his hand signaling them to stay where they were. Jesus walked to another nearby stone-thrower and said to him, "Why would you, a married man with six children, stone this woman for being a prostitute when you paid her for your pleasure two days ago?"

The man slowly backed away from Jesus, and then he dropped his stone and ran. The rest of the people who had gathered in the town square for Jesus's blessings soon arrived and wondered what was happening. The police and disciples kept them at a distance.

Jesus ignored the growing crowd and turned to another stone thrower. The painful wailing of the stoned woman cut into the momentary silence as Jesus stood before the next man. He said to him, "And you, who carried the Torah for last Friday night's Sabbath service, you visited the woman you now stone early the next morning before Saturday's Sabbath service. You are a married man. Have you not also sinned and committed adultery on the Sabbath? Should you not be stoned?"

The man's astonished face turned ashen. He dropped his rock. The gathering crowd listened intently. The stone throwers became wary with so many people now looking at them and this unknown man, Jesus, sharing, with great authority, secret knowledge of their neighbors' abhorrent behavior. Jesus pointed his finger at the man he last addressed, who now backed away from him. Jesus slowly turned in an arc and pointed his finger at each man encircling the stoning pit. He loudly declared, "I see the sins that each of you has knowingly committed. I will tell every one of your sins, and then the people can judge whether you are righteous enough to judge this woman whom you want to stone to death. If any of you can say in your heart that you are without sin, then cast the next stone."

The stunned stone throwers looked at each other with fearful and guilty expressions. They all backed away and dropped their rocks. Jesus then went to the wounded woman and knelt by her side. He tenderly stroked the side of her bruised and bleeding face, then placed his hand over her blood-filled ear. She reached up and placed her hand over his, and in a barely audible voice she asked weakly, "Is it you? My beloved Jesus?"

"Yes, Mary, it is I." He picked her up and carried her as if she were as light as a baby. He carried her past the stone throwers, who quickly parted to create a path for him. Jesus then walked toward Judas and the police, who immediately encircled him.

Judas asked, "Where are you going?"

"To the little synagogue near the square," Jesus replied.

"Who is this woman?" Judas asked.

"Ask nothing more of me now," Jesus replied as he walked on, staring tenderly and lovingly at the woman in his arms.

"What can he be doing in there?" Peter asked Judas.

"I don't know," Judas replied, "but we must respect the Messiah's request not to be disturbed. He said that he will speak to us when he is ready."

Luke protested, "He needs to know that those people outside are wondering why he has taken a prostitute onto the synagogue's grounds. Already rumors are circulating. The people also keep asking when tomorrow's healing session will begin. What are we to tell them?"

"Tell them to be patient, "Judas said. "The Messiah will let them know in due time. We must also be patient until then."

Jesus and Mary were in the bedroom of the synagogue rabbi's quarters. Judas had made arrangements for Jesus and his disciples to stay there during their time in Magdala. The Magdala rabbi who had witnessed Jesus's miracles in Capernaum had gladly relinquished his home to the Messiah and would stay with relatives for the duration of Jesus's visit. The disciples continued to speculate about what Jesus and the prostitute were doing in the bedroom for two hours.

Jesus sat on the edge of the bed and looked at Mary's face as she lay asleep. She started to dream again. Jesus was able to see her dream images and feel the feelings of her life's most intense experiences.

With Jesus's ministrations, Mary's skull and brain injuries were rapidly healing. Her fractured arm had already mended. Jesus placed his hand gently over the injured side of Mary's face and head. Still asleep, she stirred slightly and placed her hand over his, murmuring, "My beloved Jesus"; then she rested peacefully and continued dreaming.

The trauma and shock of her stoning brought up deep memories from her aura of when she was a sweet-faced but severely traumatized seven-year-old girl. Jesus saw the images of her aura and dream blending together. The little girl's wrist was being grabbed by a man's strong hand. He pulled her into a room and punched her arm forcefully, knocking her off her feet, but he held her wrist tightly, preventing her fall, and jerked her up to her feet. The shocked little girl cried out, "I didn't do anything!"

The man raised his fist as he held onto her wrist with his other hand and said, "I know. But you must be taught to respect me and my family. You must obey us or you'll be beaten far worse than what will happen to you now. This is the first lesson I teach to all my slaves." He punched her hard on the side of her head – the same side that had just been stoned.

The sleeping Mary winced and pressed her hand over Jesus's more securely. Images of "little Mary" and her family appeared in her aura of the day before the beating. Two Roman soldiers stood at her family's front door. Her mother and father were crying and hugging her tightly. Her sisters and brothers were also in tears and very frightened.

Mary's father had previously claimed that he had been unfairly taxed for a crop that had failed and left the family penniless. The tax collector said it wasn't true and demanded payment. The family had no money to pay; subsequently, a Roman court ruled that all their land would be confiscated unless the tax was paid. The tax collector knew a Roman family that needed another slave girl. The father of that family wanted a "pretty little slave girl" and would pay handsomely for the right one, and the tax collector would receive a hefty fee. The tax collector persuaded the family to sell Mary to settle their debts or lose everything. The parents vehemently protested, but in the end they had no other means of providing for the rest of the family and remorsefully had to obey the court order.

The two Roman soldiers walked toward little Mary, who clung fearfully to her parents. Her mother held Mary's face in her hands, and with tears streaming down her cheeks, she said to her daughter, "Whatever happens to you, know in your heart that we have always loved you and we always will."

"Enough," one soldier said. He took hold of the little girl's arm, yanked her away from her mother, and pulled her out the door.

Little Mary cried hysterically and screamed, "No! No!"

Jesus grimaced at the heart-wrenching scene he viewed. He sighed compassionately as he experienced Mary's terror and anguish. After that first night's merciless beating by her new Roman master, more images and feelings of oppression emerged of her seven-year-old self working strenuously for long hours doing laundry, cleaning the house, and performing endless chores. Then images appeared of her master's family humiliating and beating her on a multitude of occasions. Mary now cringed as images of the little girl being molested and sodomized by the new family's father and his young sons appeared in her aura. Jesus felt the intensity of her terror and humiliation. He also felt the entrenched hate and anger she had harbored from her hopeless state of enslavement.

Jesus spoke to Mary in her dream state, *"What happened to that little girl was terrible. That little girl is a part of you, but she is not the woman you are now. I will help cleanse you of your hate, anger, and fear so that your heart will be able to receive love. Please allow me to help."*

Mary's dream voice replied, *"I'm afraid. It's too difficult for me to trust anyone."*

Jesus sat back and stared at Mary. Her physical injuries had healed completely, but her emotional injuries from the past were a more complicated matter for him to minister to because of his previous intimate connection with Mary. Jesus knew from his experience with his mother in Nazareth that in spite of his desire to help, his intervention could not be successful if her beliefs were in opposition. He yearned to connect Mary to the Light.

After hearing Jesus's voice, Mary's dream turned to images of the time when they had first met when Jesus was on a break from rabbinical school. As a teenager, Mary had managed to run away from her captivity; she changed her name and was in hiding, ever fearful of being found by the Romans and arrested for being a runaway slave and then tortured and killed. Jesus glimpsed images of their then evolving relationship and of their moments of closeness. Her desire for him was as powerful as his had been for her, yet her inner demons of fear, anger and hatred of men were so instilled in her psyche that those overwhelming emotions had prevented her from opening herself to receiving love in the complete way that Jesus had then yearned for. Her childhood sexual experiences had tainted her and only allowed partial intimacy with Jesus.

Jesus shook his head at those frustrating early days with Mary. He felt then, and reaffirmed his feelings now, that there had been an undeniable chemistry – an attraction so powerful that they seemed destined to be together. It was a time in young Jesus's life that had given him the greatest pleasures and the most acute pains. Mary had been his first and only love.

Images then appeared of the time after he and Mary had parted. To provide a living for herself, Mary had turned to prostitution, yet her body was devoid of any sexual pleasure. She had developed a powerful resentment of all men although now Jesus could discern a long-buried flame of love and desire for him. Mary would soon awaken. Jesus turned away from her to compose himself and to commune with his heavenly Father. He sought to look at Mary's thought-form images as his heavenly Father would – with ineffable understanding, without judgment, and with unfathomable acceptance and divine love.

———

Nicodemus stood with Samuel in a corner of the Sanhedrin's conference chamber, which adjoined the Jerusalem Temple council's court. He whispered to Samuel, "I'm leaving tonight for Capernaum. I must meet with the Messiah."

"But tomorrow is the vote to decide how the council will officially decide the best way to react to Rome's new tax increase." Samuel placed his hand on Nicodemus's shoulder and implored, "Your wisdom and guidance are needed. The council will listen to you. A tempered response to the new taxes is vital if we're going to prevent an uprising of our people that Rome will ruthlessly crush."

"There are always pressing matters that must be attended to," Nicodemus replied, "but now I feel compelled to speak with the Messiah and ask his advice on how I can best help all concerned. If he was able to feed over five thousand people, he will surely know how to lead us to a new age."

"Your presence at the council will be sorely missed. What shall I tell everyone?"

"Tell them I have gone to visit my infirm uncle, which I will do also, but say nothing of my seeking the Messiah. To help him, I must maintain my neutrality with the council."

Samuel agreed, "I will do as you request."

———

Mary stirred. Still sleeping, she tossed her head side to side. Her lips formed a faint smile of peace, then a grimace. She clenched her hands into fists. She thrust a protective hand out in front of her and cried out, "No! Please. No more! Please!"

Jesus saw in her aura's images of the stone throwers about to hurl more rocks at her. Mary bolted up and sat wide-eyed facing Jesus. In her panicked and confused state, she asked, "Where am I? Who are you?"

Before Jesus could answer, she started to get off the bed to leave. Jesus said, "Wait."

Mary ignored him and in her state of fear, made for the door. She had taken two steps when her knees buckled from her recent trauma. Jesus caught her in his arms and carried her back to the bed. "You need to be still. You're too weak to move about."

As Mary stared at him, her expression softened. "Is it you? Can it be?" she asked in an incredulous whisper.

Jesus took her hand and kissed it, "Yes, Mary, I am with you now."

She was overwhelmed. "How is it possible," she asked, "after all these years?"

"It doesn't matter how; we're together now."

Mary reached out her hand and touched Jesus's beard, "It is you. Your beard has filled in nicely." She smiled. "It is you!" Her eyes welled with tears.

Jesus gently placed his hand on the side of Mary's face. "I see you as I first saw you," he said softly. He smiled. "It brings pleasure to my heart."

Mary put her hand over his. "Your hand feels so warm and soothing." Then her body stiffened. "I remember now." She grimaced again. "They were stoning me. The first rock broke my arm." She raised her arm up and moved it about. "It feels fine now. How long have I been here?"

"Long enough to heal. Please, tell me what else you remember."

She pressed her hand over his against the side of her face and head. "The second rock hit my head. I heard my skull crack; then I couldn't see anything." A tear rolled down her cheek and onto Jesus's fingers. "But I heard your precious voice."

Her brow furrowed, "You saved my life. How could you have known of those men's sins?"

"My heavenly Father has given me the gift of divine sight, "Jesus replied.

"I don't understand," Mary said.

"It doesn't matter. You're safe now. That's what's important."

Mary put her arms around Jesus, and they embraced. She pressed her body hard against his and cried. She whispered, "It's really you."

They sat silently and looked into each other's eyes, connecting once again. Mary said, "After you left me," she lowered her head shamefully, "I lived a life... a life that would disgust you."

"I know of your life," Jesus replied. He kissed her forehead, "There is nothing that you have done or could do that would disgust me. I accept you fully as you are now."

"How could you know of my life?"

"I told you that my heavenly Father has given me the gift of divine sight. Believe me, I know."

The way Jesus spoke and her memory of his naming the sins of the stone throwers convinced her that what he said was true. "Then you must know of the terrible things they did to me as a slave-child," Mary said, her face contorted painfully with anger, hate, and resentment.

"Yes, I do," Jesus replied in a soft, compassionate voice.

Mary sobbed while Jesus held her. She wrapped her arms around him, then pressed against him, and between her sobs said, "They made me do anything they desired! Anything! Any time they wanted!"

Jesus stroked her back, comforting her as she cried. He said, "As a child in your circumstances, you did nothing wrong. When you were able to run away, you did."

Mary's tense shoulders relaxed with the relief of having finally shared her dark secret with Jesus; her tears decreased. "I loved you so much," she said, "I thought if you knew of my past, you would leave me."

"My beloved Mary. Know that I love you in blessed ways, more than ever before."

Mary leaned away from Jesus, looked into his eyes, and said, "You always told the truth." Jesus tenderly wiped the tears from her cheeks. She smiled weakly and said, "I believe you. Then, I could not bring myself to trust a man." She embraced him again, and he hugged her lovingly.

After a few moments, she asked, "But if you know that I've become a prostitute, how can you still love me? I've lived such an unclean life."

"My sweet Mary, you've done what you felt you had to do to survive. You sold your body, not your heart and soul. I am truly grateful that you have survived so that I can be with you now. I don't judge you. I accept you with my love as I know my heavenly Father accepts you with His unquestionable love."

"Hold me," Mary implored. "Please, just hold me."

Jesus drew Mary to him and held her in his arms. They remained embraced in peaceful, silent union

Peter stood up in the main room and said, "We shouldn't have to wait any longer. We haven't seen the Messiah in months, and now," Peter pointed down the hallway toward the bedroom, "he's in there with her. I'm going to knock on the door and ask him to come out."

Peter started to walk down the hallway. As he passed Judas, Judas grabbed Peter's robe and pulled him back. "Do not disturb our Master! When he is ready to be with us, he will come."

Peter scowled at Judas, but Judas pulled more firmly on Peter's robe. The other twenty-three disciples sitting on chairs and on the floor stared at the two of them. Finally, Peter backed off and said, "Okay, Judas, I'll wait. But our Messiah being with that prostitute for so long isn't right."

Mary and Jesus reminisced about how they had first met in the marketplace. She had been carrying a bucket of water to her one-room home. As she was walking by him, he caught her eye; then he tripped and stumbled against her, spilling the water over her shabby dress.

Mary's tears had now dried. She laughed at that recollection and said, "I thought you were clumsy and inconsiderate."

Jesus smiled affectionately. "And you told me so. Very curtly, as I remember."

"You were just another man. I hated all men. But as I got to know you...you were so different from anyone I'd ever met. Later on, I was thankful that you had accidentally bumped into me."

Jesus replied, "I know now that it wasn't an accident. All events have a purpose. Our 'accident' was a divine connection that was destined to happen in our time."

"You've become quite a philosopher," Mary teased.

"You'd be surprised at what I've become," Jesus teased back.

Mary hugged him tightly and said, "I don't care. I'm just glad you're here now. Thank you for saving my life. Thank you."

She leaned back against the small headboard and held Jesus's hands. She studied his face and then said, "You've become more attractive with age." She smiled. "But I still see that – almost boyish – sweet kindness in you."

Mary sighed, "I was mean to you sometimes. Can you forgive me for being a silly girl then?"

Jesus replied, "I felt fortunate to be with you in all your moods. I know now that it was your pain and anger that were speaking harshly, not your heart."

Mary squeezed Jesus's hands. "You were always so gracious and forgiving."

"Certainly not to everyone then, but I had loved no one as I loved you. Nothing you could say or do could destroy that love."

Mary embraced Jesus again. She closed her eyes and felt his muscular chest against hers. Silent and still and at peace, they remained in each other's arms.

The sergeant of the temple police knocked rapidly on the door. Luke opened it, and the disciples looked on as the sergeant spoke. "The people keep asking when the Messiah will come back out. They want to know what's happening. They're restless and getting unruly. What should we tell them?"

Judas came to the door and told the sergeant, "Go back to your post. We'll be right out." The sergeant nodded and left. Judas turned to the disciples and said, "John, Luke, Matthew, Simon, Seth, come with me. The rest of you – keep your faith in our Master."

Jesus sat against the headboard alongside Mary. They held hands, and their legs lay straight out on the bed. Mary sighed and said, "I regret I couldn't have been more intimate with you. Maybe you wouldn't have left me."

"You were very intimate with me when we just held hands lying down in a meadow, watching the clouds by day or the stars at night, never saying a word, but feeling the closeness of sharing God's majesty. That was a sacred intimacy I wouldn't have experienced had I not been with you. I realize that we had countless shared moments of true intimacy – and I cherish them all."

"You're so sweet. I cherished those times also. But I meant that I regret that I couldn't feel more sexually intimate. You were young and so eager... and so easily stimulated...and so disappointed when I couldn't respond to you."

Jesus laughed, "That's how most young men are. It was all very confusing to me then. I thought you were rejecting me because you didn't love me as I loved you. I know now that the abuses you suffered as a child caused you to feel revulsion toward sex and to harbor anger, hate and resentment toward all men. Like demons, those wretched feelings possessed you and governed your judgment."

"I did resent you as a man, but your love and kindness toward me melted much of that away." Mary stared at the empty air before her and said, "But..." as a tear formed in the corner of her eye, "I know deep inside, I wasn't able to cast off those painful experiences of my past. They stood in the way...I'm sorry."

"Please, don't be. You've given me the blessed privilege of having loved you. There were times of pain, for no true love is without those moments. But my heart would race with joy just knowing that I was going to see you at a certain time. All I could think about was you. It may have been confusing and frustrating at times, but that was a small price to pay to have shared those treasured moments with you that stirred my soul like no other."

Mary sighed, "I wish I had known then that you felt that way."

"I also wish I could have known that then, as I do now. Please have no regrets, especially since we did share love as best we could. I'm grateful for that!"

Mary sighed, then said, "If we had married, your life would have been miserable with me. You did the right thing to leave."

"Please don't feel that way. Unfulfilled desires are usually frustrating to a young man, but in our relationship, much of my frustration came from the failure of my efforts to comfort you. I loved you and wanted to make you happy."

"You made me laugh at times, more than I had in years," Mary offered.

Jesus smiled fondly. "We both laughed. Sharing laughter is a gift."

Mary sighed with deep remorse, "I had so much sadness then, I wish I could have laughed more."

"So did I wish that for you. I felt inadequate for you. I realize now that no one can make another happy, they can only provide the opportunity. I also felt sexually inadequate to satisfy you as a man. That was painful then; now I know that it was the demons from your past and not me that prevented our complete union."

Mary rested her head on Jesus's shoulder and said, "We were so young then. You were the only one I ever felt close to, and I was never as intimate with my feelings as I was with you, especially my feelings of anger."

Stroking Mary's hair, Jesus said, "I thought then that you were angry at me, that I had done something wrong. As a man who loved his beloved, it was my impulse to make things right for you. I felt your anguish but didn't know the source and thought it was me. I know now that you projected your hurt feelings of the past onto me." Jesus squeezed Mary's hand reassuringly. "That was because we shared an intimate connection as best we could and you were able to express your feelings with me as best you could."

Mary squeezed Jesus's hand in response and replied, "You tried so hard in so many ways. You spoiled me, and I took you for granted... until you left. I felt so lonely and empty without you. You'd wipe the tears from my eyes when I cried, and then you'd make me laugh."

Jesus gently brushed away Mary's tears. She kissed his hand and said, "After you left, it felt like a part of me was missing – like when I lost my childhood and became a slave. Before that, as a child, I took everything for granted, that I would be fed and loved and could play forever. As a slave, I craved the simplest joys of childhood but was denied. And when you were gone from my life, I craved the simple loving and kind things that you did for me – a pretty flower, a strip of cloth that you tried to tie to make into a bird." Mary giggled, "It sure was a funny-looking bird!"

Jesus replied, "I didn't know how to make it fly then."

"You sure knew how to make me laugh…I missed that so much." Mary looked at Jesus's profile. He had closed his eyes as he listened to her. "What are you thinking?" she asked.

Jesus opened his eyes and turned to her. "I wasn't thinking as much as seeing and feeling."

"What do you mean?"

"As you spoke your thoughts of our time together, I was able to see those times as they occurred. I was able to know your thoughts at that time and mine. More importantly, I was able to experience the source of our emotions – why we felt certain ways that governed our actions. Looking back through the eyes of time, I know that we loved each other then the best way that was possible for us then."

Mary let out a deep sigh and asked, "If you loved me so much and didn't leave me because of my sexual inadequacies, then why did you leave?"

Jesus again stroked Mary's long hair. "I will tell you what I know now. There was no doubt in my heart that I loved you. Before I met you, I had made a promise to a very wise rabbi. His name was Stephen, and I respected and loved him. He was from an aristocratic family, yet very humble. Despite objections from his peers, he was steadfast in his beliefs that the truth of the Torah should be interpreted for the needs of today's times and should be taught to all people in a universal manner. Just before I made a commitment to become a rabbi, I had a dream in which I was a healer and a counselor helping others and teaching God's Truth. That's what a rabbi should do. And the rabbi I most admired said that he would sponsor me for rabbinical school. I told him of my dream. He said that he had had a dream that very night before…that a student of rare abilities would come before him who was seeking those very same things. And he knew that I was the one. He dedicated himself to teaching me in his more insightful ways.

"I was honored and thrilled. I felt that with his teachings, I could fulfill the desires of my dream – which I know now were needed to fulfill my destiny, and I made a promise to him."

Mary placed her hand on Jesus's shoulder. "You always seemed inner-guided, and I am truly happy for you that you've succeeded in becoming a rabbi and a healer." Mary waved her healed arm. "And I'm happy for myself that you've been able to help me. And with your gift of inner sight, maybe you should join forces with that other Jesus everyone is talking about. They say he's the Messiah who has come and will change the world forever."

Jesus nodded. "I have joined forces with God."

Mary asked, "Is it possible for me to help you?"

"All things are possible," Jesus replied.

Mary sighed. "That's encouraging. Please, tell me what you promised Stephen, the rabbi."

"I promised him that I wouldn't let anything prevent me from achieving that goal and would never disappoint him."

"But what has that got to do with the reason why you left me? If you loved me, then even with our problems, I would have married you and you could still have gone to rabbinical school."

Jesus sighed, "It was the way I loved you that was my problem then." Jesus took Mary's hand and kissed it. "I was so deeply in love with you that being with you, or even the thought of being with you, dominated my mind. I was ruled by my feelings... my feelings of love for you."

"Was that a bad thing?" Mary asked.

"Certainly it was not a bad thing. That feeling gave me the greatest pleasure I had ever known at that time. To be able to feel such love is divine. But I also realized that our relationship would interfere with my becoming a rabbi."

"How?"

"Because I needed you so desperately when I was without you. Above all, a rabbi is meant to be a man of God, and a man of God's true spirit cannot be a desperate man. To possess God's true spirit is to have an undying faith that leaves nothing to be desperate about. It was a choice I made to pursue God's work and to no longer pressure you to love me in ways that I yearned for but that you were unable to fulfill. There were times I just wanted to hold you in my arms, to feel the closeness of your body – not in a sexual way, just a loving, tender embrace. You would push away from me as if I were a nuisance that you resented. I was young and wanted to be your hero, not an annoyance to you. It broke my heart to leave you even though I thought it was the best thing for both of us at the time."

"My sweet Jesus. You are a hero to me now. You saved my life. It was those inner demons of mine that treated you horribly. My heart broke when you left, but the demons lived on. After I turned to prostitution, my resentment and hatred of men increased tenfold. I have never experienced sexual satisfaction."

Jesus held the sides of Mary's face. He looked into her eyes. "I think I can satisfy you in a way that you've never experienced."

Mary grimaced. "Forgive me, but much to my disgust, I have already experienced everything imaginable."

Jesus smiled, "Not like what I now have in my heart for you. But first, if you'll allow me, I will exorcise those demons from you that kept us apart."

"If that will bring us closer together, please cast them off from me; they've separated us for too long."

Jesus stood up beside the bed and said, "Lie down flat on your back."

Mary did so. Jesus raised his hands over Mary's body and began to cast out her seven demons of anger, fear, anxiety, resentment, despair, anguish, and hate to facilitate the healing of her emotional body.

<hr/>

Judas had not yet come back with the disciples who had accompanied him. They were still trying to placate the huge crowd that had massed around the synagogue grounds. The disciples in the house were debating whether they should disturb the Messiah to ask him what they should do. Most of the disciples cast aspersions on the prostitute he was with and what might be happening in the bedroom. Joseph refrained from speaking.

Suddenly they heard a loud, fiendish howl from the woman in Jesus's room. Bartholomew was closest to the hall and was the first one to get to the bedroom. The others quickly followed. Bartholomew was about to knock on the door when Joseph warned, "Remember what Judas said: 'Do not disturb our Master. When he is ready to be with us, he will come.'"

Peter said, "Something terrible may have happened. Go ahead and knock."

Bartholomew hesitated. He looked at Joseph, who shook his head "no." The other disciples were lined up in the hallway anxiously waiting for Bartholomew to act. Instead of knocking, Bartholomew pressed his ear against the door to listen. He heard Jesus say, "Your demons have been cast off. You are free. Now rest."

Bartholomew kept his ear against the door but heard nothing more. He turned to the others and said, "Our Master exorcised demons from the woman. That's what the scream was about."

The disciples were temporarily relieved. John said, "Let's maintain our faith in the Messiah. Leave him be." They all went back to the main room except for Peter and Bartholomew, who sat down outside the bedroom door.

<hr/>

Mary opened her eyes. Jesus sat next to her. She took his hand and said, "I feel so...different, so light. Before, I felt as if I had been buried in sand up to my neck, unable to move about and express myself." She took a deep breath and exhaled with relief, "Now I feel free." She cried, "Oh my sweet Jesus, you've unlocked the chains that have bound my heart and mind. I'm free!"

Jesus caressed her face and said, "Yes, you are free. I see your innocence now as the child you were. You're no longer enslaved by your past. You're free to choose a far better life for yourself."

"I want to be with you," Mary immediately replied. "I missed my opportunity to truly love you and receive your love. She sat up and embraced him. "Can we be together again? This time I know it will be different and wonderful for both of us."

Jesus smiled tenderly. "We can be together, but in a different way from before. I said that I could satisfy you in a way that you have never experienced, and now, if you allow me, I would like to do so."

Mary hugged Jesus tightly. "Yes, yes, please. I'm ready. Anything you offer, I'm ready to receive."

Jesus said, "Close your eyes, and think of the times when we were young and together."

Mary did so. She excitedly said, "I can see you in my mind as you were when we were young."

Jesus held Mary's shoulders and faced her. She opened her eyes and saw Jesus's younger image as she had just seen it in her mind's eye.

She shrieked loudly with surprise.

Bartholomew and Peter sat up straight. They looked at each other and then pressed their ears against the door. The other disciples near the hall also heard Mary's shriek, and all of them crowded into the hallway to find out what was happening.

40

Mary had calmed down after the initial shock of seeing the young Jesus she had known before her. She touched his face. "I can't believe it. Even your beard is the same as it was then. How is it possible?"

"For now," Jesus replied, "just accept what you see."

Mary closed her eyes and inhaled deeply. "You even smell as you did then. I loved it." She opened her eyes.

Jesus smiled, "I always thought that I smelled bad."

Mary replied, "After you left, there was no part of you that I didn't love and yearn for." She looked into Jesus's eyes. "And now we are together again."

In the hallway, Andrew whispered to Peter, "What are they saying?"

Peter put his finger to his lips, made a "shush" sound, and whispered, "They're talking too low. I can't make out what they're saying." He pressed his ear against the door again.

Jesus said to Mary, "I see you also as I saw you then, through the eyes of love."

The gleam of young love came into Mary's eyes, and her face glowed and radiated with new life. "I feel closer to you than ever before. I want to be intimate with you – to feel what I have never known."

"You shall," Jesus replied. He looked into her eyes, and she stared back. She felt his power embrace her. Within that envelope of love, she closed her eyes. They pressed closer together. The fibers of her body tingled with an abandonment so intense and free that she shivered ecstatically. They communed in a divine, holy intimacy that she never could have imagined. A flood of Light and bliss swept over her. She gasped and then moaned loudly. She made swooning sounds and then let out a very loud, rapturous *"YELP!"*

All the disciples heard Mary's orgasmic yelp. Peter shook his head and said, "How could he?" The other disciples were dismayed.

Mary lay limp on the bed. Jesus kissed her forehead, then went to the door and said, "You need to sleep now so that all that has occurred can integrate in the best way. I must attend to other important matters."

"I do feel tired, but also exhilarated." Mary reached out her hand toward Jesus and said, "Please stay with me a little while longer, until I fall asleep."

Peter and Andrew heard Jesus's remark at the door. They gestured to the other disciples that he was coming out, and they all scurried back to the main room.

Jesus went back to Mary's bedside. He took her hand and said, "Close your eyes. Sleep will come."

She kissed his hand and looked at him in drowsy contentment. Soon her eyelids closed. Jesus stayed with her until he saw that she was sleeping peacefully.

As Jesus walked to the main room, he felt even more evolved and empowered by The Light. At the end of his forty-day retreat in the Wilderness of Judea, where he was imbued with the exalted energy of the Holy Spirit, he had realized that his physical body could not contain its awesome, majestic power beyond that time without disintegrating. Now he realized that The Light of the Holy Spirit that had remained within him had gradually continued to grow more powerful and evolve as more people acknowledged him as the Messiah.

As more people recognized and affirmed Jesus's inner forces of divine truth, the outer forces of people's new beliefs combined with Jesus's forces to initiate a powerful and unstoppable shift in mankind's thinking and psyche. The intertwining of those inner and outer confirming forces resonated together, increasing exponentially, and their effects would continue to carve an indelible path through mankind's evolving history.

Now, after his divine communion with Mary, he felt a surge of even greater empowerment. He also realized that a time would come when The Light within him would manifest itself to the point where his physical body would fade away and he would become a being of pure Light. That thought caused him to feel a greater urgency to complete his mission before that time arrived.

Jesus entered the main room and saw all the disciples kneeling and praying. At a glance, he saw what their minds were struggling with. Philip looked up and was startled to see Jesus. He exclaimed, "Master!"

The other disciples turned toward Jesus. The front door opened, and Judas, John, Matthew, Simon, and Seth entered. Judas addressed Jesus, "Master, in your absence, I've announced that your healing session for the people will be at noon tomorrow when you usually plan it. Do you wish to change the time?"

"You've done well, Judas. I am pleased with you."

Judas saw the deep concern on the other disciples' faces and asked, "What's going on? Is something wrong?"

Peter blurted, "The Messiah has been fornicating with a prostitute."

Thomas added, "We're praying for his forgiveness."

Judas looked at Jesus and questioned, "Master?"

Jesus held up his hand. "Say no more, Judas. Let these men speak their minds." He turned to Peter and said, "Say what you think."

"We thought that you were above such sins. We held you high over the lust of the flesh," Peter replied indignantly.

"Are you so righteous, Peter, that you have not sinned?" Jesus turned to the others and said, "Are any of you without sin?"

Andrew replied, "But we are mortal men; you are the Messiah."

"And my message is to forgive and to love. Yet you have condemned the woman as a prostitute and cast her in an immoral light because she received money to satisfy the lust of men. Could a prostitute ever be a prostitute without the carnal demands of men? If men feel that prostitutes should be shamed, should not men also share that shame?"

The disciples looked down at the floor. Then Philip said, "But, My Lord, what if you have a child, a child of the Son of God with a prostitute for a mother? What would your followers think?"

"You mean how would they judge me?" Jesus replied. "If they were true followers of my teachings, as you should be, then they would forgive me and love me and accept me, no matter what appearances may seem to be."

Luke spoke, "But, My Lord, why a prostitute? If you have carnal needs, why not choose a wholesome woman?"

"You judge her as a prostitute; I see her as a soul in a woman's body. From a young age, she was forced into slavery and woefully abused sexually as a child. In later years as a runaway, to support herself, she turned to prostitution and gave her body for money but never felt pleasure or fulfillment. But her soul yearned to give and receive love. I tell you this because there is a valuable lesson for you to learn. You have misinterpreted what occurred between Mary and me."

The disciples looked at each other, puzzled by what Jesus said. He continued, "As you secretly listened at the bedroom door, your ears deceived you. If you truly believed in me, your heart would not have deceived you."

The disciples stiffened, surprised that Jesus knew they had listened in on his privacy. Judas looked at them scornfully.

"When I looked upon the woman in the bedroom, I saw beyond her flesh and viewed her as patterns of light and color. I saw the pain and suffering in her life, and I extended my Light to her. It filled up the empty spaces of her soul, and she became complete. She yearned to be whole, and I provided an intimate connection to my heavenly Father, and she was fulfilled. The only physical connection was a hug, an embrace of spiritual love, not lust."

Still skeptical, Peter said, "But what we heard sounded...well, orgasmic."

Jesus shook his head disapprovingly and said, "O ye of little faith. It was not sexually orgasmic; it was the sound of the rapture of God-love – a moment of divine bliss that fills one up with an exquisite indescribable feeling of fulfillment and ecstatic joy. She cried, she quivered and swooned. She moaned, and she yelled with abandoned pleasure, but not from a sexual union. She experienced 'agape' – a sacred love that resonates with God's gift of life and oneness. And so you needn't worry; I can assure you that there will be no child."

Judas could hold his tongue no longer. "I told you not to disturb the Master!"

Simon said to the disciples, "You m-m-must always r-r-respect and honor our b-b-benevolent and loving M-M-Master."

Jesus smiled at Simon and said, "This occasion is not without purpose. It demonstrates that most of you are projecting your own thoughts and feelings upon me and still think of me in terms of the flesh. By now you should know that my dimensions are beyond that. I have nothing more to prove of myself than to be who I am. You have only to open the eyes of your hearts to see me for who and what I am."

Philip spoke with guilt. "Forgive me, for I have let you down."

"I forgive you. I forgive all of you, and you must forgive yourselves and learn that from this moment on, you must have undying faith in me, for I speak and act in the name of my heavenly Father, the Lord of all lords. If I accept Mary, the woman whom you condemn as a prostitute, as my companion, who among you has the right to judge me?"

The disciples stared at Jesus a moment; then Bartholomew said, "Not I."

James, his brother John, and Thomas chimed in and said, "Not I."

The other disciples also agreed, and all said "Not I."

Jesus replied, "That is good. From now on, you must demonstrate your suspension of judgment by honoring and respecting Mary as you do me."

Jesus looked upon the kneeling disciples and saw their resistance to accepting Mary. He said, "Before you pass judgment on a prostitute, pause, for truly I tell you that one of you is the great-grandson of a prostitute. If it were not for your great-grandmother and her part in your conception, you wouldn't be here now."

The disciples glanced at each other, wondering who it was. Then each wondered if it was he. Jesus nodded, seeing that they understood. But he also saw that their cultural prejudices toward women as subservient to men remained deeply ingrained. Many of the disciples still clung to the impression of Jesus engaging in sexual activity with the woman.

Jesus addressed the men, "It is understandable that common reason would lead you to believe that illicit activity was occurring behind the bedroom door when you listened but could not see the source of your impressions. However, you've been called to take on an uncommon mission that requires your faith to be greater than your reason. For a man to walk on water or raise the dead defies reason. It is my faith in my heavenly Father that supersedes reason and guides me to accomplish His bidding. And so you must rely more on your faith in me and trust my Father to guide you on your mission."

Jesus bid the kneeling men, "Now go out and be with the people. As my disciples, speak to them of my teachings and judge them not. Reassure them that I am safe and in God's guiding hands and speak His words. And as they follow The Way, so there lives shall be richer."

<hr />

The sun had set. He held her shoulders as she leaned against the synagogue's back wall. "Are you sure?" he asked.

"I should know. I'm pregnant. I've missed my period for two months – and I've always been on time." She took his hand and placed it on her belly. "Feel. I'm getting a little bigger there."

Joseph stared at Seffira. His mouth opened, but he was speechless. Seffira's forehead furrowed, "Well? What are you thinking?"

Joseph continued to stare a moment as the idea of his becoming a father took hold. Again she prodded, "Well?"

Joseph grinned nearly ear-to-ear and replied, "If the baby is like you, we will be blessed!" He drew her into his arms.

"But I want our child to be like you, Joseph."

Joseph squeezed her tighter. "It won't matter. It will be our child – and that is a blessed miracle! I'm so exited!"

Seffira pulled away. As her forehead furrowed once more, she said, "I'm worried about my parents and what they'll say."

"I'll ask the Messiah to marry us as soon as possible. What can they say if the Messiah marries us and gives us his blessing?"

She smiled, "Only good things…I hope." Seffira put her hand over her belly and said, "I'm hungry."

Joseph held her face tenderly. "When I look at you, I am nourished. I don't need food, for I want nothing more then to be in your presence."

Seffira grabbed his hand and pulled. "Come. We have a baby to feed."

It was nearly midnight. Herod secretly stood behind a curtain listening intently as Octavius questioned the trembling man in a brownish-black robe, the assassin who had been sent to Magdala to kill Jesus. "Yes," he replied, "I remember his words exactly. He said, 'Arise. You need not spend time kneeling in false pretense. Go now to Herod and tell him that I am here.'"

Herod clenched his fists.

Octavius asked, "What happened then?"

"There was no doubt in my mind that he knew I had the poison-tipped dagger in my hand. The temple police were by his side. He knew!" The assassin's hands were shaking. "I ran. The police started to chase me, but he called to them and said, 'Come back. He is doing my bidding.' I kept running and then rode here as fast as I could. He knew! The Rabbi looked right though me. How could he know?"

Herod hit his hand with his fist. The assassin looked toward the curtain at the sound's source. Octavius said, "You were right to report back immediately." He took the assassin's arm and led him to the door. Octavius said to the sentry at the door, "Take this man to the guards' mess hall and get him something special to eat. Stay with him."

As the sentry led the assassin down the hall, Octavius closed the door. Herod came out from behind the curtain, his face flaming with anger. "This Jesus mocks me! He sends my assassin away to tell me where he is. Then he taunts me by telling his police that my servant is doing 'his' bidding."

Trying to placate Herod, Octavius offered, "The assassin's food will be poisoned. No one will know of the failed plot."

Ignoring him, Herod said, "This Jesus must be highly clairvoyant. He knew what the man was thinking. Does he know what I'm thinking? Spartus was thwarted. This one also failed. Is this Jesus charmed? Or is it just luck? Or is he really the Messiah? What is this magic that he has that can produce five thousand loaves of bread out of the air and cause fish to jump out of the sea?"

Octavius replied, "He is a force to reckon with."

"No!" Herod yelled. "He is a force to be eliminated! He will never become the King of Israel while I still live. This time you will send the archer. He can hit a tossed coin in the air ten out of ten times from fifty yards."

"Maybe this is a time for us to reconsider our strategy," Octavius offered. "There is enough unrest since John the Baptist was beheaded.

Again I must suggest that it may be better to form an alliance with Jesus than oppose him."

"No! An alliance will only give him greater credibility. After the archer plants an arrow in his heart, the archer will be slain immediately. We will claim that we tried to protect the rabbi from being harmed, but it was too late."

"The people will still blame you for his death."

"I know, but it will still create some doubt. When Jesus travels on the road to wherever he is going next, that is when the deed is to be done. There are too many people around him in Magdala."

"As you wish, my Lord," Octavius replied and then stroked his beard. "It's ironic that your father tried to kill the Messiah when he was supposedly born in Bethlehem. If Jesus is the Messiah, then all those Jewish babies your father had slain were for naught."

Herod grinned devilishly. "If Jesus is the Messiah, then I will accomplish what my father could not do."

41

The crescent moon hanging over the pre-dawn horizon shone brightly against the pale, yellow-orange sky. Five long gray fingers of cloud sleepily rested above the silver moon. Jesus stood alone in the synagogue courtyard. In the stillness, he saw the black silhouette of palm trees against the soft pastel sky. Three large birds flew past the trees; their wings, silhouetted black, appeared like small flapping palm leaves, a sign that palm leaves of welcome would soon be laid before him.

He turned toward the door of the rabbi's quarters. A moment later, Judas opened it and walked toward him. Jesus greeted him, "It is a good morning, Judas."

"I hope it will turn into a good day. I'm troubled, Master. All of the men still grumble about you and Mary. I've accepted what you've told us, and I will accept Mary and extend my respect and honor to her as you have asked us to… but most of the others have yet to do so."

"I know, and I also know that you are the most faithful. The others have yet to fully bloom, but they will soon change their attitude toward Mary, and in doing so, they will become more enlightened and more worthy to carry my message and spread The Word."

Jesus looked at the palm trees and smiled. Judas asked, "Master, why do you smile?"

"You look at a tree and see its trunk, branches, and leaves. I see that also. But I also see my heavenly Father's vital life-force surrounding the trees." Jesus pointed to a distant mountain and said, "I see His life-force over the mountains." He turned to Judas and told him, "I see His life-force in every rock, in birds, in insects, and in you – all are of God's creation, and his gift of life dwells within; God's life-force surrounds and connects all things and gives vitality to all life."

Judas looked at the trees and the mountain, "I see the beauty in nature, but I don't see what you do."

"To see the beauty of all of God's creations is to see with gifted eyes. Be thankful for your sight and for what you do see. People see me as they must see a physical being, yet I have become much more. My time on earth moves quickly; and I have much to do, for I will soon leave."

"You have spoken of your leaving many times to me. It always causes me to feel a deep sadness."

"You must be happy for me when I'm gone from this body; for as John left this plane of existence not long after his baptism of me, so too will I leave when my mission on Earth has been completed. When that time comes, be not sad for me, for I will have a heavenly existence, and my influence will become greater than anyone can imagine."

"I cannot imagine life without you." Judas looked dismayed.

"Devote your feelings to the road ahead, Judas. There's much to do and little time left."

"What is the time schedule that you speak of?"

"The exact time is yet unknown, but I do know that the approximate time will be during Passover in Jerusalem."

Judas was aghast. "That's only six months away! How can we reach enough people by then?"

"I have already been working in the dream state to herald God's calling for mankind to enter a New Age. More and more souls are becoming open to that possibility. Trust the power of my working in the dream state, for as you now know, my dream communications have proved fruitful with you."

Judas replied, "I pray that it will be so for others."

Jesus spoke softly. "When I pray and work in the dream state, I affirm with my Father that those souls will see the Light; and He reveals to me that in time, with their desire and my teaching of His Word, all souls will know the Light." Jesus stared at the new dawn sky. The grey clouds had turned pink against the pale blue backdrop. The moon was dimmer as the glowing red ball of the sun rose above the horizon, illuminating the land and sea.

Jesus turned to Judas. "Awaken my disciples for our morning prayers. There is much to do."

Seth shook her shoulder again. Mary sat up in the bed with a start and asked, "Who are you?"

"My name is Seth. John told me to bring you breakfast. The Messiah said to awaken you one hour before his healing session."

"The Messiah? John? Who is John?"

"You can see for yourself by the village tower in one hour. I've got to go."

Seth left in a hurry. Mary looked at the food on the tray that Seth had brought. She felt her hunger and ate.

Two thousand people crowded around the landmark tall tower of Magdala. Jesus's protective circle surrounded him. To maintain order, his disciples escorted those wishing to be healed to the inner circle. Mary approached the periphery of the crowd but was too short to see above the mass of people. The crowd let out a gasp, and a tall man next to Mary said, "Did you see that? Unbelievable!"

"No. I can't see above everyone's heads."

"The Messiah just healed a leper," the man snapped his fingers, "just like that. He's done it for the lame, the blind, and he has exorcised demons." The man snapped his fingers again. "Just like that. He healed them!"

Mary walked around the periphery of the crowd, but the people stood too close together for her to make her way toward the front. Again the crowd gasped. Mary heard yells from them: "Heal me!" "Save me!" She made her way across the street to a stone house with a low stone wall. She climbed up on the wall to see. She gasped also, not because of the healing deeds of the man in the center, but because she saw that the man was Jesus. She nearly fainted and had to quickly sit down on the wall for fear of losing her balance. She trembled and whispered to herself, "My Jesus is the Messiah!"

<hr/>

After the healing and blessing session ended, the disciples and temple police tightened their protective circle around Jesus. They struggled to clear a path through the crowd. The people pushed and shoved to touch Jesus. Mary realized that she would be unable to approach him, so she returned to the Rabbi's quarters and awaited his return.

<hr/>

Jesus sat in a chair in the main room. The disciples sat on the floor, once more in awe of the day's miraculous healings and the way that he captivated the people and lifted their spirits with his message of hope and love and how the people fervently proclaimed him their Messiah and Savior.

Jesus looked around the room and then said, "John, you wish to say something. Please speak."

Simultaneously both Johns started to answer. "No, I have nothing to say," said the older John.

The younger John, the brother of James, deferred to the older John, and then he replied, "Yes, I am new and uncertain of the healing ways and that you've told us that we will also be healers. I ask your guidance."

Jesus pointed to the older John and said, "He is the first John to join with me in Jerusalem." Jesus then pointed to the younger John and said, "I will call you Jude so there will no longer be any confusion."

Jesus breathed in deeply, closed his eyes, then breathed out and opened his eyes. He replied to Jude's question regarding healing, "As you and I breathe, we share the same air of life. When I heal, I share the person's aura as they share mine although I do not take on their ailments. You must feel the oneness of God that you share – that all life shares. A way to help you do this is to breathe in harmony with the person seeking healing and to think in terms of oneness as if you and that person were one. When you do so, you must also have the intent to heal those parts of yourself that need improvement – although your area of need may be different from those you seek to heal; for all are one and each is a part of the other; and as one is in pain or sickness, so it is shared by all to degrees, though few consciously realize it. To help another is to help yourself as well. To best do that, you need to accept and forgive the faults and sins of all people, especially those whom you desire to help heal. And you must also forgive your own faults and sins. That is accomplished with divine love and forgiveness, for you are acting as an agent of God and need to act in a godly way."

Jesus held his palms out toward the disciples. He inhaled deeply again. As he breathed out, they felt a gentle, palpable force enfold them. He said, "As you heal others, you will realize that there is no empty space between you and the person to be healed. Your auras will be intertwined with the person's desire to be healed and your intent to heal. Know that God's divine power to heal is flowing through you rather than coming from you. That way you won't feel tiredness or a loss of energy or take on another's ills. As a vessel of God's Light flowing through you, you will feel uplifted and energized. Step away from your own emotions and the onus that it is your responsibility to heal others, and allow God's Light to take its course. Direct your desire to heal from the love center of your heart and not from your gut or from your ego or from your mind."

Jesus put his hands in his lap and saw that although most of the disciples understood his instructions, many still doubted their ability to do as he said. He closed his eyes again in deep thought. The room was silent. He opened his eyes and said, "Within the week, we must move on. More people will want to come here. Many are already on their way. This town doesn't have the capacity to house or feed everyone. All of you need to leave and again go to as many towns as possible to heal and to spread the good news as I have spoken to my followers. More people will listen to you than before when you traveled from town to town. You've shared the power of my aura during my healings, and the knowledge contained within it has blended with your auras. As you help to heal others and speak The Word, your new abilities will become more instilled in you, and you will automatically say and do the naturally right things. Keep the faith in me that you now have, and that faith will guide you."

The men felt a little more confident and encouraged by Jesus's words, but Peter sat up stiffly with a look of scorn as he stared toward the hallway as Mary came into the room. She carried a small basin of water. Jesus turned toward her and smiled. He extended his hand to her and said, "Come."

Jesus then addressed Peter. "Your traits are as solid as a rock, strong and consistent. It is wise to be strong and consistent in that which is true, but it is foolish to be so under false convictions. I shall call you The Rock."

Jesus turned to Mary and smiled glowingly at her. He took her hand and said, "It was a blessing to reunite with you in this town of Magdala. I shall call you Mary Magdalene in honor of our place of meeting again."

Mary's eyes stayed fixed on Jesus as if he were the only one in the room. She nodded humbly, kneeling at his feet with lowered head, then looked up at him. "Forgive me. I didn't know that you are the Anointed One, our Messiah. I spoke to you as if you were just a man. Please forgive me."

Jesus replied, "There is no need for forgiveness, for you have blessed me with the grace of your soul."

Mary reached into the top of her robe for a vial attached to a leather cord around her neck. "Please allow me to anoint you with this myrrh."

"I will be pleased if you do so," Jesus replied.

Mary's eyes welled with tears. As she reached up to Jesus's head, he bowed toward her, and she poured a few drops onto his hair and lovingly rubbed it in. She then took off his sandals and began to bath his feet in the basin of water. The tears from her eyes dropped into the water as she gently rubbed and caressed his feet. Strands of her long hair fell from her bowed head over his feet, and she tenderly rubbed his feet with the strands of her long hair, then cleaning between his toes. The men looked on; some with curiosity, some with acknowledgement of her devotion to their Messiah, and some with disdain.

Mary's tears continued to flow over Jesus's feet as she cried in silent devotion. After Mary had dried Jesus's feet, she retired to her bedroom. When Jesus finished speaking with his disciples, he joined her there. He sat on the side of the bed as she lay on it. "Why do you still cry?" he asked.

"I have so many buried emotions that have come to the surface."

"If you speak of them, it will help you."

In a barely audible voice, hesitantly at first Mary replied, "As a child, when I was being sexually abused, I would speak to God. When I did, I didn't feel what they were doing to me. Even when they whipped me to work faster, my body moved, but it was as if I weren't there when I spoke with God. That is how it also was when I made my living as a prostitute. I spoke to God and was not in my body when men did what they wanted." Mary sniffed to hold back her tears. "Is it possible to sin and speak to God at the same time?"

Jesus stroked her hair as a father would endearingly stroke his little girl. "You were taken as a child to become a slave to pay a tax debt. In those times, people's bodies could be bought and sold, but not their hearts or their minds or their souls. When speaking with God during those times of your early abuse and when you were supporting yourself by selling your body, you were able to retain your sanity and spirit. Those times are past. You are not the 'you' that you were. Before I came to Magdala, you had already made a decision to leave that life and rejoin your family. Do so, and continue to speak to God, and He will comfort you."

"I feel that I am speaking to God when I talk with you," Mary smiled weakly. "It gives me great comfort."

"God dwells within you and outside of you. When you speak with God with a sincere heart, He will always answer you."

<hr>

After dinner, Jesus and Judas went into the synagogue courtyard. Judas said, "I've seen a golden glow around your head many times today."

"That's because your inner sight is opening up to see what others cannot, as I told you it would. Your consciousness is evolving, and so is the power of my aura. When I was giving the blessings today, I felt the emotions and thoughts of the true believers in the crowd and their fervent desire to receive me. That allows my power to increase because more of the Holy Spirit can flow through me to them."

"Once again, Master, you have helped so many people. They seem to respond to your words more than ever before. I don't know where all those people came from. I heard it said that they just knew you would be here. How is that possible?"

"Those who have come are the faithful who believe in me and have received me in their thoughts, visions and dreams. My work goes on day and night when people sleep or are awake."

Matthew, Mark, Luke, and John came into the courtyard. "Thank you for joining us," Jesus greeted them. "Please, sit."

The men sat and asked where they should travel to next so that they could best serve Jesus's mission. Jesus replied, "Have faith that you will be guided to the appropriate towns and places. Then we shall meet in Jericho, and go on to Jerusalem for Passover."

Luke said, "Passover is not that far off."

Matthew said, "We can go to the many towns in the area of Jericho, then go on to Jerusalem for Passover in a few days' travel. But when do we meet in Jericho?"

"One month before Passover at Moshe's synagogue, "Jesus replied.

Mark asked, "Are there any towns that you would prefer that we visit?"

Jesus sighed, then smiled. "No, Mark, no matter which towns you go to, each of you will serve my heavenly Father differently. Each of you, according to your individual perceptions, will see these times through different eyes as the people you meet to teach and heal will see each of you through their different eyes. You will have to adapt the ways you teach in different ways so that The Word will be heard and understood by different people."

Jesus chuckled, "Each of you will tell your own different story of these days and the days to come. Others will tell your stories to others in different lands in different languages so that different cultures can relate to your stories. I laugh because there will be obvious distortions to your stories in the decades to come, yet the stories will carry many of God's truths even with those distortions." Jesus became very serious. "So my dear Matthew, Mark, Luke, John, and Judas, it doesn't matter which town you go to. Men and women will see things differently and interpret the intent and meaning of your words to suit their needs, whether it is to help others grow or to destroy them."

Jesus saw the disciples' concern that their message might lead to destruction. He said, "Those who align themselves with God's ways of love, kindness, and forgiveness shall be called the meek. The warlike will destroy themselves, and those called the meek, with their boundless courage to hold on to their convictions of God's eternal love, peace, and non-violence, they shall remain – and blessed be they – for the meek shall inherit the earth.

"But fear not, for when you speak The Word, you are doing God's will. And when it is that time for your final breaths of life, by my words, I tell you, you will have become Apostles who have sown the seeds of God's truth so that in time those seeds may flourish. So take heart, and do not worry about how men may react; it will be their choice and their destiny. You must be steadfast to The Word and speak it to all who will listen. That is your task."

The next day after morning prayers and breakfast, Jesus sent all the disciples out of the house to be among the people. He bade Mary go to her home to collect her belongings and then return to stay with him. Many of the disciples were displeased and grumbled amongst themselves that a woman was going to live with them. In synagogues, women were kept separate from men and sat in the back or at the sides of the congregation as a symbol of their stature as inferior to men before God. Generations of cultural influence had firmly rooted those traditional beliefs when the men were growing from children to adults.

The disciples returned for the noon meal as arranged. When they entered the main room, they saw Jesus sitting in a chair facing the corner of the room. The hood of his red-brown robe was pulled over his head so that his face was hidden. His hands were folded under his sleeves on his lap. He sat silently, his head bowed as if in prayer. The disciples sat respectfully behind him on the floor in silent devotion. Twenty minutes passed. Jesus did not move or say a word. The disciples looked at each other with concern. Finally, Andrew felt compelled to ask, "Master, are you all right?"

The figure on the chair remained still and did not respond.

Bartholomew asked, "Master, is there something we can do for you?"

Again, there was no response. The disciples were puzzled but remained sitting and waiting. After ten more minutes, Peter said, "Master, please speak to us."

There was no response. Peter stood up and said to the others, "I must see if he is well." Peter went to the chair and leaned down to face Jesus. A look of shock filled his face. "What is this?" he angrily demanded. "How could you?"

Peter pulled down the robe's hood and forcibly turned the chair toward the disciples. They gasped in shock. They all stared at the strange woman wearing Jesus's robe. Peter grabbed the woman's shoulders to pull her up and yelled, "How dare you wear the Messiah's robe! Take it off immediately and leave this house."

The woman resisted and grabbed Peter's wrists. In a deep, penetrating voice – the voice of Jesus – she said, "Peter the Rock, sit down."

Peter froze in disbelief. The firm, strong voice of Jesus spoke again. "Sit, Peter."

Peter released his grip on the robe. "Who are you?" he demanded.

The disciples stood and backed away in fear, rejecting what they beheld.

"Sit ye down," Jesus's voice commanded with great authority. The men hesitated but then sat with reluctance and uncertainty. "The voice you hear, is it not my voice?"

The men silently and slowly nodded.

The timbre of Jesus's voice changed and penetrated the silence with an echo-like vibration that resonated in the heads of the disciples. "I speak to you now not as a man, nor as a woman, but as the Christ Consciousness that supersedes form and speaks to man as God's prophet and messenger. Whether you perceive my Essence to be that of a man or a woman can in no way diminish me, and each gender is equally capable of teaching you, even the woman I appear to be now."

Jesus spoke firmly. "Should you reject the truth of God because it is spoken by a woman, then the wisdom of my words will be like pearls cast before swine that would trample upon that truth. Shed your prejudices and listen with your hearts, and I will reveal to you what no eye can see, what no ear can hear, what no hand can touch, and what cannot be conceived by the human mind."

Jesus felt the men's hearts quivering with fear at what they beheld and uncertainty as to how to react. As the men's eyes widened in shock, he saw their auras open as well.

Jesus, perceived as a woman, extended her palms toward the disciples. She breathed in deeply. With her outward breath, they felt a gentle force like a calming breeze pass through their bodies. They sighed and relaxed. They also felt an unfathomable love that softened their prejudices and opened their hearts. Jesus said, "You have been touched by the mystery of God's power. You now have a feeling within you that has no words; nonetheless, I will speak to you in words so that in time, you may form beliefs based on God's Truth."

"Know ye that God speaks not only through a man or a woman, but my heavenly Father speaks through all life – the animals, the plants, the stars, even a single grain of sand in the middle of the desert."

Jesus quickly surveyed the disciples' thoughts and said, "As you first rejected me in this form as a woman, so mankind turns a deaf ear to the knowledge of life that freely speaks the essence of God, for 'All That Is' is God's creation and expresses God's Essence."

"If I choose the body of a woman in which to fulfill my mission, who, in these times, would listen to me, even if I speak The Word? As I speak to you now, have I changed who I am beneath the flesh, or has your perception of me changed? Do not let your eyes deny the knowledge of your inner sight to know and feel what is true. To be a true teacher of my ministry, you must look beyond the color of people's skin or their nation of origin or their gender; instead, you must see their souls – for it is their souls that you must help to see the Light."

Again Jesus surveyed his disciples' thoughts and saw a slight shift in their prejudices. Their auras had received the Seeds of Light; now he had to attend to their minds' thinking. He continued, "If you think of God as a man, then you diminish God. God is neither male nor female; God is 'All That Is.' Because it is hard for most of you to think otherwise concerning women, respond to this question: If you had to make a choice between cutting off your right arm and cutting off your left arm, think of which would you choose?"

The disciples became quite disturbed at the question.

Jesus commanded, "Raise the arm up that you would choose to cut off."

The men were perplexed. Hesitantly, those who were right-handed raised their left arms, and those who were left-handed raised their right arms.

"I see," Jesus said. "Now raise your other arm up if you think it would be much harder for you to go about your life with one arm rather than both arms."

The men raised their other arms up.

Jesus nodded, "Now if you had a choice of cutting off one arm or keeping both arms, put your arms down, and clasp your hands together if you would chose to keep both of your arms."

All of the men quickly lowered their arms and clasped their hands together.

Jesus nodded again, "As you now have thought about how valuable both of your arms are to you, it is obvious that it would be foolish to cut off either arm. God treasures both men and women more than you treasure both of your arms. Both men and women are a part of God and have been created to express His magnificent creative Essence. Your two hands clasped together signify their union and completeness with each other because men and women are intended to complement each other rather than be in opposition. To diminish a woman's standing is to diminish a part of God. All men and all women are precious and sacred to my Father; thus, you must learn to think, feel, and act in harmony with God's ways. God is love – honor and act godly with love toward all people, be they man or woman of any race, color, or nation."

Jesus put his palms down on his lap and looked upon his disciples. Mary opened the front door and stood there holding her belongings in a large basket. The men turned toward her. Jesus smiled as he saw a more accepting light in his disciples' auras. When they turned back to Jesus, he appeared as they knew him.

<hr>

Later that night, Jesus asked Judas to bring dinner to Mary and speak with her. Jesus planned to spend his nights in the courtyard alone in communion with God. He told the disciples that Mary was to occupy the bedroom as her place and that he no longer required sleep. He also told them that he had work to attend to in the dream state while everyone slept. Jesus said, "I am preparing the groundwork for pathways that will connect me now and in the future to whoever asks for my guidance and help in their prayers or dreams."

———

Mary was finishing her meal in the privacy of her bedroom. She and Judas had shared their experience of seeing Jesus's various images – hers of Jesus becoming the young man she had known and his of Jesus's recent appearance as a woman and its effect upon the disciples.

"I can tell a lot about men," Mary said as she sat back from the dinner tray on the bed. "When I came into the room with my basket of clothes, they looked at me in a different way. I knew something had happened; now I know what it was."

Judas replied, "After the men saw you, when they turned back to the Master, he appeared as he always has, and again we were shocked by how quickly he can change his image. They are still marveling at what he can do."

"What you have told me of his miracles shows that he is indeed the Son of God. He is my Savior. He saved me from being stoned to death and then healed the wounds of my body and heart. And most important, he saved my soul."

There was a light knock on the door. Judas went to open it. Jesus was there and asked, "May I come in?"

Mary sat up straight and said, "Of course. I am here to serve you."

Jesus smiled and said, "I see that you are both comfortable with the way that I appear to you now."

"I am," Judas replied.

"Master," Mary replied in a respectful and admiring tone, "I am pleased with both of your appearances to me."

Jesus sat on the bed next to Judas and said, "It's my message that must live on beyond these times, not my image. My heavenly Father's message is for all people in all lands. It doesn't matter what face is painted of me in people's minds because what is important is how open their hearts are to receiving the truth of God's message and His love. Even as you see me now, others will perceive me differently. So that my teachings will be accepted universally, people will create their own impressions of how I should look. During the lifetimes of all who see me as I am now, there will be no artists' paintings or sculptures of me to be seen in the future except those images in people's dreams and imaginations. Those personal images will have a greater reality than paint or stone. It's better that way."

"I love you just as you are," Mary replied.

"As do I," Judas followed.

Jesus nodded, "Then that is how you shall see me...most of the time."

"What do you mean by 'most of the time,' Master?" Judas asked.

"Tomorrow you'll see. That's when I have to leave."

"Leave? So soon?" Mary was upset.

"Master, it's been only a short time since you came back," Judas protested. "You said that we would all be leaving when the moon is half full. That won't be for days."

"I said that you and the others would leave then. I must go tomorrow. I want both of you to escort me out through the synagogue gate. Then I will be on my way by myself."

"Master, you haven't been out recently. The people will mob you. Many are already in a frenzy over what they have heard about you and seen for themselves. They constantly plead and clamor for you. You cannot—I know I should not say that 'you cannot,' but there is no doubt that the people would mob you and wall you off from any movement."

Jesus chuckled, "Fear not, Judas, because no walls, whether stone or flesh, can contain me."

Mary spoke sadly. "If you leave, when will I see you again?"

"I will see both of you on your travels to Jericho. When you leave, Judas, I want you to take Mary, Matthew, Seth, Joseph, and Seffira with you. Instruct the others to form their own small groups or go alone. All of you will have people following you. Be their good shepherds. When you announce to the people that you'll be leaving to teach my ministry, that's when you'll tell them that I've already left. Tell them to not to be dismayed, for I will be in Jerusalem for the Passover Pilgrimage."

When Jesus left the bedroom, James saw him in the hallway and exclaimed, "Master, with your words, I have been able to help five people change their outlook on life from misery to hope! Jude also has helped others. You not only created for us the most bountiful catch of fish in Capernaum to feed the masses, you have now made us fishers of men as you said you would. It feels so fulfilling to help and heal others. Thank you."

Jesus put his hand on the young man's shoulder and said, "James, you are a natural healer. You have now begun your mission. I am pleased with you."

42

The next day, Peter and Simon left the house first. The temple police opened a narrow path for them, but the people pressed toward them in hopes that the Messiah would follow. The temple police had to push as hard as they could against the surge of people. When the people saw that it was only the two disciples, they eased off. Peter and Simon finally made their way to the edge of the packed crowd. There, they began speaking with an eager group who sought information about the Messiah. A few minutes later, John, Jude, and his brother James walked out. Again, the crowd surged toward them but then backed off as before. Then John, Jude, and James also moved to the periphery of the crowd. Soon Matthew, Seth, and Andrew emerged, and once more, the crowd surged toward them to see if it was Jesus. They also repeated the pattern of going to the periphery of the congealed mass of people. Luke and Thomas appeared a little later and followed suit. The other disciples soon followed and passed through the synagogue's front gate at different time intervals. As each set of disciples came into view, the crowd surged less toward them, becoming conditioned to not seeing the Messiah. The Roman cavalry observed all events and recorded all the comings and goings on their clay tablets.

Then Judas, Mary, and James came to the gate. The people saw the Messiah was not with them either. One of the temple police looked at James curiously and thought that he had already passed through. Suddenly a man pointed his finger at Mary and yelled, "She's the prostitute!"

The people next to the man hissed at Mary. A temple policeman quickly stood between them and Mary. He warned, "Let these people pass freely." The accusatory man backed off. During the distraction, James quickly melted into the crowd. When Judas and Mary looked for him but did not see him, they knew that Jesus appearing as James had left safely. The disciples returned to the synagogue as the sun was setting. The crowd continued their steadfast watch throughout the night.

The morning after the night of the half moon, the disciples announced to the clamoring crowd that the Messiah had already left. The people's disappointment began to turn into riotous talk. The temple police drew their swords and held their shields in battle stance. Luke asked for quiet, and after a while, the crowd was finally stilled. Luke said loudly to them, "Be not dismayed, for our Messiah, Jesus of Nazareth, will be in Jerusalem for the annual Passover observance. It is his desire that you be with him then."

There was much protesting and grumbling. Luke pointed toward the other disciples and said, "We will be traveling to many towns and villages so that we may teach others his message. The Messiah has told us to invite all of you who wish to join us to please do so. We will be leaving today at noon."

Many in the crowd groaned with disappointment; however, when noon arrived and the disciples headed off in different directions, many of the believers with the greatest faith followed them. Among those followers were spies seeking the whereabouts of Jesus.

———

In the weeks that followed, Jesus visited the towns of Caesarea, Philippi, Gennesaret, Cana, Nain, and Decapolis, among many others. Being by himself and not having to account to anyone, Jesus had the freedom to change his appearance as easily as one who wears and then discards his or her clothing at the end of the day. In various towns, he appeared as a rich man or a poor man, a young attractive woman or an old wrinkled woman. He once again marveled at the irony of people's reaction to his teachings in each of his different appearances. Although his words were the same, his message was accepted or rejected more by the way he looked than what he said, as he had noted before. In some towns, without identifying himself, he appeared as his normal self and performed many healings and exorcisms; in those cases, people acknowledged him with greater favor although he did not reveal his identity as the Messiah.

Once again Jesus reaffirmed to himself that he had to maintain the male image to be accepted by the culture and beliefs of those times to best give birth to his message. He was acutely aware of the sting of being belittled, regardless of all that he had to offer, because of people's impression of his physical appearance rather than the Christ consciousness behind his mask of flesh. He realized that the time period in which he was living – the painful, growing years for mankind – held the hope for his vision of peace, love, and harmony for future generations. Then there would be challenges and dangers, but there would be greater opportunity that his message would become a reality.

———

Mary, Judas, Joseph, Seffira, Matthew, and Seth had traveled with only thirty followers, mostly single women who had been orphaned, abused, divorced, or were widows. Because of Mary's reputation as a prostitute, many people from Magdala avoided going with their group. Because Mary had been enlightened by Jesus, she was able to counsel those women who had chosen to accompany them as they traveled onward to a small village. Along the way, Mary and Judas shared with each other their experiences with Jesus, and a strong bond developed between them.

When they arrived at a small village, the people had already heard of the Messiah and his miracles and were very receptive to Mary and Judas's group. After a week of teaching, having been warmly received, they prepared to leave. A little boy, five years old, was near the wagons that were being loaded with gifts of food from the village people. He climbed onto one of the wagons and declared to Joseph and Seffira, "I'm going with you."

His father, who had been looking for his missing son, came up to the wagon and sternly said, "Where have you been?" He grabbed the boy under his small arms and yanked him off the wagon.

The little boy started to cry. As he sobbed, he adamantly declared, "No! I want to go!"

The father became perturbed. He angrily said, "Stop crying! You can't go!"

The boy cried louder. The father yelled at him, "STOP CRYING!"

The boy cried even louder. His father raised his hand and threatened, "Stop crying or I will hit you!" He yelled again, "STOP IT!"

Seth approached the father and tapped him on the shoulder. The man snapped at Seth, "What do you want?"

In a calm, steady voice, Seth said, "May I please speak to you for just a moment?"

The man, very annoyed, barked, "Leave us alone." His son continued to bawl.

Seth persisted, "It will only take a moment. Please."

Seth's politeness and mature demeanor impressed the man. He said, "You're Matthew's son. He has helped my family. What do you want?"

Seth tugged on the man's sleeve and said, "Come over here with me." He led the man away from the hysterical child. As the man reluctantly followed, he turned to his frantic son and again yelled, "STOP CRYING!" The little boy cried louder still.

When Seth and the man were twenty feet away, he asked Seth again, "What do you want?"

Seth replied in a low voice, "I know that you love your son very much."

"Of course I do. That's why I want him to stop crying."

"Please don't be upset with me," Seth said, "for what I am about to tell you."

"Well, what is it?"

"When your son is upset and you yell at him or threaten to hit him, it only makes him more upset."

The man looked at Seth with scorn. "What do you know? You're only a child yourself."

Seth calmly replied, "Please stay here a moment."

Seth walked over to the little boy and whispered in his ear. The little boy shook his head "no." Seth whispered again, and the boy nodded "yes." In a few moments, the little boy caught his breath and stopped crying. Seth walked back to the disgruntled man.

The man asked, "What did you tell him?"

"I said 'Your father loves you very much. He was concerned that if you left on the wagon, that would make him very sad.' I then asked your son if he wanted to make you feel sad. Your son shook his head 'no.' Then I asked him if he loved you. He nodded his head 'yes.' I then told him that you would feel much better if he stopped crying and that you and he could ride on the wagon together for a little while."

The man looked at his son, who looked back at him with wide, pleading eyes. The father's stern expression softened, and then he sighed. He smiled at his son and walked back to the wagon with Seth. He said to Seth, "He's a good boy. I love him with all my heart. I didn't want his crying to make an impression of bad manners on strangers."

Seth replied, "We know he's only a little boy. That's how they are. He can't make a bad impression; he can only be a little boy. Because you love him, whenever he's upset, don't yell at him, but speak gently and lovingly to him, and he will respond much better to your wishes than when you yell and make him even more upset.

The man looked down at Seth and said, "For being only a boy yourself, you speak wisely."

"That's because Jesus has taught me how to work with the grain of people's nature as a wise carpenter does with the grain of the wood and to be mindful not to work against the grain. Your son's nature is that of a little boy." Seth whose height had gained three-quarters of an inch now stood taller and proudly said, "You should also know that I'm going to be a rabbi!"

The father nodded and said, "You have the makings of a great rabbi." Then the father sat on the wagon next to his son and hugged him. The little boy hugged him back and in a quiet voice said, "I'm sorry for crying and making you mad."

The father replied, "I'm sorry for yelling at you. You are a wonderful son. I love you so much."

Joseph snapped the reins over the horse's back, and the wagon headed out.

After three weeks of travel and having visited two more towns, Judas's group was camped in a small cove a quarter mile from the main road. Three women and a strong young man who kept to himself had joined their group from the last town.

The next morning Judas and Mary both rose before sunrise while the rest of the encampment still slept. They looked at each other from across the encampment from their segregated male and female sections. Without a word, they quickly headed up the hill. At the top, they stared silently at each other for a full minute. Their breath was rapid, more from what they had just experienced than from the uphill climb. "I know that you had the same dream that I did," Judas finally said.

Mary replied, "It was of The Light."

Judas sighed. "Yes it was. I'll never forget my first time of being in The Light. It was in a dream but more real than life. For many minutes after I awoke, it left me terrified, blind, and unable to feel my body or even the room with my hands. I didn't know who Jesus was then, but I was compelled to search for him that very day. In my dream, his image comprised patterns of brilliant white light. Later that day, I found him— or rather, he found me."

Mary said, "My first experience of Jesus since his transformation was that day he found me and saved my life. When I let out that howl in the bedroom that the others talk about, it was when I became infused with The Light. I wasn't terrified – it was ecstasy! I wish it could have lasted forever."

"It's strange that it felt so different for you, Mary."

Mary nodded and then said, "It was powerful, confusing and enlightening all at once, and yes, it is strange that last night we both shared The Light in our dream again. I knew before you spoke that you had had the same dream also."

Judas agreed and said, "The Light somehow imparts profound knowledge without words. It's more than strange; it's mystical. The second time I saw The Light was when John baptized Jesus. The River Jordan boiled with steam and ice. That wasn't a dream. I knew it was the divine and holy hand of God blessing our Savior."

"So it's true," Mary affirmed. "The water did boil with ice as people have said of that day."

"Yes, Mary. I was there. It happened, unquestionably."

"And is it also true that he resurrected a dead girl in Jericho?"

"Yes, it's true—that and so much more. Jesus is indeed a true performer of miracles. I may not understand him at times when he speaks of God's ways that are unknown to man or if he asks me to do something that may not make sense at the time, but I have learned to have undying trust and faith in him and will always do whatever he asks of me. Later on, I always see the wisdom of his words and actions. I no longer doubt him as I first did when I didn't know that he was the Messiah."

Mary smiled at Judas and said, "When I first spoke to Jesus after the stoning, I spoke to him as if he were just a man. Like you, at first, I didn't know that he was the Messiah. There are many men named Jesus that when people spoke of his miracles, I couldn't conceive then that it was the Jesus I had known."

Mary took Judas's hand, squeezed it, and then said, "He's coming to see us soon!"

Judas smiled widely and replied, "Yes, he is. I feel it also."

<hr />

Later that morning, Seffira leaned against Joseph as he drove their wagon toward Beth-Shan, a town located twenty miles south of Galilee where the Jezreal and Jordan Valleys meet. Joseph held the reins with one hand and put his other hand on Seffira's belly. "Our baby is growing bigger," he said with a big grin. "Its a miracle! I still can't believe it."

"Being with you, my beloved Joseph, is a miracle."

"My sweet Seffira, our life together is a miracle. And for you and I to be married by the Messiah, that will be a miraculous blessing. We are so fortunate."

Seffira's forehead furrowed, and she asked, "Do you love me as much as you love the Messiah?"

Joseph removed his hand from her belly and held the reins with both hands. Perplexed, he remained silent.

She asked, "Why don't you answer me?"

Joseph sighed and then said, "God is above all things."

Seffira looked disappointed and turned away. Joseph gently grasped her chin and turned her head toward him. With a soft, endearing voice he said, "You are a creation of God...and I love you as much. I see God's light in you, and it's magic to me."

Happily, Seffira kissed Joseph's cheek and then told him, "I don't pretend to compare myself in importance to the Messiah or to put you on the spot. It's just silly thoughts in my mind."

"That's all right, my love. You can ask me anything."

Seffira put her hand against her cheek. "There's something else that's crossed my mind."

"What is it?"

"You once said that you loved me so much that you would die for me."

"I did and I would. You are everything to me."

"Would you die for the Messiah also?"

Joseph turned away and looked toward the horse. He snapped the reins, and the wagon lurched ahead at a quicker pace. "Why do you ask me that?" he said.

"I worry about you. I don't trust Herod. People say he will try and kill Jesus. I know that you would try and protect him with your life. What if Herod's soldiers killed you? I wouldn't know how to live without you. What would become of our baby and me?"

"Seffira, we must have faith that being in the Messiah's presence will protect us. Nothing bad will happen if he is with us. Please don't worry about such things. Think about how much we'll love our baby instead and how happy we'll be."

"I do think about that. I'm excited to give birth to our baby. It means the world to me. I just worry sometimes."

Joseph pulled on the reins, stopping the wagon. He stood up and pointed at a distant figure standing on the road ahead. "It's him! It's the Messiah!" He turned to Seffira. "Worry not, my beloved; the Messiah is here. We'll soon be married."

Judas and Mary's wagon pulled past them and sped ahead to greet Jesus.

$\Longleftrightarrow$

Later that afternoon, Jesus and Judas's group arrived in the town of Beth-Shan where some of Mary's relatives lived. Preparations were made for Jesus to address the townspeople the next day. That night, the strong young man who had joined Judas's group stole a horse and rode out at a full gallop to inform Herod of Jesus's whereabouts.

$\Longleftrightarrow$

Octavius entered Herod's dressing room, where the palace jeweler was fitting a new necklace of gold and jewels and matching wristband on the King. "We know where he is," Octavius declared.

"Leave us," Herod ordered the jeweler, who left immediately. Herod then asked Octavius, "Where is the Rabbi?"

"Jesus is in the town of Beth-Shan with some of his disciples and a group of thirty-two followers. I know you are determined to kill him, but it is my duty to warn you once more of the possible consequences."

Herod raised his hand to Octavius, "Say no more. Send the archer."

"Yes, My Lord. I shall do as you wish."

After four days, Mary had met with her relatives in Beth-Shan, and Jesus had completed his work. They planned to leave the next morning. Joseph and Seffira walked nervously past Jesus twice as he spoke to two women. They soon returned, lingered a moment, but said nothing and walked away again. Seffira nudged Joseph in the side, "Why didn't you ask him?"

"He was busy, Seffira."

"You are too shy. Ask him. It's important."

"I'm not shy. It just didn't feel right. Let's try again."

Joseph took Seffira's hand, and they approached Jesus once more. The two women he had been speaking with departed with glowing looks on their faces. Jesus turned to Joseph and Seffira. He smiled at them and said, "Yes, I will marry you two days after we leave Beth-Shan."

Joseph and Seffira were thrilled and surprised that Jesus knew what was on their minds. Joseph exclaimed, "You will? That's wonderful! Thank you, Master. Thank you."

All had gone well in Beth-Shan. Through his disciples' travels and his own work in the dream state, Jesus's ministry was taking root in the lands of Judea. The night before they were to leave the town, Jesus, Judas, Joseph, and Mary sat under a group of Cedars of Lebanon trees near the outskirts of Beth-Shan discussing The Light.

"As you know, Judas," Jesus replied, and turning to Mary, said, "and you are learning, The Light encompasses and connects all things in all times and all places. It is the force that God uses to give the gift of life to all of His Essences. Because you both have seen The Light and felt its awesome power, you are now carriers of The Light and you have been called to help me to enlighten the world."

"But, Master, what of my many sins?" Mary asked. "How can I ever be worthy to carry The Light?"

"You already carry The Light, and you've already begun to spread The Light to others. The Light has given you salvation, and now you are fulfilling your calling to bring salvation to others." Jesus put his hand on Mary's shoulder. "And please, my beloved Mary, do not call me Master; call me Jesus." He smiled fondly. "It gives me pleasure when I hear the way you say my name."

Mary nodded respectfully.

Jesus turned to Judas, who asked, "I'm not sure I understand the meaning of God's 'Essences.' Could you tell us more?"

"All of life is a part of God's Essence. You, my dear Judas, and you, dear Mary, are a part of God's Essence although you are not God. As I've said many times, all of nature and the stars are also of God's Essence, and to God, each star, each grain of sand, and every person are a part of His Essence. And the Essence of each person and each Essence of everything live eternally as a part of God. One's Essence can never be destroyed and exists before one's birth and after the death of one's physical body. Each Essence is distinctly unique. No two Essences – even those of identical twins – are the same. All Essences are inviolate and add to the collective completeness of my heavenly Father. Those who know and love God should also love their neighbors and enemies, for they too are a part of God."

"But how can we think of the Romans' cruelty toward us and feel love for them?" Mary asked.

Jesus saw the images of her thoughts and the inhumane treatment by her Roman masters and her suffering as a slave-child. He answered, "When the Light in you grows brighter, you will know that God dwells in All That Is, and you will feel the indescribable grace of God's love for you. And that recognition will allow you to extend your light of love to God's Light within another, no matter what their sins or transgressions have been."

"Hmmm…" Mary said, "I need to think about that."

"Know that all things have a purpose, even the darkness. There are no coincidences or accidents. Accept all people and all circumstances no matter how dire. They are part of God's mystery that presents challenges and opportunities to ascend to higher levels of consciousness." Jesus said, "I say to you, although you may not understand now, act with love toward all things, for that is the way of The Light. The love of God enfolds your soul. Your love of God is your true salvation."

"What more can you tell us about The Light?" Judas persisted.

"Bless your curiosity, Judas," Jesus replied. "Our Hebrew ancestors, those who came into The Light, felt God's Holy Presence. It moved them in such a powerful and unearthly manner that they could not even utter God's sacred name, for no words could describe their glimpse of God's never-ending unknowable Being and the infinite oneness and wonder of

His glorious majesty. Having experienced The Light as you both have, you know that that 'feeling' is beyond the physical senses of sight, smell, taste, touch, and hearing. It is an ineffable spiritual sense of God's Essence that one may experience that words cannot describe.

"I see that it will take more time for you to understand," Jesus added. "Perhaps it will help if I tell you how I work with The Light to serve my heavenly Father. In the dream state, where time and space operate differently, I extend my Essence to all who desire to receive it. I am a Light in the darkness of their dreams. I know of their suffering, their pain, and their agony. It would be too burdensome and too overwhelming a cross to bear if I were not in The Light. The Light sustains me for my mission, which, if not for the grace of my heavenly Father's Light—The Holy Spirit—would be beyond imagination and too torturous for a mortal to remain sane."

"Are you immortal?" Judas asked.

"I am not the body that you see with your eyes. I am a force that for now must appear incarnate. There is very little time left for me to do what must be done. Each day, the intensity of The Light in this body grows more powerful, and soon enough, this body will no longer be able to contain it."

"What will happen to you?" Mary asked anxiously.

"That is something I shall find out when the time comes. For now, I have been building dream pathways to navigate in my Father's dimension of Light. I strive to bring His love and message of hope to those who yearn for salvation and a renewed life with which to create a new civilization. Fear not for me, for I have supreme faith that my heavenly Father will guide and protect me on my path that He has created."

Mary sighed, "I wish I could see things more in The Light as you do."

Jesus smiled and stared into Mary's eyes. Mary gasped and covered her eyes. She backed away, then took her hands down and exclaimed, "I see a golden-white glow around your head!"

"I see it too!" Judas exclaimed.

"It is an affirmation that your inner eyes are opening to The Light. Be comforted by what you perceive; it is a sign that The Light grows stronger within you."

<hr/>

After his morning's work, Herod bathed in soothing lavender-scented water to relax himself, but even after half an hour, he remained tense. It wasn't his workload that kept his mind engaged, or even putting his palace guard on battle alert for a possible attack. Vexed, he whispered repeatedly, "Why are they coming here?"

Octavius entered and said anxiously to Herod, "The general has arrived." Spotters had earlier reported that the general's large contingent of soldiers had been making their way to Herod's palace since disembarking at the seaport.

Herod's disgruntled expression mirrored his feelings as he dressed hurriedly, assisted by his attendants. He and Octavius headed toward the huge royal reception hall. There, Herod sat upon his throne, Octavius standing at his side. A Roman captain, dressed in his finest shining armor, marched through the hall's great entrance and walked up to the throne. He drew his sword and pointed it up high over his head. In a loud, distinctive voice he announced, "General Fabius Maximus Scipio, Supreme Commander of the Roman Army, will have an immediate audience with King Herod." The captain brought his sword's shaft down to the front of his face, holding the handle over his heart, its sharp point gleaming above him.

Herod sat erect with a stone-cold expression that masked his annoyance at this surprise intrusion as well as his deep concern and puzzlement over what the urgent matter could be that Rome's highest ranking military commander—feared because he had the sole power to turn the Roman army's might on the Empire's rulers—would come to see him without notice. Herod was also insulted that the general did not ask for an audience, but announced that he *would have an audience with him.* Before Herod could raise his hand in acknowledgement and say, "Let him enter," the general entered in regal battle dress and a spectacular, highly polished breastplate, dented from past battles, and marched up to the throne. His stare burned into Herod's eyes. Without breaking eye contact, Fabius raised his hand toward the captain and bluntly ordered, "Go." The captain obediently sheathed his sword, turned, and left.

The general's stern expression was heightened by the presence of a long battle scar running from his ear to the corner of his lips and another scar over his eye. "We will speak privately," he ordered.

In an icy voice, Herod replied, "As you request. I will dismiss my guards."

"No," the General retorted, "we must go where the walls have no ears."

Herod stared at the general a moment and then said, "Perhaps you are right. I feel like walking in my garden."

The general snorted and nodded his head in amusement at Herod's weak attempt at trying to make it appear that it was his idea to change the venue. "Very well," the general scoffed.

As they approached the verdant royal garden, the general pointed to Octavius, who had followed them to the garden's entrance, and said, "He leaves. I said 'private.'"

Herod, controlling his temper, spoke in a calculated, matter-of-fact, dismissive tone, "Octavius is my most trusted advisor. You can trust him also."

The general stopped walking. Herod stopped also. The general curtly replied, "I said 'private.' When I am done, you may appreciate that." Fabius walked on before Herod could respond. Herod turned to Octavius and waved him away, then followed after the general.

Fabius walked to the only chair under a shade tree in a small clearing and sat down. With no other seating available, Herod stood in front of him, feeling humiliated as if Fabius were the king and he was a subject. Herod said, "It's unusual, but nonetheless an honor to have…"

"Cut the camel crap," the general interrupted. "I'm here to accomplish two things. First, I will be taking an additional half of your remaining battalions."

"That's impossible!" Herod exclaimed. "That's more then Sejanus said he would need. It creates a huge vulnerability for me."

Fabius raised his hand to silence Herod. "I need your soldiers to conduct a successful campaign. My reconnaissance of the mountainous area of Germany where we will be engaging indicates the necessity for more troops than previously expected. I do not intend to fail; I intend to overwhelm. As of now, your soldiers are under my command. Alert them accordingly."

Herod backed away a step and gnashed his teeth.

"As for Sejanus," Fabius continued, "he and I have spoken long and hard about you, and that is the subject of the second matter. He warned you that, with regard to the increased taxes, it was imperative that you not take any action that would cause further unrest, which would lead to a revolt and require military intervention with soldiers that you will not have."

Before Fabius could continue, Herod interjected, "Sejanus gave specific instructions that the one called Jesus of Nazareth who pretends to be a Messiah not be harmed by me and…"

Fabius held up his hand to quiet Herod and said curtly, "Speak not." The general stood and removed his armored breastplate. He laid it on the ground by the chair, then sat again and pointed to the breastplate. "It gets hot and bulky, but it has saved my life in battle many times." The general gazed around the exotic garden. Herod, outwardly calm, was fuming inside.

Fabius's gaze returned to Herod, and he said, "I'm sure you love your garden. It's as exquisite as your palace. I don't understand why you foolishly risk all of this."

"What do you mean? I have complied with Sejanus's request for my army, and I have not harmed the Jesus personage."

In an angry voice, Fabius bellowed, "I don't give a rat's ass about Jewish gods or Messiahs. You were told that unrest must be avoided at this precarious time. And what do you do? You beheaded John the Baptist, a man revered by a large portion of the Jewish population. Did you think that would curry favor with the people? And why did you behead him? At the request of a girl, in exchange for a night with virgin flesh! Only a fool would risk bargaining away half of his kingdom for a dalliance."

The general thrust his fist at Herod. Herod's head jerked back reflexively; then he stood his ground. The veins in Fabius's neck bulged as he spoke and pointed his finger at Herod, "You had better keep your eye on your kingdom and keep your sex poker under your royal robes, or you will lose both."

The general sternly continued, "Concerning the second matter, of Jesus the Rabbi, this is what you will do…"

Octavius stood at the periphery of the garden, trying to make out what was being said by his king and the general. He could hear only a few words that Fabius barked, but he knew all was far from well.

After a few more minutes, the general stood and put his breastplate back on. He walked briskly away as if he had just slain one enemy and was off to slay another. Herod followed six paces behind. The general stormed past Octavius, Herod stopped beside Octavius, who grimaced when he saw Herod's ashen face. "What did he say, My Lord?"

"Listen very carefully, Octavius. There are two things you must attend to. Rome is taking another half of our remaining battalions. You need to notify our commanders."

"My Lord, that will weaken your power."

"The second matter must be attended to immediately. It is of the highest priority."

"What is it? It shall be done."

Herod grasped Octavius's shoulders and stared at him. Octavius saw the desperation in his king's eyes as Herod said, "You must call back the archer before he completes his task. No harm must come to the Rabbi."

"But, My Lord, by now, the archer must be very close to finishing, if he hasn't killed the Rabbi already."

Herod squeezed Octavius's shoulders harder and shook him. Herod demanded, "You must stop the archer at all costs. My rule depends on the Rabbi's safety and well-being. Go immediately!"

<hr>

Octavius dispatched the captain of Herod's royal palace guard to go immediately to Beth-Shan, where Jesus had been spotted, then to proceed with the king's rescinding of his assassination order.

The next day, the captain of Herod's royal guard and his soldiers arrived in Beth-Shan only to learn that Jesus had left. Now alone he raced his chariot across a plain and was nearing a hilly region. He slowed to study the tracks of Jesus's party that had merged with other travelers' tracks as the path narrowed. It was still easy tracking. He knew the archer would be nearby – if only he could get there in time.

The captain looked back toward Beth-Shan and saw two small dust swirls in the distance. He nodded, knowing that his men had procured fresh horses and were headed toward him. There was no time to wait for them. He took a lance from his chariot and wedged it into the ground pointing in the direction in which Jesus's party was headed. A moment later, he sped away.

<hr>

"Thank you, Master. This is the happiest day in my life. Seffira's also. Thank you again for marrying us," Joseph said, as the after-wedding celebration – as meager as it was – began.

"You're welcome, Joseph. I believe that today is the most joyous day in your life. Your glow of happiness and pleasure is unmistakable."

At the base of a small hill in a remote area between towns, Jesus had given a stirring benediction of hope and faith at the wedding's end. Jesus said afterward to Joseph, "It would be best for everyone if I stepped away by myself for now."

Joseph wasn't sure what Jesus meant, but like Judas, Joseph had learned to accept Jesus's ways. Joseph replied, "I know that you need your solitude at times. Thank you again for sanctifying our marriage." Joseph hurried back to be with Seffira.

The morning breezes had stopped, and the air was dead still. A flock of white doves flew across the clear blue sky and alighted on a cluster of hilltop trees surrounded by dense shrubs. Jesus walked about a hundred yards away from the wedding group to a quiet spot fifty yards below the hilltop. There he stood in his white tunic, looking at the distant auras of happiness that the distant wedding celebrants shared. He had his back to the hill.

A mile away, Herod's captain of the royal guard spotted the two chariots and two centurions near a hilltop cluster of trees. He cracked his whip over the sweaty hides of the two panting horses that pulled his chariot. The chariot surged ahead only a little faster as the horses had already been running at full gallop. He yelled out to the centurions near the hilltop, "STOP! NO! STOP!" but they were too far to hear and were staring intently in another direction.

In the tall shrubs below the trees, the archer pulled back on the razor-sharp arrow with the string of his longbow, aiming upward at a forty-degree angle. His sight was fixed perfectly on his target – the back of Jesus's tunic over his heart-spot. The archer breathed in. He had no doubt that his arrow would fly true to its mark. His father – a master archer – had taught him as a small child how to hit the center of a bullseye. He had since done so tens of thousands of times. He could easily hit a tossed coin in the air at fifty yards. This target was perfectly still. He was fully confident that Herod's reward of gold coins would soon be his. The archer started to exhale slowly. He relaxed his fingers and released the powerful, taut bowstring.

The arrow arched upward on a true course toward Jesus's heart. The archer smiled, knowing that the arrow could not miss. Suddenly, the archer's head involuntarily snapped upward. He felt a stinging pain in his back. He looked down at his chest and saw the point-tip of a crossbow arrow that had pierced him from behind.

At the same time, the archer's launched arrow dipped downward, speeding true in the windless clear-blue sky. Jesus stood motionless, his back fully exposed. He sighed. Three doves flew wing-to-wing and transversed the arrow's trajectory. In less than a second's time, the arrow had passed completely through the three doves. The doves twirled lifelessly to the ground. A moment later, the arrow pierced the ground between Jesus's feet. The arrow's feathers were brushed with tinges of fresh blood from the doves that had altered the arrow's path.

Jesus turned around and picked up the arrow. He made three mournful *"cooing"* sounds and bowed his head. Then in a whisper he said, "Thank you, Father, for the grace of your protection."

The captain of the royal guard finally approached the centurions as one of them was replacing his crossbow in his chariot.

Jesus placed the arrow on the ground and covered it with dirt so that others would not see it and worry needlessly. He then walked back to the wedding group. Five minutes later, the captain, two centurions, and their three chariots approached the wedding group. In great fear, all in the wedding party huddled around Jesus. Joseph hugged his trembling bride tightly to him. The captain announced to everyone, "Under orders of King Herod, we will be escorting you to offer protection. We will not interfere with your activities."

The other two chariots of the captain's detail raced into view. The wedding party looked at each other in concern and disbelief. Jesus reassured them, "There is no need to worry. These soldiers speak the truth and will not harm you. Maintain your faith that when I am with you, you will be protected."

43

Jesus, Judas, Mary, Mathew, Seth, Joseph, Seffira, and their group of followers traveled to many towns and villages over a three-month period. Along the way, two hundred and twenty additional followers joined them. Two-dozen Roman cavalry members joined the captain of Herod's personal royal guard and his detail to further protect Jesus from harm. The Roman cavalry were to ensure that Herod's soldiers maintained protection for Jesus and his followers, or else the Romans would.

The time had come for Jesus to meet with the other disciples and their followers in Jericho as planned. Jesus and his inner group stayed at Moshe's synagogue in Jericho as before. A large contingent of temple police surrounded the synagogue. Herod's guards and Roman calvary and troops surrounded the temple police. Jesus's followers set up a tent city on the outskirts of the city for those who could not afford refuge in Jericho's inns. Many slept on blankets under the night sky. Within three days, Mark, Thomas, John, Andrew, Luke, Philip, James, Jude, Simon, Peter, Bartholomew, and other disciples arrived with over five hundred more followers who had joined them along the way.

When Jesus's group first arrived in Jericho, the city's people were stunned and mystified that Herod's and Rome's soldiers were escorting Jesus and his followers.

As word spread that the miracle worker Messiah who had resurrected Zacchaeus's daughter was now back in Jericho, thousands more from the city and nearby areas came and congregated near the synagogue. Travelers going to Jerusalem and other areas in Judea carried the word that the Messiah was in Jericho. More Roman troops were called to maintain order. A mass gathering was planned for Jesus to address everyone, most of whom yearned to be in the presence of the Savior.

Judas spoke with Jesus in a corner of the main room of Moshe's quarters. Mary came by and stood next to Judas as he said, "Master, my money reserves are almost gone. There are too many people to feed and care for. I've sent a message to my family to borrow funds and to send someone to bring the money, but I don't know if they'll get my message and come in time to help."

Without hesitation, Mary said, "I have resources that I've saved for a long time. They are yours to help feed and care for the people." She reached into a small pocket inside the top of her dress and pulled out a small cloth pouch. She opened the pouch and poured a handful of precious jewels into the palm of her hand and offered it to Jesus.

"I don't think that will be necessary, Mary," Jesus replied. "Keep your jewels. You'll need your savings for future travel to teach others The Word and to help your family. All will be well here. Today it's important for you to leave and be with your sister, Martha, and your brother, Lazarus. They need you."

"Is it so important that I must leave today? I want to be here with you," Mary pleaded.

Jesus gently squeezed Mary's arm and told her, "It's best to leave as soon as possible."

Mary became very concerned. "If you say I must, then I'll go as you request, but here with you is where my heart is."

When Bartholomew opened the door in response to a loud knocking, a temple policeman announced, "Zacchaeus, the tax collector, is here to see the Messiah."

Bartholomew looked toward Jesus, who said, "Have him come in."

A moment later, Zacchaeus, dressed in fine cloth and an elegant robe, entered and approached Jesus. He knelt before Jesus and said, "Welcome back to Jericho, My Lord. I have come to offer my help."

"Thank you," Jesus replied. "There are many people who need food and shelter. Your help in caring for them will be greatly appreciated."

"Whatever you wish is yours."

"I see that your spirit of charity has blossomed."

"You have shown me the way. You are my Savior."

"How does your daughter, Isabella, fare?"

"Isabella is well and very happy. You have blessed me with the gift of her life. I know that I cannot do enough to repay you."

"Just keep the spirit of charity alive for those less fortunate than yourself. That is a gift to yourself and others."

Judas said to Zacchaeus, "There is much that needs to be done with your help."

Jesus took Zacchaeus's arm and helped the short man to his feet. "Go with Judas now," Jesus instructed. "He will tell you what needs to be done."

Zacchaeus replied, "It shall be done. You have changed my life for the better. Thank you and blessed be your name." Then he and Judas left.

Jesus turned to Mary, "You too must go now. Your family awaits you in Bethany."

The day was warm. Joseph and Seffira escorted Mary to Bethany in their wagon. Suddenly Seffira grabbed Joseph's arm and squeezed sharply. "What is it, Seffira?" Joseph asked after he saw her wince in discomfort.

She placed a hand over her pregnant belly and then smiled. "At seven months, our baby's kick is getting stronger. It startled me." Her smile grew wider. "That's a sign of our baby's good health."

Joseph held the reins with one hand and put his other hand over Seffira's hand on her rounded belly. The baby kicked again. "I felt it! It was very strong!" Joseph exclaimed and smiled broadly. "It won't be long before we can hold our baby in our arms. I can't wait."

The baby kicked again. Seffira winced once more and replied, "It won't be soon enough."

Mary sat in the back of the wagon. She heard Joseph and Seffira's words, but her mind was filled with thoughts concerning her sister Martha and her brother Lazarus and why Jesus had felt it was so urgent that she leave so soon. Bethany was less than ten miles from Jericho, and they were halfway there.

"Father, I'm worried. There was so little attendance at our morning service."

Zadak, the head priest of the Pharisees, replied in a huff, "Why plague me with what I know? More of our people leave each day for Jericho to see the one they call their Messiah. He attracts people like nectar attracts bees. He's a growing threat to our existence. His interpretations of the Torah are a curse."

"He is a heretic," Zadak's son replied. "Our people say they have dreams and visions of Jesus offering them salvation for the asking. What can be done about that?"

Zadak clenched his fist. "He will be taken care of in time. Mark my words, the day of justice will come."

Pontius Pilate stared at his noonday meal. Zena asked, "Why don't you eat? It's your favorite food."

"My thoughts are not of food." Pilate frowned. "Why has Herod given protection to your sister's savior? What is it that Herod is so worried about that he would do such a thing?"

Zena replied, "It must be because of the tax increases and his beheading of John the Baptist. Rome has also taken most of his battalions, and he wants to prevent any revolt if something unfortunate happens to the Jews' Messiah."

"I've thought of that already. But I'm not sure those are the only reasons. I don't trust Herod. I also don't like the people's attraction to their new 'King of the Jews.' It vexes me."

"Be patient, my husband. Any 'King of the Jews' will soon die, as have those before him."

"It won't be soon enough, Zena.

<hr>

John and Mark escorted a man to Moshe's bedroom, where Jesus was. The man wore his hood draped over his forehead and the sides of his face. He pulled down his hood, revealing a kind and wise face with a well-manicured white beard. John said, "Master, this is Nicodemus. He is a highly respected member of the Sanhedrin. I know of him, and I believe that he can be trusted to help us."

Jesus smiled at Nicodemus and said, "Yes, I see. You have come secretly in person to verify what you have heard of me."

Nicodemus's eyes widened. "Already you speak with great insight."

Jesus turned to John and Mark, "Please allow us to speak alone."

"Yes, Master," Mark replied. The two left, and Jesus and Nicodemus spoke together for some time.

<hr>

Two days later, Mary, Joseph, and Seffira returned to Jericho and went straight to the synagogue. Mary ran ahead to Moshe's quarters, where Jesus was counseling a small group of disciples. She stood to the side, her eyes red from weeping. She trembled and looked ashen. Jesus dismissed the disciples and opened his arms to Mary, who walked weakly to him. They embraced, and then she burst into tears. "He's dead," she said between sobs. "Lazarus is dead."

"It's a blessing that you were able to be with him before he died," Jesus consoled.

Mary continued to weep profusely; then she calmed as she felt Jesus's comforting energy envelop her. She said softly with deep sadness in her voice, "He had the fever for months. Martha said he'd get better for a week or two; then the fever would return." She broke into tears again. "I was able to talk to him, to hold him. He was so thin and weak." She began to sob again, then caught her breath. "He died the next day. I had so little time with him."

Jesus hugged her tighter. Tears welled in his eyes, and he said, "I truly feel your sorrow and pain."

Mary took a half step away from Jesus and then took his hands in hers. She looked into his eyes and pleaded, "I know you have the power to resurrect the dead. Please! Please come to Bethany and bring my brother back! Please, I beg you. Let's go now!"

Jesus sighed. He kissed Mary's hand and then said, "Tomorrow I must fulfill my commitment to address the mass gathering that has been planned."

"Please. Can't you change the day and come to Bethany now? I know you can bring Lazarus back to me."

"I will go with you after my sermon. Then I will do what I can to awaken your brother."

Mary collapsed at Jesus's feet. In a weak voice she murmured, "I pray that it won't be too late for you to help."

―――――

The next day, Jesus spoke with great authority to a mass gathering of thousands. As he spoke, Jesus saw hundreds of angels hovering over him and the multitudes. The people were captivated by Jesus's words of hope and his promise that his heavenly Father's kingdom was open to all who truly repented their sins and desired to enter. Jesus saw The Light above the crowd grow brighter as the people's minds resonated upon hearing his words and parables. Jesus was able to crystallize the people's feelings and desires with his hallowed passion and phrasing to give greater meaning and purpose to his listeners' lives; and in turn, their minds and hearts radiated with sympathetic vibrations that enhanced The Light. A thrilling sensation spread among the people. Many in the huge assemblage spontaneously yelled out "hosannas" of jubilation, exclaiming their joy at the feeling of having received divine help and salvation. Many others declared that their ailments had left them just upon hearing Jesus's message. He also saw the doubts of some people who wanted to believe but needed more than words to be convinced of The Truth that Jesus had ardently proclaimed would give them the gift of a new life.

Afterward, Jesus felt The Light of the Holy Spirit increase within him once again. He knew his powers were becoming ever greater than before. He also knew that the time remaining to complete his mission was growing much shorter. Plans had been made the night before that he would leave for Bethany after his sermon. This was announced to the throngs of people, and they were invited to join him in Bethany. Because of the short notice, only about fifteen hundred people were able to accompany their Savior.

Markus, the Roman tribune assigned to protect and oversee Zacchaeus and his tax collections for Rome, proudly led the procession of hundreds of wagons and carts filled with the people from the mass gathering in Jericho. They and the temple police traveled with Jesus and his disciples to Bethany, followed by Roman cavalry and soldiers. Markus's regal chariot with its Roman flags and Herod's cavalry and their chariots led by Herod's captain of the royal palace guard closely accompanied Jesus and his followers. To all who witnessed the procession, such an astounding escort was an acknowledgement of Jesus's status as the recognized Messiah.

Jesus, Mary, and his disciples went directly to Martha and Lazarus's home in Bethany. There, many mourners had gathered to grieve for their beloved Lazarus. Mary's brother had been a pillar of the community. He was known for helping the downtrodden and giving the rabbis in Bethany and Jerusalem wise council to keep their synagogues flourishing even in hard economic times. Bethany was less than two miles from Jerusalem, and hundreds of Jewish leaders from that city had come to pay their respects to the memory of Lazarus. At first, the dignitaries were all stunned at the throngs of people and the soldiers who had also arrived and wondered if a revolt were taking place. But when they learned that the soldiers had accompanied the Messiah to Bethany, they felt less trepidation and greater wonder.

Mary and her sister, Martha, embraced upon Mary's arrival, both weeping profusely at the shared loss of their brother. Jesus stood beside them and looked upon the Jewish leaders and friends who were wailing with grief so strong and true of heart that he also wept. Martha had been informed during Mary's last visit that Jesus's miracles were real. Martha said to him, "Lord, if you had been here, my brother would not have died. But I know that even now, for Lazarus's sake, God will give you whatever you ask."

Jesus replied, "I am the resurrection and life. He who believes in me will live, even though they die; and whoever lives and believes in me will never die. Do you believe this?"

Martha replied with solemn respect, "Yes, Lord, I believe that you are the Christ, the Son of God, who has come into this world."

"Then let us go to where you have laid your brother."

"I will take you to where Lazarus has been entombed for four days."

As the mourners followed them to Lazarus's entombment, word quickly spread among the people who had accompanied Jesus to Bethany of Lazarus's death four days ago and that the Messiah was going to resurrect him. They all wondered how that could be possible.

When everyone arrived at a nearby cave in a small valley, the local mourners and those who came from Jericho totaled over two thousand people. They gathered on the surrounding hills and looked down upon Jesus as he approached the cave that entombed Lazarus. Jesus raised his hands toward the crowd; and in a few moments, the people became still, and the valley was hushed in silence. Jesus pointed to the large stone that covered the entrance to the cave and said, "Take away the stone."

Martha meekly protested, "But, Lord, by this time there will be a terrible smell, for Lazarus has been dead for four days."

"Did I not tell you that if you believed, you would see the glory of God?"

Weeping, Martha nodded. "Yes, I believe you."

The stone was rolled away. Those near the cave recoiled at the stench of rotting flesh. They covered their noses and backed away. Jesus looked up at the sky and then, in a loud voice that echoed throughout the valley, said, "Father, I thank You that You have heard me. You always hear me, and You always know my thoughts; but I say this aloud for the benefit of the people standing here that they may believe in You and that You have sent me as Your Son."

The multitude of witnesses were transfixed in an unfathomable state of anticipation. Jesus then held his palms out toward the cave's open entrance and called out in a loud voice, "Lazarus, come out."

Moments passed. Everyone waited, motionless and silent. More moments passed. Jesus maintained his stance with his palms directed toward the cave. Then Lazarus was standing at the cave's entrance. He was bound in burial clothes with his head muffled in a linen swath. Many people in the crowd screamed; others fainted. Others stared wide-eyed at what they had witnessed. Many "ohhs" and "ahhs" were heard. Jesus loudly declared, "Lazarus lives among you again. Unwrap and clean him."

Jesus looked at the crowd, who stared at him in awe. When he cast his sight on the doubters who had once needed something more to be convinced of his authenticity, they spontaneously shouted, "Hosanna! You are the true Messiah!"

Later that evening, at Martha and Lazarus's home, the disciples had gathered around Jesus as he answered their many questions regarding death and the afterlife. Jude asked, "When I die, will I be resurrected in heaven, and if I am, will I be a disciple or a fisherman, as I have been both?"

Jesus smiled. "You have had many more identities than just those two: you were a small child and a teenager; you are the brother of James, the son of Zebedee, and on and on. But in my Father's Kingdom, you will be not any of them, yet all of them will be a part of the Self that is your Essence. You mustn't think of yourselves in terms of the flesh or of the roles that you have played or the status you may have achieved in your present life. Those are all passing things of this earthly world's experience."

Jesus pointed to James and said, "In my Father's Kingdom, this man will not be your brother, nor Zebedee your father, nor will you be a fisherman."

Jesus saw that his disciples were having difficulty in understanding his full meaning. He said, "Have all of you not read the book of Exodus in our Holy Scriptures, about Moses whom God spoke to from the burning bush? God said to Moses, *'I am the God of Abraham, and I am the God of Isaac, and I am the God of Jacob.'*"

Jesus saw that the disciples were still puzzled, so he explained further, revealing his insight into the Scriptures. "God was telling Moses that these men, though dead for centuries, were still very much alive, as you will be; for He did not say, *'I was the God'*; He said, *'I am the God'* of those who no longer live in your world, which means that in God's eyes, those men exist as Angels of Light in His eternal domain – as will you. As Angels of Light, your Essence will retain the wisdom gained from all of your earthly experiences, especially as my disciples; but you will be much more, for in my Father's Kingdom, you will also be one with 'All That Is.'"

The disciples discussed this revelation among themselves until they understood the deeper meaning of those Scriptures. In their discussion of Moses and God's Ten Commandments, Philip wondered which Commandment was the most important. Jesus knew his thoughts and said, "To answer your question, Philip, the commandment that is most important is the one that says, 'Hear, O Israel! The Lord our God is the one and only God. And you must love him with all your heart and soul and mind and strength.'"

Jesus continued, "The second most important commandment is a part of the first: 'You must love others as much as yourself,' for as I have said before, others are a part of God as you are – and all parts of God are to be loved."

Again the disciples discussed the Oneness of God's boundless creation and how He viewed all of His creations with eternal love. Finally Jesus was satisfied that they not only understood why "love for all" was critical in their spreading his Good News, but having been under

Jesus's grace, they were now also able to sense that divine "agape" love of which he spoke.

Then Jesus surprised everyone when he announced, "One week from this Sunday, I will give my last sermon. There will be a much greater number of people there than have ever attended before."

Thomas asked, "Why will that be your last sermon?"

"There are many reasons," Jesus replied, "but know for now that future sermons would attract too many people to hear my words. For next week's final sermon, you must organize many more 'voice relay' teams than you did in Capernaum so that the tens of thousands who attend will hear and understand my messages. And you shall convey those messages with the feelings of divine love that you have now experienced. After the sermon, we will all be going into Jerusalem for the annual Passover pilgrimage."

The dark night sky had started to fade to faint violet just before Sunday's dawn. It was one week later, and thousands of people were already being directed to a gentle slope on the Mount of Olives, located just a thousand yards east of Jerusalem. The year before, fire had burned the five-hundred-acre slope of olive trees, and the slope had been cleared for replanting the next year. Thousands had camped out on the slope the night before the Messiah's sermon. Word of the noontime sermon had quickly spread among the hundreds of thousands of Jews who had made their annual Passover pilgrimage to Jerusalem. As the morning progressed, delegations from the Zealot, Sadducee, Essene, and Pharisee communities who had been sent by their leaders to monitor Jesus's sermon were grouped among the crowd of the poor and oppressed as well as the wealthy. Many Gentiles felt a calling to be there, and some were there simply out of curiosity. The spring morning air was cool and breezy. Strong, palpable levels of anticipation and excitement had spread among the people like a wild brush fire. Their dreams and visions had presaged this day of the Sermon on the Mount.

By ten o'clock, over forty thousand people had assembled. They had been directed to settle in a fan-like arrangement below a rock outcropping just above the gently graded slope. The breeze had turned to a steady wind, and the people covered themselves and their children with blankets and robes. Thousands of Roman infantry soldiers, cavalry, and archery artillery units surrounded the area, ready to respond to any insurrection.

By eleven forty-five, another ten thousand people had arrived. The winds became stronger.

Before noon, seventy-two disciples fanned out among the multitudes in a much larger pattern than they had for Jesus's sermon in Capernaum. As noon approached, the disciples began to quiet the din of the people's fervent conversations about the Messiah's many miracles and announced that soon he would be in their presence. In short order, the huge crowd had quieted. Jesus, clad in his white tunic, stepped onto the rock outcropping and looked down upon the masses, who looked up to him with faces filled with wonder, hope, and awe.

Jesus held up his hands to the sky and closed his eyes. With his inner sight, he saw Four Archangels posted at the four corners of the Earth. They began to hold back the Four Winds of the Earth to prevent any wind from blowing on the land or the sea. For that moment, it was as if the Earth stood still. Jesus opened his eyes. The cool winds had stopped, the people taken aback with Jesus's gesture hushed and marveled that he was able to still the wind; only the sounds of some chirping birds and tweeting insects could be heard in the quiet stillness of the warming noon sun.

Then Jesus saw tens of thousands of angels over the masses of people, Another surge of the Holy Spirit's power coursed through him heightening his power. In a clarion voice he began his sermon, "I am the Son of God. I say to you, with all that is holy and sacred, that you also are sons and daughters and children of God's family and that God dwells within you. You need not get permission from a priest or rabbi to be connected to God. Although many formal prayers and rituals honor God, you do not need them to be connected with God, for with or without your recognition, God has always been intimately connected to you, as he is to all life and all things. God dwells within you now!"

In the quiet stillness, those close to him heard Jesus's voice clearly, and his disciples, who were fanned out in the assembled crowd, relayed his words as before in Capernaum. Jesus continued, "My heavenly Father has chosen me as His shepherd to lead you to His divine springs of living waters, where He will wipe away every tear that your eyes have ever shed. If you choose me as your Savior to help you bridge the connection to my Father, then I am humbled and glad to help you open your inner eyes to the fact that you have never been separated from the Oneness of our Lord, our God, the Creator of All That Is. So close your outer eyes now, and open your hearts and your inner eyes and experience God within yourself. Take a deep breath. Feel what makes you breathe the breath of life; hear with your inner ears what makes your heart beat, for I say again, know ye that God dwells within you now."

Most of the people closed their eyes and became aware of their breath and heartbeat. Many from the religious delegations looked upon

Jesus with disdain for his claim that he was the Son of God and that their rituals might not be necessary, although a few of those in the delegation were moved by his words. Jesus saw that ten of thousands of additional angels had joined the ones already there. They all hovered now above the masses, adding more intensity to the auric white light and the growing brightness that had already formed above those gathered.

The people opened their eyes, and Jesus continued, "I am from and of the Light of God, the Almighty Lord of lords, King of kings, my heavenly Father. Unbeknownst to most of you, you are also of that same Light – His Light – and I now inform you that you are also guardians of God's Light. As His Son, I bring this message of Good News to you. He wants your light to grow brighter with the rest of His Creation of Universes. But too many of you have allowed your light to dim by not recognizing His Light that dwells within you. Too often you shroud that sacred Light with fear and worry, jealousy, hate, and other dark thoughts that dim your Light."

Jesus looked upon the masses and saw many with dark thoughts. He said, "My Father knows that the darkness is a natural part of life, but you are not intended to dwell in the darkness, for as night changes to day, you too, with faith and trust in God's Light, need to let go of your dark thoughts as the black of night must give way to the dawn of a new day. The way to do so is to forgive yourself for your sins and the regrets of yesterday and to forgive the sins of others, for the sins you forgive will be the sins that you will be forgiven for."

Jesus paused and then saw a mass "letting go" of the darkness in the auras of the majority of people who had heeded his instruction; the darkness dissolved over them. The angels above quivered with delight as God's Light within the people shone outward and the white glow over the crowd grew brighter. Then Jesus triumphantly continued, "I am here to herald in a New Age of love and tolerance, forgiveness and brotherhood. Verily I say, you are all needed to play your parts in making this opportunity for a New Age a reality. To help bring this about, I say that in your relationship with others with whom you differ, seek dialogue rather than violence; do not exclude them, but include them whoever they may be, for although they may not know it, they too are of the same Light as you – and you must honor, respect, and love all of God's Light. And, as guardians of God's Light, you must also honor and respect the nature of the land and the animals and be mindful caretakers, for All That Is within His universe is a part of Him and of His Living Light.

"This is not an impossible task, for to rise above your present state is a natural impulse of life; not to do so is peril. Balance your opinion of others by seeing the good things that they do as well as their errors. Before you can live a righteous life, you must become aware of the plight of others. Be willing to listen with an open and sincere heart to their viewpoints, for when you have walked for years in their sandals, you will realize that your first judgment has changed into a different and more understanding and compassionate impression."

Jesus continued to speak passionately with stunning examples and parables conveying his Father's message in ways that most understood and accepted. Even when he was not understood, the manner and dynamic conviction of his speaking penetrated the hearts and defensive emotional armor of the majority in attendance. "Be happy for those who are happy," he said, "and give joy to those who are joyous, for then you will feel happiness and joy, and that will enrich your life and the lives of others, and your light and theirs will shine brighter. That will please my heavenly Father, and He will be pleased with you."

Jesus spoke for an hour more. Instead of fidgeting or tiring, the people remained riveted on his every word – the One whom they now revered as the Christ who would change their world for the better. As Jesus spoke, he continued to see the white aura of enlightenment above the masses further expand upward and outward. As the Light from the crowd and angels intensified, he also felt the Light of the Holy Spirit become ever more potent within him. Jesus took a deep breath and continued, "You have heard it said before by God to men of old that 'Thou shall not murder.' I say to you that it is not enough to just refrain from killing. To honor God, you must take the initiative to reconcile with those with whom you are in conflict and to act generously toward those less fortunate than yourself. Devote your energies to works of mercy, not as a means of public recognition, but to humbly serve God's intention for mankind to help each other. Each hour of each day and each moment of each hour, God's energies surely work for you when you align your heart and actions with His.

"When you think, feel, and act in harmony with my Father's ways, you will receive spiritual nourishment that will feed your soul for eternity. These divine gifts will be yours as you accept God's will into your life. Blessed are those who are poor of spirit, for your wealth awaits you in my heavenly Father's Kingdom, and there you shall reap Heaven's treasure. Blessed are those who hunger now, for you will be nourished and satisfied."

Jesus turned his gaze toward the Pharisees' delegation where the head priest, who was at the Jordan River during Jesus's baptism, sat with the tall, thin priest and the short, portly priest and their twenty assistants. He said to them, "Woe to you who are well fed now, for you will go hungry." They frowned, seething with resentment. Jesus nodded to them and said, "Woe to you who are rich in things that are material and give you comfort now, for if your heart is poor of true spiritual richness, you will suffer." The Pharisees' delegation bristled at his insinuation.

Jesus turned toward the soldiers who stood ready for battle and said, "Those who are warlike shall bring destruction upon themselves and leave those who are loving, kind, and meek to inherit the earth." He addressed the people again. "To those who strike you, turn your other cheek, for in their ignorance and fury, they act to strike a part of God, although God cannot be hurt. To strike another back in revenge, or to smite him, is also to strike and smite a part of God."

The cadence and charismatic power of Jesus's delivery and message captivated the huge crowd. The disciples' harmonized, chorus-like repetition of his words served to reinforce his message and crystallize the Seeds of Truth deeper into the psyches of the listeners. Jesus continued with great conviction, "And so I say again, there is only one God, creator of All That Is and creator of the human family. The family of man, though of many nations and tribes, is but one family. My hope and prayers for the one family of man is that you will act in balance and harmony with each other for the good of all. To do so is to love thy neighbor as thyself and to do unto others as you would have them do unto you. Act with love! That is the Golden Rule that will guide you to fulfill God's vision for mankind, to become true guardians of life on earth, and to act as co-creators with Him."

The people were mesmerized by the lofty goals that Jesus set before them and the spirit of love that they needed to embrace to achieve those goals. He spoke more emphatically, "Make the Lord your shepherd, and you shall not want. With sincere faith, surrender to God's infallible wisdom, and He will clear a path and make a way for you when no way appears possible."

"I know it is hard for many of you not to feel oppressed, for surely you have been, but I say to you now, believe in your minds that the rights and privileges of freedom for all are God's will, and in time, God's will will prevail. Have faith and hope that that journey to my Father's intended destination for mankind's glory will prove fruitful and become a reality on Earth as it is in Heaven. And as that road is paved with the love of men's hearts for one another in a true spirit of brotherhood and the knowledge that all creation is One Creation, I tell you with certainty that you will fulfill your roles within our Lord's creation and all are intended to play their parts in harmony with God's will. To do so, you must act as One. For you are the salt of the earth and are meant to be the Light of the World. Only you can do as no fish or bird or beast can do. It is your gift and responsibility to create Good with your powers and avoid violence.

"Whoever heeds my words is like a man who builds his house made of stone on a deep foundation of rock that will weather times of storms and floods. Those who listen but do not obey build their houses without that blessed foundation, and they will suffer damage in times of strife and storms and will be swept away in times of fear and flood.

"Once you truly work with God's love, you will experience the 'divine connection' and begin to know the unimaginable vastness and never-ending domain of my Father's glorious kingdom."

Jesus raised his hands to bless the multitudes as he gave his benediction. "Be the best of yourselves, and know ye all that when you enter my Father's Heavenly Kingdom, all are blessed, and in their own way, all are equal, for all are a necessary part of God, and no part of God is lesser or greater than any other part. Act in harmony with God's way of love for the benefit of all of His creations, and you will be blessed with His grace. Amen."

Jesus looked above and saw the sky completely covered by angels. In that hallowed moment, he felt his Light and the Light of the angels bathing the people in a blessed state of grace. Most of those in attendance felt a tingling on their skin as the high frequency of the angels' vibrations elevated their Essence once Jesus's words had opened their hearts and minds.

Jesus closed his eyes and with his inner sight was able to see the Four Archangels at the Four Corners of the World. Intertwining streams of jasper and carnelian-colored Light emanated from the Archangels' hands and encircled the globe. When a band of their Light passed over Jesus, the hundreds of thousands of angels above the crowd funneled the Light stream toward him. It dipped down in a vortex and encircled him and changed to a pure white Light that radiated brilliant sparkling flashes of pure red, orange, yellow, green, blue, indigo, and violet. The white vortex then rose above and away from Jesus and transformed back to the shades of jasper and carnelian. The Four Archangels drew the streams back into their hands and then vanished. Jesus opened his eyes. He had blinked for less than a second.

Jesus beamed joyously. He felt as if he had been kissed by his heavenly Father's Holy Spirit and was now blessed with a superluminal surge of enormous power. Jesus knew it was a sign that his Father was very pleased with him. He also knew that his time as a quasi-incarnate being his body of flesh could not last much longer than another week.

The vast majority of the people accepted his message, which greatly encouraged Jesus. He held the thought that there was hope that enough time was left for mankind to heed the wisdom of his Father's message and that enough people could make the changes to unite as one people and advance mankind's ways before they destroyed themselves in a distant apocalyptic Armageddon.

After Jesus's benediction, the disciples announced to those assembled that the Messiah would be entering Jerusalem later that day. Jesus was then quickly escorted along a trail behind the rock outcropping from which he had spoken. He told his escorts to leave him as he walked into an olive grove and seemed to disappear from their sight, blending as one with the grove. Without being asked, people went to his disciples and gave them so many alms that soon the disciples' pockets and pouches were stuffed full. The disciples then formed cloth receptacles by holding their arms under their robes like baskets, which were also soon filled. The scornful Pharisee delegation jealousy watched as people lined up to make donations.

Afterward, the disciples met at a pre-arranged, secured area where tents had been erected, and they began to gleefully count the money. Jesus walked into the large tent, now wearing his heavenly Father's robe, and saw his disciples making stacks of different sized coins. Matthew exclaimed, "Master! Look and see how much people have given in appreciation for your sermon." Matthew pointed to the stacks of gold and silver coins and said, "The rich have given generously."

Peter pointed to the stacks of small copper pennies and said, "Some people didn't give much at all." Two copper pennies lay beside the neatly piled stacks.

Jesus picked up the two small coins and said, "These two pennies were given by a poor widow. They were her last two coins. She has given more than all of the greatest donations, for those with wealth and abundance have given a little of what they didn't need, but this homeless widow, poor as she is, has given everything she had." Jesus stared silently at the men.

The disciples bowed their heads shamefully in acknowledgement of Jesus's words.

Then, to be more encouraging, Luke said, "Master, we have all come to the conclusion that rather than traveling the land to teach The Word, it would be far better to build a temple in your name."

"A very large and glorious temple," Thomas added.

"Yes," Luke continued, "a very large and glorious temple where people can come to us rather than our needing to travel to them. They will come from all over to see and hear you speak."

John said, "We will not want for money to build the world's most spectacular temple in your honor."

Jesus stared coldly at his disciples. He studied the multiple thought-forms expanding in their auras and said, "I see what you have in mind: a grand temple of marble and granite, massive columns supporting a magnificent roof, splendid gardens and reflecting pools that would make even Herod envious. I foresee a necessarily large force of temple police guarding over all your imaginings. But I also see arguments among the many committees that you would form to manage such a large and grand temple and its functions and maintenance. I also see more arguments amongst yourselves about how the vast sums of monies collected should be spent."

Jesus paused and then adamantly shook his head in a resolute No! He said, "I also see that the abundant food bought with people's donations that you will eat will make you fat and your high status will insulate you from the pain and suffering of the poor and oppressed. Have I failed so miserably in my mission that those closest to me have not learned that each person is his or her own temple because God dwells within them? And that each person is also his or her own intimate connection to my Father? The temple that you envision will fail as many grand temples of the past have."

The disciples were first disappointed; then a feeling of shame came over them. Jesus lamented, "No temple or building of stone can house almighty God, for He is in all people and all things and cannot be housed in a physical structure. If you are my true disciples, then just spread The Word – the Good News – to people in all lands: that God dwells within and each is responsible for living an honest life and helping one another in unity with a spirit of brotherly love."

"But, Master," Mark said, "people need a place to honor and worship you and God."

Jesus's voice became stern. "I have never asked any of you to promise me that you would do as I say. I have made my desires known and always honored your free will to act out of love and devotion to fulfill the wishes of my heavenly Father. But I ask you now to give me your promise that you will not build a synagogue, church, or temple in my name, for God's sky and this Earth are my place of worship where I feel most connected to my Father.

"And yes, Mark, people do need a place to honor and worship my Father – a place where people gather in a spirit of community to share their love for God, to praise His works and His ways as examples of how they should live their lives, and to help each other in the spirit of His love. But a true house of God will always preach that God dwells within each of its members and will make its rules to honor that Holy Truth rather than forming allegiances to a structure or organization, for when two or more are gathered in my name, that is what matters most, regardless of a grand or humble house of worship. Let others build temples and name them to honor my Father, but live your lives spreading The Word."

The disciples were all humbled by Jesus's words, and they all promised not to build any temples or churches, but to do as he bade them, to travel the land and preach his message to all people.

Judas had paid little attention to the counting of the money, for his wealthy family had dealt with large amounts of money many times before. He remarked, "Master, your reddish-brown robe has become much lighter in color."

The other disciples noted the change for the first time. Jesus said to them, "Keep your eyes open to God rather than fixed on counting money, or you will not see the signs of His presence."

———————

As final preparations were being made for Jesus to make the short walk from the Mount of Olives to Jerusalem, Joseph was helping Seffira, with her cumbersome, swollen belly, onto their wagon. He then climbed up and sat next to her and was about to take the reins when he heard her sniffling. "What is it, Seffira? Are you in pain? Has our baby kicked too hard?" he asked.

She bent her head and held her hands over her belly, then shook her head.

"What is it then? You look...so worried...so pained. Please tell me!" Joseph implored.

Seffira looked up and into Joseph's eyes and said, "I don't know. I just have this terrible feeling."

"About what?"

"I don't know. But it makes me feel sick."

"It must just be part of being in the last stages of your pregnancy, Seffira. It will soon pass."

She shook her head many times and then murmured, "I'm not sure what it is. I just know that it's a terrible, dreadful feeling that something very bad will soon happen." Then Seffira began to cry uncontrollably.

THE FINAL DAYS

44

The procession at the Mount of Olives was organized and set to leave for Jerusalem, waiting only for Jesus to come out of his tent, which the temple police from Jericho steadfastly guarded. Herod's infantry and cavalry surrounded the entire procession, and tens of thousands of onlookers stood around them. Judas and Mary walked out of the tent first. All eyes waited for Jesus to follow. When he came out, all those in the procession and the crowd hailed him with jubilant "Hosannas" and welcomes to "the King of Israel."

Simon led Mary, Judas, and Jesus to a regal stallion that stood at the front of the procession. It had an elaborately embroidered leather saddle with gold and silver adornments. Jesus looked at the majestically groomed horse with its intricately braided long tail and said, "What's this?"

"Th-Th-This is f-f-for you, M-M-Master, for you to r-r-ride into J-J-Jerusalem. Za-Za- Zacchaeus gave th-th-this horse to you as a g-g-gift," replied Simon.

Jesus turned and looked past the procession and the soldiers, and then he smiled. There, twenty yards away and unattended stood Star, the same small donkey with a simple wooden saddle and rolled-up blanket that Judas had seen when he first encountered Jesus at Jerusalem's gate. On its forehead, a white star stood out against the surrounding brown fur. Jesus and Judas walked joyfully toward the donkey, surrounded by the temple police.

Jesus stopped and turned to a man holding a folded garment. The man stood only a few yards from where the donkey had appeared. The man, like the others in the crowd around him, had been vying for Jesus's attention. Jesus extended his arms to the man and said, "James, come."

The soldiers and temple police allowed the man through, and he came and embraced Jesus and then kissed him on the lips. He said, "It is good to see you again, my brother."

"Come and walk with me now to Jerusalem. Later, you will tell me of the things that are on your mind."

Judas, Jesus, and his brother James, surrounded by guards, walked to Star, the patiently waiting donkey. Jesus patted the small donkey's neck. The donkey nuzzled the side of Jesus's robe. Jesus and Judas walked to the front of the procession with the donkey standing next to Jesus. James stepped back into the procession with the other disciples.

"Aren't you going to get on your donkey?" Judas asked.

"It is only a thousand yards to Jerusalem's east gate. I will get on my four-footed friend when we near it. Today is a good day to walk."

The donkey brayed. The two men chuckled.

"The Rabbi Jesus will be here soon," Octavius said to Herod in the tower of his king's Jerusalem palace.

"Are you sure my palace guard is still on battle alert?" Herod asked.

"Yes, My Lord, they are, although I still don't think that it's necessary."

"I don't care what you think. With all the unrest at this time and with over a million Jews here for Passover and this Jesus..." Herod shook his head in disgust. "I still can't stomach that they are calling him the 'King of Israel' – am I to be regarded as salted fish? He needs to die – and it's absurd that I have to protect him!" Herod grimaced in anger and frustration.

"It is absurd, My Lord. But we must be patient. There will come a time when the circumstances will present an opportunity to eliminate him, after Passover ends. For now, it would ignite a riotous calamity if any action against him were linked to you. Rome would doom your throne."

Herod paced nervously. "How could he have attracted over fifty thousand people to his sermon on such short notice? He disappears, then reappears with crowds hailing him as their savior. His head also belongs on a platter."

"His end will come, My Lord. For now, let's take some comfort in the fact that he will soon be in Jerusalem."

Herod's consternation eased. He smiled slyly. "Yes, Octavius, you're right. This is a moment for comfort. Make absolutely sure that my orders are followed when Jesus enters Jerusalem."

"It will be done, My Lord."

Herod grinned, "Now Pilate will boil in the rotting stew of his domain."

When Jesus's procession was halfway to the city's east gate, he looked back at the line of wagons following him and the throngs of his followers surrounding them. He caught Seth's eye and waved him forward. Seth gleefully jumped off his wagon and ran to Jesus's side. Jesus picked him up and placed him on the donkey's saddle. Seth beamed proudly to be leading the procession.

After a few minutes, Seth said, "Teacher, I have a question to ask about your sermon. If God creates a path before people, then why is there so much suffering? Why doesn't everyone have a better life?"

Jesus replied, "God creates many paths for people to take. God has given man free will to choose which path he will travel on. It is only ignorance of spiritual laws that causes man to choose paths that bring him woe." Jesus smiled at Seth. "Be not dismayed, for whether one chooses the right road or the seemingly wrong road, in time, all roads lead home to my Father."

Seth smiled and then pointed ahead, "I see that God has created a glorious path before you now and that you're taking it."

As before, the impressive number of soldiers who accompanied Jesus and his procession suggested a highly important figure being honored and escorted to the holy city rather than their intended tasks of protection and oversight.

When they were two hundred yards from the east gate, Seth saw a huge crowd massed by the entrance. He got off the donkey and said to Jesus, "You need to get on now. The people await you."

Jesus smiled, "Yes, Seth, it is time." Jesus mounted the young donkey, and they continued. Most of Herod's soldiers went through the gate first, then immediately proceeded to Herod's palace. As Jesus reached the last hundred yards, the people who had gathered palm leaves laid them on the ground in a symbol that Jesus and his donkey would maintain their exalted status and that neither their feet nor hooves would touch the earth.

With the thousands of peoples' new hope and affirmed faith in their belief that the Christ, their Messiah, had now come to fulfill the prophecies of the scriptures, shouts rang out, and choruses of "Hosanna" and "Hail to the King of Israel" reverberated throughout the crowd. Many danced to the celebratory sounds of flutes and drums. The palm leaves were layered so thick that the ground could not be seen on that glorious Palm Sunday.

Seth pointed at a large waiting caravan of over sixty camels near the side of the crowd led by one enormous camel. "Look, there!" he said to Jesus. "It's Razur, Omar's camel that you healed."

Jesus looked and nodded. He pointed to the people gathered by the gate. "There's Omar."

Seth smiled. "He has two hands full of palm leaves!"

The cheers of jubilation and praise grew thunderous as Jesus neared the gate to enter Jerusalem. The contagious excitement had already spread to all who lived in the city and those who came for the Passover feast.

After Jesus had passed through the gate, there were even more people lining the path with more palm leaves to welcome their Savior into the holy city of Jerusalem. The balance of Herod's troops from the rear of the precession made haste to his palace.

⸺

Pontius Pilate paced nervously around his large marble conference table for the third time. "Try and relax, my husband," Zena implored. "It makes me uncomfortable to see you upset in this way."

"Maybe you should share my discomfort," Pilate glared at her. "Why are Herod's palace guards on battle alert? What is he planning? Where have his battalions gone? Is he or Rome plotting to take Jerusalem from me?"

"My husband, you are not easily replaced. Rome needs you."

The commander of the Praetorian Guard entered. "What news have you?" Pilate demanded.

"My Lord, Herod's soldiers have abandoned the Jews' Messiah at the east gate and gone directly to Herod's palace. They too now stand at battle alert. The Rabbi Jesus is being hailed as the King of Israel in most areas of the city. That is all that is new to report now."

"Double our guard. As soon as you know anything more, report it to me immediately. Go now," Pilate ordered.

"Yes My Lord, it shall be done."

As soon as the commander left, Pilate exclaimed, "Damn Herod! That's why he hasn't killed the Rabbi. He made sure that Jesus lived because he knew he'd come to my city for Passover. Now that Herod has delivered the Jews' Messiah safely to me, he thinks he has rid himself of a thorn in his side. He knows that I will not tolerate any Jewish disruptions in my jurisdiction. And if I act against their Messiah now, a million Jews could rise up against me. What else could Herod be planning?"

Zena replied, "There are so many ears listening that if that sly fox farts, all of Jerusalem will know of it."

⸺

"It's outright blasphemy! He's a heretic, and by his own words, he deserves to die!" Zadak adamantly interrupted the three priests as they were recounting to him the opening words of Jesus's Sermon on the Mount when he had claimed to be the Son of God and said that believers do not need priests or rabbis to be connected to God.

The tall, thin priest replied, "He's trying to destroy us. He hypnotizes the crowds. We will lose our members. He must be stopped."

The short, fat priest said, "After his sermon, the people gave so much in alms that his disciples could barely carry it all. In a year's time, we have not received a fraction of what he collected at just one sermon."

Zadak squinted his eyes, "And you said that no one was even asked to give. He is a trickster and has fooled the people into believing his false promises."

"Not only that," the short, fat priest added, "he insulted and threatened us directly and said that 'woe' would come to us for being 'well fed' and that we would go hungry."

Zadak grew angrier. "So he thinks that he can attack us directly and go unpunished. I promise you, these next days will bring great woe to that sinful accuser. I will have him condemned, arrested, and put to death."

The head priest, who was also in attendance at the sermon, responded, "But the law does not allow us to murder him."

Zadak raised his hand to silence any more talk. "I am well aware of Moses's commandment. We cannot kill him, but Pontius Pilate can. I will meet with him later tonight. Now go and follow that heretic's moves and listen carefully to his words, which we will use against him."

When the priests left, Benjamin, who had remained with Zadak, said hesitantly to his father, "I saw Joseph at the Sermon. I learned from one of Jesus's disciples that Joseph has a new bride and she's pregnant. Joseph has also become a disciple of Jesus."

Zadak smiled sardonically. "Good. That rodent-worm Joseph is in Jerusalem. He'll soon know his fate for betraying me. You bring me some good news among the bad, my son."

———

Jesus and his inner circle had made their way to Judas's home in Jerusalem. The crowds had followed them, but as they neared Judas's residence, the multitudes were turned away by the Praetorian Guard. The Guard had already searched and evacuated all the residences in a three-block radius surrounding Judas's home and denied passage on nearby streets to all of his followers. The area was now heavily surrounded by soldiers, thus effecting a quarantine. The temple police from Jericho were allowed through with Jesus's inner circle and stood guard by the outer walls of Judas's home.

Once everyone had entered Judas's house, Jesus's brother James, who still carried the folded garment, approached Jesus, who was speaking with Judas and Mary. He and Jesus embraced again. "Please forgive me, my brother," James said. "I feel so ashamed that I pulled on your robe to sit down and bid you not speak at our synagogue in

Nazareth. I thought then that you would embarrass our family again. When the townspeople took you to throw you off the cliff, I tried to help you, but they held me back. I saw your sermon on the mountain, and now I have no doubt of your greater identity. Again, I ask for your forgiveness."

Jesus smiled, "Of course, you have my forgiveness and my love."

"Thank you," James replied. Then he held out the folded garment to his brother. "This is the robe that our mother has made for you to wear for the Passover Seder. You know how painful her hands are, yet she was determined and struggled with her twisted fingers to spin the finest thread and weave the cloth perfectly to make what she called the most splendid garment that she has ever woven. Please take it."

"I cannot, James, for I wear my heavenly Father's robe. He is the one who has given me my life."

"Please consider wearing this robe," James pleaded as he again held it out to Jesus. "Our mother is making the Passover pilgrimage to Jerusalem as she has done her whole life, but this will be her last time. Her hip is so painful that the wagon that brings her must go slowly and carefully, for each bump in the road causes her to wince. She realized that she might not make it in time for Passover to give the robe to you for the Seder. When she heard that you were here, she sent me ahead to give it to you. I must leave right away to get back to her and help escort our mother. Please, take her gift she labored to make for you, and wear it for Passover. It is her fervent wish."

Jesus pulled the sides of his robe closer around his neck and stared at the offered robe but did not take it. Mary took the robe from James and said to him, "I will keep the robe for your brother for when he decides to wear it."

"Thank you," James said; then he embraced Jesus and said, "I must leave now." He embraced Jesus again and kissed him.

Jesus said, "Go safely and come back safely" as James left.

Roman cavalry continually patrolled the empty streets surrounding Judas's house. As night fell, the city was jubilant and percolated with the excitement that the Messiah had come at last. The cavalry and Praetorian Guard remained on edge and on high alert.

Two days later, Pontius Pilate walked briskly along the aisles among the fifty money counters' desks in the large accounting room. Huge piles of assorted coins filled half the desktops. Coins that had already been counted were stacked neatly on the other side. The head accountant followed a half step behind him. He said to Pilate, "Our tax receipts so far have surpassed our best year. Rome will be very happy. It's a good thing you have authority over the Jews' temple treasury."

Pilate smiled, pointing to the piles of coins, and said, "Now I can easily afford to build the new aqueduct. Make sure all the counters are double-searched before they leave."

"As always, My Lord."

The commander of the Praetorian Guard entered the accounting room. He caught Pilate's eye and waved him toward a quiet corner of the room. Seeing the commander's worried and angry expression, Pilate hurried. The commander spoke quickly in a low voice. "That first killing was not random. Three more of my Guard were killed in three different quarters of the city. They were attacked from behind when alone, and their throats were slit. We captured one of the assassins. His name is Barabbas. He's a rebel who has been linked to others fomenting a resurrection against us. He claims his group will continue to murder Roman soldiers unless you allow their Messiah to be released from quarantine and be with his people."

Pilate's eyes bulged with fury. "First torture the murderer; then we will put him on trial and crucify the snake as an example to anyone, especially a Jew, who kills a Roman and threatens me."

"It will be done."

"Make sure that your patrols are in groups of four or more. That will prevent further attacks. If not ambushed alone, just one of my Praetorian Guard can easily slay ten Jews in less than a minute."

"My Lord, we haven't enough men. With the doubling of the guard on battle alert for your Praetorian fortress and the contingent needed to quarantine the Rabbi, combined with the overflow of crowds for the Passover feast, we are far short of the manpower needed to quadruple single foot patrols." The commander looked into Pilate's eyes. "More importantly, these calculated killings could escalate into a full scale revolt if the Rabbi is denied access to the Jews."

Pilate seethed and turned away. He knew that the commander was right. He fixed his eyes on the money counters a moment and then turned back to the Commander. "Allow the Rabbi to move about the city. Guard him closely and monitor his activities. I want to know what he's doing, where he goes, and who he's with. After the Passover feast, when the Jewish Pilgrims have left, we will have ample forces. Then the Rabbi will disappear forever. I will crush any opposition as I would swat an insect. For now, reduce the single patrol routes by half and double the men. That should reduce the risk from this Barabbas assassin's group. We can't afford any disruptions in our revenue flow."

"It shall be done, My Lord."

The Commander turned and left as Pilate's appointment secretary entered the accounting room. He walked up to Pilate and said, "Forgive me for causing any interruption. Zadak, the head priest of the Pharisees, again requests a meeting with you. He knows you are extremely busy this time of year, but he says it's urgent that he speak with you."

"Give him an appointment tonight – after my dinner."

<hr>

That afternoon, Jesus and his inner group made their way to the temple of Jerusalem. Herod Antipas's father, Herod the Great, had built the temple on the Temple Mount, which had become the heart of Judaism. Its high walls were fifteen hundred feet long, towering in height, gleaming white as snow—an impressive sight to behold, especially to people who lived in simple and meager rural areas.

Colonnaded courtyards of huge columns seventeen feet in circumference encompassed the temple area of thirty-five acres. Located in different areas of the temple grounds were sectioned sanctuaries designated the Court of Women; the Court of Israel, only for men; the Court of Priests; and the Court of Gentiles, which was open to people of all nations. Within the Court of Women was the Chamber of Oils, the Chamber of Nazirites, the Chamber of Wood—where wood to be used for altar fires was inspected to ensure it contained no worms—and the Chamber of Lepers. This chamber was for those afflicted who claimed they had been cleansed. They were inspected by the chamber priests for verification and were later given purification rites. Many visitors brought goats, lambs, rams, pigeons, doves, cows, and oxen to be sacrificed in hopes that God would be pleased and answer their prayers. These animals could also be bought in the temple marketplace. The sounds of the bleating animals, the men and women talking, some chanting reverently, created a cacophony of sounds that mixed with the odors of incense, blood, and charred animal fats from the sacrifices. Above one high walled platform was the impressive large meeting hall for the Sanhedrin council of seventy-two ruling priests that gave final religious opinions and rulings.

With his entourage, Jesus stood by the bathing area at the outer base of the temple by the council hall. They took off their sandals and went inside for their required ritual bath before entering the temple gates. The Jerusalem temple police did not permit the temple police from Jericho to enter. The captain of the Praetorian Guard dismounted and led a contingent of soldiers from the larger force that had surrounded and escorted Jesus and his group from Judas's house into the temple. A buffer zone was cleared and manned by soldiers so that very few people could see Jesus; however, when he passed certain sections, some of his admirers got a glimpse of him. Jubilant shouts of "Hosanna," pronouncements of "King of Israel," and loud cheering erupted and echoed through large areas of the temple.

Once inside the temple, the Jerusalem temple police followed Jesus and maintained order around him, the Praetorian contingent following closely behind. Persistent cheers from the throngs of temple visitors, already there for the Passover holiday, expressed their exuberant joy and awe. Jesus walked around the temple grounds, taking in the atmosphere amid the clamoring conversations about the Messiah's arrival. After a while, he neared the market area and stood still. His disciples looked at him as he stared at the moneychangers, who converted currency from the many nations of the visitors into local currency. Behind them stood Roman overseers who calculated the portion in taxes they would collect from the exchanges. Jesus turned and frowned at the vendors selling their wares. His disciples also looked at the vendors, but they didn't see anything wrong. Judas saw on Jesus's face an expression that he had never seen before – anger!

In a rage, Jesus stared again at the moneychangers and then deftly made his way past a combination of temple police, visitors, and the Praetorian Guard, who immediately cleared a path for him. Jesus glared angerly and silently at the moneychangers behind their table. Within moments they stood up and backed away, leaving their money piles unattended. Jesus's nostrils flared. He bent under the long table and placed his palms below the tabletop and then lifted it with its heavy coinage high above his head. The crowd became stone silent. The Roman soldiers and temple police stood still. The moneychangers and their Roman overseers backed much farther away.

With the table over his head and his arms locked straight up, Jesus rebuked them, and all heard, "You take money from honest worshippers and cheat them in what you give back. And you, who oversee and know that they cheat, care not, for your take becomes greater with their dishonesty. And why? You do it for greed!"

The moneychangers and overseers froze, fearful as they looked at Jesus's inflamed face. Jesus bent his knees and lowered his arms, bringing the long heavy table to an inch above his head. Then, in one swift powerful movement, he pushed up and straightened his legs and arms, thrusting the table into the air toward the cowering men. They scrambled away as the table rotated and came crashing to the ground. The jingle of coins flooding the area drew simultaneous gasps from the stunned onlookers, who marveled at Jesus's strength and audacity. Some children stepped out of the crowd to pick up loose coins that had rolled their way, but their parents quickly pulled them back.

Then Jesus turned and stomped to a nearby vendor's stall that sold doves. The vendor immediately stood and backed away. Jesus opened all the cages of doves, and they quickly flew out, up, and over the temple walls. He pointed his finger at the vendor. "You would knowingly sell sick birds that are unknowingly bought by worshippers to use as a holy sacrifice to God. And why? For greed!"

Each time Jesus pointed his finger at one of the other vendors and accused, "And you!" another one backed away. He loudly declared, "Each of you who cheats in the house that is intended for worshipping our God insults and mocks my Father! My Father's house shall be called a house of prayer for all nations. You have made it a den of thieves!"

Jesus thrust his arm straight out to his side and clenched his fist. He walked briskly in front of each vendor's table and with his extended arm, knocked down the poles that supported their overhead shade tents, which floated slowly to the ground in successive sections.

After the last shade cloth dropped, the crowd cheered jubilantly. Jesus walked back to his disciples and stood before them. "Is this the kind of temple you were going to build to honor me? It's better to build nothing."

Twenty temple police led by a high priest dressed in a white robe and a white mitered head covering, accompanied by his finely robed attendants, quickly approached Jesus from behind.

Jesus turned and faced the high priest, who said, "I am Caiaphas, the head priest of the Sanhedrin. You have created havoc in my temple. You call yourself a holy man and a rabbi. You should rebuke all those cheering for your destructive acts in God's house."

Jesus stared solemnly at him and said, "If these people were to keep quiet, the stone floor beneath your feet would sing."

The crowd cheered louder. Jesus walked away and led his disciples out of the temple. The crowds followed. At the temple's gate, the Jericho temple police accompanied him back to Judas's house. The Praetorian Guard escorted them, and the throngs of people in the streets cheered with glee and praise for their hero and Savior.

<hr />

In the back yard of Judas's house, Jesus sat on the garden bench that he and Seth had made. Andrew, Philip, Seth, Matthew, Joseph, and Judas sat at his feet on the carpet of vibrant grass sprinkled with yellow flowers, which had been barren earth before Jesus first arrived there. The fig trees on the sides of the stall where Star, his donkey, stayed were bearing fruit, as were the sapling pomegranate trees. The disciples had remarked on how unusual it was for them to bear fruit in the early spring instead of later in the summer. Beautiful red and white camellias blossomed along the back wall. The once dried-out palm tree had grown many feet taller; its green fronds were now shiny and full. The well that had once been nearly dry was now filled to the brim with water.

It was nearing time for the dinner that Mary, Seffira, and John had prepared for the thirty house members. Jesus had been giving those seated before him final instructions on how to best fulfill their missions after his pending final departure. The disciples were solemn and saddened as he spoke of that time. "You see," he said, "my Consciousness, which is the Christ Consciousness, was born into this body, and I have experienced a life of these times, but all the while, I dreamed at the same time that I was awake. My dreams and my intimate connection to my heavenly Father's Kingdom have now become a greater reality to me than my waking life. The two are fast becoming one as my time in this body will no longer serve my Father's purpose, and my consciousness will be able to work with far greater freedom."

Andrew asked, "Teacher, are one's consciousness and their soul the same thing?"

"No, one's consciousness is like a marvelous living tool that the soul uses to operate in the physical world. It has a unique identity attuned to an individual's personality and can connect to all possibilities that could potentially become realities in the world. What one concentrates on is what his conscious mind becomes aware of, for one can only be aware of so many things without being overwhelmed. Consciousness is used by one's soul to help make choices and to create anew. Once an individual consciousness exists, it exists eternally and can be accessed and shared by the consciousnesses of others for their growth and creative abilities, as any thought created can likewise be used by those who seek to do so.

"What you know of me will soon become pure consciousness with no physical body. My soul lives eternally not only from this point in time to the never-ending future, but also from this point back to the beginning of time, as I am the Alpha and the Omega. As mankind has come to be, I, as the Christ Consciousness that you know now, have always acted to guide man's progress when called upon. I have been sent by my Father to come at this time in the flesh to initiate a New Age. You have been chosen to help that New Age take root, and after I leave this body, my consciousness will remain with you to give you guidance. My soul is of the Light, as your souls are. It is difficult to explain in physical terms how the Light of one's soul can be in many places and in many times simultaneously because in this Earth life, one's mind must be tightly focused on the physical world to physically survive. During times of prayer or meditation, you may feel moments of enlightenment when unforeseen knowledge and ideas mysteriously comes to you. That is when you have made soul-contact with your conscious mind."

Philip asked, "It is written in the scriptures that God separated the Light from the Darkness and created the universe. Are our souls of that same Light?"

"Yes, Philip, and there is truth in that concept of darkness and light if you think about it in these terms: first, there was only the Light and not the Darkness. The souls of mankind were and are a unique part of the Light. Human souls, as they become more aware of being connected to the Light, become overwhelmed with the infinite possibilities of existence. The collective Over-Soul of mankind fervently yearned to experience itself under circumstances that would allow for distinctions among its male and female soul-selves to know itself, to grow and evolve as the human earth-family, and to become co-creators with The Word, which is God. At this point in time, for better or worse, man is a co-creator and must grow in balance and harmony with 'All That Is' or cease to be of this world.

"God granted mankind's desires to know itself and evolve, and from a divine portion of All That Is, He created Darkness around a concentrated area of Light within that divine portion. That Light within the Light continued to concentrate and became denser. This may or may not be understood, but I shall say it anyway. Within mankind's divine portion of God's all-loving womb, what man calls empty or dark is still filled with the Light although man has yet to register that truth. The Light is always within and without in physical forms that man can see and also in forms that man cannot see."

Mary urgently called out from the back door to the men in the garden, "Joseph, Seffira needs you. She's feeling very weak."

Joseph got up and walked toward the kitchen where Seffira was having contractions that turned out to be false labor. A short time later Mary then announced to the others, "Dinner is almost ready," and returned to the kitchen.

Jesus said, "I have said enough for you to think about for now," and then stood. Andrew, Philip, Matthew, Seth, and Judas also stood and started walking toward the door for dinner. Jesus said, "Judas, Matthew, please stay a while longer. Seth, please get the water bag from Star's saddle."

Seth obediently went to the donkey's stall.

Jesus said to Matthew, "You are honored to have a brilliant and faithful son such as Seth."

"Yes, Teacher, he is a good boy."

"Matthew, do you think that because an adult has lived a decade or more than a child that the adult understands the mystery of the soul better than the child?"

"Well, children play with dolls and toys. The more one has experienced life, the more one should know."

"That is not always so. Children have an innate understanding with their unbridled imaginations and sense of play that actually better connects them to the nature of the soul than older men and women."

"Why is that so, Teacher?"

"Because, as one grows older, that sense of play and imagination is too often lost by the culture of one's peers. When a man talks of 'spirits,' he is often deemed foolish, but a child can freely talk with 'imaginary friends' and be considered normal. The child has a truer sense of the soul than most adults, for the soul has unlimited imagination and loves to play."

Matthew stroked his beard in thought. "I suppose that I have lost my sense of play. In these times, when life has become so challenging, it's difficult to have a sense of play."

"Yes, it is. That's why it's important to pause in life to see the world through the eyes of a child, where simple wisdom often prevails over the complications of men's actions. We must share in the moments of joy that a child experiences. Go and join the others. I'll be in shortly."

"You always give me much to think about, Master," Matthew said as he walked back to the house.

Jesus and Judas went to the stall and saw Seth stroking Star's neck. Mary came out of the house, and she went with Judas and they spoke together by the bench. Jesus stroked the other side of Star's neck. The donkey rubbed the side of its nose against Jesus's robe, then against Seth's robe in appreciation of their loving strokes. Jesus said to Seth, "It's time to say good-bye to Star. This will be his last night here."

Seth's face became sad. "Where will he go? I can take care of him." Seth hugged Star's neck.

Jesus smiled fondly at the donkey. "Star came to me as a gift from my Father." He gently rubbed the star on the donkey's forehead, then looked up to the sky above. "Star is going back to be with the stars in heaven. He will be there for me when I visit."

Seth laughed, "I'm no longer a little boy who believes in fairy tales." Seth stared at Jesus's face and saw that his Master was serious. Then Seth saw a golden-white glow around Jesus's head. He declared, "I absolutely believe in you." Both knew that Seth was able to see Jesus's aura.

The glow around Jesus's head grew larger and brighter. "Thank you, Seth. Your faith in me gives me comfort."

Seth's eyes were wide with delight and wonder. He said, "I see."

Mary and Judas also saw Jesus and Seth's auras as they embraced. Jesus pointed to the house and said to Seth, "I know you're hungry. Go in and I'll be there shortly."

Seth left with the goatskin bag of healing living waters. Jesus patted Star's star once more, then kissed it. The donkey brayed softly, and then Jesus walked to Judas and Mary. Judas said, "We saw your 'connection' with Seth. It was a beautiful moment."

"He's a special young man." Jesus put a hand on Mary's shoulder and on Judas's. "You are also both special to me."

Jesus saw that Mary was still troubled by some of the disciples' prejudiced feelings toward her. He said to her, "Do not be dismayed by what others think. For all the violations of your body, your soul remains virgin."

A tear rolled down Mary's cheek. "Thank you," she softly acknowledged.

Jesus brushed her tear away and tenderly kissed her cheek where the tear had been. "Seffira needs your help," Jesus said. "Go to her. I'll be in shortly."

As Mary walked toward the house, Judas saw Jesus looking at her with a tender fondness. "Does the Magdalene woman make you happy, Master?"

"Yes, she's been very good for me. When I'm in her company, it's her sense of childlike comfort that gives me a feeling of being more settled within as chaos percolates all around me. She's also a good balance of feminine emotions and viewpoints against the preponderance of men's ways of thinking that saturate the atmosphere."

"Then I'm glad for you, Master. There certainly was a lot of chaos at the temple today. I've never seen you angry like you were."

"That was 'righteous anger,' Judas. It served its purpose, yet no one was physically harmed. It was a display of 'divine outrage' against men worshiping the false idol of money in a place that had been designated as my Father's home. No one should dare to mock my Father's ways in His house with their greed and not receive some form of justified retribution. Now it's time for you to go in and leave me to reflect in this garden in solitude."

Judas nodded and went into the house. Jesus knelt beside the bench and prayed. Twenty minutes later, Simon came out and said to Jesus, "T-T-Teacher, w-w-we all await you f-f-for dinner."

Jesus stood up and said, "I tell you, Simon, do not believe that he who looks like me is truly me. You will know what I mean when the time comes."

Simon did not understand but nonetheless said, "As y-y-you say, M-M-Master."

They both went into the house for dinner.

Pontius Pilate scoffed at Zadak, "You want me to arrest the Jew Jesus because he knocked over some stalls in the temple? Why do you bother me with Jewish problems? You have influence in your Jewish temple; Jesus is a Jew, and you have your Jewish temple police there. You can take care of your own problems. I can't be bothered with your petty Jewish politics."

Zadak retorted, "He has gotten popular enough to lead an uprising against you."

Pilate mocked, "I suppose he will attack me with his cavalry, who will ride on cows and oxen, and legions of infantry who will wield pitchforks and large kitchen knives. You know that neither Rome nor I will ever tolerate such a foolish act. It would be immediately crushed. Don't bother me anymore."

Zadak seethed. "You underestimate the sentiment of the people. Those who protest your authority have already murdered members of your Praetorian Guard.

Pilate growled and pointed to the door. "Get out of here now!"

A little later in Pilate's bedroom, Zena suggested, "Maybe you should arrest the Rabbi Jesus so he won't cause any more trouble."

"If I were to do that now, it would appear that I'm acting on Zadak's wishes. Besides, my Guard surrounds the Jews' so-called Messiah. I will make my own move against that Rabbi when the time is right for me. The Jews already hate me. So what? Damn them!"

Later that night, Zadak spoke with Caiaphas, the high priest of the Sanhedrin, to persuade him that Jesus should no longer be permitted to disrupt the workings of the temple and that he should be arrested immediately. There was no doubt in Caiaphas's mind that Jesus's actions and his growing popularity as a force against Roman oppression of the Jewish people would, in time, cause a severe Roman retaliatory response against the Jewish leadership and the people of Israel. He remembered what the head of the secret seers' council had warned about great turmoil to come. As Zadak was about to leave, Caiaphas said, "I will order his arrest only on temple grounds if Jesus comes to the temple again."

The next day was a cool spring morning in Jerusalem. Seth had gone to the courtyard well to get water for the preparation of the breakfast meal. He looked toward the stall and saw that it was empty, as Jesus had said it would be. Star's saddle and blanket that Seth had hung over a rack the night before were also gone. Seth felt saddened at Star's absence and that his beloved teacher and friend would also be leaving. He stood at the gate to the stall with the filled bucket of water in his hand, and then he burst into tears. He put the bucket on the ground and continued to weep until he could cry no more. He looked up at the sky and remembered Jesus's words that Star would be in Heaven waiting for Jesus to visit him. That thought gave him some comfort, but his heart still ached. Seth composed himself, determined not to show his distress to the others. Then he carried the bucket of water into Judas's kitchen.

Mid-morning, many meetings were taking place at the Jerusalem temple to decide what to do about Jesus. Caiaphas and Nicodemus met privately in the high priest's chambers. Nicodemus said, "I've seen Jesus's healings and witnessed the miraculous resurrection of Lazarus. Before that, I had met privately and spoken with the Holy Rabbi. He is truly a man of God – or, I should say, if anyone has a right to call himself the Son of God, Jesus is the one to rightly do so."

"You are one of the most respected men who sits on the Sanhedrin council," Caiaphas replied. "Many will listen to you and take to heart what you say. From all I have seen and all the reports that I've heard, there's no doubt that the situation for all of us has become highly dangerous. The crowds will soon crown him king. The Romans would ban such a crowning as a move against their authority to choose who shall reign over Judea. It would usurp their choice of Herod, and they would come down on us brutally if we support Jesus. Herod would also waste little time in moving against us. All that we've gained over the years will end with our spilled blood. The masses of Jesus's followers would most likely rebel against the Romans at the removal of their Messiah. Roman swords, in turn, would butcher them. We must put a stop to our people's growing mania for Jesus as their Savior. I can only see one solution: Jesus must disappear or die in order to save our nation, or we will suffer greater oppression and the slaughter of thousands upon thousands of Jews."

Nicodemus sighed with reluctance. Then he said softly, "I agree with what you say about the political climate. But it goes against my heart to act against such a personage, even if my mind tells me that for now, it's what appears best for our people."

Nicodemus closed his eyes and sat in silent reflection for a moment. Then he said, "When I've seen Jesus, he's dressed as an ordinary man, yet he does extraordinary things. He is proclaimed ruler of a kingdom, yet he has not one house to call his own. He has no temple, yet he preaches to more people than a temple can hold. When I spoke to him, I told him that many people of authority wanted him dead – even many who sit on the council. He foretold what is happening now and said that the day would come when I would have to make a choice in the matter of which we now speak. You see, he is prescient, and he has the gifts to lead our people; yet he abhors bloodshed and said that his life is meant to save people, not cause their murders. I asked him, 'What should I do?' He looked at me with his kind, loving eyes and said, 'You must do what you think is best, Nicodemus.'"

"What will you do when it comes time to vote?" Caiaphas asked.

"I don't know. I just don't know."

Zadak led the meeting of the council of his Pharisee priests. He proclaimed, "This Jesus will surely bring the wrath of Rome upon us. He already has committed many sins that he should be condemned for. He breaks the laws of the Sabbath for his own aggrandizement. He calls himself a rabbi but keeps company with a prostitute. He should not know her or let her touch him because she is polluted. But most sacrilegious of all, he has no shame in saying that God is his Father and that he and his Father are One. He is calling himself God! That is a sin of blasphemy! He seeks to be our king, and in doing so, he mocks our God, who is King of all Kings. Jesus must die for his sins."

"He's a heretic!" one priest exclaimed. The other priests loudly agreed, and the Pharisee priests agreed that at the Sanhedrin council meeting, they would vote to put Jesus to death.

The head Sadducee priest presided over the gathering of his aristocratic council of priests. One of them stated, "We have concluded that the claimed resurrection of Lazarus was a hoax. We know that 'resurrection' is not in God's plan. Lazarus never died. He stayed in the tomb, as Jesus planned, until he was called upon to come out. It was a fraud against the people to make them believe that Jesus has a power that he does not have."

The gathering of Sadducee priests all nodded their agreement. Another priest said, "He's attempting to make our followers his followers."

Another said, "We also know from our scriptures that there is no afterlife. But this shrewd would-be Messiah promises that if people follow him, then in the so called afterlife, he will deliver them to Heaven and God's glory. He is a false Messiah and should be put to death for his false claims and crimes of sin."

All the priests voiced their agreement. The head priest said, "Then it's unanimous. We will all vote at the council meeting to condemn Jesus to death."

<hr>

The Herodians – who were not a religious group – supported the Herodian rulers, especially Herod Antipas, who wielded the most power. They were officially designated leaders with status and given valued jobs by the Herodian rulers; thus, that is where their allegiance lay. They readily viewed Jesus as a threat to their status quo because their personal welfare was dependent upon the Herods continuing reign of power. They also readily agreed to use their sway to condemn Jesus to death.

<hr>

The Essenes and Zealots also had their objections to Jesus's claim and resented his popularity, but they didn't have significant power in the Sanhedrin council. Some members in their groups posited that if Jesus were put to death, he would become a martyr and they could lead his followers in his place. All the while, the masses of Jewish people brimmed with new hope and excitement that their Messiah had finally come as the prophecies had long foretold. They, the overwhelming majority of Jews without a political agenda, enthusiastically welcomed Jesus as their hero, savior, and King.

<hr>

At one o'clock that afternoon, Jesus and his inner circle were about to leave Judas's house for the Temple of Jerusalem. The captain of the Praetorian Guard had been informed two hours earlier, and the streets leading to the temple had been cleared and secured. The crowds of people were informed by the disciples and had been anxiously awaiting the Messiah. A palpable electrified current of excitement streamed though the streets of Jerusalem. Fervent talk that the Messiah was soon coming out attracted greater crowds, which spilled over into the streets near Judas's house beyond the protective perimeter.

In the main room of Judas's home, Jesus had just finished reviewing his final instructions of the plan to his inner circle when Seffira, who had been standing against the wall, cried out in pain. She put both hands over her large, round belly. "It's coming! The baby is coming!" she frantically announced.

Mary was by her side in a flash. She put an arm around Seffira and helped her to lie on the floor. Joseph made his way to them from the other side of the large room, adroitly stepping over and in between the other disciples who were sitting or reclining on the floor. He held his young wife's hand. "Are you sure this time?" he asked.

"I've never given birth before," she grunted as she caught her breath, "but I know our baby wants to come now."

Mary said, "It certainly seems so. There's no doubt that you're due soon." Mary gently patted Seffira's belly and smiled. "Very soon."

"It could be false labor, like last night," Joseph said.

"I don't know," Seffira responded. "It just hurts – a lot!"

The disciples became edgy. All were ready to leave, their minds fixed on implementing their plan. Having a birth occur now was a hindrance. Mary understood everyone's feelings and said to Seffira, "It doesn't matter if this is the start of your labor or not. You're in no condition to stay here alone." Mary squeezed Joseph's wrist and then said to him, "You must take Seffira to a midwife's house and stay with her. The rest of us must leave now. You are the only one she has."

Joseph looked at his wife with the compelling urge to help that a new father-to-be has; then he turned to look at Jesus, then back to Seffira. With glazed eyes, she said, "I know how much you want to go with the Messiah, but I need you now."

Mary squeezed Joseph's wrist harder. "Your wife needs you. After the birth, if you can safely get away unnoticed, you can meet us for the Passover Seder."

Joseph looked at Seffira, who implored him with desperate eyes, "Please, I need you now."

Joseph stood, looked at Jesus, and firmly stated, "I need to go with Seffira."

Jesus replied, "I understand. Come to me, Joseph."

Joseph stepped around and through the disciples and stood before Jesus. Jesus embraced Joseph, then kissed him on the lips, as was the custom when men greeted or took leave of one another on special occasions such as weddings or funerals. Jesus said to Joseph, "I will be with you in our dreams."

John went to Joseph's side and told him of a nearby midwife whose home was safely away from the Guard. Joseph brought his wagon to the front gate, Seffira joined him, and they left for the midwife's home. Minutes later, Jesus and his nervous entourage departed for the temple.

———

Tumultuous cheers and praise rang out as Jesus passed by the crowds, seemingly led and protected by the Praetorian Guard. Those on the farther side streets and the back streets, hearing by word of mouth that Jesus was nearby, also cheered with the contagious jubilation of the newly uplifted spirit of the people. As Jesus made his way to the temple entrance, multitudes gathered behind Jesus's detachment of police, soldiers and cavalry escorts and followed his procession. Once at the entrance steps to the temple, Jesus and his disciples once again removed their sandals and went to the baths for the ritual cleansing before entering the temple. The crowds massed in the temple's outer courtyard and spilled onto the adjoining streets. The mood of the people in Jerusalem for the Passover festival was not only much more festive than usual, it felt historic and intensely exciting.

A smaller detachment of the Praetorian Guard led by the captain went inside the temple with Jesus as before and escorted him as he walked toward an unoccupied portion of the large west wall. There it was announced that Jesus would give his healing blessing to those who asked. In a short time, many areas in the temple Courtyard of the Gentiles emptied as the people massed in a wide arc around Jesus, who was encapsulated by his disciples and a protective row of Praetorian guards. To prevent overcrowding, the outer temple gate guards limited the number of people allowed in.

An hour of healings took place rapidly as Jesus's power and abilities had continued to escalate. He became more energized as he worked and, in turn, received the sanction of the people that he was the Messiah. The "ohhs" and "ahhs" of the crowd when Jesus healed those who were crippled, deaf, blind, and demonized loudly echoed throughout the temple's massive courtyard.

When lepers revealed themselves and then were healed, there were screams and fainting in the crowd.

Each time a male leper was healed, a disciple from Jesus's inner circle accompanied him to the Chamber of Lepers to make sure the former leper would receive clean clothes once there. Mary accompanied a female leper to the chamber after Jesus had healed her sores. Jesus continued for another half hour as those who sought healing filed past the security perimeters and were healed. The mere presence of the feared Praetorian Guard maintained order.

⬯

Zadak had left his meeting in the Jerusalem temple and was walking across the Court of Gentiles with his group of chief priests, eight attendants, and four temple policemen. He was impressed by the crowd's loud reactions and was curious about what they were responding to. His attendants made a path through the people for Zadak and the priests to Jesus's outer security perimeter.

Jesus raised his hands for the benediction at the end of his healing service. The crowd became silent. His voice resonated against the high stone wall and penetrated the skin of the listeners as he said, "My Father has sent me, His Son, to bring the Light of His Truth to the world. Whoever follows my Father's Words will never walk in darkness, but will enjoy the Light of life."

Zadak stood at the Praetorian Guards' perimeter and saw Jesus as he said those words. A man standing near Zadak said to him, "God has given us a King. Blessed be the King who has come in the name of the Lord."

Zadak sneered at the man, then stared at Jesus contemptuously, and in a loud voice challenged, "Who is your father?"

The crowd turned toward Zadak and his entourage as he spoke and then turned back to Jesus for his answer.

Jesus replied, "You have no idea where I come from. You do not know me or my Father."

Zadak fumed in anger. He pointed a finger at Jesus and yelled out to the crowd, "He speaks gibberish!" Then he grabbed the arm of a temple policeman and barked, "Arrest that man. It has been ordered by your high priest, Caiaphas."

The temple policeman hesitated. Zadak pushed him forward. The other three policemen started to follow him toward Jesus when the captain of the Praetorian Guard stepped between the police and Jesus. The captain drew his sword and held it casually pointed at the ground. The policemen stopped in their tracks. They had seen the guards bludgeon, whip, and murder temple resisters and quell riots in the temple. Zadak shouted, "Execute the order for arrest or be severely punished!"

Jesus quickly walked between the Praetorian Guard and the temple police and addressed Zadak. "There is no need for my arrest nor of your plots to kill me, for I will soon be going away."

"Where are you going?" Zadak asked tauntingly.

"I will be going home to my Father."

"Where does your father live?"

"Where I go, you cannot come. You are from below; I am from above. You are of this world; I am not of this world."

"Enough! Arrest him!" Zadak yelled. "Arrest him!"

Instead, the temple police stepped back. In a frustrated rage, Zadak grabbed the corners of his elaborately bejeweled vestment and tore it down the center. He turned and stormed away with his entourage in tow. Jesus and his remaining disciples soon left the Court of the Gentiles and made their way to the temple gate, where they had entered. On the outer steps of the temple gate, Jesus bade farewell to his remaining disciples, who then dispersed into the crowd. Many spies from the Herodians, the Sadducees, the Pharisees, the Roman Empire, and Pontius Pilate's security team followed them. It was later noted that not all of the disciples were accounted for.

Many more spies mingled in the huge crowd that followed Jesus as he walked alone without his disciples – alone, except for the temple police from Jericho and the protective procession of the Praetorian Guard. Jesus had told the captain of the guard that he was going to a small synagogue nearby to pray. The captain ordered several details of cavalry to clear the synagogue and cordon off the surrounding area. They sped away to fulfill their orders. Clouds were moving in, graying the sky.

When Jesus arrived at the small synagogue, he requested that he be left in solitude to commune with his heavenly Father. His request was respected, and Jesus sat by himself, alone in the synagogue. Hundreds of soldiers' eyes stared at the synagogue's outer walls. Within minutes, the sky darkened with thick clouds. An intense bright flash of white light suddenly illuminated the inner sanctum of the synagogue. Rays of the light beamed out through the sanctuary windows, stunning the onlookers' eyes as if the sun had burned them. The light vanished, and the sanctuary darkened as before. When their sight returned, the temple police and Praetorian Guard raced into the sanctuary to see what had happened. They searched and double-searched every corner of the synagogue and the surrounding buildings – but not a trace of Jesus could be found.

During Jesus's time in the synagogue, the Sanhedrin Council held its meeting to officially decide his fate. When Rome had annexed Judea as its province, it had appointed seventy-one priests and elders of the Jewish sects who acted as Judea's seat of authority, giving them power over judicial, religious, and administrative matters concerning the people of Judea. One of the main religious purposes of the Sanhedrin was to investigate and punish heretics who were accused of teaching contrary to the Torah; such teachings could lead people astray. Alliances between the sects to vote to have Jesus condemned were made prior to the meeting although there were many members in the minority who had witnessed Jesus's healings and believed that he could be the Messiah. Yet the dangers that Jesus posed to the Jewish population's security overshadowed all other considerations.

Near the end of their discussion and debate, one member said, "On the matter of blasphemy, Jesus has said that he will sit on a throne at the right hand of God. By his own words, it is clearly evident that Jesus has committed blasphemy."

A resounding chorus of "yes, yes" followed.

One of Jesus's sympathizers said, "But what if he is the Messiah? The people are enthralled by his miracles. How can we condemn such a man?"

The majority shouted him down. The seventy-first member and chairman of the Sanhedrin was the High Priest Caiaphas, who had listened to all who spoke and then addressed the council, "You know nothing at all! You don't understand that it is better for you to have one son die for the people than to have the whole nation of Israel destroyed. Jesus should die for our nation, and not only for our nation, but to gather together into one the dispersed children of God, our brothers and sisters. I now call for a vote on this matter. We will start with Nicodemus."

All eyes turned to the most respected member of the Sanhedrin. Caiaphas asked him, "Do you vote to condemn Jesus or not?"

Nicodemus stood and said, "It is my conviction that Jesus has come to us as the prophecies said that he would. I have no doubt that his presence here at this time is divine and is meant to serve a great purpose for our people."

Nicodemus paused and bowed his head in a moment of silence, then looked up and said, "I know that if all of our people, rather than just this elite council, had the power to vote, they would readily choose Jesus as their King. But such is not the case, and it is left to us to decide. I acknowledge the grave dangers that our people will face if Jesus lives. But in my heart, I know that he is the one – the Anointed One – who has been sent to us." Nicodemus's eyes grew teary. "So I will not cast a vote that will bring countless deaths to our people. He paused, then said resolutely, "Nor will I cast a vote to condemn a man who preaches love and forgiveness and offers healing to all who come to him. I therefore abstain from voting."

Nicodemus sadly turned away from the council and with lowered head, walked out of the Sanhedrin chamber. Heated discussion ensued, and then the voting continued. Jesus was condemned, and his arrest was officially sanctioned. After the meeting, plans were made to arrest Jesus at night when he was away from the sleeping crowds that they knew would otherwise protest and protect him.

The "Inn of Lepers" – that's what Jesus had called it when he first described his plan. The holy holiday of Passover attracted more lepers than any other time of the year. They would come to the temple in Jerusalem for cleansing and purification rituals. A group of twelve male lepers who had become friends had made the annual pilgrimage from different distant lands for the last three years. They always stayed together at a private inn outside Jerusalem's gates, where people would not shun them. The inn's owners, the Gethsemanes, were kind and compassionate to the lepers because their beloved parents had died horrid deaths from leprosy. For those twelve lepers' Passover Seder, the owners always prepared the traditional Seder meal with fresh matzoth – the traditional flat, thin, unleavened bread made without yeast. The owners never stayed for the Seder dinner. Instead, the Gethsemanes would leave before the lepers arrived so that they could be with their relatives for the traditional and most important Jewish family dinner of the year. The lepers always left money to reserve the inn for the following year.

Jesus's plan had unfolded as he healed each of the thirteen lepers at the temple; after each healing, a disciple had accompanied each one to the Chamber of Lepers. When Jesus first told his disciples the next part of the plan, many of them had cringed and protested in repugnance. James, the son of Zebedee, asked Jesus, "Isn't there another way?"

Jesus replied, "You will be wearing clothes that were cleaned that day, worn by someone who had bathed just before coming to the temple, and was healed of their leprosy and blessed by me."

That quelled the resistance that Jesus had seen in the disciples' auras. The disciples accepted their roles in the plan, but many still felt repulsed. They also knew that spies were always around, and many disciples were worried that Jesus would be assassinated. Nonetheless, with their apprehensions, they proceeded with the plan. After escorting each healed leper separately, once in the Chamber of Lepers, each of those thirteen disciples - the twelve men and Mary - exchanged clothes with the thirteen healed lepers. The disciples had also brought clean but soiled-looking bandages to cover their faces. The healed lepers were so elated by their healed affliction that all of them agreed they would, for the first time in years, celebrate Passover Seder night with their families in Jerusalem and not stay at the inn.

The "leper-appearing" disciples easily walked out of the crowded temple gates unrecognized as Jesus's disciples and were instead shunned as lepers. They made their way to the inn, which was located in a remote corner of the Mount of Olives known as the Gardens of Gethsemane because of all the flowers that the Gethsemanes had planted around the inn. So as not to distract from the area, the locals had named it "The Gardens" rather than have it falsely known as a leper colony. The locals stayed clear of the area.

Prior to entering the temple, Seth had donned a girl's robe and carried his own rolled robe and the goatskin bag of healing living water, holding them in front of him like a girl rather than as a man would. At first he had protested when Jesus told him what his gender role would be, but then Seth said, "I will do it because I know who I am. Donning a feminine outfit for a higher purpose makes me no less of a man." The disciples nodded their approval. Seth then stood on his toes and pranced over the reclining disciples in an exaggerated feminine manner. The disciples all laughed, including Mary and Jesus.

After Jesus's temple healing session, Seth had held the water bag and folded robe high enough to cover the bottom of his face as he easily passed though the guarded Jerusalem gates.

Mary safely passed through the gates as well. She wore the robe that Mother Mary had made for Jesus underneath the long robe of the larger female leper who had been healed. By late afternoon, after buying a few things along the way, one by one, the disciples had made their way up the hill to a heavily wooded, narrow path, and all finally arrived at the secluded and homey Inn of the Lepers, where Jesus would eat his last supper.

⬯

On the second floor of the inn, Jesus and the disciples reclined on the floor around a low, long table that had been set with the traditional Passover Seder accouterments that were used to tell the story and explain the significance of the Seder. On a plate in the center of the table sat the symbolic egg, lamb shank bone, bitter herbs, parsley and choarsest – a combination of apple, nuts wine and cinnamon. Each was to remind the Seder participants of the story and meaning of Passover, such as the bitter herbs that were in remembrance of the bitter times when the Pharaoh of Egypt enslaved the Jews.

The fresh matzoth was placed next to the symbolic plate of herbs and signified the time after the ten plagues that Moses had rained down upon Egypt's people to convince the Pharaoh to let his people go free from their harsh enslavement. The first plague had turned the Nile River blood red. Then Moses sent plagues of frogs flooding the land, then vermin, followed by beasts, cattle disease, boils on the people, hail, locusts, and finally, a darkness that frighteningly cloaked the land during the daylight hours. However, after each plague, the Pharaoh still refused to let Moses' people go. Moses then unleashed the final and crushing plague on the Egyptians: their firstborn sons were slain by the Angel of Death. The children of Israel, however, had been instructed to place lamb's blood upon their doors and thus were spared because the Angel of Death "passed over" the Jewish homes and did not enter. That is how the celebratory holiday came to be called "Passover." It was this last plague that caused the Pharaoh - in his weakened moments of deep grief when his own firstborn son died - to finally relent and let the enslaved Jewish people go free.

Moses then bade his people to leave Egypt quickly before the Pharaoh could change his mind. There was not enough time to leaven their bread with yeast so the flour dough was quickly mixed and baked, producing the thin, flat bread called matzoth.

Pharaoh did change his mind. His grief soon transformed into anger and revenge. He sent his army of chariots to slaughter all the Jews to pay for his son's death. Moses had already led his people toward the Red Sea. In the distance, they saw the long trails of dust rise from the desert floor as many hundreds of the Pharaoh's chariots sped toward them. Through Moses, God parted the Red Sea, and the Jewish people safely passed through to the other side. The charging chariots closed in, and once they were on the dry sea floor, the waters of the parted Red Sea flowed together again, consuming all of Pharaoh's pursuers of the Jews.

The disciples now began their Seder to commemorate those times. Large jugs of wine had already been placed by the innkeepers on the floor near the long, low table. Jesus and the disciples sat on floor pillows. Peter uncorked the jugs and poured the wine into two large pitchers. Then John poured the wine from the pitchers into the goblets that had been placed on the table.

Everyone sat silently around the table and waited for Jesus, who, as a rabbi, sat at the head of the table and was about to conduct the traditional Seder dinner. Jesus looked around at those waiting for him to begin, but he did not pick up his goblet of wine. Instead, he said, "There are to be no weapons carried by those who follow me." Six of the disciples looked at each other guiltily.

Young James blurted "But, Teacher, we want to protect you."

His brother said, "There is talk that many are jealous of you and wish you harm."

Jesus laughed, "I have no fear for my life, nor should you fear for me."

Philip protested, "But some people are insane. Some hate you so intensely that you can feel the air thicken black around them."

Bartholomew said, "There's talk of plots by the chief priests to have you murdered."

"Enough!" Jesus said. "Show me your weapons."

The six disciples reluctantly laid on the table four daggers and two short swords that they had purchased on their way to the inn. Jesus said, "You have heard me say that those who refuse to take up the sword shall inherit the Earth. Those who live by the sword shall die by the sword. If you are true followers of me, you will not bear arms."

Jesus gathered the weapons and went to a window and threw them out. They *clanged* to the ground two stories below. He looked up at the night sky and saw many angels gathering above the inn. He smiled and returned to the table.

Then he firmly addressed the disciples, "You must all understand that when groups of Jews bear and use arms while living under Roman authority, there is a great chance that they will die. If any of you do the same, there is a likelihood that you will be perceived as a threat, especially when you teach and attract many followers. To refuse to bear arms—although others may view that as lacking courage—will help to ensure your survival, which is far more important, for you are needed to carry my message to the world." Jesus picked up his goblet of wine and said, "Now we shall begin in a proper manner."

"B-B-But, T-T-Teacher, w-w-what if you d-d-die?"

"Do not be concerned, Simon. I can only leave this body by God's will, not by man's desires."

"But, Master," Andrew pleaded, "you say that you will be leaving us. What if for some unforeseen reason you were to die?"

"Again I say, if it is my Father's will that it be so, then so it will be, and it would be my honor to serve His divine purpose."

"I want to follow wherever you go. If you die, where will you go?" Thomas asked.

"Even if that could come to pass, then in less time than Lazarus was resurrected, I too would return, if that should be my Father's will. In any event, I know that in time I will always return to His kingdom, and you are all invited to follow me there when your time comes to do so. Now I must remind you of things that I have spoken of before. If you understood, you would not be asking questions about my death."

"Please, Master, help us to understand," Luke pleaded.

Jesus replied, "In my Father's Kingdom, all Essences of everything and everyone that have ceased to exist in this world are resurrected at once and are instantly manifested in our Lord's blessed eternal domain. Let us have no more talk of my leaving now, but know this: no weapons of man can keep me from leaving, and no weapons of man will make me leave if I choose not to. Now it is time for our Seder."

Jesus then said the prayer over the wine. "Blessed art thou, Eternal our God, Ruler of all the Universe, Creator of the fruit of the vine." All present took a sip of their wine, and the Seder began.

After more prayers and the ritual washing of the hands, came the breaking of the matzoh and the recitation of the story of Moses freeing the Jewish people from slavery. Jesus also emphasized that the Jews' liberation from their enslavement was more than a physical freedom; it was intended to be a spiritual liberation from heathen authority and to consecrate man's service to God.

<hr>

At first, Zadak, conducting the Passover Seder, was incensed that his family and honored guests, the chief priests, were being interrupted. The attendant who had interrupted whispered into Zadak's ear, but after he had heard the attendant's news, Zadak smiled with fiendish delight. He abruptly excused himself. "There is an urgent matter that I must attend to. There is no need to be concerned." He told the tall priest to finish conducting the Seder and quickly left.

When he entered the basement jail chamber of the Pharisees' quarters, he saw Joseph tied to a chair. Seeing Joseph's face bloodied from having been beaten, Zadak's smile broadened. Seffira sat across from the crude wooden table where Joseph was restrained. Pharisee interrogators surrounded them. Seffira was sobbing profusely and held one hand over her eyes, the other on her large belly. "Please. I can look no more. Please don't hit my husband again."

A burly interrogator standing behind Seffira pulled her hand away from her eyes and held her wrist tightly. He said, "If you want us to stop, tell us where he is."

Seffira looked down and said nothing. The lead interrogator said to Zadak, "We have learned that they know where Jesus is, but we have not yet made them tell us."

"Fools!" Zadak scowled at the interrogators. He grabbed a dagger from the sheath of a nearby guard and stood behind Joseph. He grabbed Joseph's hair, sharply jerked his head back over the chair, and looked down at him. Zadak held the dagger's sharp blade against Joseph's throat.

He ordered the interrogator behind Seffira, "Hold her head up so she can see the blood flow from her husband's throat."

The interrogator held Seffira's head firmly in place against her futile resistance. Zadak pressed the blade harder, causing a thin bloody line to appear along Joseph's throat. He spit down on Joseph's face and said, "You are a lowly worm that should be fed to the fish. Tell me now where your Jesus is, and your wife and child will live."

Joseph knew Zadak only too well and knew that he and Seffira would die whether he told or not. Joseph spit his bloodied saliva back into Zadak's face. Infuriated, Zadak pulled harder on Joseph's hair until a tuft of it was ripped out. Joseph refused to cry out in pain. In disgust, Zadak thrust Joseph's head forward, releasing his hair. He walked around the table, stood behind Seffira, and grabbed her hair. He held the knife to her throat and said to Joseph, "Is your foolish loyalty to your Jesus higher than the value of your wife's life?"

Joseph grimaced but said nothing. His tears mixed with the blood on his beaten face. Seffira, even though her wits were frayed with fear for themselves and their baby said, "Don't tell him Joseph. Our Master's life is more important."

Joseph admired Seffira's brave resolve to protect their savior at all costs. "I love you with all my heart – forever!" he cried out.

More frustrated, Zadak plunged the dagger into the table in front of Seffira and sneered at Joseph, "Death would be too quick. But can a despicable worm like you tolerate your dear pregnant wife being tortured in front of your eyes?"

Zadak walked back behind Joseph, grabbed the side of his head, and held it fixed on Seffira. Joseph strained at the bonds on his arms but could not free himself. Zadak ordered the guard standing beside Seffira, "Cut off her fingers one by one until this insect tells us what we want to know. If he still won't tell us, then we'll cut off her hands." He looked down at Joseph. "If pain to your body will not make you speak, then the pain in your heart for your beloved will."

The interrogator standing over Seffira drew his knife. Seffira and Joseph's eyes reflected their shared terror and deep love. She could not be certain that Joseph could remain silent if she were tortured so Seffira quickly pulled the dagger from the table and plunged it into her heart.

"No!" Joseph cried out.

Seffira, shocked by the pain, looked back at Joseph and gasped, "I love you more than my life. Don't tell him where our Master is." Then, with the dagger still in her chest and a trickle of blood flowing from the corner of her mouth, she put both hands over her belly and cried out with a different pain. "Joseph! Our baby is coming. Now!"

Zadak's anger at their defiance overwhelmed him. He took a sword from a guard and thrust it into Joseph's abdomen. Joseph cried out from the burning pain, but he never took his eyes off Seffira. She slid her pelvis forward on the chair. With each sharp contraction,, the blood from her chest spurted out more forcibly. Joseph felt his body becoming colder with the loss of his own blood.

Seffira gave a yelp of pain and looked down. In a very weak voice she said, 'It's a boy, Joseph! It's a boy!"

The infant lay on the floor, its umbilical cord still attached to Seffira. She looked back up at Joseph. Their eyes were starting to close for the final time. In a fading voice, Joseph said, "We will be our son's angels."

Those were the last words that Seffira heard and the last words that Joseph spoke.

46

As their Passover meal and closing prayers of gratitude were coming to an end, Jesus said, "Let us now pause for a memorial prayer."

The disciples looked at each other at the highly unusual pronouncement of a memorial prayer at that particular point in the Seder. When Jesus bowed his head to pray, the disciples followed and bowed their heads. Jesus, in his expansive mind, held the thought-form images of Joseph and Seffira and their infant son and of all the other disciples who were not present.

Jesus solemnly said, "Dear Father, Lord of all lords, King of all kings, we give thanks for the blessings of the bountiful food and the fruit of the vine that have been provided for us. We also give our blessings and ask that You give Your blessings to those who are connected to us in spirit but could not be here with us tonight and to those who have departed from this world and live again in Your kingdom. We thank You for all You have done, for all that You do, and for all that You will do. Though we may not know all Your reasons for that which You do, we must trust in Your eternal wisdom. With undying faith, we know in our hearts that Thy Will will be done with Your merciful love for us and to serve your great purpose. Amen."

The disciples responded with "Amen."

The disciples' bellies were full, and their heads were filled with the copious amounts of wine that they had drunk during the festive meal. They sang joyous songs in unison and ended with great contentment and an uplifted spirit. Mary, Judas, and Seth also felt uplifted although they had only sipped small amounts of wine. Mary rarely drank wine, for within her former profession, she never wanted to lose control of her senses when engaging with men.

Jesus stood up from the table, took a chair from against a wall, and placed it in the center of the room. Then he put a basin at the foot of the chair. Jesus took off his outer clothing and wrapped a cloth around his waist. He looked at Judas and said, "Please come and sit here." The disciples were puzzled.

Judas obediently stood up, walked to the chair, and sat on it. Jesus turned to Seth and said, "Please bring me my heavenly Father's goatskin bag of healing living water."

Seth sprang up and went to the side of the room where everyone had placed their sandals and brought the water bag to Jesus. Jesus knelt at Judas's feet and poured the healing living water over Judas's feet. The other disciples' jaws dropped open. The jealousies that they had harbored toward Judas as being favored by Jesus surfaced in their shock that their Messiah would lovingly wash his feet, even between his toes. Judas also was taken aback but said nothing. When Jesus was done, he told Judas to go back to the table, then said, "Matthew, please come and sit here."

Matthew got up hesitantly, not sure of the meaning of Jesus's actions, and sat in the chair. Jesus knelt before Matthew and washed his feet as well. Then he called Mark to the chair and washed his feet, also lovingly, with the healing living water. The disciples marveled at what Jesus was doing in such a humble and caring way. In succession, he called Luke, Peter, John, Simon, James, his brother Jude, Philip, Andrew, and Bartholomew and performed the same ritual washing of their feet for all.

Each time Jesus poured the healing living water onto a disciple's feet, they felt a pleasant tingling sensation run up their legs to their spine and outward to their abdomen, chest, and arms. Then a feeling like a high-frequency vibration radiated out from their hands and the tops of their heads. When the disciples got up from the chair, they experienced a lightness in their bodies. The disciples also felt euphoric and could hear a high-pitched angelic sound, and they also felt the effects of the copious amounts of wine consumed with each of the Seder's numerous blessings. As they walked back to their places, many looked down at their footing as if they weren't sure where the floor was.

Jesus looked at Mary and bade her come forward. She did, and Jesus cleaned her feet as well. Many of the disciples frowned at their Messiah cleaning the feet of a woman. Jesus then bade Seth come forward. Seth bounded toward Jesus and proudly sat in the chair and thrust his feet out toward his teacher. Jesus smiled widely and cleansed Seth's feet. Everyone wondered why Jesus was doing what he did.

After everyone had returned to their places, Jesus put on his tunic and robe and then stood silently before them. He closed his eyes and bowed his head in prayer. Jesus felt the energy of the hundreds of angels and two Escort Archangels that were arriving to join the angels that were already there. He sent a thought to them, "Thank you, and bless you all."

Jesus looked up at his disciples and said, "Do you understand what I have done for you?"

They were still puzzled and shook their heads.

"You call me 'Teacher' and 'Lord' and rightly so, for that is what I am," he told them. "Now that I, your Lord, have washed your feet, so too should you wash one another's feet. I have set you an example that you should do for each other as I have done for you. I tell you the truth: no servant is greater than his master, nor is a messenger such as myself greater than the One who sent him. Now that you know these things, you will be blessed if you do them. You must love one another as I have loved you."

The disciples understood and nodded.

Jesus smiled, "Now that you understand, it remains for you to do. Know also that not only have your feet been cleansed, you have been anointed with my Father's healing living water. The pleasant feelings and the sounds of angels that you hear are a heavenly connection to His kingdom that His healing living water on your flesh has made possible for you. For tonight, two great souls have been sent to visit here, and I have prepared the way for your senses to see what others cannot."

Jesus looked to the empty space beside him and then bowed his head to it. In an excited voice, Peter exclaimed, "I see it! I see two bright white figures by your side!"

James exclaimed, "I see it also!"

His brother Jude said, "Me too! They're getting brighter!"

The other disciples also began to see the figures of Light. Jesus said, "In our Seder prayers tonight, we all said, 'May the all-merciful send to us the prophet Elijah, of blessed memory.' God, as the scriptures have told us, also promised Moses that He would rise up a prophet like him in the future and that God Almighty would put His words in the prophet's mouth. I am that prophet. The two beside me who have come tonight to visit are our two most revered prophets of centuries past, Elijah and Moses."

With Jesus's last words, his face then appeared brighter than the sun. The figures beside him turned dazzling white, as did Jesus's body. The disciples turned away from the intense brightness. As their eyes adjusted, they turned back and saw the images of the faces of Jesus, Moses, and Elijah in a bright opaque light; their bodies were pulsing white radiance.

"I am Elijah," said one figure. "I have come from a time now past. Then I spoke The Word, but the people knew me not. They debased me in every way they wished. I am here to warn of what has become of prophets past and to give my encouragement and blessings for our new hope, that the Christ in Jesus and his message will be heard and followed. I bid you, as his disciples, love, honor, and support him always. Greater love has no man than to lay down his life for his friends. You are Jesus's friends if you do this."

"I am Moses," spoke the figure next to Elijah. "I too have come here on this Holy Passover night to give encouragement and hope to you and also to bring warnings. The Lord Almighty God gave me powers to make Egypt's Pharaoh free our people from slavery. I performed miracles and brought plagues on the Pharaoh. I parted the Red Sea for our people's safe passage. I received the Lord's Ten Commandments on

Mount Sinai, but when I gave God's Commandments to our people, I was received not by open arms, but by the sight of their praising a false idol made of gold. As time has passed, our people have come to know God's Commandments, but too few follow His Laws in the ways God intended. Now Jesus has been sent to this time and place, he has performed many miracles, and he has spoken The Word of our Lord as Elijah and I have. You, as his disciples, must carry forth The Word when Jesus, your Messiah, is no longer here to do so. The masses of people must change their ways or horrible, unimaginable destruction will be their future. You are our hope to carry forth His Word."

Elijah spoke again, "We have come to bless this holy gathering and, as Moses has said, to warn you of the dangers ahead. It matters not how pure the Truth that a prophet brings if those who hear it fear that Truth. They may be afraid that the truth will make them less rather than fulfill the truthteller's intention to set them free from their false pretensions. They will seek to destroy the teller of Truth, but the Truth cannot die. You must carry that Truth to the world. Be vigilant and stay true to The Word."

Jesus lifted up his eyes to heaven. His radiance brightened. He prayed for his disciples. "Sanctify them in the Truth: Thy Word is Truth. And for all those who will believe from the teachings of these disciples before me, may they all be one, even as Thou, Father, art one in me, and I in Thee. May they also be in us so that The World may believe and be as one with You in love and harmony."

The disciples sat transfixed in a hypnotic state. The whole room turned a bright white, and within their heads they heard the words of God: *"THIS IS MY SON, WHOM I LOVE. LISTEN TO HIM AND GO FORTH AS HE SAYS."*

The bright light became whiter and more intense; the whirring high-pitched sound in their heads became extreme. They closed their eyes but could not diminish the sight of the blinding light or the penetrating sound that resonated within.

Suddenly, the sound stopped, and the blinding white light was gone. The disciples opened their eyes wide. They felt groggy, as if they had been awakened from a deep sleep. Jesus stood alone as before. He felt an acceleration of the Holy Spirit's power that he had received from the Holy Prophets and that had flowed through them from the Escort Archangels. He knew that the flesh of his human form could not contain that energy much longer than another day or so.

Jesus held his palms out toward his disciples and said, "This evening's meal has been consecrated and blessed by our most revered Jewish prophets to sanctify my last supper in this body that has clothed me. Our glorified prophets have also warned of the danger that may befall you. From the times of Pharaoh's enslavement of our people to the present oppression by the Romans, our people have suffered hardships, but our faith in Almighty God, the one God of All That Is, must always survive. You must prepare for personal hardships, but know that this hallowed evening you have been infused with the power of The Light to go forth and spread The Word. The Good News of our Creator is the salvation of mankind. You are on a holy mission with great peril before you. But know that the forces of the prophets and the Lord, our God, will be by your side. No matter what pain and suffering you may endure, The Light will sustain you on your mission, and your place in my Father's Kingdom will await you."

The disciples sat in awe and pondered what they had just experienced. "Master," Philip said, "I fear not for myself, but I fear for you. When will you leave us?"

"I know that it will be very soon. I don't know when or how; that is for my Father to decide. I tell you that Elijah came in the past as a prophet, but he was not recognized and was badly mistreated, as they did to him everything they wished. In the same way, John the Baptizer, as a prophet, also suffered. And now, as you have heard, plots have been set for me to suffer as well."

"But, Master," Bartholomew said, "surely your miraculous powers will be able to overcome any dangers mere men will try and bring upon you."

"My divine powers have been given to me by my Father's graces as the circumstances for their need arose. It will be my Father's will when and how he will take me home to His Kingdom. I do not fear or worry for myself, for I have absolute faith in my Father's wisdom and His ineffable ways. But the supreme reason that I am comfortable with my fate is that I have undying trust in His eternal and boundless love for me and unshakable faith that the path that he creates for me will be for the greatest good. To have faith is to believe in and be certain of what cannot be seen. I know that it is my Father's divine love for me that I feel intimately and that sustains me. I know without doubt that His divine Love gives me that belief, faith, and certainty."

The disciples admired Jesus's convictions. Luke asked, "When you do leave us, will you visit us as Elijah and Moses have? What will you look like?"

"Some of you will see me again although I may not be clothed in this body. You shall know me by my Light."

Mary stood and announced, "My Savior, you have cleansed and anointed our feet on this holy night. It is only fitting that your feet should be cleansed as well."

The disciples were taken aback at Mary's boldness. They thought, *Who is she to determine what should be done for the Messiah?*

Mary walked to Jesus and took his hand. She led him to the chair in the center of the room and sat him down. Jesus smiled because he knew what Mary's intention was. Many of the disciples felt indignation at Mary's actions.

She knelt before Jesus and poured the remaining healing living water from the goatskin bag over Jesus's feet. The water then flowed into the basin. With her hair, as she did before, Mary tenderly and lovingly cleansed his feet and between each of his toes.

Some of the disciples felt jealous of Jesus's appreciation of her devotion. After Mary had cleansed Jesus's feet, she said, "Now your feet have been anointed as you have done for us."

Jesus stood with his feet still in the basin of water. He extended his hands down for her to grasp. She took his hands, and he gently pulled her up until they stood facing each other. Jesus looked deep into her eyes; she saw the same gleam of light in them as she had in their younger days together. He said, "Remember me as we are now, and you shall know me this way again."

Mary sighed, and then from around her neck, she pulled a small alabaster flask attached to a leather cord. She uncurled the thread at the top of the flask that held the wax seal and then pulled it off. Mary held the flask toward Jesus and said, "This precious spikenard ointment has come from a plant in the Indian Himalayas by the pathways of our Lord to this inn on this Holy Night to anoint you as our Savior and Lord. This has been a tense and trying time for all of us, and you have led us with love, hope, courage, and conviction. But who has had concern for the stresses that you have faced? This ointment is to ease your heart of the pains of people's hearts that you have touched with your love, the minds that you have reached with your words, and the bodies that you have healed with your hands."

Mary raised the vial over Jesus's head and poured out the full contents. Then she ran her fingers through Jesus's hair with comb-like strokes, rubbing the ointment into his long hair. She knelt again and rubbed his feet with the ointment that still coated her hands. Jesus closed his eyes and took in a long, deep breath of the soothing, earthy fragrance as he savored the marvelous feelings of Mary's hands massaging his feet. He let out his breath with a deep, relaxing sigh. His shoulders relaxed and lowered as if a heavy burden had been removed. Then, Mary kissed Jesus's feet.

The scent of the rarely used and very costly spikenard that had been copiously massaged into Jesus's hair filled the room with the herbal ointment's calming fragrance. Mary and Judas saw a bright golden glow around Jesus's head. It was the brightest and largest aura that either had yet seen.

Peter pointed at Mary and blurted, "Why do you waste a year's worth of a worker's wages on expensive perfume when that money could be used to feed the poor?" Venting their baser emotions, many of the disciples also began to rebuke her harshly.

Jesus opened his eyes and held up a hand to silence them. In a calm but firm voice he said, "Leave her alone. Why are you berating her for doing something good and beautiful for me? You will always have the poor among you, and whenever you will, you can help them, but I will not be here much longer. This woman has done for me what she could. She has anointed this body that will soon be no more. And I tell you this in solemn truth, that whenever the Good News is preached throughout the world, this woman's deed will be remembered and praised. As my disciples, you should teach others not to be critical or oppressive of women, but to praise their ways, for when you appreciate their mysterious differences, you will be richer for it."

Jesus reached up and tenderly held the sides of Mary's head. He gently pulled her to him and kissed her lips for a long moment. Judas saw one large, golden glow around Jesus and Mary's heads blend into one as they kissed.

After the kiss, Mary stepped away and humbly bowed her head to Jesus. She held back her tears, trying to maintain her composure, knowing that her Jesus would soon leave her life. Only the wetness in her eyes betrayed her deepest feelings. She turned and said to the disciples, "After I left the temple today, I traded my precious red ruby for this costly ointment to honor and anoint our Lord." Mary turned to Jesus, bowed, and then looked at him and said, "You, My Lord, are a more precious jewel than all of the precious jewels in the world."

Jesus smiled and bowed his head in gratitude to Mary, his eyes moist from connecting with the deepest of her sacred feelings for him. Jesus then returned and sat on the floor at the center of the low dining table. The disciples sat up from their reclining positions around the table. Mary resumed her place at the table next to Seth. Jesus said, "Seth, please pour the wine for everyone." Seth stood slowly with a heavy feeling of sadness because his best friend, whom he loved so dearly, was leaving his world. He took the large pitcher of wine and began filling everyone's goblets. His tears flowed as he finished filling the last disciple's goblet, and then he came to Jesus's side. Seth sniffed to stifle his tears and stumbled slightly as he bent to pour the wine into Jesus's goblet. Some of the red wine spilled onto the sleeve and side of Jesus's robe.

Seth felt awful and began to apologize. Before he could, Jesus said, "Do not be dismayed, Seth. Wine will not ruin my Father's cloth. It will come clean. All things have a purpose, even though we may not understand why."

Mary got up, stood over Jesus, and said, "I'll clean your sacred robe. Please give it to me."

Jesus took off his robe and handing it to her, said, "Thank you for your concern. Please clean it later, for I have important things that must be said now." Mary took the robe, sat down next to Seth, and placed it by her side.

The men frowned disapprovingly at Seth, who still felt embarrassed for soiling Jesus's robe. He humbly bowed his head in shame as their eyes looked upon him.

Jesus lifted his goblet toward Seth and said to his disciples, "One should not frown on another who stumbles as he strives to live a righteous life, for all of you will, at times, stumble on your journeys. Know this: whoever seeks to be the greatest among you should be like the youngest, such as Seth, who has lovingly and loyally served me. For you men of older ages who aspire to rule, you should rule as the one who serves. Sip now your wine in recognition of Seth as an example, and aspire to be of like spirit with him." Jesus did not sip, but put down his goblet.

The disciples sipped their wine. Seth sat up tall and beamed proudly. Jesus saw Seth's glow become brighter and larger. Jesus smiled broadly and relaxed his arms on the table.

Looking at Jesus, Judas saw that his Master's demeanor at last reflected deep peace and contentment - a peace and satisfaction that comes with having done with all one's heart and soul all that one is able to do with all of his God-given abilities, a peace that comes when one has met all of the challenges that have been placed before him.

The oil lamps flickered; the fragrance of spikenard and the copious amounts of wine that the disciples had drunk left them deeply relaxed. The room was silent, all eyes on Jesus. He then breathed the Holy Spirit upon the disciples, and they involuntarily swayed and swooned. He bowed his head in prayer and said, "Dear Father, who art in heaven, sanctify those here in the Truth; Thy Word is Truth. And may those whom they teach all be one, even as Thou, Father, art one in me and I in thee, that they also may be in us, so that the world may believe."

Jesus looked up and said, "You must trust that the Holy Spirit – the Counselor of Truth – will guide you after I have left, and so you will be guided. Know that those you teach of my teachings may or may not believe in me as their Savior; that is of lesser concern if they accept the truth and wisdom of my words that will benefit their lives and the lives of others. Know also that many people who live their lives with the spirit of love, tolerance, forgiveness, and brotherhood are Christ-like although they know it not, and they will enjoy the privileges of my Father's Kingdom even though they may never have heard of me or my teachings or even though they may have religious beliefs that differ from yours. Fear not to point to them as those who live The Word for others to follow, for they are in harmony with the Christ-Consciousness even if they do not believe in me. It is far better for people to act Christ-like and not believe in me than for people to profess belief in me but not act Christ-like, for they are hypocrites."

Jesus made eye contact with each person individually, then continued, "Always remember to be inclusive of all people. Do not establish rigid rules or demand strict allegiance, but do speak of The Word and that the gates to God's Kingdom are open to all who seek Him. They shall know that God is good and that the true nature of God is good and that the seeds of goodness dwell within all people. So it is for you to awaken those seeds of goodness – the Christ – in those you preach to and to reaffirm and inspire that natural goodness. If you do this, then you have served my Father, your higher purpose, and me. You have heard me speak of these things in other ways, but before I leave, because of its importance, I have said it again."

The disciples sat in a solemn, transfixed state as they absorbed Jesus's words. After a while, Philip said, "Master, you are my example as my teacher, but I still don't feel that I am able to teach others as you have taught me."

Jesus replied, "Do not try to be perfect. Just 'be,' do good things, and give thanks to your Lord for being able to do so – as all of you should."

<hr />

Caiaphas, Zadak, and a Sadducee high priest all sat in silence as Pontius Pilate stared at them, evaluating their pleas. Prior to their meeting with Pilate, Zadak had gone to Caiaphas in a demanding frenzy to convince him that they needed Roman soldiers to accompany their temple police when they learned of Jesus's whereabouts to arrest him.

After experiencing Joseph and Seffira's unremitting resolution to protect Jesus with their lives, he feared others would also fight passionately against their Messiah's arrest and that a riot could start between the temple police and Jesus's supporters. Zadak felt that such a turn of events would turn many of Jesus's recent followers against Zadak's own Pharisee rule and that more of his Pharisee followers would reject him and join Jesus.

However, Zadak presented a different danger to Caiaphas. He adamantly made the point that the entire Sanhedrin would be threatened because they had issued the arrest warrant and that if a riot occurred, Roman soldiers would move against all parties, resulting in many Jewish deaths and the probable dismissal of the present Sanhedrin appointees.

Although it was still during his Passover meal, Caiaphas acknowledged the urgency and insisted that a Sadducee priest accompany them to secure Pontius Pilate's Praetorian Guard that night to show a unified front because Zadak insisted that Jesus's arrest was imminent.

After hearing the high priests' reasoning, Pilate continued to stare at the trio of Sanhedrin Council Jews. Finally he said, "I cannot give you all of the soldiers that you ask for. The guard is already on double shifts and overstretched. But because you, Caiaphas, are here as the Roman appointed head priest of the Sanhedrin, I will assign a sergeant and a platoon of foot soldiers to accompany you when you arrest the Rabbi. They will have my written orders to show to any of my guard or Jerusalem soldiers that will instruct them not to interfere with your arrest or any interactions between Jewish parties. Your Jewish factions can fight among themselves, and for now, I will not interfere. But I warn you, do not let your actions precipitate any adverse reactions toward my rule of Jerusalem, or you will surely know my unrelenting wrath. The sergeant and platoon will be stationed at the temple, to be notified if and when you are going to make your arrest."

<hr/>

Jesus picked up his goblet of wine and raised it toward his disciples as a toast. As they picked up their goblets, Jesus said, "Take a sip of your wine." All took a sip, except Jesus. He then said, "Truly I tell you, one of you shall be called my betrayer, one of you who have sipped your wine."

The disciples all looked aghast. One by one they said to Jesus, "Surely, not I?"

"It will be one of you who have dipped his bread with me tonight. The Son of Man will go as it is written. But woe to that man who betrays the Son of Man! It would be far better for him if he had not been born."

The disciples looked at each other in disbelief that any of them could ever do such a thing. Then, because their Master had said it was so, they became suspicious of each other.

Jesus then said, "Sip again from your wine as if it were my blood that is poured for the many." Hesitantly, they did as they were told.

Jesus nodded his approval, but he did not sip his wine and set his goblet on the table and said, "I will not drink again of the fruit of the vine until that day when I drink it anew in my Father's Kingdom."

The disciples fell into a state of despair at the finality of Jesus's words. Jesus comforted his disciples and said, "Do not let your hearts be troubled. Trust in your Lord, your God; trust also in me."

The saddened disciples sang a hymn in Jesus's honor. When they finished, Jesus said, "Many of you will fall away, for in the scriptures it is written, 'I will strike the shepherd, and the sheep of the flock will be scattered.' But after I have arisen, as I have said before, you shall know me by my Light."

Peter replied, "Even if all others fall away, I never will."

"I tell you the truth," Jesus answered. "This very night before the rooster crows for the new dawn, you will disown me three times."

Peter declared, "Even if I have to die with you, I will never disown you." And all the disciples said the same.

Jesus replied, "That remains to be seen." He then took a large piece of the unleavened bread, broke it into smaller pieces, and passed it among the disciples. "Take and eat this bread in remembrance of me, as if it were my body."

The disciples hesitated. Jesus reiterated, "Eat of the matzoth as I say, for it is in remembrance of me – and know that the substance of this bread is of the same God-substance that clothes me." Slowly, the disciples ate the unleavened bread as they were told, but in their despair, it tasted like parchment.

When they had finished eating the bread, Jesus said, "Now drink all of your wine, knowing it is my blood of the covenant." Again the disciples hesitated. Jesus bade them, "Do as I say." They obeyed and drank until their goblets were dry. Jesus then said, "Now my last supper with you has been completed. I see that you're all weary from this long and trying day. You have all done as I have told you, and you should find contentment in that. Now it is time to sleep, and many of you will sleep deeply and long."

Jesus stood and then the disciples stood, and all made for their night's retirement in the bedrooms below. With the copious amounts of wine they had drunk, the long stressful hours of the day, and the extraordinary and powerful effect of Moses and Elijah's visit, their exhaustion was great; and they readily fell into a deep sleep. Even Jesus, for the first time in months, slept.

Only Mary remained awake. She took Jesus's wine-stained robe and dutifully and lovingly cleansed it and then hung it to dry on the back of the chair in the center of the upper room next to the basin of healing living water that remained at the base of the chair. Mary then took the robe that Jesus's mother had made for him to wear on that Passover night and tenderly laid it over Jesus's slumbering body. She then lay down next to him, and she too fell into a deep sleep.

<hr />

In a kaleidoscopic sequence, Jesus dreamed: *In the middle of the night, temple police and Roman soldiers arrested a man called Jesus. He was mercilessly beaten, then handed over to Pontius Pilate to be sentenced and crucified. Pilate's soldiers brutally punched and kicked him, then whipped him and flayed his back into bloodied flesh. They made a large ring from a sharp thorn bush and plunged it into his scalp in the form of a mock crown. Blood streamed from his head, covering his face. They insulted and cursed him, then laughed and spat upon him. They bowed down before him and mocked him again as a pitiful wretch who would be "King of the Jews."*

Then Pilate sentenced him to be crucified on a cross. The bloodied man was made to carry his own cross through the streets of Jerusalem to Golgotha, the Place of the Skull. Many cried for him as he painfully struggled to carry his heavy cross. Others cursed him as a false messiah. On the Mount of Golgotha, they crucified two thieves; then between the crosses of the two thieves, they prepared to crucify the man called Jesus. They laid him upon the cross that still lay on the ground. The Roman soldiers held his hands and feet. A soldier took a long spike and held it over the man's right wrist. With a heavy hammer he forcefully hit the spike. The man on the cross screamed out in agonizing pain as the spike pierced the man's wrist and was driven into the wood of the cross. The soldier then hammered the spike deeper into the wood. Then the soldier did the same to the left wrist. The soldier stepped to the man's feet that were held tightly together by other solders. The soldier with the heavy hammer raised it high; then with great might, he brought it down on the spike that was placed over the man's heels. The long spike pierced one heel and went halfway though the other as the man's screams of torment filled the air. The soldier raised the hammer overhead once again, and with a strong downward thrust, he hammered the spike's point through the rest of the heel into the wood. With three more blows of the hammer, the large spike securely pinned both feet to the cross.

The soldiers then nailed a signboard written in Greek, Latin, and Hebrew that said, THIS IS THE KING OF THE JEWS. There was a priest who had accused the man of sins against God and had called for his crucifixion. The priest mocked the man being crucified and laughed. He sneered at the agonized man lying on the cross and said, "You were so good at helping others. Now let's see you save yourself if you are really God's chosen One, the so-called Messiah."

The soldiers raised the cross and set it with a thump into a posthole that had been dug earlier. As the cross was set into the ground, the man screamed in horrible pain as the weight of his body pulled sharply down on the spikes that pierced him. There, on the Mount of the Skull, stood the three men on the three crosses suffering an excruciating death.

It was after midnight when Jesus awoke with a shudder from the horrible and amazingly realistic dream. He rolled over face down, put his face in his hands, and began to cry. Mary awoke next to him. She, too, was terrified, having experienced the same dream. She hugged his back and cried with him. Judas came to their room, panting with fear. He too had experienced the same horrifying dream. "Master!" Judas exclaimed. "I had to see you." He didn't know what to make of Jesus and Mary's crying. Judas blurted, "I had this dream, so horrible that I am shaking."

Jesus rolled over to face Judas. Mary sat up and pointed to the bloodied bedding where Jesus had lain. She picked up his hand and saw blood on his wrist and cried out in pain for him. Judas saw that Jesus's other wrist was also bloodied, as were the heels of his feet.

Judas began to cry also and said between sobs, "The dream – can it be true? My Lord, tell me it is not so."

Jesus sat up and his crying eased. With the bottom edge of Mother Mary's robe, he wiped away the blood from his wrists and feet. The wounds beneath the blood rapidly disappeared. Jesus's composure returned to his normal state although Mary still cried disconsolately.

Jesus placed his hands on Judas and Mary's shoulders. In a soft, solemn voice, he said, "Cry not for me, for my Beloved Father who has sent me, do you think that he would allow pain and suffering caused by men to befall His Beloved Son? You should think that my Father would do all in His power to protect the One who has pleased Him. Be not dismayed for me, for I am certain in my faith that my Father has only the best intentions for me and will do what is necessary for me to fulfill my mission."

Mary's crying abated, but Jesus's words could not console her.

"But, Master," Judas asked, "if that is so, then why have you bled and cried?"

"My dear, Judas, I bleed for the sins and sufferings of all mankind. I cried not for myself, but for man's inhumane cruelty to his fellow man, for neither beast nor plague can cause man the torture that man's invented crucifixion can. I felt the indescribable pain and excruciating suffering that the one on the cross felt. I experienced the horrible reality of the spikes piercing the flesh, the gasping for air while on the cross, bleeding slowly from the body's weight pulling on the wounded flesh where the spikes impaled his limbs on the cross. And it is for him and all the others for whom crucifixion brings pain and death designed by man's inhumanity to itself that I have wept. I have no desire to experience that degradation with this body. I do not believe in self-sacrifice or torture to one's self. It serves no purpose for me."

Mary stopped crying and caught her breath. "My Savior," she said in a barely audible voice, "you've said that you're leaving us. We know there are plots to kill you. In the dream, it was so real. You were beaten, humiliated, a crown of thorns was pressed into your head, they drove spikes into…" Mary's voice trailed off, and she again began to sob.

Dear beloved Mary, I am the Son of God, and that that I am can never die."

Judas said, "But you have said that the prophecies will come true."

"Romans may kill a man, but they cannot kill the God within me, for that Essence shall live forever." Jesus squeezed their shoulders in a reassuring manner and said, "You must keep in mind the time when my Father tested Abraham's faith when He told him to sacrifice his son, Isaac for Him. Abraham loved his son dearly, but because of his faith in God, he followed God's command to slay Isaac to prove that faith. As Abraham was about to plunge his blade into Isaac, my Father stopped him because there was no need for Abraham to actually kill his son: Abraham had proved his intent to do so if that was God's will. In so doing, Abraham proved to himself how strong his belief in God was. My Father is a loving and merciful creator, and He would not allow a father who loved his son so dearly to make such a sacrifice in His name. Do you not believe in God's blessed mercy and unfathomable wisdom as I have told you time and time again?"

Mary weakly replied, "I do believe in you, and all that you say. But …" She began to weep again. Between sobs she said, "That dream…it was so terribly real."

Jesus wiped the tears from her cheeks and said, "Then if you believe my words and what I have said about my Father's ways with Abraham and his son, how can you think that my Beloved Father would allow me, His Beloved Son, to be flogged, mocked, and then put horribly to death on the cross? In my heart, I could not will that for anyone, and because I am certain of my heavenly Father's love for me, I know that He would not will such a thing to happen to His Son." Jesus squeezed Mary's hand and said, "I have heard my heavenly Father's words. He has said 'Have faith in Me, and I will always protect and provide for you.' I have had that faith in Him, and He has always protected and provided for me. I still have that undying faith, so fear not for me; I am protected."

Judas and Mary felt a little more relieved as Jesus's absolute faith and sincere reassurance comforted them, but they remained shaken from the terrible, vivid dream that they had all experienced.

Jesus stood, pulled his mother's robe over his shoulders, and said, "Please stay here. I now need to go into the garden by myself and commune with my Father."

Jesus walked among the flowers in the cool night. He looked up at the stars and sighed, and then he knelt and prayed, "O My Father, let this cup of life pass from me, not as I will, but as You will, for Your will is my destiny. What may I do to please you?"

Jesus closed his eyes and heard, *"BE WHO YOU ARE, MY SON."*

Jesus reflected on his Father's words and the dream that he had had. He prayed again, "Abraham offered his one and only son for You as a sacrifice. You did not desire sacrifice and offerings, but You prepared a body for me; You were not pleased with burnt offerings and sin offerings at the temple. Here I am – it is written about me in Your eternal scroll – I have come to do Your will. O God, my heavenly Father, would you sacrifice me, Your Son, as an offering to cleanse mankind of their sins?"

"YOU ARE MY BELOVED SON WITH WHOM I AM PLEASED. GO FORTH WITH YOUR FAITH IN THE LOVE THAT I HAVE FOR YOU AND TRUST THAT ALL WILL BE WELL."

Jesus bowed his head and said, "I will follow the path that Thou will create before me."

Jesus closed his eyes and felt the Holy Oneness of himself with his Father. Greater insights and awareness of All That Is flooded his mind with wonder and amazement. He reveled in that eternal moment. The power of the Holy Spirit surged even stronger within him as he felt God's grace securely embrace his soul. He opened his eyes and stood. He then walked back to the inn to Judas and Mary.

"I feel that you have come to say good-bye for the last time," Mary said to Jesus. She didn't sob, but constant tears fell.

"Fret not, my beloved Mary," Jesus replied, "for when I am gone as you know me now, I will still be with you as I am now, but without this body that clothes me. And in time, when you have shed the body that clothes you, we shall be closer than we are now. Time may soon seem to separate us, yet in time we'll be united."

Jesus hugged Mary. She clung to him tightly and said, "It's unbearably hard to let you go."

"Don't let me go from your heart, for there I will always be."

"My Savior, you will be in my heart forever."

Jesus stepped back and held Mary's hands. He looked deeply into her eyes and said, "Remember me as you do now and as you did when we were younger." Jesus's image changed as it had before to the earlier times of their youth. His beard and face were younger, as they were then. She breathed in and said, "I will never forget you and your scent from those days." She stroked his young beard, and more tears fell.

Jesus kissed her lips tenderly and then stared into her eyes for what seemed a long time. He squeezed her hands and said, "Now I must go with Judas to Jerusalem. You are not to follow us or leave the inn tonight, but know this – you and I will be together again in my Father's Kingdom."

Mary said nothing but looked longingly at Jesus. He turned to Judas and said, "Come, my loyal friend; it's time to go."

When they left the room, Mary lay down on the bedding where Jesus had slept. She pressed her face where his head had lain and breathed in deeply. She smelled his scent mixed with the spikenard, and then she wept with soul-wrenching sorrow.

Before Jesus and Judas left the inn, Jesus went to where Seth slept. Jesus knelt down and kissed Seth's forehead, then placed his hand on Seth's head and said a silent prayer. Judas saw the golden glow surround them as before. Then Jesus and Judas left the inn at Gethsemane for Jerusalem.

47

Jesus and Judas walked past the flowers in the garden. No words were spoken.

The late night air had grown colder. When they entered the narrow, tree-lined path leading down from the Mount of Olives, Judas asked, "Why do you want to go to Jerusalem? We'll be walking into the mouth of the lion."

"I see your fears and worry, Judas. Why does what I do still seem so strange to you? Do you really think that the Son of God would be deaf and blind to things that scream out glaring danger? Of course I know of the fearful possibilities that are clouding your mind. Perhaps your mind will shift to more glorious thoughts if I share with you some of the mysteries of my Father's greater Kingdom – His Kingdom beyond all universes – that I experienced when I communed with my Father in the garden tonight. His Kingdom is a great and boundless realm, which no eye of an angel has ever seen, no thought of the heart has ever comprehended, and it has never been called a name. To be in that Kingdom of all kingdoms is to be everywhere at once, spontaneously and instantly. One thought spawns infinite offshoots of possibilities, including all that is called 'good and bad' and all things in-between and beyond. And, Judas, there's so much more that words can no longer define their implications. Man cannot fathom the depths and meanings of their every thought or action, much less pass judgment on what is good or not. That is for our Holy Creator to decide."

Jesus pointed up at the stars and said, "And the 'One Great Creator' that I speak of is not even the God that created this universe, for the 'One Great Creator' created that God."

Judas sighed, "You seem enthralled with your expanded insight. I am glad to see you so buoyant, but my insides ache with worry and concern for your fate. Although what you speak of sounds glorious indeed, dread fills my thoughts at this time. There are so many forces that seek to destroy you."

"Dear Judas, do you still not realize? No one can take my life from me, but I will lay it down myself if my Father wills it, for I have the power to lay it down, and I have the power to take it again. I have already offered this body to sanctify man's sins if that is my Father's will, just as Abraham offered his son's life to God. It is the sincere intent of offering that pleases my Father, for He seeks no ill for man, only that man do good unto himself and others."

"Master, I hear your words, but still, I tremble and fear for your life."

"Judas, do you believe that I am the Son of God?"

"Yes, I do. There is no doubt, for I have witnessed your miracles that only a god can perform."

"Then, dear Judas, how do you suppose that the priests or Romans can kill God? God is mightier than the sun and the universe that He created. Would the Roman army throw all of their spears at the sun to kill it? Would they shoot all of their arrows and catapult thousands of huge stones at the sun to harm it? They could try, but they couldn't harm it one iota. And all the spears, arrows, and stones that they would launch would only fall back upon them. God cannot die, nor can that which I am die."

Judas sighed again. He wanted to feel more reassured that all would be well, but deep in the pit of his belly, he still felt a dread and foreboding that he couldn't shed. They continued toward Jerusalem's gate. A hardwood walking staff lay at the side of the path. Jesus bent down, picked it up, and continued walking.

"Master," Judas said as he sniffed the air, "when we pass by the guards at the gate, they will smell the costly spikenard, and that will raise many questions."

Jesus winked at Judas, "Fear not; it will be of no concern."

As they approached the gate, Judas slowed his pace. The guards stood at their post and looked at the two men approaching. When Judas turned to Jesus, he saw instead an old man hunched over, limping and supporting himself with the walking stick. Judas grinned. When they got to the gate, one of the guards ordered, "Halt. Identify yourselves."

Judas's posture stiffened. The other guard sniffed the air and smelled foul, stale urine and feces. He looked at the soiled clothes that the bent-over old man wore. He exclaimed to his fellow guard, "Let them pass quickly. I can't bear this old fart's stench."

The other guard backed away two steps and with repugnance, waved the two on.

Once inside Jerusalem, after they had walked around a corner, Judas turned to Jesus and saw him as himself again standing erect, having shed the image of the old man. Judas's eyes widened. He exclaimed, "My Lord! There is a very bright golden-white glow around your head and body. People will see you, and they'll know that you are the Messiah."

"Only you can see my glow, dear Judas." Jesus's glow grew even brighter and larger. With the excitement and joy of a child anticipating a grand birthday present, Jesus said, "I feel lit up inside with my Father's Light, like a candle that has all of its center's wick joyfully aflame at once. The candle appears whole from the outside, but it is all aglow from the growing flame that burns within."

"Teacher, what happens when the flame consumes the candle's wax?"

"Then it would be consumed," Jesus smiled broadly with great anticipation. "Judas, I tell you, I am glowing brightly within this body that has clothed me."

"Master, you're still here."

"Yes, I am still here, and I am with you now in Jerusalem on this Holy and Good Friday so that you can help me to fulfill the prophecies."

"You are my Lord, and you know that I'll always do whatever you ask of me gladly."

Jesus stared into Judas's eyes and then said, "Perhaps not this time."

"What is it that you need of me?"

Jesus pointed to the Pharisees' head priest's quarters, where they had just arrived, and said, "I bid you go there and tell those who seek me that I am here."

Judas was stunned. He adamantly replied, "No! Not I! Never could I betray you!" Judas's body shuddered, "That dream! I know what they'll do to you. The dream was so real; I could feel the spikes driven into your flesh as if it were my own wrists and ankles. It was excruciatingly real. This one thing you ask of me – to betray you – I cannot do."

"Surely you know, Judas, that at my will, I can seem to disappear before any soldier's eyes who would come to arrest me."

"But the dream? The crucifixion?"

"If it is my Father's will that I go with them, then so my Father's will shall be done. I am His, and He will do what is right and best for all concerned."

"But if that dream were to come true and I were the one who betrayed you, our beloved Messiah, then I would be hated forever as I would hate myself. No! That would be too much for me to bear."

"It's your choice, Judas. It is true that you would become the Apostle who will be cursed by all the others. But if you do as I ask, it is possible for you to reach the Kingdom of Heaven, though in this life, you will have merciless pain and grieve greatly."

"But what good is it for me to be hated by all those who love you?"

"Judas, as time unfolds, all will not be as it seems. Your star's brilliance will eclipse all the others. You will be greater than them all, for it is you who shall be called the one who sacrifices the man that clothes me."

Jesus pointed up at the night sky to a star that shone brightest among twelve smaller stars. He said, "Judas, that star that leads the way is your star."

Judas stepped back from Jesus and shook his head vigorously 'no' many times.

Jesus smiled compassionately and said, "My beloved Judas, in the temple, the blood of goats and calves is ceremoniously sprinkled to make those who are unclean seem cleansed, for they think God is pleased by an animal's sacrifice for their sins. If afterward, they truly repent and live a righteous life, then the poor animal's blood will have served a purpose. But do you really think that my Father would allow His beloved Son to be beaten and painfully slaughtered as a sacrificial lamb? God would surely not make a scapegoat of His Son whom He loves dearly and with whom He is pleased."

Judas frowned, "I don't know what to think. I tremble at the thought of that horrid dream and your suffering."

Jesus put his hand on Judas's shoulder, "Again I say, fear not for me. I know of all the plots of those who wish me dead and what they're doing at this very moment, although neither I nor the angels in Heaven know what the next moments will be nor of the hours that will follow – for you, my beloved and loyal friend, are the one who now must decide whether to accept your role and do as I bid you. That will determine what will follow."

Judas was still deeply shaken and deathly concerned. Jesus continued, "I ask you again, as an act of love and sacrifice for me, please go and tell the Pharisees that I am here. And remember what I have said before: there is no greater love for a friend than to lay down one's life for him. Know also that our heavenly Father is not vengeful, for He is all forgiving and understanding and His message is one of love – and that which I ask you to do, when you do it, will be your greatest act of love for me."

Judas bowed his head and again shook it slowly "no" many times. He looked up into Jesus's eyes – then Judas cried.

Jesus stared back at him and slowly nodded "yes" many times.

Judas sighed, his shoulders slumped, and with great reluctance and surrender he whispered, "My sweet Lord, whom I love with my life... I cannot refuse you ... I shall do as you ask."

"Thank you, Judas. In your heart, know that you doing as the scriptures have prophesied. Hesitate no more. What you are about to do, do quickly." Jesus hugged Judas tightly and kissed him on the lips. "Go, my friend, go now. You have my blessings and those of my Father."

Judas turned to go, tears flooding his eyes. Jesus called out to him as he walked away, "You must ask for money so that they will believe you and not feel fooled."

Judas replied, "I will do as you bid me do, for you are the one whom I love and obey."

<hr/>

Seth fitfully tossed and turned in his sleep. His disturbing dream caused him to sweat heavily, dampening his nightshirt. Then he bolted up with a start. He shivered and sat wide-eyed, looking all around. He got up and went to Jesus's room only to find Mary sleeping alone. He woke her and asked, "Where is our Messiah? Do you know where he is?"

Mary answered in a sleepy voice, "He's gone to Jerusalem with Judas."

"We must help him! Come with me to Jerusalem."

"I can't, Seth. Jesus told me not go there tonight, and I gave my word to him that I wouldn't."

"Then I'll get the others to come with me. I must go help him."

Seth hurried out of Mary's room to where Peter was snoring. Seth shook Peter's shoulders and urged, "Get up! Get up! We must help the Messiah!" But Seth could not awaken Peter from his deep sleep. He tried to awaken his father Matthew and the other disciples, but they too could not be awakened. Frantically, Seth ran out into the cold dark wearing only his nightshirt. He ran as fast as he could to Jerusalem's gate.

Jesus stood alone on the narrow street awaiting Judas's return. He breathed in the cold night air and with it the essence of the city's centuries-old history of turmoil and opposing factions. He felt the horrors of times past, and with his prescience, he foresaw the possibilities of future perils that might come to be. Jesus closed his eyes and prayed, "Dear Father, may this holy city, one day at last, become a city of peace in which men live in harmony as one."

Jesus opened his eyes and saw a lone figure staggering toward him, clad only in a torn and soiled tunic tied with a leather belt. The gaunt man had a drunken, glazed look. He approached Jesus and stopped a few feet in front of him. Jesus nodded at the man and said to him, "So it is you who comes at this moment in time."

The man glared at Jesus and then pointed his finger at him. He spat out the words, "And it is you whom the people worship and wrongly call the Messiah, and not me. I saw you at the Mount of Olives and how you captivated the people with your wordy sermon, yet they know little about me, Jesus of Jerusalem!" He placed his hand over his heart and exclaimed, "I am the one to be glorified!"

Jesus raised his eyebrows with a new understanding of his Father's master plan. "I see," he said. "You should know that there is no true glory in the sadness and torture of a crucifixion."

The man looked confused; then he smiled in realization and said, "Ah, then if it is to be a crucifixion and then glory comes, so let it be; for I know that I am the one. God has revealed it to me in my dream. I will choose death, and it will be my salvation and pathway to resurrection."

Jesus compassionately replied, "You have experienced some revelations of truth, but your insatiable desire for self-aggrandizement has distorted your mind and the meaning of what has been revealed to you."

"Of this I am certain," the man replied. "I am Jesus of Jerusalem, the chosen one. It is you who are distorting the minds of the people. It is you who are stealing away those who would follow me. After your sermon, the few followers I had left me for you. Now I am alone, hungry, and cold."

The man reached behind his back and pulled a dagger from his leather belt. He pointed it at Jesus. "Give me your robe. I deserve its warmth, not you."

Jesus said calmly, "I would gladly give this robe to you, for I have another. But I don't want to give it to you. For if you take it, you will suffer greatly. I have come to relieve needless suffering and wish you no harm, so it is best for you not to have this robe."

The man thrust his dagger closer to Jesus, exposing a long, curved red scar on the back of his hand. He said, "How does the price of pain for a few days compare to an eternity of glorious life?"

Jesus held his ground and replied, "Again I warn you, if you take this robe you shall die a horrible death."

The man's face filled with anger. He lunged with his dagger toward Jesus's chest. In an instant, Jesus stepped to the side, easily avoiding the dagger. The man's forward momentum almost caused him to fall as he stabbed at the empty air. He turned to lunge again. Jesus held up his hand and said, "A man who would kill for a cloth is one who has lost his sense of humanity. If you insist in such a drastic way on having this robe and the woe that it will bring you, it is yours. There's no need for violence."

Jesus laid down his staff, took off his robe, and handed it to the man. The man returned his dagger to its sheath and put on the robe. He then bent down and picked up the hardwood walking staff. "I will take this also," he declared.

"It is yours if you choose to have it. I found it only a short while ago; but if you take it, that staff will also bring you pain and woe."

The man raised the staff to strike Jesus. He sneered and brought the staff swiftly down toward Jesus's head. Jesus easily stepped away again. The forceful momentum of the swing caused the man to stumble forward and fall. Disgusted with Jesus, he said, "To hell with you."

Jesus replied, "Be careful what you wish for others, lest that wish becomes your fate."

The man got up and raised the staff to strike again and yelled, "Leave me! Go!"

Jesus was about to try once more to persuade the man to change his mind when, twenty feet away in the street, he saw a bright star-like pattern of blazing light the size of a person. Jesus stared at the brilliant, radiating crystalline light. The man still held the staff high above his head ready to strike but turned to see what Jesus was staring at. He saw nothing.

Jesus heard his Father. *"FOLLOW THE LIGHT, MY SON."*

Jesus backed away from the man and said simultaneously to the man and to his Father, "I shall do as you wish."

The dazzling pattern of Light moved along the street away from the man. The Light took the form of an angel with its outstretched arms resembling a cross symbolizing the four directions that destiny can go in. The angel beckoned Jesus to follow as it floated away from him down the street.

Jesus, wearing only his white tunic, followed the Angel of Light. The man wrapped Mother Mary's robe tightly around his body and pulled its hood over his face to contain his warmth against the cold night. He smiled triumphantly and said, "This is as it should be." Then he walked toward the Pharisees' Quarter.

Heavy sweat further drenched Seth's linen nightshirt as he ran through the streets of Jerusalem searching for Jesus. As he approached the Pharisees' Quarter, he saw Judas leading a group of Pharisee priests and elders accompanied by temple police and a platoon of Roman soldiers. They carried lanterns, torches, swords, and clubs. Without their knowledge, Seth followed them down the dark street. He saw a man he thought was Jesus, who was clad in his teacher's robe, walking toward the menacing group. Judas stopped and pointed toward Jesus. The group of men walked faster, then stopped twenty feet from Jesus of Jerusalem, who also stopped walking.

Judas then walked on alone, his head bowed. Deep sadness filled his soul as he approached the man. Judas could not bring himself to look directly at his Master, whose face was cloaked by the robe's hood. Judas bent over and took the man's hand and kissed it; then he turned away and walked back to the group of men. One of the priests handed Judas a pouch of coins. Judas took it and walked quickly away so that they would not see his stream of tears.

As Judas walked away, Jesus of Jerusalem pointed his finger at Judas and yelled, "I have condemned you to eternal damnation once before, and I condemn you again."

Seth heard the man's words although, oddly, it did not sound like his teacher's voice.

When Judas turned a corner of the street, he opened the pouch and spilled the thirty silver coins out upon the ground; then he threw the pouch down in disgust and kicked it away.

Seth edged closer to hear what was being said as the threatening group encircled Jesus. One of the priests announced, "We have a warrant for your arrest. You are to come with us."

The sergeant leading the platoon, who, like his men, was tired and grumpy from their double shift said, "Wait. I need to verify this man's identity." He faced the man and asked, "Are you Jesus the rabbi healer and preacher who calls himself the King of the Jews?"

The man replied, "I answer you with the truth of my soul: yes, I am him." Then the drunken deranged man spit in the sergeant's face and said, "You should kneel before me."

The sergeant instantly grabbed the man's staff and began beating him furiously about the head and shoulders. The man fell to the ground. The other soldiers gathered around and viciously kicked the man's face and body. Seth spontaneously ran toward the group yelling, "Stop! Stop! He's the Messiah!"

The soldiers looked up and saw a boy in his nightshirt running at them. Seth approached a soldier near the fallen man and pushed the soldier away from the bloodied man on the ground. Another soldier grabbed Seth by his nightshirt to seize him. Seth frantically pulled away. His nightshirt tore off of his body, and he turned and ran away as fast as he could – naked into the night. The soldier threw the boy's nightshirt to the ground, and again, the soldiers began to savagely beat the man who had affirmed that he was Jesus.

When the soldiers tired of beating the man, they propped him up, and two soldiers held him under his arms. They marched the man to the Courtyard of the Pharisees. There, Zadak looked out of his window at the bloodied man who appeared to be Jesus. Zadak smiled broadly at his priests' success and called out, "Now take him to Pontius Pilate as planned."

The Angel of Light led Jesus further away from the Pharisees' Quarter. After Jesus followed it around a street corner, the Light of the angel again extended its arms out to its sides and transfigured into a blazing silver and gold cross. Jesus acknowledged the symbolic meaning of the cross's shape in human form – its arms extended outward with no facial features further denoted the surrender of the ego-self, creating a transformative path to one's higher self, leading to the greater Light, Love, and Glory of his Father's Kingdom.

And then it faded away. In the street ahead, a sleek black stallion came toward Jesus. Riding upon the regal horse sat a Bedouin. He sat tall and proud in a fine saddle that held his sheathed sword. His dark robe was open, and a dagger's red and black zigzag handle could be seen attached to his belt.

Jesus stood still and smiled. The Bedouin approached Jesus and halted his horse. He too smiled broadly, his white teeth shining brightly against his dark olive skin. The assassin looked down at Jesus and said, "My friend, the Rabbi, you look as you did when we first met at the tavern."

"As do you," Jesus replied.

"You also look like you might need a ride." The Bedouin extended his hand to Jesus, indicating that Jesus should come up and sit behind him.

Jesus took his hand, and the Bedouin pulled as Jesus easily climbed up and sat comfortably. "Thank you," Jesus replied.

"You're sitting on folded blanket," the Bedouin said. "It's a cold night, and you're welcome to cover yourself with it."

"No, thank you. I am quite warm within."

"Where are you going at such a late hour? Perhaps avoiding arrest?"

Jesus replied, "It seems that I am going with you now."

The Bedouin chuckled, "That you are. I am going back to the desert for some peace and for a special celebration day that my tribe is holding to honor me. This time of the Passover Feast in Jerusalem is too crowded and hectic for me."

"Wait up!" came a call from behind. Jesus smiled again and turned around to see a very large white horse laden with stuffed cloth sacks and baskets. The rotund merchant sat upon the horse and waved to Jesus. "Wait!"

The Bedouin slowed his horse to allow the merchant to catch up. "Ah, the Rabbi," the merchant greeted Jesus. "It's good to see you again.

I witnessed your sermon on the Mount – very impressive. And now you appear as just a common man."

Jesus grinned at the merchant. "You seem happy to be up and about so early."

"We just came from the tavern," the merchant replied and then sniffed the air. "Rabbi, you have acquired an expensive taste in fragrances. That spikenard smells marvelous!"

Jesus replied, "I see that your senses still appreciate the finer things in life."

"That I do. And I see that you are still wearing that fine woven tunic."

The merchant leaned over and rubbed the edges of Jesus's sleeve between his fingers. "It is as I remembered. I've never seen a weave like this before – and fabric of such fine quality. Where did you get it?"

Jesus replied, "It was a gift from my Father."

"Do you know where it was made?" the merchant inquired.

"Yes, it is from beyond this world."

The merchant laughed. "You still have your sense of humor and still speak in mysteries. Have you made any more of your superlative wine lately?"

"Not from any of the unique ingredients that you gave me to work with that night in the tavern."

The assassin laughed, "That was an amazing feat."

The merchant added, "I still haven't tasted a drop of wine finer than that night."

Two patrolling Roman soldiers on horseback approached them from the far end of the street. The assassin's demeanor stiffened. He nudged his steed forward, the merchant silently following.

"Halt!" commanded one of the soldiers. The assassin ignored the command and maintained his pace.

"I said halt!" the soldier yelled angrily and started to draw his sword. The other soldier put his hand over his compatriot's hand to still his sword.

The assassin sat tall and proud, staring defiantly at the soldiers, and continued moving forward. The other soldier kept his hand on his partner's sword hand and said to the assassin, "It's okay. You may proceed."

The assassin looked straight ahead, maintaining the same deliberate pace as if the soldiers were not there. The merchant followed and nodded "Good evening" to the soldiers as he passed them.

When the trio was out of earshot of the soldiers, the merchant and the assassin burst out laughing. The merchant said to Jesus, "Those soldiers know that a Bedouin's reaction can be unpredictable if he's harassed, and tonight all the soldiers in Jerusalem are spread thin and weary from so many shifts."

The assassin added, "They know that we will fight viciously and mightily to the death – and we are excellent fighters. There were only two of them."

Jesus nodded in agreement and said, "I can see that you accurately projected that to them."

One of the soldiers turned to look back at the three men as they rode away. He said to the other soldier, "Do you think that could be the Jews' Messiah?"

The other replied, "I'm not sure what he looks like. He did resemble the description, but so do so many." Then he laughed. "It's unimaginable to think that a Bedouin would be giving a ride to the Jews' Messiah." They rode on.

As the three continued, the merchant halted his horse and said to Jesus, "I have to turn off here. I wish I could continue with you, but this is my busiest time of the year, and as you can see, I have a lot of wares to sell and need to put this horse in a stall near the Temple."

Jesus smiled at the merchant, "I see. It has been a pleasure for me to be with you."

The merchant laughed. "And for me to be with you," he said, and then he nodded to his friend the assassin, who nodded back. The merchant turned his horse and rode down a side street. The assassin nudged his horse toward Jerusalem's outer gate and onward to his desert tribe.

———

Seth arrived back at the inn. He was panting heavily from his run and the terror of what he had just witnessed. He went directly to Matthew and shook him violently. "Wake up! Wake up, Father! You must wake up!"

Matthew opened his sleep-heavy eyes, emerging from his deep slumber. "What? What is it, Seth?" he said in a half-awake voice.

"They arrested our Master! And they beat him!" Seth replied, still panting from his run.

"What are you saying, Seth? Where are your clothes?"

"Hurry! Judas betrayed Jesus. Help me awaken the others. We must help our Lord!"

———

"What can be so urgent at this hour?" Pontius Pilate asked the captain of the Praetorian Guard, who stood at the door to his bedroom. "He's here," the captain whispered. "They arrested the Jews' Messiah. Zadak sent him here for you to decide his fate."

Zena called to Pilate from their bed, "What is it, my husband?"

Go back to sleep, Zena. It's just a Jewish nuisance problem. Don't be concerned." Pilate pulled on his night robe and went to kiss Zena.

She said, "Please don't go. I've been having troublesome dreams."

"I'll be back shortly. Go back to sleep." Pilate kissed her and left with the captain for the Praetorian dungeons.

Pilate once again circled the chair that Jesus of Jerusalem was strapped to. The prisoner's face was bloody and badly bruised; swollen skin puffed around his eyes. Pilate scoffed and said to him, "They say that you are the Messiah, the Son of God and a god yourself. You don't look like a god to me." Pilate leaned closer. "Are you the Messiah? The Anointed One? The King of the Jews?"

The prisoner gazed straight ahead but said nothing.

"Has your god got your tongue?" Pilate prodded. Jesus of Jerusalem remained silent. Pilot felt empowered. "Where is your almighty God now that you need his help?" Jesus remained silent. He coughed and blood dribbled from his mouth. Pilate sneered at him. "You look like a pitiful lamb half-slaughtered. Tell me that you wish that almighty Zeus would set you free, and I will let you go."

Jesus said nothing. Pilate paced back and forth and then said, "You won't say a word, not even to save your life. Why?"

Jesus rolled up his eyes to Pilate; then his head dropped, almost in a faint. Pilate circled the chair. "What should I do with you? Dead, you may become a martyr. That could prove harder to control than if you stay alive. I can make you a priest on the Sanhedrin Council, and like them, you can judge others – as long as you follow Roman law. What do you say? Don't you want to live?"

Jesus remained silent. Pilate spoke his thoughts aloud. "Personally, I don't care if you live of die. I wish to keep order in my domain. If you die, your followers will be angry at me and at Rome and cause disturbances, and Rome will then be angry with me – and that we must avoid. What to do with you?"

Pilate got back into bed with Zena. She awoke and hugged him tightly. "I had a dream about the Jewish Messiah. It was terrible and disturbing."

"I just saw him," Pilate replied. "He's been arrested."

"What are you going to do with him?" Zena asked, sitting up straight.

"I'm not going to do anything with him," Pilate laughed. "He is a Galilean Jew. Herod is in Jerusalem for the feast, and he is the King of Galilee." Pilate chuckled, "As we speak, my men are making ready to take the Jews' Messiah to Herod's palace for him to decide the Rabbi's fate since Herod has jurisdiction over Galilee. Now the Jews' Messiah will be Herod's hot coal to handle. He is no longer my problem."

Zena turned away. She covered her face in her hands.

At first the disciples were incredulous at the news that Jesus had been arrested and that Judas had betrayed him. Mary believed that Jesus had been arrested, but she couldn't accept that Judas would betray him. Quickly, everyone made haste to Jerusalem. Near the Pharisees' Quarter, Seth pointed to the blood on the ground where he said Jesus had been betrayed, beaten, and arrested. Seth's torn nightshirt lay nearby. The disciples became fearful, accepting that what Seth had told them was true, especially when Seth said that Jesus had condemned Judas to eternal damnation. They knew that Seth never lied, and in this matter, he had spoken with especially intense conviction.

The men soon decided to have Mary go alone to the Pharisee guards at their compound gate and inquire about Jesus's whereabouts rather than have the men go, which might arouse suspicion. Mary had abandoned her vow not to leave the inn when Seth told her that Jesus had been arrested. She went to the gate, and ten minutes later, she returned and said, "They have taken our Lord to the Praetorian. Pontius Pilate is to decide his fate."

Andrew said, "We will never be able to get into the Praetorian; it's in a fortress."

Luke said, "What else can we do? We must go there."

As the disciples raced to the Praetorian, six chariots, a wagon, and twenty foot soldiers of the Praetorian Guard came toward them. The disciples split up and moved to the sides of the wide thoroughfare that led to Herod's palace. First the soldiers passed them, then the three chariots that led the wagon. When the wagon passed by, a man lying on it sat up. His hands and feet were bound, his face puffy and bloodied. He looked side to side at the disciples, then collapsed back down on the wagon. The man who resembled their Savior was wearing their Master's robe. Peter was shocked and devastated at what he saw. He whispered to John, "It's him. Now they will be coming after us. We must hide."

The other disciples reacted similarly, except for Mary and Seth. Mary had crumpled to the ground, thinking that her beloved Jesus had been severely beaten and was now doomed. Seth stood on his toes trying to get a better look at the man. He saw the curved red scar on the back of the man's hand, but the man's face was covered by blood-clotted hair and by the robe's hood.

After the two chariots following the wagon had passed, Seth knelt next to Mary and said, "I'm not sure that man is our Lord."

"But he's wearing the robe his mother made for him. I know for certain because I put it over him last night," Mary sobbed.

"Let's follow them," Seth said. "Maybe we can get a better look." He helped Mary to her feet. The other disciples had already dispersed in fear. Mary and Seth followed the chariots to Herod's palace until the escort passed through Herod's palace gate. The man on the wagon did not sit up again, and they could not get a glimpse of him. Seth and Mary stayed near the palace gate, waiting.

———

Even in the very late night, just hours before the sun was to rise that Friday morning, Herod was gleeful as he pointed to the bound and bloodied man huddled on the cold stone dungeon floor. Herod turned to Octavius and asked, "Are you sure this is him?"

"Yes, My Lord. It has been confirmed. One of his own disciples betrayed him."

Herod let out a long sigh of relief. He stood beside the weakened man and stared at his sordid state. He cleared his throat and then said to Octavius, "I have had nightmares and worry over..." Herod pointed down at the man, "... over nothing. This wretch can perform no miracles. He can't even untie his bonds, much less be a king."

Herod knelt to the man's ear. "What say you? Are you the King who would replace me? The real King?" Herod scoffed and affirmed, "I could raise my little finger and have your head removed from your body."

The dazed man stared ahead and did not reply. Herod stood and ordered Octavius, "Send him back to Pilate with the message that I have no need to bother with this pitiful creature."

Herod stood and sighed again. "I shall sleep very well the rest of this night."

Outside of Herod's palace, Mary and Seth tried to get closer to the cart that just left and carried the beaten prisoner, who was now bound in a sitting position on the cart's floor, but Herod's soldiers maintained a twenty-yard radius of protection that prevented them from getting a closer look. There were many people in the street near the palace who were beginning this day of the Passover feast in the pre-dawn hours. Mary and Seth ran ahead to a narrow street and waited to get a better look. As the cart passed them, the bound man looked directly at Mary. She stared at his eyes. Mary shook her head and whispered to Seth, "That's not our Jesus. He looks like him, but I know his eyes, and I'm certain that's not him." Tears of relief streamed down Mary's cheeks.

Seth replied, "I got a good look too. You're right – it's not him! What could have happened? Where is he?"

"I don't know, Seth, but I'm going back to the inn. I never should have left, but I was so worried about our Savior, I had to come to help him."

"I'm going to follow the cart and see where they're going. I'll try and meet you back at the inn later and tell you what's happening."

"Thank you, Seth. "Mary walked back to the inn wondering where her Jesus could be. Peter approached a group of servants near the Pharisees' gate who were warming themselves by a fire pit on the side of the street. They were waiting for dawn so they could pass through the gate and begin their long day's work. Already word had spread, and everyone was talking about Jesus's arrest. Peter held his palms near the fire to warm his cold hands. He overheard that Jesus had been taken to Herod's palace and then brought back to Pontius Pilate's Praetorian. He anxiously listened for more news about his Master. A young servant girl standing next to Peter stared at him and asked, "Aren't you one of the Messiah's disciples? I saw you at his sermon on Sunday."

"No, I'm not him," Peter replied curtly. The young girl studied Peter's face. He pretended to ignore her but became more worried about being discovered but yearned to learn what news there was. The girl went to her mother, who was also a servant and was refolding some mended clothing and putting it into a basket. She told her mother about Peter, and then they both came to Peter's side. The mother looked closely at Peter and said, "You're Jesus's disciple. I saw you with my daughter at his sermon. You were a speaker repeating his words." Peter became very uncomfortable and adamantly said, "Surely you're mistaken. I know who I am, and I am not the one you speak of."

As Peter turned to leave, the head servant came out of the Pharisees' Quarters to tell the guards at the gate that it was time to let the waiting servants in as the sun would soon be rising. Peter felt relieved and stayed by the fire for warmth as the servants gathered their things to leave. As they entered the gate, the mother told the head servant that she thought that the man at the fire was Jesus's disciple. He went directly to Peter, who started to turn and walk away. "Wait!" the head servant called to him. "You're a disciple of Jesus the Messiah."

Peter backed away and said, "I don't understand what you're talking about." Peter turned and walked faster. Fearing for his life, he yelled back at the servant, "I am not he! I don't know any Jesus." Peter started to run; at that moment a rooster began to crow. Seconds later, the sun's red-orange crest rose above the horizon, heralding the dawn of a new day.

"Are you sure you want to go to *that* oasis?" the assassin asked Jesus as they rode over the desert sands. "I know for sure there's no water there. I passed that oasis last week. It's been bone dry for a long time. The palm trees are long dead, and their leaves are brown and lifeless. Not a blade of grass remains. I know of a better place for you to stay."

"That is where I need to be," Jesus firmly reiterated. "I need to go to *that* oasis."

"Then that is where I shall take you if you insist."

"Thank you."

The two rode along in silence. After a while, the Bedouin said, "I don't believe it was coincidence that I met you tonight."

"I see," Jesus said. "Do tell me why."

"I had a 'job' to fulfill last night. He was old and sickly. His son-in-law paid me to remove the old man from this life so that he and the father's daughter could inherit the old man's wealth. It would have been an easy kill. I stood behind him with my dagger in hand. At that moment, I thought about you and what you had said to me."

"What was that?"

"You said that taking a life was a mistake and that in the afterlife, I would become more enlightened and would have to judge my actions from your God's point of view. I don't know if I believe in your God or not, but your words made me think about how I make a living. You spoke of a time when my heart would become open and I would feel an interconnectedness with all life." The assassin took in a deep breath and let it out with a sigh.

"Do go on," Jesus encouraged.

The assassin spoke softly, "That night at the tavern, after you left, I began to feel that interconnectedness, although I didn't change my ways. But as time passed, I began to feel guilty for taking lives for money although I continued to earn a living that way - until last night."

Although Jesus knew, he asked: "What happened last night?"

"That old man was so feeble and wretched looking – I felt that he would soon die anyway, but I also felt a sudden deep remorse for all the lives that I'd taken for money. At that moment, I put my dagger away and left the old man as he was." The assassin nodded his head in thought and then said, "I've saved enough money so that I no longer need to do any more 'jobs,' but more importantly, I realized that I've lost my taste for murder. Last night I decided to devote myself solely to helping my tribe as I have been doing only part of my time. And that's why they're honoring me today."

The Bedouin sat tall in the saddle, chin high, and said, "It's a good feeling that I like very much. I want to teach my people to help each other so that we can be better – better people than the Romans, the Jews, and the Gentles, who think it is they who are superior. And now, here you are, riding with me so I can tell you about this."

"You've made a good choice to repent for your murderous ways, and indeed, I foresee that your life and the lives of others whom you help will be more rewarding to you in this life and in the afterlife."

"Perhaps. But for now I believe it's the right thing to do."

"I assure you, it is the right thing to do."

The Bedouin abruptly halted his horse. The blazing orange-red sphere of the full sun had fully risen above the horizon. He exclaimed, "It can't be so!" He stared ahead and said, "I don't believe it. It must be a mirage." He slapped his reins against the horse's neck and they sped ahead.

As they got closer, the black silhouette of twenty palm trees could be seen against the early morning sun. "It's impossible," the Bedouin said. He kicked the sides of his horse and rode faster. As they neared their destination, he slowed his horse and then stopped at the edge of the oasis. A deep pool of water was in the middle of the area, and a side well was full to the brim. The palm trees were lush and verdant. A carpet of deep green grass surrounded the pool. Desert flowers bloomed in myriad colors.

The Bedouin got off his horse and went to the pool of water. Jesus followed. The Bedouin picked up a small stone and tossed it into the pool. He watched it sink to the bottom ten feet below as ripples from the center radiated toward the edges. He turned to Jesus, who stood at his side. The Bedouin raised his black gull-wing eyebrows in amazement and said, "In all my life, I have never seen so much water here. But these palm trees, so many, so green, could not have grown in one week."

A songbird flew by his face and then onto a palm tree with other songbirds that sang jubilantly. His horse nibbled on the succulent grass. In awe, he said, "This is a miracle! I've heard of miracles that you've performed – they were hard to believe – but this," he pointed to the trees and water, "this is an undeniable miracle that you've performed."

Jesus replied, "I know nothing of this, only that I had to come to this spot in the desert."

"Then you are indeed the Son of the King of the Universe."

The Bedouin walked around the oasis, examining all of its aspects while his horse drank from the well. He reluctantly said, "I wish I could stay with you longer, but I must be on my way. My people await me."

"And that is where you need to be," Jesus replied.

"I don't want to leave you here with no horse," replied the Bedouin.

"As you can see, my Father has provided a safe haven for me, and He will continue to do so. Go to your people and follow your new convictions, for they will bring you great fulfillment."

After the Bedouin got on his horse, he said to Jesus, "I have a feeling that I won't be seeing you again."

"Perhaps not in this life, but we may meet again in my Father's Kingdom. Keep doing good things and act with love."

"I intend to. Wherever you're going, I bid you safe passage."

"And I bid you the same. God be with you."

The Bedouin nudged his horse forward. Jesus watched him ride away into the rising sun until he disappeared into the vastness of the desert. Jesus bowed his head and said, "Dear Father, thank you for giving me the privilege of fulfilling my destiny. An assassin and other sinners who repent and become benefactors to those in need are no less a miracle than a resurrection of the dead. These miracles are of a resurrection of the forgotten spirit of love that You gave to mankind at their birth. I have been honored to serve You by sowing the seeds of Your Truth into the hearts and minds of man so that in time, those seeds will have the opportunity to blossom. I thank You, dear Father, for Your divine guidance that has led me to this moment of my fulfillment."

The sky, the sand, and the oasis suddenly turned into a flash of white light so bright and brilliant that the sun paled. Then a moment later, all was as it was before. Jesus acknowledged, "I know, it's time for me to leave." He walked to the edge of the deep pool of healing living water and saw his earth-body reflection – the reflection of a man wearing a white tunic. Jesus gave thoughtful thanks for the divine blessing that his earth-body had been to him. He gave thanks for his earthly sight, to have been able to see as man sees. He looked to the east and saw the early morning yellow-orange tinted sky around the sun; he looked to the west and saw the fading indigo of night. He looked at the lush palm trees, the vibrant green grass, and the multi-colored desert flowers. He breathed in and smelled their perfume mixed with the spikenard in his anointed hair. He felt the pristine air fill his lungs and energize his body, and he savored the simple pleasure of breath. He breathed out and sighed, "I thank You, Father, for Your grace and all that You have given me."

Jesus smiled as he remembered the tastes of fine wine and the delicious foods that had delighted his body's tongue. The sounds of songbirds filled his ears with their merriment and glory. A gentle breeze caressed his face, refreshing his skin. He touched the features of his face and felt their shape and textures. He gave thanks to have had the opportunity to appreciate man's five senses in ways that most people rarely do and that he was able to derive the great pleasure from those senses that his heavenly Father intended.

Jesus closed his outer eyes and gave thanks for his inner sight, which allowed him to have seen man's endless and creative thoughts and the many possibilities that lay before all mankind. Jesus winced as he thought of mankind's enduring pain and sorrow, and then he smiled with peace as he also thought of mankind's exquisite moments of accomplishment and bliss. Jesus bowed his head and said, "Thank you blessed Lord, my Father, for All That Is."

And then he fervently prayed that mankind would choose their paths with love in their hearts for one another, which would lead to their salvation.

Jesus then thought fondly of Mary and their times together. He opened his eyes and once more looked into the pool of healing living water.

<hr>

Mary finally walked up the stairs of the inn to the large room where they had shared their last supper. Earlier, she had gone up and down many times calling out Jesus's name to see if he had come back and might be in another part of the inn. She had also gone out numerous times to see if he was coming up from the wooded path, but he was never there. She lay on the bed once more where they had slept and smelled his scent mixed with the spikenard. Mary was haunted by where he might be or what might have happened to him.

Not knowing what more could be done, she knelt in front of the basin of healing living water with which she had washed Jesus's feet the night before. His white robe was now clean and dry and hung on the back of the chair in the center of the upper room where she had anointed her Savior.

Mary looked into the basin of water and saw her reflection. She reached in and cupped her hands. She sat up and brought the water to her face and slowly let it cascade down over her face and body. All the while, Mary's thoughts were fixated on her image of Jesus. She sat on her heels, eyes closed, and remembered her last days with him. Then she leaned forward and looked into the basin of water again. Mary saw her reflection, then remembered Jesus's face when they were young. The surface of the water rippled very slightly, distorting her image. As the ripples smoothed, Jesus's face appeared with "that gleam" in his eyes that he had had when they were young. She rubbed her eyes in disbelief. *Was it a wishful illusion?* she thought. Mary felt overwhelmed as an avalanche of memories and feelings from those times swirled within her. She stared at Jesus's face, wishing that he were with her now, if only for a moment more. She reached down to touch his face, but her touch disturbed the water and erased his image. He was gone. Mary closed her eyes, still leaning over the basin, and cried.

When she stopped crying, she sat up to wipe her tears. When she opened her eyes, she gasped - Jesus was standing before her as he had been the night before, wearing his white tunic; his feet stood in the basin of holy water. Jesus extended his hands for her to grasp. In a trance-like state, Mary took his hands and stood facing him as she had the night before.

She heard Jesus speak although his lips did not move, "My beloved Mary. Peace and love I leave with you; my peace and love I give to you. I do not give to you as the world gives. Do not let your heart be troubled, and do not be afraid. Be glad for me, for I am going to my Father, and my Father is greater than I."

Before she could say anything, Mary felt Jesus squeeze her hands tightly. He smiled with loving tenderness. Then he was gone. The robe on the chair was also gone. Mary fell to her knees and looked into the basin of still water. She saw only her own reflection.

<hr />

A breeze blew over the oasis pool, rippling the images of Mary that Jesus had just witnessed. He ran his hands over his Father's glowing white robe that he now wore and felt the divine comfort of its texture once more. No trace remained of its reddish-brown. A flash of intense white light filled the desert landscape as before, then vanished. This time, in that moment, Jesus felt the exquisite rapture of God's boundless Love as never before. Jesus looked up toward the heavens and saw hundreds of thousands of angels gathering and hovering above the oasis. He looked down at the deep pool of healing living water and then stepped into it. The Holy living water began to churn as his legs disappeared beneath the surface. Jesus continued into the water until he had submerged himself completely at the bottom of the pool. The water began to boil with steam and ice.

⬯

Saul of Tarsus had been riding his horse alone on the road to Damascus. Conflicting thoughts flooded his mind. He had not yet heard of the crucifixion, but he had received letters from some of the disciples confirming Jesus's miracles and pleading for him to join them in their mission to spread the Good News of the Messiah. Saul shook his head and affirmed aloud, "I know what I have witnessed. That Rabbi from Nazareth has become a deceiver of the masses."

Then he thought to himself, *I must find a way to expose this scoundrel. Eventually the truth will come out. The people of Israel will appear as fools. They will feel tricked when the real Messiah comes; people will refuse to accept him. They will doubt and not want to be fooled again.*

Suddenly, a flash of blinding Light, brighter than the sun, caused Saul to lose his balance and fall from his horse. He landed sharply on his hip and thought he heard a cracking sound. Saul reached for his hip but couldn't feel his hands or hip, or even the ground. His senses were numb except for the blinding Light that appeared to be in all places at once—the Light that now permeated his body and surroundings.

Then he perceived patterns within patterns of the Light. Within the patterns of pulsating intensities of the Light, a dazzling image of Jesus appeared. Saul cried out "No! No!" All of his muscles automatically contracted as if to prepare for a blow from a heavy club. Instead, he felt a wave of euphoria that filled him with an exalted peace. Paul thought, *I have died. This must be God's domain.*

Then, what can only be described as a powerful swirling vortex of "revelations" merged with his Essence. He saw glimpses of his divine mission to weave a path through the beliefs of all people—the pagans and the Jews—and to create as sure a path as possible for them through the complicated politics and brutal authority of Rome, a path that was intended to be The Path of The Word.

It was overwhelming for Saul to contemplate such a daunting task, yet he also felt imbued with a divine energy that gave him a surge of confidence and a passionate desire to fulfill the Creator's Master Plan. It was as if he had been asleep his whole life and was now awakened by the torrent of holy revelations.

Once again, Jesus's pattern of Light intensified as Saul realized his perceived transgression of forsaking the true Messiah. He heard Jesus ask, *"Who do you say that I am?"*

Saul replied, "You are the one in me, and I am the one in you."

Jesus's words resonated within Saul's soul. *"You have been touched by the Holy Spirit as John the Baptist and I have been. That is the "One" within me. I have carried the Torch of Light, and now it has been passed to you to go forth and fulfill your intended destiny."*

"I swear on my life that I will go forth with all my will and with all my heart and soul, and with all I have to give," Saul solemnly pledged. Then, with the knowledge of his revelations, he asked, "I beg you to forgive me for denying you."

"I forgive you because I am in you and you are in me. You will be known for your deeds. Verily I say to you, if you truly love and believe in God's divine ways, forgive yourself, for you are within me, and to forgive yourself is to love me. Again, I bid you go forth and fulfill your destiny."

Saul replied humbly, "I will, for I see the Light and that you are the Christ. And I shall go forth as Paul, for that is the name you call me by."

The radiance of Jesus's Light patterns became more intense, the brightness becoming almost unbearable to Paul; then suddenly it was gone. Paul lay transfixed and trembling on the ground. All that had transpired with Paul took a fraction of a second when the Light in the desert had flashed.

$$\Longrightarrow$$

Within that split second of the desert flash of Light, Mary knew that she would never see Jesus in the flesh again. The only thing that she could now touch of his was the water that was left in the basin. She reached into it and held her hands there thinking of her Jesus. Then, as before, she cupped her hands, filling them with water, and then poured the water over her head. She took two more handfuls and did the same. The water ran down her hair and over her face with a delightful and penetrating sensation. The top of her gown was wet with the runoff.

$$\Longrightarrow$$

Submerged in the water of the pool in the oasis, Jesus felt the glorious and overwhelming intensity of the Holy Spirit within him peak. Another bright white flash of light filled the desert landscape. Below the surface, Jesus's flesh vaporized. His Essence rose above the water. The expansive multitudes of angels above awaited him. The Four Archangels that were at the Four Corners of the world came forth and circled around his Essence four times and then encapsulated it. The blazing and dazzling grouping then ascended with Jesus's Essence into the magnificent vortex of countless gathered angels and then onward to the glory of his Father's Kingdom.

The healing living water in the pool and all of the greenery and life forms of the oasis instantly evaporated into the arid desert air, and their essences also ascended and mixed with the Four Winds that carried the Essence of Jesus throughout the world.

<hr>

Mary felt the tingling from the water on her face and hands intensify. She looked down at the basin and saw the water glow bright white – then it instantly evaporated before her eyes. She felt her hair and face. She felt her clothes. There was not a trace of dampness from the wetness that had been there a moment ago. The sound of a sudden wind caused her to look out the window at the trees that were swaying gracefully back and forth.

Simultaneously, within the same split second of that flash of Light, the Bedouin, upon his black stallion, turned his head toward the oasis and saw the flash of Light, not unlike the brilliant flash of Light that Judas saw the day of Jesus's arrival in the desert. The Bedouin's head jerked back from the intense Light that seemed brighter than the sun. As the afterglow of the Light still burned in his eyes, he solemnly said, "You are indeed the One."

<hr>

Jesus of Jerusalem had been delivered back to Pilate and held in the Praetorian jail. The Roman soldiers taunted the prisoner with phrases such as "King of the Jews." They stripped him of his clothes. They spit on him and cursed him. They whipped him with leaded thongs and beat him with a cane, mocking him all the time. Finally, they made a crown of branches with large, spiky thorns and pressed it deeply into his scalp; rivulets of blood trickled down his face.

<hr>

After having been dressed for the day, Zena dismissed her handmaidens. She stared at herself in the mirror and nodded her approval that her hair, make-up, jewelry, and gown were in perfect order. She looked at her favorite vase next to the mirror. It was made of delicately blown glass with decorative threads of gold and silver. Zena picked it up as she had many times before and admired its unique shape. She walked to the window to see the vase's artistic designs in the morning sunlight. A beam of golden light reflected off the glass and into her eyes. The light stirred her senses, and she felt as she did when she had heard Jesus's Sermon on the Mount. It was more than the words that he spoke that had stirred her soul and touched her heart in a way that she had never experienced before – rather, it was a mystical feeling that she had felt that she could not describe in words.

At first, when her sister Lydia had coaxed her to go with her to the Sermon on the Mount, Zena laughed at how ridiculous it would be for the wife of Pontius Pilate, the Prefect of Jerusalem, to attend a sermon by a rabbi. Now, she remembered Lydia's words, "I promise you – just to be in his presence will make you more radiant. Look at how much more vibrant I have been since I touched his robe."

Zena had once again looked enviously at her sister's glowing health and attractiveness and thought of the possibility that she too could become more radiant. She had been visiting at Lydia's house that Sunday, and when Lydia said she was leaving to go to the sermon and asked Zena one more time to come with her, Zena laughed to mask her curiosity and then told Lydia that to satisfy her, she would go. They changed their clothes and covered themselves with common hooded robes, then sneaked out a back door, leaving Zena's guards and escorts waiting in the courtyard as usual, unaware that their charges would be attending the Sermon on the Mount.

Zena now held the vase high in front of her and stared at it as she walked back to the dressing mirror. She thought of her vivid dream of the night before. *"Ouch! Ooow!"* she yelped suddenly as she stubbed her toe against the hard corner of a footstool. As she lurched forward to keep her balance, the glass vase fell from her hands and shattered upon impact with the marble floor. Zena sat on the floor holding her painful toe and mourning the broken vase she had loved. "No, no, no," she repeated in angst. When she reached over to pick up the delicate pieces of glass, Pilate entered. She looked up at him, and at that moment, she cut her finger on a glass fragment. "Oh no! This is terrible!" she gasped.

Pilate came to her side; Zena grasped her finger to stem the blood that had dripped onto her fresh gown. "What happened?" Pilate asked.

In between sobs, Zena replied, "I stubbed my toe, broke my favorite vase, cut my finger on a glass sliver, and now I've ruined my gown. My terrible dreams last night have cursed my day."

Pilate helped her to her feet and walked her to a couch as she hobbled along. They sat and Zena cried; Pilate tried to comfort her. "Your toe will be better; you've got many other gowns, and we can replace that vase."

"No, no, no. That vase can never be replaced. It's one of a kind, like that Rabbi, Jesus," Zena shed genuine tears.

Pilate was taken aback. "What do you mean? What are you saying about the Rabbi?"

"It's my terrible dream about him."

"You won't have to dream about him anymore. I was just with him, and I can tell you that he will not be alive much longer to be a bother."

"No, my husband! You don't understand!" Zena put her hand on Pilate's knee and squeezed it firmly; then she anxiously rubbed his leg and said, "I may have my womanly ways, but I am smart enough to know a man's character – even men such as Tiberius and Herod – and I know that that Rabbi is no threat to Rome, or to you, my dear husband."

"How would you know such things?"

"At his sermon on Sunday..." Zena, remembering not to mention her own attendance to Pilate, cleared her throat and then said, "Lydia heard him say to his believers that if their enemy strikes them, they should turn the other cheek."

Zena tenderly stroked Pilate's cheek and said, "A submissive man like that isn't going to declare war on Rome – he preaches non-violence." She grabbed his shoulders. "He's an innocent man!"

Pilate raised his eyebrows suspiciously at her reaction. "You said you were with Lydia all day. If Lydia was at the Sermon on Sunday, were you with her?"

Zena's posture stiffened, and then she blurted out with frustration, "Oh, Pontius, it's not what you think."

"What is it, then?"

"Well, it was just curiosity. Lydia wanted to go – you know how she claims that the Rabbi made her healthy and glowing - so, yes, I went with Lydia out of curiosity. No one recognized us the way that we were dressed."

"You changed your clothes?" Pilate said incredulously.

Zena caressed Pilate's thigh again, held his cheek gently with her other hand, and said, "Pontius, my husband, please do not fret that I have heard the Rabbi speak. Rather know that he is a king to his followers, but one you could work with to make Jerusalem more prosperous. It would be far better than having to deal with those Jewish hypocrites like Zadak. You could form an alliance with a Jewish king who is loved by his people."

Pilate pushed Zena's hand off of his thigh and pulled his face away from her other hand. "That's unthinkable! Why do you defend him so?"

"It's my dream, my husband. I dreamed that he was crucified and that he was an innocent man on the cross. It disturbed me in ways that I can't describe."

"I know this, Zena: the man I saw is no threat. Herod also deems him not to be a threat. It is the Jews in the Sanhedrin who are demanding his death, but they are only a minority. The majority of Jews see the Rabbi as their King. It has become a politically treacherous situation."

"Then, my husband, if he is no threat and an innocent man, let him be free." Zena leaned against Pilate and pressed her breast against his chest, causing her soft flesh to bulge over the top of her gown. She hugged him sensually and whispered in his ear, "Let him be free."

Pilate begrudgingly replied, "I don't know if that's possible."

"My husband, you are the smartest and most powerful man in Jerusalem. Surely you can figure out a way." Zena sensuously embraced Pilate again and squeezed him tightly as she thought about Jesus.

<hr>

During the Passover festivities, it was the custom for the Governor of Jerusalem to release a prisoner chosen by the crowd. Pilate knew that the majority of Jews claimed the Rabbi as their Messiah, so he thought that if he gave the crowd a choice between releasing the Rabbi or a notorious thief and murderer such as Barabbas, they would surely choose their Messiah; thus, Pilate would avoid conflict with the Sanhedrin priests who had voted for Jesus's death because it would be the people who had made the choice, not him.

Pilate's public judgment of Jesus was scheduled to take place in the Praetorian Courtyard of the Antonia Fortress adjoining the Temple Mount. Zadak and his priests had used their own guards to keep those Jews out who loved and supported Jesus and allowed only those under their influence into the Praetorian Courtyard for Pilate's judgment of Jesus. Zadak had gotten wind of Pilate's plan to release Jesus; thus, Zadak's people were prepared and ready.

As governor of Jerusalem, Pilate sat on the formal Chair of Judgment above the crowded courtyard. Zena sat behind him, and Pilate's high officers of the guard and his court flanked them. Jesus and Barabbas were paraded out in shackles and led by strong-armed guards. Pilate stood and addressed the crowd and announced that it was the custom to release a prisoner on this day of the feast. He pointed to Jesus of Jerusalem and then presented the choice to the crowd, "What then shall I do with this man you call the King of the Jews?"

"CRUCIFIY HIM! CRUCIFIY HIM!" the prepped crowd shouted back in unison.

Pilate was taken aback and asked the crowd, "Why? What crime has he committed? I find him innocent, and he should be freed."

The crowd shouted back louder, "CRUCIFY HIM! CRUCIFY HIM!"

Pilate turned to look at Zena. She shook her head. He looked down at the crowd and saw Zadak ordering his priests to do something. They started yelling, "If you let this man go, you are no friend of Caesar. Anyone who claims to be a king is a traitor and opposes Caesar." The crowd shouted the accusations again and again.

Pilate frowned at the implications and complications that could arise with Rome that were now voiced by so many people. He weighed those implications against the possibility of a rebellious backlash by the general Jewish population if he acquiesced to Jesus's crucifixion. He walked next to the man, Jesus, and spoke into his ear, "For the last time I will ask you, are you Jesus, the one who claims to be King of the Jews?"

Lines of dried blood remained on his face, having dripped down from the crown of thorns. The man feebly answered, "Yes, I am Jesus, and I claim that right to be mine."

Pilate stared at the man a moment, then said, "So be it." He motioned to an aide who quickly brought an ornate hand basin of water and held it in front of Pilate.

Pilate held up his hands to quiet the crowd's chanting. When the people were hushed, he said to them, "The choice to crucify this man for treason because he calls himself your king is your choice, not mine." Pilate dipped his hands into the basin and rubbed them together. He took them out and dried them with a towel handed to him by another attendant. Pilate proclaimed, "I have officially washed my hands of this matter."

Pilate turned away from the crowd and looked at Zena, who stared back at him with seething contempt. She stood and slipped off the golden serpentine amulet that the Emperor Tiberius had given to her. She continued to stare at Pilate as she tossed it to the floor in a gesture of disgust for Roman justice. She turned her back on Pilate and stalked away.

<hr />

Seth had gone back to the inn to tell Mary of Pilate's judgment. Mary told Seth of her mystical contact with Jesus and how he had come for his robe and what his words were to her. She told him how the water had evaporated and how she felt when the wind had rustled the trees and that she knew it to be a sign of God spreading the basin's vaporized holy water of Jesus's anointing to the world. They hurriedly left the inn and made their way to the path that led from Jerusalem to the Place of the Skull, the path that the man sentenced to crucifixion would take.

Jesus's mother Mary and his brother James had arrived in Jerusalem as Pilate's judgment was occurring. Afterward, word of Jesus's pending crucifixion spread quickly throughout the city. Mother Mary, who lay atop cushions on the wagon floor, was already weak and pained from her tortuous travel. Upon hearing the news from a passerby, she trembled and then fainted, realizing that her long-held fears of her son's crucifixion were soon to become a reality. James and the wagon's driver quickly came to her aid.

In anticipation of the crowds that would gather, a heavily armed military contingent was assembled to escort the sentenced man to the Place of the Skull at Golgotha, located one-third of a mile from the fortress where Pilate's judgment had occurred. More troops were sent directly to the crucifixion site. They cordoned off a wide perimeter around the Place of the Skull so that no protestors could interfere and so that the crucifixion could only be viewed from a distance. From the Antonia Praetorian Fortress, the streets of Jerusalem were cleared of spectators to the outer west gate along the path on which Jesus would be escorted.

Most of the disciples were still in hiding. But Simon, thinking that it was his true Master who had been condemned, now stood near the gate from which Jesus would leave Jerusalem for the path to the Place of the Skull. Simon feared greatly for his own life, but his passion to help his Master overrode his own fears and gave him the courage to stand closer to the path than all others in the crowd.

The gates opened, and two Roman chariots exited first. On both sides of the chariots marched soldiers who held sharp-tipped lances pointed toward the people lining the path. The crowd quickly parted to make a wider path. A platoon of Roman infantry followed the chariots, metal shields up and spears pointed in a fanned-out array at the people. Behind them, the exhausted and bloodied Jesus of Jerusalem struggled to hold the pantibulum – a wooden crossbar he was forced to carry upon which he would be crucified. A soldier escorting him prodded the condemned man forward with a hardwood cane. An infantry company followed them with Roman cavalry alongside and behind them. Priests and members of the Sanhedrim Council followed.

After arduously struggling for twenty feet, the nearly lifeless man again fell to the ground under the one hundred-and-twenty pound weight of the six-foot-long crossbar. The procession halted, and the soldier yelled at him, "Get up, Jew!" The man did not move. The soldier brought his cane down hard on the man's back, causing his bloodied robe to billow. "Get up and carry your cross!" the soldier barked. The man did not respond.

The soldier brought the cane up and was about to strike the man again when Simon stepped out from the crowd and cried out, "Wait! He's too weak. I'll carry the cross for him." Simon bent down to pick up the cross.

The soldier shifted his stance with his cane now aimed at Simon. Other infantry soldiers quickly surrounded them. Simon paid no attention to the threatening soldiers and lifted the cross upon his own shoulders. The soldiers saw that there was no threat from Simon. "Who are you?" asked the soldier with the cane.

"My name is Simon."

The soldier pointed to the prisoner on the ground and asked, "Do you know this man?"

At that moment the man on the ground looked up at Simon. The man sighed and smiled strangely, suggesting satisfaction and contentment. From his dazed eyes, the fallen man saw a beautiful blue-white glow of compassion around Simon. Simon was baffled at the man's expression, but nonetheless, he knew that it was definitely not his Master, Jesus. Simon answered the soldier, "No, I do not know this man."

"Then why do you act to help him?"

"Because he is a soul in pitiful need of help," answered Simon.

The soldier stared at Simon and was about to strike him when a cavalry captain brought his horse alongside them and ordered the soldier, "Move it! Get going!"

The soldier pointed to the fallen man and replied, "He is not able to carry the cross. This is the second time he has fallen since leaving Antonia."

"Are you going to carry it?" the captain retorted.

The soldier looked at Simon and then said to him, "Go ahead. But don't lag." The soldier grabbed the bloodied prisoner's arm and pulled him to his feet, then prodded him in the back. The man staggered forward. Simon walked beside him, carrying the cross. As he walked, Simon realized that for the first time in his life, he had spoken without stuttering. He also remembered Jesus's words, "...the one who would look like me, but would not be me." The man with the crown of thorns resembled Jesus, but it was not he.

Simon then heard the words in Jesus's voice say to him what he had said before: *"There will come a day when you will courageously participate in an extraordinary event. Your act of great compassion will overcome your shyness and the fears that cause your stuttering."*

Simon realized that although he had greatly feared being recognized as Jesus's disciple and then being arrested and crucified, he acted out of his deep compassion and lay down his life for another. When he had spoken to the soldier, he hadn't realized then that he was not stuttering. It was also the first time for as long as Simon could remember that he felt a sense of true pride, self-respect, and satisfaction. The burden of the cross on his shoulders became lighter. He felt Jesus's presence and heard his Master's voice speak to him again: *"You are a good and worthy soul, Simon."*

Simon closed his eyes as he walked and savored the feeling. He then heard Jesus say to him, *"Simon, whom I love, I am pleased with you."*

Simon felt the weight of the cross significantly lighten as he recognized his own greater inner strength and the confirmation of his worth in Jesus's words.

Since his last savage beating and after many more strikes to his head, Jesus of Jerusalem had fallen into a stupor-like, out-of-body trance. He had been in so much pain from the blows to his body that he had reached the point of numbness and now felt no pain. The kicks and strikes to his head had also clouded his sight and hearing.

As the soldiers were beating and caning him, he remembered his childhood, when he had often been caned. He had been orphaned and was raised by a group of strict orthodox rabbis. They had adamantly preached the woes of sin to him but never balanced sin with the blessings of love. The rabbis had high expectations of him because they had recognized that he was highly perceptive and intuitive; however, they constantly and harshly criticized his naive "growing-up" mistakes. They beat him cruelly and often. In the eyes of the elders whom he strove so hard to please, he always fell short and was a constant disappointment.

His whole life he had tried to please people, but he had adopted the harsh ways of the elders who raised him, which in turn caused people to turn away from him. He yearned for recognition from others for what he felt was his inner calling – to be a spiritual leader and receive the recognition and praise that he craved. The gift of his powerful perception and intuition and his ability to see people's dilemmas had initially attracted followers to his rabbinical teachings, but the harshness of his ways soon turned people away and caused even deeper feelings of rejection and unfulfillment to fester within him - until, this day, when Pontius Pilate had pronounced him "King of the Jews." He did not feel his painful body or worry about his fate; he felt elation and deluded grandeur because the Governor of Jerusalem and thousands of people were all focused on him. It did not matter that many booed and cursed or shouted at him; for once, multitudes of people had made him the center of their attention. A euphoric feeling of aggrandizement swelled within him; and in his demented state, he was determined to savor his moment of glory regardless of the pain or the death that he would have to endure.

In his trance-like stupor, his altered state of consciousness allowed him to see Simon's blue-white aura of compassion – a compassion for him - that was deep and genuine. Jesus of Jerusalem felt blessed as if by an army of angels. Then he saw it, what looked like a being of light, perhaps an angel? He didn't know for sure, but whatever it was, the light gave him a feeling of comfort and the strength to continue.

It was the presence of Jesus as the Christ, a Being of Light, who escorted Simon and Jesus of Jerusalem along the path to the Golgotha hilltop site where the crucifixion was to occur. The Christ was aware of the despair and the loss of hope that his followers were feeling and how they were suffering from their belief that their Messiah, who had come at last, was now doomed. Those believers were shrouded in very thick clouds of despair that did not allow Jesus's Light of Hope to fully enter their spirits. However, he was able to give his love to all, and those who were able to accept it felt the awe of Holiness within their grief. Some of his followers felt guilt because they believed that their Messiah was being taken from them because of their own sins. Jesus gave them his forgiveness. Although they didn't know why, they felt degrees of relief.

After Jesus's Ascension, he sat symbolically on the right-hand throne next to his heavenly Father and then ascended beyond the beyond to become One with All That Is. As on earth when in the flesh, Jesus served as a "Guiding Light" to teach mankind to live in love and harmony with each other; now that the body that had clothed him had been shed, Jesus's abilities to serve were multiplied beyond imagination by the power of his Essence to be in unlimited places in time and space simultaneously. At all times, he steadfastly maintained his infinite tolerance and readily gave his heartfelt forgiveness, guidance, and love to all who sincerely asked for it, whether in verbal prayer or in thought.

As the crucifixion procession moved on, the gray sky darkened, and the sense of doom increased. Simon carried the cross past a wagon carrying Judith and Samuel, whom Jesus had married. Judith was holding her blanketed baby son. With them were Miriam and her two children, Dustine and Sophie. The adults' faces showed their shock and deep sorrow. They could not refrain from crying mournfully. Sophie cried because of her mother's palpable anguish and from the wretched sight of the bloodied man who struggled to walk. Dustine stared blankly at the man to be crucified.

The soldier slammed his hardwood cane against his prisoner's back. The man lurched forward six inches from the momentum of the cruel strike but did not fall.

Dustine squeezed Miriam's hand and asked, "Mommy, why are they doing that to Jesus?"

"Because...they don't understand."

Dustine was puzzled. "Don't they know how special he is?"

"No, my sweet son...they do not."

"But, Mommy," Dustine said painfully, "it hurts me to see him being hurt." Tears streamed down the little boy's cheeks. He clutched his mother's side. "Mommy, I love him." Dustine's shoulders shook as he sobbed.

Sophie said between her sobs, "I... love... him... too." After hearing the children's heart-rending cries, the heavy weight of Judith's emotions was becoming overwhelming. Then she thought she heard Jesus speak the words to her that he had spoken after her father, Nathan, had been murdered, "... weeping may tarry for the night, but joy cometh in the morning." Judith remembered how moments of tragedy could feel insurmountable at the time, but that God's "favor is for a lifetime." That thought brought her a small measure of comfort but could not dispel her deep sadness over what she was witnessing, even though Jesus's Essence stood by her side and held her shoulders.

Jesus's glowing ethereal form also stood simultaneously behind Sophie and Dustine. Such is the power of the Light of the Holy Spirit, to be in many places at once. He placed his hands on their shoulders and infused their auras with the rose-pink tones of unconditional love that a parent gives to a beloved infant child, as he had before when he had told them the story of the butterflies and love.

Once again the soldier prodded his cane into the back of the staggering Jesus of Jerusalem to keep herding him toward the Place of the Skull.

48

From the summit of the Golgotha crucifixion site, a panoramic view of Jerusalem and the surrounding landscape was visible. However, the Romans chose the elevated site for a different reason, so that travelers to Jerusalem had to view those who were crucified there. People readily saw those who were condemned and on the cross, stripped of their clothes, laboring to breathe with tortured faces, tormented by insects crawling on them and biting the insides of their nostrils and ears and armpits and crotches. Birds pecked at their eyes and flesh before and after they died, and often only a skull bone remained. That is why the crucifixion site was called "The Place of the Skull." Anyone viewing the bloodied summit's site of those condemned to crucifixion by Roman law became very mindful of adhering to those laws.

For this day's crucifixion, at the base of the site, a large perimeter of Roman soldiers and cavalry were stationed to prevent the crowds from accessing the hilltop. On the hilltop, set in the ground, were three upright "stipes" – the heavy wooden post beams that the crossbars being carried by the condemned would be nailed to, thus securing their wrists. Jesus's Mother Mary, his brother James, Mary Magdalene, and Seth waited where the path at the base junctioned with the path leading to the hilltop. Unbeknownst to one another, they had all sought that spot but came to it from different directions. When Mother Mary and James encountered Mary and Seth, James recognized Mary and told his mother about her and the robe that Mary said she would give to Jesus to wear.

In a strained and weak voice, the first thing Mother Mary asked was, "Did my son get to wear the robe that I made for him for Passover?" Mary replied, "Yes, he wore the robe for Passover last night."

"Thank God," Mother Mary muttered. She then dropped to her knees from exhaustion and unrelenting horrid anxiety.

Mary knelt beside her and put a comforting arm around Jesus's grief-stricken mother. Mary then whispered in his mother's ear so that nearby soldiers could not hear, "The man they will be crucifying is not your son."

Mother Mary pulled away. "Why do you say such things?" She pointed to James and said, "He is Jesus's brother. He saw him at Judas's house. How can my son not be the one who will be crucified?" Mother Mary became angry, and she said, "Since my son was born, I have feared that this day would come. Look around you at these soldiers. Nothing can stop it now."

Mary blurted, "No! You don't understand." Then she leaned closer to Mother Mary and spoke low, "What I have told you is true. He is not your..."

A sudden roar of anger erupted from the crowds lining the pathway from the Jerusalem gate a hundred yards away. Mary stood to see what was happening. James stood on his toes, but neither could make out more than that the crucifixion procession was at the point of the angry shouting and moving toward them. Seth kept asking what was happening. No one answered because they all were straining to see above the heads of those in front of them. Seth became very frustrated and said loudly, "Would someone please tell me what is happening?"

All of a sudden, a pair of powerful hands grasped his sides and lifted him high in the air. The tall, strong man wearing a dark hooded robe and holding Seth bent forward slightly and placed Seth's legs over his own wide shoulders; then the man straightened. Seth, still surprised and very pleased with the view, exclaimed, "Thank you!"

Mary looked at Seth and asked, "What is happening?"

"The one carrying the cross is coming this way," he replied.

<hr>

Jesus the Christ made many individual and mass contacts as his multidimensional Essence moved through the crowd. He gave his blessings and love generously to all who grieved for him. Among those in the crowd were Zachaeus, his daughter, Isabella, and Markus. Even Salome, Herodias's daughter, was present and felt deep sorrow for Jesus's plight. She wore no make-up and was dressed in a plain gray robe. She cried when the beaten man passed by.

The man carrying the cross looked up at the three upright stipe-beams on the hilltop. Seth saw his face and said to Mary, "It's Simon! He's carrying the man's cross."

Mother Mary strained to stand. James helped her to her feet, but she was too short and hunched over to see anything. She tried to stand on her toes but in her weakened state quickly dropped to her knees again from despair and torment. The big man whose shoulders Seth sat upon said to the boy, "Hold on."

In one swift, flowing move, the tall, strong man reached down, picked Mother Mary up in his arms, and then stood tall again. She glanced at him but quickly turned away in revulsion. Looking over the heads of the crowd, she was able to see clearly. She muttered, "Bless you," to the man.

When the man had bent over to lift up Mother Mary, Seth had held on to the top of the hood that covered the man's head. When the man stood again, the hood shifted, exposing half of the top of his head to Seth. Seth gasped at the scarred disfigurement of a badly burned scalp. Seth quickly covered the man's head with the hood.

When Jesus of Jerusalem was within ten feet of Mother Mary, she pointed at him and shrieked with horror, "It's my Jesus!" The man stumbled and fell to the ground for the third time.

Mary Magdalene said to her, "Believe me, it's not what you think."

Mother Mary angrily retorted, "That's the robe that I made for my son. I would know it anywhere." She then cried out, "Jesus, my sweet love!"

The fallen Jesus of Jerusalem rose up on his elbows and turned toward her. His face, bloodied from the beatings and the crown of thorns, made his features difficult to recognize. The soldier with the cane whacked him between the shoulders. "Get up!" he hollered.

The man crumbled to the ground. Mother Mary fainted again. Her head fell back and hung limp over the big man's arm. He gently moved her head against his shoulder and tenderly cradled Mother Mary closer to his chest. The strong man felt soothing warmth between his shoulder blades. He felt the warmth pass through to his heart and then pass from his heart to the woman in his arms. It felt like divine love was sent from his heart to hers. He felt a goodness within himself that he had never before experienced.

Jesus's Light-Essence form had placed one hand on the large man's back and his other hand over Mother Mary's heart. Jesus had completed an energy circuit of divine love between his earth mother and Spartus, the man who had tried to kill him. Jesus blessed Spartus and acknowledged the man's true repentance and simultaneously blessed his earth-mother for the caring love and passionate protection that she had undyingly given him. Tears of bliss and sadness streamed down the tall man's grotesquely scarred cheeks - sadness for what he was witnessing and bliss from the feeling of love from Jesus, the one who had led him to salvation.

At the same time, Seth felt a strong presence behind him and looked down. He saw Jesus's face and his robe, both dazzling white, one hand on Spartus's back, the other on Mother Mary's head. Seth felt elated and relieved to see the presence of his beloved teacher and friend. Seth heard Jesus's thought to him, *"You are wise to know that the one to be crucified is not me. Take heart and also know that you will see me again."*

With that, Jesus's image faded. Elated, Seth felt graced, and he remembered Jesus's words at his last supper, "You shall know me by my Light."

Simon had also looked at Mother Mary when she cried out. He saw Seth, Mary, and James. Seth waved to Simon, but Simon shook his head "no" to avoid recognition and continued walking. Seth understood and lowered his hand. The escort soldier again pulled the fallen man to his feet and forced him to proceed. The row of soldiers guarding the perimeter stepped aside to permit Simon, Jesus of Jerusalem, and the escort soldiers to proceed up the hill to the Place of the Skull. The remaining soldiers and cavalry fanned out to reinforce the perimeter against the large crowd that had followed from Jerusalem's gate. The priests and officials who were at the rear of the procession were allowed inside the perimeter but were made to stay near the hill's base. The air grew cooler, and the sky turned grayer with heavy clouds.

When they reached the top of the hill, Simon put the crossbar down in front of the upright stipe-beam and was then made to leave and stand outside the perimeter. The soldiers laid the condemned man upon the crossbeam and held his arms outstretched over it. Large pointed spikes were driven into his wrists. With each blow, the man involuntarily screamed horrifically in pain as the spikes crossed the median nerves in his wrists. Mother Mary remained unconscious, women in the crowd wailed and cried, and men cringed with a soulful chill. The massive crowd watched intently although some turned away at the horror.

Seth heard a commotion behind him. He turned and from his high vantage point, saw two other condemned men carrying their crossbars with their soldier escorts making their way to the Place of the Skull.

On Golgotha's crest, Jesus of Jerusalem was crucified with two others, one on either side of him. Many hours later, as the dying men on their crosses struggled to breathe and suffered dehydration, a centurion raised a sponge of liquid to the mouth of the man on the middle cross, but the man did not drink of it. Pontius Pilate had wanted Jesus to die before sunset to avoid a lingering death that might last for days and cause great ferment among the growing crowds. The sponge of liquid that was offered contained hemlock to hasten his death.

The centurion made haste on his horse to Pilate, who ordered the centurion to go back and lance the Rabbi's side so that his death would be immediate.

While waiting for the men on the cross to die, the soldiers below them gambled with dice. They saw the robe that Mother Mary had made, and thinking it to be of unusual quality, gambled for it. Although Jesus offered comfort and peace to the men on the cross, the men had rejected his offerings.

The centurion returned from Pilate to Golgotha and stood beneath the man hanging from the middle cross. He grasped his lance firmly and was about to thrust it into the man's side. The centurion and the three men hanging from their crosses heard Christ's Essence speak, *"They know not what they do."*

The bewildered centurion looked around but saw no one where the distinct voice had come from. Suddenly the earth quaked. Huge boulders on the nearby mountainsides split and rumbled down the slopes, loudly cracking off large tree limbs. The centurion froze at the startling quaking and the frightening sounds from the mountainsides. He looked up at the man on the cross again, who now appeared lifeless. After a few more moments of hesitation, the centurion grimaced and then thrust his lance into the man's side. Quickly withdrawing it, he left a long gash. Immediately, copious amounts of blood and water spewed out of the wound from the hemorrhaging organs that had suffered from his many beatings and kicks. The copious fluid spilled down onto the arms and chest of the chagrined centurion. He cautiously backed away from the cross with shaking hands and threw down his lance. The sky blackened, a frigid wind swept across the land, and the earth trembled again. The centurion looked upon the man whom he had pierced and said, "Truly this was the son of God."

Jesus of Jerusalem died on the cross. Above his head, the titulus-sign read:

Jesus of Nazareth

King of the Jews

49

Soon after reporting, the centurion had left Pilate again to return to the Place of the Skull, three priests from the Sanhedrin met with Pontius Pilate. They were Caiaphas, Nicodemus, and Joseph, a Sanhedrin council member from Arimathea, which was known as the "City of the Jews." The three men requested that they be allowed to take Jesus's corpse so that they could prepare a proper burial for it. Joseph of Arimathea had firmly believed that Jesus was the Messiah - the Anointed One - whom he and most of his city's people had long hoped and prayed fervently for. Joseph was one of the minority who did not agree with the decision to have Jesus crucified and had argued strongly against it.

Pilate gave permission for the group of highly respected council members to remove the body. Later, the men took the corpse down from the cross and with the women who accompanied them, wrapped it in linen cloth. Joseph of Arimathea had recently built a large tomb hewed from the inside of a stone mountain for his wealthy family. No one had yet been laid in the tomb. A beautiful garden surrounded the tomb's entrance, freshly planted with many colorful flowers.

They took the body into the tomb and laid it upon a stone ledge. Mary, Seth, Mother Mary, and James had followed Joseph's group and watched as two strong men with a long lever rolled a huge, round rock to seal the tomb's five-foot entrance as the sun was setting. In obedience to the sundown Friday night tradition, everyone left according to the rules of the Sabbath's observance, which did not allow them further time to prepare the body with spices. The women planned to return the morning after the next day's sunset ended the Sabbath. The two large men took the long lever with them. The blood-red setting sun fell below the horizon.

Three days later, as the first rays of sunlight shone on Sunday morning, the earth beneath the large, round stone trembled. The stone rolled to the side, allowing fresh air into the entrance of the tomb in which Jesus of Jerusalem had been laid. A being of dazzling white Light surrounded by a dozen radiant white angels entered the tomb. The light-form approached the rock ledge on which the linen-clad corpse had been laid. A refreshing breeze swirled into the cave-like tomb and removed all of the foul air emanating from the corpse; in its stead, the fragrance of the new day's awakening of the morning dew on the bountiful flower garden, now filled the tomb.

In the stone quiet of the tomb, a faint sound of breathing emanated from the light-form. As the light-form's breathing grew deeper, the being of Light began to assume an opalescent shape. The form became that of a man in a brilliant white tunic and robe. At the apex of his inhalation, just before his exhalation, there was a momentary pause; and as he breathed out, the man's face became that of Jesus Christ. He breathed in deeply once more and then took a step closer to the corpse. His dazzling white robe and tunic returned to a normal appearance. The angels vanished.

Jesus reached down and unraveled the linen cloth that encased the body of Jesus of Jerusalem. He bent over the corpse, placed his open palms on the dead man's palms, and breathed into his nostrils. The corpse gave a sudden shiver and then lay still. Jesus breathed life into the corpse three more times. With each breath, the man's horrendous wounds healed a bit more. With the third breath, the man's heart began beating, and color returned to his pale face and body.

Jesus stepped back, held his palms toward the reviving man, and sent the miraculous life force of the Holy Spirit into him. When all the man's cells and organs had rejuvenated, Jesus put his hands down and said to him, "Awake."

The man's eyes opened. He blinked repeatedly and then stared at the ceiling of the cave.

Jesus said to him, "Arise."

The man sat up, perplexed. He looked around and asked, "Where am I?"

"Your body was laid here in this tomb. You are now healed from your wounds and have been made whole."

The man looked at his legs, then held up his hands and wrists to his face and examined them closely. There were no wounds from the crucifixion to be seen. He made fists and opened and closed them five times. He felt his unblemished chest and abdomen and then sat in wonder and awe. He no longer had a dazed appearance. "How is this possible?" he asked.

"With God, all things are possible," Jesus replied.

"Why have you come to do this?" the man asked.

"I have come so that you may have life."

"But I don't want the life that I had."

"You can start a new life from this moment on."

"I want nothing more to do with the wretched people who dwell on earth. I have seen God's Kingdom, and that is where I belong. I have found peace there, rather than pain here. You had no right to bring me back."

123412341

"You and I have resurrected in the flesh on this day to fulfill the prophecies and future scriptures."

"I don't care any more about prophecies. I have been hailed as the people's savior and have fulfilled my dreams and destiny."

"And for the role that you have played and all that you have suffered," Jesus replied, "you have now been rewarded with an opportunity to live again."

The man looked with scorn at Jesus and spoke with anger. "My reward is in my heavenly Father's Kingdom, not here in this stone tomb."

Jesus took the man's hand and said, "Please, come with me."

The man reluctantly took Jesus's hand and followed him outside into the bright morning light. "Take a deep breath," Jesus instructed. The man breathed in deeply and then exhaled. A faint smile formed on his lips. "What do you feel?" Jesus asked.

"The air is the freshest and sweetest that I have ever breathed."

"That's a good thing. In your renewed life, your senses are now capable of enjoying the many pleasures that you could not enjoy before."

Jesus knelt down on one knee, pointed to an array of beautiful multi-colored flowers, and said, "Look upon God's earthly creations and the magnificence of his glory."

The man looked, his faint smile widening, and said, "The colors appear dazzling, like none that I have seen before."

Jesus smiled back and pointed to a purple flower. "Kneel here and smell this flower's exquisite fragrance, for it too will be grander than any that you have smelled before."

The man folded his arms defiantly across his chest and stepped back. "You tempt me like Satan, offering me earthly pleasures to entice me to accept the new life that you have offered. But I tell you again, I want nothing more to do with this wretched world and its people. I must return to my Father's Kingdom, of that I am certain."

Jesus looked up at the man and studied his aura and thoughts for a moment. He accepted the man's resolute desire to reject a "born again" life on earth and his fervent wish to return to where he had felt the solace of peace and love.

Jesus had offered peace and comfort to him when he was being crucified on the cross, but the man's essence had stubbornly rejected Jesus's help then as he did now. Jesus replied, "I see. So be it; thy will be done."

Instantly, the man's body vaporized into a fine mist, then evaporated in the warmth of the morning air. Two women soon approached; one walked with a limp but no pain. They were carrying spices and ointments to prepare the body. The women - Mary Magdalene and Mother Mary - walked past Jesus as he still knelt by the flowers, for they thought that he was the landscaper tending to the garden. They had planned to leave the spices at the tomb's entrance and then get the two strong men to move the heavy, round stone, but they were surprised that the stone had already been moved. They entered the tomb and were shocked that no corpse was to be found.

The two mystified women exited the tomb and again passed by Jesus, who had remained kneeling on the ground. Jesus called out, "Mary."

Mary Magdalene instantly recognized Jesus's voice and turned to him. Jesus stood and smiled at the two stunned women. "My Lord!" Mary exclaimed and fell to her knees.

Mother Mary took a step back in disbelief. "Can it be?" she gasped and almost fainted. "How?" she murmured.

"Yes, it is I. Why do you look for the living among the dead? He has arisen. The Son of Man was delivered into the hands of sinful men, then crucified; and on the third day, he was resurrected from death."

The two women remained frozen as Jesus spoke. "Go now and gather my most valued disciples. I will meet with you and them tomorrow morning at Lazarus's home. With that, Jesus's image faded and disappeared before them. They remained stunned for a few moments; then both cried with rapture, realizing that Jesus was with them once again. They soon left to gather the disciples as they had been bade.

<hr />

Mother Mary took sick afterward. The heart-wrenching trauma of the crucifixion and the reappearance of Jesus at the tomb and then his disappearance again had been too overwhelming for her emotions to cope with. Her son James tended to her in Jerusalem.

At first, when Mary Magdalene and Seth looked about for the inner circle of disciples, they thought it would be highly unlikely that they would find all the scattered men, many in hiding, before the next morning. However, by the end of the day, they had crossed paths by chance or divine providence with eleven of the disciples, but Judas could not be found. By late evening, all had gathered at Mary's brother Lazarus's house in Bethany.

<hr />

The next morning, all of the disciples except Peter were eating a breakfast of bread and broiled fish. When Mary had told them that she had seen the arisen Jesus, none of the disciples had believed her. Instead, they viciously spoke of Judas's betrayal that Jesus had prophesied. They had also spoken harshly of Judas's despicable deed to many of Jesus's followers over the Sabbath, creating a fierce hatred for Judas in the mourners of their beloved, crucified Messiah.

Peter came back into the house and hurriedly locked the door behind him. He came to the breakfast table still panting from running and exclaimed to everyone, "I went to the tomb where our Master was laid! As Mary said, the stone covering the entrance had been moved away. I went in. The tomb was empty except for burial strips of linen cloth on the floor. I don't understand. Where could our Lord's body be?"

"I am here. Peace be with you." The words resonated in the room, and everyone turned to see who had spoken. Inside, Jesus stood by the locked door, as he had appeared at their last supper together. The startled disciples became frightened and stared silently in awe and disbelief as Jesus approached the table.

Finally, Luke said, "Master, you are aglow and look healthy and well, as if you had never died."

Jesus smiled, "That who I am lives."

John got up and then knelt at Jesus's feet. He kissed his Master's robe and then said, "Of course, God cannot be killed."

"You are right, John," Jesus replied. "God cannot be killed. I can change my form, but I cannot die."

Thomas protested, "But I know that you died. I saw them drive the nails into you, and I saw a lance slash your side. Blood gushed. You were dead."

"Come to me, Thomas," Jesus bade him.

Thomas came to him. Jesus held out his hands and wrists to him and asked, "Can you see any wounds?"

Thomas hesitated to look, but then he had to examine Jesus's hands and wrists. Although Thomas was filled with disbelief, he could find no wounds. Jesus pulled up his tunic and exposed the smooth, healthy skin of his abdomen. Thomas backed away and exclaimed, "No! It can't be. I saw you crucified and taken down from the cross for dead."

Jesus stared at his disciples a moment and then said, "I stand before you now. How can any of you still have doubts?"

"I have no doubt now, Master," Thomas replied. "I know that you live again, for I see you now."

Jesus addressed the others, "Blessed are those who have not seen and yet believe. Why do you still lack faith and remain stubborn in refusing to believe that I have arisen? Here I am in the flesh for you to witness my return as it has been prophesied."

Seth boldly stated, "It is our Lord. He's real!"

"The youngest among you recognizes me," Jesus stated. "Except for Mary and Seth, no one knew that my presence was with all of you during the crucifixion of the son of man."

Jesus pointed to Peter and asked him, "Do you truly love me?"

"Lord, you know all things, and you know that I love you," Peter replied.

Jesus rebuked him, "At Golgotha, you hid under a blanket in the back of a wagon for fear of being discovered and arrested. You peeked out to see a crucifixion take place, and you quivered in fear and horror at what you saw."

"How could you know that?" Peter asked in shame.

"I told you all when you accepted your roles as disciples that my presence will be with you always. No longer should you think of me in the flesh that clothed me. On Friday, I ascended from that body in which you knew me, and on the third day I arose in this body so that in one way or another, everything must be fulfilled that is written about these times. However, my Essence-spirit was with all of you on that Friday's crucifixion although except for Mary and Seth, you did not see my Light. Simon did feel my presence, and I blessed him for his magnificent courage in carrying the cross and his resolute belief in me."

In a clear voice, without stuttering, Simon said, "My Lord, I did feel your presence by my side. It lightened the weight of the cross that I carried."

Jesus turned to Peter and asked him again, "Peter, do you love me?"

"Yes, Lord, I have said so," Peter responded meekly.

"When you were fearful for your own life and denied me three times to save yourself, you put your needs and fears above your word that you would never deny me."

"Please forgive me, Master. I lost my mind and panicked. I never thought that your powers could be overcome."

"I forgive you, Peter. Do you truly love me?"

"Yes, yes, yes, I do truly love you."

"As you have learned, fear can rob your heart of faith. But I see that my presence here has restored your faith and made it stronger than before. Most of my followers have acted like sheep that scattered because they thought their shepherd had been slain. Henceforth, I want you, Peter the Rock, to be the shepherd of the flock and never again lose your faith in me or in my words."

"I never will again, My Lord. I will faithfully and undyingly do as you bid."

"So be it," Jesus replied. He sat down at the table to join in the breakfast and ate a piece of the broiled fish to demonstrate the reality of his body. The disciples sat in wonder and awe as they watched. As he ate, Jesus told them of visits with his other disciples when he was in different body forms that he was able to assume.

When Jesus finished eating, he said, "My time in this body is only for brief periods, for the almighty power of the Holy Spirit that allows me to incarnate cannot be contained for longer times because the flesh would disintegrate. My Essence-spirit is God's instrument with which to use His forces to establish His Kingdom on earth and to guide mankind to fulfill its destiny."

Jesus stood and said, "I want all of you to learn a prayer and to know and sincerely feel its meaning. Repeat after me, 'Our Father, which art in the heavens, Hallowed be thy name. Thy Kingdom come. Thy will be done on earth as it is in heaven. Give us this day our daily bread. And forgive us our trespasses, as we forgive the trespasses of others. And bring us not into temptation or trial, but deliver us from evil: for thine is the Kingdom, and the power, and the glory and the Light, forever. Amen."

The disciples repeated each phrase after Jesus had spoken it. Then he said, "Now repeat it again by yourselves."

They repeated it perfectly, in unison. Jesus then said, "Now that you know it, say it each day and feel its meanings, for they are vast, and teach it to others, for that is a prayer that I have often said for mankind's sake."

Peter enthusiastically said, "You are our Lord. Let us call your prayer the 'Lord's Prayer.'"

All at the table readily agreed. Jesus held up his palms toward everyone in a sign of benediction and said, "I endow all of you with the power on high as Moses and Elijah did unto you at our last supper together. With that power, you are all to go forth to all nations and preach The Word and all that you know of me, and know that you go forth from your true heart and soul with the Essence of the Father and my Essence as His Son and the Essence of the Holy Spirit. Do that, and surely I will be with you always, even until the end of ages.

"Always strive to seek the best ways and take the best paths to benefit All That Is in the spirit of love, for that is God's way, and God is love. My heavenly Father blesses you all."

After Jesus had spoken, his form became a blinding white light and then disappeared from their midst.

50

Time passed. A gray-clouded sky cast an ominous pallor over the barren landscape. On a hilltop a mile away from a small, remote village stood a lone tree in otherwise desolate surroundings. Most of the tree's branches were rotting or had been broken off by violent storms. An emaciated man stood alone at the tree's base. He took off his sandals and then struggled to climb up to the one remaining high branch, which he then straddled. His sorrowful weary face and long, unkempt black beard with patches of gray reflected the harshness of wretched suffering. He wore only a ragged tunic covered by a tattered robe.

He sat still for a moment and looked around the forsaken land. He sighed mournfully and shook his head in sad resignation. From around his waist he unwound the circled rope and then laid it on the branch. He removed his robe and let it drop to the ground sixteen feet below. A cold breeze cut through the air; the man felt its chill, but it didn't matter to him. He tied one end of the rope into a noose, and then he tightly secured the other end of the rope to the tree branch. All the while, his face was expressionless, as if life had gone out of it.

He surveyed the land once more but saw nothing worth looking at. The man slipped the noose around his neck and tightened it against his throat. He closed his eyes and sat as still as death. The words came out of his mouth in a weak monotone, "If you loved me... as you said you did, why has my doing your bidding become such a torturous punishment to me? I had led a life of searching for truth and helping the poor. I devoted myself to you; and for that, I have become hated... despised by all I cared for... and scorned by those who never even knew me. Why?"

The man stared blankly at the empty air before him; then the wind stilled, and he heard, "I still love you, Judas, and I always will."

Judas sat up straight. It was Jesus's voice that he heard from within. Judas angrily replied, "So you have come to me now in my final moments. What good is it now?"

"I have always been with you, but you denied me. It is only now that you have opened yourself to receive me."

"I couldn't bring myself to call upon you before. I felt betrayed by you. You convinced me that no harm would come to you if I told the Pharisees where you were. I believed you. I felt deceived. I hated you. I hated myself. Now I am the one who suffers the blame for your crucifixion – the death of the beloved Messiah. I am in constant torment; I cannot sleep or eat because of you."

"My poor dear Judas, no harm has come to me. My Beloved Father's intention was, and is, to protect me always. It was never His intention that I, His Beloved Son should be crucified on the cross. It was never my intention to be crucified."

Judas frowned in puzzlement.

Jesus continued, "The one who was crucified was not I. My death, which they think they caused, occurred in their error and blindness. They nailed a man to his death, but it was not I. When they thought they struck me with a cane, it was another. When the Romans thought they made me bear the cross, it was another. It was another upon whose head they placed the crown of thorns... and I was laughing at their ignorance."

"But if it was another and not you, what happened to you? Where did you go?"

"I ascended to my Father's Kingdom. And now I continue to serve Him."

"Surely you were crucified. Everyone knows that! The people all say that you, the Messiah, prophesied at our Passover Seder that I would 'betray the son of man,' as I and the other disciples heard you say. Now I have become the one blamed for your death."

"Dear, Judas, I have not died. I live now, and I am with you. It is true that you brought the Pharisees and then pointed to a 'son of man,' whom they arrested and crucified. But I tell you again, it was another and not me, for I am the Son of God – and you, dear Judas, did not betray me."

"If that's true, I say again, what good has it done me? I am still the one blamed for your death, and I have suffered the horrible consequences. I have become Judas the scapegoat – the poor beast that others have placed unforgiveable sins on and have driven me out to die in the wilderness. "

Jesus's voice became soft and compassionate. "On the day that we first met in Jerusalem when you were searching for me, you felt pity for an innocent goat that had become the 'scapegoat' for the sins of others. Now you have become the innocent 'scapegoat' for man's misdirected hate, and you suffer for the sin of others' hate. But I say to you, Judas, that in time the truth shall come to light and mankind will see the error of their ways. They will have the opportunity to forgive you, and in their forgiving of you, they will be forgiven for hating the one who is innocent."

Judas's eyes welled with tears, but then his face turned bitter. He was about to cry but held back and said, "I don't care if those who hate me are forgiven. I can no longer take this unbearable pain. People curse and spit upon me. They throw rotten garbage at me. I've been beaten and peed on. Tomorrow only offers more rejection and greater suffering for me. Everyone says that the Messiah's own disciple betrayed him," Judas pounded his chest with a fist, "and that I was the one who was the betrayer. It's so unjust. I can no longer stay in this life of endless torment."

"I understand your dismay, Judas. But you should know that your sacrifice for me served a great purpose, and your ultimate fate will be a rich reward in my Father's Kingdom, for as I have told you, your star will shine brightest of all of the apostles'."

Judas scoffed, "People will never believe that I am innocent. Their hate is too vehement and hard-set like dried mortar."

"Never is a long time, Judas. In the future, when the truth is known, at first people will doubt and refuse to accept that truth. Then many authorities will acknowledge the possibility of that truth, and mankind will have an important choice to make."

"What would that choice be?"

"To truly practice my teachings of The Word, most importantly those of love, tolerance, forgiveness and brotherhood. Those who call themselves my true followers must in time realize that they cannot hate selectively, but must love universally; they cannot judge and condemn, but must forgive – even extend forgiveness to you, dear Judas, who they think is responsible for my death, a death that never was nor ever could be, for I cannot die."

Judas violently shook his head and then said, "Your followers will not listen to the truth. Their intense hate has deafened their ears."

"That is tragically unfortunate for these times, but there is hope – hope that when enough people of the future acknowledge the possibility that you are my hero and not a villain to be despised, then I will come again – in the flesh – and do all in my power to bring God's magnificent Light and Love to earth as it is in heaven."

Jesus's voice became affirmative and strong. "And when my true followers correct the error of their ways and truly follow my sacred teachings of love and forgiveness toward all – especially for you dear, Judas, who suffers so from the ignorance of others – then at that time, you will be vindicated, and your innocence and sacrifice for me will be heralded. For that is my prayer for the people of tomorrow to fulfill and for them to overcome their hatred."

Judas stood up on the tree branch. He sighed mournfully and then said, "I no longer care what the people do or do not do."

"Know this, dear Judas: I love you, and I honor the choices that you made to enable me to complete my mission. Of all whom I have known on earth, you have not only been the one most loyal to me, you have also made the greatest sacrifice. You deserve peace, not torment. My Father and I are pleased with you. Be not dismayed, for what you have done by laying down your life for me has already opened the gate to my Father's Kingdom for you."

Judas looked up at the dark gray sky. A cold wind again cut through his frail body. He looked down at the ground that was the brown-rust color of dried blood. Judas whispered, "There is nothing left in this world for me."

Then Judas heard Jesus's last words to him, "I am with you until the end of your time in this world, and I will be there for you in the domain of my Father's Kingdom. Peace be with you."

Judas tightened the noose around his neck until he nearly gagged. Then he stepped off of the high branch. Like a falling knife in the air, his body plunged toward the earth below. He looked down at his feet and saw a brilliant white image of Jesus standing on the ground below with his open arms reaching up toward his falling body. At the moment that the last slack of rope snapped taut, Judas's flesh vaporized in a flash of light and his vacated ragged tunic floated softly to the ground. The empty noose swayed back and forth in the cold wind.

Made in the USA
San Bernardino, CA
02 July 2015